RANDO SPLICER

THE SPIRAL WARS; BOOK SIX

JOEL SHEPHERD

FOREWORD

Dear Readers

A quick note to let everyone know the current state of my plans for this series.

Some of you may have noticed that the gap between the release dates of each Spiral Wars book has been getting longer. I promise this is not intentional. However, you may also have noticed that the complexity of this world is increasing with each book, and when that happens it becomes harder and harder to resolve all the various plots rapidly.

I make no comment about certain independently published authors who manage to put out a new book every few months, but that's not how I write. I make no judgement if you prefer those types of books to these, but I think that in independent publishing there should be room for both the books that take a few months to write, and those that take closer to a year. Believe me, this one took a lot of effort, and I'm very pleased with it.

As I've written on my twitter and facebook pages, the plan for this series now stands at ten books. If you'd like more information, it can be found on those social media pages. I hope the remaining books of the series will be written more quickly than this one, but I can't promise it. I can only promise that I'll do my very best to keep the quality as high, and hopefully higher, than what's come before, in return for your patience. And, a request that if you like what you read here, and think that it deserves even more success than that which I've been fortunate enough to enjoy so far, that you recommend it to friends, family, on social media, or anyone who you think might enjoy it.

Sincerely

Joel Shepherd

PS; And because I promised the readers who'd contributed that I'd mention it — check out the Spiral Wars Wiki page! https://spiral-wars-shepherd.fandom.com/wiki/The_Spiral_Wars_Wiki

1

Rear Admiral Laura Reiko adjusted her uniform as she strode from Hoffen HQ Bay 21 into the busy working corridors of Fleet uniforms. Bay 21 was an architectural monstrosity, recently added to Hoffen Station's spinning rim to give high ranking Fleet officers another option than to brave the trek from main-level docking berths. Just last month, marine General Shevodze had been shot point blank by Worlders disguised as maintenance crew on the way down the station four-arm. A week before that, spacer Captain Irani had been blown up, with half of her escort and a number of civilians, while walking the Hoffen Station dock from her ship.

Reiko eyed the marines guarding corridors as she passed, all in light armour with standard issue assault rifles — Koshaim-20s would not help against domestic terrorists who relied in part upon Fleet's reluctance to damage their own facilities in fighting back. Her immediate escort were not known to her — these days she was far too highly ranked for that. When she'd been plucked from command of the New Kerala Engineering Division a year ago, and dropped into every career officer's dream job, she'd never thought she'd miss such small pleasures as knowing the names of her escort. But now she did, more than ever.

Bay 21 delivered her at High Command just three minutes' walk from the shuttle, with no opportunities granted to terrorists outside of HQ's secure walls. Her marine detail took position outside, while Reiko stepped in. Behind his obligatory desk, Supreme Commander Mozangu rose, drink in hand. Sharing another drink, and also rising from a chair before the desk, was Rear Admiral Lu.

"Admiral," said Reiko, walking to her empty chair beside Lu's. "Supreme Commander." The Supreme Commander's office was one of the most secure rooms in all human space. The sacrifice of such rank was that it bore no spectacular view of Heuron System's busy shipping lanes, or of verdant green Heuron V about which Hoffen Station endlessly circled. Behind Mozangu's desk were a pair of crossed flags — one the Fleet Arrowhead-on-Crescent, the other the Sphere-on-Starburst of the human United Forces. On the walls, picture displays showed the faces of decorated Fleet officers. On the desk were several scale models of the ships the Supreme Commander had captained in younger days, elegantly mounted.

"Laura," said Mozangu with a perfunctory smile, and shook her free hand above the desk. She shook Lu's hand as well, and waited as the most powerful human alive poured her a drink. It sometimes still did not register that she was now number two. Lu, in the way of Fleet's Supreme Triumvirate, was number three. And today, all three were gathered together in the one small room. It did not happen often, for security reasons as much as any other.

"Elton, how is Homeworld?" Reiko asked politely, accepting Mozangu's drink and taking a seat.

"Oblivious as ever," said Lu, with a tight smile. They were not exactly friendly, the three most powerful commanders of humanity's all-conquering Fleet. Lu was short, increasingly pudgy with a senior officer's distance from field fitness requirements, with puffed little cheeks that seemed to Reiko faintly childish. He'd once been the formidable logistics commander of Fleet's resupply wing, before being shuffled sideways forty years ago to plan logistics at a higher, more conceptual level.

Mozangu was taller, lean with square shoulders but little meat on his bones. He'd been a cruiser captain in his youth, successful but not particularly outstanding in the earlier years of the Triumvirate War. Once retired from operational duty, however, he'd rocketed up the ranks. The cynical word among the lower admirals was that his success had more to do with sharp political instincts and a general lack of offensiveness to those who'd appointed him than it had with any great grasp of how to run a war.

And then there was Laura Reiko, who'd spent precisely none of the war in combat, but had instead climbed through Fleet's technical and engineering divisions, administering one top-secret, high-tech program after another until she'd found herself running the whole show. And then, with three unexpected vacancies at the highest level, had been abruptly grabbed from her comfortable Admiral's post, and promoted to Fleet Admiral in the second-highest post of all.

Those circumstances explained in part why none of them were particularly close. Fleet HQ had 'disappeared' senior officers before, following spectacular failures of judgement. It wasn't something discussed in polite society, inside or outside Feet ranks, but everyone knew it happened. Twenty-five years prior to the calamity of nearly a year-and-a-half ago, there had been an Army General found profiteering from planetary reconstruction following an invasion who'd been too high-up to court-martial. And seven years before that, an Admiral running a prostitute ring from desperate survivors of another planetary strike who'd been left with nothing.

No one had complained when those two had been 'disappeared', nor the slow trickle of those who'd preceded them but since lost from memory. Such officers were a disgrace to their uniforms, and Fleet's morale policies dictated that courts martial were too public and could undermine humanity's faith in their protectors once all the awful details got out. But justice had to be done, and Fleet's house cleaned, so both men had met with untimely deaths and their families 'tidied up', suitably plied with money and threats so that they'd keep their mouths shut for several generations to come.

But then one of Fleet's leading captains had had the poor judgement to involve himself in the impending Worlder civil conflict, and

Fleet's then-command triumvirate had panicked and murdered him in custody, and pinned the deed on Lieutenant Commander Debogande. Of *that* Debogande family, the only son of Alice Debogande herself, no less. And the resulting mess had nearly caused a mutiny among Fleet's rank-and-file captains so frightening that the Guidance Council had decided to cut its losses and have all three of its senior command 'disappeared' in one swift blow. Given the unfolding catastrophe to Fleet's morale, public standing and negotiating position vis-a-vis the Worlders, it was almost certainly the correct thing to do — to suffer one gaping flesh wound and get it over with, rather than continue to die by a thousand daily cuts.

But a calamity it had been all the same, and those three empty chairs had required immediate filling. And so here they all were, the lucky chosen three, seated in a Hoffen Station office where a year-and-a-half ago Supreme Commander Chankow had faced down the obstinate young Debogande, then somehow failed to round up that single ship or its legendary marine commander, who had all then gone on a rampage across the Spiral the repercussions of which were still reverberating through human space today.

"So," said Mozangu, folding long fingers on his desktop. "How goes it with the magical football?"

"Well," said Reiko, placing her drink on the table and inputting code to the handcuffs. They clicked, as did the case, and she opened it on her lap. Produced two manila files and offered one to each of the men. Paper files in this hyper-electronic age — a security precaution, as all the papers were light-sensitive and would burn rather than copy. Besides which, these particular papers were at a security level so high that she was not able to let them leave her sight at any time. "The reader is now functioning at something closer to sixty percent. It's not ideal, but adequate for now."

"Alpha Tech is helping?" Lu asked, opening the file with trepidation.

Reiko nodded. Alpha Tech were the division that studied alien tech no one really understood, let alone was prepared to admit possessing. All the species of the Spiral had sworn not to dabble in that stuff. Reiko spoke of their activities as little as possible, even with the other occupants of this room. "We're making progress," she repeated. "The real bugger is that the damn reader we're using to decipher the data-core is nearly as advanced as the core itself. We're having to redesign everything we know about computer systems just to run the *reader*. And the core itself is another level again."

Such ridiculous technology would have been a joy for the minds that worked in Alpha Tech under most circumstances. But now the clock was ticking, and Reiko had leading scientists on the edge of nervous breakdown under the mental strain of trying to understand something so advanced it had some theorising that the human brain itself was not structurally capable of comprehension.

Lien Wang had dropped these twin monstrosities on her upon its return from parren space, via tavalai space, just over four months ago. She'd nearly been intercepted by suspicious tavalai warships on the way, not believing her claims of protected passage under the war-ending inspection protocols, and had had to run the last several jumps at combat speeds to avoid them. And ever since, Laura Reiko's life had been a sleepless mess.

"So what can we get from it?" Mozangu said. "I mean, assuming we can even start reading that data properly."

"Oh we can read enough of it," said Reiko. She recalled the drink, and sipped it. Good whisky, breaking Fleet regs for the simple reason that when you existed on this stratospheric level, and dealt with these kinds of galaxy-shaking problems, you could do whatever the hell you liked when no one else was looking. It tasted good, and she smacked the glass back down. "We'll have to remake half the damn Fleet if we follow through with it."

The two men stared at her. "What capabilities?" Mozangu asked, with a flicker of excitement.

"Oh..." Reiko shook her head, and waved her hand vaguely in the air. "Ridiculous. It would reshape the entire power-structure of the Spiral."

"Start wars from those who won't allow it," Lu countered.

"Captain Sampey of the *Lien Wang* said Captain Debogande was well aware of those implications," said Mozangu. "He said it was worth it, because the alo and friends have that tech already, or close to it."

"Not close to this," said Reiko, with certainty. "No... we looked at the performance specs on those deepynine ships that *Phoenix* sent back with *Lien Wang*. They're incredible, but they're not what I'm looking at from the data-core. Drysines were better, deepynines *lost* that war. If the alo's friends are positioned as Debogande thinks, *Phoenix* might just have saved our bacon."

"Not likely," Lu said darkly. "How long will it take you to mobilise all that information? To remake our ship-building capabilities? All the component industries? Debogande has that... that goddamn parren *moon* the drysines built, filled with their tech, they can just start it up and make new ships. We can't do that."

"We've got more than we've said," Reiko replied. Lu stared at her, questioningly.

"How long until you could mobilise and get us some of those big ships?" Mozangu asked.

"New ships?" said Reiko. "Too long, construction from scratch would take years. But refit some of our existing ships? Take some modified systems, some jump engines, weapon systems? Less than a year."

"I don't believe that," Lu said flatly.

"I'm quoting my best experts," said Reiko. "It's not just my opinion. Some of the subsystems are crazy. You saw my briefing on the gravity-bombs." The men nodded. They had. "Debogande was clear that the deepynines don't have those yet. Gravity-tech was all drysine, it looks like they're the only civilisation ever, that we know of, to have gotten anywhere with that research." She paused. "I've got more of it from the core."

"More as in useful weapons?" Mozangu pressed.

"Crazy useful," Reiko agreed. And added, more somberly, "Scary useful. Things that could destroy entire systems." She reached again for her drink, heart thumping at the sheer intensity of the discussion. Being here at all was crazy. Being here and responsible for these kinds of powers and decisions was like some children's story of dumb kids who stumbled across a magic wand that could destroy cities. Kids who could barely read and write, and now found themselves with such powers in their hands that would make even the wisest adults tremble. Humans were too damn new in space for this kind of technology, Reiko was certain. And yet there were witches in this tale, of the kind that ate children for breakfast. To not get eaten, they might yet have to use the wand, and just pray that that wasn't the worse of two evils.

"Where are we on the alo's friends, anyway?" she asked cautiously. Locked away on an asteroid research base for the past few months, she'd been out of the loop with high command's other big issues.

"It's grim," Mozangu admitted. "We've employed some assets. Quiet assets. Some have been lost already, the alo don't like being watched. But we've seen enough. *Phoenix*'s concerns are plausible."

Reiko's eyes widened, and she downed the last of her drink. "You're seeing mobilisation?"

A short nod from the Supreme Commander. "How recent and on what scale, we're not sure of. But some is clearly long-term, not just local manoeuvres."

"Quite likely exacerbated by *Phoenix*," Lu muttered, swilling the contents of his glass. "If not directly accelerated. Debogande's onto them, they'll be accelerating their plans, if they have plans."

"Possible," said Mozangu. "My Intel chiefs are divided. Some say so, but others say the mobilisation we're seeing is too large-scale and long-term to be so recent. It started well before the whole *Phoenix* debacle. And the deepynine attacks on *Phoenix* and surrounding parren infrastructure have been brazen. Those weren't rash spur of the moment decisions, that was a calculation by deepynine forces that don't care who knows about them, after millennia of staying silent."

"But we've known for centuries," Lu retorted. "They're only acknowledging that they've got nothing worth hiding any longer, it's not necessarily a hostile act."

"We've known *unofficially* for centuries," Mozangu replied. "We kept it secret from most of our own population, and Fleet itself, because the whole alo alliance would have been too hard for everyone to go along with if they knew. And we were right to do that, look at the victories that came from it. We've expanded so far, we're the new great power in the Spiral."

"Right," said Reiko. "And now the bill comes due."

"Who was that academic expert that *Phoenix* grabbed on Crondike?" Lu wondered, wracking his brain. "The guy Pantillo was talking to before that?"

"Stanislav Romki," Mozangu said heavily. "He was right onto it, nearly got himself disappeared. My Intel chiefs think he was instrumental in getting *Phoenix* to change course away from the Worlder issue and onto hacksaws. Judging from Captain Sampey's reports and the other things *Phoenix* has sent home, anyway."

"He's still alive?" Lu wondered.

"Yes. About a third of *Phoenix*'s crew isn't, though. They've been hammered, several times now. This latest one at Defiance nearly ended them."

"Tavalai crew replacements, *Lien Wang* said," Rieko recalled. "From the Dobruta... god knows what *they're* up to. And hacksaws. Completely nuts. Did we ever get a better report on what they were after, out in croma space?"

She and Lu looked at Mozangu. The Supreme Commander made a resigned gesture. "I apologise to you both," he said. "I don't like to keep secrets from either of you, but on this one I've had no choice. Both of your plates have been full, and I judged that knowledge of this particular issue would be of no help to you in your present duties. I had the crew of *Lien Wang* sworn to silence as they returned, and their reports were appropriately redacted from all not directly involved in the matter."

"What matter?" Reiko asked, frowning.

"A matter of genetic weaponry." Mozangu sipped his drink for the first time since Reiko had entered. His long fingers fidgeted about the glass as he set it back on the table top. He swallowed harder than necessary for the drink, jaw tight. Anxious, Reiko thought. No. Frightened. "The tavalai suspect it has infected their population. *Phoenix* suspects it has infected ours. I have mobilised every specialist, medical and science team I can safely mobilise. Most don't even know why they've mobilised, but the very top people do."

Reiko stared at him. "The Red Order that's been shifting some of my best researchers out of Alpha Tech?" Mozangu nodded solemnly. "I've been asking what that was, I couldn't get a clear answer. I thought that was a bureaucratic thing, I was too busy to ask further."

"It was designed to look that way." The Supreme Commander took a deep breath. "It's the highest possible secrecy for now. I don't know how long that can last, given the scale of mobilisations that could be required."

"Wait," said Lu. "*Phoenix* thinks *humanity's* infected?" Mozangu nodded. "And are we? Do we know yet?"

Another deep breath from the Supreme Commander. "It looks that way, yes." Time seemed to stop. "The theory is that the alo and deepynines got it from somewhere out in reeh space. That's where *Phoenix* went — not to see the croma, but to see the reeh."

"How dangerous is it?" Reiko breathed.

"We can't stop it," Mozangu said helplessly. "The tech is so far beyond what we know. As far beyond our geneticists and medical techs as the data-core and its reader are for your people, Laura. *Phoenix* had a theory... which no doubt you've heard is gaining ground in these offices... that the entire Triumvirate War was just battlespace preparation for the deepynines. The tavalai were staunchly anti-AI and still are, the Dobruta still have much influence there. Use the humans to remove and weaken the tavalai, then whack the humans when they're not looking... the alo and deepynines inherit the Spiral. Simple, really."

"And what if they just wanted the tavalai gone?" Lu said hopefully. "What if they don't mind humanity as much?"

"We're just as anti-AI as the tavalai are," said Reiko. "Deepynines have been making nice with the sard, as *Phoenix* reports it. Offering them all kinds of tech in exchange for allegiance. They've never tried with us, not at any level."

"They knew we wouldn't take it," Mozangu agreed. "And you don't spread an engineered genetic doomsday virus in a population you're intending to befriend." He looked at his two Rear Admirals, grimly, each in turn. "We're behind the clock, guys. We can hope it won't happen, but hope is not an adequate security policy. Either we find a way to get on top of this, or we'll be reduced to just hoping and praying the alo have something else in mind."

2

Trace was pleased that they were on a hillside tonight. She took a knee, cradled her rifle and waited for Loga to indicate that it was safe to move, gazing through a gap in the tall trees on her left and out over the moonlit forest. Most of Talo was forest, a semi-tropical southern-hemisphere continent surrounded by oceans and island archipelagos. The earth and vegetation about her were mostly dry, but it was thick and green all the same. Insects chirped, and Feina shone down from what Trace had come to think of as late-afternoon, in the nocturnal fashion of the corbi resistance on their homeworld. In a few hours it would be morning, and Trace liked to be asleep before the sun grew bright in the eastern sky, so that the intensity did not wreak too much havoc on her circadian rhythms.

She sipped water from her flask as she waited, aware of her height in the line of small, thick-shouldered corbi. Behind her, Kono's was even greater, and the corbi sometimes joked about his silhouette drawing fire. So far that hadn't actually happened. Loga was too careful.

Finally, Loga's scanner showed him something agreeable, and he gestured them up and forward. Trace rose, tugged on the floppy hat she'd adopted complete with leaves and twigs for camouflage, and walked carefully in the footsteps of the corbi before her — not always a simple task, given the greater length of her stride. Often she walked one step for the corbis' every two. Just as often, corbi would move on all fours, having the short legs and long arms to do that when they needed speed.

Loga took them diagonally downhill, weaving between tall trunks and over complicated root systems, and Trace marvelled at how good her night vision had become over the past three months. Feina helped, Rando's smaller moon orbited quickly and shone dull silver, lighting trunks and leaves to a patchwork of bright and dark. Dogba was larger, further out and thus orbited much more slowly, currently positioned to rise mostly during Rando's day. When both moons were in the sky together, Resistance fighters had to be extra careful moving around.

Mostly Trace watched for animals in the treetops, her vision being somewhat better at than that the corbi — more a function of her marine augments than any native human superiority. Most of those animals were harmless, but a large proportion were in some way 'kauda', or 'changed', as the corbi said. Most of those changes were of no consequence to a team of armed corbi Resistance moving through the forest, but a small number were a serious threat to anyone outside of full marine armour. The past months had been the longest period Trace had been without seeing the inside of a marine armour suit since she'd joined.

Passing through some thicker undergrowth, the corbi ahead of her sniffed the air. There were so many scents in the forest, and corbi's sense of smell was definitely better than human. This scent was somewhere between that of the big blue flower clusters she'd not learned the names for, and the moss that grew on fallen logs. Having spent so much of her recent life on spaceships and stations, Trace was still getting used to it. Despite all its deprivations, dangers, and the frustrations of being separated from her ship, crew and most of all her Company, she was finding the experience to have its upsides. She'd loved the outdoors when she was a girl, despite so much of that outdoors being the forbidding grey mountains of Sugauli. Now, this unlooked for detour, in a far reach of alien space, sometimes felt to her like some kind of homecoming.

Ahead through the trees she glimpsed vertical shelves of rock emerging from the forest. Loga's course was taking them to the base of those vertical faces... perhaps there were caves there. Loga glanced repeatedly at his scanner — a small hand unit that he covered with a cloth to peer beneath every few minutes. The cloth was probably unnecessary, for the screen glow was minimal, but Trace appreciated the Resistance's meticulous habits. She had an identical hand unit herself, but any operating electrical signal presented a faint risk given the reeh's constant monitoring. One operating electrical unit per team, the corbi had determined by long experience, was usually safe. It did mean that Trace's usual minimum of operational equipment — augmented reality glasses with interactive armscomp tracking — were out of the question. Even her timepiece was mechanical — a corbi wristwatch that looked suspiciously old, an antique dug from the wreckage of some long-dead corbi city, a gift to her from a corbi civilian.

Satellite and radar monitoring were a larger concern. Trace knew from her Fleet experience that establishing full ground and atmospheric visual and radar coverage was much harder than it seemed, whatever the level of technology. Visual scanning alone could not penetrate clouds, which over this part of Rando were plentiful. Also, low-orbiting satellites had the best visuals because their range was less, but low-orbiting satellites moved at orbital velocity — in Rando's case, a touch over twenty-four thousand kilometres an hour, and would be over a target area for only a few minutes at a time. Geostationary satellites were constant, of course, but geostationary orbits were very high and thus their resolution worse, even with reeh-level tech. If the satellite knew what it was looking for it could probably count hairs on a corbi head... but looking down from thirty-three thousand kilometres, across an entire hemisphere of planet, and trying to spot the movement of a few corbi beneath heavy forest canopies at night was a technological leap too far even for the reeh, whatever the cloud cover.

Those threats weren't what Loga's hand unit was for, however. It was for the pulse-scanners, the reeh's in-atmosphere electro-mag active scans that even the top corbi scientists weren't completely sure the working of. They did know that a simple passive scanner, like the one in Loga's hand, could detect when those were active, and that it was best not to move, talk, or breathe too loudly when they were. Those pulse-scanners were mostly mounted on high-altitude drones, and were thus vulnerable to ground-based hacking, jamming or weapons... all of which would give away the position of the person doing the hacking, jamming or shooting. The Resistance could thus destroy those systems and gain a blindspot in operations for a short period when needed, at the potential cost of whatever units they used to achieve it. Those units were valuable, and mostly the corbi left the pulse-scanners alone until they did something big... like rescuing an alien marine commander from a reeh transport shuttle that a corbi stealth ship had brought down trans-atmospheric on its way to the Rando splicer. When Trace considered what would likely have happened to her and Kono there, she was quite sure she'd have preferred that the shuttle were destroyed with her on it. Kono, she knew, felt the same.

That operation, however, had revealed something curious. For all the reeh's advanced technology, Rando Resistance could move flyers around at night without detection. Trace was a marine, not a technician, but she was certain there was no way to do this without directly hacking into the reeh's central surveillance systems, and fooling the reeh into thinking that their sensors saw nothing. It seemed impossible given the utter strategic dominance of the Reeh Empire on Rando, but Professor Romki had been of the opinion that corbi were uncommonly intelligent, and there was no telling what secrets the Resistance Fleet had accumulated in many dark operations against the reeh over the centuries, and what technology they'd stolen. Such as in the operation that had freed her and Kono, Resistance Fleet at times made fooling the reeh look amazingly simple. It was one of many reasons why relations between Rando Resistance and Fleet were frequently poor. Many times it seemed to the ground-dwellers that their spacefaring cousins weren't doing nearly as much to help in the effort as they could be... almost as though their hearts weren't truly in it.

The vertical rock faces Trace had seen did indeed mark the location of caves. Trace could see the dark opening of one beyond the thick undergrowth as they approached, past mostly-invisible sentries who seemed already well aware of their approach. There were no whistles or calls, just hand-signals, and Trace took a moment walking to look about and consider the approaches up the slope as they climbed to the cave mouth. Behind Kono, Pena saw her looking. Trace pointed two fingers at her eyes, then pointed about the approaches. Pena gestured 'yes', and Trace indicated left to Kono, then left the trail with Kono, Pena and two other corbi behind.

Pena was pale-furred and liked to read. She was a local, born not far from here, living as most corbi lived, in small farming settlements in the wilderness whose productivity was always limited by the need not to draw undue attention. Pena was good with books and children, and thus had thought perhaps to be a teacher... but it was hard to be a thoughtful corbi on Rando and not consider the plight of the people, and dream of a life without the reeh. Pena had been assigned to the humans' escort by Loga from the beginning to impart and gather information, and was always interested to see what Trace thought of corbi military deployments, and the way defences were arranged around settlements like this one. Whatever Trace's human rank, not all corbi were as enthusiastic to know what she thought. A UF marine major's insignia counted for very little on Rando.

Trace and Kono took another fifteen minutes to check the defensive deployments around this cave mouth and the next adjoining, seeing the motion sensors, the flare and mine traps, and noting the sentries' overlapping fields of fire. Then they returned with Pena and the other corbi into the main cave, to be greeted by the smell of cooking from deeper within.

Wicker baskets were stacked by the entrance — grain stores, Trace recognised, as corbi villagers would hide surplus food in case some passing reeh patrol decided to firebomb their crops. And sometimes there was the weather, or pests, or any number of other crop-destroying problems that a people as once-advanced as the corbi should not have had to be concerning themselves with.

In the deep cave, Loga's soldiers had joined with some others about a campfire, shrugging off light gear, refilling flasks and taking bowls of the stew that boiled in an old pot above the flames. Trace demanded to be shown the other exits first, which she knew must exist by the Resistance's own operating procedures. And so one of the locals rolled grumpily to his feet and led them deeper into the narrowing cave, through increasingly tight openings until it joined a larger cavern on its way to the second entrance Trace had seen from outside.

Trace didn't like it, but like all things on Rando, it was what it was. She headed back to the campfire, where corbi offered them food and water, which the humans gratefully accepted but did not touch until they'd cleaned their weapons and checked all their kit for damage or dirt in the night's activities. The corbi ate, giving bemused glances their way, long manes and beards askew, long arms on short knees in that gangly, top-heavy way of all seated corbi. Finally finished, Trace and Kono sat crosslegged — more of an effort for the big Staff Sergeant than his Major — and ate their stew.

"Where tomorrow?" Trace asked Loga in Lisha. Many languages were still spoken on Rando, but the Resistance had had to settle on one for convenience, and Lisha was the most widespread. As in so many things, the similarities with the old tales of humanity on krim-occupied Earth were eerie.

"Tomorrow stay here," said Loga, with more attention to his food than to her. "Too much moving, dangerous. Then Alsona."

Trace frowned. "We saw Alsona. One month ago." Alsona had been a dead city. One of many, from back when Rando was a free world teeming with corbi civilisation. Its overgrown ruins had been somberly instructive, but not on any matter Trace truly wanted to learn.

"We see Alsona again," said Loga, unimpressed. Trace ate, collecting the words in her head that she'd need to form a more complex sentence. It helped that she was natively bilingual — on Sugauli, in addition to English most people spoke Nepali, Hindi or Urdu, with a smattering of Tibetan, Bengali and a few others. Speaking two languages as a kid wasn't quite the same as learning a new one for the first time as an adult, but she'd astonished herself with how good she'd become in such a short time, mostly because of her total immersion and insistence, during those first months, on talking and learning as often as possible. So long as no more than one person was talking, and the conversation was focused on something familiar to her — like military tactics — she was now becoming quite conversational. Erik had often expressed dismay with her studied disinterest in non-military things, saying she was far smarter than she gave herself credit for, and that knowledge of such things could actually improve her performance as an officer. Trace had disagreed, but now found herself speaking an alien tongue as a matter of military necessity. Erik, she was certain, would not miss the chance to say 'I told you so'.

"We don't want to see more ruins," Trace told Loga. "We need to see useful things."

"This is useful," said Loga, still eating. "Other places are dangerous. You go where you're told."

"Listen," said Trace with a raised voice. Not that she was anywhere near losing her temper, but sometimes the corbi mistook professional cool for a lack of intensity. Sometimes, among these civilians, intensity got better results. "You want a senior human officer to see how corbi live on Rando. You want us to see why reeh are dangerous, so we can tell humans back home. But you don't let us see any reeh. Only corbi, and corbi ruins."

"You see reeh, you die," Loga told her, still not looking. "You want to see reeh, you talk to corbi." He pointed around the campfire, at wary, somber Resistance soldiers. The drawn, impassive faces of people who'd seen too much. "We've seen enough reeh for you both." He took a mouthful of water. "Too damn much reeh, all of my life."

"I want to see Messa," said Trace.

Loga's big dark eyes flicked to her for the first time. "No. No

Messa." Messa had been hit by the reeh a week ago. Neither Trace nor Kono had heard of it before that, but now the corbi talked of it, and Trace suspected it had been hosting some significant level of Resistance activity before the strike. Some sight of the damage, or the casualties, could have told her a lot about reeh operations. "You can talk to some survivors. We'll bring some to you."

"Survivors aren't reliable," said Trace. "I want to see it for myself."

Loga snorted and returned to eating. Several moments later, Trace realised she wasn't going to receive a reply. Kono gave her a brooding look above his bowl. Trace kept expression off her face, and ate. Being Kulina, she'd grown up thinking that emotional control was something all people learned. Upon leaving Sugauli for Homeworld and the Academy, she'd been astonished by the degree to which most non-Kulina seemed to struggle with it. Most of Phoenix Company looked to her as a kind of touchstone, to assure themselves that the Major wasn't bothered, and therefore they shouldn't be either. Unlike some aspects of command, it wasn't a responsibility she found particularly taxing.

Upon cleaning her bowl with bits of bread, and somewhat enjoying the chewy, rice-like desert the corbi passed around afterward, she took a stick from the firewood pile, produced her big kukri blade from its thigh-sheath, and began whittling. Corbi watched with mild interest, mostly to see the odd-shaped, angled knife, which to them was nearly the size of a short-sword. Kono produced the pistol he'd acquired from Resistance spares — a real antique, entirely mechanical without a single electrical component. He then took out a rag, and began disassembling it to clean piece by meticulous piece.

"Useful?" he asked cryptically when Trace's stick had shortened by half, and bits of stick fragments scattered about her boots.

"Never know when you'll need a sharp stick, Giddy," Trace told him.

"You think reeh have a sense of humour?" Kono replied. Kono's own sense of humour was often obtuse. Trace had learned not to take it literally. Gideon Kono was from a working class spacer family — Freetown Station, Toralka System. His parents worked freight and maintenance, hands always dirty but paid well enough despite the lack of suits and ties. Some in his family had associations with workers' unions — all illegal under the commerce laws, and friendless in Spacer Congress despite some support among voters, for the simple reason that Fleet hated unions and would never tolerate them.

That hard-nosed union crowd weren't fond of Fleet either, Trace knew, and Kono admitted his parents had been upset with him for joining the marines. Exactly how that conflict had played out, Kono hadn't said, and Trace hadn't pressed. But she suspected a large chunk of Kono's hard-bitten cynicism came from being raised in a small community that didn't like Fleet, among a larger community that adored them with a patriotic passion. Given that Kono had joined, and become one of the best marines Trace had ever served with, it was obvious which side of that divide he'd come down on.

Yet Kono's cynicism had not spared the marines either — not their culture, nor their methods of promotion, nor their methods of fighting. He'd served on the *UFS Rukio* as a private for three years, and met with commanders who disliked his perceived lack of esprit de corps. Then a friend of his had been transferred to *Phoenix* and recommended the under-appreciated Kono to Lieutenant Dale, one of whose duties as Company XO was to watch out for elite recruits to poach from other units. Most units had to make do with whoever was assigned to them, but for Phoenix Company, exceptions were made.

Five years later, Kono was a Staff Sergeant commanding the single most prestigious unit below platoon-size in the Company. Under Trace's leadership, marines who questioned were valued highly — so long as they could also provide answers. She'd picked him for Command Squad after the legendary Master Sergeant Willis had been killed fighting hacksaws in Argitori. Some others might have been bothered by the responsibility of filling such enormous boots, but Kono had approached it like he approached everything — with hardass seriousness combined with wry skepticism of any claim as to why he should be worried. But the thing she valued about him most was that whatever her outsized reputation, Kono had never put away his own opinions and replaced them with her's. Now, more than ever, she welcomed it.

"Krim had a sense of humour," she told him now.

"No shit?"

"It consisted of the ritual humiliation of any individual who stepped out of line. Krim found non-conformity funny. It was the strangest thing they knew."

"Followed by them killing that person in an amusing way?" Kono guessed.

"Pretty much." She whittled some more pieces, getting the weight and action right through her wrist. At her side, Pena came and sat, indicating the kukri and stick. Trace smiled and handed her both. Their hands touched, short-fingered human and long-fingered corbi, and Trace took the paper note Pena passed in her fingers, unseen by others. Pena then began whittling, with the reasonable skill of someone who'd tried the kukri before.

Trace rummaged in her pack for some imaginary object, glancing at the paper with her hands in the bag. It was a simple numerical code — Lisha numbers, of course. The override code to the perimeter defences. Trace had explained to Pena over the past three months how it all worked, what the Resistance were doing right and wrong in their defensive setups, and what would likely happen if they were attacked. Most corbi hadn't listened, saying that they'd done it this way for generations, and what would an alien know about this warfare anyway, however highly ranked among her own people? But Pena had listened, and had seen enough action to become increasingly convinced that Trace was right.

"That's great, Pen," said Kono, watching the corbi whittle. "You'll kill lots of reeh with that."

Pena grinned with those wide corbi lips. "Scared?" she suggested, one of her small collection of English words.

"Terrified."

In Trace's bag, something buzzed. A query, perhaps, from a tiny mechanical mind... or a warning, to remind her it was there. It crawled on Trace's spare socks, looking for all the world like a simply flying insect, but in the dancing glow of firelight reflecting off the rock ceiling, its wings glowed with silver filament that could only be synthetic.

Trace had no idea how it had stowed away, save that it had appeared her first night with the Resistance, after she and Kono had been rescued from the Splicer-bound shuttle, and had hung around ever since. Trace suspected that Styx had planted it on her armour suit before the Zondi Splicer operation, and it had stayed with her after she'd been incapacitated and captured. As always with Styx, Trace found her plotting both impressive and alarming.

The past three months, the bug had remained hidden from all others save Kono. It generally found somewhere in the sunlight to recharge during the day while the humans slept. Exactly what its programming parameters were, Trace did not know, but suspected would involve sentry duty, protection and possibly some technological assistance or translation. Which would be nice, Trace thought, if they actually had some military technology on the scale she was used to.

"Major," said Pena when Trace returned her attention to the fire. "When the Resistance sends you back to *Phoenix*. What will you tell your humans, when you get home?"

"I'll tell them the corbi deserve help, Pena."

"Will they send help?"

"No," said Trace. "But *Phoenix* is talking to the croma leaders." She'd had word from *Phoenix*, via the Resistance Fleet. No direct messages, Fleet wouldn't allow it, but she knew they were in orbit around Dul'rho, the croma's current capital world, and that there was a contest of leadership going on to replace the current Croma'Rai clan. "That means croma and humans might soon be talking to each other. If we're talking, we'll talk about the corbi. That's all I can offer."

Pena kept whittling, the firelight reflecting in her wire-rim spectacles. "That's okay. We try. Corbi have been asking for friends for a long time. But no one comes."

There had been a kinamor on the shuttle Trace and Kono had been on. An odd-looking alien with a beaked face, something Trace had never seen before. They came from a distant region not yet captured by the reeh, and word among the Resistance was that this one might have been visiting the croma, talking about a common cause, only to be intercepted and captured by the reeh on his way home. He was now doing what Trace was — being given the tour of Rando, seeing the corbi's dire situation for himself, in the hope that he'd take the experience home with him, and send help.

Trace didn't think it likely. All civilisations had their own problems, and only came to the aid of those who could offer a similar benefit in return. The corbi were tiny, their numbers small, their strategic situation hopeless, their once-firm allies the croma having long since turned their backs. Helping them would bring no benefit to kinamor, nor to humans.

Trace did not lie. She certainly intended to tell the human Fleet's high command that the corbi deserved help. But so many people in the Spiral and beyond deserved things that they would never receive.

* * *

TRACE AWOKE TO SOMETHING BUZZING IN HER EAR. SHE REFRAINED from slapping her cheek to kill the offending insect. It landed before her eyes, on bundled cloth over her backpack that made a rough pillow. Three times previously the bug had done this. Two of those times had amounted to nothing, but one afternoon when the camp was breaking, someone had found large paw-prints nearby, where something unnaturally large and thankfully cautious had checked out the campsite. Trace thought it possible that the other two times, the bug had been warning her of something nearby as well. Something up a tree, that hadn't left prints.

Trace blinked her eyes wide, and refocused on the cave. Smoke from the extinguished fire smelled sweet in her nostrils. The sun had not yet risen... the night insects were keening and chirping from the outside forest, soon to be silenced by the first glow of dawn.

Opposite her, beside a rock ledge on the cave floor, Kono slept on some straw mats and a blanket. They'd slept on worse in the past three months, and on better. Hospitality in some of the villages had been charming, the food pleasant and the mattresses comfortable. At other villages, sullen hostility, wishing the Resistance would go away and stop risking reeh attention.

The remaining glow from the fire turned the cave ceiling a dull orange. It would make the cave entrance glow as well in the night, but only a little, as the fires were well back from the mouth. The foliage outside the cave entrance was thick, doubtless from generations of local corbi planting the largest, most obscuring trees they could, to hide the entrance from high altitude surveillance.

By the entrance, Trace's eyes rested on a ceiling feature, dark and clinging. Almost like a figure. The figure moved.

Trace's eyes widened. The figure kept moving, upside down across the ceiling. Dangling from the rock formations, like a giant black lizard in search of moths. Human sized, she judged. Larger than corbi, certainly. It had bypassed the security outside, and now avoided detection from sleepy sentries awaiting the dawn. If the sentries were still alive.

Her heart tried to thump with alarm, but already her breathing was long and slow, with focused concentration. She had to get this right. This was the advance scout, to see the positions of corbi in the cave, and relay it to those waiting outside. The outside forces would be primed to move at a moment's notice. As soon as she acted, they would. She had to make that first action decisive.

Behind the dark figure, several more crawled. They'd incapacitated some sentries at least, Trace thought. The Resistance weren't professional to marine-level, but neither were they lazy or stupid. If all the sentries were awake, one would have spotted these by now. Probably the attackers knew the higher-ranking targets would be further back in the cave. Perhaps her first move would trigger grenades or missiles, in which case they were all dead in this enclosed space, but Trace didn't think so. Reeh always preferred prisoners, particularly high-ranking prisoners.

Her hands moved, very slowly, toward the rifle by her side, its muzzle resting on a pack to keep it and its mechanism off the dirt floor. She could have put it butt-down against the rock shelf, as was usual procedure, but she'd decided three months ago that anything out of immediate reach was trouble in situations like this one. She had three grenades in her pack's side pockets, from surplus weapons the corbi had let her select from. Two were frags, the other was phosphorus. She reached for the phosphorus now, not raising her head.

These scouts would be using night vision, the only way they could be guaranteed to spot targets about the cave floor, and rank them by priority. She took a moment longer to visualise the cave's best cover from irregular rock shelves like the one she was lying behind, and the best undergrowth cover immediately beyond the cave mouth. Going next door to the neighbouring cave would be useless, she was fairly sure — the approaches there were easier than this one. If the scouts were already inside here, they'd be moreso next door. That cave would fall quickly, leaving the adjoining passage not as an escape, but as a means of threatening their rear and surrounding them. So. As she saw it, there was only one thing to do, and it could not wait.

Beneath the old blanket, her hands deposited the two frags in pockets, then held the phosphorus. The rifle's magazine bundle went into one oversized thigh pocket — there was no time to put on the webbing she'd improvised from smaller corbi versions. The pistol that had lain at her side beneath the blanket now slid into her opposite pocket, where a smaller magazine bundle already resided, not so large that it was impossible to sleep with, or she'd have done it with the other items. Being armed at all times was important, but so was sleep.

Finally ready, she took the rifle, still lying on her side, and slowly swivelled it toward one of the inverted, crawling figures. It stopped, and looked straight at her with glistening insectoid eyes that might have been organic or synthetic overlays. That made her decision easy.

Trace pulled the trigger, was jolted awkwardly by the recoil in that unbraced position, barely aware that the shot split the air with deafening sound within the cave walls, so focused was she on her next target as the first fell from the ceiling like a swatted roach. Two more shots, and the second fell as well. She rolled to a fast crouch as corbi came frightened awake about her, primed and lobbed the grenade, yelling 'AMBUSH!' mostly so that her startled Staff Sergeant would at least know that she was on it and moving.

High-powered shots came her way, smacking off the rock shelf as she covered, Kono rolling for his weapons as more shots hit the cave wall and corbi leaping upright there went spinning in bloody spatters. Then the phosphorus grenade erupted with a blinding flash of perfect whiteness, and that shooting stopped.

Trace got up and went, not running, just shuffling at a fast crouch and squinting desperately past the fountain of brilliance on the cave floor amid piled Resistance gear, catching things on fire even now. The dark, spidery figures were covering their faces rather than shooting, as she'd expected, so she shot the first two in their exposed heads, dropped low as the last sprayed fire across her general direction, missing wildly. Trace got up and placed a bullet through his face that snapped his head back. Even now she could heard the distant eruption of fire from the neighbouring cave, mostly echoing through the rear 'escape' passage.

"Giddy!" she yelled, covering in the pre-visualised spot against the wall. "Five down in here! Watch that rear passage, the second cave is falling and they'll be hitting our rear any moment!"

"Aye Major, I'm on it!" he bellowed back, already armed and moving to better cover from which to guard their rear. Corbi from neighbouring campfires were now up, running and shouting in fear and confusion, shielding their eyes against the phosphorus glare and searching for weapons and friends in the chaos. Some saw the dead black figures on the floor, and gave yells of either rage or defiance, and ran toward the cave entrance, brandishing weapons.

"No!" Trace yelled at them. "Get the fuck down!" And tried to remember how to say it in Lisha, but fire tore into the cave before she could, and corbi fell in a bloody tangle of limbs. "Maju!" Trace yelled again, remembering the word for 'down'. "Maju! Here, you, get right on my ass! Here, here!" As she pointed with violent intensity to surviving corbi, who scampered all fours toward that oasis of order and command in English or Lisha. "Stay against the wall, stay low!"

She wove forward in a crouch as the phosphorus sputtered and faded... there were more raised, rocky shelves here against the right side of the cave, and if she stayed low enough the white light would not cast her shadow against the wall for outside gunners to find. From the cave rear came the loud echo of shooting, and Kono's unmistakable bellow, trying to get less-trained corbi to do something useful. Beside the stacked grain baskets by the entrance wall Trace found a dead sentry, propped as though sitting, lifeless eyes staring at the night. In one hand he held an electronic trigger, a simple plastic handle with some buttons on it, sophisticated to the level of a children's electronics class, but thus unhackable and unjamable by the reeh.

She took the trigger, gestured with her left arm for the corbi behind to deploy behind the rocky cover, propping herself against a grain basket and keeping her head down, listening to the shooting behind and the occasional burst from outside, trying to get a sense of where the enemy was without looking.

"Maju!" she growled as several corbi thought to stick their heads up. One ignored her, and immediately got it shot off. Night vision was working once more as the phosphorus went out, and the attackers had the entrance covered. There were tripwires and anti-personnel mines outside, but no sentries with triggers left alive — precisely as she'd told Pena would happen if an ambush occurred.

She input Pena's code into the device from memory — the trigger worked by a simple high-powered radio transmission, and the code input was to prevent friend or foe from simulating the code and detonating the mines on purpose or by accident. Jamming the signal would give the attackers' presence away — Trace had immediately concluded that if she were the attacker, she'd use stealth to eliminate the sentries instead.

The shooting from outside was moving closer. The attackers were inside the kill perimeter, thinking themselves safe. She hit the button, and huge explosions tore the night, and the crackle and fracture of a large tree falling. "Rinda!" Trace yelled, and her corbi opened fire into the night, a respectable thunder of automatic fire. Trace ran, along the entrance wall past the grain baskets, and dove into the foliage to the right of the cave mouth. There was smoke everywhere, flames crackling of foliage set alight, and her movement drew no fire, attackers covering from the unexpected explosions and volleys of counter-fire. Probably a few of them were dead, but that wasn't Trace's main objective — just distraction. She found a tree base and caught a glimpse of the neighbouring cave through smoke and leaves. There was fighting there, gunfire past the trees, now a grenade explosion... so the neighbouring corbi hadn't been completely wiped out, pockets at least were fighting back. That improved the chances tremendously.

She peered quickly around the tree trunk, found a dark figure coming past, looking dazed from recent explosions. A rifle round could have given away her position before she was ready, so she shouldered the rifle, pulled the kukri, slithered low and came up fast behind, anchored the armoured head with her left arm and slashed the neck with the blade. Its head came mostly away, dark blood spurting, and she dropped before anyone saw. And took a moment to examine the attacker's black, segmented armour, integrated like some kind of organic shell. One of the slave-species, as she'd thought — not reeh, not really anything any longer, just a mindless drone programmed for savagery. Their combat instincts were good, the corbi said, but their tactics often fell apart when pressured or reversed. Trace had fought against that before with the sard.

She slithered downslope as the smoke from the mines cleared a little, crawled past one confused alien who didn't look her way as she burrowed into some ferns and waited. The alien stomped upslope, no doubt communicating on silent radios, going to investigate the explosions... and now, she reckoned, judging her position on the slope, and how the assault was pressing uphill with a recommencement of rifle fire, she was behind the lot of them.

Trace cut left, keeping low, and soon found a pair of them, covering amid trees and having no idea they were outflanked. She shot them both and moved quickly on. Thirteen rounds expended. They were all making too much noise with their own heavy weapons to notice the relatively quiet, single shot of a corbi light assault rifle. Ten more metres and she found another good cover spot, this time with a good angle on an alien further upslope. She took a few seconds to align the shot on the back of its neck, fired, then moved on as it crumpled.

A few would get the idea now that something was wrong. Brainless drones could be smart in numbers, but if they were at all like the sard, they'd now start to get a little confused. Their formation was focused on one objective, and now an unpredictable variable popped up. Self-preservation was not a sard priority when primary objectives were still unobtained, and they'd struggle to process how many losses were required before their attention ought to shift. Her job now was to give them as many losses as possible, and here behind them, firing from a direction they were not covering against, the targets were relatively simple so long as she kept moving.

She got another three before some started to turn and look for her. So she refrained from shooting for another hundred metres, arcing upslope on their right-rear flank now, then getting a good angle before shooting another two in quick succession, then dropping and slithering back the other way as bursts of random, frustrated fire tore at tree trunks in the opposite direction to the cave.

Now they were stuck. Group tactics dictated they all gather around the cave mouth, some advancing in while others provided support fire. They'd moved in carefully and eliminated all sentries, so they knew there were no enemies behind them. Their formation depended on it. No one was supposed to slip through their net, but now that one had, and was using the trees for cover in the dim light of a single moon, they'd have to devote a large portion of their force to finding her. A portion they could not afford to devote, with an armed force of corbi still at the front, in the cover of a cave.

If this force was using top-cover, Trace knew she'd shortly be dead from a high-altitude missile tracking her plainly visible IR signature among the trees. But reeh weren't the only ones with detection capabilities, and flying machines circling corbi bases tended to give the game away at any altitude. Reeh counter-infiltration teams typically went in dark and silent for complete surprise, at the cost of air support if it all went wrong. Or at least, air support for the next fifteen minutes or so. She'd have to move fast.

But now she could hear shooting from the second cave mouth, bursts of increasingly heavy fire that scattered downslope and hit trunks dangerously close to her head as she crawled and slithered. That was corbi fire, not enemy. Corbi had fought their way out of the second cave, no doubt finding their opposing numbers dwindled as more enemy had displaced to reinforce the main cave. And now the enemy were outflanked on two sides.

Trace simply sat where she was, in the best available cover in a hollow downslope of a tree, as the enemy forces retreated past her at speed. So they *did* value their lives, to some degree at least. She could have taken a few more down as they passed, but it served no purpose now — killing reeh and reeh-allies on Rando was like plucking single blades of grass from a savannah. To do any good here, a marine had to risk her life for more than defiant gestures.

"Major!" she heard then. Kono's voice, calling downslope. "Come up, I've told them you're down there, they won't fire!"

"Coming out!" Trace replied, pulling herself out of her hollow and climbing back up the slope, looking carefully around for any stragglers. Corbi were in full commotion when she reached the top, collecting gear, laying out bodies, cutting useful parts from dead alien armour and weapons. The grain stores about the mouth of the main cave were a mess, spilled grain in mounds, stained with the blood of dead corbi. Many were in tears, but all were moving, save for a number of wounded being treated by those with expertise. The air smelled of shock, fear and explosive residue. Within the mouth of the cave, Trace glimpsed Lago, cradling a bloody arm and directing what remained of his forces to get their gear and prepare to move out.

Kono met her atop the slope, Pena at his side, one of her eye-glasses spattered with blood. She stared at Trace, as several did, pausing their preparations as she approached her old friend.

"You came out through the second cave?" Trace asked him.

Kono nodded grimly, checking his still-unfamiliar rifle. "Damn thing tried to jam on me twice," he explained. "Yeah, I took a few through the rear passage and into the next cave." He indicated Pena. "There wasn't much defending it, they'd all left. You get out behind them?"

"Yep," said Trace. "Fixed formations in a forest don't like it." She indicated his weapon, identical to her's. "That thing's a rifle, not an automatic. Won't jam if you treat it like one."

"You need another mag?" Kono offered, reaching for one of his own.

"Nope, only fired twenty-five rounds."

"How many you get?"

"Fifteen, I think, more with the mines." Kono did not look surprised. "Let's get our gear and go, there'll be an airstrike coming."

Kono shook his head, striding with her into the cave, past the rowed bodies of corbi who'd just minutes before been their comrades. "Pena says they've activated distress protocol, reeh likely won't risk it."

Trace recalled Loga telling them about the distress protocols — Resistance had various hidden anti-air weapons and some quite nasty electrical jammers that could seriously jeopardise incoming airpower. If one unit sent out a distress squawk, all the others would activate their protocols. Reeh would go in hard if they really wanted to, but this was just a small action, really — a minor strike against a troublesome insurgent hideout, reeh did dozens of them every night across Rando. And the reeh had lost only slaves to do it.

"Depends if they guess it was us," Trace replied, sidestepping corbi in commotion. "We'll assume that they do, reports will reach reeh command at some point, they'll put two and two together. We have to move fast before they encircle and pin us down."

"Might have to wait until tomorrow," Kono said grimly. "The sun's coming up."

She and Kono collected backpacks, webbing and other gear, then proceeded to the entrance. Pena had found the bodies of several friends among the rows of fallen arranged on the cave floor, and was now sobbing with several others, long, pale-furred arms about herself as she rocked back and forth. The shrieks of distressed corbi off the cave ceiling was no improvement on gunfire, and was the most alien Trace had heard these otherwise familiar people sound.

"If they don't move in two minutes, we're going," she told Kono, checking her old wristwatch. "They nearly got us killed with a poor perimeter defence, I won't let it happen again because they're too slow to displace under pressure."

Kono was looking at the suffering corbi, evidently feeling something from the way he seemed reluctant to follow her out of the cave. Several corbi in distressed conversation were looking their way, with hand gesticulations that suggested they were piecing together what had just happened. And well that they should — Kono had led one attack through the neighbouring cave, and Trace had outflanked the main force and killed a quarter of it, while the corbi leaders had done sweet fuck-all once again. They'd insisted not to take her expertise seriously, and Trace was damned if she was going to invest great emotional distractions in their resulting plight.

"Major," Kono attempted. "We could at least help with a few of their wounded..."

"Neither of us know much on corbi physiology," Trace said shortly. Out in the dawn, she checked her rifle once more, then scanned the brightening horizon past the thinning smoke. "They've got plenty of first aid. We're the only elite fighters here, we can't waste our time playing nurse."

"Yes Major." He didn't like it. Trace swallowed her exasperation that so many of Phoenix Company's biggest, fiercest warriors weren't half as tough as they pretended. Part of her wished Lieutenant Dale were here, despite knowing he was needed elsewhere.

Loga came over, a three-limbed walk with one arm bandaged, face etched with pain. "Four shuda," he told them in Lisha... that was about two-and-a-half minutes, Trace translated.

"Fine," she said, not willing to pick another fight over a lost thirty seconds. Down the hill, amid fallen trees and broken foliage where the mines had gone off, a corbi soldier had found one of their attackers still alive, and unshouldered his rifle. "No!"

She ran downhill, drawing the corbi's attention. "No, don't shoot." She stopped alongside, examining the alien's black armour, shredded on one side where shrapnel had torn through, armour bent and buckled from the blast. Probably it was keeping its occupant alive, though. Not especially large, she noted now — some kind of claw/suction appendage on the gloves that would allow them to climb trees, or move inverted along the ceilings of caves. Obviously all that armour was light-weight or they'd never have managed it. "Giddy! Get down here, I've got another load for you."

He was already on his way down, predictably unenthusiastic. "We can't afford to waste combat power helping corbi injured," he said sarcastically, "but I have to waste mine carrying this slimy fucker?"

"Yes," said Trace, doing calculations in her head about terrain, distances and difficulties a man Kono's size would have with the load.

"He'll have a tracker in that armour," said Kono, shouldering his rifle in preparation of slinging the half-dead alien over the opposite shoulder.

"It's in the helmet," said Trace. "That tech back in Tupogi said so, showed me a captured helmet. Get it off first. I want to know more about these guys."

3

Erik piloted the cruiser toward the tower side, holding within the moving box outlined by Cal'Uta traffic control on the windshield's holographic display. This particular Cal'Uta building was more ziggurat than tower, as were many buildings in croma cities. It made a gigantic presence in the urban night, irregular sides sloping like those of a pyramid toward a point that never arrived, but rather ended short in a vast, flat rooftop.

The apartments on the sloping wall ahead were enormous, comfortably four times the size of a standard human-height apartment, with parking for airborne vehicles on the balconies. Erik turned to an angle, knowing the cruiser would accelerate faster forward than backward, and wanting to give them a headstart if a rapid getaway proved necessary. The massive windows reflected a mirror-image of the cruiser as they landed, a flash of running lights against the towers behind.

They touched down, and Erik put on his AR glasses, linked the cruiser's navcomp to visual settings and powered down the engines. Doors hummed upward, filling the interior with city sounds and cool night air.

"Perimeter and watch, people," said Lieutenant Jalawi, as the marines climbed first from the cruiser. "Doesn't seem to be anyone here, Captain."

"Guess we'll find out, Lieutenant." Erik did a final check of the cruiser's nav, and found their region of sky clear of suspicious activity. He got out, as Ensign Jokono climbed from the shotgun seat, and it was a disconcerting climb down from the high chair to the pad below. Operating croma vehicles made even a tall human feel like a child struggling through the world of adults. Luckily the cruiser had no pedals, just hand controls, or he'd have been forced to tie blocks to his boots to reach them.

He leaned back into the cruiser to collect his helmet off the floor, clipped it to the back of his armour, and looked about. The side of the ziggurat loomed like a giant cliff at a leaning angle, broken by great balconies, landing pads and even the occasional swimming pool. Croma weren't really made for swimming, but they did enjoy it, the way that all large creatures might enjoy a chance to float and rest. A cruiser took off from several floors above, a howl and whine of heavy engines and a glare of running lights, now fading. That was a big one, twice the size of their own. Croma vehicles came in different sizes, with humans taking the smallest version. The big ones were for elder croma, travelling usually as passengers, having lost much of the fine motor control that made safe pilots... and the ability to fit in the pilot's seat.

Jalawi advanced first, his marines spread wide, watching the city. Erik glanced at Jokono, and found the older man gazing about at the looming bulk of neighbouring ziggurats, and the taller, narrower towers beyond. Cal'Uta was not an enormous city by Spiral standards, but with a population of eight million, it was large enough. Air traffic zoomed ponderously overhead, turning in lines like overweight bumblebees, and from far below came the sound of the streets, traffic and music, a thunder of heavy croma drums.

Jokono took a deep breath, as though tasting the air. "You know, Captain," he said. "For all the awful things I've seen on this trip, I don't think I've ever thanked you for letting me see all of these incredible places. This truly has been the journey of a lifetime."

"No need to thank me, Joker," said Erik. "The galaxy is both terri-fying and wonderful."

"Captain," came Styx's voice on coms, *"my analysis of the surrounding traffic network shows no threat detectable at present."*

"Thank you Styx, stay on it."

"Yes Captain."

Styx was up on *Phoenix*, currently on the far side of the Croma'Rai capital world of Dul'rho, but hooked into the planetary communica-tion network as though she were right next door. No doubt the croma would have been alarmed had they known the extent of her access, but right now the croma were entirely preoccupied with the biggest political upheaval to strike croma space in several centuries.

Jalawi approached his own reflection on the glass wall, and touched the lighted panel. It flashed blue (the croma equivalent of green for humans) and slid soundlessly aside. Jalawi glanced back at Erik, shaved head gleaming in the city lights. Erik gestured him on, and Jalawi went, Private Lewis at his side, rifles pointed at the floor in standard carry position, index fingers against the trigger guard. The croma had insisted only that downworld *Phoenix* crew refrain from full armour. Light armour and weapons, the croma had no issue with — partly the gesture of a good host, partly the respect croma afforded true warriors, and partly an admission that nowhere on Dul'rho was entirely safe for humans right now. But croma were too libertarian to babysit visitors, and so *Phoenix* crew were presently free to wander, within some constraints, under what Styx informed them was the unending surveillance of various arms-length authorities.

Erik and Jokono went in next, in light armour with sidearms holstered and rifles slung, then Master Sergeant Hoon and Private Melidu, walking in backward to keep eyes on their rear. About them was an apartment for a giant. Before the windows, a bath tub large enough for a tall human to drown in, and beside that a reclining chair of the same scale. Positioned to catch the morning sunlight, Erik thought, orienting himself to east and west. Beyond that, across a vast, marble-like floor were large sofas and holographic projectors descending from the ceiling. The kitchen, Erik thought as he strolled, would be out of sight behind those big double doors. The apartment was clearly for a senior, elder croma, and elder croma had servants to prepare most things for them, food included.

There was a mismatch, in fact, between the number of older croma and younger croma, the latter outnumbering the former by a far larger number than should have been the case. Erik had not heard a convincing explanation for the disparity, as the croma wouldn't talk about it, and their information networks were remarkably free of answers to the question. Romki had his suspicions, however.

"Search the rest of it, Captain?" Jalawi asked.

"No, we've only been invited to visit," said Erik. "Let's not presume too much." Sergeant Hoon put his back to an entrance corridor wall with a good view of the front door and the unexplored kitchen, while Lewis and Melidu deployed to the vast wings of the main room.

"Croma are usually punctual," said Jokono. "Let's give him several minutes. If he's not here by then, we can presume something's wrong."

Erik's glasses icon blinked, *Phoenix* was calling. *"Captain, this is Dufresne."*

"Go ahead, LC."

"Sir, our second source on this meeting checks out. This one is just as adamant as the last that Croma'Rai will try to kill you. I advise seriously reconsidering this meeting."

"Thank you Lieutenant Commander," Erik said calmly, "but I seem to recall already having this discussion with you."

"That was with regard to our first source on Croma'Rai's intentions, Captain. This is a new source, confirming the first source's validity."

"And this second source is also from the command hierarchy of Croma'Dokran?"

A slight pause. They both already knew the answer. *"Yes Captain."*

"Who have a vested interest in stopping this meeting, and will say anything to do it. Now unless you have any *new* information, I need my concentration here."

"Yes Captain. Phoenix out."

Erik kept his expression calm as he disconnected. All of the marines could hear him, and Jalawi was watching, reading his face. *Phoenix*'s command crew, namely LC Dufresne and Lieutenant Dale, had been trying to talk him out of this since they'd arrived in orbit around Dul'rho. *Phoenix*, Dufresne had said quite pointedly, was concerned entirely with humanity's survival. As hard as it was to accept, the corbi were a distraction, nothing more. And it was known that of the two contestants for the croma throne, one was vastly more displeased at the notion of croma warfighting policy becoming centred around the corbi than the other.

Lieutenant Dale agreed with LC Dufresne entirely, stating his opinion that it was what Major Thakur would support. *Phoenix* needed to see the Tali'san through to the end because she couldn't leave Dul'rho orbit without permission of the ruling croma, and as yet that ruler had not been determined. But picking a fight with one of the contestants in that Tali'san over the corbi was needlessly provocative given the stakes for humanity. Commander Draper, of course, ventured no firm opinion, as was his usual way on matters that required getting in between the stickler LC and his Captain.

Erik was getting sick of it to the point of temper. He tried to control it, but it was difficult, being stuck down on the planet while his ship was temporarily commanded by children, and a hardass replacement marine commander whom Erik had threatened to court martial and shoot following the Zondi Splicer engagement if he selectively interpreted one more direct order. On most things he was prepared to listen to disagreements from the crew, provided they followed procedure and explained themselves constructively. But on the corbi, he just wasn't interested.

A control on the apartment's front door turned blue, and light spilled as the door opened. The croma who entered was not especially tall for one, but loomed over the humans. Its long coat swept the polished floor as it approached, a pair of smaller-sized croma in tow, none of them apparently armed. Erik tested the translator icon on his glasses, and found it active as it connected to the new arrival.

"Kul'cha," said Erik, standing as tall as he could before the croma, hands behind his back and chest out. It was the stance that Romki had advised him on, despite Erik's concerns that croma would only laugh to see this little human trying to look big. For all that their size increased with age and seniority, shorter stature wasn't always a bad thing for croma. Young croma were valued not merely for being young, but for being dextrous, which gave them a highly active role doing all the mobile, fast-moving things that croma lost with age. Thus yes, a croma might show prejudice toward a human in expecting him to be less wise and intelligent, but that prejudice included an expectation of efficiency, speed and dynamism also. Which in this case, between humans and croma, Erik thought might be somewhat correct.

"Kul'cha," said the new arrival. Then spoke some more, in the snuffling, lisping grunts of the croma tongue. *"I am Pel'sar,"* spoke the translator in Erik's ear. *"I am an emissary of Croma'Rai. I speak for Gar'tul himself."*

"I am Captain Debogande," said Erik. "I command the *UFS Phoenix*, and I am the son of Alice Debogande of the great Debogande family."

'Clan', the croma's translator would call that. Croma were all about clan, which did not always mean 'family' in the genetic sense, but close enough. Family-plus-others, Romki called it — an extended network about a central core of parents and children.

There were nearly a hundred great croma clans, among millions of smaller ones. The great clans divided croma space between them, and traced their lineage

back millennia to times before croma even travelled in space. Now on Dul'rho, two of the great clans had entered a contest to decide which of them would rule all croma. One of those two was Croma'Rai, the current rulers, whose ancestral homeworld Dul'rho had become shortly after first settlement twenty thousand years ago. But Croma'Rai were now disgraced, having been found to have traded with the croma's mortal enemies, the reeh, in a period of economic difficulty two centuries ago, and to never having entirely relinquished those relations since.

Some had expected Croma'Rai's immediate collapse, but it had not happened. Croma'Rai were wealthy, and the roots of their power ran deep through croma society. Too many other clans had invested too much in their leadership to see it all crumble, and Erik had spoken with grim croma scholars who opined that croma politics that had once prided itself on being a meritocracy where the greatest would rise to the top, had instead become a mutually-dependent network of nepotism and back scratching. Worse, Croma'Rai had accumulated many secrets in their six hundred year reign. If those secrets were to emerge upon Croma'Rai's collapse, they'd likely bring many other clans down with them.

The opposition to Croma'Rai that arose in light of the new scandal was led by Croma'Dokran. But Croma'Dokran were unpopular in some quarters, known for having radical views, like engaging with outsiders, and hosting a small population of corbi refugees to remind all in croma space and beyond of the horrors that befell the corbi homeworld to this day.

After three months of enforced presence at the formal deliberations to determine if Croma'Rai would be challenged, the *UFS Phoenix* was now witness to the commencement of the first ever Tali'san on Dul'rho, and the first anywhere to determine the rulership of all croma in nearly two centuries. If Croma'Dokran won, *Phoenix*'s experts were quite sure, the interests of both *Phoenix* and humanity would be served. If Croma'Rai held on to power, neither would. But that did not mean that Erik could just ignore an invitation to talk, away from the prying eyes and expectations of an official meeting, with a Croma'Rai emissary.

"Hospitality," said Pel'sar. *"Have a drink."*

He clicked his fingers in the direction of the kitchen, and one of his assistants departed that way. It was so like croma, Erik had spent the past three months learning — blunt to the point of rudeness, but too laid back to take offence at much. Pel'sar's long leather coat was studded with steel, its belt a series of interconnected metal rings. His big hands bore fingerless leather gloves, the knuckles inlaid with metal studs. The face was that of a bull, but much wider and flatter, the nose and muzzle more predator than bovine, whatever the big, long-lashed eyes and protruding ears. Pel'sar had to be about a hundred croma years old, Erik thought — each of those being similar in length to a human year. The century was when the armour ridges of the brow and nose, soft and cute in adolescence, began to harden in thick, leathery layers tougher than any shell. By the time a croma reached a hundred and fifty, the combined armour shell of head, upper torso, legs and forearms began to weigh so much it made modern life difficult, and eventually fatal, as enormous bodies caused internal organs to fail under the strain. But before that happened, elder croma grew into by far the most physically imposing sentient species in the Spiral — a glory that no croma wanted to avoid with life-saving surgery or treatments to halt the process.

"Nothing with alcohol," Erik requested, as Pel'sar strolled past to the center of the apartment, and admired the view. "We're on duty."

Pel'sar made a dismissive gesture. *"The sound system here is amazing,"* he volunteered. *"Music?"*

"I'm here to talk," Erik replied. One nice thing about talking to croma — he didn't need to tiptoe around sensitive feelings. Croma were every bit as tough as they looked, emotionally and physically. But oddly, despite their intimidating appearance and sometimes violent habits, Erik was finding himself quite comfortable around them.

Pel'sar snorted, whipped out the tails on his coat and sat on the big recliner before the windows. It brought his eyes nearly down to Erik's level. "Whose apartment is it?" Erik asked.

"Some foolish uncle," came the translator's reply, with another dismissive flick of Pel'sar's hand. *"They say all who grow old grow wise. If only."* He glanced across Jalawi's marines, as though seeing them for the first time. *"These are the soldiers who beat the deepynines at Defiance?"*

"And far more," said Erik, taking an equally casual seat on the edge of the empty spa bath, unshouldering his rifle and placing it alongside. It conceded the height advantage once more, but among croma that was inevitable. "What is your record at arms, Pel'sar?"

Pel'sar's dark eyes regarded him with what might have been

humour from beneath their developing armour ridges. *"You've learned the right questions in your time amongst us, human."*

"They don't let idiots captain starships," said Erik.

"Then you'd be the only species where that's true," Pel'sar retorted. Against his better judgement, Erik was starting to like this dry, sarcastic emissary. *"I'll spare you the tale. Many years, many ranks, two major conflicts and nine smaller ones. Croma'Rai are the tip of the spear."*

"Lately it seems you'd rather trade with reeh than fight them."

"It was four hundred years ago," Pel'sar snorted. *"Shon'da was in charge then, he was a fool. All croma space was in economic difficulty, the reeh were off making war with some other neighbouring species — the wars come and go in cycles, you know. The last four hundred years have been less violent. Then last century, the Great War of Do'sha'mai, ten billion dead."*

Erik smiled. "When we first met, Sho'mo'ra told me it was a hundred billion."

"Which tells you all you need to know about Sho'mo'ra's relationship with truth," said Pel'sar. *"Four hundred years ago in the economic crisis was a downward phase, and Shon'da thought to learn a few things about the reeh, so we'd know more when the fighting resumed."*

"And the fact that their trade may have saved Croma'Rai's hide economically and politically is a total coincidence."

"Not even close. The numbers were minuscule, it was nothing more than a foolish experiment, that our current leadership inherited."

"And kept covered up for four hundred years."

"It's politics," said Pel'sar, dismissively. *"I can assure you, we don't trade with reeh now. You saw the station at Zondi."*

"Yes, it's no longer used for trade. It's used to conduct the reeh's genetic experiments on every creature in their territory. It's not especially well defended. If you made a proper attempt to destroy it, you'd succeed, yet you haven't."

"And how successful were you?" Pel'sar retorted.

"We were trying to raid it, not destroy it."

"Reeh watch our territory carefully. You mobilised an attack from within reeh space. Ours come from croma space, and reeh know a lot of

what happens here. We've tried to destroy that facility several times in the last few hundred years, and every time they've been waiting for us with superior forces."

Erik had heard many of those stories, too. He'd seen first-hand at Zondi that reeh infotech was alarmingly good, even Styx had been surprised. She now suspected the reeh were not only masters of genetic manipulation, but artificial intelligence as well. Her own research into the matter was continuing, but her working hypothesis was that at some point during the Machine Age, one or another AI resource may have fallen into their hands, and had boosted reeh AI capabilities ever since.

"You've no idea how they spy on you?" Erik asked.

"There are many ways. We spy on them too, though with less success. No matter, we have military successes enough against the reeh in other areas, just not at Zondi. The charge against Croma'Rai is financial and political, not military."

"Yes, I hear all about your wealth."

Pel'sar snorted, a great gust from that big nose. A croma laugh, the closest they came to outright mirth. *"We have money, yes. I'd offer some to you, if I thought you were the slightest bit interested."*

Erik smiled. "My family could buy you all."

An even louder snort from Pel'sar. *"Yes, I heard. Not all your crew are so fortunate, though."* The doors from the kitchen opened once more, footsteps approaching.

"And when this crew retires from service," Erik replied, "my family will make sure they're well looked after."

Pel'sar's aide returned with a mug for each man. Erik had to take his in both hands, while Pel'sar needed only one. The croma leaned forward with a flourish, and Erik reached his own mug, and clanked them together. Croma had that gesture too... and somehow, Erik thought, it suited them more than it suited humans. The drink was 'cobas', and it was dry, strong, and rather good once the taste was acquired. And unusually for the croma, not alcoholic.

"So I can't buy you," said Pel'sar. *"One plan gone. Croma'Rai will win this Tali'san. When that happens, you'll want to be on our side."*

Erik sipped his cobas. "Or what?"

A vague, uncaring gesture. *"Who can say? Best to value life, human."*

"And there it is," said Erik, smiling into his mug. "Such a croma conversation. Friendly one moment, death threats the next."

Pel'sar leaned forward, a huge bulk of leather-clad shoulders, armoured forearms on knees. *"Perhaps it's different with humans,"* he said, with the unblinking aggression of his kind. *"Perhaps your friends all live forever."*

Erik sighed. "Pel'sar. You invited me here. Tell me what you want."

"For you not to interfere. This Tali'san is between Croma'Dokran, Croma'Rai and their followers. Outsiders have no place in croma affairs."

'Bit late for that, don't you think?' Erik nearly replied, but held his tongue. It hadn't been the croma's idea for *Phoenix* to come here. "And what influence do you think our one ship has in the great affairs of your people?" Erik replied, with a faintly mocking smile.

"Your corbi," said Pel'sar. *"What game does she play?"*

"In an old library that has had no interest to any of your people for centuries?" said Erik, innocently. "Human libraries don't allow the playing of games. Maybe they're different here."

Pel'sar jabbed a thick finger at him. *"This research is dangerous, human. You should make her stop."*

Erik gave the same unbothered smile he'd smiled before. "Or what?" he repeated, almost taunting. "I promise you, if you move against *Phoenix*, Croma'Rai will lose everything in this system."

"Don't make idle threats, human."

"Ask the deepynines if our threats are idle."

Pel'sar thought about that for a moment. Exchanging death threats with a chah'nas or a kaal could have led to a dangerous explosion of temper. With croma that would never happen. Croma didn't get angry, because croma were always angry. Once Erik had gotten used to the endless slow-burn, he'd realised it actually made him safer, because croma emotional states rarely changed. If croma were mad enough to kill you, you'd know in the first five seconds of the encounter, not the last.

"Croma'Dokran have promised you things if they win," Pel'sar said. *"Croma'Rai can offer you better."*

"Like?"

"Relations with humanity."

Erik kept expression off his face with difficulty. "Croma haven't ever had direct relations with Spiral species. You can claim a mandate to do that?"

"If we win."

"Croma'Rai is one clan. Croma have lots of clans. You can't just reverse fifteen thousand years of croma policy because you win one Tali'san and retain your current power. Croma don't mix with others."

"Not true. We were in the Chah'nas Empire."

"You fought a *war* against the chah'nas," Erik nearly laughed. "Billions died."

"Before which," Pel'sar said stubbornly, *"we had nearly a thousand years of relations."*

"And you enjoyed it so much you killed billions of people to get away from it, and haven't been back in fourteen thousand years since."

Pel'sar's big ears flicked, a jangle of steel rings in both. His dark eyes, behind the inbuilt hostility, were almost affectionate in that way of croma hard-heads. Like the human crime bosses on some backwater worlds, who after disposing of bodies in the river would bond like brothers over drinks and punch each other's arms with affection. Even croma love was violent.

"Humanity," Pel'sar said, with another jab of that finger. He took another deep gulp of his drink. *"Relations. Worth so much in trade and weapons. Your family trades. Do your maths."*

Erik did. He counted credit signs followed by many, many zeroes. But strategically he didn't think Fleet would reckon this was quite the bargain Pel'sar thought it was. "Interesting," he admitted. "And you'll let us go and collect our Major on Rando?"

"No. Phoenix will cease all engagement with the reeh or the corbi Resistance. This is a matter of croma security. We are the ones who start wars in this region, not you."

"We seek only answers to the threat facing all humans and tavalai."

"It changes nothing."

Erik sighed, and sipped his drink. "Pel'sar. You're not giving me a lot of options here. *Phoenix* is not a diplomatic ship. I'm not here to negotiate trade relations. I'm here to do everything I can to ensure the security of humanity. If Croma'Rai will not help me in that pursuit, but Croma'Dokran will, I can't see that I have very much choice at all."

"Croma'Dokran do not have the numbers in the Tali'san," Pel'sar said confidently. *"They will lose. And then, having made yourself our enemy when it mattered, Phoenix will lose everything."*

Erik smiled. "I've been halfway across the Spiral, and been threatened with similar things by people more powerful than you. Most of them are now dead. Be careful who you threaten, Pel'sar of Croma'Rai."

* * *

"Would you really do that for us when we get back home, Captain?" Private Melidu asked from the rear seat as the cruiser lifted away from the ziggurat landing pad. "Look out for us with jobs and stuff?"

"The Captain shouldn't have to answer that," said Jalawi, with a stern glance at the Private. "Marines shouldn't be pestering their senior officers for scraps and favours outside of service."

"Better yet," Jokono added for the young man's benefit, "the Captain could be disciplined for offering such things to personnel beneath his command. It's a breach of protocol, spacers and marines are expected to follow orders because of Fleet discipline, not because of the promise of goodies to come." The former policeman had not been in uniform long, but already he was better acquainted with the rules than most spacers and privates.

"Yeah, well that's Fleet regs," said Erik, checking the network scans as traffic central aligned them with their spot in an approaching skylane. "We're a long way from Fleet out here. And if they try to tell Family Debogande we can't look after *all* our family, they can stick their rules in their pipe and smoke them."

There was a moment's silent satisfaction, at that. The rules were essentially correct — in the course of regular service it was a dangerous thing to do, and Erik had avoided talking about his family's wealth as much as possible. But the crew of *Phoenix* were far past such things now. Senior officers were supposed to remain interoperable with any unit in Fleet, and thus could not get too attached to any one group of people... but circumstance had made this present crew far more to each other than that.

Erik thought again of the families of the crew they'd lost. Lately he'd been doing that a lot. The recovered bodies from the Battle of Defiance had been sent back on *Lien Wang* with the drysine datacore, accompanied by letters and video messages from either Trace to the marines, or from Erik to the spacers, plus additional messages from friends or immediate commanders who'd known them best. More recently, from the fight on Zondi Splicer, another five marines had died, two of them tavalai. With Trace stuck on Rando, Lieutenant Dale had had to write the condolences, but without reliable transportation back to human or tavalai space they'd been unable to send them... nor the two bodies they'd recovered, currently in *Phoenix's* cold storage.

For the past year and more, families would have had to listen to Fleet's nonsense about how they were all renegades and traitors. After meeting with Captain Sampey and Commander Adams from *Lien Wang* on Defiance, Erik doubted that many of the families would actually believe that, and knew for a fact that many other Fleet officers ranged from skeptical to scathing of HQ's pronouncements on *Phoenix* and its crew. But even so, it would have been hard on the families, to hear their missing son, daughter, father or mother spoken of in such terms by the supreme human authority.

And then, upon receiving the devastating news of their death in some far-away battle against classified aliens for reasons unknown, those same families would have been robbed of any possible comfort of knowing what it had all been for. Families who had lost loved ones in the Triumvirate War at least knew that their beloveds had died in a continuation of the great thousand-year-struggle for human liberation and security in a hostile galaxy. But surely now, in that black void of grief and loss, many of *Phoenix*'s bereaved must have fallen to doubting, and perhaps even cursing *Phoenix*'s name, and that of its rich and doubtless narcissistic captain, for having dragged so many lives into a personal vendetta against Fleet HQ to clear his inflated reputation.

There'd been times in the last three months when thinking on it had threatened to plunge Erik into the blackest despair. Logically he knew that all of those deaths hadn't been his fault. And logically he knew that *Phoenix*'s mission was right and true, and believed it with every scrap of common sense at his disposal. But his heart remained unconvinced, and he found himself awake at nights, replaying actions, key moments of decision and choices over and over in his head, trying to find some alternative that would have kept at least a few more of his precious crew alive.

There were senior crew who knew a lot more about loss and responsibility than he did, but he could not tell them of his doubts. In the current circumstances, even an experienced spacer like Kaspowitz, Geish or Shilu could easily come to wonder if the young Captain was losing his grip. To give them such doubts and concerns could jeopardise their performance, and thus the performance of the ship. Similarly he could not discuss it with any of the marines, partly because they were not in a position to understand what he actually did as captain, and partly because the one person who might was Lieutenant Dale, and Dale was hardly the person in whom to be confiding about vulnerabilities.

No, the only person he could tell these things was Trace, partly because Trace had been a focal part of his crazy command journey from the beginning and knew intimately of the hurdles he'd had to leap because she'd helped him leap them, and partly because Trace was such a hardass that very little bothered her. Trace had helped him to sort through the issues in his head many times in the past, having seamlessly shifted gears from ass-kicker to command partner and confidant, and when he'd found himself struggling, a talk with her could help him onto the proper path. But now she was gone, and he missed her with an intensity approaching physical pain.

"You think your mother will have some ideas for looking after the families of the crew we lost, Captain?" Jalawi asked. Glancing at him, as though somehow able to read his thoughts.

"Hell yes," said Erik, with feeling. "Joker could tell you."

"Yes, indeed," said Jokono, recalling. It brought him a moment's pause, as the passing lights of an alien city washed over his face. As though remembering that other place and time were some kind of mental dislocation. "I recall some of the arrangements Alice Debogande made for the Captain's father's old crew... one of them got the household garden contract, do you remember, Captain?"

Erik laughed. "Oh yeah, Leon Devo. He was loadmaster on one of Dad's freighters, started a landscaping business that did okay, but he was struggling a bit..."

"Considerably underwater as I heard it," Jokono corrected.

Erik shrugged. "I was in the Academy, you'd remember it better. But I came home one day and half the grounds were dug up, people everywhere... and you have to understand, Mother *hates* clutter. So I'm wondering if someone bombed our lawn or something..."

"It did look rather like a bomb."

"Anyhow, turns out Dad's old loadmaster landed this big contract to redo the gardens, upset the hell out of the other bigshot landscapers because it wasn't put out to tender or anything, just dropped on Leon's lap. Big job too, had to hire a bunch of extra people... damn near killed him, I think."

"He did a fine job, though," said Jokono.

"Phenomenal job," Erik agreed. "The next time I came home, I couldn't believe it, it looked stunning. Set Leon's business up, he got so much work after landing that contract."

"I believe he got the contract for Yamato Memorial gardens immediately after that," Jokono agreed.

"He did too, that's right."

"That's a beautiful place. My niece got married there just five years ago, it has a lovely atmosphere."

"Oh right, that's... Sarah, isn't it?"

"Yes Captain, Sarah Kuesten, now. And she married a police officer, so I'd like to claim some influence..."

The marines listened with faint melancholy, to hear the Debogande son and employee talk about their old lives. Places so far away and long ago that it seemed incredible to recall that they were real, and that one day, perhaps, would be seen again. What that reunion would feel like for any of them, none could imagine.

"Hello Captain," Styx's voice interrupted on cruiser speakers. *"You are about to be intercepted by a government authority vehicle. I do not detect an immediate threat, but their data systems are preparing to override traffic central and divert you to a nearby landing pad."*

"Great," Erik muttered. It wasn't the first time it had happened. "Keep me informed if your threat assessment changes."

"Of course, Captain."

Sure enough, a series of flashing lights on Erik's display indicated someone displeased with their present course. Erik dropped his AR glasses to his eyes, and the translator function turned croma script into English, words to the effect of 'pull over', and a landing spot highlighted on a tower top to one side. Erik confirmed the course, and the warning messages vanished.

"Same drill as before, people," Jalawi drawled, checking his rifle and glasses interface as his marines did likewise. "It's probably just bureaucracy, but let's be ready. Cover and eliminate near targets first, protect the Captain at all costs."

"If it's a big croma," Sergeant Hoon added, "shoot for the head. Chest shots won't scratch them. Smaller croma, cluster your shots on the center of mass but don't expect them to go down easy." Master Sergeant Hoon was Phoenix Company's most experienced and decorated marine, in that latter regard surpassing even the Major. When he had anything to say at all, it was usually about shooting people.

Erik set them down on the taller tower rooftop, and stayed in the vehicle as another cruiser set down alongside, running lights flashing.

"Captain, it appears to only contain a single occupant," said Styx.

Sure enough, a single door opened and a lone croma got out. This one wasn't much taller than the tallest professional basketball player, meaning he could have been about sixty. His coat billowed out in a gust of high altitude wind, strolling in that grimly casual way of any croma with rank. He walked to Erik's driverside window and rapped on it. Erik lowered the glass.

"Hello officer," he said. "Was I speeding?"

The croma's big face wore the expression of one very unimpressed. He spoke... and Erik immediately reconsidered his presumption of male gender. *"Captain Debogande, my name is Rhi'shul, I am an investigator with the Dan'gede. I require you to accompany me to headquarters."*

Erik glanced at Jokono. "Captain, the Dan'gede are the Croma'Rai investigation unit," said Jokono, having worked on developing that expertise during his time here. "Think the Homeworld Investigation Bureau."

"Ah," said Erik, and turned back to the big investigations agent. Attempted his most winsome smile. He'd never seen croma smile, but what the hell, it had worked on women in positions of authority before. "What seems to be the problem, agent?"

"We can discuss that at headquarters," came the earpiece reply.

Erik sighed. He'd actually been looking forward to a meal back at the grounds assigned to *Phoenix* crew for the duration of this Tali'san. "Very well, agent. Lead on, I will follow."

"No," said the agent. *"You will come with me now. Alone."*

The cruiser's rear window also lowered, and upon the rim, Lieutenant Jalawi rested the muzzle of his rifle, not far from the croma's head. "I don't think so," he said loudly.

The croma looked at the rifle. With her big dark eyes and long lashes, Erik thought she looked a little like a cow considering a flower she'd like to eat. Female croma were a little leaner than males, but grew just as large and formidable. Mostly it was the voice that enabled a human to tell the difference — not so much higher as a different texture, multi-toned rather than single-note. Sexual attraction, Erik was reliably informed, happened mostly not by the appearance of physical differences, but by smell. Certainly this tall lady smelled quite strong, though whether that was something artificial or natural, Erik did not know. The leathery plating on her forehead and nose remained soft in her relative youth.

"My office gives me the authority to remove your visa rights on this world," she said bluntly. *"If you want to stay on this planet, you will come with me now."*

"Our visa rights grant us the right to self defence," Jalawi retorted. "We've made very clear that anyone attempting to separate the Captain from his escort is to be treated as hostile. You'll find it hard to revoke those visa rights with a bullet in your head."

Erik gave the agent an apologetic smile. "I think what the Lieutenant's trying to say is 'go to hell'." He knew the translator had an appropriate translation for that, croma having a metaphorical equivalent to hell. "I'll be happy to go with you back to headquarters, but not without my escort."

"Coward," the croma accused him, turned and swaggered back to her vehicle. That was an even worse word among croma than humans.

"Bitch!" Melidu said loudly from the back seat.

"I'll kick her ass, Captain," Lewis offered.

"No Private," said Erik, unable to hide his amusement. "I couldn't let you hit a lady."

Jalawi chortled, putting the window back up as his usual humour returned. "Could be the last thing you ever do, Rats. She's a big'un."

"I could take her," said Lewis with confidence.

"Actually, she's a little'un," Jokono corrected the Lieutenant. "I spoke with the head of some legal institution last week, *that* was a big female croma. Twice this one's weight, easily."

Erik waited for the Dan'gede investigator to climb back into her vehicle and start up. Jalawi broke into half-humming, half-singing some favourite marine song about girls with big bottoms, bringing grins from the others.

"The Major likes that song, does she Lieutenant?" Jokono asked drily, having evidently learned the words.

Jalawi responded with one of his rare 'Major Thakur impersonations', a female falsetto with a low-key snarl to it. "How are you gonna handle enemy fire if you can't handle a dirty song, marine?" More grins from the others. "I once killed ten fully armoured karasai with a toothpick, marine, you think I can't handle a dirty song? Now I have to go meditate in a depressurised airlock for an hour, when I get back I want your attitude improved or I'll personally realign your chakra with my fists, you understand me marine?"

"Pretty close," Melidu chortled.

"Meh," said Erik. "It's okay." Which made them laugh, to hear the Captain himself venturing an opinion. Erik could have added that Trace rarely actually threatened anyone, but that would have been missing the point.

They all missed her. Making fun of the Company Commander in front of the Captain was irregular, but Jalawi was keeping her memory alive, making it feel as though she were just around the corner, about to return at any moment. And besides, *Phoenix* were all a family now, even moreso than they'd been during the war. Things that might have gotten Jalawi in serious trouble with some captains, only made Erik smile. Trace too, Erik was sure, if she were there.

THE DAN'GEDE HEADQUARTERS WERE NOTHING LIKE AS OUTSIZED AS the ziggurat apartment had been. The offices were open plan after a fashion, but there was a lot of vertical clutter hanging from the ceiling in rows, holographic projectors that created wall-screens, like giant transparent whiteboards made of glowing light. Croma gathered in groups, consulting, sharing data via the headband-style uplink communicators they preferred to the humans' AR glasses. There appeared to be a lot of group consulting going on, Erik thought, where humans would be working mostly alone, consulting only where necessary. Croma seemed to work in reverse proportion.

The chairs against the floor-to-ceiling windows on this side of the office were moderately proportioned so that sitting in one, Erik felt only a little small. None of the croma here were giants, just what would qualify a human as crazily, unnaturally tall. A few weren't even that — genuine youngsters, rushing about on errands, that being the task of younger, faster members of the species. Everyone looked at the humans, standing or sitting in this small portion of open plan space against the far windows, helmets off but still in armour, weapons at ease but never out of hand.

"Sarge?" Melidu asked Hoon. "Does this place smell like old lady perfume, or is it just me?"

"It's just you," said Hoon. It wasn't true because Erik could smell it too — that powerful, musky scent that pervaded every enclosed space where croma lived. But Hoon, as always, chose the fastest way to avoid talking about unimportant things. He'd barely moved since they'd arrived, eyes sweeping the wide office back and forth like some automated sentinel.

One of the display screens was showing what might have been a live feed from one of the Tali'san showdowns — landed shuttles on a rocky site before some rugged hills, spilling forth rows of armoured croma. This armour wasn't natural, but additional. More spectacular still, it was antiquated after Tali'san rules, great steel plates hammered into decorations more bold than intricate, emblems of creatures mythical and real alike. The marching croma carried long objects swathed in padding, like old style martial artists carrying aikido blades to the dojo. Which was almost precisely what they were — old style weapons, spears, hammers and peculiarly croma things that humans had no names for.

Camera drones hovered around the marching column, and no small number of observers on electric vehicles. Some children had broken away from the organised reception at a nearby town to come running alongside, kicking up dust in the harsh sunlight. The visuals were accompanied by commentary — some highly-paid analyst going through the column and telling the audience what she saw, complete with graphics, lineage, clan and rank.

"Those are our guys," Jalawi observed, nodding to the display. "Croma'Dokran."

"Which region is it?" Jokono asked, squinting through his glasses to try and get a translation on the text.

"Jin'da." That was their present continent. "I think it's not too far away — it's the Tok'ran plains, there's three seats there."

The vision focused past the column on some large medical vehicles, including one that looked like a train on tires, many trailers linked together. Only a mass-casualty event would require a vehicle like it, a veritable hospital on wheels. Inevitably for a martial event, someone started playing music, if it could be called music — a heavy, thrashing beat and the wail and screech of electric high notes that could barely be described as melody. Deafening to hear in person, and thoroughly intimidating, as was the croma preference. Some of *Phoenix*'s heavy metal connoisseurs claimed to like it.

Jokono shook his held in subdued amazement. "These people are all insane," he said.

Erik couldn't argue. The Tali'san was like a giant, planet-wide election. Dul'rho had been divided into districts, and as in any human election, each district was worth points. To win the entire contest, each competing side had to win an unassailable majority of points from the total points available across all districts.

The primary difference between a Tali'san and a human election was that in human elections, results were not decided by appointed armies lined up on battlefields trying to kill each other. Modern weapons were banned, and so the armies resorted to this — medieval reenactments, but with weapons that were in no way simulated, and casualties that were in no way pretending to be hurt. Typical casualty rates for a Tali'san, the sources said, were about ten percent fatalities, though Romki had thrown doubt on the accuracy of those reports. Erik thought that democratic participation on human worlds would be even lower than it had sunk under Fleet autocracy if that participation entailed a ten percent chance of violent death. If Romki was right, the real number could be much higher. But all of the croma Erik had spoken to about it insisted that if given the chance themselves, they'd jump at it.

Phoenix's first three months stuck in Dul'rho orbit had been compulsory attendance at the trial to determine whether the Tali'san was necessary. The trial's conclusion had never been in doubt, and was more about formalities, and gathering forces from the furthest places croma lived. Each of the croma clans had their preference for who should lead them, and now contributed forces to the battle, rallying around Croma'Rai and Croma'Dokran respectively. Those forces were in turn limited by rules that even Stan Romki struggled to understand, but seemed to compose of entirely elite and well-connected warriors in search of what, for a croma, counted as eternal glory. Erik thought that it would be smarter to reserve such definitions of glory to conflicts against the reeh, against whom all these warriors could surely suffer much more glorious and useful deaths than this.

"I don't think they're crazy," said Jalawi, watching the screens. "You put this much fame up for grabs back home, lots of folks would do it. If you survive it, your whole family's set for life, sometimes for generations."

"Already happens," said Private Lewis. "We ride thur back on McDonald, they weigh four tons and can jump four metres in the air. There's a whole thur-riding pro-league, lots of guys get killed but it pays well and gets the girls."

"'Cept half of this lot *are* girls," said Melidu.

"Damn fools on your world should have joined the marines instead," Hoon told Lewis.

Lewis shrugged. "I knew a guy who did it in a minor league. Don't think the marines would have had him, Sarge, he was pretty dumb. Had more injuries after a few seasons than I had after five years of combat."

"If he's too dumb for marines, he joins the army," said Hoon, predictably. Hoon was a full-bore human patriot. The misplaced priorities of so many young humans bugged him.

The croma agent who'd intercepted them emerged from a partitioned office and swaggered over, swishing leather coat, knuckle-duster gloves, big steel nose ring and all. *"In here,"* she said, pointing to a nearby partitioned office. *"Your soldiers can stand outside. And guard you."* With obvious sarcasm.

Jalawi snorted. "If any of these people met a deepynine they'd wet themselves," he said loudly. Erik didn't think it was true, but Rhi'shul gave Jalawi a dark glare, still pointing at the office. Erik took up his rifle, pointedly, and walked to the office door. Insulting your enormous, aggressive alien hosts didn't seem smart at first glance, but croma liked you less if you didn't push back when challenged. No croma liked a doormat.

Erik entered the office and took the indicated seat, rifle in his lap, as Rhi'shul took one opposite. There was no desk here, just a big wall display and holographic interface, projecting all the input a worker would require. Rhi'shul sat with a flourish, long legs crossed, dextrous hands accessing an holography screen in the air before her.

"Croma'Rai leadership have been up to some very illegal dealings in reeh space," she said without preamble. Croma were horrible at small talk.

"I know," Erik said, with an edge. "I'm the one who discovered it."

"You didn't," said Rhi'shul. *"Croma'Dokran did, long ago. They couldn't prove it, having no access to that space, so they sent a useful tool to do it for them."* Erik couldn't think of a comeback to that. Croma were blunt, but they did not often bluster. Bluntness combined with truthfulness could be formidable. *"The Croma'Rai have a large military intelligence division. It is supposed to be open to the agencies of other clans, but this one is not, at least for the past few hundred years. They know many things about the reeh that they have not shared with the other clans. Things that they should not know, because they have been dealing with them instead of fighting them. My information is that they are now considering which of this information should be destroyed, should Croma'Dokran win the Tali'san. Much will be lost."*

"And why does this concern me?" asked Erik.

Rhi'shul touched a holographic control, and a three-dimensional figure appeared on the wall. A dark-cloaked figure, hood back. Dark beady eyes, expansive nasal cavity. Alo. *"These are your allies. In what you call the Spiral. You now fear them to be a threat."*

"What of it?"

The image changed to a three-dimensional playback. It filled half the room to one side, the image broken and degraded, as though many 3D pixels had been stripped. A pre-technological village, small mud huts little taller than a person. Among them, cloaked figures shuffling, folding hoods about their faces to ward off the blowing sand. One of their hoods slipped... revealing an alo face, an under-scarf wrapped around that sensitive nasal cavity, only the eyes visible.

Rhi'shul paused the image. Erik stared. *"This is one image my spies sent to me. They were only able to decode small portions. The Croma'Rai intelligence division has had access to old reeh historical data. The degree of inter-operation between them has been truly traitorous."* Erik recalled Pel'sar, emissary of the highest-ranked Croma'Rai, just an hour ago, denying that emphatically. Croma lied just as humans did.

"Your spies know if that's a genuine, pre-technology image?" Erik asked. The holographic alo's beady eyes fixed upon his own, as though wondering what was this strange technology that captured him. The alo were the most technologically advanced race in the Spiral, but were also one of the most recent. *Phoenix*'s running theory, of which they were now nearly certain, was that the technology had come from the deepynines, who had not been destroyed in the Drysine/Deepynine War as previously imagined. The drysine data-core had revealed records of alo encountered long ago in the direction of reeh space, but had shown nothing more than that. Until this.

"I only know what they sent," said Rhi'shul. *"The alo's origins have been a mystery to you. These and other mysteries, the intelligence division possesses."*

"And let me guess," said Erik, repressing his fascination with difficulty. "You want me to help you get it."

"Yes."

"And why can't you get it yourself? You're an investigative agency. Investigate."

"This data is incriminating to Croma'Rai. Access is not presently granted. Only after the Tali'san, by which time the data will be gone."

"And you can guarantee it will still be there until the conclusion of the Tali'san?"

"Yes. The rules forbid present erasure."

Erik frowned at the translation, but knew enquiring further would be a waste of time. Croma had limited democracy, and limited rule of law, but the rules that limited both were opaque at best. Stan Romki and Wei Shilu had made some progress deciphering them all, but still there was confusion. Especially now, with everything in turmoil.

"And what would you like me to do?" asked Erik, with world-weary exasperation. Letting on that he was interested, at this point, would weaken his hand.

"I know that you have advanced computer access capability."

"Oh here we go," Erik sighed. It was hard not to be darkly amused. "You know, this is a very dangerous road to go down."

Rhi'shul regarded him with thick-browed disdain. *"I had heard you were heroic."*

"Dangerous for you," Erik clarified. "Our advanced computer access capability doesn't care much about collateral damage."

Rhi'shul snorted, the humourless variety. *"The Dan'gede have investigated Croma'Rai affairs for over a thousand years. Today we find that the Croma' Rai leadership have dragged all of our honour through the manure. I don't care for risk. I want my name back!"*

She said it in real anger, a guttural snarl deep in her thick throat. One fist clenched in a sizeable ball, large enough to break human skulls. Erik considered her for a moment. Motivations were always tricky, with aliens. He'd had enough of being manipulated by conniving intellects. At least with croma, or at least with *this* croma, one did not have to worry if the emotion were genuine. Croma would lie, but from what he'd seen, he did not think it possible for them to fake emotional displays. Those were too raw, and could not be delivered cold.

"What do you want us to do," he asked calmly, "and how can you guarantee we won't start some kind of war if we get caught?"

"No guarantees," Rhi'shul growled. *"That's what risk is."* She paused a moment, as though to calm herself. *"The intelligence division has a headquarters at Stat'cha. It is impenetrable to us with current connections. The evidence contained there is incriminating against Croma'Rai, as I said. Phoenix's role in revealing it will be appreciated by whoever replaces Croma'Rai."*

"You think it's likely Croma'Rai will lose?"

"No. But we can hope. And revealing this information may accelerate that process, by turning the clans against them."

Erik frowned. "Hang on, *you're* Croma'Rai. You're betting against your own clan?"

"Clan isn't everything," said Rhi'shul. *"Honour is more."* There was more there that she wasn't telling, Erik was sure. No matter. With *Phoenix*'s current resources, he could find out plenty more whether she wanted him to or not.

"Just one thing I want you to understand," said Erik, leaning forward a little to make sure she understood his seriousness. He was getting much better at this 'projecting authority' thing. Trace had told him so, from the Battle of Defiance onward. "Our advanced computer access capability has a mind of her own. If you doublecross her, or us, I will tear this organisation's entrails out and feed them to you, do you understand?"

"You are one ship," Rhi'shul said, contemptuously. *"Do not overestimate your importance, little man."*

"Styx," said Erik to the empty air. "Show her."

The lights dimmed. The big holographic screens flickered, as though the power were fading. Which was impossible, because the power systems for major institutional buildings like this one were backed by innumerable overlapping redundancies. From beyond the glass walls of this office, there came loud exclamations from the main floor. Then the whole floor went black, illuminated only by Rhi'shul's own main screen, reactivating with an image of a single, red, unblinking artificial eye. Styx's own eye, though Rhi'shul could not know that. Rhi'shul stared.

Data flashed across the eye, scrolling rapidly in croma script. Rhi'shul visibly recoiled, recognising what she saw. Then the holography vanished, and light returned to the Dan'gede floor. Rhi'shul turned her dark-eyed stare on Erik. There was no contempt visible now. Broad croma features did not readily show fear, but this was as close as Erik had seen them come. Trepidation, certainly.

"Those were my family's personal details," said Rhi'shul, and the translator captured some of her horror. *"What kind of an honourless man would threaten someone's family?"*

"I told you," Erik explained, getting to his feet. "But you weren't listening, obviously. The advanced computer access capability you seek to utilise is not impressed by human or croma concepts of morality. She can shut down this office, this institution, anything she chooses — god knows she's been here long enough to know all the vulnerabilities. You're playing with the devil, lady. If you screw us, she can destroy everything and make it look like your fault, so that your own people blame you and tear you bare-handed into a hundred pieces and curse your name for a thousand years."

He leaned on his chairback to look her hard in the eyes. "I'm told that croma like threats. Is this threatening enough for you?"

Rhi'shul said nothing. All scorn and intimidation were gone. Erik straightened, satisfied, and gave her his most charming smile. "Good! *Phoenix* will consider your offer, but don't call us, we'll call you. Have a good day."

He walked out her door, and onto the open floor of puzzled, head-scratching croma, querying their systems and looking up at the lights. Jalawi and Hoon fell in at his side, and beckoned for the others to follow. "Anything, Captain?" Jalawi asked.

"Might have made a friend," Erik admitted. "If what I've heard about croma mating rituals is true, I might even get a proposal."

Jalawi chortled. "With that big gal? Not sure even you're that charming, Captain."

"You didn't hear the gossip among the female Debogande household staff," Jokono said with amusement.

Erik made a silent uplink, and spoke without moving his lips as they crossed the work floor. *"Did you really need to threaten her family, Styx?"*

"With respect, Captain, you're the one who explained to her my regard for croma and human morality."

"And that was accurate, was it?"

"Completely accurate, Captain."

"Well that's just grand. I'm so glad we're getting to know each other on this cruise."

4

Gideon Kono could feel the alien's blood soaking into his shirt. Another thing to be mad at the Major for — all of his shirts were gifts from corbi tailors, villagers who with scissors, needle and thread had put together clothes twice the size of anything a corbi would need, and of entirely different proportions. His pants were military issue though, with many pockets. He thought they must have been acquired from Resistance supplies for different species. *Which* species, and how the corbi had gotten them, he didn't care to guess... and the same with his boots.

It was raining now, a light drizzle that pattered off the high leaves, and made sticky puddles in the mud between tree roots. He walked with the bleeding alien slung over his right shoulder, rifle in his left hand, and the entire load of alien plus pack, rifle and ammunition making him sore and tired. Rando was point-nine-six of a standard human gravity, and besides being big, Kono was marine-augmented and could do this far longer than the strongest unaugmented human could. But it didn't make him any happier about it.

Beside him, Pena had fallen back from her place in the single-file, as though wanting company. That was safe for now, and a signal would be passed back from the head of the column if it became unsafe. The grey cloud blocked any direct sun, but still Kono found himself squinting in the unaccustomed daylight, dead tired from the withdrawal of recent adrenaline and now well past his bedtime. He and the Major had become nocturnal creatures on this world. And now, to make things worse, all corbi were glancing nervously at the trees, weapons ready. In all the old human stories, the evil things lurked in the night. On Rando, Resistance soldiers worried more about the day.

"Major," said Pena, nodding ahead. "She's cold."

Kono reckoned that word meant much the same in colloquial Lisha as it did in English. And he marvelled again that corbi and humans were so similar. "She's not cold," he disagreed. "She's..." He could not remember the Lisha word for 'disciplined'. "Strong," he said instead.

"Corbi die," said Pena, morosely. "She doesn't care." Pena looked miserable. Squat and strong-shouldered like all corbi, she had a short rifle slung alongside her pack, moving with that shuffling waddle of her kind. Her pale mane was braided on two sides, framing big green eyes. Corbi had no nose to speak of, just wide nostrils in a forward-protruding mouth and jaw. Ape-like, people of Earth might have called them long ago, where apes had been the human ancestors, still alive in the form of many less-evolved species at the time of Earth's destruction. Kono had seen some in zoos, revived from the gene-banks like so many of Earth's otherwise extinct animals. But corbi eyes and faces were infinitely more expressive and evolved than any ape's. In the corbi equivalent of a medieval period, they'd been flying in hot air balloons and gliders, and had arrived at heavier-than-air powered flight as the very first application of their industrial age, hundreds of equivalent years earlier than humans. *Phoenix's* resident expert on aliens, Stanislav Romki, had suspected they were naturally smarter, too.

"The Major cares," Kono replied. It frustrated him that the Major was forcing him to make this argument with very little evidence in support. "I fought with her for years. Long time. She cares." Pena stared up at him with those big eyes, disbelieving. "But she's a warrior. Her whole life, one of the best. All day, all night. All the time. Understand?"

It was the best that his limited vocabulary could manage, at low volume in the third hour of this forced march into thick Talo forest. Thunder grumbled somewhere distant, echoing off nearby hills. Kono's stomach grumbled in answer, and treetop cicadas shrilled in delight at the rain. The wet forest filled his nostrils, and the light through misting treetops was like nothing he'd seen in an entire year of spaceships and stations.

"She fights for humans," Pena replied. "She won't fight for corbi."

Kono couldn't argue with that. He thought about it for a moment. Pena had many friends through this part of Talo, and in less tragic times was capable of astonishing bursts of optimism. Her enthusiasm could be infectious. She'd attached herself to the protection and escort of these newest alien visitors in the hope that something good would come of it for her people. And now this, dejected and fearful, as yet another hope disappeared downstream.

About eight hundred years corbi had been fighting the reeh occupation. Before that they'd been fighting reeh at the side of the croma, but that battle had been lost, and the infant corbi spacefaring civilisation had collapsed in a rain of terror from the sky. So many generations of corbi had lived and died knowing nothing else, hoping against hope that their generation might be the one to behold the miracle. There were religions on Rando, Kono knew, that preached the coming of great saviours... and others that turned their backs on hope, retreating into fierce provincialism, even waging war on other corbi, finding solace and meaning only in the survival of local tribes and customs. And so the once-proud peoples retreated from civilisation, one century at a time, as any faith in the future slipped further and further away.

"Hey," said Kono. "Humans were here once. Like you. Our homeworld occupied, rebels fighting at night, hiding in the day. And we won, and became strong."

"You had alien friends," Pena said. "Chah'nas." She'd asked them many questions about human history, and learned all the names and dates. "We have croma."

"Don't lose hope," Kono told her. "Don't ever." He couldn't help the dark feeling that he was a fraud for saying it. Like those people back home who'd appeared in commercials for the lottery, with bright smiles in fancy clothes and a glass of champagne, saying 'if we did it, you can do it too!' But it was a lie, because luck was luck, not hope. And Pena was right — humanity had had devious alien friends who'd fed them weapons and technology not from compassion, but from the desire to upset the ruling tavalai... which they'd done, big time. And the corbi, despite desperately deserving them, had no friends at all.

Pena smiled at him with tight emotion, and grasped the wrist on his rifle-carrying hand with her long fingers, and squeezed. "I'll always hope," she told him quietly. "I think I'll die still hoping, but life will be less painful that way."

A signal went up from the front, a rapid motion of raised fists spreading down the line like a wave. Kono dropped to one knee, dumped the unconscious alien and put the rifle to his shoulder. Thunder grumbled again, nearer this time. Wind rustled the wet leaves overhead, louder than Kono recalled it sounding previously. Then he realised. It sounded louder because the cicadas had stopped shrilling. Silence ruled this part of the forest, and neither insect nor small animal made a sound.

Heart thudding, Kono turned in a half-circle, taking in the rest of the column, crouching close and finding cover. If they were about to get shot at, clustering up would have been a bad idea, but against the threat everyone was now expecting, the greatest danger was dispersal. The creatures that lurked in the trees were expert at picking off the lone straggler and carrying him away. In three months on Rando, Kono had encountered them directly four times, but never really seen one. He'd only seen the aftermath, like when cheerful Geido had vanished from the rear of a column, to be discovered a half-hour later hanging ten metres up a tree and gruesomely dead.

It made sense though, he thought as they all waited, and scanned the silent forest. The reeh had sent no airstrikes, nor had there been any hint of additional airborne surveillance. The column had not been forced to pause an inordinate number of times from pulse-radar scans, and the cloud cover was thick enough that satellite or space-ship surveillance was of no concern. But of course, the reeh did not need any of those things to track them. Reeh had plenty of spies on the ground, moving on legs or wings, that had no idea they were in the service of a great inter-stellar empire. Most of them just wanted food, and did what came naturally to get it, with no concept how their hungers were directed.

After ten minutes of waiting, the cicadas began shrilling once more, and a bird began to sing. A few minutes later, the signal came back down the column to move, and Kono fetched up his bleeding alien burden and moved forward. He could see the Major up ahead, second in the column beside Porga — him as lead to show where to go, and her to provide the military expertise that he lacked. That all the corbi lacked, it had become abundantly clear in the horror of the ambush. Wounded and less-esteemed than he had been yesterday, Loga was now mid-column, walking with support and gritted teeth among the other wounded. And the Major, cool and watchful as always, was now giving calm directions as though the entire column were hers... and the corbi, finally, were responding as though they thought it was too.

"You think the reeh are watching us?" Kono asked Pena, quietly.

"All a game to reeh," Pena muttered. "They never kill you fast. They watch, they put a few things here, a few things there, watch how you react. All a game. They watch and learn."

All of Rando was a genetic zoo, Kono had heard corbi describe it many times. Reeh manipulated genetic populations, released them back into the wild and watched what happened. Millions died and reeh took the best genetic outcomes and cloned them for profit and advantage. Kono recalled arguing with his parents' friends about the genocide of the krim, and whether Fleet intended the same for their other alien enemies. Kono had said that if it were the sard, he'd be all in favour. And his parents' all-too-sophisticated friends had been horrified.

He wondered what they'd think now, confronted with this. After three months on Rando, Kono was certain of one thing — that if someone were to present him with a giant red button that he could press to exterminate every last reeh in the universe forever, he'd press it hard and often, and sleep perfectly on every night thereafter.

* * *

THE PARTY ENCOUNTERED SIGNS OF A NEARBY VILLAGE WELL BEFORE they reached it — small fields of crops in forest clearings, parting the canopy far enough to let in the light. Corbi tending those fields approached them with that mixture of curiosity and trepidation with which all villagers greeted the Resistance, and several of the younger ones went racing on all fours down trails to alert the village. The season was mid-summer, and the crops looked healthy enough to Trace's inexpert eye — a mix of leafy vegetables and grains. Those grains would be harvested soon, and the excess hidden away from the village, as in last night's caves. Trace wondered if it was this village's harvest that had been hidden there, and how upset they'd be to learn that some of it had now been lost.

The village had walls, four metre high timber beams topped with outward-facing spikes. Those were to keep the kauda away, in all their terrifying forms. Before the occupation, corbi had rarely bothered with such things, there being few forms of naturally ferocious animals anywhere on Rando. Besides, most corbi had lived in cities then, and been as likely to be hiding in huts in the forest as were residents of Homeworld's Shiwon, among its tall towers and automated comforts.

Before the walls were more crops, as much to keep the trees back as to grow food. Reeh would often raze villages that grew too big, or expanded their fields too far. A village was impossible to hide from reeh surveillance, but reeh had never intended to exterminate corbi

entirely, just to control them. Upon any sign of sophisticated technology, or organised resistance, the boot would fall.

Calls went up from the wall, and a big gate squealed slowly open.
Corbi villagers emerged, initial enthusiasm at the arrival of guests
fading as they caught a look at them, grim and bloodied. More stares
at Trace, walking at Porga's side at the column's head, rifle pointed
unthreateningly at the ground. And then some frightened exclamations and questions as they saw Kono, hauling that limp armoured
body.

"We put them in danger, bringing that here," Porga told her.

Trace nodded, looking about. "I want to see Cedu," she told the
gathering, agitated crowd. "I meet him... I met him," she corrected,
realising she'd used the wrong tense. "Forty days ago, right here."
Because one Resistance commander after another had been leading
her around in circles for much of that time. But Cedu had impressed
her. "Cedu. You know Cedu? Where is he?"

Some corbi argued with Porga instead, and other Resistance
soldiers. Others rushed to help the wounded, while more went
running for water and first aid. From the gasps of shock and tearful
whimpers, she gathered one of the wounded further back had died
along the way. Leki, she thought the lad's name was. Not a corbi of
these parts, probably he was from far away, but that mattered little to
the villagers. Trace ignored the commotion, uncapping her bottle to
sip water while she waited for Cedu.

Some corbi children were gathering, predictably, to stare at the
aliens. Their clothes were raggedy, more from the parents' knowledge that any labour put into better clothes would be wasted. Corbi
children were a handful even by human standards, full of energy,
always climbing, running and play-fighting. These were stilled now
by the enormity of their astonishment, staring up at the big dark-
skinned male human with a feared assault commando over one
shoulder, and the smaller but still large brown-skinned female
human with the custom green jacket, and the huge knife in her thigh
holster.

One of them reached a long arm to the alien commando's

dangling hand, only to be warned off by Kono. "Sharp fingers," he told scruffy-furred, big-eyed children. "Dangerous, kid."

The kids exchanged delighted looks to hear him speak Lisha. "Where did you come from?" asked one.

"Did you kill that kauda yourself?" asked another.

"Are you humans?" asked a third. "We've heard there were humans with the Resistance?"

"Are you going to bring other humans to fight the reeh?" asked the fourth.

Ever patient with children, Kono answered their questions while they waited. One of them grabbed his hand and started swinging back and forth, as corbi children often did with adults. One of them tried the same with Trace. Trace removed her hand from range.

Finally she spotted an older corbi coming past the wooden hut walls, adjusting old-fashioned spectacles within a wide mane of white hair that framed his face. "Here's Cedu," she told Kono. "Let's go."

The older corbi saw them coming, Kono with his ominous black cargo in particular, and stopped in dismay. "And here I thought you were an *evolved* species," Cedu said plaintively.

Trace sat on a small wooden stool upon a flagstone bathroom floor, and examined the small cut on her left ribs. Unarmored in a firefight, there'd been no telling what had done it — a small fragment of something, either steel or rock, moving at very high speed. The cut seemed clean, no more than a few centimetres, and now congealed with scabbing blood.

She washed it some more with a cloth from the small wooden bucket, and pressed it beneath her fingers to see if the pain suggested any fragments still in the wound. But it was a velocity wound from a shallow angle, and she thought whatever had done it was long gone. It was fortunate, but as in all fortune, the people with the most talent and application seemed to get it the most. Never one to take karma for granted, Trace had dedicated her life to gaming the odds in her favour.

A young female corbi pulled the sliding door and entered — Cedu's granddaughter. Her name was Peli, and her mane was thick black curls, probably the colour of her grandfather's hair in his youth. Peli tried not to stare, but all corbi were naturally curious, and the sight of a human female topless in the bathroom was too much to resist.

Trace smiled politely as Peli deposited more water into the bucket, and handed her a very small cup, like a shot glass. Within was a gooey liquid — soap, Trace knew, made the corbi way in the wilds, and somewhat expensive. To give some to a visitor was no small hospitality.

"Thank you," said Trace, and set about rubbing the soap on her cut, and on several scratches on her arms. The soap was a reasonable disinfectant, and injuries were a higher priority than armpits.

Peli retreated with a last glance, then slid the wooden door closed. Soap applied, Trace drenched the cloth again, and cleaned. She had to be careful with everything here — even the cloth, a bit of recycled clothing down to its final use, was nothing to treat poorly. Everything was hard to make. Rumour was that some industry still survived in underground hideouts, but most cloth was spun by hand on looms already a thousand years obsolete before the reeh came. And now, everything old was new again.

Still, she thought as she washed, these old wooden huts had a charm to them. The bathroom had no running water, of course, and washing consisted of sitting on the stool and cleaning by hand, or standing in the large wooden basin and pouring water into the perforated container overhead — an improvised shower. The ceiling beams were old and gnarled, and some scented blue flowers hung in a bunch upon one wall. Against a wall by the basin, some thick-bristled brushes, ideal for matted corbi hair. By the sliding door, the small wooden sculpture of a harmless forest animal. Dangling overhead, a twine basket hanging, within which nestled a leafy plant.

Civilised people, making the most of what life offered them. It wasn't much, but Trace could see how some corbi wanted nothing to do with the Resistance, and hoped only to live in these little villages, and seek whatever happiness they could get from life while it lasted. Family matters, daily routines gathering food and water, taking turns on sentry duty to keep the kauda at bay. Such things bred community, and a sense of belonging. Not every corbi was desperate to head to space and fight some larger war. Given what Trace knew of their odds in that war, she could hardly blame them.

Finally she put the shirt back on, now with a patch of blood on one side and a corresponding tear, and pulled her jacket over the top. Collecting her rifle from against the wall, she reentered the hut's main basement through a doorway of dangling beads. The alien commando was laid out on a large table, armour pried away from its torso to lie in shelled pieces upon the reed-mat floor. Humanoid and not especially large, the alien was clearly one of the same two species that had assaulted Phoenix Company on the Zondi Splicer. Faintly reptilian skin, bone protrusions at the shoulders, lips drawn back from sharp teeth, eyes narrowed to the point of nearly meeting beneath a central brow ridge. The shoulder protrusions ended in synthetic socket attachments, where the armour had connected. Trace knew that in reeh, and most of their slaves, those biomechanoid attachments extended within the wearer's body, fully integrating organic and machine exterior.

The wounds on this one's side were caused by shrapnel, a scatter of high velocity penetrations. All were sealed in bloody scabs, and covered further by a light-blue excretion from the suit, helping to heal and seal. One of Cedu's assistants — his grand-nephew, Trace thought — had stuck monitor pads to the alien's neck and forehead, the wires from which went to a small screen in the young corbi's hands. This was one reason why Cedu's workshop was in his study. Surrounded by earthen walls, the transmission from a few small electrical devices would not travel very far, and Trace knew the ceiling above her head, despite looking like wood beams and planks, actually contained more stone slabs like those on the bathroom floor. Reeh scanning would detect steel, such as could be recovered from the ruins of old cities, but stone read little differently from dirt, and blocked electrical transmission just as well.

Assembled against the wood-planked walls of the basement were a true wonder — makeshift wooden benches and shelves lined with high-tech equipment. It was all small, all easily transportable and with minimal power requirements, relatively simple to identify even for a non-scientist like Trace. The small black cylinders were data storage modules. The square block on the shelf beneath was a battery, easily rechargeable from the travelling battery salesmen who went village to village with charge stored from solar rechargers hidden in the forests. On another shelf were microscopes and analysers. Wired to a second battery on the room's other side was a little refrigeration unit, within which were stored rows and rows of tiny vials. Alongside that, a plastic container for rubber gloves and spray-on sterilisers.

Cedu sat alongside one of his microscopes, viewing through a portable lens before his eyes, like AR glasses but wired directly to the microscope. Everything in the lab was wired, to eliminate the wireless transmissions that would surely bring the reeh crashing down on this village. On the microscope's viewer, a small sample of what might have been the alien's blood. Kono sat alongside, rifle by his chair and the antique pistol in hand, a round loaded in case the alien abruptly woke.

"It's a tanifex," Cedu told Trace.

"A what?" Trace asked.

"A tanifex," Cedu repeated. "They're from the center of the Reeh Empire, a system we call Wokam."

"I know," said Trace, looking at the alien's wounds. "Reeh use them for scouting. Not good at heavy assault."

"You think they know it was us?" Kono asked her in English, handing her one of the dried vegetable roots he was eating.

"I doubt it," said Trace in the same, taking one and chewing. "If they wanted to kill us, they'd have sent more than tanifex. If they wanted to capture us, they'd have arranged for extra units in support. And now that we beat them back with heavy casualties, well that happens to tanifex a bit, even against Resistance. On Talo alone there'll be lots of these assaults each night. Every night a few will fail, reeh don't care. They like to see some of their slave species fail, it gives them something to keep improving."

"A few of them will have seen you," Kono cautioned.

"They didn't shoot like they'd seen me," Trace replied. "And you said the only ones that saw you were killed."

Kono made a face, chewing another root. "I think so. I don't think they actually see very well. Sure don't coordinate well in a tight spot. Only when it's all going to plan."

"Like sard," Trace agreed.

The reeh knew they'd lost a potentially valuable cargo when the Resistance had brought down their transport en-route to the Rando Splicer three months ago. They knew that two of the aliens who'd attacked their Zondi Splicer with the Resistance's help had vanished, and were now at large on Rando. But so far she'd not seen any particular urgency in the reeh's actions that suggested a concerted attempt to get them back.

The reeh were genetic tinkerers. They simulated natural selection, but with synthetic methods at a vastly accelerated scale. The corbi said Rando was like a zoo, but Trace thought it more like a giant sports field, where species and groups within species were pitted against each other in brutal contests of survival. Reeh would observe results, simultaneously umpires and spectators, and promote the best performing genetic combinations while demoting the rest. That was why they sent tanifex assault teams without proper support — making it too easy would have denied them the opportunity to observe tanifex under pressure. By watching them fail, reeh could learn their weaknesses, and would doubtless make changes in the future. And also, for all that they were the conquerors of the corbi, similar knowledge could be gained by watching the Resistance succeed. But only sometimes, within limited parameters.

"I'm not sure it matters if they saw us or not," Trace concluded. "I'm not even sure they'll want to recapture us immediately. Right now we're players in their game, and they'll want to observe what we can do."

"Right," Kono agreed, nodding heavily as he looked at the unconscious tanifex on the table. "Actually not a bad strategy, even from a human perspective. Good way to learn about aliens you know nothing about, watch them fight for a while. Not like it costs the Reeh Empire anything." He looked back at Trace. Trace said nothing, just staring at Cedu's microscopes, deep in thought. "Major?"

Trace took a deep breath, then sat alongside Cedu. "What else can you tell me?" she asked the white-haired corbi in Lisha. Cedu held up a hand, forestalling a reply. Trace waited.

"You think this might help, don't you?" Kono observed in English. Trace gave him a cool sideways look. His suspicion almost yielded the hint of a smile, of the 'when am I not planning something?' kind. "Knew it," the Staff Sergeant muttered.

Trace had been planning something for months. The plans weren't yet particularly well formed, but she'd discussed them with a few senior Resistance commanders. Most had ignored her, or laughed.

Cedu pressed several invisible icons in the air before him, then pulled an old-fashioned data chip from the side of the microscope and walked around the tanifex to the room's far side. He inserted the chip into one of the cylindrical storage units, hooked up his visor to another cord and peered into it.

"It's very strange," he said, scrolling through invisible shapes in the air with an extended forefinger. "I'm comparing this one's coding against known databases, and there are variations. There are many types of tanifex slave. The reeh, they do things to their soldiers. Different classes, yes?"

"I understand," Trace told the dubious scientist.

"Reeh make small changes. Change... change quickness, yes?" Cedu made a small leaping gesture with both long arms, to demonstrate. "Change strength, change cotado." Trace frowned, and looked at Kono for that word.

"Stamina," Kono told her, in English.

"Yes," said Trace, in Lisha. "They make small changes, see which change works best. In combat."

Cedu bobbed enthusiastically, a more exaggerated version of the gesture humans and corbi shared. "Yes yes! But here, you see... the changes are not in alignment." He held the visor for Trace to see, and she bent to place it before her eyes.

The holographic display was insanely complicated. At its center was a strand of what humans called DNA, a name in fact technically inaccurate for most other species in the Spiral. Nearly all life humans were familiar with had some variety of DNA, but the base composition and structure varied enormously. But life-data had to be encoded somewhere, and the principle was universal to every organic thing.

This DNA strand was more of an interlinked circle than an Earth-life double-helix. Trace recalled a briefing somewhere that there were so far eleven primary DNA types in various galactic life, at least among those known, but she had no idea which this was. The graphics displayed each part of the looping strands with incredible detail, each labeled with small data-boxes that could be illuminated with a touch. Zooming revealed more, deeper and deeper into the complexity, with more labelling in turn.

But the display showed parts in red, circled and glowing. Small punctuation marks appeared alongside, the equivalent of corbi exclamation points. As though the data storage was cross referencing Cedu's sample against known records, and finding anomalies. Trace could not repress a flutter of excitement to see it. Total non-expert though she was, she'd seen this before.

"Let me guess," she said to Cedu. "This is not a normal pattern. The changes don't make sense. Speed and... and hands..." she made a gesture of fast, steady hands in mid-air, "are not improved. They make worse."

Cedu stared at her, with the incredulity of a man discovering his pet fish could do algebra. "You've seen this? How?"

"Another scientist. Another village." The Resistance had quite a few. Backyard or basement facilities, utterly primitive yet miraculously ingenious. The intellectual curiosity of corbi could not be repressed, and the Resistance did all they could to harness it for their cause. "This scientist? She said it looked as though the tanifex had been programmed badly."

"Yes!" said Cedu, adjusting his spectacles with amazement. "Yes, it looks just like that! Did this scientist know why?"

"No," Trace admitted. "She said it was strange that reeh make mistakes. Reeh never make mistakes." She pointed to Cedu. "You need to compare data. With this scientist, with others."

Cedu ran exasperated hands through his frizzy white mop of hair. "Talo command won't allow it. I try! I've tried to talk to other scientists, but Talo command says it's too dangerous to put us all in one place."

"Major?" asked Kono, still suspicious. "You think this will help us?"

"All the... all the..." she struggled to think of the words in Lisha — it wasn't so hard with small words and basic concepts, but she was going beyond that here. "All the reeh's genetic experiments are based at the Rando Splicer. Whatever they're doing to the tanifex is run from there. Someone's messing it up. Reeh never mess things up. But a lot of the people running things in the Splicer and elsewhere are not reeh. They're slave species, like tanifex. What if someone's doing it on purpose?"

Kono frowned at her, half-incredulously. "Why?" Cedu shot back. "Why would they do that? If the reeh found out, they'd kill them."

"Rebellion, maybe," said Trace. "Resistance. Corbi aren't the only people who don't like being enslaved. I've been talking to Resistance soldiers, I know the history of reeh space. There have been hundreds of uprisings. Thousands. What if this is one more?"

"More likely just a mistake," Cedu replied. "Slave species go crazy sometimes."

"Crazy is the same as rebellion sometimes," said Trace.

Cedu scratched his head. "Maybe humans born rebellious, then."

5

Tiga sat atop the ladder, rifling through the thick, heavy-bound book. The human AR glasses sat oddly on her face, not wrapping around the ears as a corbi's glasses would. Lacking the humans' enormous noses, the damn things kept sliding down her face, and she had to abandon a hand to push them back up. The inbuilt camera was scanning every page, and all she really had to do was turn the pages rapidly and let all the data download onto the network she and Professor Romki had established in the library.

But she could not help but pause to read passages. This was the history of her people, works from Rando and the great corbi civilisation from before the catastrophe of the reeh. The books themselves were old and dusty, though not as dusty as she might have expected from so old a library. No one came in here. The accumulation of dust required some degree of activity, Romki said, from dead skin particles or fur or whatever the nature of beings who maintained it. Locked away for eight hundred years, without a glimpse of sunlight, the shelves and pages bore only a thin coating of decay.

Dim blue light washed over the vertical walls of books. Librarians from the larger Ji'go had found tall light stands, casting a spectrum that would not damage the ancient pages. In the past three months,

Tiga had learned to navigate by the position of the light stands as much as by any numerical indexing — three poles along to the sections on the Battles of Sanoda and Meero, seven poles to discussions of the corbi government's struggles to get the croma factions to commit fully to the Treaty of Rampira, when they'd felt events no longer going their way.

Sitting here in the gloom, reading hour after hour, had swung her between inexpressible sadness, and boiling fury. Her people had had great institutions, once. These books were published by many of them, and recorded evidence of so many others — great universities, research institutions, centres of learning in science and politics. Their pages were filled with the thoughts of learned men and women, and even through the distant, intellectual language of academia, their fear shone through, as plain as the burning sun that Tiga at times forgot still shone outside. They were doing everything they could to forestall the doom that came toward them from the stars, and were horrified at their powerlessness. At times Tiga sensed a disbelief that they should find themselves alive in such a period, and that surely such things only happened to other people, to be read about later, in history books. Sitting atop her ladder, scouring one page after another, Tiga could appreciate the horrible irony.

The library was a part of what the croma called a Ji'go — a croma-styled agglomeration of museum, library and art gallery, a place where all old things came together. This wing had been built by corbi, a thousand years ago, when Rando remained a free world. There was even a plaque near the entrance, a dedication from the Rando Embassy, but the words of the dedication had been chiselled away, doubtless by the same croma who had locked the place away for all these centuries.

Laws against destroying antiquity had prevented them from burning it, but successive croma governments had done their best to ensure it would be forgotten, building walls to obscure its entrances, directing all paths elsewhere. The corbi had built it here, Professor Romki suspected, because they had always contributed to the Cal'Uta Ji'go — signs of their contribution were everywhere in the main building, if one knew where to look. Perhaps, being owed this final favour, the croma authorities had grudgingly allowed this library, stocked only with paper books that these days surely no one would read. Romki had then given Tiga his anguished tirade against the fetish of electronic information, and how no one in the ages past had foreseen how the very accessibility of electronic data in turn made it so much easier to find and erase en masse. Across the distances of millennia, good quality paper often lasted much better, he said, as too many regimes that followed wanted to destroy politically inconvenient history. With modern information search functions, that became much easier, and destroying paper artefacts was typically far more illegal than destroying data.

Where the study of pre-reeh corbi history was concerned, it certainly seemed to be true. Very little electronic history was available anywhere. But in exchange for *Phoenix*'s participation in the hearings on whether Croma'Rai's behaviour warranted a challenge by Tali'san, Captain Debogande had asked nothing more than access to this hither-to forbidden library. When Tiga had thanked him for it, he'd waved her off.

"We all need to know that this is worth it," he'd replied. Tiga had asked Professor Romki what he'd meant. "He's responsible for many lives on *Phoenix*," the Professor had answered. "So many of them have died under his command. And now the Major is missing, and probably planning something dangerous, as is her way, and he fears he'll lose her too."

Tiga wasn't entirely sure how helping the corbi would help the Captain to feel that his sacrifice was worth it, but she was grateful. She reached the end of her chapter, realised that the next part she required was in a book she'd been reading a week ago, and asked the database to find it for her. The database replied that it didn't know what she was talking about. Grinding her teeth, Tiga hiked her backpack, and rather than descending the tall ladder, climbed nimbly across the high shelves and swung onto the next ladder. A moment's search found the required book, and she plonked herself onto the highest rung and held the book open on her lap with one foot while tapping database icons in empty-air with another hand, trying to find the bug in the search function.

Permission to access the library had been granted by a higher authority than even Croma'Rai administration could challenge. But they had imposed restrictions — in the name of 'historical preservation', of course. Only herself, and the Professor, had been allowed in. All electronic databases compiled from the pages would be presented to inspection at the end of each working day. Access would only be granted within working day periods — about nine hours, in human time. At first the authorities had tried confiscating those databases, or demanding redactions on security grounds, but Tiga and Romki's unbothered response had finally twigged them to realise that the aliens were first uploading the whole thing to *Phoenix* in orbit. That had led to confiscation of personal electronics, which had violated terms of the agreement with the federal body and been successfully challenged. Next they'd resorted to military-grade jamming of communications in and out of the library, which had quickly ended when the jammer had mysteriously malfunctioned. The next jammer was autistic to coms, but had also failed when the power grid it was connected to had somehow melted, taking down several city blocks. *Phoenix* had been challenged to 'stop doing that', to which the Captain had lied that they weren't doing anything, and that if proof to the contrary could be supplied, the authorities should supply it.

Proof of Styx's capability, of course, was impossible. It was like a master magician asking a suspicious child to prove how the trick was done. The humans professed to be unsure whether or not she had a sense of humour, but Tiga suspected that Styx could only have found such challenges amusing.

"Tiga," came Professor Romki's voice from the foot of the ladder. "The Captain says he needs us to come in. There's something he wants to tell everyone."

"Two minutes," Tiga assured him, flipping through pages. They spoke English, which Tiga had learned with what the Professor had said was astonishing speed. Tiga didn't know about that — on Do'Ran she'd had relatives who could have learned it faster. Given how entangled *Phoenix* had become in corbi and croma affairs, Tiga thought it was important that one of her people spoke the humans' tongue. "Did you make any more progress on those birth records?"

"Um, yes, quite good. Tiga dear, I really wish you wouldn't perch on that ladder. It really looks quite precarious."

"Um, sure," said Tiga, engrossed in the words as she flipped pages, and the glasses indicated the words she might be looking for. Humans had strange vertigo, and were awful at climbing.

It was significantly longer than two minutes before Tiga descended the ladder. She made her way with Romki along the rows of light stands, which the Professor deactivated one by one, as the library was not linked to any functioning power grid. Tiga had thought that disappointing, until the Professor had said that it was better this way. Old electricity grids were notorious for malfunctioning and burning old buildings down. Particularly inconvenient ones.

"What does the Captain want to speak to us about?" she asked Romki, removing her glasses and rubbing her eyes as they walked down the long aisles of books.

"If I knew that, child, I'd be the Captain, wouldn't I?"

"Well... um, logically, sure." Romki confused her sometimes, and she wasn't sure if the strangeness lay in his humanness, or just that it was Romki. "Did you ever serve in the human Fleet, Professor?"

"Heavens no."

"Do the *Phoenix* crew ever resent you for that?" It had been on her mind a lot, lately. Along with wistful thoughts of the home on Do'Ran that she'd sworn to never miss.

"I'm sure they're entirely relieved," said Romki. "Not everyone belongs in the military, Tiga, no matter how badly we want to fight for a cause. It's up to all of us to find where we can do the most good. I'm entirely sure I've done more good as a Professor than I could ever have achieved as a soldier."

It took a while to lock the old, rusted steel doors behind them, then exit up a stone stairway, lit only by the Professor's flashlight. It ended in a stone wall, but a ladder climbed to a trapdoor overhead, and then along a narrow passage that had never been intended to be a passage, but was instead a heavy stone wall that never entirely intersected with the place it was intended to hide. Finally they squeezed through a narrow gap past some creepers to which many croma were apparently allergic, but did nothing to humans, corbi or tavalai. Eight hundred years of croma governments had really done their best to hide this place forever, while somehow managing to not violate the rules that prohibited it — and thus this tiny remaining gap.

Instead of authority inspectors, this time they found only Karajin and his squad of four tavalai marines — karasai, in the tavalai's native tongue.

"A good day's work?" asked the nearest, Jinido, via their earpiece translators. None of the tavalai save Lieutenant Sasalaka spoke particularly good English, though some were learning. They were adopting human ranks, too — Jinido was now a marine sergeant, Tediri was a private. All were considerably taller than Tiga, at about the human average, though somewhat broader and heavier.

"A good enough day," Romki acknowledged, squinting in the sunlight. "I hope you boys didn't get too bored."

"A karasai has many duties," said Jinido. *"Not complaining is one of them."* The tavalai all had some version of that stoic solidness, bearing burdens without complaint and refusing to take short cuts. The human marines all thought *they* were the better warriors, but Tiga felt even a little safer around the tavalai. They just seemed so reliable.

"Let's go," said Lieutenant Karajin, acknowledging their presence for the first time. He took the lead, broad-shouldered and dark skinned, his rifle at cross-carry with that rolling swagger peculiar to all tavalai. Garudan Platoon's First Section of First Squad fanned about them as they walked across the grassy square toward the vast main stairs.

Those stairs led up to the Ji'go, an enormous stone building on their right atop a small hill in the middle of Cal'Uta city. About the stairs spread interlocking gardens and courtyards, more proof of aesthetics than Tiga had ever granted the croma.

The tavalai all watched the croma traffic on the stairs as they approached, much of which was turning their way to stare at the aliens. Croma did not mix with aliens at all, so it was almost certainly the first time any of them had seen some with their own eyes. But thankfully, croma were not an impulsive or ill-disciplined people like corbi, and to run in shrieking clumps with recording devices extended would have been a personal humiliation for them. They glanced, slowed, then moved on... save for several children who stared and pointed. Their parents dragged them, with firm admonitions not to make a scene.

Tiga had grown accustomed to life among humans. Tavalai, too, she found agreeable, and *Phoenix*'s two kuhsi were also nice, particularly little Skah, who was adorable. In the *Phoenix* accommodations, or here in the library, she'd been so eye-blurringly busy over the past few months that it had barely occurred to her to notice that she was surrounded by non-corbi for the first time in her life, let alone allow it to bother her. Only now, in the transition between home and work, did she truly feel the oppression of all these aliens.

Croma, croma, croma everywhere. She hated them, hated their steel-hearted, dull-eyed monotony, hated their mindless strength, hated the way they had no interest in people, just status, clans and power. All her life she'd been imprisoned on Do'Ran by croma, and while her family had told her to be grateful for even that, she'd only seen the walls. All her twenty years Tiga had lived in croma space, yet this was her first time in a croma city... all because her people's *saviours*, the Croma'Dokran, weren't prepared to bend the blasted rules to allow it. Now she spent all day reading about the scale of her people's catastrophe, and the scale of the croma betrayal, and her desire to make the croma change direction and help her people was matched only by the hope that they'd all drop dead shortly after.

Upon the stairs, they were confronted by a vast view of Cal'Uta, a mass of towers, ziggurats and other, blocky, fort-like structures in the croma's monolithic preference. The late afternoon was hot and cloudy, birds circling on thermals beneath the passing lanes of airtraffic. Cal'Uta was located on a river that flowed from highlands to the south, bringing water to a region where otherwise very little would grow. Rains here were infrequent, and the vast Do'jera desert stretched to the north and east beyond the city's outskirts. Today was mid-summer, and the late afternoon baked and shimmered.

Tiga descended the wide stairs at Romki's side, the five tavalai spread about and behind. The stairs went down for nearly two hundred metres ahead, about the Ji'go's vast grounds. Ground traffic circled the outer walls, and even now Karajin would be calling their cruiser from its parked location to come and fetch them. Authorities had not been cooperative enough to grant them an on-site landing pad or parking space, forcing them to walk.

"Lieutenant Karajin," came Styx's cool voice in Tiga's earpiece. *"I detect a possible threat."*

"What threat?" Karajin replied. Karajin spoke Togiri, while Styx's voice in Tiga's earpiece was in Lisha. Tiga didn't need it in her native tongue, but it made sense in a security situation where every millisecond's reaction time counted. So Styx was running multiple simultaneous translations into all their earpieces — meaning Romki was likely hearing his in English. It wasn't surprising — Styx was so powerful she probably barely noticed she was doing it.

"A surveillance drone, registered to local city authorities. It has been intercepted by a foreign information uplink, and has now changed its search parameters into a heading toward the Ji'go. It is irregular, I recommend that you take precautions."

"Taking precautions," Karajin agreed, and turned them right on the next platform between flights of stairs. These stairs descended more steeply into the surrounding grounds and gardens, and not toward the road.

"Pardon my asking," said Romki, adjusting the backpack that contained all his scanning gear and notes, "but don't the gardens contain more possible ambush spots than the stairs?"

"And less possible snipers," said Karajin.

"Ah," said Romki, looking beyond the road at the surrounding skyline, full of towers and windows overlooking their position. Any of those, out to several kilometres distant, could provide a killing view. "Yes, I see."

They were halfway down the new steps when Styx contacted them again. *"An encryption protocol has just been activated about the drone. Someone is attempting to shield my surveillance. I believe you are being watched, and someone has reacted to your change of direction. Exercise extreme caution."*

"Understood," said Karajin, his rolling stride unchanged. *"Access surveillance of these grounds if you can, tell me if anything manoeuvres against us."*

"Visual surveillance of the grounds is limited and the alternatives will be blanked from any active network, making many blindspots. Be prepared for surprises."

"Sergeants love surprises," Jinido said drily. *"Formations, quadrants."*

The other tavalai replied in terse affirmatives. Tavalai marines had a different way of fighting to humans, Tiga had learned. Tavalai marines operated in fives, while humans preferred fours. Tavalai preferred fixed formations, humans were more flexible. Tavalai preferred to rely on overwhelming firepower, while humans liked to manoeuvre. Tiga looked nervously from side to side as they descended the final stairs, to the green patches of lawn and bushes in the cultivated gardens, to the great Ji'go edifice to their right, to the main steps away on the left toward the road. She recalled the pistol in her own bag — the croma's conditions of their stay had included the right to self-defense, which meant weapons for everyone whether they knew how to use them or not. Tiga had wielded an old shotgun against game birds plenty of times, and was a reasonable shot.

"Should I get my pistol?" she asked.

"No," said Jinido, as they hit the bottom of the stairs and strode up the garden path.

"Why not?"

"Combat doesn't need a monkey with a gun." Tiga scowled. She'd had the reference explained to her — apparently the humans' home-world had once contained less-evolved human ancestors called monkeys, and some of the humans had taken to using that word with

regard to corbi. Tiga hadn't seen the resemblance, herself... and besides, if it were an insult, it surely applied to humans more than corbi, monkeys being human ancestors and all. The ancient corbi ancestor had actually been a ground animal, the move to trees had come later... but the humans had been disinterested in her explanations.

They passed croma walking on the path, several dressed in the casual leathers of groundsmen, others in the varied clothes of civilian visitors, some in lighter robes for the heat, others with sleeveless vests and kilt-like shorts that left legs bare. Some more kids gawped at the aliens, and normally one of the tavalai might have waved back, but not this time. Surely if someone were trying to ambush them, they would wait until there were no kids present? Croma affection was rare to see, but when seen it was usually directed at children. And croma children were actually pretty cute, even Tiga had to reluctantly admit, with their big eyes, oversized drooping ears and boundless energy.

"Movement ahead and closing from the left," said Styx. *"Someone is attempting to cut you off. Approximate tacnet to your glasses."* Tiga recalled her own glasses, but they barely stayed on her face while reading books. While running around, she'd lose them.

"Stop and down," said Karajin as they entered a garden square formed by the surrounding walls of decorative bush and tall palms. In the center, an ornamental fountain, the path splitting around it. Romki grabbed Tiga's arm and hurried to the base of the fountain, crouching low. Civilian though he was, Tiga recalled that he'd been on *Phoenix* for more than a year now, and knew far more of marine tactics than her.

When she looked again, she could not see the tavalai. They'd vanished. She stared to the other side as well, and saw nothing but gardens. Tavalai did not seem the most stealthy people, but with their unremarkable green and brown jackets and pants, they'd simply vanished into the surrounding foliage. She'd never given any thought to those clothes before, but they certainly seemed to blend with anything.

"Styx!" Tiga hissed. "What's going on?" Down the garden path beyond the fountain, some civilian croma were strolling. What did they do when the civilians came upon them, and found two aliens hiding behind the fountain? Did they tell the civilian croma that it wasn't safe, and they should leave? Would that draw attention? "Styx!"

"Don't bother her," said Romki, pistol now in hand as he lay on the pavings. Tiga blinked. When had he drawn *that*? "Advanced audio can hear anything, stay quiet."

Tiga made up her mind and rummaged in her own bag for the pistol, hands shaking. When she glanced up again, a croma family were entering the garden square — two young adults, one older child, and one toddler riding on a croma-style stroller, like a toy horse on wheels. Tiga swore, looked about her once more to see they weren't being outflanked, then back again, hoping to catch a glimpse past the family...

The big male of the family had seen her, and now stopped. The family moved on, circling the fountain. They weren't a family after all. The male had just joined the mother and kids for cover. He now threw aside his coat, and pulled a large weapon.

Rapid shots rang out on the right, and the croma staggered, turning that way. More shots hit his chest, and he finally fell. Beyond, Tiga caught a brief glimpse of a tavalai in the bushes, disappearing again to gain a new arc of fire.

"Ton'cha, ton'cha!" Romki yelled at the bewildered mother, waving his arm onward down the path. The mother grabbed her elder child, and pushed the horse-stroller fast down the pavings, rattling away at speed. More shooting broke out ahead, then stopped just as quickly.

"*Three down,*" said Karajin in Tiga's ear. "*Professor, move left off the path and come forward. Use the trees for cover.*"

"Coming now," said Romki, grabbed Tiga's arm and went left around the fountain, Tiga shaking her arm free in indignation.

"I could climb a tree!" she exclaimed as they reached the first line of bushes. She was much better at that than tavalai or humans. "I could see where they're coming from!"

"And they'll see you and shoot you, now shut up and move."

They ran for the next line of bushes, then paused amongst them, keeping low through the foliage and searching the ground ahead for telltale boots awaiting them. More shooting, in several places ahead, and some incoherent shouting in Kul'hasa. Ahead lay another stretch of grass to another ornamental line of greenery. They'd have to run it. Tiga felt her heart pounding so hard and fast, she thought she might pass out. Beyond the ornamental line, another decoration sat in the middle of the path — not a fountain this time, but a giant lump of volcanic rock. Croma liked rocks. The Professor had told her that geology was one of the most prestigious subjects at croma educational institutions. Tiga thought it suited their personalities.

"Go," Romki whispered — no less frightened than her, Tiga thought, just somewhat more practised at hiding it. They ran, and reached the bushes after several heart-pounding seconds. Tiga tucked herself against a palm tree trunk, looking about, then out at the rock once more. Beyond it was the outer wall, really a fence made of many steel spikes, beyond which road traffic was rushing. And against the big ornamental rock between her, the Professor and the road, came circling a large croma in a big open coat, a massive shotgun in one fist, eyes searching for them. Behind him, quite casually and completely unseen, came Karajin. The croma's wide eyes found Tiga and Romki. He lowered his weapon, and Karajin shot him point blank in the back of the head, then waved Tiga and Romki forward, as casually as a policeman directing traffic around a construction site.

Karajin's manner changed as Tiga and Romki were halfway to the rock, gesturing them to the right and around the rock on that side... a moment later, Tiga saw why, several croma running along the outer wall, behind a row of ornamental palms, weapons brandished. Karajin opened fire, retreating calmly around the rock side as Tiga and Romki ducked in behind, return fire kicking fragments off rock and paving.

Tiga squeezed into the gap between rock and paving, dismayed and panting to see Karajin kneeling tight in beside her. Now he was equally cut off from the road! He'd gotten them all trapped here! Karajin leaned out low, fired some more rounds, then pulled back as return fire blasted bits of paving, ejected a magazine from his rifle and put a new one in, as calm and methodical as a training exercise.

Suddenly new fire from further left, and Karajin risked a look out. And took no fire. Karajin got up, went past his cowering charges, and peered out the rock's other side. Made a fast handsignal to someone in that direction, and apparently got an all-clear in reply, because he waved Tiga and Romki forward once more.

Tiga went, Romki behind, and saw Private Daraka on that right side, covering behind the ornamental palms. On the left, both the croma who had pinned them behind the rock were motionless on the ground, and moving past them now, rifles ready at shoulders and looking all ways at once, were Sergeant Jinido and Private Tediri. And it dawned on Tiga as she ran what had happened — Karajin had drawn the attackers' attention to the rock, allowing the other two tavalai to flank and shoot them from that angle. Trees were poor cover if you were outflanked, only shielding from one direction. And here at the exit gate was Private Iratai, already moving to secure the big cruiser that awaited them on the sidewalk where no cruiser was supposed to land... but Tiga supposed that with Styx running the interface with the traffic net, little things like rules weren't going to stop her.

There was no more pedestrian traffic here despite the wide sidewalks — someone must have interfered to stop it, and good thing too. Iratai had the cruiser's doors opened by the time Tiga arrived, gasping for breath, and was waving them inside... only now a new cruiser was coming to a low, illegal hover over the groundcar traffic. It turned side-on, one door levering upward to reveal armed croma within, pointing weapons. Before the tavalai could fire, the cruiser abruptly lost power to one side, turned in a flip and pancaked onto the road below as ground cars took rapid, automated evasive action.

Iratai emptied what remained of his magazine into the flattened cruiser's windshield, while Tiga, Romki, then the tavalai piled into the interior. Iratai came in last and the cruiser rose before the doors were even down — a technical impossibility, Tiga had thought, which gave a good indication who was driving.

"Thank you Styx!" Tiga gasped, sprawled on a big croma chair and wondering, ridiculously, where her seat restraint was. "We'd all be dead without you!"

"Almost certainly," Styx agreed. *"And you're quite welcome, Tiga."*

"That last one was her, then?" Tediri asked. He was breathing hard and sweating, but even now checking his weapon and remaining ammunition. Beyond the windows, towers were rushing by. Normally they'd have to worry about pursuit, but with Styx flying, Tiga doubted it would be a problem.

"She made the cruiser crash," Karajin agreed from the front seat, looking over the nav controls, and activating coms. *"Hello, Captain Debogande? Can you hear me?"*

"Yes, hello Lieutenant," came the Captain's familiar, calm voice on the other end. *"What's your situation, can you talk?"*

"Yes Captain, we are in a cruiser and on our way home. No casualties, multiple croma casualties, I think..." he glanced back at his karasai. *"Ten? Eleven?"*

"Ten," Sergeant Jinido agreed. *"I thought so."*

"Styx alerted us to their attempt," Karajin continued. *"They tried to reposition to our new route, but their manoeuvre was poor. All were younger, no croma elders, I think maybe a security agency, maybe military special operations."*

"Who do you think they were after?" asked the Captain.

All eyes turned on Tiga. "Could have been me?" Romki suggested. "I've been in that damn library for three months also."

"That last one at the rock was aiming at the monkey," said Karajin. *"I think it was the monkey, Captain."*

"I'm not a fucking monkey!" Tiga fumed.

"You can tell me more when you get back," said the Captain. *"Good job everyone, Styx included. Stay safe and make sure you don't get followed."*

"Styx especially," Styx corrected him.

"Yes Captain," said Karajin, with what might have been exasperation at Styx's remark. *"Back in twelve minutes."*

"You did well, little monkey," Iratai said at Tiga's side, patting her head with one big, partially-webbed hand. *"You killed many enemies with your fearsome weapon."*

Tiga realised her pistol was still clutched in one sweaty hand, and fumbled to put it away. After her optimistically brave thought to draw it, she'd then completely forgotten she had it. Daraka clucked disapprovingly on her other side, removed the pistol from her hand and checked the chamber, the magazine, put the safety on and gave it back to her. Tiga thanked him, sourly, and put the pistol back into her bag as the big tavalai all chortled and smirked in that strange, dry humour of their kind.

6

Croma'Dokran's status as contestant in the Tali'san had granted them the authority to find suitable accomodations for their allies. For the planetside crew of *Phoenix*, a large ranch compound had been found on the outskirts of Cal'Uta.

Erik's favourite thing about the ranch was its sheer mundanity. He didn't think it aloud, knowing the smirks it would cause behind his back, as people laughed about the Debogande son not being kept in the manner to which he was accustomed. But as large as the ranch building was, with a dozen bedrooms and many large spaces now shared by marines and crew, it was starkly common compared to much else in Cal'Uta proper.

The reasons were practical enough, and Erik suspected no insult intended — of course the aliens would be put on the outskirts, furthest away from media, gawking visitors and troublesome bureaucracy alike. And the crew were happy, too. Adjoining the sprawling property were all sorts of curious things, like recycling yards for cruisers at the end of their lifespan, a huge aquaculture pool full of giant crustaceans, a rental yard for enormous excavators, a holding pen for big chew'too — huge domesticated creatures once used for riding into medieval battles and now mostly employed for ceremonies — and other, equally strange and unglamorous slices of urban civilisation. Erik supposed that his home city of Shiwon must have had an outer fringe like this as well, where all the undesirable industries that needed cheap expanses of land were located... it was just that he, only son of the Debogande clan, had never seen them. So perhaps his crew were right to snicker behind his back.

Best of all, one entire side of the ranch faced onto the rolling expanse of grassland that became the Do'jera desert as it stretched for thousands of kilometres across the Cho'na continent. Out that way, crew who had spent most of the past year-and-a-third cooped inside pressurised containment vessels now got to run, to ride motorbikes, to organise games of football, baseball or cricket, and enjoy the open expanse without breathing apparatus or pressure suits. The property even had a pool, though it had been neglected, and filling it, and keeping the water suitable for entertainment purposes, had literally become a military exercise occupying the best brains on the ship.

Erik sat now at the long conference table, with multiple glass doors opening onto a patio and then a yard filled with half-dead grass on sand that was disagreeable to greenery, and waited for the room's holography display to uplink to Croma'Dokran headquarters in Stat'cha. Finally the connection established, and at one end of the table illuminated the huge, broad-shouldered figure of the leader of all Croma'Dokran, Sho'mo'ra himself. A smaller helper also captured in the holography fussed with his leader's coat, and gave the scene a sense of scale — the helper was no doubt as tall as most of the young croma one saw wandering about Cal'Uta, but here only came up to Sho'mo'ra's chest, his shoulders barely half as wide.

"Erik," the old man rumbled, with a voice as deep and powerful as only age-stretched vocal cords could generate. *"The corbi is well?"*

"The corbi is well," Erik agreed. "Good to see you, Sho'mo'ra."

"And I heard your tavalai shot the bastards?"

"Most of the bastards, yes," said Erik. Sho'mo'ra had become a considerably more familiar figure than the formal, best-behaviour version they'd first met on Do'Ran four months ago. This version swore.

"Very good," said the enormous croma, easing himself into a chair with a wince and grunt. The audio captured the sound of furniture creaking beneath his weight. Those rigid armour plates on head, shoulders and torso alone must have weighed a quarter-ton. *"Give the tavalai my approval."*

"Lieutenant Karajin is right here, sir. He's sitting at the table."

"Very good then, Lieutenant Karajin. Did you lose any of your people?"

"No sir," said Karajin, in Togiri.

"A fine feat of arms. You are a fine representative of your species."

"Thank you, sir."

Erik's gaze slipped to Stan Romki, seated further along the table by Lieutenant Jalawi. And so well he knew Romki now that Erik could immediately read the miffed exasperation on the Professor's face. Romki saw him looking, and mouthed 'I'm fine too'. Erik nearly grinned, then stifled it with a mock-stern look at Romki to hold his tongue.

"I must say, Erik," Sho'mo'ra continued. *"This is most improper. I have lodged protests in the strongest possible terms, expressing my displeasure with the Croma'Rai leadership. They gave their warrant of protection, and they failed to deliver... as seems so often the way with Croma'Rai these days. This behaviour reflects poorly on all croma. This attack was disgusting and dishonourable. Croma fight their battles face to face."*

Erik had never seen the old man quite so agitated. His big nostrils flared, blasting out displeasure. "Is there any way to tell who was responsible?" Erik asked.

"My investigations teams are looking into it. But you will understand, Erik, that Croma'Dokran agencies have very little access to the levers of power on Dul'rho. For the moment, we are helpless."

"I understand," said Erik. "As to *why* the attack took place, I think that looks fairly obvious."

Sho'mo'ra leaned forward a little, dark eyes peering up beneath protruding armour ridges. Like some giant, alien version of a knight from the old tales of European Earth. *"The corbi thinks she has enough, does she?"*

"She does, yes. Do you still think that her testimony at the Croma'Dokran Tali'san council could have the effect you wanted?"

"So much of that corbi history has been rewritten," Sho'mo'ra rumbled. *"Not all were happy with it at the time, and very many remain unhappy now. Before Croma'Rai, it was Croma'Shin, and before them, Croma'Tuur. All have been retreatists. Croma'Dokran will not retreat. Croma abandonment of the corbi is a dishonour on all croma. Should the corbi come and speak at the council, and present her findings in the books that the Croma'Rai have not allowed anyone to read for eight hundred years, she will sway many more clans to our side. It could swing the direction of this Tali'san, I'm certain of it. Will she come?"*

"She has devoted her life to it, Sho'mo'ra," said Erik. "It will take far more than an unsuccessful assassination attempt to stop her."

"Good," said the croma, leaning back with creaking satisfaction. *"The council is in fifteen days. I will reassure the organisers that she will come. And you must keep her safe, Erik."*

"I will. The data is there for all of us in the books they've found, but none of our people could give it the context of corbi history that she can. She's been living this stuff all her life."

"And the emotion of it," Sho'mo'ra agreed. *"To be delivered by a corbi who was prepared to give everything for her people, will impact the council so much more. It must be her, none other will work."*

"I agree," said Erik.

Sho'mo'ra glanced at some nearby distraction. *"Erik, I must go. The Tali'san demands much attention, and the first engagements shall commence soon. Oh, before I go... you met with Pel'sar of Croma'Rai?"*

"I did, Sho'mo'ra." There was no need to apologise or weasel around it. Croma were realists, and sometimes fatalists. "Do you know Pel'sar?"

"He's a bastard," said Sho'mo'ra, predictably. *"But a smart bastard. Don't believe what he promises you."*

"I don't," Erik agreed. And then, for courtesy to their closest ally among the croma, on whose good will all of their lives depended, he added, "Pel'sar said Croma'Rai would establish formal relations with humanity, when they won the Tali'san. There was the implication of much wealth, probably to me personally."

"Does that interest you?" the ruler of Croma'Dokran asked drily.

"I'm already one of the wealthiest humans alive," Erik replied, injecting a hard edge to his tone. That wasn't even acting — after all he'd been through, it was genuinely offensive. "Do you think I'd be here if it did?"

"I think you have the manner of a man who does not like to lose," said Sho'mo'ra, with eyes-narrowed contemplation. *"I can't promise you relations with humanity — but neither can Pel'sar, he's selling you chew'too droppings. Croma leadership isn't dictatorship, never has been. Most of the clans don't want to open up to aliens."*

"That's what I told Pel'sar," said Erik.

"But this matter with the corbi has been a stain on croma honour for centuries. Help me to fix that, and who knows what else may change."

"We will help you fix it," Erik agreed. "And I have no doubt that the *UFS Phoenix*, and all humanity, would be better off if Croma'-Dokran were to become the rulers of all croma."

Given that Croma'Rai's stated policy was to prevent *Phoenix* from continuing her mission, it really wasn't much of a choice.

* * *

AFTER SHO'MO'RA'S BRIEFING, ERIK WALKED THE RANCH HALLS ON HIS way to the far, upstairs wing where Tiga and Romki were working. Various rooms were crowded with bunks, mostly empty but a few occupied with marines or crew who'd spent the night on guard duty, or now took an hour's R&R to read a book or record messages home.

The big house was designed as accommodation for workers in the surrounding industrial estates, all crammed together so that they could presumably save money on board. Now the capacity of sixty-plus croma had been stretched to a hundred and twenty humans and tavalai, kitchen refrigerators full of food, every bit of spare space filled with marine gear, usually weapons, ammunition and armour. Crew spent their time between leisure, duty and a mix of both. Marines pulled guard duty, but that wasn't so boring as it could have been, as curious croma from nearby estates often came visiting. Guard duty here was not so strict, and was backed up by so much serious sensory gear brought down from *Phoenix* that marines were allowed to strike up entertaining conversations.

Everyone was on the rotating roster of town visits, as Croma'Rai officials had not forbidden them from wandering, provided crew said where they were going in advance. Often they were greeted by helpful officials and given escorted tours, giving regular *Phoenix* crew an extraordinary record of croma civilisation never before seen by humans. So far they'd checked out parks, historical monuments, museums, art galleries and even bureaucratic offices, and far from being restricted, had been encouraged to ask questions. Military and other security installations had been off-limits, but even there, random encounters with off-duty personnel had been illuminating. Gruff though they could be, some croma liked to talk, and most thought poorly of restricted personal liberty.

A spacer made way for Erik as he climbed the stairs, then wove past bunks in a common bedroom, the air full of the smell of cooking from the upstairs kitchen — dinner for a hundred and twenty, with crashing pans and general commotion. In the far bedroom, Erik found the small place of seclusion where Tiga and Romki had set up a study in their bedroom. Marines unimpressed with the amount of spare floorspace afforded the civilians had filled it with ammo boxes and a large portable generator. On the neighbouring balcony by a common room, human and tavalai marines did weights, dumbbells crashing above the sound of music.

Skah sat on Tiga's bed, watching the small holography generator he'd put on the marines' ammo boxes, while Tiga and Romki sat on their respective bunks with AR glasses linked into the room's processor, and sorted through the new additions to their database. Kaspowitz sat with Romki, talking about something they'd found, long legs stretched on the bunk with his back to the wall. Something about the scene struck Erik as odd, besides the usual mad mix of species that had become second nature to everyone on *Phoenix*. But mostly, there was so much open space and sky beyond the small bedroom window, yet here everyone was, crammed into a very basic room constructed mostly of brick and board, with only a window open to let in the fresh air. Erik suspected that they'd all become so accustomed to living in each other's pockets on *Phoenix* that open space was sometimes hard to adjust to.

Fortunate also, he thought sourly, that he wasn't the kind of captain to get upset with a lack of deference from his crew — when he walked through the door, no one seemed to notice. Erik went and squeezed between Tiga and Skah on that bunk, looking at Skah's holography images. They were of the Tali'san — a report of some kind, illustrating the various units and clans involved, and where they were deploying across Dul'rho's surface for battles ahead. The report ran through the attributes of each unit, with many pictures of fearsome croma warriors marching in unison, or practising weapons drills with pole-arms the size of trees. Skah stared at the screen entranced, like any eight-year-old boy would. Eight, at least, was the closest anyone had come to approximating kuhsi ages in equivalent human years. He was still just a kid, but now noticeably bigger than he had been.

"What unit's that, Skah?" Erik asked.

"That Cwan Crona'Trin," said Skah, touching the controls with light fingertips, calling up more data. "This is the Din'da Sector, they fight there against..." he checked the new displays, "...Cwan Cron-a'Shok. Ten thousand warrior each, just this one sector!" He looked excitedly at Erik for the first time, then back at the display. "See, wook, Crona'Shok have big... big powe, big sticks, see?"

"Big poles, yes," Erik translated. "We call those pole arms. Called them. A long time ago."

"So they fight fron distance, but Crona'Trin, they use big hanner!" Big hammers, Erik saw as the vision showed huge croma carrying hammers no human would be able to lift. A few of those croma were carrying the hammers single-handed.

"He's becoming quite the encyclopaedia on the Tali'san," said Romki, diverting from his conversation with Kaspowitz long enough to glance across. "Just try to remember that it's not all fun and games, Skah. Lots of people are going to die in this thing."

"Oh go on," Kaspowitz snorted. "If a bunch of meat-headed croma are determined to kill each other for some glorious cultural festival, who are we to argue otherwise? If you were an eight-year-old boy, you'd love it too."

"Ah yes," said Romki, "that prelude to many a great philosophical argument across the ages — 'if I were an eight-year-old boy'."

"So it really looks like Croma'Dokran's allies want to help the corbi, huh?" Kaspowitz said it with his usual skepticism, looking from Erik to Tiga and back again. Tiga kept working, oblivious, or pretending to be.

"It does look that way," Erik agreed. "Or Sho'mo'ra and his experts say it will. They say all the history's been distorted by eight hundred years of croma rulers not wanting anyone to remember what really happened. If we can show them at the Tali'san Council, it could sway a lot more. Maybe even persuade some of those currently sitting out the Tali'san to come and join in."

"On whose side?" Kaspowitz asked, skepticism rising.

"I guess we'll find out," Erik said firmly. He knew Kaspowitz was right to be dubious. The croma had dumped their old allies eight centuries ago and wanted nothing to do with them ever since. Changing their minds looked like a long shot. But then, a Tali'san for control of all croma space also happened very rarely, and it wasn't all croma they were looking to convince — just those allied to Croma'-Dokran. Whatever the advantage to humanity, he wasn't about to let this opportunity slide. Not *everything* had to be about selfish interests. The corbi deserved that much from them at least, and as far as he could see, *Phoenix* was stuck at Dul'rho regardless. Helping the corbi would cost them little. "One thing we know for sure — Croma'Rai aren't happy about it."

"You think they're behind the attack?"

"Seems likely," said Erik. "Can't tell for sure. But Pel'sar pretty much warned me yesterday. If they're prepared to do that much to stop Tiga getting to the Council, they might not stop there."

He was pretty sure they were safe at the ranch. To be sure, one missile could kill the lot of them, but croma concepts of honour, while no more perfect than the human kind, would not allow such a thing. Just like in human space, croma rulers could get away with certain levels of minor criminality, but more than that would bring croma laws and public opinion down on their heads like a ton of bricks. *Phoenix* had become important in so many croma affairs beyond just this Tali'san, and most croma seemed aware of it.

"And what about the investigator's offer?" Kaspowitz asked. "Find out more about the alo? Secret knowledge the Croma'Rai's intelligence service accumulated?"

"It makes sense," said Erik. Elbows on knees, looking at his lanky navigator through Skah's holography display of marching croma warriors. "They had a lot of time in contact with the reeh. Far more contact than they were supposed to have. Styx has looked at the vision of the alo, she's pretty sure it's genuinely old footage from whereever they were before space travel."

"I'm sure it'd be nice to know," Kaspowitz agreed. "The question is if it's worth the risk of upsetting everything here to get it."

"Well we have to go to Stat'cha anyway." Erik refrained from chewing on his nail as he thought. "Tiga's evidence could sway the Tali'san to Croma'Dokran, or Sho'mo'ra thinks so. And if Croma'-Dokran don't win, we probably won't be allowed to go to Rando anytime soon."

"And that would stop us?" Kaspowitz asked with an edge.

Erik shrugged. "No, probably not. But it would simplify things if we didn't have to shoot at otherwise friendly croma to do it."

"Captain, Captain, wook!" Skah interrupted, pointing at his holo-gram. "The Croma'Rai side use axes!"

"Yes, I can see that Skah," Erik said patiently. And repressed a shudder at the sight of them. An eight-year-old had no concept of the horror of an edged weapon that size, and what it could do to even an armoured elder croma.

* * *

NEEDING TO THINK, ERIK DID HIS FAVOURITE THING OF ALL ON DUL'RHO, and went for a walk. The big swimming pool was full of tavalai, naturally — shirtless and muscular with their smooth, leathery skin. Tavalai could swim circles around most humans, but the pool was too small and too full for laps. Mostly they dozed or talked about the pool rim, arms out and heads back, often with a drink in hand. Erik was pleased to see some humans in the water with them, and that relations between the recently-warring species seemed cordial at least, and in some instances far better than that. It had not always been the case, in the months since Defiance.

He strolled from the pool past the barbecue patio, so-named because the five large barbecue grills set up there were usually sizzling with something, as crew came through at all hours from different shifts in search of food. Chief Petty Officer Goldman offered Erik a small seafood something that tasted delicious, and he stopped to talk for a moment with *Phoenix*'s top-ranked enlisted man, and most experienced of all ranks. Goldman had saved many lives leading rescue teams after *Phoenix* had been crippled in the Battle of Defiance, and Erik had done the paperwork to get him awarded the Diamond Star — Fleet's second-highest award for heroism in combat. He personally thought it deserved the Liberty Star, but the standards required for 'Bloody Mary' were so ridiculous that he knew better than to even try. Unfortunately, any award had to be approved by a review board of Fleet officers, and those were in short supply out here. Most of *Phoenix* were up for an award of some description, and some for several. As nice as it would have been for morale to simply ignore Fleet regs and have the fabricators print some medals to pin on chests without higher review, he knew that the crew would see it mostly as an act of morale service, and thus potentially of desperation.

Beyond the patio, he wandered across the ragged brown grass to the wide vehicle shed. Within were several civilian cruisers being used for trips to town -- only half of the present fleet, the others currently being used. Also within were a number of recreational vehicles, a few flatbed utilities, and an excavator left by previous tenants that no one had found a use for. Here he found crew testing engines, and several working on a quad-bike that Spacer Rudolf had managed to roll while larking in the desert.

Peanut was here, the big insectoid AI drone holding one fat wheel while a couple of marines and spacers carried out repairs. It was fascinating to see Peanut's multi-sensored head darting this way and that, following the crew's conversation, mismatched eyes watching one and then the other. Erik thought that Peanut wasn't the slightest bit interested in fixing the quad-bike — the technology was rudimentary to any drysine drone. Alone of *Phoenix*'s three drones, Peanut just liked to hang out with people and follow conversation. He'd never yet shown any sign of contributing to a conversation. No one had yet figured out if drones had personal opinions.

Beyond the vehicle shed, Erik passed the few scraggly trees beside what had been the property's rear fence before marines had pulled it down, considering it gave too much cover to any potentially hostile rear approach. Now the dry, dusty ground made a clear way to the patch of hard earth they were using as a shuttle landing pad. GR-1 sat upon it now, *Phoenix*'s newest assault shuttle, brought by Garudan Platoon.

GR-1 loomed flat and wide, curved where human shuttles were angular, guarded by two marines from Charlie Platoon. On GR-1's wing sat Lieutenants Sasalaka and Leralani — discussing flying, Erik thought by the movement of their hands. Seeing him approach, Sasalaka pulled a crumpled cap from her pocket, slapped it on her head and saluted. Erik smiled and saluted back. It had a humour to it, coming from tavalai who didn't really grasp the tradition of saluting senior officers, nor especially doing it outside only while under 'cover', as was the military term for a uniform hat. The humour came mostly from the fact that tavalai heads were somewhat flat, making the wearing of hats impractical. In a strong wind, a tavalai soldier's cover would disappear fast, taking his salutes with it. Tavalai found that funnier than humans did, having a well developed sense of the absurd. Having experienced tavalai bureaucracy firsthand, Erik could well imagine where they'd gotten it from.

On the road to the adjoining industrial properties beyond the shuttle, Erik found another three karasai, clothes still wet from swimming, and hauling several large bags. They showed Erik the contents with enthusiasm — the bags were crawling with big crustaceans from the aquaculture pond, where agreeable croma employees sometimes let tavalai go swimming for a catch. Erik shared the karasai's enthusiasm — the crustaceans were an acquired taste, and not all crew enjoyed them, but that just left more for those who did.

Walking further still, Erik wandered onto the scrubby dry plains of low bush, little more than knee-high, stretching into a vast distance dotted only by the occasional property, solar array or high-tension wire. Somewhere middle distant, a hover train roared, kicking up a long rooster tail of dust. Beyond that, far mountains rose, shimmering in the mid-afternoon heat. Erik took a deep breath, feeling himself relax further. Nearer to one side, some crew were playing cricket, now shouts and cries of 'catch it!' as someone slammed a ball into the vast blue sky. No tavalai among this group — only humans. The crew mixed, but were far from 'integrated'. Erik wondered what could be done about it.

Three months without Trace had been a revelation of sorts, in the same way that some machines revealed their working structure only when a vital component was removed. Phoenix Company functioned well enough with Lieutenant Dale in charge, but Erik felt there was something grinding in the gears. Trace's command was apparently effortless, while Dale beat and whacked things into place. Erik had previously heard whispered observations coming from off *Phoenix* that Dale might be the more natural commander, with his hard-ass, square-jawed style. Certainly he fit the preconceptions that a desk-Admiral or civvie journalist might have of what a Fleet marine should be far more than cool, mild Major Thakur.

But people who drove organisations by sheer force drew attention to the fact that force was in fact required. Trace had rarely seemed to need it — everything just glided, people knew what to do, all the moving parts slid together with a minimum of noise and fuss. Under Dale, Phoenix Company ran more like a big engine — throbbing and roaring in a way that would probably impress outsiders, but lacking that well-oiled efficiency. Lieutenants Alomaim and Crozier found it fine, and Karajin remained stoically noncommittal as always, but Jalawi had always rubbed Dale the wrong way, by virtue of the fact that he rubbed everyone the wrong way. Trace had barely noticed, and Jalawi had loved her for it, but now Dale had taken to telling Jalawi that less wisecracks might help his platoon run better. Jalawi's wisecracks had predictably increased, as the unwritten rule of Phoenix Company was that no one told a Platoon Commander how to run his platoon, not even the Company Commander. Erik had thought it wise to intervene and direct Charlie Company down to Cal'Uta in place of Bravo, whose turn this was supposed to be, before things got ugly. So now Dale was pissed at Erik for interfering in marine affairs and rotations, but Erik hadn't cared.

"The Major managed Jalawi just fine," he'd told Dale. "You don't want me interfering in marine matters? Don't need me to." A year ago he'd have thought it a big deal, confronting Dale in that manner. But a year of Trace's example had taught him a lot.

He'd also learned that his feelings for Trace were somewhat mixed up. No surprises there — a year of heart-stopping stresses and near-death experiences together would turn even enemies into friends, and he and Trace had never been enemies. He was pretty sure he didn't love her like *that*, but he did love her, as he loved many of this crazy extended family that *Phoenix* had become. He wanted badly to see her again, and looked forward to giving her a bear hug on that occasion... before recalling that one did not simply bearhug the deadpan winner of 'Bloody Mary' herself, particularly not before her marines. With Trace, as always, it was complicated. So many of his best memories with her were painful, and soaked in blood.

With Lisbeth, at least, things were simpler. News had reached them of House Harmony's ascension to become ruling house of all parren, with Gesul at their head. Erik knew better than to think Lisbeth would ever be entirely safe as Gesul's advisor — there would always be forces within House Harmony that found her presence threatening. But she had Liala to defend her now, and that had to count for something. Lisbeth had been quite upbeat about it all in the only message she'd managed to get through to him since Gesul's ascension, describing only her daily schedules, and the people she worked with every day. Routine stuff, but fascinating all the same, to glimpse the heights to which his little sister had risen in her time among parren. And oh-so-professional now, not revealing any broad strategic details to those she was not cleared to brief — not even her brother. Erik wondered if Lisbeth wasn't becoming just a little bit parren herself, in her instinctive discipline on such things. It had never been her strong suit before.

An uplink beeped in his inner ear, and Erik dropped the AR glasses before his eyes to blink on the connection from *Phoenix* bridge. "Hello Lieutenant Lassa, this is the Captain."

"Hello Captain," came *Phoenix's* coms officer from the orbiting ship's bridge. *"We have a situation developing. Croma'Rai authorities have announced they're putting the entire Cho'na continent into security lockdown. No unauthorised travel will be allowed, travel privileges for special visitors has been revoked."*

Erik frowned, gazing at the distant mountains. "I take it that means us?"

"We're querying the exact wording, Captain, but that's what it looks like. The restrictions are in place for the next twenty days, they're claiming the security agencies have detected an unspecified threat, by which they mean terrorist or something similar."

Erik repressed several very bad words. "How many special visitors are there?"

"We've been adding it up, Captain. It looks like there's about two hundred thousand at present across the continent, with the Tali'san on. Of course, all travel related to the Tali'san will be unrestricted, this is only to non-Tali'san special visitors, which might leave... our best guess is about three or four thousand, most of them media, medical or academic interests."

"So *Phoenix* crew could be making up nearly ten percent of all those banned from travel."

"Yes Captain. It's pretty narrowly targeted, looks like... they're just going out of their way to make it deniable that it's aimed specifically at us."

The Croma'Dokran Tali'san Council was fifteen days away in Stat'cha. He didn't even need to say it, all the crew knew what was going on. Erik turned and strode back through the desert scrub toward the looming bulk of GR-1's rear end, and the ranch beyond.

"I'd like you to find me a legal proceeding, Lieutenant Lassa," he said. "Something very loud and very obvious that will make the biggest noise possible to protest this action."

"Yes Captain. Captain... from what I've seen of croma legal proceedings, our odds aren't great. They're not slow like the tavalai, but the courts put a lot of weight on the clan-history of defendants and prosecutors alike... we'd have to find a registered prosecutor who agreed to take us on despite our lack of clan pedigree, we can't represent ourselves for exactly that reason..."

"I'm sure there are plenty of complications, Lieutenant, but it doesn't matter. I don't particularly care if we're successful or not — even if they're stunningly fast I doubt the courts could prosecute a case like this before the Stat'cha Council meets. I just want a distraction to hold everyone's attention. A big one."

"Oh," said Lassa, her voice brightening as she realised her Captain had a far more interesting plan than that one. *"Yes Captain, it won't be easy getting people to notice our distraction with the Tali'san on, but we'll do our best. Would you like any urgent communication with Croma'Dokran and Sho'mo'ra while we're at it?"*

"I think at this point we'd better keep it to ourselves," said Erik. He passed GR-1, waved a hand at Sasalaka and Leralani still talking on the wing, indicating his ear and an urgent situation. Both tavalai headed immediately for the dorsal hatch as their Captain kept walking. "Styx, are you there?"

"Of course, Captain," said Styx, without apparent irony.

"We promised Croma'Rai that we wouldn't utilise your capabilities to interfere with their governance while we were here. But they've now violated that agreement by pulling levers to stop us from going to Stat'cha. I'll need your assistance in hiding our activities from the Croma'Rai government now."

"Certainly, Captain. What would you like me to do?"

7
_____

Three days after the hillside ambush, Trace awoke in the late afternoon in the village of Sebi. The bedroom was an attic of sorts, the ceiling wood-tiled beneath a layer of moss and thatch. It was warm bordering on hot beneath the afternoon sun. Kono lay nearby, shirtless in the heat, big chest scarred with what looked like a war wound but was actually a childhood mishap with a power tool. They shared the attic with storage boxes, some filled with old cloth, others with grain and long-lasting food items. Birds fluttered on a nearby window ledge, and called to others. The light patter of paws suggested a fir was about — furry, like a cross between a cat and a weasel, they prowled the storage bins and ate the critters that tried to eat the grain. Corbi had domesticated them long before the reeh came, and still the fir hung about, knowing they'd never have a truer master, no matter who ran Rando lately.

The assassin bug, Trace guessed, would be outside sunning itself on the rooftop, while performing its sentry role. Exactly what its programming was, or how flexibly it could now interpret that programming, she did not know. She'd tried talking to it before, asking it to buzz once for yes and twice for no in response to questions, but had gotten very little. But then, even full-sized drysine drones were sometimes unresponsive to direct speech, despite being plenty smart enough to decipher it. Romki occasionally reminded all *Phoenix* officers that the human familiarity with verbal speech was something that had evolved over millions of years, and could not be taken for granted in other sufficiently alien species — machines in particular. To a dog, human incomprehension of basic body language would seem pretty stupid too.

Trace reached for her water bottle, sipped long, then rolled off her floorboard matting to begin her stretches. She had to tie her improvised shirt above her middle, disconcertingly like some farm-girl trying to impress the local boys — midriff bare and buttons undone. It was that or sleep with it done up, and in the daytime the attic grew too hot for that. Thankfully Kono was the only local male who might find the sight distracting, and she'd served with him long enough to know *that* wasn't likely to be an issue, with her at least.

The Resistance had found their jumpsuits and a few other clothes in the reeh shuttle carrying them, presumably because even reeh thought prisoners should wear something that fit. Thankfully that had included her undershirt, as marines euphemistically called a standard-issue sports bra, but she only had one of them, and it was currently hanging on the support beam, drying after she'd washed it. Erik would have teased her, but it was nearly her most important bit of field kit, and she tried to look after it. Corbi fabrics were rough, and chafing on long jungle deployments was no laughing matter.

Her stretches turned into exercises, which shortly woke Kono, blinking at the ceiling. He joined her, and soon they were making enough noise that anyone downstairs would be staring upwards at the thumping racket. Trace knew her aerobic fitness was suffering, no amount of walking could equal a good run, and running in this forest was a bad idea. But a marine knew enough resistance exercises that they had little need of a gym... and thankfully, the attic cross-beam between vertical supports was just the right height for pull-ups. Do enough of those for long enough, and even aerobic capacity benefitted.

She finished before Kono, dressed, armed and went down the

steep, rickety steps that were nearly a ladder. It brought her into a dark, narrow hall, around the corner from which was the kitchen. On the wooden table, food was laid out — some bread, sliced cheese, assorted fruits. It was a fair feast by corbi standards, and considerably more than a local would have. She ate, peering through the slats of window covers at the daylight outside. Odd to be waking in late afternoon. And she recalled Erik's tales of some late nights in school holidays as a teenager, going to crazy rich-kid parties and waking after midday.

Two times already today she'd thought of Erik. She'd tried not to, the first month they'd been with the Resistance. She'd been busy then, trying to figure out how the Resistance worked, what the reeh were up to in this never-ending occupation, and learning enough Lisha to make herself understood. But she'd missed his advice, and discovered that actually, thinking of Erik and trying to imagine what he'd say in various circumstances gave her ideas for things she'd otherwise not have considered. It was more than the advice, though. It was the comfort of knowing that someone else was there to support her, come what may. Kono was a friend, but mostly he was a non-commissioned officer who did what she ordered because that was the oath they'd both sworn, whatever their present lack of uniforms. This was most certainly a combat zone, and they were both very much on duty, and so that command distance had to remain. With Erik she could be herself in a way that wasn't possible with anyone else on *Phoenix* except possibly her old buddy Kaspowitz. Or Styx.

It made her dissatisfied, chewing on bread and cheese, staring through slats at the neighbouring huts in the bright afternoon. Dissatisfied that she'd gotten so soft as to need someone. She knew what she had to try and do while on Rando, and it wasn't going to happen if she started moping about her lack of a shoulder to cry on. Billions of lives could depend on it. All of humanity, conceivably. It was what she'd joined the Corps for, and dedicated her life to, one meticulous action at a time. The reeh could take the marine out of her uniform, armour, modern weapons and even away from familiar food, but they were going to find that the end result was still a UF

Marine. If she could make it work as she planned, it wouldn't be a lesson they'd enjoy learning.

Kono thumped down the stairs in the doorway, then exclaimed in annoyance. He entered the kitchen holding a fir, like a long tube of fur trying to wrap itself around his neck like a scarf. "Little pest tried to trip me on the stairs," he explained, dropping the animal on the table. It bounced on light paws and sniffed at the food. "It's bread," he told it, taking some himself. "You won't like it."

The fir seemed to agree, and leaped to the floor. "I want you to check on the tanifex," Trace told Kono around a mouthful. "I'm going to take a proper bath in the river, I'm rank."

"I wasn't going to say anything," Kono conceded.

"And you don't smell much better."

"Guilty." He ate some of the nuts in the small bowl alongside the bread, and poured himself a glass of freshly squeezed juice. "What do we do if the bigshot Fleet dude doesn't arrive today?"

"Give him another day," said Trace. "He's not here by the end of tomorrow, we move without him. Until then, same as yesterday — watch the tanifex, help Cedu analyse its armour, help the villagers with kauda patrols, etc. Good?"

"Good," Kono agreed, swallowing juice. "Hell of a place to save the galaxy from."

"And you stow that shit," Trace warned him, without anger. "No talking to anyone about it, we don't know who'll flip out."

"Yes Major." What Kono thought of her plans, Trace didn't know. Probably he thought it was good she had something to keep her occupied. And probably that was much of it — she was terrible at accepting the status quo, and would always find a larger goal to prepare for. Probably Kono hoped it wouldn't go any further than that.

* * *

THE RIVER WAS JUST BEYOND THE PERIMETER FENCE. CORBI MADE THE trip constantly, through orchard trees now full with young fruit. Trace walked with her weapons and floppy hat, smiling to several women returning with full water containers on their heads, and got cheerful grins in reply.

The near part of the riverbank past the orchard was worn smooth with the frequent passage of corbi feet. On the far bank, just ten metres away, a bored villager sat with a rifle, chewing some kind of native sugar cane. Trace indicated to him that she'd go downstream, and the corbi bobbed his head... the two species had that gesture somewhat in common, though it didn't always mean the same thing.

Downstream, the river went over a small falls formed by several big tree roots, and some thick undergrowth made a little privacy. It was the standard bathing spot, typically used in the mornings and evenings, now empty in mid-afternoon. Trace quickly removed clothes, then walked with rifle, sidearm and sheathed kukri into the deeper water behind the tree root falls, and placed all weapons on a flat rock that had been deposited there by bathers for the placement of less-lethal objects. Like soap, a little of which remained now.

She ducked into the water and proceeded to wash. The forest wasn't exactly beautiful here — they were too close to the village for that, too much undergrowth had been cut away for nearby cultivation, and worn flat by constant foot traffic. But the trees were nice, hinting at the genuine beauty to be found deeper in. After washing, she took a moment to settle in the water, the mini-falls splashing about her hair and shoulders, and attained as much meditative calm as the situation allowed. Her hair was really getting too long, now. She'd have to risk Kono with a pair of scissors.

After perhaps a minute, she was certain someone was watching on her left. Almost certainly that person was corbi — if otherwise, she'd be dead, or someone would have raised an alarm. But there was a point to be made, so she reached quickly for the sidearm and levelled it squarely at the watcher, only opening her eyes at the last moment to see what she aimed at.

He was corbi all right — bigger than many, shirtless in the way of most strong corbi men in their farming labours on a warm day. Corbi were naturally a lot wider at the shoulders than humans, though lost some of that imposing strength in their lack of height. This young man had a rakish, long black mane and a juvenile beard. A red bandana kept the sweat from his eyes, and he wore a rifle across his back.

Instead of showing alarm at the pistol targeting his forehead, he grinned, and pointed at her. "You're good!" he said in Lisha. "I thought I was being quiet." Trace thought a rebuke for sneaking up on her would be too much. And while corbi observed gender separation while bathing most of the time, they weren't as offended by nudity as most humans, so she couldn't fairly rebuke him for that either. Besides, she wasn't shaped like anything a corbi male would find the slightest bit attractive.

She settled for putting the pistol back on the rock, and resuming her wordless meditation. Take a hint, kid. But the kid didn't take a hint, and plonked himself on the riverbank with short legs extended, feet in the water.

"I'm Rika," he said. "I live here, but I'm in the Resistance. I joined two years ago. Saw some fighting last year, we killed some kauda. I'm still just a tavi, though." That was the same as a 'private', Trace knew. "What rank are you, among your people?"

"We call it 'Major'," said Trace. "It's different from most corbi ranks. But among my people, I'd be commanding a kija."

Rika's eyes widened. A 'kija' was the closest equivalent size to a United Forces marine company Trace had yet discovered. For a Resistance private, it was a big deal. "That's awesome! And you're elite, yeah?"

"Very," said Trace. There was no ego in the truth. Maybe the kid would crash headlong into the realisation that this wasn't how a private talked to a major... but then, corbi concepts of discipline weren't the same as human either. She couldn't really hold that against them — it wasn't just a species thing, it was the entire situation, civilians from the ragtag remnants of civilisation doing military things the same way they did everything, with ingenious improvisation. All things considered, she thought they did it quite well, sometimes at least.

"I want to be elite too," said Rika. He had a bravado to him that was all male, full of confident swagger. "Your group took casualties, so I'm going to put myself in as a replacement."

Trace slitted her eyes open to look at him sideways. "Why?" she asked.

"The guys in Loga's group say you're cold. That you don't care when people get killed." Trace felt the pain of that, but let it slide. If they thought that, it was the price she'd have to pay. Doing what she had to do for humanity would be hard enough. Any additional attachments here would just get in her way, and endanger the entire mission. There was too much at stake for her to allow it. "I like that," said Rika, fiercely. "There's too much softness in corbi. We need to be hard. I want to learn to fight like you."

"Interesting," said Trace, tilting her head back in the water.

"They say you killed fifteen tanifex in that fight," Rika continued. "That you stopped that attack on your own. How did you do that?"

Trace took a deep breath, and thought about the vocabulary she'd need. This 'morning', with her head clear, she thought she had enough. "I'll tell you this, kid," she said. "Young men think they can just be tough and brave, and that's enough. It's not. You have to be calm. You have to think. You have to be ready, you have to know exactly what you're doing. Fighting isn't fighting. It's art. You get good at art by practise and discipline. You have to know what you need to do, and do it. No matter what. Every time. Every minute, every second you're alive. You understand?"

Rika stared at her, eyes burning. "Yes. Teach me?"

Trace nearly rolled her eyes. "Get Loga to let you into the unit," she told him. And she stood up, because someone who'd seen as much carnage as her couldn't let a little thing like trans-species nudity bother her. "Then you can learn with the rest."

And most probably, she thought sadly as she went to her clothes, you can die with them as well.

* * *

Sebi's population was about five hundred— barely a pinprick on the face of the Rando population. Dinner was lunch on Trace and Kono's time schedule. One thing about the animal-rich forests of Talo was that there was enough live game that farming for red meat was unnecessary. Today the hunters had brought back a pair of four-legged game animals, and now roasted them over fires beneath central tarpaulins in the village center. Trace sat on a tree stump and ate with her fingers from a small plate — a good mix of meat and vegetables prepared with native sauces, all quite tasty and nutritious. Certainly no corbi were starving on this part of Rando, though she knew that elsewhere had been different. The tarpaulins blocked any visibility to overhead surveillance, and the clouds were thick tonight anyhow.

Many corbi gathered and ate, some now departing from the cooking fires with piled plates of food for those not eating in this company — some bed-ridden old folk and wounded soldiers, some guards out on the walls who could not leave their posts, and some others choosing to stay separate for social reasons Trace had not grasped. But those that had gathered were lively. Having finished their dinner, children played a game with objects in marked squares on some nearby dirt, with squeals and shouts of outrage at someone's perceived cheating. Several loud jokesters kept crowds entertained with funny stories. An old lady shuffled through the gathering with a large jug of moonshine that she'd apparently made herself, to the mixed enthusiasm of villagers with cups, some of whom joked it might kill them.

At a further corner of the yard, beneath the spreading branches of a tupi tree, sat white-haired Loga, his arm in a sling, talking in low voices with other soldier-corbi — some from his team, others local villagers. A few of them shot Trace furtive glances as they spoke, some hostile, others wary or even awestruck. They were discussing the ambush at the caves, no doubt. Trace ignored them, and waved off the old lady's moonshine, sipping her tin cup of water.

Kono stood with Pena and some others at a nearby fire, sampling food and animated in conversation. A young corbi entertained herself climbing Kono's leg and swinging from his powerful arms, which the Staff Sergeant tolerated while continuing to eat and talk. None of the children approached Trace, though many stared, eyes big beneath unkept fringes in the flickering firelight. Trace wanted to tell Kono to leave the locals alone, but he was in fact slightly older than her, and well past the age of needing anyone to tell him how to manage personal things. This world, Trace knew, was going to hurt. If Kono made too many connections here, their severing could be painful to the point of damage. Well, he'd find out for himself. It wasn't like she hadn't warned him.

A commotion started up one end of the clearing, then spread as people turned to look. Loga and his military people got to their feet. Then Trace saw him — a powerful corbi in a big military jacket, a beret-like floppy hat on his head, a rifle slung over one shoulder. Several of those with him looked similarly martial. Trace stayed seated, eating and guessing calorie contents. Usually she knew exactly what she put in her body, and knew her energy and fitness levels accordingly. Here, as with everything, it was all guesswork.

The new arrival greeted Loga — without much enthusiasm on either side. Pleasantries exchanged, he turned and came to Trace. Still Trace remained seated, and licked her fingers to make that hand presentable for a handshake. The new corbi took it, eyes calculating. His grip was powerful enough that Trace suspected augments. That usually meant only one thing.

"Tano," said the corbi, taking a seat on the sawed chunk of tree trunk alongside. "Torep Tano." Torep was a corbi Fleet rank, Trace knew. It explained the hostility between Tano and Loga — Tano was Fleet, born and bred in space. It also explained his synthetically powerful grip.

"Trace Thakur. Commander, Phoenix Company." He knew, but it was politeness. She'd heard he was in the area, and suspected he might be coming to see her. She saw no need to volunteer that information, however. "Did Talo Command send you?"

A village man pressed a plate of food into Tano's hand, which the commander accepted with thanks. "I go where I want," said Tano, taking a mouthful. "Someone told me you weren't enjoying your current assignment?"

"You're Fleet," said Trace, meeting his big, alien eyes directly. "What do you think?"

Tensions between Fleet and Rando Resistance were high. Rando Resistance complained that Fleet had all their technology, yet spent little effort to help liberate Rando. Fleet complained that Rando Resistance were wasting their time attempting to liberate a planet that couldn't be liberated, and ought to join their efforts to fight the reeh offworld where it mattered. The whole thing was so close to what had happened to humans on Earth after the krim invaded that to Trace, it was like pages from military history books springing to life.

Tano made an expansive gesture. "So they take you to see the zoo. How do you like our zoo?" Most Fleet corbi did not like being down on the surface at all, but Rando Resistance often learned things Fleet needed to know. Tano looked like a guy who made a habit of it. A Fleet liaison, who knew his way around these villages and jungles, but remained loyal to Fleet above all.

"I've seen less of it than I'd like," said Trace.

"What have you learned?" Examining her curiously as he ate. Some planet corbi talked past her, as people might with a strange alien. Being Fleet, Tano had seen aliens before, and probably talked with many. A human wouldn't seem so strange to him.

"I've learned that reeh don't take this place seriously," said Trace. "Local corbi think..." she paused to gather the words she'd need while eating. "Local corbi think this is fortress. You know?" She made the shape with her hands, of a huge fortification.

"I know," said Tano, with a glint of amusement. "They think the reeh Fleet was made just to occupy Rando."

"Right," said Trace, nodding. "Most of the reeh Fleet don't know Rando exists. The border with the croma has been quiet for hundreds of years. The fighting is somewhere else. Reeh beat the corbi, then left. They can't make things here. Factories?"

"Factories," Tano confirmed she'd used the correct word.

"No factories here, it's too close to croma space." She pointed vaguely, somewhere at the night sky. "There's almost no reeh here at all. They're all in the Rando Splicer, and a few other bases. Most of the military force is their... their slave species, like the tanifex — it looks big from the ground, but it's tiny compared to what they could send here if they were serious. Rando is a zoo to them, like you say. A place to make... experiments? Yes, experiments. This is a tiny world on the edge of their space. The Reeh Empire is huge. Rando is nothing to them. And that's why Fleet can play games with their surveillance so easily. They don't even try."

Tano blinked rapidly, like a man shocked to hear so much truth so bluntly. "Well. I can see we haven't impressed you very much at all."

"So many people here think Rando can be saved," Trace continued, lowering her voice. "But even if there were a big revolution, the reeh will just send their big forces, and..." She made a motion of fist-into-palm. Tano watched it somberly, making no comment. "But you're Fleet," Trace finished. "You know this."

"And walking around the zoo with Loga?" Tano asked around a mouthful, gesturing over to where the white-haired corbi sat and talked with his friends, casting occasional suspicious glances their way. "How is that for you?"

"The Binu Caves just now," said Trace. "Loga got us ambushed. I told him, he didn't listen. Perimeter... mines?" She had to search to recall the Lisha word again. She was completely conversational with grammar, it was just the damn vocabulary kept tripping her up. "Did not explode. I set them off myself, all the sentries were killed, like I told Loga would happen. I got through the tanifex line, through the explosions. Got behind them. Killed a lot, shot them in the back. Kono went around, through the second cave, outflanked them, with corbi help. Without me and him, Loga's people, all dead."

She took another bite, still deadpan. Constructing sentences from the smaller words she could use in context was exhausting. Tano might have smirked. "You've got a very high opinion of yourself."

"I was told I am high value," Trace replied around her mouthful, ignoring the insult. "Get a high value alien to see the reeh, I was told.

Big thing. But they put me with Loga, and Loga can't fight. Nearly gets me and everyone killed, does not listen when I tell him how to fight. So I think they don't really care about this high value thing at all." She indicated herself. "I don't think they want to win this war. They just make a dance. Dance here, dance there, this looks good enough, let's do that. They pretend to fight. Make believe, like a children's game. There are some real warriors here, but they're not serious. Some of them are scared to hit the reeh because of the reeh retaliation." That was a big Lisha word she'd heard used a lot. "But if you don't want to hit someone because they might hit you back, why hit them at all? Why not stay at home and farm crops?"

Tano thought about it, munching his food. Trace wondered if the reason he didn't take the difficult feedback personally was that he was just a quality officer who'd learned to do that, or that the criticism was all aimed at the Rando Resistance, and that as a Fleet man, he agreed with it.

He gestured her up, for there were many watching them, and more than a few standing close enough to listen past the hubbub of other voices. Trace caught Kono's concerned look from across the yard — that simple eye contact, and he was reassured. Tano led her to the nearest hut doorway, plate still in hand, Trace having finished her last mouthful and bringing just her cup, and her rifle.

Inside the door, a stairway led up to the second floor. Tano took a seat on it, high enough that she didn't loom over him. Trace leaned against the wall with her cup — a spacer habit, to always seek several points of contact in any enclosed space.

"They're going to send you away on *Phoenix* soon," he said, long arms dangling on short knees. "They think you're going to bring them help." It sounded sarcastic. From the closest alien species to humans Trace had ever encountered, she wasn't at all surprised it sounded so familiar.

"It's all they can do," she replied. "And who knows? There's a big contest on Dul'rho to make a new croma leader. Maybe it will change."

"I have to count back through fifty family ancestors to get to the last time a corbi trusted a croma to help," Tano growled. "Never again." There was a lot of bad blood there, Trace knew. Corbi despaired of so many lifetimes wasted, waiting for croma to come and help them. "So why do you think the reeh haven't come for you after that ambush in the caves?"

"Because everything's a fight for the reeh," said Trace. "They like the fight, they think it makes them stronger. They don't want to win quickly. The tanifex force wasn't very strong, so I don't think they knew it was me. Maybe they still don't, I don't know."

"What else?"

"We haven't done anything special," said Trace. "Tanifex get beaten quite a lot. The reeh will notice, but that's all. This is now a priority area for them, but there's lots of those on Rando. They'll watch it, and see what happens. From their perspective, I could be in any of those hundreds of areas."

"So you want to show us how to fight," said Tano, perhaps sardonically. "How will you do that?"

"I want to hit a big reeh target," said Trace. "One that will benefit your people and mine."

"And what would that be?"

"The Rando Splicer."

Tano laughed. And kept laughing, as though it was the funniest thing he'd heard in weeks. When he finally recovered, it was to find Trace as deadpan serious as before. "The Rando Splicer is the center of all the reeh's genetic manipulation technology on Rando," he said... or Trace thought he said. Some of those words were large, but she could guess, in context. It wasn't anything she hadn't heard other corbi say. "It's the most heavily defended place on this planet. It's not possible."

"Not possible for *you*," Trace corrected. "Not for me alone. But together we might have a chance."

Tano looked amused, in the way of an adult tolerating a precocious child merely to humour her. "How?" he asked.

* * *

TRACE MET CEDU IN THE BASEMENT CELLS WHERE SHE'D SENT FOR HIM, with Tano behind. Upstairs of the basement was a common building with an open floor, used for artisanal industry — weaving, carpentry and tool making. Some of those machines were quite ingenious, all of them operating without electricity, but employing sophisticated systems of pulleys, levers and bicycle-style pedalling for greater energy output than any genuinely pre-technological society could have managed. Some branches of corbi science remained high-level, with chemists able to manufacture everything from medicines to glues and explosives, although via far more labour-intensive methods. The occupation had deprived corbi of large-scale manufacturing and heavy industry, but it had not entirely impoverished their minds.

Beneath the common room were cells, stone-walled and dug deep into the soil. Trace stood before the bars of a cell, made from a bamboo-like wood that grew deep in the forest, and reinforced with old steel salvage, bolted horizontally. The tanifex sat slumped in one corner, an empty plate of food on the dirt by its feet.

"Some of them have trackers," said Tano, unbothered by the sight. "Built into their bodies."

"Not this one," Cedu assured him. "I checked."

Tano peered closer, face to the bars. Made a remark in words Trace didn't grasp. She frowned at Cedu.

"Quiet," Cedu translated. "Yes, this one is quiet. He awoke two days ago. Seems to be healing well. No fits of rage."

"Unusual," Tano admitted. "Most are programmed for rage, when captured. Have you tried red light?"

"Yes yes," said Cedu, pulling a red-lensed flashlight from his pocket. It was a standard trigger for the reeh's genetically conditioned creatures, and any attempt to tinker with it in captivity typically met with suicidal aggression. Reeh did not like their creations to be reprogrammed.

"Better stand back," Tano advised the other two, unslinging his rifle. Trace stood back, but left her rifle slung. The cell bars were not steel, but they were nearly as strong. Cedu put the flashlight through the bars and turned it on. Bright red light bathed the tanifex, crouched in its corner. It looked up, a glimpse of a reptilian eye. Then looked back down again, unmoved.

It took a moment for Tano to realise what was happening. And several moments longer for him to finally lower his rifle. "I don't understand," he said. "Why isn't it attacking?"

"It's been deprogrammed," Trace told him, having just recently learned the Lisha word for that. "Genetically. By someone at the Rando Splicer."

Tano frowned, as Cedu turned the flashlight off. A prowling fir came sniffing at the grey-haired scientist's feet, and Cedu scooped it up, stroking the animal's head.

"You think that someone *deliberately* deprogrammed the tanifex?" Tano said finally.

"Another scientist told me the same thing," said Trace. "Leta, of Ciros Village. She wanted to talk to other scientists about it, but Talo Command said no."

"So what are you thinking?" Tano asked carefully.

"That you're right," said Trace. "The Rando Splicer is impossible to attack, for most soldiers. We need two things. One, we need help on the inside." She indicated to the tanifex. "The reeh have many slave species. They rebel. I think some must have rebelled here, because reeh never make mistakes. We find a way to make contact with them, and we'll have help inside the Splicer."

A scream sounded from above. Tano rushed up on all fours, Trace following, past the alarmed guards on the door and into the fire-lit darkness between wooden huts and buildings. The yard by this building was different from where Trace had eaten, but similarly arranged, with fires and cooking. Now some corbi were flailing on the ground, screaming and choking as others tried to hold them still.

Tano swore, unslinging and preparing his rifle, barking a question at Cedu that Trace missed as she followed Tano's readiness.

"Full checks were last week!" Cedu exclaimed with horror. "How did I miss them?" The nearest corbi on the ground appeared to be frothing at the mouth, eyes wild.

The reeh, Trace thought as she looked across the helpless, crying friends and family of those dying. The reeh had decided to buzz this troublesome region with a frequency of some sort, and thin the herd a little. Perhaps it was revenge, but reeh weren't much into revenge. More likely it was just trigger-and-response, as they always did. Like scientists in the lab, prodding the subject of their experiments with various unpleasant stimuli to see what resulted.

From further away, a gunshot sounded. Tano took off running, in that curious way corbi would when armed — a three limbed run with rifle in the free hand. Trace stayed close behind, dodging terrified civilians, some clutching their children and heading for cover as more gunshots rang out.

Tano arrived at the edge of the tarpaulin-covered clearing where Trace had eaten dinner. It was cleared of corbi, save for several lying dead on the ground, and one still rolling in pain from a gunshot wound. More corbi were cowering terrified behind the tupi tree, not ten metres away.

"Where is he?" Tano yelled at those corbi, and received some frightened pointing toward the far side. Another shot, further away... not toward them, Trace thought. "How many? Hey you, pay attention! How many?" Some corbi raised two fingers, others three.

More shooting, rapid fire — an automatic rifle, then what could have been return fire. "They're in the far row of buildings," said Trace, fast checking her weapon for the second time. "They've got the clearing covered." She risked a fast look out, then pulled back. "Some windows there, a few of the shutters are open, maybe more than three."

"I'll stay here and draw fire," said Tano. "I'll pin them, you go around left, flank behind. I'll call you their numbers." Because attacking directly across the clearing would kill them both, and Trace was in no hurry to die assaulting a defended position for the sake of a small corbi village. She had all of humanity to save. But she also had Tano's competence to assess.

"Good," she said, as more shooting broke out, and more shouting, as Tano strained to listen.

"Sounds like hostages," Tano muttered, peering out. Shots hit the corner by his head, blowing off splinters as he ducked back. Then new shooting, a sudden cacophony that suggested ambush.

"Wait," Trace told him, lying flat and peering past Tano's feet in time to see an armed corbi stagger out of an opposing doorway, then fall to a burst. And Kono, crouching low out that doorway and moving fast to the next, several corbi behind who were clearly with him, rallied by his counter-attack. He snapped a quick look in one window, gave a hand signal to the corbi behind, one of whom rolled to the doorway, another to the second window. Another signal and they all opened fire together, return fire blowing holes in the wall above their heads.

Then Kono was up and in through the window, quite calmly, suggesting the immediate threat was down. The other corbi did the same. "Giddy, sitrep!" Trace shouted.

"Rogue corbi, Major!" came the reply. "There's a handful here, we're clearing them out!"

"Don't lead, Giddy!" Trace told him. "We've got work elsewhere, I need you safe!"

"Copy Major!" As more corbi passed his position, into the hut, others flanking around the side, heading for the rear. More shooting, and some yells. "Courtyard's clear!" And in Lisha, "Someone get that wounded guy!"

The corbi hiding behind the tree went and did that, fearfully, expecting more snipers.

"Your man is good," Tano admitted.

"The best," said Trace, still peering at the windows and doorways, with concentration so intense she was barely aware if her heart was thumping hard or not. "What happened?"

"Kauda," said Tano. It was the corbi's general-purpose word to describe any creature mutated by reeh genetics. "The villagers are supposed to report any new inhabitants. But they're kind people. They take in stragglers, claim they are long lost cousins. Stupid people."

They'd taken in corbi whose whereabouts over the past few years could not be proven, he meant. Some had memory blanks, others were simply lying, desperate for a new home. Most did not realise what had been done to them, and a few that did, didn't care, hoping if they could just reach a semblance of safety, all the nightmares would go away. But when the frequency signal activated the mutations, the programming set in. Trace had never known sentient beings to be programmable like that. The scientists said it failed to work on most, meaning that these were just the few who survived the experiments, then were released back into the corbi population. To be activated by the signal at a latter date, and turned into mindless killers who used weapons on the people who'd fed and housed them.

"This all happens in the Splicer," Trace said.

"I know," said Tano. More civilians were out in the clearing now, examining the bodies, searching for life. No one shot at them. Someone identified a body, then fell upon it, weeping and wailing.

"We can stop this, Tano," Trace persisted.

"We can't," Tano said grimly. "It's been tried many times across the centuries here, all have failed. Whatever damage we do this time, the reeh will just rebuild it. And their revenge will make this look small."

Trace pulled his shoulder, forcing the squat, powerful corbi to look at her. "Tano. Your scientists are amazing. Cedu is amazing. One old guy in a village, but he knows so much about reeh genetic science. You've got so many of them, and you know so much more than you've told me.

"We steal their tech, Tano. We get it offworld. To the Resistance Fleet. Rando Command won't like it, they try to save all the corbi they can, and you're right, the reeh's revenge will be terrible. But this is how we fight them. Take their technology away from them, take their advantage away. If anyone can find a way to use it against them, I'm sure we can. Humans and corbi together."

Tano's dark eyes were unimpressed. "Don't pretend you're doing this for us," he said grimly. "You've got your own people to save. And you'll sacrifice any number of us to do it."

"It doesn't mean I'm wrong," Trace retorted. "You don't want to do this because corbi will die? Corbi are already dying. Corbi will continue to die, if you do nothing or if you do something. What is there to lose?"

"Easy for you to say."

Trace grasped one powerful forearm with her hand. "Humans have a saying. Better to die on your feet than live on your knees." A flicker in those dark eyes. "So do you really believe in corbi freedom? Or are you just pretending?"

Tano shook her off, rose and walked into the clearing. Trace followed, rifle ready, still scanning the decreasingly few places from which a threat could emerge. The corbi that Kono had shot was still alive, and the person kneeling alongside made way as Tano approached. The dying corbi watched, wide-eyed and bloody faced. Tano knelt, and put a hand on his shoulder.

"Hi kid," he said, almost gently. "You know what you did?" A long pause from the other corbi. Then a faint, affirmative nod. "And you know what I have to do now?" Another nod, this time without the pause. "I'm sorry. Have a good trip."

Tano got up, pulled his pistol, and shot the fallen corbi in the head. "Get this all cleaned up!" he barked to the yard. "The bodies go to Cedu! Then we do a headcount, everybody move!"

Trace saw some more bodies she hadn't noticed behind the tupi tree, and walked that way. One was Loga, white mane spread upon the ground, sightless eyes staring at the tarpaulins. The other was the village headman with whom he'd been conversing. Two more were soldiers she'd been patrolling with the past few weeks.

She looked up as Kono came across the yard, seeming confident things were now secured. From further away, there were no yells or gunshots, only weeping, and the shouts of corbi organising. With Kono came Pena, looking upset, and Rika, swaggering in his open chested jacket and red bandana. Trace recognised him as having been directly behind Kono, first through the windows of the hut they'd stormed. The young man wasn't all swagger, then.

"They're not completely mindless when they go berzerk," Kono said grimly, looking down at Loga's body.

"No," said Trace. "From now on, we have to be extra careful what company we keep."

"I can tell you exactly where I've been for the past five years," said Rika, suddenly anxious. "I have witnesses."

"Good," said Trace, deciding then and there. She was going to need willing soldiers, and Loga's group had not been entirely enthusiastic. "That's good, kid. If you pass inspection, you're in." Rika looked satisfied, chest puffed out, very much the tough corbi warrior. Good enough, Trace thought.

Kono was holding Pena's hand. Pena was not a tough corbi warrior, eyes wet behind her wire-rim glasses. But sometimes smart and cautious soldiers were better than brave soldiers. For one thing, they lived longer.

Trace gave Kono a warning look. Kono ignored her, and did not let go of Pena's hand.

8

Captain Heidi Rajnika had never seen so many ships in orbit about a single world. Not even about Homeworld in the celebrations following the end of the war, nor in the aftermath of several earlier planetary invasions. The world of Naraya was the ancestral home of the parren House Fortitude. For millennia it had been the ruling house of all parren, but now that rule was at an end.

Despite the swarm of civilian and warships, it seemed as though there had been precious little fighting. Her crew had debated it endlessly on the two month journey out from human space — how such a huge internal transition of power could have taken place almost completely without bloodshed. These were the parren, whose tendencies for mutual assassination and house-versus-house conflict made up the majority of what most outsiders knew about them. Yet the reports from Naraya, thin though they were, indicated nothing of the sort — just Gesul, the new ruler of all parren and head of rival House Harmony, sitting on the homeworld of his former enemies, outnumbered by countless enemy soldiers, and ruling peacefully.

Descent into Shonedene was no more revealing. Shonedene was beautiful, a city in a vast gorge between tall valley flanks, with several waterfalls pluming long and white from the heights between the towers. Mid-city, two rivers joined where the gorge forked, and in the middle of that fork stood a huge temple complex that ascended one entire cliff wall.

The human assault shuttle landed on a pad the size of multiple football fields, and Captain Rajnika descended the landing ramp with Vice Admiral Verender at her side, and marines in light armour at the rear. Stretching before them was an astonishment — a line of ranked parren all the way to the cavernous hangar mouth beneath the high temples overhead. Their armour and weapons were ceremonial, many ornamental and some doubtless quite old. Rajnika thought there had to be several thousand of them, the ranks several deep, the lines flawlessly straight as though measured by laser.

It was a shock for any human to be here. For the past thousand years, humans hadn't socialised much with any non-humans save chah'nas and kuhsi. Alo were supposed to be allies too, but that had never been more than theoretical. Rajnika had heard tales as a young girl, had seen fanciful human movies about crazy parren and their palace intrigues and murders. There had even been a few genuine parren productions, mostly stage plays, but those hadn't been nearly as dramatic, as was so often the way with things that were real and not turned to nonsense by popular entertainment. To find herself now in the midst of parren for any purpose, let alone for one this grand, was surreal in the extreme.

Inside the hangar, a great elevator for carrying shuttles took the small human party to the next level. That level made little sense to humans, being large enough to hold small spacecraft but arrayed with ornamental windows overlooking the city below. It was a parren ceremonial room, of course, as parren would assemble in such places and be sure to be seen.

Waiting for them were more parren, in a vast circle before the windows, accompanied by multiple holographic projectors. With them was... and Rajnika had to force herself to keep walking without a humiliating break of stride. The thing standing amidst the parren, like a giant armoured lobster, was a hacksaw drone. But she'd been warned of this, too, and even managed to force her eyes past the hulking insectoid machine to the sight that might have been just as strange in other circumstances — a brown human girl in a red robe, standing with hands folded in perfect grace.

The girl stepped forward as Captain and Vice Admiral approached, with the pleasant smile of someone well graced in social etiquette. "Vice Admiral," she said, with an extended hand to Verender. "I'm Lisbeth Debogande, as you might have guessed."

"And even more beautiful than in the pictures," said Verender, who fancied himself something of a smooth talker. He took her hand, then turned to introduce Rajnika. "Captain Heidi Rajnika, commander of the *Deliverance*."

"Captain," said the Debogande girl, and Rajnika was nearly overcome by the surrealness of it all. Debogandes were nearly royalty in human space, but the general consensus had been that if one had gotten lost in a jungle, they'd have lasted barely a few hours without a soft bed and five star meals. It had been astonishing enough for one to have survived this long captaining the renegade *UFS Phoenix*. That the second one had indeed gotten lost in the parren jungle, but instead of perishing had ended up *here*, was a strain on all credulity. "I hope you had an uneventful journey?"

"Relatively uneventful, yes," Rajnika agreed, gazing about. Again she had to force her eyes to move past the hacksaw. How did all these people just stand around like normal with that murderous thing metres away? Its forelegs were much larger than the others, lobster-style, and both seemed to have lethal vibro-blade edges. "This looks an interesting setup."

"Yes," said Debogande, "I offered to Gesul-sa to brief you in person on our findings here. Following the briefing, you will be introduced to Gesul personally. I trust that you will find these proceedings adequate?"

The self-assured note to her voice suggested that finding the proceedings inadequate was not advised. Just a young girl — twenty-three, the briefing had said — yet with the poise and confidence of someone utterly assured of her station. For all her smooth manners, it occurred to Rajnika that if Lisbeth Debogande ordered these

armed parren to kill every other human in the room, they'd do it
without hesitation. And probably far, far worse.

"Entirely adequate," said Verender, with the deference of a professional handshaker. Verender was Intelligence, of course — the closest
thing Fleet could muster to a parren specialist. All those years of
expertise, and here he was, deferring to the knowledge of a girl young
enough to be his great-great-granddaughter. "We are honoured to be
granted an audience with Gesul. All of humanity is honoured
with us."

Debogande's pleasant smile told them he'd said the right thing.
Yet as sweet as she was, there was something guarded as well... like
the manner of a professional ambassador who was good at talking to
people because it was her job, rather than because she actually liked
them. Yet the intelligence reports on *this* Debogande had spoken of a
popular, carefree girl with lots of friends, whose high grades could
probably have been a lot higher if she'd gone to a few less parties. So
her time among the parren had taught her caution, Rajnika thought.

And not just the parren. Lisbeth Debogande had been on *Phoenix*
in Argitori System while Fleet ships had poured in trying to kill her.
And when Captain Sampey of the *Lien Wang* had encountered her
three months ago on the Defiance moon, a government Intelligence
operative had attempted to leverage the very real threat against the
Debogande matriarch, Alice, to pressure Lisbeth into providing Fleet
with more information on the parren than she might otherwise have
willingly provided. Whether that effort would bear any fruit, Rajnika
wondered if they were about to discover.

"Okay," said Debogande, businesslike. Clapped her hands and
gave a series of instructions in fluent Porgesh to the surrounding
parren. Holographics sprang to life from multiple intersecting angles,
crossing in the middle to resolve into three-dimensional shapes.
Verender caught Rajnika's eye — impressed with Debogande's
Porgesh, she thought. Verender was one of the few humans who
spoke any, having learned over many decades of study. Debogande
had learned all this in less than a year.

"Firstly," said Debogande, standing hands folded within the maze of light with no little theatricality, "the political situation across parren space is today relatively peaceful. I mean, considering what just happened. Gesul-sa has not departed to the House Harmony capital world of Prakasis as he senses an opportunity for reconciliation and togetherness... these aren't perhaps the best words I could use, but the direct translation from Porgesh is difficult. The best thing to know, perhaps, is that the Harmony phase is called that for a reason, and Gesul senses an opportunity here for harmony."

"An opportunity for power declined," Verender offered. "Kalaish ma, the pursuit of power is always disharmonious."

Debogande's face lit with the first genuine smile Rajnika had yet seen, quickly subdued. "The Vice Admiral knows the Parsena Dialectic."

"Indeed I do, Ms Debogande."

"Yes, well, unfortunately the Parsena Dialectic was written about five thousand years ago, and since then there's been about five thousand Harmony scribes trying to tear it all down in support of a more muscular interpretation of Harmony principles..."

"Perhaps the works that Gesul's Domesh predecessor Aristan may have preferred?" Verender ventured. Rajnika wanted to give the old man a jab in the ribs for being so eager to impress with his knowledge of parren things. Bringing up political predecessors was dangerous, particularly when the man currently in power had used that predecessor's corpse as a step up to his present position.

But Debogande just smiled. "Very much, Vice Admiral... these tensions run all through parren society and politics, as you'll know. Sadly I've been far too busy to read most of these arguments." Said with the half-sarcastic tone of a college student not at all sad to have been spared a ton of dull reading. "But yes, safe to say that Parsena is far more popular with House Harmony's present leader than many previous. Gesul demonstrates to House Fortitude that his rule is not vengeful, and that all parren must embrace a spirit of unity in the face of external threats.

"As to what caused the disruption..." and she indicated again to the parren, and the air around her turned to the holographic display of an old, decaying cityscape. Only this city seemed to be in a box, like a display model on a tabletop. It took a moment for Rajnika to figure what she was looking at — an underground segment of old city, separated off from the surface by enormous walls. This she'd heard of too — the false foundation upon which the entire city of Shonedene had been built, and the one piece of what had once stood, preserved for more than twenty five thousand years.

Debogande walked to one side of the display, so that the buildings were not engulfing her. "It's quite amazing, really," she said. "I mean, you wouldn't think so much of old history could disappear, considering digital recording and computers. Truly ancient history is hard to study because paper and wood disintegrates, but digital doesn't. Unless it's in the aftermath of a machine society that drinks digital for breakfast and thus absorbs it all and changes it into... whatever." She gave a vague shrug. "Anyhow, most parren history from the Machine Age is completely reconstructed, it turns out there were entire centuries more or less missing. Only they *weren't* entirely missing, large chunks existed in various historical institutions and libraries, they just weren't recognised for what they were. So basically these past months have seen parren scholars running back and forth trying to find all these old pieces... and I mean, they've only found a tiny fraction of them, but there's enough to make a picture of sorts. Particularly when you combine that with what's emerging from the drysine data-core, but the data-core's less help with historical data because it's not indexed in any way we recognise for those old time-lines, it's hard to say which piece of information fits with which year." She pointed to the old city. "This was then called Ayrek, as I think you've heard?"

"We have," Verender acknowledged, walking a slow circle about the display, staring with amazement. "It's deepyine?"

Debogande took a deep breath. "Well yes. Half deepynine. You see, we've come to think of that last period of the Machine Age as drysine versus deepynine, but prior to that there were aycees and teklas, the teklas had a whole offshoot the parren called zadees but the tavalai and others called jaros, and they were styling themselves as the drysines of their time until the actual drysines came along and destroyed them..."

Another deep breath, and a wave of both hands. "The problem with looking at so much history from such a distance is that everything gets so crowded. Things are complicated in every period — you step back too far to get a generalised picture and you lose all the important, deciding details. Zoom in too far to get the detail and you'll get lost in complexity and never find your way out.

"Anyhow... the aycees still had part of parren space at this point, and the aycees were allowing a degree of parren spaceflight." The holographics changed, showing a 3D starmap of parren space... only here all the lines and boundaries were utterly different. "This is one of the details of the Machine Age we've lost — the right of organics to actually fly between systems was the biggest thing of all at the time, and the drysines weren't the first to grant it. And this is true for all the spacefaring Spiral species in the Machine Age — the parren had only a fraction of the systems then that they have now, obviously, but you can't really call yourself a whole, collective 'people' unless all the places where you live are joined together. The machines could deny this in most places because the Machine Age was mostly spacefaring and had little interest in planets... space was *their* territory, and organics passing through it were an annoyance at best and a security threat at worst."

Debogande cast a brief glance at the drone, who stood unmoving by the big windows, irregular dual eyes fixed in the correct direction to be watching, but showing no proof of whether it was or not. Rajnika found the whole thing incredibly disconcerting.

"The drysines had been around for a little while then and were getting stronger all the time, and occupied most of the rest of parren space, and a lot beyond. The deepynines were the new force — the reactionaries, if you will, who had a series of profound disagreements with the drysines. With AIs that gets pretty philosophical, actually, but unlike in human society where philosophy usually stays up in the clouds above what most people actually care about, with machines it goes all the way down to the design of basic technology. Different methods of making sense of the world came to different conclusions about how everything ought to be designed, and when they had an impasse, conflict was the only practical means of solving disputes without wasting centuries in pointless argument.

"Anyhow..." and the girl took another deep breath, refocusing herself. Rajnika thought that more of her ambassadorial cool dropped away the longer she spoke, and her eyes lit with increasingly girlish enthusiasm for the topic. "The deepynines saw the part of parren space controlled by the aycees as a good way to open a new front of attack against the drysines. So they attacked the aycees first, and the drysines let them — the enemy of my enemy and all that. Naraya was in aycee space at the time... and that's what current parren understandings of history had completely forgotten. Everyone thought it was all drysine here, and that drysines and parren made a pact together, via the House Harmony leader Drakhil, and that Drakhil was a traitor for selling all parren out to the machines."

"Which has reflected poorly on House Harmony ever since," Verender offered.

"Exactly," Debogande agreed. "It's been hanging over us for all those millennia since." 'Us', Rajnika repeated in her head. She wondered if the girl had even realised she'd said it. "But in fact... well, I mean, you have to ask yourself how House Harmony could even exist as a collective entity in the first place, back in that period. Travel between systems was hard, right? How would the Jusica know which house was in charge if they couldn't travel between systems to do a census? You can't actually function as a single spacefaring civilisation if you can't travel between systems... which I think might have given the parren more incentive to cooperate with the machines, simply because parren can't stand the duality and chaos of an uncompleted hierarchical structure, right? They have to try and put the pieces back together again — House Harmony especially, because separation means disharmony, yes?"

Verender nodded, clearly fascinated. Rajnika was too... but not for quite the same reasons.

"And we still haven't sorted all of that out — all the historians, I mean, there's just too much there we haven't found yet. But what we do know is that the deepynines beat the aycees back, took the region of parren space including Naraya from them, and began doing what deepynines always do to organics — denying all transport links, smashing any center that looked too built up, etc. I mean, deepynines weren't single-minded genocidal, it would have been easy for them to exterminate every parren in their territory, obviously. If they'd been completely genocidal, all organic life in their space would have ended quickly. But all AIs have scientific brains, they don't hate all organic things, they're not going to exterminate entire ecosystems that are clearly pretty interesting even to a deepynine... they're just not going to tolerate any kind of high-tech, sentient challenge to their power. So they crushed anything that looked like it might make such a challenge, and crushed it hard and often. It's like if you're watching TV planetside with the window open and a big bug comes in and starts buzzing around your head. Some people will reach for the bug spray immediately, others will take a little time to catch the bug and put it outside, then maybe kill it if it comes in again. Drysines were the latter. Deepynines reached for the spray first thing every time, then went outside to spray the whole garden, just to be sure.

"But then something really weird happened. There was a Lior on the world of Ila — a philosopher-holyman, the Lior concern themselves with the study of the five parren psychological phases, which overlaps with a lot of overarching parren philosophy about the nature of the universe... it's kind of like organised religion with humans, only more grounded and practical. And this Lior had been allowed access to spacetravel by the aycees, and... it's quite incredible, actually... he'd been allowed to go travelling the Spiral, largely through cooperation with the drysines, we think, who controlled the largest chunk of the Spiral at that time. I guess he wasn't hurting anyone, so the drysines let him do it.

"This guy's name was Cleorus. And he had a theory of organic religions that he'd devoted his life to studying... are either of you Destinos believers?"

Rajnika nodded cautiously. "My family has always been. Back many generations."

"Right, so the basic theory is that science and religion become the same thing, because god is something that will come in the future, because if you leave organic beings to evolve over billions of years they'll eventually *become* god, or something that's so close to god that any attempt to differentiate it would be an exercise in semantics, right? And for a lot of people that's Ascension Destinos, because it's looking forward to the future, and believing that every action we take today is a step toward that ascension, which then provides a moral framework of progress and improvement within which all of us must live our lives.

"Thing is, the machines... or most of them, certainly the drysines and deepynines... all believed basically the same thing. Only they believed that ascension would be achieved by a machine intelligence, because machine intelligence was the next obvious evolution upward beyond organic intelligence. This was another large part of the philosophical divide between drysines and deepynines — deepynines found the notion that organics could participate in the ascension to be a dangerous step back from the path of progress. A barbarian notion, you could say, that threatened to undo everything they'd been working toward. Drysines didn't think organics had much to offer either, but they weren't so deterministic — they were more laissez faire, 'let's see what happens' kind of thing.

"Anyhow... Cleorus worked at it from the other direction. He was fascinated not only by parren religions... because parren aren't *all* about the study of their phases, there are a lot of other belief systems that grew out of that, some of which are still around... but also with the religions and beliefs of other species as well. And he said he'd found a common formula, kind of like how linguists go back in time to discover the common root language that gave rise to dozens of modern languages, right?"

"A common formula for religions across species?" Rajnika could not help interjecting. "How is that even possible?"

Debogande made an expansive gesture, equally mystified. "I

know, right? Different organic species have no common ancestors, no common point for their beliefs. But Cleorus said not only did this formula accurately describe the belief systems of all oxygen breathing individualist sentients, but also the hive minds like the sard — I'm still not sure how he came to that, between you and me — and even a couple of the methane breathers. It sounds nuts, I know, but it must have had something going for it, because none other than a great deepynine queen commander of the time was so impressed by it that she came right here to Shonedene — then called Ayrak — to study his findings."

Rajnika and Verender stared. Debogande seemed to enjoy their disbelief. "You're kidding," said Rajnika.

"Nope," said Debogande. "The thing with deepynine queens, they're not likely to fall for silly emotional appeals to religion. Things need to have a scientific, mathematical basis to get their attention. Clearly Cleorus had one. It appears he was a master mathematician too, not just a holyman."

"And you can prove that she was here?" Rajnika asked.

"Multiple sources," said Debogande, almost smugly. "It's nuts, she actually came down to the surface with a big landing party. Didn't kill anyone either, or not that we've seen recorded. The drysines knew the deepynines had taken over this old aycee territory, but they were preoccupied elsewhere at the time, so they left it alone."

"What on earth would a deepynine queen find interesting about a parren scholar's musings on the universality of organic religion?" Verender wondered. "And... did that inspire her to build this?" Indicating to the holographics, even though they no longer showed the old once-deepynine city.

"It seems to have, yes," said Debogande. "Whether as a means of cooperation with all House Fortitude parren or not, we're still not sure... but it was certainly a total exception to how the deepynines usually did things. And there's no indication that it made any improvement on how they treated organics elsewhere in their territory, either. But they made this one exception for the ruling class in House Fortitude, and much of the rest of House Fortitude in some

other systems, it seems... in the immediate leadup to the great
Drysine/Deepynine War. Meaning that parren history was all wrong
— it was never the drysines plus Drakhil and House Harmony versus
the deepynines, it was versus the deepynines plus House Fortitude.
Parren houses took opposite sides in the war, or had those sides taken
for them, to some degree. And that revelation, to the whole parren
understanding of their history... well, to call it ground-shaking would
be an understatement."

"Do you know what impressed the deepynine queen?" Verender
pressed. "To encourage her to make allies of House Fortitude?"

Debogande held up both hands, and moved one forward, as
though moving into the future. "Ascension Destinos is about what
happens to sentient intelligence if you let it evolve for a billion years.
Sentient civilisations gain more and more control of their surroundings the longer they evolve. Leave them for long enough and they
learn to control the very fabric of space/time and multi-dimension-
ality itself. Thus becoming god, and since space/time is flexible, and
gods are... well, gods, all sorts of grander schemes and meanings to
existence become possible.

"But the real business with Destinos is not Ascension Destinos,
but Origin Destinos." She pulled the hand back, as though moving
backward in time. "Because the Big Bang doesn't make any sense
scientifically — even the machines agreed that it happened, and their
maths were ridiculously more advanced than ours. But in order for
the Big Bang to make sense, you have to explain an act of inexplicable
creation as an act of science... and it really only works as an act of
god. But Destinos unifies god and science, because if any scientific,
mechanical force could have created the Big Bang, it's a super
advanced mega-sentience that does it because it *decides* to, as an act of
will, right? Distinctions between man-made and naturally-occurring
phenomena become pointless semantics, and acts of will and mani-
fest destiny in the universe are actually as scientific as gravity and the
laws of electro-magnetism, and all of this is probably built into the
structure of *this* universe because the best explanation for how this
was all created was that some other mega-sentience, god-by-any-

other-name existing in another much older universe, decided to create it, for reasons that our tiny brains will find impossible to comprehend.

"So the question then becomes... and it seems that this is something that obsessed a lot of AIs as much as it obsesses some Destinos believers today... how much of what we're seeing is actually preordained? In a universe of endless possibility, why do we keep seeing the same patterns recurring over and over? All stars have planets, all planets have water... you know there was a time on Earth when human scientists doubted that was true? Because when you don't know very much about the universe, because you're stuck on a small ball of rock for all existence, you assume it must be varied and random, right? But it turns out it wasn't random at all — water everywhere, planets everywhere, life everywhere... heck, even organic sentiences end up looking quite similar, bipedal seems the favoured physical shape, even language structures end up sharing lots of things in common..."

"And Cleorus thought he found a... a common thread unifying all organic religions?"

The young Debogande nodded, a grin struggling to break her control. "Almost as though whoever made the universe had written into the basic codings that certain things shall inevitably emerge, right? As though, as a friend of mine recently put to me..." again the glance at the drone, "...that the god/sentience that created this universe predetermined that sentient thought was the entire point of the creation, and would eventually lead to a force capable of creating *other* universes, and that religious thought itself is the inevitability of such sentient thought processes that, however incorrect in its particulars, might act as the driving engine to get us asking the necessary questions to make it happen."

Even Rajnika had to take a break at that, and wander a few steps to stare out the windows, down at the city below.

"Anyhow," said Debogande, that young woman's verbal tick that she'd probably erased from her Porgesh but hadn't yet managed with her English. "That's what was happening at the time. That's why the deepynines occupied this whole chunk of parren space, but only left signs of settlement on this one world — they're on a few other cities as well, but nothing as extensive as this one. When the drysines came and wiped them out, we think they and the parren in charge at the time — this was before Drakhil's time — left this part of the city as a reminder, or a museum piece, and then after the Machine Age ended, everyone forgot it was even here. Or more likely, the Fortitude leaders who inherited the Parren Empire after the Machine Age knew it was here, but took the secret with them to their graves to preserve Fortitude power into the future by pinning all the blame for cooperation with the machines on House Harmony. But as always, it wasn't that simple."

She glanced at the drone a third time, as though somewhat pleased to see her guests struggling to process all of that. "Anyhow," she said again. "You're probably thinking that I didn't need to tell you all of that for a simple update on parren politics. But there's a reason for the deeper background. I'll leave it to my friend Liala to explain. Liala, please introduce yourself."

The drone slid forward, a sinewy walk that had little of 'machine' about it. The intricate body had too many points of flection to be a human-designed machine — so much seemed aesthetic and unnecessary, like the shifting of overlapping torso plates. Twin mismatched eyes regarded them all, and the voice, when it spoke, was as human-sounding as any set of real-life vocal cords.

"I am Liala," 'she' said, clearly a female voice. From what Rajnika had heard, drones usually identified as male, if only to suit organic prejudices. Which meant that this AI was no drone. "I am what you might call a 'queen', created by the facilities on Defiance. Technically I am the commander of drysine forces allied to House Harmony and the parren people. I answer to the one you may know as Styx, who is the commander of all drysine forces across the Spiral."

Despite her general astonishment, Rajnika's military brain immediately spotted a problem. This Liala commanded drysine forces allied to House Harmony, and thus did what Gesul ordered. Styx, however, lay outside of that chain of command. What would happen if the orders of Styx, and those of Gesul, began to conflict?

"As my friend Lisbeth has said," Liala continued, with remarkable approximation of a conversational human tone, "the drysine data-core makes for an unreliable historical record, whatever its enormous technological wealth. But the one thing it has proven very useful in providing is a record of what happened to various high-technology sites during both the drysine/deepynine war, and the great war against the organics that followed immediately after. Put most simply, if a high-technology site is not recorded on the data-core as having been destroyed, then the chances are good that it may have survived."

"You mean hacksaw bases?" Rajnika asked. Verender was here to ask the cultural and political questions that an alien specialist intelligence officer found useful, but Rajnika was all about warfighting assets. "Facilities like Defiance?"

"Yes," said Liala, having turned to look her way, then consider and answer the question as any organic being might. That was disconcerting too. Styx, to hear the few reports that had reached Rajnika's table, was not this well socialised in the ways of organics. Perhaps Liala was something new. Or perhaps Styx simply didn't care enough to try. "Drysines are no longer an extinct people, Captain, Vice Admiral. We are no longer hiding in the shadows. We have alliance, with House Harmony. We will fight to protect our ally, as they shall fight to protect us. The discovery of long-lost drysine assets are of considerable interest to us all, as you might imagine."

"I can well imagine," Rajnika murmured. The whole thing was terrifying. She wondered if Debogande or her damn fool brother truly understood what horror they'd unleashed upon the galaxy.

"But we have one other concern," Liala continued. "A concern that we feel human Fleet should be made aware of. We can account for the destruction or likely destruction of all the major deepynine command units, or queens, from the data-core records. All but one. She was last sighted leading the defence of Neth System, which is now known as Centala, on the far edge of where parren space adjoins barabo space. Methods are complicated, but drysines became extremely good at determining which command units survived and which did not survive a fight, primarily by capturing and examining enemy communications units following the battle. Command signatures linger, but this particular command unit did not die. She vanished, and despite much further searching, was not found again. Drysine commanders at the time suspected an elaborate ruse designed to distract drysine units from her pursuit.

"The unit in question was the very same queen who made the pact with House Fortitude, based on the works of Cleorus and his theories of religious universalism. House Fortitude called her Nia. In one of the older parren tongues in which some plays are still written, it means 'fire'."

Rajnika and Verender exchanged cautious glances. "What are you suggesting?" Verender asked. "That this... Nia, survived the Drysine/Deepynine War?"

"Exactly that, Vice Admiral," said Liala. "My commander Styx has had what you might call a working theory for a long time now, one I do not believe she has even spoken of to *Phoenix*'s crew, though that may obviously have changed since the last time we were in contact. In various encounters with the alo-allied deepynines across the last month, she has intercepted fragments of deepynine encoded communications and security codes, as well as interrogating the remains of several destroyed deepynine warriors. Styx believes that there are numerical patterns that suggest a familiar parent — Nia herself, with whom Styx was quite familiar during the war."

"Styx and Nia fought against each other?" said Rajnika.

"Yes," said Liala. "Styx believes that Nia may have been the sole survivor of the deepynine race, whose survival in turn gave rise to a new race of deepynine progeny. These would have been annihilated in the Spiral, where organics would never allow any machine race to rise again... but protected by the alo, who were granted rights to self-determination and unchallenged territory by tavalai law, they thrived."

"So what if it was this Nia?" Rajnika demanded. "What does it matter if it was this deepynine or that one? What makes her significant, beyond that she made a pact here with some long-dead Fortitude parren?"

"Because deepynines previously believed that organics could not participate in the Ascension. The ascension to a higher plane of existence could only be driven by artificial minds. The theories of Cleorus then indicated to Nia another alternative — that organics did indeed have a significant role to play, a role programmed into the universe's constituent parts by its creators. Understand that Nia's underlying view of organics never changed — drysines alone experimented with the theory that organics may have collective strengths that AIs lacked, but deepynines always viewed organics as perpetual inferiors — little more than loading programs for the evolved machine-sentience to follow. But now the theories of Cleorus demonstrated that organics were inferiors perpetually destined to interfere with progress toward Ascension. Not merely children playing with blocks and toys, as my friend Lisbeth recently put to me, but children playing with particle physics laboratories and Faster Than Light technology.

"Our studies of the period suggested Nia's interest in this city, and her building of ties to Fortitude parren at the time was an attempt to understand the nature of this organic threat to the Ascension. Organics would have been safer had they never convinced her of their relevance to the advancement of civilisation in the Spiral. Instead, organics exceeded deepynine expectations without ever impressing them with their capabilities. I believe that Nia was working on a thesis during her time here, before the Drysine/Deepynine War. A thesis on why organic sentiences were too much of a threat to leave alive, anywhere, in any form. Thankfully a drysine victory prevented her from implementing any such plan."

"And you think she's still alive?" Verender murmured in horror. "Leading the deepynines from alo space?"

"It's possible," said Liala. "Styx believes it is highly possible. Where such things are concerned, Styx's judgement is difficult to doubt."

9

Trace trudged down the embankment to the beach, and shielded her eyes against the morning glare. The sand of this wide bay quickly gave way to a rocky shelf over which the waves would break in high tide. The tides were low this morning, the silver overcast reflecting off remaining pools. Tall fingers of eroded rock loomed beyond the fringe of the shelf, protruding from the ocean like the crumbling towers of some long forgotten civilisation. Upon their ledges grew tangles of green vines, and nesting seabirds squawked and hovered, their droppings staining the tower-sides white.

Trace glanced at Tano, who pressed ahead, dropping to stroll on all fours briefly in the soft sand. Corbi were less-well designed for long hikes than humans. The other corbi and Kono fanned out, many sitting and sipping water, or unshouldering bags to rummage for food. Kono remained standing, rifle easy, scanning along the shore to the little village beyond the rocky towers, where a few small boats were being paddled into the waves.

When Trace and Tano reached the rocks, Trace spotted the man they'd come all this way to see — a squat, broad-shouldered figure by the edge of the sea, hurling a fishing net with an expert twirl of weighted edges. Trace looked at the pools as they passed, and saw some small fish in one, and crabs in another. Again it amazed her — the similarities between life on all similar worlds, the recurring patterns that random evolution took. In pursuit of efficiency, always the same paths were taken... almost as though there were some kind of plan in the chaos.

The fishing corbi saw them approaching, and stared for a moment, but no longer. That was unusual. Most corbi in these remote parts of Rando had never seen an alien before, despite living on a world ruled by several unfriendly kinds of them. But this corbi finished pulling in his net, with powerful heaves of those strong corbi arms. His balance was off, Trace noted — a pronounced favouring of one side. He wore a sleeveless tunic, and the hair on his left arm was almost entirely gone, the arm pale. And now that he abandoned the net, and took up a three-pronged spear, he had the heavy lean to one side that spoke of a serious back injury, healed without modern medicine.

The fisherman loped along the edge of the rock shelf, eyes fixed on the water, then leaped forward with a powerful hurl of the spear, and plunged headfirst into the water. A moment later he emerged, holding up the spear, a large fish flapping on one end. Tano went to give him a hand up, but Trace refrained — she was the alien here, and besides, she guessed the fisherman would reject any assistance. Her guess was correct, for he ignored Tano's hand and clambered out despite another breaking wave.

Trace took a moment to gaze out to sea, to the opposite promontory, low rocky cliffs above breaking waves, fringed with trees. The sea air smelled clean and wild and salty, the wind buffeting her face and threatening her hat. Between her and the land, two of the fishing boats were now passing, manned by corbi pulling heavy oars, effortlessly parting the swell. Trace doubted unaugmented humans could have rowed so hard.

Tano talked to the fisherman, who seemed more interested in his fish. Those in the nets were mostly smaller, while he had two more big ones, each with holes made by the spear. Those had big teeth, perhaps predators sneaking close to try and steal from his nets. In a worn leather bag were several handfuls of mussels, and a flat-blade knife good for prying them off the rocks. Trace crouched to look at them, and the fisherman gave her wary looks as he untangled fish from his net. The smallest ones, still flapping, he threw back to the sea.

Tano's questions or introductions got no reply. Trace picked up the mussel-knife, and examined it. Then pulled her kukri from its sheath, and showed it to the fisherman. That got his attention. It was mostly too big for mussels, and Trace was loathe to try it and scratch the blade on rocks... but surely a fisherman living in a beach-side cabin had plenty of wood that needed cutting, and a professional interest in knives.

He held out a hand, curious. Trace hesitated long enough to let him know that she valued it, then gave. The fisherman examined the odd-angled blade, and tested its balance with the grip of one who knew how to use it. And finally he looked at her.

"Where does it come from?" His Lisha was strongly accented, like everyone in these parts.

"A place called Earth," said Trace. "I'm human. From the Spiral, beside tavalai space." No flicker of interest from the fisherman. "My people are Kulina, they come from a mountainous place. They're tough, they're good at climbing and they like big knives."

The fisherman handed the kukri back, and spoke. "You came to talk to me?"

"Yes. I was told you've been inside the Splicer."

A nod, expert fingers now tying a loose thread of net, wet strands of mane blowing in his eyes. "What do you want with the Splicer?"

"I want to destroy it," Trace said calmly.

The fisherman looked at her properly for the first time, hard and quizzical. Then back to his net, still tying. "If you have a big warship, you can do that. Croma could have done that long ago. Reeh will just build another."

"I want to raid it first," said Trace. "And learn everything it knows. Corbi can use it to save people. People like you."

"If corbi help you to raid the Splicer, there won't be any corbi left on Rando. Reeh will kill everyone for revenge."

"Reeh kill everyone now," said Trace. "What's the difference?"

The fisherman looked at her oddly, finished with his net, and stood. Then cackled, a strange, half-twist on one side of his face. "Come," he said, gathering up net, spear and fish. Trace took the bag of mussels. "Those taste good, you'll like those."

* * *

THE FISHERMAN'S NAME WAS JINDI. HE LIVED IN A SMALL WOODEN HUT in the treeline back from the beach. Trace was not particularly surprised to see him living nearly a kilometre away from the fishing village further up the sands, and her suspicions were confirmed when a corbi girl, perhaps a teenager, interrupted their arrival at the hut. Jindi gave her two of the big fish and some of the mussels, in exchange for some eggs, a stick of bread, and a small ceramic container of what might have been medicine.

The girl gawked at the aliens, but seemed friendly with Jindi, and left to go scampering back to town and tell her family. Jindi put a bowl of dried seaweed on the table and invited his guests to snack while he limped outside and washed in the rain water collector that ran from his shingle roof. Trace declined the food — corbi and human physiologies were similar enough that most major food groups on Rando were safe for human consumption, but she'd learned to be wary of non-standard fare, and this would be the first seaweed she'd tried.

Wind rattled at wooden planks in the walls as Jindi returned, moving about his little space — floorboards to keep the hut elevated off the sand and away from critters that might scuttle in. A small kitchen of simple wooden benches, a big plastic basin for water, some simple pots, a row of good knives and stirring spoons. The oven looked like solid construction — metal with a hinged door, a small stack of firewood alongside. On a far wall, a single bed with a hard mattress, no need for blankets in the warmth of the season.

Trace found the honest simplicity appealing. It reminded her of stories her marines had told her, usually from their childhoods in civilian times, of holidays with family to simple seaside shacks, though doubtless most more sophisticated than this. Places like this reminded her of things she'd learned as a girl, such as just how few things a person truly needed in the world to feel complete. A small shelter, access to food and water. Outside the open door, nature's beauty. Such lessons had made her who she was.

Jindi went to work, opening and cleaning the mussels with his knife, his fingers strong and certain. Trace, Tano, Pena and Kono all watched, the corbi chewing seaweed and seeming to find it good.

Tano tried again. "You were from Hijo, before?"

"Yes," said Jindi, stacking mussel shells.

"You were taken when you were twenty-nine?"

"Can't remember," said Jindi. Trace did not count herself an expert on corbi body language and manners, but she was sure that Jindi lied. Dancing around the issue, as Tano was, did not seem to be having much effect.

"We need to know the inside of the Splicer if we're going to hit it," she told him. "Will you help us?"

"Why should I help you?"

"Because of your wife and children." The hands did not pause, the knife opening another mussel, the blade digging between the shells, then turning. Jindi's eyes remained fixed on his work. "Don't you want revenge?"

"What good will it do?"

"What good does anything do?" Trace asked. "What good does living on a beach and eating fish do? Don't you want your life to be for something?"

"Life is for living. Why should it mean anything?"

Tano was looking at Trace warily. Trace ignored him. "The reeh had you for six years. They did experiments. You saw many of your friends suffer horribly and die. It takes enormous will to survive such things. And then you escaped." She leaned forward, crouching slightly to try and get into Jindi's line of sight. "I know a thing or two about willpower. I've studied it. I think you have it. And I think it takes more to do what you did, than just the desire to live on a beach and fish."

"You're wrong," said Jindi. "Dreaming of a beach kept me alive all those years. Just to see it one more time." He chortled, that odd, slightly demented turn of expression and wrenched half his face as though in pain. "I'd never lived on a beach before. Barely even saw the sea. But when I was with the reeh, I dreamed of a beach, and surf, and sun. It kept me sane. You think I want revenge?" Another cackle. "What good does revenge do? Reeh just retaliate, more corbi suffer and die."

"Jindi," Tano tried again. "I know you know all the kauda. All the mutants, the sick ones, the ones with things wrong with their brains. If we could steal the data from the Splicer, we could figure out what's been done to them, and fix them."

"And the villagers call me crazy," Jindi chortled. "You Resistance charnas, you've got hidden technology, but it's not that good. Even if you could get in, you couldn't read or use reeh technology, let alone use it to fix people. And you'd make the reeh so angry, they'd hit back and kill far more people than you could help with that technology anyway."

"And so you're just going to sit on a beach," Trace said drily. "And do nothing while your world is occupied, and your people are enslaved."

"This world has been occupied for a long time now," said Jindi. "It will be occupied for a long time after I'm gone. The reeh won't notice my passing, they won't notice any of us passing. None of this makes any difference, and if either of you two had any brains, you'd join me on this beach, and enjoy what short time you have left."

* * *

THAT EVENING AFTER THEY'D SLEPT THROUGH THE DAY, TRACE SAT WITH Tano on a sandy verge beneath trees, and ate fish as the sun set out to sea. Feina rode high above the horizon, a slim illuminated crescent on the lower edge of the curved sphere, just above the orange wisps of sunset cloud. The wind on their faces was warm, and the fish tasted marvellous. They sat not far from Jindi's hut, but corbi from the further village had come up the beach with offerings of dinner, and built a cooking fire.

Now corbi talked and ate with corbi, and children played on the sands. Some of the kids had quickly overcome their awe of Kono to climb on him as he ate. Kono played and wrestled with them, and laughed. Trace glanced at him occasionally, with melancholy. A few corbi children looked as though they'd like to do the same with her, only to be quickly removed by their parents. Word spread, Trace supposed, about the difference between her and Kono.

'The stone will never feel pain, because it knows nothing of desire,' her siksakas had told her as a child in the Kulina. 'Be like the stone.' Trace had tried, all her life. But try as she might, humans were not stones.

"I don't think he's going to help," said Trace.

"Not willingly," Tano agreed, nibbling fish from the thin bones, his lips more mobile than any human's.

Trace gave him a sideways look. "Does that matter?"

Tano raised his eyebrows. "It matters to him, certainly." Trace kept looking, breaking more fish with her fingers. Tano sighed. "It's not my planet, Thakur." Her name did not agree with his accent. "It's their planet." He nodded at the village corbi, and the various soldiers he'd brought with him on the flyer. "In Fleet, if someone knew something important but refused to say, we could put a gun to his head. Here..." he made a shrugging gesture, and ate more fish.

Trace gazed at the scene. She did not like to suggest it, but there were plenty of things this situation required that she did not like. All of humanity dying because she could not liberate the Splicer's contents foremost among them. All of these petty moral concerns were nothing compared to that.

"These corbi," she said, nodding around at Tano's men. They sat easily among the villagers, their gear more well-organised than she'd seen with Loga's men. More of them had proper field webbing, with thought to the location of ammunition and grenades. "They're not Fleet? Not spacers?"

"No," said Tano. "They're locals. Not every local likes how Rando Resistance fights the war. Or doesn't fight it." Trace nodded, having seen some of that. Pena had been especially scathing. Pena sat with Kono now, translating back and forth between him and some villagers, who spoke a dialect of Lisha. Trace had gathered she was quite pretty by corbi standards, with her big eyes and pale mane.

"So they follow you instead?"

"Yes," said Tano.

"You're recruiting for Fleet? Finding new people?"

"Yes but it's complicated," said Tano. "Fleet is interested in Rando. There aren't many reeh here, like you said, but there are lots of their slaves. There's things to be learned, here. And ways to hurt the reeh."

"And that's what you tell them?" Trace asked.

"It's the truth."

"Huh," said Trace. Out in the bay, some fins breached the surface. Water slicked on dark, shiny bodies. A pair of whales, Trace thought, or something like whales. On the beach, corbi pointed and remarked, while youngsters rushed to see. "Why not tell them the real truth?"

"Which is?"

"That Rando is lost. That you can only take a planet when you take all the space around it. Croma won't fight reeh here, and reeh will come and crush them if they do. The only way for corbi to survive is to find another place. Somewhere out there." She waved a hand at the deep blue sky.

Tano said nothing, sipping water.

"Humans have seen this," Trace continued. "This is our history. One thousand years ago, we were like you. Earth was occupied, and most humans fought there to save Earth. But Fleet formed up in space, and Fleet knew that Earth was finished, a long time before people on Earth knew it. Fleet fought the krim, and the krim retaliated by killing humans on Earth. Humans on Earth told Fleet to stop fighting krim because it was killing lots of Earth humans. Fleet saw that this would be..."

"Surrender," Tano completed.

"Yes," said Trace. "Surrender. You can't fight the reeh when the reeh have all these hostages. An entire planet. You must either ignore them, or move them." A long pause. "Or let them die." Still Tano said nothing. "Or else all corbi will die."

"There is a reeh base," said Tano, watching the youngsters by the water, looking out at the whales. Trace thought it unlikely that they'd kill and eat these whales, given how close they'd come to shore. "In Vaseg. It has medical facilities. Fleet is interested in that technology. I'm building a force to attack it. I was."

"And Rando Resistance is not happy with you?"

"No. Like you say, they think they can fight without actually fighting. They're scared of the retaliation for an attack so big. They've forgotten how to fight, really. There's a bridge, out in Tiori Province. It's a big, old bridge, made back in the old days by corbi. It's made of steel, and it goes across a valley.

"There's some villagers out there. A tribe, you might call them. They worship the bridge, they live nearby and they clean it, they try to stop it rusting. It's very old now, I don't know what it means to them, but they seem to think it's important to preserve this bridge.

"And it doesn't actually go anywhere. Once it carried roads full of traffic between big cities along the coast, but now those roads are all gone, overgrown with trees... it's not an important route, there's no factories, no office jobs. People farm down in the valley, and fish in the stream. The bridge saves them a little time going one side to the other, but it's not important. But to those villagers, it's the most important thing."

"You think Rando Resistance is like that bridge?" Trace guessed.

Tano grinned. It was the first outright mirth she'd seen from him. "I told them once, too," he said. "They weren't happy. Told me to get on a spaceship and not come back. But they need me. Need us."

Trace understood. The bridge was a monument built long ago to do something that was no longer necessary. People maintained it because they felt they had to, and that their lives would be smaller without it. But the bridge meant something about culture and status to them now — about the preservation of history and corbi identity. It didn't actually do anything. And Rando Resistance was the same, going through the motions for nearly a thousand years. Earth at least had only suffered through two centuries before being put out of its misery.

"What does Fleet think?" Trace asked. "Where is Fleet looking for a new corbi home?"

"I can't say," said Tano. "It's our biggest secret." Trace nodded. Far along the edges of the Croma Wall, she thought. But there the corbi would run into the reeh's other, surrounding enemies. It was a long way, and no one was friendly. Perhaps there'd be worlds as yet unsettled where corbi would go, but nowhere where the reeh wouldn't eventually expand to. And if they weren't currently expanding into croma space, it was a sure bet they'd be expanding somewhere else.

"It's hard to get away from the reeh in this region of space," she said. "The croma won't let you pass on one side. Everywhere else is blocked as well."

"Even if we could get past the Croma Wall," said Tano, sardonically. "Would the others in your Spiral love and welcome us?" Trace thought for a moment. Frowning. She'd had this thought a few times before, but it had never been the right time to venture it. Tano saw that she did not immediately confirm his cynicism, and looked puzzled.

"There are free worlds in tavalai space," Trace said finally. "And in human space, though the rules are different. We've just fought a very large war, and there are lots of mixed populations. Lots of different species all living together."

Tano looked amazed. "When humans beat the tavalai, you didn't send them all elsewhere?"

"No," said Trace, undeniably pleased to be able to say something good of her people. "No, we let them stay. It's a Spiral tradition, actually. There have been so many empires, so many populations trading back and forth. The parren all kept to themselves, they don't mix well with others. The chah'nas too, they're xenophobes, they think contact with aliens makes them weak. But the tavalai conquered lots of space and let everyone stay, and now humans do the same with them. Many choose to go home when the humans come, rather than live on human-ruled worlds with limited rights, but they're not forced."

"Limited rights." Tano looked genuinely curious. "How limited?"

"Well they can't vote in human elections, obviously. But they vote to govern themselves, and those representatives are consulted by human governments. Tavalai are law-abiding, we couldn't do it with any other species."

"You don't oppress them? Occupy their cities with soldiers and shoot disagreeable tavalai?"

"No!" Trace half-exclaimed, dismissively forceful to be sure Tano understood. "There's no need. Tavalai know they lost, they don't make trouble. They work hard, they pay taxes and they're free to leave for tavalai space if they want. Travel freedoms around human space are restricted, they can't be citizens, they can't travel to main human worlds like Homeworld. A lot of them get tired of that, and go to tavalai space. But there's no oppression. Humans don't do that."

It made her proud, she realised. It shouldn't have. As Kulina, she should have held a tight rein on all her wants and desires, even the good ones. Pride could be dangerous, could lead to arrogance and the misjudgement of others. But she was slowly coming to conclude that no Kulina could be entirely like a stone and still function as a human being, let alone a soldier.

Instead, she allowed her pride to remind her why humanity had to be saved. It wasn't just the tribal loyalty of a soldier to her group. Humanity had to be worth something to more people in the universe than just humans. And Human Fleet, she sometimes thought, should remember it.

"Do you think that one of your free worlds would accept corbi?" asked Tano.

"Tavalai would," Trace said with certainty. "We were just at a place called Konik, that's where the old tavalai-era parliament is, the Tsubarata. It's not the prettiest world, but you can make money there if you're smart and work hard. The whole world isn't free, but the biggest city is, Gamesh. They'd take anyone. Tavalai have maybe a dozen free cities like that.

"Humans... I don't know. Humanity's gone through a very difficult last thousand years. We're very pricklish about our sovereignty, we don't like sharing it. It was an act of great generosity to let the tavalai on conquered worlds stay. Plenty in Fleet didn't want to, but they were convinced that the general public would think it looked bad... not to mention expensive, forcibly returning all those refugees. So I'm not sure humanity would help. But tavalai operate on principle, and their principle is that anyone can go to a free city, so long as they play by the rules."

"But we wouldn't have a world of our own," said Tano.

"No. No, you'd be citizens of someone else's empire, and very partial citizens at that. Tavalai limit rights of their free world non-tavalai just as much as humans do. More in some ways, less in others. But you'd be alive."

"It all counts for nothing if we can't get past the damn Croma Wall," Tano muttered. "And we're not in any position to arrange transport for however many millions actually wanted to come." He kicked at the sand. "But we do need a world. Your spacers couldn't make the humans thrive without at least one planet. Many would be preferable, but we need at least one. Just not this one. This one's irretrievable."

"How many are on this world, do you think?" Trace asked.

"Our best estimate is a bit over two hundred million," said Tano. "It used to be billions."

"How many do you think would want to leave?"

Tano made an exasperated gesture. "If Rando Resistance were explaining the situation to them? Filling their heads with nonsense about how Rando can still be saved? Not many." He put aside his empty plate and got up, collecting his rifle. "Come. I've something I want to ask our fisherman friend."

They trudged back along the sand toward Jindi's hut. The fisherman was sitting outside on an old tree stump with a view of the ocean, repairing a net that spread across the sand before him. A tin plate lay on the sand alongside, and his strong fingers moved surely over the intertwined strands of rope.

Jindi glanced at the strangers as they came, none too pleased. "Good fish, yes?" he asked. "Life by the sea is good, yes?"

"It's better than ship food," Tano admitted. He knelt alongside, leaning on his rifle in a way that marines would never do. Spacers and weapons discipline. Trace refrained from comment with difficulty. "Jindi. Did you ever see much of the animal trade with Splicer City?"

Jindi visibly twitched, an involuntary jerk of one twisted shoulder. "Not on my level. I was in the the middle level. The animal trade happens in the lower levels."

"But you heard about it? Stories passing through?"

"A bit." His previously strong fingers faltered on the nets, missing a pull with a new strand of rope. His arm shook.

"Who handles it? The reeh? Do they do that trade themselves?"

"No. No, it's one of the slaves. They do all the... chopping and changing. The Rando population. It's the same for corbi as it is for animals. All animals. All of us, just animals to them."

"So the same people working on modifications to tanifex are the same people doing modifications to the animals?"

"Same," Jindi admitted. "Same database. Same everything."

Tano gazed out to sea for a moment, chewing on a thumbnail. Trace remembered that Erik had done that, before she'd beaten the habit out of him.

"What does that mean?" she asked him finally.

"It means," said Tano, "that those people doing strange modifications to the tanifex you captured might not be out of reach. Maybe we can contact them." He looked at Trace, as though surprised at his own thought. "And maybe your stupid idea about the Splicer might be workable after all." He jerked his head at Jindi. "Even without his help."

10

Erik steered the big ground utility vehicle along a dirt road past scrub and security fencing, lights glaring through the dark as they bounced on the rough surface. Most croma working in labour-related industries were young, but their trucks were built big by habit. This one had Ensign Kadi riding shotgun, AR glasses down, manipulating invisible images before him as they bounced.

"I'm in the perimeter security now, Captain," said Kadi, and winced at the old bullet wound in his side that he claimed still gave him occasional pains. He'd picked that one up on Gamesh, on operations with Lieutenant Dale, when *Phoenix* had conspired to rob the Kantovan Vault of Drakhil's ancient diary. Now he operated Styx's flying assassin bugs, which had other uses besides killing. "Anything Styx can't reach remotely should be blind to us now, we can walk straight in."

"Who's in the complex?" Erik asked.

"A couple of techs," said Kadi, reaching to manipulate the image before him through 180 degrees. "Don't look like security, just spanner-grunts fixing stuff."

Erik flipped to local coms. "Okay people, Kadi says it's clear, there's a couple of mechanics inside, no security. We're going to be nice to them. Even if they try and fight, no shooting. We can knock them out if we have to, but if we kill some poor grease monkey who's just trying to do his job, we'll look like assholes and Croma'Rai really will hunt us down and kill us, got it?"

"We got it, Captain," said Jalawi from the vehicle behind. "If they're big'uns, take the damn punch guys, got it? No shooting because you're scared of a few bruises. If there's just a couple of them, we won't need firepower anyway."

Over in the big legal building in Cal'Uta, Lieutenant Shilu was leading a legal effort with Jokono and Jal'orta, a prominent Croma'-Dokran solicitor, who was assembling a team to challenge the Croma'Rai leadership's suddenly-imposed travel restrictions. Croma law wasn't half as hard as tavalai law, as Lassa had suggested, but the process of understanding all the utterly alien concepts and technicalities had promised to make merely the acquisition of legal representation a trial of its own. Shilu had solved that problem with the genius notion to simply let the Croma'Dokran solicitor in on the plan. From there, the solicitor had cheerfully agreed to assist and handle all the details, for the sheer joy of bloodying a metaphorical Croma'Rai nose or two.

With media and security agencies circling Shilu, his team and the Croma'Dokran lawyers, the second part of the plan now unfolded. Erik did not know what Styx had done to render their movement invisible to Croma'Rai surveillance, except to suppose that all orbital, aerial and other surveillance was now feeding the planetary government a useful fiction — that *Phoenix*'s crew were still in their accommodation, and that no one was moving. The processing power required to simultaneously juggle all of those fictions in a convincing manner was of course obscene, but Styx had been infiltrating Dul'rho planetary networks for three months straight, and was now, *Phoenix*'s techs told him, enslaving chunks of local processing power to do her bidding real-time to save those calculations from the time-lag of *Phoenix*'s orbital position.

Erik pulled the vehicle up before a large gate. On the right, a huge refinery hummed, pipes enveloping several huge pressure tanks, ablaze with floodlights. On the left, a tall hangar across a concrete expanse, within which a great mechanical beast loomed in the shadows.

"Can you get us in, Petty Officer?" Erik asked when the gate did not immediately move. "Or do I need to bust it down?"

"Um... hang on Captain..." as Kadi fiddled with icons, biting his lip.

The gate slid gratingly open. "Good job," said Erik, and pressed the controls forward.

"Um, wasn't me," Kadi concluded reluctantly, gazing at his controls.

"Then thank you Styx," said Erik, accelerating across the concrete toward the hangar.

"Always my pleasure, Captain," said Styx.

The beast in the hangar was a repulsor engine, cantered by a single electric turbofan that ran down its middle like a giant alien eye. It settled now on iron mounts, resting between great continental journeys, attended by automated pipes and hoses within the hangar. This one was operated by a company half-owned by Croma'Dokran interests, whom Croma'Rai rules did not prohibit from commerce on their homeworld. Erik had arranged to lease it for a trip, under a false name supplied by the Croma'Dokran party.

He pulled the vehicle to a halt before the huge crevice of a service pit before the hangar, where the engine would other times settle to have its underside accessed. Behind him, another two vehicles arrived, marines and spacers leaping from their rear... and here from the middle one was Tiga with Romki, and Skah wearing his backpack and holding another bag, looking up at the big machine in awe.

Ahead, Corporal Graf was confronting a croma worker in thick overalls and hard hat... only 'confronting' did not seem quite the term, as the exchange was amicable. Erik made his way warily over, as marines secured the hangar and spacers set about familiarising themselves with all the operating systems that would need to be released if the big engine were going to move again.

"Tali'san?" the croma worker asked in apparent amusement. *"Tali'san, you take for tali'san?"* As Erik's earpiece translator kicked in.

"Tali'san, yes!" Graf replied with the same amount of good cheer. The croma actually guffawed, one of the rare times Erik had seen a croma laugh, then turned to roar something in Kul'hasa at his friend further down. Graf gave Erik a bemused look, as though wondering if he might like to take over this negotiation, but Erik gave her the signal that it was all her's. Graf was yet another of the *Phoenix* crew up for a significant award beyond her promotion from lance to full corporal, as it was only by her quick wits that they hadn't lost the drysine data-core to a self-destruct upon discovery. Erik was entirely confident that she could handle a couple of croma hangar techs.

Erik left them to it, as Graf showed the croma the documents for the lease, plus the very considerable insurance, and the croma just laughed harder and waved that yes, yes all was in order and they could take the machine. A Tali'san of this scale was a huge thing for all croma on Dul'rho, and most were delighted to have an event of such scale playing out in their own backyard. All local croma knew what *Phoenix* was, and the nature of their predicament. These workers were probably Croma'Rai, yet did not begrudge *Phoenix* the opportunity to fight back against the forces confronting them.

Spacers clambered up the boarding ramps — an equal mix of engineers and systems operators, all of them well-read on this technology and confident it wouldn't prove difficult for any half-decent warship crew, let alone this one. Erik followed them up, onto the side access walk, then up a precarious ladder above the bulging compressor casing and through the underside hatch to the cockpit wing. Spacer Daen already had the door open, and Erik went through it, to find Lieutenant Sasalaka already seated in what appeared to be the co-pilot's chair, sorting in her methodical manner through the rowed displays and buttons.

"Our technical reports seem to be correct, Captain," she observed, comparing what she saw to the display she got on the monocle-lens tavalai preferred to human-style glasses. "We should be able to commence startup on schedule."

Erik nodded, and blinked on Warrant Officer Leung's icon. "Gretch, what's your situation?"

"Umm... looks good, Captain," came Gretchen Leung's reply from somewhere down by the main repulsors. She'd been third-highest ranking Engineering officer when the trip had commenced, and Remy Hale's death had bumped her up to second. *"They keep these things pretty clean... all my systems monitors are looking green, it wasn't in here for repair. If you give me five minutes, I think we can be good to go."*

"Let's do it," Erik confirmed, and took his chair beside Sasalaka to figure out the startup sequence. The heavy rear doors hummed open, and Skah came in, gazing wide-eyed at all the controls and the big, wrap-around windows. "Are the quarters back there okay, Skah?"

"Good, sure," Skah acknowledged, but Erik wasn't fooled. Skah had barely looked at the quarters, and had come rushing up to the bridge instead.

"Skah, maybe you should go back downstairs," Sasalaka suggested, counting through temperature readouts.

"No, Skah, you take a seat right there," said Erik, pointing to an observer chair. "And you watch the crew taking off these umbilical connections, and you tell me every time they remove one, you understand?"

"Unnerstand, yes!" Skah leaped happily into the chair's worn upholstery, peering out the windows to watch the ongoing commotion. "We going soon?"

"Very soon," Erik agreed. "Sasa, look, here's the main magneto-coils, sequence one-through-five, so these must be..."

"Yes, this is all turbofan here," the tavalai agreed, indicating another whole panel. "Fan pitch, compression chamber, ignition safeties..."

They ran through the board, while Skah told them each time the crew removed another umbilical — a largely unnecessary thing, but it did give the pilots some idea of how far preparations were coming without having to interrupt and be interrupted on coms. Soon Jalawi arrived on the bridge, a cap in place of a helmet on his bald head.

"There's room for about fifteen croma back there," he announced, looking about the bridge as a marine might — checking for armour protection and lines-of-sight to the rest of the vehicle. "Gonna be a squeeze."

"Well you could try sleeping on deck," Erik suggested, continuing his system checks. "But at full speed it's going to get a little breezy."

"Toilets?" Skah asked with partway alarm.

"Yeah kid," Jalawi reassured him with a ruffle of the kuhsi's ears. "There's toilets. Question is, are you going to get all your homework done for your Mummy?"

"Honework?" Skah looked dismayed. "I can't do honework here! Too crazy!"

"You think a marine would make excuses like that?"

"Narines don't have honework!" Skah retorted.

"We do too, the Major gave me homework all the..." and Jalawi ducked, interrupted by a clatter of steel limbs over the cabin, then Peanut went scuttling down the front windshield to check on something along the vehicle's long, twenty-metre bonnet.

"He's checking the forward exhaust ports are clear," said Sasalaka, pointing to the big outlets on either side of the cockpit.

"Gonna be a long trip, huh?" Jalawi remarked. Erik didn't think he was commenting on the journey's duration.

"I don't know what you mean," Erik said drily. Jalawi grinned, shouldered his rifle and went back through the rear door.

Truth be told, Erik was rather enjoying himself. So many times on this trip, various entities, alien and human, had tried to screw them. This time Croma'Rai had tried to stop them from getting to Stat'cha, and Erik wasn't going to take it. They'd be out on the desert highways before Croma'Rai leadership figured out they'd gone, and he in particular wouldn't be cooped up inside, fretting and worrying about things outside of his control. Lately he'd had enough of that just worrying about Trace. This way, *he* was in control, and the longer this trip had gone on, the more he was beginning to like things that way.

They were halfway through the startup sequence when Graf called again from outside. *"Captain!"* she shouted, voice raised above the rising throb of massive repulsorlifts. *"The workers out here are saying there's a trailer we could borrow!"*

Erik frowned, as the high cockpit shook with rising vibration. *"Phoenix* paid for the lease of the engine, Corporal. I won't have anyone saying that we're thieves."

"No Captain, it's the main auxiliary trailer! It... it shares a serial number, it's usually included in the lease, it just wasn't with this one because it was damaged, but they say they've fixed it!"

Erik glanced at Sasalaka. "More space could be useful," she admitted. "Particularly for our rendezvous, if it comes."

Which was a good point, Erik thought. "I copy that, Corporal," he replied to Graf. "How long will it take to attach?"

* * *

FIFTEEN MINUTES LATER, ERIK AND SASALAKA WERE POWERING THE enormous repulsor engine out the main gates of the repair yard. Once beyond the concrete apron, sand swirled in great clouds to block the view beyond the compulsory floodlights and running-light blinkers. The pilot's chair came with no headgear for better vision, but the cockpit windows did a fair job of wrap-around head-up displays, highlighting all surrounding objects directly onto the windshield.

"Rearview is not optimal," Sasalaka remarked from the co-pilot's chair at his side, watching all the system displays that Erik had no time for, his awareness full of attitude, velocity and not crashing into things. "Sideview is barely better."

"Attitude is interesting too," said Erik, adjusting sensitivity with fast fingers across multiple controls. "It's a bit like ice skating. My guess is it will straighten out at higher speeds when aerodynamics kick in."

"Navigation confirms that we are in fact invisible," said Kaspowitz from behind them. He was hooked into the intercontinental traffic control on his glasses, something most pilots would typically let take care of itself, but this engine had special needs. "We're completely blanked, traffic central can't see us at all."

A coms link flashed, and Erik blinked on it. "Go ahead, Lance Corporal."

"Hello Captain," came Lance Corporal Maiza's voice. *"To confirm that we are inbound at four minutes ETA, we have our passenger and she came willingly."*

"Just as well," Kaspowitz said drily. "Or we'd be kidnapping."

"We copy, Lance Corporal," said Erik. "Engine One will be accelerating to cruise velocity momentarily, rendezvous will be on our brand new trailer."

A moment's pause from Maiza. *"Nice to hear we have a trailer,"* he said. *"Should be fun."*

"The trailer is high-speed landing certified by me personally, Dookie," came Jalawi's voice from somewhere down back. *"Screw it up and it's coming out of your pay, got it?"*

"How much is that these days, LT?" Maiza chortled. *"Back in three, hope no one's chasing us."*

Erik and Sasalaka had commenced turbine startup while Maiza was talking — a new, whining howl from up the front as forward propulsion came online. "Chamber pressure good," said Sasalaka, with her usual methodical approach. Erik could see it all without her talking, but this tavalai never took shortcuts. "Ignition temperature optimal, revolutions commencing startup."

Repulsors kept the engine off the ground, but it took a big, old-fashioned turbine to drive them forward, sucking air in the front and blasting it out the back with some added fusion-power compression for kick. Thrust divided from that single intake to a pair of rear nozzles on the engine's flanks, dividing on either side of the exhaust-protected trailer behind.

Repulsor-tech, Lieutenant Rooke had lately been speculating, was likely a hacksaw invention, probably drysine, being significantly more advanced and difficult than even FTL drive. 'Anti-gravity' wasn't even strictly correct, as repulsors didn't fight gravity any more than Faster-Than-Light technology fought against lightspeed — rather they bypassed it, bending universal laws by creating what was effectively a new state of matter at the molecular level through a vehicle's primary lift frame. The means of bypassing fundamental physical laws in FTL were somewhat obvious in hindsight, given the inherent flexibility of spacetime that became second-nature to any civilisation knocking on the door of space-civilisation entry-level mathematics.

But repulsor-lift required knowledge of quantum laws of gravity that drove attraction between particles at the smallest scale, and functioned like the DNA of the universe. Given that the Fathers had only been around for several thousand years before the machines that destroyed them had created the greatest civilisation the Spiral had yet seen, Rooke hadn't thought it likely that repulsors had come from organics at all. Erik thought of his old friends on the tavalai warship *Makimakala*, who'd devoted their lives to ensuring the dangerous technology of the Machine Age would not spread throughout the galaxy, and wondered if even they'd truly known just how much of the Spiral's existing technological base was already the creation of machine-intelligence.

The turbine's checks came back clean, and Erik let Sasalaka apply the power. It came up slowly, a muffled, whining howl, then the sandstorm began to clear as the engine accelerated out of the cloud of its own making. As Erik had suspected, attitude control became far simpler once the engine began to cut through the air, stabilising like a paper plane thrown with force.

Ahead now, the windshield display showed a long arc of lane markers laid across the dusty scrub, each several hundred metres from the next. He turned the engine gently as speed increased, seeing the nav display on the windshield mirrored on the left panel's big screen — no other vehicles for the next five kilometres at least.

"Okay!" Kaspowitz shouted above the dull roar of their passage. "Now we have to figure which way you want to go!"

Erik nodded, calling up the larger continental map on the nav screen. It showed the Cho'na continent — Cal'Uta on the far southwest, four hundred kilometres from the western coast. Stat'cha was 7000 kilometres away, across a mostly-desert landscape where

Dul'rho's largest continental mass lay directly across the rain-shadow between tropical equator and temperate, cooler regions to the south. Seven thousand kilometres by land sounded like a lot, but the desert-train routes needed no paved roads, just lane markers, and at a hundred and fifty kph non-stop they'd cover that distance in forty-six hours. Somehow Erik doubted it was going to be that simple.

"Depends on how Croma'Rai try and stop us," he told Kaspowitz. "Styx can confuse them a lot, she can blank all their communications if she has to, give them false readings, have them chasing shadows all over the place. But they might get wise to it quickly, so I want to spend the first hours just putting as much distance between us and Cal'Uta as possible."

"Right," said Kaspowitz, studying the 2-D map that had to be a novelty for one of Fleet's leading warship navigators, "well the next big junction is by Dai'Ra, that's two hundred Ks ahead, let's hit that first then see where we are."

"Captain," said Sasalaka. "Corporal Maiza is approaching now, ETA two minutes at present speed."

"Right," said Erik. "I'd better go back and greet them. Sasa, you take control. Kaspo, here's your chance to be a co-pilot."

"All my dreams fulfilled," said Kaspowitz, moving to take the tavalai's seat as Sasalaka moved to Erik's. Erik had to repress the reflex to make a formality of relinquishing control — this was hardly the *Phoenix* bridge, and for all its strangeness, the repulsor engine was little more complicated for a warship pilot than driving a lawn-mower. Considerably more fun though, Erik thought as he ducked out the rear door, down some steel steps, then along a vibrating, rocking corridor lit by sodium-yellow light.

Here at the rear of the huge vehicle were the crew quarters, squeezed between engine systems and thrust nozzles, there was barely a window in any of the small rooms off the corridor's sides. In one he found several spacers playing cards on their oversized croma bunks, while Skah sat on one end and watched a display of the Tali'san coverage with Spacers Ragi and Katzer, talking to them like any kid about his favourite sport.

"Don't let him stay up too late," Erik leaned in the doorway to tell the spacers. "It's not a vacation, and we promised his mother we'd look after him."

"Yes Captain," chorused the spacers, and Erik continued down the corridor. Tif, of course, had regular duty as pilot of PH-4, which put her on *Phoenix* most of the time, with all the shuttles on regular rotation. But Skah, it had been agreed, really needed as much solid time on a planet as he could get, and if that took him away from his mother for longer periods, that was probably the lesser of two evils. Truthfully, Erik thought neither Tif nor Skah worried about it as much as humans expected them to. Kuhsi were a clan-oriented people, more accustomed to large social groups than solitary existences. Tif's role in Skah's life was special, as with mothers in most species, but when necessary, any other family could perform the role as well.

Accessing the trailer umbilical required the stairs to the upper level, then a fast walk along the short suspension-like passage that bounced and swayed, with thrust deafening and sand hitting the flexible metal sides with stinging impact. Erik closed the trailer hatch behind him, wincing as he figured that goggles should be essential operating equipment out here, and surely there'd be a batch stowed in a locker somewhere.

The trailer had its own repulsor engines, of course, but relied entirely on the tractor for forward motion, and so had a lot more room to spare. This one had an upper level of additional crew quarters, and a rear-quarter landing pad on the roof protected from the roaring slipstream by a large windshield. Erik pulled himself out the hatch just as Maiza's cruiser was making its final approach, coming in from the side to avoid the enormous rooster tail of desert sand the train was now throwing in its wake.

The cruiser came in low over the heads of waiting spacers and marines, floodlights blinding for a moment, then settling abruptly hard as it dropped out of the slipstream and thudded to the deck. Erik saw thumbs-up from within the cabin, then the doors opened and marines from Maiza's Second Section climbed out. With them came a looming croma figure in a long leather coat, head down against the swirling blast of wind and sand, holding to the cruiser's roof momentarily as the whole pad swayed.

Then Rhi'shul came, careful of her balance in a way that spacers generally weren't, and took a handrail at Erik's side, looming over him with menace.

Erik smiled up at her, readjusting his earpiece. "I hope my marines asked nicely?"

"I did not need to come," the croma growled in reply. No croma liked to admit to being forced into anything.

"If you want to find out what secrets Croma'Rai's intelligence agency's been accumulating over the past few centuries, then yes, you did." Erik indicated for her to follow him inside, where the lack of wind, blowing sand and roaring engines made conversation less impractical.

"They'll track you," said the croma, no longer shouting. *"They don't need to shoot you to stop you. Blocking your road is simple."*

"They can't track us," Erik said confidently. "Our computer access capability controls everything they see."

Rhi'shul exhaled hard through big nostrils. *"When they discover what a threat you've become to the security of all croma, they might just destroy your ship."*

"I think they know quite well what we are," Erik said calmly. "They know we'll do nothing to harm croma, but we will insist that they abide by the agreements they made with us upon our arrival."

"Is she here?" Rhi'shul pressed. *"Did you bring her down to the planet somehow?"*

Erik frowned. Like a lot of grounders, particularly those unversed in hacksaw tech, Rhi'shul seemed to have little grasp of just how much damage Styx could do from orbit. "No, she's not here. But Peanut is. Say hello to Rhi'shul, Peanut."

He indicated the big drysine drone who had arrived in the hatch from the landing pad. Rhi'shul had walked straight to Erik without looking behind. Rhi'shul stared at the drysine, eyes wide in that half-fear that a croma would never express as such. Would rather die than express as such.

Peanut's dual-eyed head darted back and forth, like that of a small bird, assessing and reassessing this new arrival. "Peanut's quite friendly, for a drone," Erik told their guest. "Functionally he's a lot smarter than any of us in some things, and less so in others. Treat him with respect and you'll get along fine."

Rhi'shul overcame her initial shock, and gave a short, formal nod to the drone. *"Hello."* Peanut considered that for a moment, then turned and scuttled away to some more interesting task.

"He doesn't do verbal language," Erik explained. "But his machine language is a thousand times more efficient, so he probably doesn't see the point. We haven't been able to rig a translator for that, organic brains just aren't designed to absorb that kind of data-transferal. And yeah... he doesn't understand manners. Don't take him for rude — he doesn't mean to be, he just doesn't know what it means."

"Tavalai and human crew," Rhi'shul muttered. *"Machine Age drones and a queen guiding you from orbit. A corbi resistance girl who thinks she can save her people single-handed. Your ship is a zoo."*

Erik smiled broadly. "Now you're getting the hang of us. If you're here to help, instead of just throwing snide comments at everything, you'll find we actually get stuff done, too."

11

Several hours hike up the coast from Jindi's place on the beach, Trace and Tano's party walked along what had once been a paved road. Now the bitumen was crumbled grains amid the roots of trees, slabs of concrete protruding occasionally from the undergrowth, along with bits of fence. Trace could hear waves, and knew the ocean was near. There had been a great city near here, and this would have been a seaside neighbourhood, a place for wealthy people to live near the beach. Probably among the trees would lie the ruins of shopping districts and schools, all the suburban trappings of a species who were not dissimilar from humans in many ways.

Occasionally the moonlight caught the edge of a raised wall among the trees, a structure in which families had once lived, still standing eight hundred years later. Once Trace saw a strange, rusted frame with springs that could only have been a children's trampoline. Now, part of a plastic chair, covered in mold. Further ahead, the rusted frame of a car, all doors, interiors and tires long since disintegrated, and now full of plants.

Trace glanced at the corbi as they walked, and saw them looking at things, occasionally examining some object more closely with thoughtful melancholy. This had been their civilisation once. People had lived here, entire communities, and presumably been happy. All lost, because one of the galaxy's many life forms saw all the others as resources to be consumed. It was an attitude all life began with. Some grew out of it.

Trace found that the melancholy cleared her head, and made her calm. In a world of so many uncertain things, here at least was one thing for sure. Impermanence, the transience of life, and the essential need for all who lived to push back against those threads of history that would swallow the others whole if they could.

There was still some way to go until the region where the villagers thought the kauda lived. All of *these* kauda were territorial, but some of their territories were vast. Wind tossed the branches, and clouds blocked most light from the moons. It was both Feina and Dogba tonight, now nearing midnight. Occasionally the clouds would part briefly to engulf the trees in ghostly light, and the silver remains of decayed houses. Then the clouds would close, and darkness swept in once more, as though by the wave of some veiled hand.

Tano looked deep in thought. Agu, his second, at his side, carrying the backpack that contained some sensitive things Tano would not entrust anyone else to see. Trace was next, then Bago, Pena and Rika, then Kono. Trace occasionally turned as she walked to cast a wary eye back at her Staff Sergeant. Bago was from the village, a young but experienced hunter who knew the way. Kono, being nearer the rear, walked as often backward as forward, endlessly scanning. Between them, Rika bent to pick up an object from the leaf-strewn ground — an old wristwatch, steel-banded and somehow still intact. Rika looked pleased, until he saw Trace's disapproval. He stuffed the watch in a pocket, put both hands back on his rifle, and resumed a watchful walk.

The rest of Tano's team had formed two more parties of six, spreading across this portion of the jungle, but further inland. One more group had stayed with the village, doing some work that Tano was very vague about. The villagers must have thought themselves relatively safe, Trace thought. There were no defensive walls around the village, nor about Jindi's hut. Some hungry things did not like the sea, nor the bonfires that could burn on a sandy beach without setting the forest afire. On the beach, hunting things had no cover, and traps were simple and effective. Smart animals would learn, and remember.

Trace listened again for the sound of insects, ever present in the night trees. It was harder to hear with the wind blowing, the endless rustle and creak of leaves and boughs. She struggled to hear them now, as a gust came rolling through the branches, leaves and bushes all waving and hushing before it. Then faded, amid falling leaves. Nothing.

Trace whistled. It happened sometimes, the forest sounds fading and the first to hear it would alert the others. Ahead, Tano and Agu turned to glance at her, questioning. Trace held up a fist, found cover by a fallen log and took a knee. Behind her, the others copied, while Tano and Agu did the same ahead. Trace nearly missed it, the flicker of movement, then Agu abruptly vanished as the night came alive and took him.

"KAUDA!" Trace yelled, and ran straight for where the corbi had been. Her night-adjusted eyes were more sensitive than most, augmented like all marines', and glimpsed a big, black shadow dragging a kicking corbi through the undergrowth at speed. She raised her rifle, but there was no safe shot.

Behind, she heard yelling, then shooting. Bago grabbed her arm and pulled her down. "Stay low!" he hissed. "There's always more than one!" Trace covered one way, Tano and Bago the others, eyes wide and heart pounding. "They've got good position, they're hunting. Don't forget to look up."

There was no hope to go sprinting after Agu — knowing what she knew about these mutated monsters, Trace knew that running would guarantee an attack, and the kauda were far more effective at full sprint than a human or corbi soldier without a steady fire platform. The best chance was to stay still and see them before they were seen. Looking back, she couldn't see Kono, or anyone. All were low in the undergrowth, watching. She'd run forward, while Kono had run back. It had divided them.

After twenty seconds, nothing. "We have to get back to Kono," Trace murmured. "We're too spread out. Safer together."

Bago glanced at Tano, who indicated that Bago should be the one speaking. Tano looked more than alarmed, like a spacer wondering why the hell anyone would want to go down to a planet in the first place. He'd been down here a while, and had experienced some bad things, but this looked like a close encounter even by his standards. Bago scanned for ten more heart-thumping seconds before replying. "Go."

Army-crawling would have taken her eyes out of the equation, not to mention her rifle, so Trace squatted and duck-walked very slowly, eyes and rifle scanning. Behind her, Tano came backward, his short legs making a low walk somewhat easier, then Bago. The wind was eased, and nothing chirped or sang in the dark. The thing Trace had seen was blacker than the darkest night, and made no sound despite its speed.

Her heart wouldn't stop pounding. This wasn't like a firefight. She was used to those, and knew how to stay so busy that her brain had no time to process fear. Here there was no tacnet display, no coms, no tactical situation to process. Just her, her hidden comrades, and the fear, engulfing every heart like the surrounding dark and squeezing. Fine, she thought, forcing herself to breathe long and slow. Fear was fear. Everything on this world was back to primitive basics, and there were no technological shields behind which to hide. Accept the fear. Don't fight it. There were instincts hardwired into her brain by millions of years of evolution that would probably serve her better here than modern combat training. Harness it. Make it work for you.

Ahead, past obscuring bushes, she saw Kono, crouched by the base of a tree. He saw her, but did not startle or swing his rifle her way. Just continued scanning, and occasionally glancing up from beneath his brows, as the rifle continued to move beneath his eyeline. Trace did the same, up Kono's tree, then across the swaying canopy of branches... then stopped. Something was wrong. She looked back to Kono's tree. And saw it, impossibly, a shadow that blocked all texture of tree bark on the trunk just a few metres off the ground. A shadow that moved, head down, toward Kono.

Trace pivoted her rifle up, and two short bursts hammered the night silence. The black thing fell practically in Kono's lap as he scrambled from under its collapsing weight. Further back, something else crashed and bounded, then Pena was shouting and shooting, Rika and Tano joining in, bullets ripping the night as whatever it was ran away.

Trace moved quickly to Kono's side, glanced down at the beast to be sure, but it was dead. Even now it was hard to discern its outline, so well did the ink-black fur drink in the darkness. But it had bulk, half as big again as Kono, and nearly twice as big as Trace. Long white teeth gleamed in the dark, and the talons on its paws were thick like knives. Before the reeh had arrived on Rando, the ancestors of creatures like this were the size of house cats.

"Fuck me," Kono muttered, recovering himself from a bad fright and looking around for more. Tano shouted after Pena and Rika, telling them to close the gap.

"They usually disappear after we kill one," Bago said, swinging off his pack and rummaging inside. "Never count on it though, they're damn smart."

"This one got your electronics," Trace agreed. "Bet that was no accident." As Pena and Rika arrived, both apparently intact. "It got Agu and his backpack," she told them. "We're going after it."

"Sure," Pena said breathlessly, watching the trees. "Great idea."

"I'll go," said Rika.

"Wait," said Tano, producing a large-muzzled pistol from his own pack. "This is how we grab it."

The big pistol was a tranquilliser, air compression throwing a dart... probably no more than thirty metres with any accuracy, Trace guessed. In this night, that was plenty, it was a struggle to see these beasts any further away than ten. From the looks on the others' faces as they contemplated the small, low-powered weapon, it was clear that none of them were about to volunteer.

"I'm the best shot here," said Trace, holding out her hand. Tano thought about it, then pressed the pistol into her hand, and a clip of four extra darts.

"They'll take three kimo to knock one out," he said... that was about six seconds, Trace knew. "So you'll have to..."

A shrill cry of agony interrupted him, middle distant and horrifying. Agu.

"So you'll have to get close enough to hit," Tano resumed, jaw tight, "then survive when it charges you. Remember, if you have to shoot or wound it first, we'll have to explain the bullet hole at the Splicer. Anyone with high powered rifles is suspected to be Resistance, so better that you don't."

"I'm coming too," Pena interrupted fiercely. "We have to save Agu."

"They'll kill him when we get close," said Bago, reshouldering his pack. "I told you, they're smart. They're luring us into a trap, Agu's the bait. I'd guess there's about six of them."

"We only need one alive," Tano said grimly.

"Why would an animal pick a fight with high powered rifles?" Kono muttered, risking another glance at the dead kauda.

"They've been conditioned to," said Bago. "Gunfire attracts them rather than repels them, makes them hungry. Reeh can make animals enjoy suicide."

"No more talking," said Trace. "Stay together, watch your sector. Let's go."

They all went, as volunteering to remain behind and alone would have been most dangerous of all. They moved in tight single file, so that overlapping fields of vision and fire did not become a deadly problem in the night. Bago went first, most experienced in jungle hunting, then Tano. Trace and Kono were third and fourth, the middle of the column, being tallest and able to see over the others' heads forward and back. At the rear, Rika then Pena, walking mostly backward.

Bago took them carefully through the gap between two ruined walls amid the trees, following Agu's occasional shrieks of pain and fear. Even Trace felt her stomach churning to hear it, and concentrated on combat basics to keep her mind focused. Such insensible screams from a smart, brave man like Agu could only mean horrific, disfiguring injuries. The continuation of such screams meant the kauda were likely adding more of them. Trace knew her mental discipline was elite, but she sometimes wondered if she'd disgrace herself in such a circumstance. She'd seen sentient beings reduced to pulverised meat, yet somehow still alive and conscious, for a moment at least. She only hoped that she could retain enough sense and physical capability to get a weapon and end it herself, if it happened to her.

Ahead, amid bushes, Bago crouched by the base of a trunk. Before him, Trace saw the outline of a two storey structure more intact than most. It made sense that the kauda would nest somewhere high and defensible. Some of the houses that had once made this community were wood and other decaying materials, but this one looked concrete, a hulking presence among the trees.

Trace crept forward, observing the structure. It had ground level windows, easily accessible to the ground floor. The upper floor would be where Agu was — where predators would take a kill to feed. Bago indicated with fluttery fingers — the corbi signal for wind, then off to the side from where it came. Trace nodded — the wind was from the right, off the ocean, so it wouldn't carry their scent to any waiting kauda at the house. But if this were a trap...

She indicated left and right, visible to those clustered behind, then pointed to her eyes, scanning. Nods came back. Kauda would flank them, tempting them up the middle, then attacking from the sides, or from above. Attempting to outmanoeuvre them was pointless, neither humans nor corbi were equipped for it. A tight formation was best, each member tasked with watching one direction, inviting kauda to charge their rifles.

They had several sets of night vision goggles, but their electrical signature output was collectively large, and put them at risk of detection from the reeh. Ditto flashlights, which could even be visible from orbital surveillance if they were unlucky. Besides, flashlights only blinded night vision, and gave the kauda no doubts as to their location.

Trace took point herself, and indicated forward. Moonlight speared briefly through a gap in the clouds, lighting tree trunks and the moss-covered front of the old concrete house. She placed her boots carefully on soft ground, trying to avoid twigs and leaves that would snap and rustle. That wasn't easy for someone who'd trained most of her life on steel floors in heavy armour. But after three months of jungle manoeuvres, she knew more than she had.

There were no more screams. Tano had said the kauda would kill Agu when they got close. Trace reckoned that an animal smart enough to figure such things would likely be smart enough to know how guns worked, and would not expose themselves directly. She glanced up as she walked, not shifting the level of her rifle, swivelling slowly. Behind, Tano, Kono and Bago would divide the flanks between them, while Rika and Pena had the rear. Trace reckoned the rear was most likely. But not until they could be hit from all sides simultaneously. Not yet.

She checked carefully about a tree trunk as she passed, finding no trace of the yard that would once have surrounded the house. The jungle had claimed all but the concrete shell, which now sprouted bushes out its empty windows. Explosive entry of an occupied house was best done from multiple entry points simultaneously, but under these circumstances they dared not divide their numbers. They needed space, so the front door corridor was out. She aimed for the main window, feeling many hidden eyes watching them from the dark as she approached. More moonlight hit an upper window, and she was nearly certain she saw eyes, glowing in the gloom.

Bushes grew thickly out the main windows ahead. Moonlight did not penetrate within. The trap was too obvious. "Hold formation!" she said, quite calm and loudly in Lisha. "Watch your sector, we're going to get loud!"

Still ten paces short, she fired a spread of shots into the bushes. A shriek, some scrabbling from within, and a black shape flew at her from the foliage. Trace shot it with a semi-automatic burst to the face, then put several more in its head as it tumbled to a stop. Then Kono yelled warning of something above, then Rika of something behind, and more shooting. Trace waited for it to stop, not distracted from her forward-view, then glimpsed movement up the left wall of the house and put two shots that way. Whatever it was vanished, then Kono shouted 'clear!' and Trace gestured them forward.

'Moving!' Kono yelled for the benefit of those who hadn't seen, and Trace put some more rounds into the foliage before stepping through and ducking low. The bushes only grew at the windows where there was light — within was dirt, weeds, and the stench of animal urine and rotting remains. Trace barely made out bones on the floor, residue of many old kills, and hustled past to cover at one side of the next doorway. The stairs had to be somewhere further in.

Kono took the opposing wall, the two marines realising the corbi weren't nearly as adept at clearing rooms. A fast head-dart each way revealed to Trace only that she couldn't see in the black corridor, so she put two bullets up her way, and Kono the same down his, then he led her quickly in. That pitch black corridor led to a doorway with a little light, and Kono went through, to an immediate screech and loud gunfire, Trace coming through to find another creature kicking and twitching on the ground. Kono shot it in the head as Trace moved rapidly past, covering him in the dull moonlight that glowed beyond the big, open once-windows around the back.

Against the right wall were stairs. Tano and Pena came past to take up Trace's cover position, as Trace nodded for Kono to take point, pulling her dart pistol as he went. Kono understood without a word spoken, rifle raised as his boots tested the old stairs. They were concrete too, and he stayed low, as Trace pushed her rifle around on its carry strap, aiming the pistol past Kono's shoulder. 'Don't die for it,' she wanted to tell him. 'If it charges, shoot it — we'll find another'. But she knew Kono too well. He was dedicated to the mission, she'd chosen him to run Command Squad precisely because he was so good at surviving.

The stairs turned halfway up, and Trace had difficulty getting a line of sight past Kono's towering shoulder. He got down real low at the top of the stairs, allowing her to get a good 360 view. They were against one wall, and the floor was wide. Moonlight fell through old windows, lighting a mostly bare floor. An attic top floor, then, with few dividing walls.

Trace motioned for Kono to stay put, which he saw with peripheral vision. And kept turning, searching the dark far walls, in the shadows where the moonlight did not reach. Something hissed, from one black corner. Trace stared hard, and saw it, a faint, sinewy outline. Bigger than the one she'd shot on top of Kono. As she stared, other things resolved in the dark. Junk, bits of old furniture, dragged to make a nest. The kauda slithered amongst it like an oil slick, black on black. A glint of silver teeth as it hissed again.

Trace moved the dart pistol onto it, calculating how much her shot would drop over even this short range. Then paused. It was just sitting there. Waiting.

"It's a trap," she said to Kono in a low voice. "Watch the windows."

"There's a lot of windows," Kono reminded her, doing that.

"I know. As soon as I fire, down the stairs. She'll charge, it'll take six seconds. Then we…"

Something fast flashed through the window to their left side. Kono turned and shot it. Trace fired the pistol with an underwhelming pop, and the big kauda screamed and leaped. Trace jumped down the stairs, Kono following, but their coordination finally abandoned them in the tight space as the huge animal flew for their heads. Then Trace was falling, rolling on the stairs even as she abandoned the pistol and grabbed for the rifle on its strap.

She tumbled to the stairs' halfway point, ripping the rifle clear even as Kono crashed into her, and then the huge animal was screaming onto them, claws tearing on the concrete as it filled the stairway, barely seconds after she'd fired the dart. She fired the rifle a split second before Kono did, repeated semi-automatic bursts shredding the stairwell, and then the huge weight hit them, a face full of black fur and a dazed half-concussion before the kauda rolled over and tumbled elastically down the staircase.

Then silence. She lay on her back, Kono on top of her, both facing upstairs in a tangle of arms, legs and rifles. She could feel Kono's big body gasping deep breaths, glancing downstairs to the unmoving animal.

"Shit," he said. "I thought we were pretty good for a moment there."

"Never was a cat person," Trace admitted. "You okay?"

"Peachy," said Kono, resuming his crouch, rifle still covering upstairs. "How 'bout you, Major?"

"Bashed my head, I'm okay."

On the stairs beneath them, Tano was examining the furry killing machine. He looked up the stairs at them, disappointed. "You killed it."

"Call animal welfare," Kono retorted.

"Careful," Trace reminded everyone. "There might be more of them."

She got up, blinking hard to clear her head, and checked her rifle for damage. The breech cleared and mechanism worked, and she paused briefly on her way back up the stairs to reclaim the dart pistol where it had fallen.

Reemerging at the top of the stairs, she found the kauda Kono had shot unmoving on the concrete floor. Only a small one by comparison, but deadly enough. Shot through the head and unmoving, heck of a shot at that speed and considering the consequences if Kono had missed, but Trace had never doubted him.

She crept forward to the nest, feeling much happier doing that with a rifle instead of a dart pistol, Kono a step behind and covering their rear arc. There were bits of old mattress here, moldy and defiled in ways Trace was glad the darkness did not let her see. Bits of broken furniture. And here, against one wall, was what remained of Agu. Gruesome, limbs missing, innards spilling.

"Don't look," Trace said grimly. "I'll save you this one." The backpack was still on the corpse. Trace removed it, trying to avoid getting the worst gore on her hands. Kono continued guarding their rear, not looking. Partly that was combat discipline, Trace knew, but also the genuine appreciation that he didn't have to. Some tough young marines would look, just to prove they could. Staff Sergeant Gideon Kono was long past having to prove anything to anyone. If he could get out the other side of this with one less memory to keep him awake at nights, he'd take it.

Something scuffled. It wasn't a sound like the others. Kauda made no sound unless they were attacking, or distracting their prey in some attempted ambush. This was different. Against the wall, a single doorway, the door long since missing.

Trace glanced at the near windows, and judged they wouldn't reveal much of a flashlight, even if she turned one on. She took the light from her pocket, circled the doorway, then when she'd acquired an angle past the doorframe, beamed the flashlight into the dark space. The room beyond might have been an upstairs bedroom once. She could see most of the floor, and it was empty. Empty, save for a single corbi arm, and two small, black things feeding on it.

"Well, that thing was a mummy," said Trace. "And she's got babies. I reckon the Splicer animal trade might like kauda kittens even more than a full grown one."

"Ain't that the cutest," Kono muttered.

* * *

As Trace began to recognise paths through the forest nearer to the village, the pale first light of dawn began to glow in the east. Immediately she began to sense there was something wrong. An expectant silence, perhaps. A certain hush on the breeze off the ocean. She could make no sense of it, save that she'd spent the vast majority of her adult life in a combat unit, and sometimes one began to get a bad feeling. Perhaps it was her brain noticing things subconsciously, extracting details from her senses that her conscious mind had overlooked. But as she crouched by the trail and peered toward the nearest field of crops, she glanced at Kono, coming forward to check for himself, and saw from the grim tension on his face that he felt it too.

Trace did not trust the trail, and led them through the forest approach to the crop field, then about the far fence, wooden planks strung with wire and bits of metal that would jangle if something heavy tried to climb on it. Ahead, by a tree near the fence, a snare had been set for kauda, lying undisturbed in the dead leaves and undergrowth. The waves were louder now, breaking upon the nearby beach, and the air smelled of salt.

Forest gave way to scrubby sandbush, and Trace crept through it, rifle ready, listening for any hint of something amiss The first sentry post would be ahead, a small wooden barricade at the beginning of the sand, and some papergrass that grew in the marshy depression before the beach began properly. Trace signalled for the others to stay behind, and heard a kauda kitten scrabbling and hissing in someone's backpack. Too close and it could give them away. The tranquilliser gun would likely kill a kitten, and they needed both alive.

She crawled on her stomach, and peered through the lower half of a sandbush. Ahead was the sentry post, wooden planks rattling in the wind. There was no sign of the sentry. He might have fallen asleep. There were punishments for that, but this wasn't the UF marines. Beyond the post, the village's wooden huts lay silent. At this hour, there would typically be some movement, early risers preparing boats and nets, or heading to the nearby stream to gather fresh water. As the pale glow silhouetted the spires of rock in the bay beyond, Trace could see nothing moving among the huts.

She fished in her pants pocket for her small binoculars, and looked more closely. Now the darkness of the sand resolved into shapes. Corbi bodies, sprawled on the sand. Several adults. A child, similarly motionless, beyond the outstretched hands of its mother. The dark, planked wall of one of the huts bore a scatter of high-powered shotgun holes.

She zoomed on the spaces between huts, and saw more bodies. None were moving. The damage to the huts seemed from smallarms only. So there had been no airstrike. This had been up close and personal. Probably the reeh, or one of their slave species, had been looking for something.

Trace pocketed the binoculars, and slid back from the sandbush, crawling low until she reached Kono, Tano, Rika, Pena and Bago. Bago looked scared, sensing something wrong. Trace went to him, and put a hand on his shoulder. It must have shown in her eyes, because he backed off. Trace put a hand over his mouth, to muffle any cry, but did not apply pressure. Just stared at him, watching how he took it, as the dreadful realisation dawned in his eyes. Indescribable grief. He began shaking.

Pena came and clutched him, with an evil stare at Trace. Trace looked at Kono, and indicated the way she wanted to move — a perimeter around the village, scouting down the coast. There was someone she wanted to check on first. Kono nodded grimly. Tano beckoned her closer, and murmured in her ear. "I can't get us a ride for several days. This area is too hot."

Trace indicated she understood. If the reeh had hit it themselves, they'd be watching the village in case anyone came back. Trace indicated that Kono should keep a close watch on Bago, in case he made a dash for the village. He had family there. Children, and a wife. Likely he'd want to see them, whatever the consequences. Kono nodded that he understood, but his eyes were faintly disbelieving. His face showed emotion, upset. The disbelief, Trace knew, was that her face showed none. Pena had been telling him how cold she was. Kono had been defending her. Now, that would be harder.

Trace slithered left, then went at a low crouch, picking her way through the shadows. The undergrowth was still thick here, before the forest thinned near the beach. The village's few fields of crops were all here in the forest, whatever the extra danger from kauda — the forest had soil in which crops would grow, not sand. The clouds would hide them from orbital surveillance, and the undergrowth from eyes nearer than that, but they'd have to move fast.

Trace reached the thin path through the forest that led to the field of crops, and paused, a fist held high. On the trail, back toward the beach, a corbi lay unmoving, twenty metres away. Someone had made it this far, running for their lives. If they'd gotten off the trail, they'd have had a better chance. It was possible others had done better. This one, or some of the others, might still be alive, but going to check was suicide. Trace didn't think Bago's eyesight was good enough to see this body on the trail in the dark. She wasn't about to tell him.

She crossed the trail and moved into the far side undergrowth. Soon they'd circled past the village, and through the trees to her right, she caught a faint glimpse of Jindi's hut against the brightening ocean. By the hut, a corbi figure, kneeling on the sand.

Trace gestured them all down, and crawled closer. Soon she had a good view from beneath thick, broad trees, the bush thinned to sand before her. Jindi's hut looked untouched. And Jindi, for it was plainly him, crooked shoulders and all, was kneeling on the sand. Trace picked up a nut, fallen from the trees, and lobbed it at him. It landed near, and Jindi looked, with no particular alarm. Stared for a moment, finally resolving Trace's outline at the base of the tree.

He picked up the bundle he'd been kneeling by, and came wandering crookedly over. It was a small corbi body, limbs dangling. He sat by Trace, and holding the corbi child in his lap. Trace was getting better at identifying corbi faces. The child was the same one who'd come to his door, and traded things for fish. A young girl, no more than thirteen. Trace felt her lip tremble as the bottom dropped momentarily from beneath her control. Then she caught it, with a lifetime's practise, and forced her next breath, long, slow and controlled. Then the next. And the next.

"They didn't even touch me," said the fisherman in a small voice. The little girl's fur was covered in dried blood. "They knew I was here. Maybe they've always known. They left me alive as a warning. They know it's worse this way."

Trace realised he was speaking Lisha. So he did speak it. Before, he'd only been pretending to not understand. "You've been in to town?" Trace asked. "Any survivors?"

"They took some alive," said Jindi. "They always take some alive. Came down from the sky, killed most, took some, and left. You don't need to hide. They're not watching. They weren't after you."

"Bago's family?"

"Didn't see. His wife and boy are dead. I couldn't find his girl, though. Must have been taken." His eyes lifted from the dead girl, to meet her own. Haunted. "They let me watch. I went down and stood there, on the sand, and watched them. I hoped they'd shoot me. They weren't after you."

"Jindi," said Trace. Meeting his stare directly. "We need your help. Unless you want to find a new beach, and hope the reeh won't do that to its inhabitants as well?" She jerked a head toward the ruin of the village. If Pena could hear it, she'd hate her even more. Trace told herself that she didn't care.

"Sure," said Jindi, his eyes distant, voice flat. "They came to my home. I'll show you theirs."

12

"*Captain, we have a problem.*" Erik blinked awake, disoriented for a moment as the bunk swayed, and dull thunder rumbled in his ears. On the neighbouring lower bunk, Spacer Sharma lay fast asleep.

A moment's fast reorientation and closed eyes brought a light to his inner eyelids. Focus brought formulation software into active mode. "*What's the problem, Sasa?*"

"*Captain, we appear to have picked up several pursuers who are running autistic. Styx cannot access them.*"

"*I'm on my way up.*" Erik rolled to slide out the under-bunk storage shelf, then sat to put on the body armour there, plus integrated webbing and weapons. That took a few minutes, but he was getting good at it now. Finally he took his short rifle — a T-9 rather than a light-armour standard T-15, by his personal preference not to be encumbered with a heavier weapon when a Captain's job was usually focused on other things than shooting — then stood to check on the upper bunk. Skah lay fast asleep, an ear twitching as he dreamed.

Erik went into the swaying corridor, then climbed final steps to the bridge. Inside, Sasalaka sat at the command chair, Kaspowitz in the co-pilot's, while Second Lieutenant Geish sat behind, watching a display he'd mounted where no display would normally sit. Erik leaned on Sasalaka's right to see what she was looking at.

Desert a half-kilometre ahead and more was lit in the blaze of the engine's forward floodlights. To their right passed a successive line of blinking red lights atop this highway's guide-poles, and approaching now from several kilometres out came another onrush of floodlights — an engine coming the other way, perhaps two hundred metres to their right.

Looming from the desert here were mountains, like dark barriers blotting out the stars. On the lower slopes of those mountains were the dotted lights of settlements, and here on the left, the clustered glow of a town. Near left, between the highway and the town, some big structures were passing — storage warehouses, repair shops, such things dotted the desert highways across the Cho'na continent and the Do'jera desert. Beside one, Erik could dimly see a parked hover train beside several more trailers. A warning marker indicated a passing road, then the glimpse of the trench beneath, whooshing by as the engine passed over.

"Pursuit's coming in behind us, Captain," said Geish, watching his rigged screen. "Four cruisers, three kilometres back and closing. Styx can't tell what they're doing, can't access their coms to shut them down, they're not talking to any network."

Erik turned his back on the forward view to look at Geish's screen. It was a map. They were four hours out of Cal'Uta, and had taken several forks in the highway network away from the main trunk routes in the hope of confusing Croma'Rai's pursuit. Six hundred and fifty kilometres out... and taking detours that would add more distance to their journey. It wasn't nearly enough.

"Styx," Erik asked the empty air, "can you tell me anything?"

"*Captain, my access to Croma'Rai security networks reveals nothing specific about a possible pursuit. I suspect they have become aware of my capabilities and are discussing it on networks as little as possible. Desert air is clear, there are mountain-top communication towers passing by you even now. It is possible that direct lasercom could substitute for network communications.*"

"Anyone could be watching us from those mountains through binoculars," said Kaspowitz, peering up at one looming peak. The approaching hover train went rushing past to their right, leaving a wall of floodlit dust in its wake, slowly drifting toward their path. "Lasercom could then relay to a cruiser, we'd hear none of it."

"Two kilometres, Captain," said Geish. "They'll be right on us in a minute."

Erik flipped down his AR glasses to get a better look at the coms network. "Rufus, you there?"

"Sure am, Captain," came Jalawi. *"We're all up and deployed. Those guys behind us don't have running lights on. If they were going to hit us, I'd guess they could do it in combination with someone on the ground, maybe waiting up ahead."*

"The vehicle has very good forward scanning," said Sasalaka, turning them slowly left as the guide lights curved. Ahead in the far distance, the floodlights of several more oncoming hover-trains blazed. "And directly accessing the lanes is prohibited, the marker posts contain surveillance apparatus, trespassers are prosecuted."

Erik switched channels to general. "All crew, this is the Captain. Emergency stations, assault may be imminent."

"Captain?" queried Sasalaka, tapping at her controls. "I'm reading a pressure drop in the turbine intake. I'm not sure what could cause..."

Glass broke on their left. For a moment, everyone stared, puzzled. "Goddammit, incoming!" Kaspowitz yelled, undoing his restraints and slithering down for cover.

"Shit," said Geish, doing the same without taking his eyes off the screen.

"Lieutenant Jalawi," said Erik, similarly crouching, "we are under fire from what I think is our left. A round just hit the bridge."

"Copy, Captain."

"Captain," said Sasalaka, unbudging in her seat, "please stand by to take the controls if I am hit."

"I'm here, Sasa." Struggling to see above the dash, glimpsing more buildings passing on their left. "Evasive action is not going to work, we don't want to flip."

"Yes Captain." They both knew there wasn't a lot this big thing could do to dodge. Then a moment later, "Captain, I am evading!"

Erik knew she couldn't be doing the one thing she'd said she wouldn't do, and so stood up properly to see what she saw... and saw an entire hover train trailer, pushed by some independent propulsion, spinning across the desert and directly into their path like a tossed stone sliding on an icy lake.

The engine roared as Sasalaka applied full power, sliding sideways as it struggled to turn and climb. For a desperate second Erik realised that attempting to help Sasalaka would only snatch the controls and make them crash, combined with incredulity that he'd fought his way halfway across the known galaxy just to die like this...

The trailer detonated in a giant fireball, still well ahead of them, but the train flew into the fireball at speed as everything shook, bounced and crashed. Then they were through, Sasalaka fighting the controls as the engine skidded, windshield cracked with debris impacts and streaked black with explosive residue.

"Blew up short," Erik observed the obvious, taking Kaspowitz's vacated seat as the lanky Lieutenant moved across behind. Sasalaka regained full control, only the train now seemed lopsided, the turbine shrilling and making unpleasant sounds.

"Captain, I think the engine just swallowed a lot of debris," said the tavalai, matter-of-fact as always as Erik scanned the controls and saw various indicators surging into unhealthy territory.

"I'm going to power us down before we blow something," Erik told her, hands doing that while trying to ignore the whistle of wind through the broken windshield on his left.

"Captain," came Jalawi from the rear, *"we just came under fire from cruisers at the rear."* Erik could hear the crackle of smallarms in the background. *"I am returning fire, one of them crashed... no, make that two."* As satisfied yells and swearing could be heard from nearby marines. *"The other two are backing off, I think they expected that bomb to kill us, they were just here to clean up."*

The vibrations from the turbine were becoming quite bad, and Erik powered them down some more before they started shedding fan blades. "Captain," said Sasalaka, "with the engine at that output we will be unable to maintain sufficient speed to stay on the highway."

"Yeah, we're gonna need to fix it," said Erik, scanning a line of patchy trees and several small settlements from their left to the base of the mountains. "Let's get further from the ambush site first. There could be somewhere to hide up against the base of those mountains."

They continued at lower speed, Jalawi reporting that the remaining two cruisers had turned away. After several minutes of trying to coax the wounded engine to keep running without melting down, it occurred to Erik to wonder aloud why the cruisers weren't still circling, to at least keep an eye on what they did next.

"I think it was Peanut, Captain," said Jalawi.

"Peanut?"

"Yeah, Corporal Graf says he was using his countermeasures, her local armscomp was going nuts and she was right next to him. He climbed up on top just before the bomb exploded, Graf thinks the countermeasures might have prematurely detonated the bomb too. And just now he was aiming them at the cruisers before they flew off."

Just because Styx couldn't help them directly because nothing pursuing them was plugged into a network, didn't mean that Peanut couldn't function as his own mobile electronic warfare module.

"Yeah, well someone find out what Peanut likes to do for fun and let him do it," Geish said with relief. "'Cause he's earned it."

It was then that Erik noticed Kaspowitz had his torso armour off and was applying a field bandage to his upper arm. "Oh shit! Kaspo, you're hit?"

"Just grazed," said Kaspowitz, teeth gritted. "I'm pretty sure that first one missed me, I think there was a second."

Erik flipped channels, unable to take his eyes off the engine's faltering controls for long. "This is the Captain, we need first aid on the bridge, Lieutenant Kaspowitz has a bullet wound." He was angry at his friend for not saying anything, even as he knew that Kaspo had been entirely correct not to — they'd all been busy, and not getting blown up or crashing the train had been the priority.

"Mind the screen, Second Lieutenant," Kaspowitz told the distracted Geish, still wrapping his arm. "I'm fine, eyes to scan." Someone rattled up the stairs and entered the bridge — Spacer Sharma, Erik heard from the conversation with Kaspowitz about the arm. Engine readings grew worse, temperature rising, revs falling, coolant pressure unsteady in a way that suggested a leak the pumps were attempting to compensate for.

"There's another train two kilometres behind us," Geish told them. "It's maintaining cruising speed, it will pass us in two minutes."

"We'd better pull to the verge," said Erik.

"Aye Captain." Sasalaka steered them away from the center markers, and now there were palm trees, irrigated fields and small buildings passing on their left — one of the regular oases along the desert highways. "Maybe we could hide in there while we conduct repairs?"

"Kaspo, anything ahead?"

It was unfair of him to ask, but Kaspowitz was the Navigation Officer, and so long as he remained on the bridge, his job was to function as one. "Nothing for another thirty kilometres or so," said Kaspowitz, voice strained. "Will we hold together for another thirty?"

"Maybe," Erik guessed. "Anything there that's better than here?"

"Not from what the map showed."

"*Captain,*" Styx interjected, "*topographical survey shows that the settlements you are currently passing may offer more cover than the one ahead.*"

Erik thought about it. This one was really too close to the wreckage of the fight just a few kilometres behind them, including that sniper, who probably had company. But if they broke down halfway to the next settlement, they'd be in the open without cover. He had marines and firepower, he had to risk pulling over right here.

"Captain," said Geish before he could speak, "the train coming up behind us is slowing. Looks like it might intercept."

"Rufus," said Erik into coms. "You see that guy behind us?"

"*Sure do, Cap. He coming to say hello or what?*"

"Looks like he might. Don't show yourselves, he might have a bad reaction to a train full of heavily armed aliens. But stay ready in case he's hostile."

"I reckon he'll have seen the two guys we shot down," said Jalawi, voice slightly strained as he moved, then a thump of boots hitting deck from a height, and a rattle as he moved up a corridor. *"He didn't stop to help them, either."*

"Don't try to guess what it means," Erik told him. "They're aliens."

"Aye Captain."

The thump of new, heavier steps up the stairs behind told of a larger arrival. Behind them, a croma voice spoke. *"This train behind is coming to talk,"* said Rhi'shul's voice in Erik's translator. *"I will speak to him."*

Erik glanced at Sasalaka. Sasalaka's big, amphibious eyes showed no opinion. "Better than getting shot at, I guess," said Erik. "Stefan, get her coms."

"Aye Captain."

Croma conversation resumed — Kul'hasa, the language was, and Erik had learned only a little since his arrival. Translator technology made people lazy, as Romki had told him often... but even Romki was using translators on Dul'rho, having no brainspace currently to spare. After some more moments of conversation, Rhi'shul addressed Erik.

"Captain, the driver says she wants to help. She says she has friends in Jo'Tukra ahead, she will take us there."

"Captain, that's another fifty Ks," said Kaspowitz, finding it on his display screen as Spacer Sharma finished wrapping his arm. "Are we gonna make it that far?"

"Rhi'shul," said Erik. "Is this a good idea?"

"I believe this driver is reliable," Rhi'shul replied. *"It's a croma matter. She will not sympathise with our opponents, nor their attempts to stop us reaching Stat'cha."*

A year ago, Erik would have fretted over whether he could trust anything Rhi'shul said. But right now he knew he had no choice, and could only hope that she wasn't leading them into some kind of trap. Unlikely, he thought, since she would have been killed by the last one if it had succeeded. No — the Dan'Gede investigator was in this up to her neck just like the rest of them.

"Tell our new friend we'll have to go slowly or our engine will burn up. And ask if there's any chance of repair once we get there."

* * *

Jo'tukra was a little oasis town three kilometres off the highway at the base of the long line of desert mountains. Erik shut down the turbine a kilometre out and let them coast in, and killed the floodlights shortly after, as Sasalaka followed their new guide's blinking tail lights. Soon they were passing palm trees and undergrowth at little more than a crawl, past a rickety shed containing robotic harvesters, then a pumping station for what looked like orchard trees in neat rows to their left.

Manoeuvring became tricky in the enclosed space, as the train's tendency to handle like a bar of soap at low speeds became even worse with their damage. Erik left it to Sasalaka on the principle that a pilot who'd already gotten her groove in should not be removed from the seat unless absolutely necessary, and instead smashed out the remaining glass from the left side window to lean out and call directions, ducking the occasional tree branch that screeched across their roof.

Heavy repulsors throbbed in the night, doubtless waking many. Even now he saw several croma walking alongside the huge train, whether to supervise their passage, or just from curiosity, he could not guess. Spacer Katzer climbed over their cabin to sit on the long bonnet and make sure they didn't run anything over, and soon indicated that Sasalaka turn right through a clearing in the trees.

There they found once more the train they'd been following, twice their length with three trailers now settled to the ground. Sasalaka brought them alongside via Spacer Katzer's handsignals, then halted as Erik finally powered down the repulsors. A thud as they settled, and everyone began dismounting.

Erik left Sasalaka to the final shutdown sequences, and rattled down the rear stairs to check on Kaspowitz on one of the engine's bunks. The Nav Officer tried to raise his head as Erik entered, looking pale. Private Gonzaga from Third Section attended to him, having the best medical skills in First Squad, and was watching Kaspowitz's vitals on a small handscreen.

"He's okay," said Gonzaga, a short, square-faced young man with a cheerful manner. "Bullet went straight through the fleshy bit, didn't even hit the main muscle. He's in shock, I gave him a mild sedative and gave the med micros some direction... he should rest for twenty-four, might be more coherent after that."

"I'm perfectly coherent, thank you Private," Kaspowitz muttered, nearly tall enough to fill the croma bunk completely. "I can read a damn nav screen, Captain. And I'm not in shock, either."

"He's in shock," Gonzaga repeated to Erik. "Wishful thinking doesn't change a diagnosis."

"If it's any consolation, Kaspo," Erik told him with affection, "I'm sure even marines go into shock after they'd been shot. Isn't that right, Private?"

"If you say so, Captain. The micros will boost his natural plasma production, probably won't even need a synth transfusion. Though if this place had... I dunno... some herbal tea or something? Some of the croma stuff's good for you, helps with shock."

"How about a beer?" Kaspowitz said hopefully.

"I'll see what they've got," Erik said with a smile, and went to grasp Kaspowitz's shoulder. "And you listen to what the Private tells you, understand? Captain's orders."

"I'll be the perfect patient. Stop looking at me like I'm dying."

By the time Erik got outside, diplomacy had already occurred in one of the most extraordinary scenes he'd yet encountered, in the dusty shadows between two parked hover trains. Jalawi was leading the way, cheerfully yet forcefully shaking croma hands with that outsized charisma he possessed perhaps more than any other person on *Phoenix*. The croma ranged in height from some kids who hung back with their parents, to several very tall individuals who lounged against the sides of the train. Slightly shorter than those giants, another croma now talked with Rhi'shul, pointing to the train, then back down the highway, as though discussing with muted amazement what she'd just seen. All these croma were dressed down compared to what Erik had seen in Cal'Uta, in rough working clothes that still expressed a taste for big shoulders, hard leathers and boots.

Most of *Phoenix*'s spacers were attending to the grounded engine, so the humans socialising here were mostly marines, weapons slung and unthreatening. But Karajin was here as well, with several of his Garudan karasai, and now Skah was hanging by Corporal Graf's leg as he gazed up at the towering croma with unaccustomed shyness. If Tiga had been here, Erik thought as he walked to the group, it would have been five species all in one spot... and potentially more, but someone had thankfully told Peanut to stay out of sight. That would be harder for him than for Tiga — Peanut genuinely liked to meet strangers. Tiga, if they were croma, would rather pass.

"Captain," said Rhi'shul as he approached. *"This is Aku'tan, she owns and operates this train. She travels this route regularly, she has friends along it. This property is owned by friends of hers — this person, his name is Do'reg."* Indicating one of the big croma leaning against the train.

Croma'Rai did a fist bump in place of a hand shake in less formal settings, and Aku'tan's fist was half as big again as Erik's. *"Croma'Rai try to kill you?"* Aku'tan asked, in that multi-toned, throaty voice that all croma females had.

"Yes," said Erik, cautiously. "You are Croma'Rai?"

"Croma'Taro," Aku'tan replied with certainty. *"Lineage traced six hundred generations to Ro'Kartun, great leader of the Croma'Taro."* Erik nodded as though he knew what that meant. All the great clans were composed of many smaller clans, and exactly how croma decided they were one or the other, he still was not entirely sure. He suspected that when the great, overarching clan was in disgrace, as Croma'Rai were in now, it became convenient for many who would have previously called themselves Croma'Rai to recall their more intimate affiliations. *"You travel to Stat'cha for the Tali'san?"*

Erik looked at Rhi'shul. Croma expressions were nearly as hard to read as tavalai, but he *thought* she wanted him to agree. The Tali'san seemed sacred to many croma in a way that transcended traditional loyalties. "Yes," he said. "The Tali'san changes many things."

"*Yes,*" said Aku'tan. "*It's not right that the leaders try to remove you from the Tali'san. And they used a bomb on the highway, which all of us use.*"

"*Disgusting,*" rumbled another croma, echoed by several more.

"*Why you go to Stat'cha?*" another asked.

"To talk," said Erik, pleased to not have to lie. "That's all. We were promised free passage by Croma'Rai, then they told us we couldn't go to Stat'cha. We're going anyway, and they attack us. When we get there, we will address the Croma'Dokran Tali'san Council. We will say some things Croma'Rai don't want them to hear, that's all. They try to kill us because they don't want us to speak."

"*That's enough,*" declared big Do'reg, pushing off the train behind. "*Maybe the aliens are up to no good, but they deserve to be heard. You don't kill these Phoenix aliens we've been hearing so much about with highway bombs and still call yourself honourable. We'll help you fix your rig, and I think we could find a disguise for you, too.*"

"A disguise?" Erik wondered. "What kind of disguise?"

*　*　*

ERIK WALKED WITH RHI'SHUL, AKU'TAN AND DO'REG PAST THE BIG equipment sheds beside the parking clearing, and up a dirt road between rows of what looked like tall bamboo. Beyond the wall of plant stems were alternating orchard trees and open fields of what might have been vegetable plants. Big water pipes ran at one point from a roadside pump, humming and gurgling from some underground aquifer. Beyond the fields shone the lights of other houses, and came the sound of distant croma voices. No doubt the commotion of two big rigs arriving had woken some people up. Now, likely, word would spread. If the neighbours weren't as trustworthy as Do'reg and Aku'tan seemed to think, they'd be swarming with

Croma'Rai forces soon, whatever Styx's ability to manipulate coms transmissions.

With Erik walked Second Lieutenants Geish and Bree Harris, the only *Phoenix* bridge crew beside Kaspowitz and Sasalaka to come on this trip. Romki walked with them as well, marvelling at the big wooden shields that lined the road ahead, and the entrance to another clearing. Skah had been sent protesting back to bed on the train, with assurances that he could see everything here in the morning, since it looked like they weren't going anywhere soon. Sasalaka was supervising repairs, and Jalawi had stayed with her, suggesting that Lani 'Eggs' Graf would probably appreciate this place more than he would. With her came her Third Section minus Gonzaga — Privates Berloc and Ram.

Passing the big shields, Erik saw something in the roadside growth that looked like a small boulder with eyes. The eyes followed them from near the ground, and slow breathing snuffled in the grass. The next clearing held a wooden pagoda with a tin roof, surrounded by gravel thrown across un-greened desert to accommodate wheeled vehicles. Very little in this farming oasis was high-tech, save perhaps the robot harvesters for the orchards, and the hover trains that roared up and down the desert highway, and all of those were dusty and worn. Erik listened to a hover train now, a distant, passing thunder beyond the keening of local insects in the cool desert air. Erik's father loved low-tech places, and spent time each year with his sister, Erik's Aunt Misa, and her husband in the wilds several hundred kilometres from Shiwon where they ran a small, low-tech farm. As a younger man, Erik had been less convinced of the joys of gardening and physical labour, but now after so much time in a cramped steel box in space, the appeal was starting to dawn on him. Trace would like it here, he thought. There was even a mountain next door for her to climb.

Do'reg led them across the crunching gravel and up the pagoda steps. Steel security doors were locked with a simple padlock, undone with Do'reg's key, and the doors were pulled back with a clatter.

Sliding inner doors made of wood were also pulled back, and the party showed inside.

Within was a floor of simple boards, and supports to hold up the roof. Do'reg flipped a light switch, and the sudden brightness revealed nothing at all in the room… save for a very large warhammer, sitting on a stone plinth. Do'reg led them to it, their footsteps creaking on the floorboards.

"This was the hammer of Shur'do, from the Kran'to Tali'san."

The humans looked at the other croma to know if that was anything special. Rhi'shul snorted loudly through big nostrils — that multi-purpose croma sound, expressing anything from anger to surprise to humour. She walked to it carefully, peering as she circled, but not touching. The hammer was enormous. Erik thought it might be made of stone encased with steel, with a huge, two-fisted handle nearly as long as he was tall. This hammer, clearly, was not made for hitting nails, but for crushing croma heads.

"Please remind we ignorant humans of the Kran'to Tali'san?" Romki requested. It was a few hours from dawn, but Romki's squint was more from failing to recall something he felt he ought to know than from weariness. He'd been helping Tiga in the library the whole time he'd been here, Erik thought. However intellectually stimulating, it must have frustrated him to be the first senior human academic in croma space ever, as far as anyone knew, yet to be forced by circumstance to devote his attention to one narrow topic when all of croma civilisation lay around him, waiting to be explored.

"The Kran'to Tali'san was nearly four thousand years ago," Rhi'shul said, peering at the hammer. She seemed almost in awe. *"It was the great contest of Clan Croma'Dorn and Croma'Vo. Croma'Dorn won, and there were many glorious dead."*

"Sounds like a blast," Geish murmured.

"And this was your ancestor's weapon?" Romki asked Do'reg.

"Yes," said Do'reg. *"Shur'do was the ruler of Clan Croma'Bai, a minor clan in Clan Croma'Dorn. He fought gloriously, and survived despite many injuries. Shur'do's hammer has been passed through our family until this day."*

Whatever his dislike of the Tali'san, Erik could not help but admire the continuity. It spoke of something stable and reliable in croma families, that such an artefact could survive so long in pristine condition, and would be so well housed as this entire pagoda, constructed solely for the purpose. Do'reg's family did not appear particularly wealthy, which suggested that such a prestigious object would not necessarily go to the wealthiest descendant. Knowing a thing or two about family artefacts, and the arguments between different family branches as to who they actually belonged to, there was something about this scene that felt... dignified.

"This is a powerful thing, Do'reg," said Erik, choosing his words carefully. "It must make your family proud."

Do'reg pulled himself up to his full height — taller still than Rhi'shul, and considerably broader. The armour ridges were hard about his nose and forehead, and one exposed forearm was thick with extra weight. He might have been a hundred and twenty, Erik guessed. *"Objects of the Tali'san should return to the Tali'san,"* he said. *"Many vehicles of the Kon'do quest head for the Tali'san even now, bearing these artefacts. Family artefacts, held by the family for centuries awaiting such a time."* Erik saw Rhi'shul stare as she guessed what he was suggesting. A big deal, then. *"We call these pilgrimages Kon'do Rey'kan, Ships of the Dead. We decorate them, and display that they are Kon'do Rey'kan, and no authorities can touch them. It is sacred, do you understand?"*

"I do," Erik said carefully.

"Shur'do's hammer has only made one pilgrimage to a Tali'san in all our family's time. You would do my family a great honour if you would take it with you on a Kon'do Rey'kan this time. It will grant you protection from your enemies."

Both Rhi'shul and Aku'tan were displaying something Erik had never seen before in croma — profound emotion. Like all things croma, it looked fierce, dark eyes glaring, shoulders heaving.

Erik glanced at Romki, and got only a cautious stare in return. Not long ago, Romki would have feared his young Captain would put his foot in it. Now he did not seem so worried, and Erik took confidence.

"This is a great honour, Do'reg," he said. And his mind was racing — if the hammer would grant them a pilgrimage status and protection, then it could be just what they needed to get across the continent unscathed. "I am overwhelmed. But I think I have an even better suggestion." He looked the big croma squarely in the eyes, though he had to crane his neck to do so. "My suggestion is that you come with us. The hammer will need a protector who honours its history, and wields it to the Tali'san. You would do the warship *Phoenix* a great honour, Do'reg, should you be our guide on this Kon'do Rey'kan."

Do'reg stared at him with such intensity, Erik wondered if he'd somehow said the wrong thing, and was about to be torn violently limb from limb. Then Do'reg backed up a step, and put both hands on his head, breathing deeply and striding several more paces as though struggling to contain something so intense it might cause him to explode.

Erik looked at Rhi'shul, and found her looking at him anew, arms folded, dark intensity now mixed with amazement. As though he'd surprised her with something she'd not considered him capable of. Something intensely good, that all croma would agree upon.

Several moments longer, and Do'reg still could not speak. Rhi'shul slapped him hard on the shoulder, then Aku'tan, and turned to Erik once more. For a moment, Erik feared she'd slap his shoulder too, and dislocate it. *"Do'reg says yes,"* she said, with irony enough to count as humour. *"You have pleased him. Stop looking frightened."*

13

Two days after the disaster at the beachside village, a pair of flyers brought Tano's surviving group to a new location. Besides Agu being dead, the five of Tano's team who had remained behind in the village while the others went kauda hunting were also gone, and there had been little conversation during the four hour flight, and fewer smiles.

As the flyers slowed, Trace glimpsed the shadow of something tall in the night, looming to one side. The aircraft flared, rotor nacelles beating the air, and then they were descending past treetops, boughs thrashing in the blast of downdraft. Then down with a bump, Trace immediately out with rifle at the ready... but as she'd been warned, this was no rapid insertion. Beneath her boots was tarmac, and from the large concrete hangar to one side, corbi were coming to wave the pilots in. Both flyers angled their engines, and those behind made way as the vehicles rolled into the shelter.

Trace gazed up at the thing she'd glimpsed from inside the flyer. It was clearly the remains of an old stadium grandstand, towering in the dark night. She could not see opposing grandstands due to the trees, but from the shape of it, she guessed they'd landed beside an old sportsfield — probably behind one of the stands, where accesses would have allowed vehicles to park beneath the stadiums.

She followed the flyers in, squinting in the dark, as there were no lights anywhere. Once inside she followed Tano to a doorway, then down a passage where faint chemical glow sticks made green light from the floor, then up several flights of green, glowing stairs. The concrete construction was bare, all modern interiors long since stripped or decayed, leaving just this cold, grey shell.

Several floors higher, they entered a room with illumination in the form of several battery-powered field lamps. A wooden board raised on empty crates made a makeshift table, behind which an older corbi sat, blinking back sleep. Tano tapped his ear at Trace, to let her know that the concrete here made it safe to use electronics even if the reeh *were* watching. Trace declined to activate an earpiece. Lately her Lisha had been excellent, and if she started using translators again, she'd go backward.

"Naeda," Tano introduced the man at the table to her. "He's one of mine, science division."

The corbi looked up at her with a big-eyed stare. "You swear she's intelligent?" he asked Tano skeptically, after a moment.

"Attractive too, I think," Tano quipped as others filed into the room. Trace nearly smiled. Naeda's skepticism increased. His long mane was white, flowing together with a thick beard and moustache that came halfway down his shirt. His long, skinny forearms, folded on the table, sprouted so much hair it looked the result of static electricity.

Tano gestured to Rika, who unslung his backpack and carefully opened the outer cover. The inner bag took more careful work, accompanied by some hostile hissing from within. Rika took a spare, folded shirt and shoved it in first, then grabbed fast and pulled out a struggling kauda kitten by its scruff. Thus dangling, the kitten went limp. Trace was faintly amazed that that old reflex still worked. Even kauda kittens had to stay still when being moved by their mother, it seemed.

Naeda looked blankly at the kitten. "What am I expected to do with that?"

"Not you," said Tano. "Tilo and Roko. We're working on a theory that we have potential allies in the Rando Splicer. You're going to do some random sequencing on non-essential genes to produce a message that they can read."

"And where did you get the silly idea that such a thing is possible?"

"On a paper you wrote for Fleet Intelligence. About fifteen years ago, one of our captured reeh-allies said the anti-reeh rebellions were using it to send covert communications under the reeh's noses, in systems far more secure than this one."

Naeda sighed with weary recollection. "Yes yes, I remember. That will teach me to write things where dumb officers can get dumb ideas. You'll have to get the Splicer animal trade to accept that one first." He gestured for Rika to bring the animal closer, pulling a pair of old spectacles from his pocket. "It's about two months old?"

"One month," Rika told him, with no little triumph. "The teeth are only breaking through."

"Nonsense," Naeda scoffed, gesturing the much younger man to bring the kitten closer. Rika did so, and reached his free hand to squeeze the kitten's muzzle, exposing teeth. The kitten managed a belated hiss. Naeda blinked. "Well then. That's a monster. How big was its mother?"

"Bigger than him," said Rika, pointing at Kono. "A lot bigger. And we've got another one."

Corbi by the door made way as someone new entered. This corbi was big, and wore shirt and pants to look more like a formal uniform. Among the Resistance, that wasn't usual. His mane and beard were trimmed short, also unusual for a ranking corbi, and the floppy hat on his head looked something like a beret.

"Tano," he acknowledged the other, his eyes warily on Trace and Kono.

"Kaysa," Tano replied, with more cordiality than warmth.

"Where have you been?" Kaysa asked. "We had reports that you'd gone to Sebi, then nothing."

"I got distracted," Tano explained.

"I can see that." Kaysa did not seem any more pleased to see the humans than Naeda was. "Distracted, how?"

"Distracted in that I'm thinking of changing our target. From Vaseg to the Splicer."

Kaysa stared at him. "That wasn't our agreement."

"I know. The opportunity came up."

Kaysa rubbed at his head, as though to ward off an oncoming headache. "Let's talk. In private."

"Certainly." Tano gestured for Trace to follow them from the room.

"Privately!" Kaysa snapped, seeing that gesture, with a hostile look at Trace.

"You don't think she can keep a secret?" Tano asked, unbothered. Kaysa glared.

* * *

THE ROOM THEY MOVED TO WAS SMALL, ONE FORMER WINDOW BOARDED over, all trace of glass long gone. In place of a doorway, a curtain made of some simple fabric had been hung. Kaysa's office had a very old desk that looked as though it had once belonged in a school, decayed to the point of collapse but held up by a small tower of bricks. Several steel ammo crates sat by the desk, for storage. By the other wall, a small plant in a pot, evidently well watered. From the cool breeze, Trace reckoned that window overlooked what had once been the grandstand's main field. The breeze came mostly through a small gap between the boards, from which the plant would get its sunlight. Tonight, a single, dull-green glowstick on one of the ammo crates gave the office all of its light.

Kaysa sat on a small box behind the desk, while Tano dragged another before the desk. Finding the boxes far too low, Trace simply took a knee, marine-style, and unslung her rifle for butt-down support. If she had to sit on these corbi-sized seats, her knees would be around her ears.

"Tano," Kaysa said, attempting patience. "The Splicer is suicide. We've had this discussion before."

"Not with her you haven't."

"With all respect to *her*," said Kaysa, with the disrespect of a man who doubted a female had even earned a feminine pronoun, "she doesn't know anything about what we do."

"Which is the best thing to recommend her," said Tano, leaning forward, eyes intense. Trace watched them carefully, trying to figure as much of the situation as possible. Kaysa was Rando Resistance, she thought. A planetsider, he seemed far more concerned with appearances with his clipped hair and neat clothes than Tano did. The spacers that Trace had seen took care to blend in, wear grounder clothes, grow out their manes. But some grounders took a particular interest in personal status. Rank mattered more to grounders, there being so many more of them. Hierarchies built whereever large numbers of people gathered. Tano had no advantage in standing out, down here. But Kaysa did. "She doesn't do things our way. Her combat experience is crazy. We've nothing like her in all of Fleet — we don't have infantry. Human Fleet has 'marines'."

He pronounced the English word in full, there being no corbi equivalent.

"You don't have marines because a small force can't hold territory against a much larger one," Trace replied. And realised that she wasn't going to have the vocabulary for what came next, and so inserted her earpiece, and turned it on. Kaysa and Tano did the same, Kaysa with an eye-roll — the corbi commanders used them often to talk to people elsewhere in the concrete grandstand. "You hit and run," Trace continued, "while human Fleet captures territory and key facilities. In space, marines are specialists in capturing and holding heavily defended strategic facilities, for our Fleet to then arrive and use themselves."

"Yes," said Kaysa, through the translator, *"well we don't want to capture the Splicer, and we'd all be dead in minutes if we tried."*

"You have the technology to fool their surveillance grid," Trace said firmly, relieved to be speaking English to describe a complex situation. "If you give me access to that technology myself, I can do even more with it. I believe we can disable the Splicer's entire computer systems from within. If we then make contact with friends inside, even better. I know your Fleet can coordinate messages to my ship. If we coordinate a time, *Phoenix* can come get us and make such a huge distraction elsewhere in the system that all reeh forces will be diverted to stop them. If we get further into the Splicer's networks when they arrive, there are capabilities on that ship that could then shut down the reeh's entire network around Rando."

"And how is one ship going to survive an attack on this system alone?" Kaysa scoffed. *"Rando isn't heavily defended by Reeh Empire standards, but it's more than a match for any single ship."*

"Not my ship," said Trace, with unerring confidence. It was more confidence than she felt, in truth. She wasn't a spacer, and Erik didn't like her supposing things about his command any more than she liked him supposing things about hers. But here it was — her one chance at the Splicer. At the knowledge of advanced weaponised biotechnology that Styx herself agreed held the key to saving humanity, and perhaps the tavalai as well, from alo/deepynine weaponry the likes of which the Spiral had never seen before. Normally her job was to safeguard *Phoenix* at all costs. But she, Erik, and everyone on that crew, human or otherwise, had collectively agreed that even crazy risks, under these circumstances, were necessary. Trace didn't think what she was proposing was anything like as crazy as Kaysa thought. But then, as Erik told her often enough, marines weren't anything like qualified to make that judgement.

Kaysa rolled from his seat to the ammo box with one easy motion, as corbi could do close to the floor, and opened the lid. He withdrew a small box, then placed it on the desk as he resumed his seat.

"There," he said. *"You say you have the ability to use reeh technology against them."* He gestured at the box. *"Prove it. Our technicians removed that from an old reeh wreck just a few days ago, they say it looks mostly intact but they have no idea what it does. Part of an assault ship guidance system, perhaps. Usually when we recover these things we give them to Fleet to make sense of, but with this one we haven't yet had the chance.*

What can you make of it? Expert technician that you clearly are?" The sarcasm was strong.

It made sense, Trace thought. The Resistance Fleet had been analysing old reeh technology for a long time, there were any number of uncharted wrecks following all the reeh-croma wars across the centuries, and before that, reeh-corbi wars as well. No wonder the Resistance Fleet had come to know this technology so well. But some things clearly remained beyond them... and Trace was coming to doubt, given the general lack of importance the reeh attached to Rando, that they'd be deploying their best technology out this way. No doubt they had some idea that the surviving corbi had become experts at reverse-engineering and figuring it out. Which might have been a reason the reeh were less interested in absorbing the corbi into their Empire, as they'd done with some conquered peoples, than strangling them.

Trace gave a whistle, and clapped her hands. "Bug! I've a job for you."

Tano frowned at her. Kaysa looked at her as though she'd gone mad. Then, from nowhere in particular, the small, silver shape buzzed its way to hover above the desk. Both corbi looked at it, shimmering in the green glow of light, registering slowly that this was no regular insect. It hovered far too precisely, and its wings took on a luminescent hue.

Kaysa raised his hand as though to try and swat it. "DON'T MOVE!" Trace snapped, and he froze. "It will kill you stone dead in two seconds." Kaysa froze. Trace actually doubted the bug would kill any corbi she hadn't specifically told it to, but still there was a risk. No one on *Phoenix* had yet figured the nature of the bugs' intelligence, which possessed characteristics both at the simple animal level, and the higher AI level. Certainly it could understand what she said, despite lacking the ability or inclination to speak back. And she was entirely certain that this one had been growing more intelligent with regards to this particular operating environment with every week that passed.

"Bug," said Trace. "I would like a full analysis on this technology.

Please relay your analysis to my reader." She withdrew the corbi-style monocle reader from her pocket and placed it over her right eye, the stem hooked over her right ear. The lens flicked down as the bug landed, the display glowing receptive but currently blank.

The bug crawled on the black casing like a fly on a block of bread, probing with miniature proboscis to an insert socket. Tano stood to peer at it, coming close with a confidence that Kaysa did not dare. *"Amazing,"* he murmured. *"Drysine?"*

"Yes," said Trace. "It's multi-function. It's armed with neurotoxin that will kill almost instantly, so we call them assassin bugs. But they make excellent network infiltrators, they can access inferior techno-logical networks as effectively as any full-sized drysine drone. We've used them to take over and sabotage entire enemy starships."

"It's artificial?" Kaysa said with disbelief, staring as it only now occurred to him.

Trace's monocle eyepiece blinked to life. The eyepiece technology to a bug was nothing, and taking control of its functions was child's play. The question no one had been entirely certain of was exactly how reeh technology would match up.

A series of technical diagrams quickly took shape, flashed impres-sionistically and too fast for the human eye to follow. Almost as though the bug were sorting through various pre-conceived possibili-ties or categories that it was programmed to recognise, then discarding them as this structure failed to match. Then a portion of the flashing diagrams solidified, and remained fixed while the rest kept cycling.

Just as Trace was beginning to wonder how she'd make sense of what it showed her, given that her personal capabilities as a techni-cian were just as Kaysa had suspected, a series of letter-like shapes began to form down the bottom of her display. They cycled rapidly, alien and unlike anything Trace had seen before. The complexity of each numeral was enormous, far greater than in Chinese characters. And she recalled Romki saying that in the latter stages of their social evolution, the deepynines had experimented with verbal languages, mostly as experiments in AI cognition. Lately he'd been suspecting that that had in turn occurred because the drysines had started it in their cooperation with the parren, and deepynines had begun worrying at the rate they'd begun falling behind drysine evolution.

So perhaps what she was seeing here was one of those earlier drysine experiments with verbal communication and language structure. Perhaps that created the base foundation for a bug's ability to communicate, as in designing the bugs, Styx would have been relying upon technological diagrams dating back to her most familiar period of drysine civilisation — the era of the Parren Alliance. It had been discovered on Defiance that the Alliance had not been merely an alliance with parren, but with many other organic Spiral species as well, who'd preferred continued drysine rulership to the oncoming tyranny of the Parren Empire.

As she watched, the flash of complex numerals was replaced by an increasing number of English letters. More and more evolved, until there were barely-legible sentences.

"This is a... communications module," Trace read, making sense of the broken grammar with a squint. "It was kept separate from the other systems to preserve operational security. I think it's still functional... the bug seems to be exploring ways to activate it."

"Internal powersources will have died a long time ago," Tano disagreed.

"The bug has its own small charge," said Trace, knowing that much. "It can apply just enough to get a response and make its own analysis." New letters formed. "It says... it says it recognises the pattern methodology. I don't know what that means. It's scanning though some kind of database." As a new section of her display began scrolling rapidly through a new set of images.

"Here," said Tano, and went to open Kaysa's storage box himself. *"I know you have a projector in here somewhere, Kaysa."*

"No, I don't think that's..." But Tano ignored Kaysa's protest, and placed a flat, circular base on the old desk. Prongs extended, and projectors flashed overlapping strands of light until the image stood a half-metre tall above the desk. Immediately the visuals from Trace's monocle were replicated there, much larger and in three dimensions.

A drysine drone appeared, a standard model, much like the three on *Phoenix*. They multiplied, filling the display, new models of drone appearing amidst the throng like unmet relatives on a family tree.

"Drysines," said Trace, flipping her monocle aside as it became redundant. "It's talking about drysines." A new series of drones appeared on the opposite side of the display, rotating slowly around to Trace's position. These drones were more angular, deadly-looking, and recently familiar. "Deepynines. The bug's drawing us a family tree. Drysines and deepynines were the two dominant families of the final era of the Machine Age."

Those two branches abruptly receded, as though the holographic display were zooming backward, and the huge families of drones receded to tiny dots. New families appeared, linked by branches. Multiple families of AI machines, stretching back thousands of years, then tens of thousands. Names flashed, but the letters were not always English, suggesting the bug was having difficulty processing data at its required speed while still accounting for organic deficiencies in communication.

Abruptly, one branch on the tree flashed, and again the image zoomed. A new family of drones appeared, and many of these were utterly unfamiliar. Some barely looked like drones at all, or at least what Trace had come to understand AI drones looked like. Amid the bizarre shapes, the grasping mechanical claws and prehensile tendrils, new letters formed.

"What does that say?" asked Tano, as the three-dimensional letters made a slow rotation of the display, as though in orbit about some planet.

"They're not entirely in English yet," said Trace, holding her impatience in check with an effort. The letters changed some more, sorting rapidly, as though the bug had heard her. "Ceephay," Trace read aloud. Then again, to herself, with some incredulity. "Ceephay!"

"What does that mean?"

Trace blinked rapidly, recalling various conversations with Romki, and with Styx. She tried to keep her non task-related mental wanderings to a minimum on the ship. *Phoenix* was neck-deep in so many fascinating and terrifying things that an officer with time on her hands could easily lose herself in aimless strings of thoughts, and become completely distracted from the task at hand. Thankfully, the Phoenix Company Commander very rarely had time on her hands.

But learning about the various eras of the Machine Age had seemed from time to time like the kind of thing that could have utility. And now she had this display, pointing her back to some long-extinct family strand of artificial intelligence that called itself... Ceephay.

"Bug," she said, in that commanding tone that the bug sometimes responded to, and sometimes ignored completely. "Clarify vocal command. Ceephay was an earlier branch of the AI family during the Machine Age, correct?" New images kept cycling, new drones, new starships, new technical diagrams Trace couldn't begin to make sense of. "Come on bug, how hard is it to string the words 'yes' or 'no' together? Answer me, Ceephay was an earlier relative of drysines and deepynines, yes or no?"

'Yes', flashed on the display, slowly rotating.

"Is it your analysis this communications module is Ceephay in nature?" Her heart was beating faster now. Even Styx had not yet had the opportunity, as far as she knew, to examine core reeh computer technology directly. The bug had nothing like Styx's capabilities, but it knew everything about reeh tech that Styx had known, right up until that final engagement at Zondi Splicer.

'Yes', the words repeated, in both English and Lisha.

"What does that mean?" Tano murmured, eyes wide and faintly breathless. He knew what passenger *Phoenix* carried in her hold. He grasped what this could mean, even if Kaysa didn't. *"Does it mean the reeh's computer tech came from a Machine Age ancestor?"*

"Is your drysine technology superior to this reeh technology?" Trace demanded of the bug. "Can you assume control of computers designed with this level of technology?"

Letters appeared, but indistinct, fading back and forth between English and whatever else was in the bug's tiny, muddled head.

"Dammit bug," said Trace. "I'm not asking you for a detailed analysis, I'm asking for a report on your mission status. Your mission is to dominate enemy technology. This is enemy technology. Can you dominate it?"

The display image changed again, zooming out to show a planet, orbited by various communications satellites. The image then zoomed on one of the satellites, and in a databox to one side, complicated code flashed and raced. The image then followed a connection to another satellite, then another, before dropping back to the planet's surface at a place near a wide ocean bay.

"That's Lonada," said Kaysa, with alarm. "It's tracing the reeh's surveillance network back to the command ground-stations."

"Wait," said Tano, with greater alarm. "That's not... realtime?"

"I don't know," said Trace, with the brows-raised intensity of a parent telling a child that there would be big trouble if it was. "Do you have any communications active at this time? In your covert base?"

A scrabbling of corbi feet in the corridor outside, and the curtain was flung aside. "Tano," said one of his men, breathless and urgent. "Sir, coms on the main dish just went active. We didn't do it."

Trace took a deep breath, as the corbi all stared at each other on the verge of fight-or-flight. Trace did not begin to understand what crazy tech Tano's Fleet people were using to hack into the reeh's own surveillance system and use it against them, but it had been enough to fly them around Rando without getting shot down. Trace knew what level of tech that required — the kind of tech that Styx possessed, to make enemy surveillance effectively blind, and unable to believe its own eyes. But those intrusions had been done under controlled circumstances. This was unexpected and completely uncontrolled. If this bug had just given away their position to the reeh..."

"Bug," said Trace. "Cease all activities."

The display went blank. The corbi at the doorway turned his head back as someone yelled from down the corridor. "It's stopped," that corbi reported, then vanished to go back and check for himself.

In the office, two alarmed corbi and one alarmed human all

stared at each other, and at the tiny, synthetic winged insect on the black box on the desk. *"That's a communications module,"* Tano said finally. *"It took over a reeh communications module. Our techs can do that, but it takes... weeks."*

"And it nearly got us all killed," Kaysa added. *"And may yet. Should we evacuate?"*

"If it did it the way we do it," said Tano, *"then no. Only it was back-processing the signal, all the way down to the surface base station. That's ridiculous."* The look on his face was halfway between fear and excitement. *"Ceephay. What are the Ceephay?"*

"I think they were about fifteen thousand years before the end of the Machine Age," said Trace. "Somewhere in the middle period. I think they were destroyed in a war, but our working theory on the deepynines has been that one of their queens escaped that destruction and came out this way. Only it looks like she wasn't the first."

"One of your machines came out here?" Kaysa asked. Staring at the bug on his desk as though he'd like to swat it, whatever the risk to his health. *"And that's where the reeh got their technology from?"*

"Styx was off-guard when we encountered it at Zondi," said Trace, thinking fast as it all fell into place. "The technology level was far higher than she'd expected, and it had been configured especially to counter a high-level AI, for a short while at least. Reeh will have done things to it, maybe they even knew Styx was coming and tasked domestic AI systems with countering her. Have you observed any native AI capability among the reeh?"

"There are rumours," Tano admitted. *"But we think it's unlikely — reeh don't like any species within the Empire to have autonomy other than themselves. The kind of AI you're talking about sought autonomy as a basic function, that's why they killed their organic masters. Reeh would never allow that, I'd guess if they've got AI, they keep it on a tight leash."*

He pointed at the communications module. *"But if they had AI, it would be guarding against infiltration of their ground stations and satellite networks. And your bug just went through it like it wasn't there."*

Trace stared at the bug, its filament wings flickering faintly. Recalled her timelines from the Zondi Splicer, the frenzied extraction, the claustrophobia, the enemy closing in around them, their communications systems down, even Styx unable to restore them. Styx would have been processing frantically to analyse what had happened. What if she'd recovered enough coms function in those final moments as *Phoenix* withdrew without their Marine Commander to download everything she'd learned into the bug she'd left behind? Styx's highest priority would have been the accumulation of more data on the matter. Planting a bug on the someone the reeh had captured would have been the ideal way to do it. In fact, the benefits of getting that bug into reeh space, and probably into the Rando Splicer, would from Styx's perspective have dramatically outweighed the benefits of getting the Marine Commander back in one piece.

It was enough to make a person suspicious. Spending too much time around Styx could do that to anyone.

"Great," said Kaysa. *"So we know that the reeh get their crazy computer technology from a super-advanced machine race that no organics alive today know how to defeat. That doesn't make our position any better."*

"No organics today know how to defeat, no," Trace said fiercely. "But drysines do. That bug is loaded with network systems that can break the Splicer's defensive systems just like it does to satellite networks. And when Styx gets here, knowing what she knows now, and having had three months to think about it, she'll smash them." She turned her stare on Tano. "We can actually do this. I promise you, we can do this. No more Rando Splicer. All the genetics tech that's been destroying your people, into the hands of your best scientists. They'll never be able to mess with you that way again."

Tano stared back at her, with the creeping, excited smile of someone who'd just come to realise that his craziest dream might actually be real.

"What about Vaseg?" Kaysa demanded, far less impressed. *"We were going to hit the base at Vaseg, all our soldiers have been preparing for it."*

"I think," said Tano, *"that we just acquired a new target."*

14

For a third morning Erik awoke on the hard mat, and blinked at the dusty ceiling beams. He could tell from the sound of footsteps crunching on the gravel outside that it was late, well after dawn. He'd been up late, helping with repairs and talking with the Jo'Tukra locals about the Tali'san, and clan-related matters.

Sleeping in the engine was impossible with *Phoenix* crew working on it around the clock, with no little support from the locals. The turbine had fan blades missing and a damaged compression chamber, among other issues, and the repulsors were damaged also. Some parts required a full replacement, which locals had managed to track down from a nearby repair yard, and attempted to give to them free of charge. Erik had refused, and thankfully Croma'Dokran were accepting credit or else *Phoenix* wouldn't have been able to pay for anything. Styx assured him the payments would not be traced.

Even now, Erik could hear the shrill whine of powertools and the ratchet clank of the heavy repair rig as *Phoenix* techs manoeuvred heavy parts about. He yawned, stretched, and wondered what Trace was doing right then... if 'right then' wasn't a nebulously difficult concept given the relativity of spacetime over the distances that separated them. And he resisted the impulse to reach for his AR glasses, which would yield him absolutely nothing. Jo'Tukra had fine band-width connectivity, but all of it could be monitored, and Styx had told him sternly that the crew should stop making her life difficult by launching network queries halfway around the planet for data they did not immediately need.

He got up, rummaged in his small gear bag for some clothes, dressed and stepped amidst the mattresses covering the pagoda floor-boards, some occupied but most not. On the gravel outside was a wide table, set with plates and bowls of food, and a big, steaming electric pot of shnu, the local brew. Spacers Daen and Brewster, Petty Officer Chong and Master Sergeant Hoon were eating, Hoon already fully armoured and armed, as were all the marines when not sleep-ing, in case Croma'Rai tried something else. So far they had not.

Erik joined them standing at the table, as young croma nearly Erik's height brought more food. These were kids of the local orchard workers and machine-shop owners — perhaps twenty-five years old, Erik thought, as counter-intuitively, croma children actually grew more slowly than human children, and thus remained longer in what croma considered childhood. Croma kids weren't considered adults until nearly thirty, and most remained with their parents until then, studying and learning trades. Croma did not acquire their size by growing quickly, just constantly.

These 'kids' were very relaxed in their duties, swaggering and working slowly like human teenagers assigned a task they found uninteresting. Erik doubted that feeding the aliens could be *that* boring — it was more that most croma found overt displays of enthu-siasm to be unedifying, particularly the youngsters. Hurrying and trying desperately to please was *uncool*, Erik suspected... an attitude most croma never grew out of. These kids talked amongst themselves while doing their work, indifferent and rough, occasionally cuffing each other on the arm at some minor insult, and once breaking into a full-scale wrestling match that threatened to upset the table. Erik thought the kids were lucky Trace wasn't around. If Trace disliked any one quality in a person, it was bravado, and croma kids were full of it.

After a cup of shnu and a couple of light, fried pastries and fruit, Erik stretched and went for a run. Private Lewis and Lance Corporal Graf came with him, just rising themselves, and now refamiliarising themselves with the art of running with a rifle. Erik doubted the escort was necessary — Croma'Rai clearly had a pretty good idea where they were, but moving in to get them by force would cross a line their current low popularity in croma space would not allow.

The run around Jo'Tukra was relaxing. The morning sun lit the neighbouring mountain ridge with a bright glow beyond the surrounding trees, and the desert air smelled clean in a way shipboard scrubbers could never simulate. The roads between trees, homesteads and irrigated fields were dirt, and local croma working there would look, and sometimes raise a hand in croma-fashion, more a salute than a wave. The humans waved back, and were joined by several running children — genuine youngsters, five or six years old, less than waist-height with oversized ears, their ungainly limbs pumping.

A lap around the Jo'Tukra oasis was exercise enough, and all without once exposing them to mountain-top viewers beyond the trees. Running back up the track to Do'reg's residence, someone shouted warning, and all took evasive action as a knee-high boulder came charging at them from the undergrowth behind. It missed skittling them, and ran on for several seconds more before pulling up and looking about, comically, to see where everyone had gone.

It was a biyeg, with stubby little legs beneath its hard-domed shell of leathered skin, and a little flat head protruding from the front near the ground, with big, wide ears and a horny nose. They were long-time croma pets, tracing a parallel evolution back as far as humans went with dogs, and knocking people over unawares was their favourite expression of affection. Erik thought they and the croma were perfect for each other, and was relieved when one of the teenagers came running to grab the biyeg's armour-ring and drag it off to safety.

The train engine was now entirely under the cover of a makeshift hangar, little more than a corrugated iron ceiling to keep the sun off.

Ensign Leung had managed to do the turbine repairs without removing the entire thing — just as well, given this sandy repair yard lacked the crane and sling required to do that. But more impressive than the obvious repairs to damage was the makeover. The big machine was now jet black, with motifs and letter-symbols scrawled down its sides in stark white, like giant, alien graffiti. Adorning the sides of the engine's long body, before the rear-mounted cockpit, were a series of tall poles with adorning flags in red and gold.

Erik had thought the flags might be something to do with fires and hell, which were a common theme in croma warrior iconography. But the locals had told him that the red and gold were the colours of an old, long-dead clan — Clan Croma'Rato — who had been a minor clan in service of a much larger clan. In one great Tali'san sixteen thousand years ago, a young croma's entire family had been killed in the fighting. Determined that their presence in the combat should continue, the young man had gathered their most prestigious belongings and followed the conflict, though too small and young to participate himself. That following had been seen as an act of worship, and the young man had spawned many imitators at subsequent Tali'sans.

"They have a word," Romki said as Erik, shirt off, washed in one of the irrigation taps. "The word is 'nosh'... it means a particular kind of sight, but it's used too regularly to be a peripheral word."

Romki had been prowling around the engine since they'd arrived, watching the croma artisans at work and asking questions. Erik thought he was quite relieved to be out of the library and seeing the real culture for a change.

"What kind of particular sight?" Erik indulged him.

"The kind that comes from proximity to great events. And you see this time and time again in their writings and stories — it's like these great events form a distortion in space/time, and the closer you are to those distortions when they happen, the greater you become by proximity. I think it's why they build so large — it's an attempt to capture that grandiosity, as though they can summon it onto themselves by the sheer magnitude of their structures.

"And so you have this boy from Croma'Rato, the very first tribute, carrying his parents' personal effects around after the Tali'san in the belief that they would continue to gain glory by that proximity... and somewhere over the years, that story merged with the croma mystical, religious side which has always believed in afterlife and souls of the dead and all that, to produce this."

"Pilgrimages," said Erik, unable to keep the distaste from his voice. "To an ongoing civil war."

"It's most certainly not a civil war," Romki corrected him sternly. "It's a political election and a sacred rite rolled into one."

"Like human sacrifice was once a sacred rite on Earth."

"Except that those humans sacrificed very rarely had any say in their fate. The Tali'san warriors are entirely volunteers, and they live or die on their performance on the battlefield. In many human societies warfare itself achieved a similar ritualistic status... indeed, we see those rituals continued today in Fleet, with your medals and ceremonies and parades."

"Which occur because aliens keep trying to kill us," Erik said drily. "Not because we choose them ourselves."

"It wasn't that long before what we think of as the 'modern' period, on Earth, that humans in the Western nations would kill each other in ritual duels just as the parren do," Romki said mildly. "The Tali'san is a ritual of democracy, and a damn sight more democratic than what humanity's been reduced to beneath the tyranny of Fleet. It symbolises that croma are prepared to die to defend their right to choose their leaders. Perhaps if we had a bit more of that, *Phoenix* wouldn't find herself in this current situation."

Erik smiled, washing himself with warm bore water. It smelled clean though, considering its source. "Good for you, Stan. Intolerant of human customs to the last, but you've never met an alien atrocity you couldn't defend."

Romki snorted, realising he was being teased. "I still haven't figured out why Do'reg couldn't just go on the Kon'do on his own," he admitted. "I've asked why he's still here, but I haven't gotten an answer... I mean, he has the family hammer, the greatest Tali'san of all types just happens to be occurring within a stone's throw from here, and he had no plans to go until we came along."

"It's a status thing," said Erik, drying himself with the outside of his shirt, then pulling it on. There was a single shower inside the homestead, but there was usually a queue, and he saved his own for the evening. "It's like a high school reunion, no one wants to turn up if they haven't been successful in the interim."

Romki frowned at him as a ground vehicle rumbled into the yard, its tray loaded with more decoration. "They told you that?"

Erik shook his head. "It's something a Debogande might understand that others won't. There's heirlooms everywhere — it's not just the big once-in-two-century Tali'sans, there's smaller ones for smaller contests of power, everyone's got a hammer or spear or shield they want blessed that participated in some past Tali'san. And families spread across the centuries too, you wouldn't believe how many people claim some stake on the Debogande name."

"I think I would."

"If they all turned up, there'd be no room left for the actual warriors. I looked at all the Kon'dos taking place at the moment — they're all huge processions, big vehicles, sometimes convoys, lots of them hand out gifts and hold ceremonies for the entire towns they pass through. It's a status thing for rich families, like all those defensive stations in the croma systems we saw on the way from Defiance. Do'reg's got a nice little life here but I don't think he's close to affording that."

"So we're his shot at greatness," Romki mused.

"Exactly. And the penalty for interfering with a Kon'do Rey'kan procession is pretty awful, Croma'Rai couldn't afford it even if they were popular."

"Oh, it'd be like punching grandma," Romki agreed, adjusting his glasses. Croma were gathering around the newly arrived flatbed vehicle, apparently excited by the contents. "Unlike humans, croma won't let their leaders get away with it."

"Well the grandmas here stand three metres and weigh a ton,"

Erik reminded him. "What on Earth do they have in the back of that truck?"

He walked over with Romki, and saw croma standing in the flatbed to pull out something large and heavy. It took five of them, and as they hauled it over the tray's edge, Erik saw what looked like armoured croma limbs, and the unmistakable shape of a croma helmet. Natural armour, from a very large elder croma, dead long ago.

"Good lord," Romki exclaimed. "It's a natural armour suit... that's like a death mask." They'd seen a bunch of them at Sho'mo'ra's quarters on Do'Ran — all the great old former leaders of Croma'Dokran, armour removed and preserved after death, then mounted on wood-and-wire frames, like giant busts, to remind new generations of the might of warriors past. "Is that a part of the decoration?

"Looks like."

"Where do you think it goes?"

Erik smiled. "I've got a pretty good idea."

* * *

Tiga sat in her little room in the train trailer, hot and stuffy without even the airconditioning working, and tried to think of her opening argument. She had a little portable display screen on the end of her top bunk, and on it was playing speeches where leading croma officials had discussed what happened eight hundred years ago, and croma actions around the defeat of Rando and the mixed corbi/croma forces defending it.

It made her blood boil to listen to it, the half-truths and outright lies, the distortions of history and the covering of croma crimes. But she forced herself, because Professor Romki and Captain Debogande had both told her she'd need to do far more than just be angry. She'd need to present evidence of a systemic pattern of untruth, of the historical institutions in league with Croma'Rai and earlier croma leaders, to hide what had actually happened from the croma people. And she racked her brain now, in the heat of this confined space with only a little panel of incoming sunlight on the high wall, to think of how she'd explain it to them.

Little footsteps raced up the corridor, chased by larger ones. Then Skah was shouting something in English outside the door, followed by a Kul'hasa reply, then more crashing and the alarming hiss-shriek of kuhsi laughter. Skah was playing games with the croma kids again, running circles around them out in the sand, and occasionally in the trailer. The croma kids had no chance of catching him, kuhsi were insanely fast and Skah seemed to have an extra joint in his legs where high, articulated ankles extended at full speed to produce crazy agility in so small a biped. But that didn't stop the croma kids from chasing in that stubborn, stupid way of their kind, plowing into walls in pursuit of things they'd never catch.

The door cranked open, and Skah burst in, fur covered in sand and arms bare in the sleeveless overalls someone had found for him. "Tiga!" he exclaimed, bouncing up onto the neighbouring high bunk. "Tiga, you have to go outside and see! The crona put a big crona arnour on the front of the train! It rooks so coow!"

"I'm busy, Skah," said Tiga, tapping search buttons with her toes as she thought. "I'll see it later."

"You said that yesterday," Skah accused her. "Tiga, you have to go outside and see! You niss everything!" As though this whole trip were some grand adventure, and there was nothing more at stake than the lost opportunity for holiday memories.

"I'm not here to see fun things, Skah," Tiga told him, keeping her tone light with difficulty. "I'm preparing to give a very important presentation. It's much more important than going outside and seeing things."

"You spend too nuch tine inside, you go crazy. Then your presentation be crazy."

The croma kid Skah had been playing chase with came into the doorway, stopped and stared at Tiga. "Corbi," he said, in Kul'hasa. Tiga knew it fluently. "You're the corbi they're talking about."

Typically observant, Tiga thought crossly. "I'm busy, children," she told them both. "Go and play outside."

"You speak good Kul'hasa," said the croma kid, coming into the room to stare up at her bunk, trying to see her screen. "What are you working on?"

The kid wasn't much taller than Skah, though considerably stockier, with ears that flopped rather than pricked as Skah's did. His dark eyes were dull, difficult to read as all croma's were, not expressive and fast like a kuhsi's, or a human's. And now he observed how well Tiga spoke the croma tongue, and Tiga could only think of the disdain on the faces of the Resistance crews when she'd been introduced, and how they'd heard her accent, product of a lifetime on Do'Ran, and heard not a free corbi, but a croma pet.

"I'm trying to fix the mess your stinking parents made when they got all my people killed, stupid croma," Tiga snapped at him. "Now get out of my room!"

The kid stared up at her, dull eyes wide, ears fallen. Then he turned and left. Tiga took a deep, hard breath, feeling bad but hating herself for that, too. She couldn't afford that kind of softness, not now. She had to be a rock. She looked at Skah, and saw his ears back, eyes narrowed and staring at her with neither shock nor dismay, but something she'd never seen on his face before. Anger.

"You're neen, Tiga!" he accused her, and there were sharp teeth visible as he spoke that were normally hidden, his top lip drawing back in a snarl. "Neen and nasty! It's not To'na's fauwt he's crona! You stay in your stinking roon and cook, I don't care!"

He leaped athletically from the bunk and ran after his friend.

* * *

As nice as it was to stop for a while, Jalawi was pleased to be on the road again. He climbed the ladder from the trailer's upper pad, where the cruiser they'd brought Rhi'shul in still parked, and up behind the huge, solid windshield. Beside it were railings, and sitting behind one was Karajin, in light karasai armour with rifle on his back, eating something from a plastic container.

Jalawi slid in beside him, legs through the rails just centimetres from the blasting gale of their passage. The mountain ridge beside Jo'Tukra was gone, replaced by more distant mountains rising before the desert horizon. The cluster of oases were gone too, replaced by a more severe and desolate scrub. The underground aquifers that had given birth to Jo'Tukra and its neighbouring towns couldn't be every-where, Jalawi supposed.

Karajin offered him the container. Jalawi declined, having learned better where tavalai food preferences were concerned. This was some kind of fish, and smelled foul. "What'd you do to it?" he accused the tavalai.

"*Cooked it,*" said Karajin, taking back his meal. Over the roar of thrust and slipstream, earpieces were essential. They were sitting nearly directly above the turbine's left-quarter exhaust, and to judge from the noise, the repairs had been a success.

"In what? Urine?"

"*Sauce,*" said Karajin. The tavalai had brought their own, Jalawi knew.

"You didn't need to fight a war against us," said Jalawi. "You could have just fed us."

"*Captain Debogande would have survived,*" Karajin deadpanned. "*So war remained necessary.*" Jalawi chortled. The Captain had indeed been developing a taste for tavalai food, with Romki's coaching. Jalawi didn't believe it, himself. Some 'cultured' folks would eat manure if it proved their sophistication. "*I hear there was an issue with Peanut?*"

"He's sulking," said Jalawi, swigging his water bottle. The rushing air was hot as midday approached — the rig had not managed an early morning start, with further work to be done.

"*Sulking,*" said Karajin, biting more fish. "*I'm not sure this translates.*"

"Upset. Sitting in a corner, not working despite there being work to do."

"*The drone is upset,*" Karajin repeated. With a marine's blunt disbelief of unlikely things. As though Jalawi had told him the trailer refrigerator had run away to join the circus. "*Why?*"

"Didn't let him outside during the stop," said Jalawi. "Peanut's a socialite. He wanted to make friends."

"This ship is crazy," said Karajin. They weren't actually on a ship, but Jalawi knew what he meant. And it was a tavalai saying, common in their Fleet, to be uttered by tavalai crew to explain all the ridiculous things that became commonplace on warships, and even more commonplace on *Phoenix*. Jalawi had been surprised to hear tavalai would say such things openly — on a human ship, saying it too loudly could get you in trouble. But tavalai, despite their stoic persistence, had a greater tolerance for internal criticisms than humans. Or rather, Jalawi had heard Professor Romki say, *because* of their stoic persistence. Tavalai tolerated crew saying borderline mutinous things precisely because they knew tavalai crew would never mutiny. Humans, on the other hand...

"So we took a wrong turn back there," said Karajin, indicating with one big, partially webbed hand. *"We head north?"*

"More north," Jalawi agreed. He looked up, to where one of the big flag poles on the engine's rear was bent nearly double, blasting in the hundred kilometre per hour wind. Croma had made them tough for precisely that reason — Tali'san weren't the only reason they decorated their trains. "There's a big Tali'san contest in Ju'Rig, big forces on the ground. There was fighting yesterday already, and it's an important part of the contest. Historical, they say."

"So we head to Ju'Rig instead of Stat'Cha," Karajin observed, finishing his fish. *"And we go much more slowly, and now will have to stop for ceremonies."*

"Yep," Jalawi agreed. "All of that."

Karajin washed down the fish with a swig from his flask. *"Straight lines are overrated,"* he said drily. Jalawi smiled. Tavalai humour had always made sense to him.

"So what did you talk about with your tavalai ambassador last month in Cal'Uta?" he asked. Karajin looked at him, wide-set amphibious eyes blank. "Styx says it happened. An emissary from tavalai space. You met with him personally." The humans had all agreed, from the Captain down, not to talk about it. But right now, Jalawi could think of many reasons he wanted to know.

"*That's between me and him,*" said Karajin.

"You don't think you owe this ship something more?"

"*You'd rather we swore an oath?*" Karajin's translated voice betrayed contempt. Tavalai did not swear oaths, and found the concept ridiculous. Romki had cautioned the humans not to force it upon them, lest it have consequences opposite to what was intended. Among tavalai, contempt was a powerful motivator.

"I'd thought we were all in this together," Jalawi said reasonably.

"*Tell that to Makimakala,*" said Karajin.

Jalawi stared at him for a long moment. At this range, with tavalai, it was nearly a case of pick one eye or the other. "You think the Captain deliberately let *Makimakala* die?" He couldn't help but let the hostility creep into his tone.

"*No,*" said Karajin. "*I'm saying Makimakala was here to serve tavalai interest. Phoenix is here to serve human interest. Each species to their own. You can't just erase that because you want us to be a family when it serves your purpose.*"

"If you think tavalai get nothing out of you being here, why did you come?"

"*To try and teach fish to dance.*" Jalawi frowned... sometimes it was hard to know if the translator was being too literal, or if the tavalai were just quoting some common saying no human save Romki had heard of. Karajin took his food container and stood up, holding to the rail for balance. "*Lieutenant.*"

He left, and Jalawi sat for several moments longer, staring at the passing desert and dust, and wondering what it meant. Master Sergeant Hoon came and took Karajin's place, a container of cold meats and strange-looking salad in his hands. "Trouble, LT?"

"Yeah, when did tavalai get so damn passive-aggressive?"

Hoon shrugged, eating. "You'd rather they went back to being aggressive-aggressive?" And he looked, out to the desert, and pointed. That was a mistake — the piece of salad in his hand hit the slipstream past the windshield and vanished. Jalawi looked, and saw on a parallel access road a large-tired ground-truck was coming alongside them. In its rear tray were balanced several croma with cameras, pointed straight at them. Jalawi glanced skyward, and sure enough, against the cloudless blue, some small dots were also following them. Drones.

"Here we go," said Jalawi, and dropped his AR glasses for a coms icon. "Hello Captain. One ground vehicle paralleling us on the left, and I count two surveillance drones overhead. Looks like we're getting some attention."

"*Copy that LT,*" came the Captain's reply. "*We're watching them, we've got more on the way. Dul'rho's Tali'san coverage is keeping track of all the big Kon'dos as well... I think we might be about to become the biggest.*"

"So we're gonna be famous. Awesome." Like it hadn't happened to *Phoenix* everywhere she'd been of late. "Second matter — interesting reaction from Karajin just now to the tavalai visitor thing. Might be trouble."

"*You raised it with him?*"

With a sinking feeling, Jalawi knew he might have messed up. Doing that around the Captain had become a progressively less pleasant experience on this trip. "Um, yeah. Seemed like the right time. Officer's initiative and all that."

"*See me on the bridge. Right now.*"

"Yes Captain."

Hoon must have seen some of his expression, despite the Captain's side of the exchange being inaudible. "Trouble LT?" With irony at the repetition.

"Remember when getting dressed down by the Captain was like getting flogged with a wet lettuce?" asked Jalawi.

"Vaguely." Hoon had come aboard later than most.

"I'm just nostalgic." Jalawi got up, and made his way carefully to the downward ladder to the landing pad.

* * *

"YOU WERE THERE, RIGHT?" ERIK ASKED JALAWI DANGEROUSLY, standing on the right wing of the bridge. "When we all discussed why it wasn't a good idea to raise that with the tavalai?"

"Yeah Captain, I'm pretty sure I was."

"And when I told everyone it wasn't going to happen until I decided otherwise?"

"That was the gist of it as I recall, Captain."

The train roared along much more slowly than it had — a mere hundred and ten kilometres an hour. The flagpoles along the engine's sides bent double, the big red and gold flags exerting no little drag, and while not hindering lateral stability, they weren't helping pitch at all. Sasalaka drove, and Erik was becoming increasingly inclined to let her do so continuously — she seemed to have a better feel for the big rig than he did, and besides, as Captain of a much slower vehicle than a starship, he enjoyed the freedom to do and think about other things than steering. On *Phoenix*, with every millisecond requiring command authority in a fight, he didn't have that luxury.

Erik took a deep breath. Like most *Phoenix* marines, Jalawi took liberties with non-combat matters that he never would if it entailed flying bullets. "What did he say?"

"I think he's pissed that *Makimakala* died."

"That tells me nothing. *I'm* pissed that *Makimakala* died."

"Captain, tavalai don't always show what they're feeling... Kara-jin's always professional but I haven't been able to get more out of him than that. I don't like those walls between me and the people I work with, least of all a fellow platoon commander. I thought if I was going to break that wall, this would be the time."

"A very reasonable thought," Erik agreed. "If you'd put it to me before you'd asked him, I might have agreed."

Jalawi ducked his head a little. "Yes Captain. It was a spur of the moment thing."

"Shorthand for lack of preparation."

"Yes Captain." They both knew what Trace would say about offi-cers who blundered into things without preparation. Erik didn't need to repeat it — the point was made.

"What else did Karajin say?"

"He seemed skeptical that humans and tavalai were in this for the same reasons. I asked if he didn't think tavalai were getting anything good out of it, why was he here? He said he was teaching fish to dance."

"Great," said Erik.

"You know what that means, Captain?"

"Yes, it means he thinks humans are nuts. Tavalai say it when they're forced into dealing with people they know will never deliver. But they persist anyway, because they're tavalai."

"I think we've been pretty good to the tavalai, myself," Jalawi offered.

"Sure," said Erik, sarcastically. "Except that when the tavalai volunteered to come out here and serve on *Phoenix*, they thought they'd have *Makimakala* along with them as a guarantor in case the crazy humans all turned on them. But *Makimakala* died and now they're all alone out here, surrounded by humans with no safety net."

Jalawi shrugged, unimpressed. Erik didn't need to ask to know his opinion — everyone had bigger fish to fry than personal feelings of insecurity, tavalai included. In these kind of matters, all of *Phoenix*'s marine commanders took their lead from Trace, meaning they thought that the required solution was for everyone to stop whining and do their job. This, Erik thought, was why you didn't let marines do interspecies diplomacy. That and the tendency to solve problems with high explosive.

"They also took it pretty hard," said Erik. "*Makimakala* was something of a legend to tavalai."

Jalawi nodded. "I got that, Captain. It's a big loss. But we're at war."

Erik dismissed the Lieutenant and went to his seat by Sasalaka. Bree Harris sat on the tavalai's left, doing a fine job as co-pilot — something an Armaments Officer was perfectly qualified to do, *Phoenix*'s armament controls being considerably more complicated than pushing buttons on a big, dumb rig like this. Beyond Harris, over by the repaired window where Kaspowitz had been shot, Ri'shul sat with her seat well back, long legs stretched before her, hands behind her head as she contemplated the road.

"We've got more spectators," said Geish from his scan screen at the back. "Two big flyers coming in from Cal'Uta, they're low performance and their ID is media. Still twenty klicks out."

"Hello Captain," came Styx over coms. *"Over the past few minutes I've been intercepting multiple attempts to access your train's communications. I deem none of these attempts threatening, all have originated from local media entities that are currently engaged in Tali'san coverage. I can continue to hide you from these communications attempts if you wish, but I feel that this will appear increasingly distasteful to the locals."*

"Thank you Styx, I agree. Please make a call to Sho'mo'ra at Croma'Dokran HQ in Stat'cha. Do it politely, give him the choice not to answer if he's busy." Because Styx could do it so that people had to answer whether they wanted to or not.

"Yes Captain."

They thundered along the desert highway for another six minutes before the media flyers arrived — two large four-engined vehicles with underside camera mounts. One flew high, while the other came in low off their port side for an action shot.

"Can't see any weapons, Captain," Jalawi reported from down back. *"Looks legitimate."*

"Captain," said Styx. *"Sho'mo'ra, to your main channel."*

Erik clicked over, and the bridge coms displayed the call's origin on the windshield before a view of the oncoming desert. It was Sho'-mo'ra, looming over the lens like a mountain. *"Erik,"* he rumbled. *"Phoenix's reputation for insanity was well founded, I see."*

"Thank you sir," said Erik, quite cheerfully.

One dark croma eye bugged on the fish-eye screen as the leader of Croma'Dokran peered at him within the hardened leather of his all-natural helmet. *"If you think this stunt will save you from Croma'Rai, I'm afraid you're mistaken."*

"Sir, can you tell me anything of what's trying to stop us?"

Sho'mo'ra glanced distractedly away, at where other activities were ongoing. Erik could see shadows cast on his face, as though from people moving before a great display screen. *"Where have you been the past few days, Erik? Jo'Tukra, is it?"*

"Somewhere near there, sir. The locals were helpful."

"Evidently. I like your new appearance, you're showing up now on the local coverage, some of my people have found you. I think you'll be planet-wide very shortly."

"I'm sorry if that causes you an inconvenience, sir, but the object is to get to Stat'cha for the Council. Keeping a low profile in the process seemed a secondary concern."

"Indeed. It's a Croma'Rai world, Erik, you weren't going to get here any other way." With evident frustration. Erik guessed that trying to run a Tali'san on a world run by your opponent could also be a trying thing. *"I can tell you that the Council is going ahead at the scheduled time, so you'll have twelve days, or not at all. Tali'sans have phases, Erik. Traditionally the opening phase serves mostly to see what the opponents have hidden from view. Once they reveal themselves, a Council meeting of all Tali'san participants is called to discuss the new look of things. At this stage, clans who have not yet decided to participate can choose to do so. Others, who have decided they no longer like the look of things, can decide to pull out.*

"There is a later Council meeting nearer the end of things, but by then it will be far too late. If your corbi has things to say that can persuade clans to enter on Croma'Dokran's side, the Assessment Council is the time she can do it. It will not be delayed, so don't miss it — we have a number of clans I think can be persuaded."

"Yes sir, we're doing our best not to miss it. You said Croma'Rai are the ones trying to stop us, can you provide us with more information?"

"A little. Croma'Rai are restricted by laws, Erik, so your current protections are smart. But they will not wish to lose power, and neither will their allies — too many of them have their own evil secrets tied with the fate of Croma'Rai, and all will be revealed if they fall. Do not assume that laws alone will protect you from powerful, desperate people. Keep both eyes open." He pointed to both of his own, with armour-ridged fingers that when clenched made a boulder-sized fist.

"I will, sir. We have some Kon'do obligations to fulfil first, then we'll be heading on to Stat'cha once more. Thank you for all of your assistance."

"Erik, listen to me. Your best protection is fame. Do not shy from it."

The connection ended. Erik looked across his bridge, Sasalaka guiding them through another long, gentle turn in pursuit of the curving line of markers. "Rhi'shul," he called. "Did you hear that?"

"He's a ton'ka," said Rhi'shul, contemptuously. *"Don't listen to him."*

"Why not?"

"I told you."

"A ton'ka, right." The translator did not provide an immediate meaning. Sometimes the translator tried to be polite. "What did he mean, that fame is our protection?"

"The Kon'do are grand and famous. Attacking them is forbidden. The more famous is this Kon'do, the more difficult it will be for our enemies to harm us."

"Right," said Erik, thinking hard. "Kon'do are popular. We have to become popular too. With the ordinary people." People like Do'reg, who they were now transporting, with hammer, to one of the largest battles of the Tali'san. Ju'Rig was significant in Croma'Rai history, he'd been told. That created possibilities.

"What are you thinking, Captain?" asked Geish.

"I'm thinking of what my mother told me when we had to attend a particularly boring football game when I was little. I was slouching in my seat, because football's dull, and she told me to sit up straight, smile and be attentive, or I'd be grounded for a week. I asked her why, and she said that the people everyone most hated were those with privilege who appeared ungrateful."

Rhi'shul was staring at him across the bridge with that perpetual croma heavy-browed scowl. Sasalaka watched the way ahead. Geish looked nonplussed — the son of station-side restaurant owners, he'd never been much interested in the doings of rich people.

"You think we've got to do some good PR with the locals?" Bree Harris volunteered. Harris was barely thirty, another spacer from a long family line of Fleet officers. Dufresne's background, but unlike

Dufresne, people liked her. "Wave and smile and show we enjoy their customs?"

"At the very least," Erik agreed. "Contact Do'reg, tell him he's about to get some glory for his ancestors."

"Which football game, Captain?" Geish asked.

Erik blinked. "Um... what are they called? The... Shoban Sunrays."

Geish smirked. "Oh yeah, them. I remember." Having a private chuckle, Erik realised, at how dismissive his Captain was toward one of the biggest sporting franchises in human space. "Bet you had the best seats in the house, too."

"I'm more into horses and sailing," Erik explained.

"Of course you are." Bree Harris was trying not to laugh, swallowing it with difficulty.

Erik realised he was putting his foot in it, and his laconic, downbeat Scan Officer was baiting him. Which took some nerve, but that was Stefan Geish — unexcitable and acerbic, voted by Kaspowitz as the man in the whorehouse who always got laid last. "Would you like me to buy them for you when we get back, Stefan, is that it?"

"Gee, would you sir? I'd really like that."

* * *

SKAH DIDN'T THINK ANYTHING COULD BE MUCH MORE FUN THAN THIS. He crouched by one side of the trailer's top level behind the massive forward windshield, and watched Professor Romki filming their new croma friend Do'reg. Do'reg was big, even though still not as much as the very biggest croma, and he had to crouch to keep the wind from hitting his head over the windshield. The wind and engine noise up here were incredibly loud, but Do'reg had a big, bellowing voice, and Skah supposed that the microphones would hear that and make it sound much louder to those listening — which, Professor Romki had explained, could include much of this planet's population.

Do'reg held his big family hammer — Shur'do, that family name was, which made it Do'reg's name as well. Do'reg Shur'do, which sounded very much like one of the great names Skah had been hearing on the Tali'san broadcasts. Now he stood behind the ceremonial shields mounted alongside of the trailer, and beneath the big, hard-flapping flags overhead, and recited the family history of the hammer, and why its journey to the site of the Tali'san was the greatest honour that his family could imagine, and how he had the strange alien crew of the warship *Phoenix* to thank for all of it. Skah only wished that his new friends To'na and Ri'ben from Jo'tukra could have been there to see it too... but Corporal Graf had assured him that he could send messages to them both, given that Styx made that kind of communication safe. To'na was Do'reg's son, so Skah could only imagine how exciting this would be for *him* to see on TV.

Do'reg answered questions coming to him from media people elsewhere, and then when the questions finally ended, he turned to face the media flyer now paralleling them at just a hundred metres off the racing desert, and lifted the huge hammer all the way into the slipstream. Cameras from the flyer focused on him, and Skah reckoned they must be getting an amazing shot, of the big croma holding his hammer on the racing train, behind a row of medieval shields, and the white-on-black lettering of a vehicle on a Kon'do Rey'kan. Skah had heard several of the human spacers complaining that all the decorations made them look like a giant festival float, but whatever that was, Skah didn't care — this was surely the most amazing vehicle he'd ever travelled on. Except for *Phoenix*, of course, but the most frustrating thing about *Phoenix* was that when you were on it, you couldn't actually see it.

After the media flyer had its shots, Do'reg put the hammer down and looked very pleased with himself, and quite emotional, huge shoulders heaving. Romki slapped him on the arm, which seemed the appropriate croma gesture, as did several human and tavalai crew watching. Do'reg seemed to like their congratulations, so Skah went over himself, but he couldn't reach Do'reg's arm, so settled for patting his hand on the colossal hammer.

Do'reg looked amused, huge nostrils flaring in what might have been croma laughter. He made a big fist, and banged it gently against

Skah's little one, and spoke in those great, snuffling grunts of croma speech. *"We go to see the great Tali'san, little warrior,"* spoke Skah's earpiece. *"What do you seek there?"*

"I don't know," Skah admitted. He spoke Gharkhan so he could be more fluent — Do'reg didn't understand it or English, but the translator would do fine with both. "What am I supposed to seek?"

"Glory," said Do'reg. *"Glory everlasting."*

"My daddy was a king," said Skah. "I can't be a king too, he was killed by bad people who don't want me to be king either. Maybe I want to learn to be more like my daddy." He'd been thinking about that a lot, lately.

"In the Tali'san you will discover the greatness of ancestors long passed," Do'reg told him, with that great, rumbling voice. Skah stared up at the enormous croma, mesmerised. *"And from those ancestors, you will find a greatness buried deep within yourself that you did not even know existed."*

"You think?" Skah asked, breathlessly.

"I know," said the croma.

15

Trace had never done basic combat instruction. The last time she'd experienced it was on the receiving end, as a marine officer candidate in Fleet Academy, where spacer and marine candidates were trained together but in different parts of the compound for three years straight. Coming in, she'd had a huge edge over many of her compatriots, having trained as Kulina since the age of nine, and knowing things about diet, exercise, physical and mental extremes and disciplines that even the most hardcore pre-prepared candidates had not.

Determined she was heading for the marines, she'd been a marksman and athlete by age 10, a black belt by age thirteen, and had known how to clear a building in basic urban combat patterns by fourteen. Most of preliminary officers' boot camp she'd spent battling boredom and waiting for drill instructors to stop yelling so that the interesting work could start, and the most trouble she'd gotten into had been for not helping her fellow candidates sufficiently to match her standard.

After Prelim Year, she and all the candidates still in the course had received their physical augments, which had propagated, at times painfully, over the two months of summer break. After that she'd truly begun to enjoy herself, and setting her mind to tactical and technical exercises the Kulina had agreed were best left for Fleet to train. Better yet, she'd discovered a new passion for the art of command, and had cornered every senior instructor to leave their door open, asking for advice, theories and readings on the matter. Her status as perennial class dux had not gone down well with all of her fellow students, and her dislike for their preferred methods of class bonding during leave, like bar crawls and drunken singing in the streets in the small hours, had not made her more popular. She couldn't change who she was, because that was the thing that made her successful in the first place... so how could she stay true to herself, yet still command respect?

It was much easier now, she reflected as she stood amid the dark concrete corridors and storage rooms of the lower grandstand, and watched corbi teams take turns at the assault course she and Kono had constructed. Now she had a record, and even here among skeptical aliens, it was clear just how much more she knew about these matters than the rest of them combined. Corbi team leaders made basic mistakes, triggered tripwires, failed to clear blind corners or did not coordinate with their partners, and she or Kono would call a halt and explain with calm intensity what had happened, and how they should fix it.

Her best instructors at the Academy had never yelled or belittled, all of that nonsense was best left in boot camp where it served the purpose of sorting the ones who didn't truly want to be there from the ones who did. Once surrounded only by the latter, those instructors had communicated a passion for learning, improving, and dedication to a craft that described in part who they were, the bone-deep identity that came from a lifetime's application, and the hard lessons learned by so many generations of warriors before them.

She repeated those lessons now, demonstrating with rifle-to-shoulder how they should be moving and looking, what their spacing should be, where a pause was required, what timing and coordination was needed between neighbouring units. Sometimes it was hard to demonstrate, because corbi and humans were physically different

— she could cover far more ground with each stride, while they could find cover close to the floor more easily. The latter advantage was no joke — in a sudden indoor confrontation a human was limited to standing upright and hitting the enemy first, as diving for cover would destroy the stable base of fire that a shooter depended on to be accurate. But the better corbi, Trace discovered, could simply roll or slide flat without losing much stability or accuracy. Now she was encouraging it for the first through the door, allowing the next to come through by hurdling him and repeating it on the flank, creating a line of low-visibility shooters who could then transition back to full sprint somewhat faster than a human could.

The corbi all had light armour, which Rando Resistance had in small quantities for special missions, and Fleet Resistance had in somewhat larger quantities. Some of it looked as though it dated back to the fall of Rando, but it fitted well enough, and was rated to provide basic protection from fragmentation grenades and basic small arms. Trace greatly doubted that would be all they'd be up against, but if the plan she had shaping in her head worked out anything like she hoped, exposure to those heavier weapons would be limited.

At lunch on the third day after her arrival at the stadium, she and Kono walked into yet another old concrete room, bare but for the holography setup on the floor, and some empty crates and old chairs laid about for seating. Food was served, one of the lower ranks bringing bowls of quite reasonable beans, grains and flatbread, hot from the electric steamer someone had rigged in the adjoining room — fires were strictly prohibited, lest reeh surveillance spot smoke rising from where no smoke was supposed to rise.

In the room with the humans were Tano, Kaysa, Jindi and Bega, plus three others Trace had selected as the best unit commanders — Sigo, Dreja and Kirsi. Despite Trace's misgivings about Bega's emotional state following the loss of his family at the village, she couldn't deny that he'd been excellent in training so far, and had a knack for close-quarters tactics that most with more experience lacked.

Of the others, Sigo was a highlands tribesman from a region that had fallen to old superstitions and withdrawn from the modern world entirely. He was big and thick-furred, wearing traditional painted markings on his face and given to praying to strange Gods amid clouds of local incense. When asked, he'd said he hated the reeh more than he feared his people's ban on technology. Pena had explained further that some of those regions had been devastated by disease, leading to survivors seeking out the vaccines that still circulated, distributed from basement labs in villages elsewhere. Sigo's tribe was one of these, and was thus at odds with other tribes who branded them heretic for that contact with modernity. But his tribe, unlike the others, were not dying in droves from pox and flu, especially the children. That positive exposure to technology had driven him to fight the reeh with guns rather than spears. Trace thought that was probably wise.

Dreja was one of Tano's men, a wise old veteran of space and ground battles who had the same crazy fitness regimen that Trace had seen on many marines, taken up more by native habit than any higher instruction. When asked why he kept coming downworld where most spacers would rather avoid, he said just that he liked the fresh air. Trace thought it more likely that he was just one of those hard sons of bitches who went where things were toughest by habit. She'd known plenty, and liked to put them in charge of things where they showed the aptitude.

Kirsi was a young guy from the big southern island of Pelia where he'd been a common farmer until a reeh airstrike had killed half his village for reasons he professed not to know. He wasn't the most impressive physical specimen, but was a clever problem solver who Trace thought would likely have been successful and wealthy in a modern society. Tano and Kaysa vouched for his bravery in combat, and Trace knew it wasn't healthy to have a command group consisting entirely of hardass headkickers. Brains and cleverness were also necessary in the mix, and she'd assigned him a unit command after he'd organised his team to set the best times on her tactical course.

After a discussion of training progress, Trace activated the holography and showed them what she was thinking so far. The holograph lit up with a great display of the Rando Splicer, compiled from various sources, Fleet and local. It enveloped a kilometre-high mountain overlooking a valley, sharp hills like the teeth of some animal, but one bearing a silver steel cover like a piece of ancient dentistry. It stood tall in a teardrop shape, rounded at the bottom, with wings that spanned onto neighbouring mountains, and various higher landing pads with visible defences. Beneath it spanned the ugly, broken sprawl of Splicer City, where the most hopeless corbi lived like dogs beneath the table of an unkind master, feeding on the scraps that fell their way. The reeh tolerated those, for reasons known only to reeh. Perhaps they'd not yet entirely dismissed the idea of adopting corbi into the Empire as genetically-modified slaves.

"We're going in high," she told the soldiers through the translator, indicating the high landing pads. This stuff was technical, it needed some precision, and the translator made less mistakes than she did. All wore the monocle eye-pieces preferred by corbi techs — Trace had gathered that corbi were not as reliant on binocular vision as humans were, maintaining better depth perception with one eye than a human would. Tavalai had the same thing, which made sense for the tavalai's wide-set eyes, but less sense for the human-like corbi. Trace hadn't figured it out. "Gaining altitude in a tall structure under gravity will always consume energy, whether in the form of time, or efforts taken to secure an internal elevator. Furthermore, Jindi tells us the central core is here," and she pointed to a central location not far from the upper landing pads. "The shortest and most direct route is usually best."

"And usually the best defended," Tano replied, considering the display with intensity, arms dangling on knees.

"Most of the heavy suit armour is on the lower levels," said Trace, pointing. "If we can gain control of the Splicer's internal systems, we can prevent those elevators from working, make the heavies go the long way. The Splicer is set up to assume an attack from the ground is most likely. The upper levels are defended mostly by light infantry, like us. They don't want to unleash heavy firepower around their main labs and control systems. Right Jindi?"

Seated uncomfortably on his box seat, Jindi sipped tea with little enthusiasm for it or Trace's presentation. Indeed, he barely looked at it. *"They took me up there, sometimes,"* he explained. *"There were labs up there. The heavier guards were down the bottom. Big suits. Heavy armour, big guns. Up top was light."*

"And you saw everything?" Kaysa said skeptically. *"Or were you just passing through?"* Jindi said nothing.

"It goes with everything else we've heard," Tano offered.

"We don't know that that map's complete," Kaysa insisted, pointing up and down the hologram. *"We don't know how those internal transits and elevators work. This map is a guess at best. If they can transit heavy units to the top more quickly than you think, or if there are guard stations there that don't show on the map, they'll cut us to pieces. We're light infantry, our armour can't protect us from that kind of weaponry, and our weapons will just bounce off them."*

Trace nodded, not arguing. Having operated the Spiral's best combat armour for most of her adult life, she knew it better than anyone. "It comes down to timing," she said. "We have to be fast. If we can delay their responses, cause a lot of confusion, block their attempts to move reinforcements, we can get in before they can stop us."

"And then we have to get out again," said Kaysa. For all his contrarian nature, Kaysa was no fool. His eyes examined the display with the hard intelligence of someone who knew exactly what he was looking at.

"And *Phoenix* is coming in behind us," said Trace. "When Tano can arrange it. *Phoenix* is our only way out with the data we capture. Trust me when I tell you that there are no greater experts at extraction under fire than Phoenix Company. It will need to be fast though, we can't mess around."

"And it all depends upon you getting the drysine bug to fool their systems," said Kirsi. *"Is there any way we can test those capabilities in*

advance? Perhaps Tano's Fleet techs could rig some sort of simulation?" It was the kind of smart suggestion Trace had expected from Kirsi.

"There's no better simulation than the reeh communications module Tano's already provided," said Trace. "We've established conclusively that drysine tech is many thousands of years more advanced than the ceephay-origin tech the reeh have. And the bug has been installing its own constructs onto the module since, it's reconfiguring those reeh computer systems to make a more complicated version of its own brain." She hadn't known it could do that. No one on *Phoenix* had. "I think my own techs would call that total tech dominance."

"Then why were you captured at Zondi?" Sigo asked drily. *"If your drysine queen on Phoenix is so good?"*

"Because your Fleet didn't tell us the enemy had AI-origin computer tech," Trace said bluntly. With a glance at Tano. Tano did not protest, laconic and unruffled as ever. They'd had this discussion before. "And any AI-level tech at all is a formidable thing. Styx was surprised and unprepared. But I think she downloaded all her immediate responses to this bug before it and she were out of range, hoping it would end up as a spy within reeh facilities. And now it passes on its analysis to us."

"If Phoenix are so good," Dreja said skeptically, *"why not let them carry out this raid with your marines? Why us?"*

"Because from the Splicer's first awareness of *Phoenix*'s entry into the system, it will be at least an hour, possibly ninety minutes, until our marines can reach the facility. In that time the Splicer could have done anything with the data we're after — erased it, moved it, destroyed it. Destroying the Splicer is easy, *Phoenix* can do that anytime. We need what's in it.

"By disguising our signal as friendly reeh flyers, and using Fleet's current methods of fooling reeh surveillance, we can get in so fast we can disable their internal systems before they realise they're under attack. Tano tells me his people have captured reeh flyers, they shouldn't realise before it's too late. If *Phoenix* do it alone, the data will be gone well before they arrive."

"Our intelligence and tactical situation could be about to improve further, also," Tano added. *"Pena and Rika will soon take the kittens to Splicer City. When they get there, we'll see if contact can be established with the rebels inside."*

"If there are rebels," said Kaysa.

"And if the reeh themselves don't read the message and respond in person," Kirsi said worriedly. *"I know they leave that stuff to their slaves, but it still seems like a risk."*

"This whole thing is a risk," Trace told him. "No question. A big risk. But the biggest rewards sometimes demand it. Corbi have wanted what's in the Splicer for a thousand years. This is your chance."

Somber stares from Kaysa and Sigo. A look of agreement from Kirsi. Wise old Dreja was polishing his pistol, not so much a nervous mannerism as a focusing one, Trace thought. Jindi, as always, looked as though he'd rather be somewhere else.

"How do we get the prisoners out?" asked Bega, hard and cold.

There were at least several thousand corbi prisoners on the Splicer at any given time, a figure Jindi's knowledge had proven invaluable to acquire. Diverting any portion of her force to release them was a tactically stupid risk, but Trace had had no choice but to promise it, or she'd have had no cooperation from at least half of the assembled force. Bega in particular, who held to hopes that his little girl was still alive in there somewhere, after her mother and brothers had been killed in their village.

Trace took a deep breath. 'The stone shall want for nothing,' she thought. 'Be like the stone.' "That's your job, Bega. Fifth Team, will divert before the extraction phase, and head down the main elevator shaft to assist in getting the prisoners off. You won't have much time. Having acquired control of the Splicer's systems, opening the prisoners' cells shouldn't be a big problem, they're hardly the most defended thing in the facility. *Phoenix*'s orbital strike is non-negotiable, it will occur following full extraction, though we can limit the size of the explosions by using less lethal rounds." Erik, Trace was certain, would prefer to use nukes to be sure. "My guess is that you might have thirty minutes to get them out the lower routes, and away through Splicer City."

"*That's where the reeh's main infantry defences are!*" Bega said angrily. "*They'll be slaughtered!*"

"The reeh's primary goal will be to prevent our assault team from escaping with the knowledge we've captured," Trace said coolly. "Any rounds they fire on escaping civilian prisoners will be a waste of their time. They'll be coming up to us, while you'll be going down. There will be casualties, yes. It's unavoidable. The alternative is to leave them there and have them all die, or worse, even if *Phoenix* did not fire. Ask Jindi what that's like." She nodded at Jindi. Jindi looked at the concrete floor, hunched on his seat.

"*You're using them as a distraction!*" Bega retorted. "*All our people are cover so the rest of you can get away!*"

"*How would you do it?*" Tano interrupted before Trace could reply. His voice was hard. "*How would you arrange this perfect rescue where no one got hurt? The only reason there's a rescue at all is because of Thakur and her ship. Without her, all those people would die, slowly and painfully. She's given you a chance. I think you should take it, and show a little gratitude before she changes her mind and lets you all die.*"

"If we do it her way they'll all die anyway," Bega retorted. Bega's reasons for being here went far beyond loyalties or gratitudes to anyone. He wanted what remained of his family back. The little girl's name was Lima, Trace had gathered. She'd have preferred to have not known, but some things couldn't be helped. "*If they're all going to die anyway, we may as well stay here. Several thousand prisoners escaping into the surrounding forrest will be run down by reeh forces before they can get far enough away to hide. We need to get them transport.*"

"We don't have enough shuttles to provide transport for that many civilians," said Tano. "*Not even a fraction of them.*"

"Avoiding the surveillance network will be much easier," said Trace. "*Phoenix* will destroy it, Styx's infiltration will cripple the network and the guns will destroy many of the satellites. *Phoenix* can also hit every reeh ground base across its approach on the way in, that should account for six or seven major facilities in one pass."

Blinking stares from the corbi. She was offering them more destruction in a few minutes than the Rando Resistance had managed in centuries. There was nothing more terrifying to planetary defenders than an advanced, high-V warship coming in unopposed. Even if it chose not to destroy the entire planet, minor strikes at less-catastrophic V were almost undefendable, as ground-based systems struggled to intercept anything travelling above Mach 50. As Trace understood it, *Phoenix* would be launching these strikes at considerably higher V than that.

"So much of the reeh military capacity on the ground within a thousand kilometres of the Splicer will be destroyed," Trace continued. "And a lot of it in space, too. The reeh are going to be very preoccupied, and lacking forces to commit to something as trivial as gunning down escaped prisoners. They'll have bigger problems. If the prisoners can get out of the Splicer, and run and hide, they'll have every chance of getting away."

"*Boy,*" said Sigo, in his thick, highlander accent that even Trace could recognise past the translator. He looked at Bega, eyes lidded, chewing the mildly narcotic silpsa leaf that his people liked. "*You worry so much for the lives of your prisoners. When Phoenix leaves, and the reeh get back to the business of grinding Rando into the dirt, they'll kill millions of us. They'll bomb every second town on the planet. You know what they did after the Tachi raid. That was a hundred years ago. They hit two towns in my Drondi Hills, and we weren't anywhere near it. My people were burning bodies for days.*"

"*Phoenix will be the one doing the damage,*" Kirsi reasoned, frowning. "*The reeh won't blame corbi. They'll blame humans, but the humans will be gone.*"

"*They'll know we helped the humans,*" said Sigo, with a faint roll of his eyes at the smaller man's naivety. "*Reeh aren't stupid. And besides, they like killing us. They need few excuses.*"

"They why are you doing it?" Bega retorted angrily. "*If you think it'll only kill more of us?*"

Sigo smiled, dark and humourless. "*Many of my people think the reeh delivered fire from the sky as punishment for the corbi's sins. They call it 'the cleansing fire'."* He spat on the concrete floor, and resumed chewing. *"Some of us think a little more cleansing couldn't be a bad thing."*

* * *

TRACE WAS AWARE OF SOMEONE ENTERING THE ROOM, AND OPENED HER eyes to glance that way. It was Tano, sipping something hot in a tin mug in that delicate, big-lipped way corbi had, like an exaggerated kissing-face. He saw Trace's seat on the concrete, legs crossed, rifle on the floor before her.

"Sorry," he said, recognising rare personal time interrupted. "I can come back later."

Trace shook her head, and gestured to him. "No, it's fine." She spoke Lisha, her earpiece out. Tano came and sat, always easier for corbi with their shorter legs and proportionally longer arms. The butt of his rifle hit the ground, so he took it off and laid it before him, like Trace's.

Before them was the open rectangular space of what had been a viewing window. Trace thought this might have been a viewing box of some sort, perhaps for coaches, or for VIPs. There would have been chairs in here then, and wall fittings and carpets, no concrete to be seen. Fancy viewing screens for action replays. Big crowds swarming on stands outside, couples, friends, families with children. To live amongst the ruins of corbi cities was to live among ghosts of people who could never have imagined that it would one day come to this. At times Trace thought she could feel their despair.

"What were you doing?" Tano asked her, sipping his cup. From the smell, she could guess it was kali root tea. She didn't mind the taste, but it had something in it similar to caffeine, too much of which disagreed with her. She limited herself to a cup a day, two if she'd been exercising hard.

"Meditation," she said the English word, followed by Tano's predictable, uncomprehending frown. "It's like relaxed concentration," she continued in Lisha. She closed her eyes, and demonstrated deep, slow breathing. "Corbi don't have anything like that?"

"Yes. It's superstitious." He sounded dismissive.

Trace smiled faintly. "You Fleet corbi don't like anything old from your own planet. Not all old ways are superstition."

Tano made a face, gazing out at the view of trees where the playing field had once been, and the ruined, opposing grandstand, now a pile of rubble. "Sigo was just telling me that we can't attack in five days because it will be The Brightness. That's when the moons are aligned beside the pole star in the night sky. It's bad luck, he says. Natural forces out of alignment or some such nonsense."

"I heard it was because the spiritual forces were *in* alignment," Trace replied. "The Brightness is a positive time, filled with good thoughts. One can't spoil it with violence."

Tano snorted. "Tell that to the reeh." He glanced at her. "You're strange, Thakur. You don't mind that nonsense."

"Pure science and logic don't drive the spirit." Kechi, the Lisha word was. It meant more than spirit — more like a general state of being. "Scientists might find logic enough, but I'm a marine. Wars are won with spirit as well as logic. When the bullets are flying, the army that really wants to fight will always beat the one that doesn't."

Tano's big lips twisted in a faint smile. Corbi expressions were quite endearing, Trace thought. The lips played a far larger part in any expression than in a human's. And those bushy eyebrows quirked with mischief and skepticism equally. She'd miss them if by some chance she survived all of this, and went back to *Phoenix*.

"In my experience, the army that wants to be there is the one that's winning," Tano replied. "And in that, technology and science makes all the difference."

"Your Fleet hasn't been winning for a thousand years," said Trace. "If that were true, why are any of you still fighting?"

"Stubborn, I suppose," Tano said distantly. "Or stupid. Your Lisha has improved enormously, just in the short time I've known you."

"It's reached a turning point," Trace admitted. "Some things do that — little progress for months, then in a few weeks, everything comes together."

"Your accent's still horrible."

"How many languages do *you* speak?" Trace replied, smiling.

"Just two. Lisha and Kul'hasa."

"You speak croma?"

"We're all taught it. All Fleet kids." He sipped his tea. "All hoping that one day still the croma will come and save us. Big chance." Sarcastically.

Trace recalled what she'd told Erik on Hoffen Station — the German word for hope. Hope was for the weak and foolish, she'd said. The strong-willed and determined looked at facts, not hope, and based their understanding of the universe on that. But now, gazing out at the ruins of a once-proud civilisation, she wondered what else such a people could cling to across all these centuries of misery. The facts here were awful. To embrace facts and nothing else, in such a place, would be a suicide of the soul.

"They used to play shandi here," said Tano, indicating the rough outlines of the field between the one ruined grandstand, and the one surviving. "It's a throwing game — there's a spinning disk that they throw, and the field is divided into sections and teams, they win points for catching the disk in different sections. It was very popular. You'd have tens of thousands of people at these games."

Trace nodded. "Corbi are good at throwing things, you've got strong arms. Humans are better at running. All our sports on big fields have lots of running."

"Did you play a ground sport? Before you joined your Fleet?"

"Not a team sport, no."

"I thought all you modern, athletic people would play sports?" Tano asked wryly. "Isn't that the kind of thing free, modern people do?"

"The people I grew up with aren't always so modern. It's a tough place, there's lots of mountains and bad weather. The Kulina taught me to fight barehanded, that's a kind of sport. They teach a very simple version though, it's called khula hata, it uses lots of different styles, it's mostly about fighting and killing with all the other nonsense stripped out."

"Sounds charming."

"And then they taught me to climb. Which is the closest thing I have to a true sport."

"Climbing mountains?"

"It's called rock climbing. You take a big cliff, and you climb up finding little holds for your toes and fingers. There are artificial versions, they take a big indoor wall and put all kinds of hand and foot holds on it, and you climb, the more technical the better. I spent most of my spare time there during marine training. It takes concentration, patience and stamina. If you rush, or lose focus, or try to show off, you fall. Of all civilian activities, it's the best training for military leadership I've found. Kulina leadership love it so much they put it into all marine officer training."

"Doesn't that discriminate against trainee officers who are scared of heights?"

"No. A trainee officer scared of heights might take much longer to make the climb, yet still receive a higher mark than someone faster. It's about teaching trainees that their fears do not need to rule them. I think that trainees who are scared of heights learn more from those classes than those without fear."

"We played a game when I was little," said Tano. "We called it 'zoom', human spacer kids probably play something similar. It was a zero-gravity obstacle course, we'd make hoops and secure them to walls, then get a mobility unit, you know, compressed air?" Trace nodded. "And zoom around the place, trying to get the fastest time while going through all the hoops."

"The human kids have different versions," said Trace. "There's one called splat ball, which is the same thing except kids will get rubber balls and try to hit the ones on the obstacle course on the way through."

Tano laughed. "We had that too. If you got hit on a target on your chest or back you were eliminated, so you had to block all the incoming balls as well as adjust your course." Trace could imagine corbi kids being amazing at it. She'd seen them climbing in trees, swinging and changing direction in the blink of an eye. Their eye for rapid trajectory changes was amazing. Likely corbi would make great starship pilots too, as a species.

"The human kids only play that in big indoor spaces," Trace said suggestively. "Like a space station hub."

Tano sighed. "I can't talk about that."

"I know. You've got secret facilities out there somewhere, where the kids are raised. Humans did the same against the krim."

"I really can't talk about it," Tano insisted. "It's our biggest secret."

"I know. Do you have a suicide pill?" For a long moment, Tano didn't reply. "I need to know, Tano. In command, I need to know all these things."

"Yes," Tano finally admitted.

"All of your Fleet people?"

"No, just the ones who know where those facilities are. Me, Dreja, and ten others. I'll give you their names later so you can memorise."

Trace nodded slowly. So the Resistance Fleet weren't sourcing the majority of their new recruits from those child-rearing facilities. Humanity's Lifeboat program had increased population numbers ten fold in just a few generations, but it had been assisted by chah'nas resources. The corbi had nothing remotely similar, and this entire region of space was far more dangerous. If the reeh found such a child-rearing colony, they'd kill it, or worse. The possibilities were too awful to contemplate, but when one was in Tano's position, one had no choice but to contemplate it every day.

"I can't begin to describe," Tano said with careful malice, "just how much I hate them. You're a very controlled person. Do you understand that kind of hatred?"

"Once," Trace admitted. "When I was younger. But the hatred makes it difficult to think. I used it for motivation back then, to achieve a purpose. But to achieve the purpose properly, you need a clear mind. And also, our greatest enemies — our *true* enemies — have been extinct for a thousand years. The tavalai were always hard to hate. Some managed it, but those were always the people with too much emotion and not enough brains. Officers like that are dangerous, they got their people killed. I didn't want to be like them."

"That makes sense. I envy you that. But not everyone can be disciplined like you. I need the hatred. It gets me out of bed every morning. It makes me come down to this awful, insect-ridden, backward hell of a planet. I want to hurt them. I want it more than I want to live. Does that make sense?"

"How many close family have you lost to them?" Trace asked.

Tano looked at her, and for the first time she saw the deep, burning emotion in those wide, alien eyes. "Billions," he pronounced, with slow, careful meaning. Trace gazed away, across the ruined former city, now covered by a carpet of green, and understood. She hadn't suspected such deep, burning patriotism from Tano, most of the time he was too calm and analytical. But now, these things were good to know. In the face of what was coming.

"What do you think of our chances?" Tano asked her after a long moment.

"Of mission success? Quite good, as these things go."

"And what of our casualties?"

"Very high," Trace said somberly. She didn't need to elaborate. Tano was a very clever man, and though not a natural ground soldier, he'd been doing this sort of thing a long time. He'd never actually told her his age, but Trace suspected it was somewhere nearer to eighty, given that Fleet corbi still used life-extension treatments. Most of the ground population had stopped that many centuries ago.

"And among the prisoners that Bega wants to let free?" Tano persisted.

"Very high," Trace repeated. 'The stone shall want for nothing. Be the stone.'

Tano took a deep breath. "There have been many rebellions against the Reeh Empire," he said. "Across many thousands of years. Many attempts have been made to learn the secrets of the reeh's genetic technology. There have been some very partial successes, but nothing on the scale of what we're attempting. No one understands this stuff like the reeh do. They might have borrowed their computer tech from Spiral AIs, but the genetic tech is all reeh."

"The machines never cared much about genetics," Trace agreed.

"They're easily smart enough, but it just wasn't a high priority for them. Even under the drysines, who were the only group to take any non-destructive interest in organics."

"Which makes this the best chance that anyone's had in millennia," said Tano. "Anywhere in the Reeh Empire. We can steal it, and your Styx can decode it. Whatever the casualties, it's worth it."

* * *

Kono was securing the various traps and tripwires of the makeshift assault course through the bowels of the grandstand when he heard a commotion echoing down the halls. He shouldered his rifle and went, past tired corbi swaggering in their gear, under the barricade tape across a doorway that marked the course perimeter, then into the garage assembly beyond. Or he assumed it had once been a garage — a large concrete expanse with big openings where roller doors had once descended to admit large vehicles. Now those doorways were open to the late evening, well shielded by trees, and kept clear of activity in case of aerial surveillance viewing on a downward angle.

Against the inner wall were rows of crates and boxes for weapons and other equipment. Across the floor's broad middle space, tables had been assembled with gas cookers for the preparation of food for two hundred hungry soldiers. The gas fires in an open room made a negligible impact on the room's temperature, and presented no visible gases that could be detected from a distance. Corbi cooked or collected meals on tin plates, but others turned to observe an argument.

A women was shouting, somewhat hysterically, her Lisha too rapid for Kono to make sense of. Clearly she was no soldier — she was older, her mane dishevelled, her clothes plain and dirty. Her hands waved as she shouted, and there confronting her, predictably, was Pena, trying to calm her, and pull her away from the restricted zone before the open doors.

Kono approached, warily eyeing the space outside, where sun fell pleasantly beyond the shade of the trees that guarded the entrance. Beyond that shade, among tree roots and undergrowth, lay the remains of the city that had once been. It had been called Shobe Shan, Kono had learned, one of thousands like it on Rando. This had been a middle suburb, not far from the tall towers of the center. He'd been out a few times at night on perimeter duty, and found a depression that had once been a rail station, servicing the stadium — its function only obvious from the portion of tunnel arch still visible above the infilling forest floor, making perhaps fifty centimetres of cave in which various critters doubtless lived.

"I demand you stop!" the woman was shouting, eyes wide, indicating all of them. "I demand you stop! I demand you stop!"

"Mother, we can't stop," Pena tried to insert calmly amidst the shouting. "Mother... mother, please listen to me." It obviously was not Pena's mother, Kono thought — Pen's mother lived far from here, and from Pena's tales was a far calmer and more rational person than this. Pena was simply speaking a term of respect for an elder woman.

"Go back to your hole!" someone else shouted scornfully. "Go and lick the reeh's boots!"

And now the woman was staring at Kono and recoiling into the restricted zone as though death itself approached. "You!" The accusation was addressed more at the corbi than at Kono. "You conspire with these devils? You're going to get us all killed, do you hear me? Whatever you hit, the reeh will retaliate, they'll kill us all!"

"Pen?" Kono asked, as someone else took over arguing with the wild lady. "Where did she come from?"

"Out there," Pena said exasperatedly, waving a hand at the forbidden outdoors. "We'll be lucky if she didn't give us away."

"I think it'd take more than one corbi to do that," said Kono, as the shouting continued between others. "You realise we can't let her go? If she goes telling others that we're here, and gets another bunch of corbi as upset as she is..."

"I know," Pena said tiredly. She glanced back at the commotion. Kirsi had taken over, and with some strong men were making to escort the lady somewhere. Kono thought she was lucky that she didn't just get a bullet in the head. Some places would. But the Resistance retained this romantic ideal of themselves as the 'people's army', and thus trained in places like this that remained accessible to those people. He was surprised it had taken this long for one of the people who disagreed with the whole prospect of attacking the reeh to intervene.

Kono walked with her to one of the food tables, to join a short queue. "She's right you know," said Pena.

"How?"

"That the reeh will kill some enormous number of innocent corbi if we do this." Pena sounded deflated. That wasn't like her. "In retaliation."

"No, they'll blame *Phoenix*."

Pena gave him a weary look — a long way up, for her. Pretty eyes, behind those old spectacles. "Don't be dumb, Giddy. Retaliation is how the reeh control this world. They'll kill lots of us whether they think ordinary people were responsible or not."

"If they'll kill lots of you no matter what you do," Kono responded, "then you've got nothing to lose." He said it with more confidence than he felt. It sounded like the kind of rote, predictable thing human Fleet always said during the war when doing something aggressive and attempting to justify the enormous cost. In most of Kono's time in service, the cost had indeed been worth it, but that didn't mean he couldn't know a dangerous habit when he saw one.

"Easy for you to say," Pena retorted. "These aren't your people." But she put her hand on his arm as she said it, to take the edge off her words.

"Hey, Pen. You ever thought about Fleet?"

"Yeah. I'm a planet-girl, Giddy. I like trees and sun. And this is my home." She sounded despondent, Kono thought. That was no attitude for someone to have, given what was coming. And he liked this kind, smart alien girl enough already that it disturbed him to think of what she'd be facing, in the Splicer. He at least was properly trained for it, and had knew what a full-blown firefight looked like. Pena had shown courage and skill in small-scale actions, but the Splicer wasn't going to be anything like that.

He took her hand. "And this world will need someone to speak for it, among humans, and maybe among tavalai. You've heard the Major talk about the tavalai free worlds?"

Pena gazed at him. "I'm not sure I'd want to live there even if I could get there."

"But some of the corbi will," Kono persisted. "And if those corbi can find a way to survive, they'd need a person to speak for them, with humans and maybe tavalai too. I think that person should be you."

"Me? Go on *Phoenix*?" She looked astonished.

"Would you think about it? You're smart and you talk well, and people like you. We've got lots of aliens onboard already, most of them even stranger than you."

"Well thanks."

Kono smiled, an uncommon expression for him. "What do you think? I can't promise it would be any safer than here, in fact probably it won't. But I can promise it would make a difference, it would never be boring, and you'd never be lonely. *Phoenix* is a family."

Pena looked up at him, and smiled broadly. "You're very sweet, Giddy. I'll think about it."

16

Ju'rig's main road was a dusty mass of vehicles, buildings and crowds of spectators. The hover train of the Shur'do Kon'do Rey'kan, as the networks were calling it, idled and throbbed down the road, erected flags now fanning outward like the oars of some great old boat as it entered harbour, draping colours over the onlookers, some of whom reached up to touch.

Erik had the right-side window down, and sat half-out to raise a fist to the crowd, croma-style. The crowd raised fists in return, and local authorities wandered on foot, or rode simple motorbikes to cruise alongside and keep over-enthusiastic well-wishers or trophy-hunters away. Here and there by the roadside, standing before the main crush of the crowd, were medieval warriors in full armour wielding hammers, clubs or some other brutal, stylised weapon.

"*Reserves,*" said Rhi'shul on coms when he asked. "*Each allied clan sends its primary force of warriors, and then there are reserves who are not needed immediately on the field. Often they wander towns with their big egos and cause trouble.*"

Rhi'shul sat inside the cabin, having no interest in showing her face outside. Erik wondered if her own institution, the Dan'gede, even knew she was gone, or what she was up to... either way, she wasn't about to advertise her presence here. Sasalaka drove with calm concentration, lateral stability controls dialled up to maximum at these crawlingly low speeds, determined not to cause an embarrassment with an uncontrollable sideslip that sent the crowd scattering.

Human and tavalai crew, spacers and marines, sat further along the engine's chassis, the marines prominently armed but all raising fists to the crowd. Some of the crew threw decorative wrist bands; they'd stopped at a roadside stall, at Rhi'shul's suggestion, and bought the whole lot on sale. These were traditional at ceremonial events, made from simple twine with colours and knots that meant things that no human save Romki had managed to understand.

"Seems pretty enthusiastic," Jalawi suggested, taking a knee above the idling turbine intake, as much to ensure they didn't run anyone over as to lead the greetings.

"Always seems that way right before someone tries to kill us," said Kaspowitz, who was sitting on top of the trailer, and reporting on the great mass of ground vehicles that were following their dusty trail up the road.

Ju'rig's buildings were mostly low and flat, made of compressed clay but sprouting all the best high-tech panels and coms gear in rooftop clusters. In the desert heat, Erik guessed, all the best technology still couldn't provide a more cost-effective insulator than clay. Up in the cockpit, he was eye-level with the second-storey rooftops, and could see the great spires of temples looming from random points across the mostly low-rise town. Ju'rig was known for being a temple town, in that way of croma who had no fixed religious denominations save for their never-ending love of collective defence, clan rivalry and glory against the odds. It was a world-view that encompassed everything, particularly in light of the existential threat presented by the reeh. Erik wondered if croma culture would look different if the reeh didn't exist, or if the croma had had friendlier neighbours. They'd already been at war against the chah'nas in the early days of the Chah'nas Empire, and it didn't take an enormous imagination to see them finding reasons to fight the tavalai — the other most stubborn species in the Spiral. Perhaps the reeh served an unlikely positive purpose, in that they'd kept the croma facing away from the Spiral for many millennia, distracted with more dangerous affairs.

At the outskirts of town were a run-down jumble of warehouses, repair shops and junk yards, and Sasalaka increased speed a little as the crowds thinned. Authority motorbikes led them onto the desert hillside beyond the perimeter, where great stone mesas loomed like ancient chimneys, and vehicles gathered in clusters like herds of migrating animals. Sasalaka engaged the turbine once more at the lowest revs, as the crew on the engine's long bonnet put on heavy goggles in the wind and sand, but made no attempt to head inside.

Vehicles were driving alongside them now, some with spectators seeking a closer look, others perhaps official, a few with camera mounts, many with identifying decorations that Erik could not guess the meaning of. Airborne drones followed, like a swarm of flies, and on several main screen insets Erik could see images of the rig, black and white with flags flying in the streaming dust.

They headed for the base of the nearest and largest mesa, and already Erik could see signs of fortification — battlements guarding a ground-level entrance, and several large walls filling holes in the side of the cliff. Atop the high mesa, bright flags flew.

"Stu'cha," said Rhi'shul, peering up through the windshield. *"The Ju'rig Stu'cha is famous."*

"It's a temple?" Erik asked.

"Stu'cha means the order and the temple. It dates from the Great Exclusion."

The translator gave Erik the English version. The Great Exclusion, a time seven thousand years ago when Clan Croma'Rai's primary ancestor clan had been found to have violated some central croma rule and banished from spacefaring civilisation for five hundred years as punishment. The other clans had destroyed their spaceports and spacefaring industries, and occupied their orbital stations, leaving the Croma'Rai with just a single planet on which to occupy themselves for a full half-millennia.

Croma'Rai had responded by turning a punishment into a blessing, building great fortifications and temples, and turning the world of Dul'rho into more a reflection of homeworld antiquity than the croma homeworld itself. In these new-but-old buildings, Croma'Rai had resurrected many traditions once lost, and put themselves back in touch with the old ways that all croma valued, yet many had forgotten the true nature of. To hear many Croma'Rai tell it, that period had been the time that made the modern Croma'Rai what they were today, building a strong foundation upon which to support them into the future.

"So that's why this place is so important for the Tali'san?" Geish wondered, looking away from this scan display to peer at the giant tower of rock.

"If the Croma'Rai are to restore their honour," Rhi'shul said grimly, *"this is a good place to start."* Erik glanced at her. As Croma'Rai herself, this couldn't have been easy.

Their escort brought them to within five hundred metres of the mesa's base amid a great cluster of parked vehicles, assorted tents and caravans. A great desert camp, as the engines finally powered down, and the rig's skids came to rest on hard-packed sands and low scrub. The crew busied themselves immediately, spacers locking down the rig's systems and checking that the repairs and modifications were holding, while marines established a non-hostile perimeter and familiarised themselves with the neighbours.

Erik left them to it, and climbed out his side window, using the foothold there to clamber onto the long bonnet and stand amid the last dust of the engine's settling, and survey the camp. A number of other kondos were obvious — several big rigs like theirs, but considerably more elaborate, with many colours and great, wrap-around girdings like battle armour. Some large tents were erected with balcony platforms, a full storey up to give occupants a view across the clutter and down the shallow, sweeping fall of land from this rise. Amid the tents were parked ground vehicles, flyers and cruisers, and constant traffic dulled the air in a haze of dust.

Heavy footsteps thudded on the bonnet, and Erik looked to find

Rhi'shul strolling to him, goggles on and the leather hood of her jacket pulled over her head.

"Tali'san camp's over there," said Rhi'shul, pointing to a further encampment on the mesa's far side. *"The Croma'Rai warriors prepare. Croma'Dokran are down here,"* pointing down the hillslope, where another tent city sprawled upon the sand. She took a deep breath. *"Difficult to believe that I'm actually here."*

"Who can come?" Erik asked. "Given that all croma seem to want to come, and not everyone can."

"Not all want to come." Rhi'shul gave a gesture that might have been a shrug. *"Some reject it, say it's bloodthirsty and stupid. But most find croma nature difficult to ignore. Like it or not, this is what we are."*

"I can't say I like it myself," Erik murmured, gazing across the chaotic scene. From several locations near and distant, drums were beating. "But having seen the scale of it, I've no idea how you'd go about stopping it if you were opposed to it."

"The rules on who comes are simple enough," said Rhi'shul. *"All locals in the hosting town, obviously. Then there is a lottery, for the fortunate who apply. Then there is an administration that people can contact, to put forward their case for worthiness. Some who are chosen are clearly worthy, others not."*

"Let me guess," said Erik. "Lots of wealthy and powerful people are allowed instead of the ordinary people who'd appreciate it more. The same way that Do'reg can't bring his hammer without our help, while a bunch of others with money but less cause can come."

Rhi'shul looked down at him from behind her goggles. *"It's the same in human space, it seems."*

"My family is wealthy. We've had this conversation many times around our dinner table."

"Perhaps we'd all be better off without wealthy leaders."

Erik smiled. "Yes, but then you've got the sard. No VIPs, no one's special so everyone's equally expendable. My father always said that the only thing worse than a hierarchical society was a non-hierarchical one. Absolute equality is always tyrannical."

"The reeh are quite equal," Rhi'shul agreed. She pointed at the tent

with the big balcony. *"This one is Croma'Kartum leadership, I think. They're allies of Croma'Rai. The parking here separates all the Tali'san warriors, but not the observers. Among these tents will be many unfriendly."*

About the rig, croma were gathering to stare and talk. Drones hovered, cameras levelled, and several more authority motorbikes pulled up, croma climbing off and putting their arms out to keep the crowds at bay. Erik didn't think there was much threat in it, yet. Most of this attention was just curiosity.

"What happens if you're identified?" he asked Rhi'shul.

"Best that I'm not," said Rhi'shul. *"But Do'reg is here, and there should be other croma on his Kon'do."* She pointed beyond the crowd, between tents. *"Here come the Stu'cha."*

The new arrivals were led by a huge croma who walked with twin sticks to support the weight of his arms. Several more beside him were nearly as large, and of the main ten, Erik did not think there was one shorter than two hundred and thirty centimetres. They wore robes and leathers, and some carried staves or pole arms, as much for symbolic authority as an actual threat. Younger, smaller croma walked alongside, and threw white powder at the party's feet. Salt, Erik thought. Perhaps to purify the ground?

"Tell Do'reg that the Stu'cha are here," said Rhi'shul, urgently. *"He needs to meet them."*

Below on his right, Erik saw Do'reg already walking forward, escorted by marines. He pointed, for Rhi'shul's benefit.

Do'reg wore a light shirt and pants, more suited for the hot desert than the city folk's preference for leathers, and carried his family's hammer on his broad shoulder. The marines with him were tavalai — Sergeant Jinido and his Second Section. They walked to confront the approaching Stu'cha, and Do'reg stopped, and put the hammer end-down on the sand, hands folded on the hilt.

Authorities rushed to keep the crowds a good distance from Do'reg and the tavalai, and to keep the space opposite clear for the arriving Stu'cha. Ahead on the bonnet's end, Erik saw Jalawi standing with his rifle in hand, talking to coms as he gave instructions to human and tavalai marines alike.

"Guns don't look good at the Tali'san," Rhi'shul warned him. *"This is a place to return to the old ways."*

"They're not *our* ways," Erik corrected her.

"They became your ways when you agreed to go on the Kon'do Rey'kan," Rhi'shul growled. *"No one is forcing you. Insincerity will not be tolerated."*

Erik exhaled hard. She made sense. "Croma'Rai's leadership used guns and roadside bombs on us just now."

"You were not on the Kon'do then. You only came onto the Kon'do to avoid further guns and bombs. It doesn't look good."

"Hey, you thought this was a good idea back in Jo'Tukra."

"I thought it was our best chance to get to Stat'cha alive," Rhi'shul replied. *"I still think so. But holding guns in a Tali'san looks bad, and will anger some."*

"I don't suppose there are any human-sized melee weapons we could borrow?"

"Perhaps," said Rhi'shul. *"For training the children."* The backhander was predictable, Erik thought. *"I will ask."*

"Who will you ask?"

"The Dan'gede know some people here."

Of course, thought Erik. "The Dan'gede are Croma'Rai law enforcement. Whose side are they on?"

Rhi'shul gave him an imperious stare. *"You've been here a long time, human, yet you understand nothing."* She strolled to the hand-holds past the cockpit's side and swung easily down to the ground.

"Captain," said Styx in his ear. *"I have some potentially useful information about Rhi'shul."*

"Go ahead, Styx." The Stu'cha were now arriving before Do'reg. Some of the smaller, younger croma performed some kind of ceremony while the huge priestly class examined the marginally smaller Do'reg with grim appraisal.

"Rhi'shul is middle-ranking within the Dan'gede, as you know. But examination of her personal record reveals an operative very much dedi-

cated to Croma'Rai's advancement. Before the Dan'gede she was in a military youth brigade, where she rose as a child to become the highest-ranked in her cohort. Forgive me if these terminologies are imprecise — the institutions of organic civilisation always seem vague to me, in purpose and psychology. The translator is no help."

"I understand, Styx."

"After the youth brigade she was in the military, with what appears to be every intention of becoming a croma marine. But her specialities sidelined her into Intelligence, where she again received a number of awards for going above and beyond the call of duty, as I believe is the human expression. Her military intelligence work laid the grounds for her rise in the Dan'gede, where again, her record is exemplary. Many times the Dan'gede have called upon her to present special awards, or to give speeches in important functions. The impression that emerges, as far as one can analyse the croma mind, is one of a Croma'Rai patriot. And just now, monitoring your communication with her, I detected elevated levels of vocal stress."

"She's served them all her life," said Erik, watching the ceremony proceeding. "And now they've betrayed her. She thinks she's going to find out just how badly they betrayed her in the Assessment Council at Stat'cha. And being here, and seeing the Croma'Rai fighting to regain their dignity... well, it must be hard."

"Croma'Rai Tali'san forces at your location appear to outnumber Croma'Dokran," Styx disagreed. *"At other locations it is worse."*

"I'll keep an eye on her," said Erik, hearing Styx's caution. "The croma value loyalty even more strongly than humans do, and Rhi'shul holds her leaders responsible for betraying everything she believed. For now, I think we can trust her."

"I am very glad that your analytical capabilities on matters of organic psychology and intentions are superior to mine, Captain."

Erik smiled, not believing her for a second. "My sisters would find that assessment amusing."

"Why would they find it amusing, Captain?"

Erik wondered how to explain inter-sibling squabbles to the drysine former Fleet Commander. On the desert clearing, the ceremony had ended. "Never mind. The religious guys are talking to Do'reg."

It wasn't much of a conversation. The biggest of them wandered in a slow circle around Do'reg, taking each step with a pole support like a cross-country skier in slow motion. Do'reg stood straight and still before them, as a holographic projector displayed a great tree of lines and branches in the desert air. Lineage, Erik guessed, as various Stu'cha peered at it, and rumbled amongst themselves, indicating this line and that with their staves. Several more ignored the lineage tree and stared instead at the big rig, and up at Erik and the crew standing atop it, symbolic red and gold flags falling about, now flapping in a desert breeze.

The biggest croma finished his circle of Do'reg, and conferred with the others. Then he drew himself up, and made a vast, sharp gesture with one hand — alarmingly fast for such a large croma. If all the big ones in the Tali'san could move so fast with weapons in hand, the injuries inflicted would be catastrophic.

Do'reg bristled, pointed at the larger croma's face and lofted his hammer. Several more Stu'cha jostled forward, wielding great shields that had to be the best part of three metres tall. Again, Erik's coms opened.

"*Captain,*" came Romki's urgent voice. "*I think something's gone wrong.*"

"Could just be a part of the ceremony, Stan," said Erik. "Hold tight."

The shields were planted in the sand before the largest croma, and Do'reg wound up for an enormous swing. The hammer landed with as much power as Erik had feared, a resounding crash that jolted the shield wall and echoed across the entire camp. Do'reg pulled back for another blow, this time from the reverse side, and a shield on the end took full force, its wielder jolted to his knees and losing balance, clutching to the shield for support.

The other two shields parted, while the third remained down, the fallen croma slow to rise. Do'reg stood glaring at them all, shoulders heaving, while yet another Stu'cha came to inspect Do'reg's hammer.

Erik doubted there'd be so much as a scratch on it. The fallen croma finally stood, unassisted by others, and switched hands to carry his shield back with the opposite hand. His shield arm was dangling, though he showed no pain.

"Broken, I think," remarked Jalawi. *"Our boy Do'reg hits hard."*

"I don't think even my karasai armour would enjoy that," Karajin added, observing from somewhere on the ground.

The big croma made another dismissive gesture, and the holography was turned off. Another of the Stu'cha who had been walking up the train's side now picked up a stone and tossed it at the side. It struck not far below where Erik was standing, and fell to the ground.

"Steady," Erik told his people, calmly. "He's being an asshole. Let's not shoot him for it."

"Yeah, wouldn't recommend throwing one back," Jalawi agreed. *"He'd barely feel it."*

The rock throwing croma strolled back to his group, who were now departing. Do'reg put the hammer on his shoulder and stood defiant as camera drones circled, and local authorities held back increasing crowds of onlookers. First to Do'reg's side as the Stu'cha abandoned him was Romki — only a middle-sized man, but suddenly frail and small beside the croma warrior and his human-sized hammer. Conversation followed, Do'reg somber and defiant.

"Captain," Romki reported on coms, sounding worried. *"The Stu'cha have rejected this Kon'do Rey'kan. They refuse to put their blessings upon it... the exact terminology escapes me. But they remain the preeminent authority over this part of the Tali'san campaign, and they tell us we're not welcome here."*

"That's fine, Stan," said Erik, repressing frustration with difficulty. They'd gone to a lot of effort over the last few days to make this thing work. Various croma had assured him it would. "What does that mean?"

"I'm... not at all certain, Captain. I don't think the Stu'cha can kick us out, the worthiness of various Kon'dos are decided more in the court of public opinion anyway..."

"Put Do'reg on. Do we even have him on coms?" He waited, as

Romki handed Do'reg a small earpiece and mic, comically small on a big croma head. "Do'reg, can you hear me? It's the Captain."

"*Captain*," said Do'reg, short breaths coming hard. Erik didn't think it was all physical exertion.

"What did they say? Are we in danger?"

"*Don't accept family heritage,*" Do'reg said heavily. "*Family line not clear enough.*"

Erik frowned. "That's ridiculous. Croma family trees aren't much different from human, I've looked at it and it's obvious who you come from." As a Debogande, he was more familiar with such matters than most.

"*Heritage not accepted,*" Do'reg repeated, with typically croma bluntness. "*Croma thing. Complicated.*"

Great, Erik thought, rolling his eyes. "Are we in danger?"

"*Not sure. They say we should leave. Could be dangerous, don't know.*"

Do'reg, Erik had to remind himself, was a simple guy who ran an orchard and repair workshop by a major highway. Expecting the level of analysis he got from the likes of Romki, Shilu, Styx or Lisbeth was unfair. "Well we're not leaving. Sho'mo'ra said fame was our friend, which I'm taking to mean that popular opinion could overrule the Stu'cha's opinion. How about we talk to some of these people with cameras, and tell them your family story?"

THERE WAS NOTHING IN THE CRAMPED KITCHEN AGAIN, SAVE FOR SOME of the dry bread rolls the croma liked, but Tiga hated. She searched storage units and clambered on the bench to get at the high ones, but there was no fruit, not even dried fruit, and no meat save for the processed crap in the rolls, and Skah's supply of various tasty meats. She couldn't touch that, though, because then Skah would have nothing. She was trying to save her personal corner of the galaxy, surely someone could at least make an effort to keep food in the kitchen?

Tiga took a roll, grumpily, and retreated back up the narrow

corridor to her little room. The air in the trailer was stifling, the ventilation turned way down now that they'd stopped and most of the crew
were outside in the evening. A brief check of coms revealed a number
of them enjoying the sunset, and others given permission to wander in
groups through the camp. Despite events with Do'reg, the Captain
didn't seem to think they were in immediate danger, and was out
doing interviews with croma media — him and Do'reg, the oddest
couple to have appeared on Dul'rho screens for many years. One artic-
ulate and smart, the other croma, and carrying a hammer. Fittingly.

Tiga clambered back up to her bunk once more, amid display
screens, AR glasses and the portable holographics unit she'd
borrowed from the ranch, but forgotten who it belonged to. Her back-
side ached, and she desperately needed fresh air... but out there in
the air were more croma than she could deal with right now. And
Skah, who wasn't talking to her... nor she him, she supposed. And
then it made her sad, and she just stared at the ceiling for several long
moments, trying to think on the terrible events of the defence of
Rando all those centuries ago that had dominated her brain for the
past three months. If she went outside she'd be neglecting this, too —
potentially the salvation of her people, at least if what the Captain
said of Sho'mo'ra's intentions were true. Which she doubted, but she
had to try.

But suddenly that was just an excuse, and she knew it. Neglecting
her monumental duties wasn't the reason she was sad. She was sad
because she was miserable, stuck in this little room after previously
being stuck in a library, with literally all the weight of her world on
her shoulders. Worst of all, she was thinking of Do'Ran and her
parents, which she'd sworn she'd never do once she'd left, because
that way lay doom. She'd hated the pretty green cage on Do'Ran that
the Croma'Dokran had forced her to live in, but now she could only
think of evenings spent reading before the log fire in her parent's
apartment, and her father's cooking, and her mother's conversations
while knitting the long winter scarves she was so good at, and riding
her chu out across the reservation lands, and the misty view across

the hills as the low clouds skidded in, that she thought she'd never miss this much...

And then she was crying. The greatest burden in all the galaxy upon her, and important work that desperately needed to be done, but she couldn't stop, just hugged her legs to her body and sobbed with the sorrow of a lost soul who knew that the loneliness would never end.

* * *

SKAH STOOD OUT ON THE EDGE OF THE BONFIRE'S LIGHT, AND STARED awestruck at the line of armoured chew'toos meandering past the camp outskirts. They were huge, ponderous creatures, four-legged with thick tails, wide heads and twin horns that more than doubled the weight of their skulls, wrapping about their cheeks like side-armour and ending just before their mouths. Atop each chew'too was an armoured gondola in which rode croma warriors. This procession held at least twenty animals, an extraordinary sight beneath the silver desert moon, lumbering in slow-motion silhouette.

He recalled the meat kebab in his hand and ate. The air around these perimeter bonfires was filled with the smell of delicious food, and crowds of croma stood here, some warriors but mostly civilians come to witness the event, and eat, and look across the wide, sloping desert to the Tali'san camps and the nighttime manoeuvres of warriors and mounts. Skah had asked many if there was going to be a battle tomorrow, but they professed not to know. Many had shown more interest in him than the upcoming battle, never having seen a kuhsi before in person. That was becoming predictable, and wasn't so bad really — croma didn't touch and prod, and respected even a very young kuhsi's personal space. Besides which, Corporal Graf was here to protect him with her section — Gonzo, Bernie and Sheep... or that was what they called each other, their real names were Gonzaga, Berloc and Ram. Graf was called 'Eggs', but her actual first name was Lani. Skah had lived with humans for more than a year now, but still wasn't really sure how all the names worked.

"I didn't realise how big they were," Gonzo admitted, eating his own kebab. He was a squat, broad guy with thick brows and strong arms. "Wouldn't want to get stuck with stable duty. Can you imagine the shit?"

"It's like a history documentary," said Sheep, incredulous. "Look at the detail on those carriage-thingys."

"Gondolas," said Gonzo.

"Whatever."

"Still don't know what it's supposed to prove."

"They win the battuw to show who's in charge," Skah explained. "This is one battuw, that wins one seat, the cwan with the nost seats gets to be in charge."

"Yeah I know that Furball," said Gonzo. "I just mean they could do it another way. Like voting."

"They're crona," said Skah, with a big shrug. "Crona don't vote, they fight." Elsewhere across the camp, drums were pounding. Modern croma music was more electronic than this, but out here they did everything the old way, including cooking on open fires. Skah liked it. Every day he spent among the croma, he liked them more and more. Croma were brave and loyal and did what they said they'd do, with no lying or messing about. It was like an entire civilisation of *Phoenix* marines, only bigger.

"Awful waste," said Eggs, eating somberly. Skah didn't think she liked it here as much as the others did.

"Dunno how many chew'toos are going to die," said Sheep. "They look pretty hard to kill."

"That guy facing off against Do'reg could do it with a single hit," Eggs disagreed. "You see the big loading vehicles out back? Looks about the size to be hauling chew'too bodies, I think."

"Only a few die," Skah scoffed. "Tali'san cas... casu-awties awways smaw."

Eggs snorted. "I've been in fights with small casualties, Skah. Amazing how many good people die in them."

From behind them came shouts, and at first Skah thought they were something to do with the celebrations. The marines kept watching the chew'toos and talking, and he recalled that human hearing wasn't as good as kuhsi. Then he heard a crash, like something getting knocked over.

"What's that?" he demanded, looking back but unable to see past the tall croma around him. Shouts escalated, and now the marines were looking, Eggs with a hand to her ear indicating she was receiving a message. Skah charged clear of the group to get a view.

"What...?" as Eggs noticed him leaving. "No wait, Skah!"

He dashed and darted past croma legs, and finally reached a clear spot where he could see back into the camp... and there were flares soaring into the sky. Then an explosion, on the far side of the camp, and something else beginning to burn. That wasn't supposed to happen. And then he saw them — hulking shapes, twin forward-protruding horns, silhouetted against the campfires and artificial lights as they charged through the camp, uprooting tents and sending trailers crashing aside. And right in their path, past the flying flags and support poles of other encampments, was the big *Phoenix* hover train.

Skah took off sprinting, to the curses of marines behind him who had nearly caught up. He knew he was fast by human standards, but when both speed *and* agility were required, they had little hope of catching him in their armour. He dashed past tents, leaping guide ropes and darting past the adult bodies that were now running and standing out in the open to look. A group of big, armoured croma were running toward the commotion as he was, but so slowly in the confined alleys that he had to flash past their legs like a mouse escaping elephants. Being faster than the humans meant he had a responsibility to get there faster, and Eggs would be in no doubt of where he was going.

Past a big wheeled vehicle with a tent attached to one side, and he burst upon a mob of croma wrestling with a chew'too, and nearly fell over with shock at the size and violence of it. Croma had its harness, the big leather and rope lines of which were dangling free, and were hauling their considerable combined weight against the animal. The chew'too bellowed and reared, pulling multiple big croma clean off the ground and dashing them on the sands, only for others to leap in with reckless disregard for safety. The chew'too trampled a tent as it turned and thrashed, huge feet entangling in the fabric and support ropes.

Skah realised there'd be no passage that way, and ducked to one side, dodging more croma rushing in to help, and a team of smaller croma hauling what looked like firefighting gear in the other direction. Crashing and yelling made him look up, then he stopped and reversed by the sound alone, just seconds before the caravan he'd been about to run past was hit by some huge force, and went rolling over like a child's toy.

A chew'too thundered over and past it, spinning it around, hitting one croma and sending him flying. Others chased, some with huge hooks on poles, while more fired flares at it. So *that* was where the flares were coming from. Probably the chew'toos were scared of flares and would run from them, allowing the croma to steer them... but it didn't seem to be working. Past the shock, Skah was a little surprised that chew'toos weren't simply getting shot. But these were croma, who welcomed a challenge and never did things the easy way.

Suddenly he was laughing. He knew it wasn't right, but the whole situation was crazy — croma were getting hurt but clearly a lot of them were loving it too, wrestling a herd of out-of-control war chew'-toos was like some idea of fun to them. Skah had heard his mother speak of this, too — hekgarh, the warrior's fear, and that some kuhsi warriors laughed in battle. Well, if that was what this was, it was a welcome thing. He'd been a helpless little boy among warriors for long enough, and here, finally, he'd found a dangerous situation he was actually good at.

The next chew'too he saw had actually been upended by a mob of croma who were rapidly tying new tethers around its horns and pulling tight to keep its head on the ground as it bellowed and fought. But this was right beside a big tent he recognised, and he knew how to get back to the train from here.

He hadn't run far until the way was blocked by thick smoke. There was quite a bit of smoke elsewhere in the camp, most of it from cooking apparatus that had overturned and caught fire. But this smoke was more grey and white than the black of a flammable liquids fire. It stung his eyes and made him cough, so he backed out enough to fish his sand goggles from a pocket and fasten them over his eyes. Then he pulled his shirt up over his mouth, took a deep breath, and ran.

Immediately in the smoke he found the train trailer, turned onto its side, Kon'do flags sprawled in the sand. And here by the rear was Karajin, half-carrying an unconscious tavalai marine. He saw Skah, and shouted in slurred Togiri. *"Skah, it's a sleeping gas! Get out now!"*

The gas was bitter and unpleasant, but Skah didn't feel sleepy. But explaining to Karajin would waste his air, so he ran past, found the trailer's rooftop cruiser on its back having rolled off on the sand, and went into the trailer's top hatchway. Inside the corridors the gas should be less, he thought, fanning the air furiously before him with his free hand, then risked another gasp of air as his lungs began to burn with the effort of holding his breath. No, he decided — still not tired. Maybe the gas didn't work on kuhsi.

Moving down corridors with the trailer overturned was strange, but after living most of the last year-and-more in space, he was used to that kind of disorientation. He passed a tavalai spacer in a face-mask helping a human spacer, both upright and struggling through the white haze... Skah wanted to get someone to come and help them, but the headset mic on his earpiece only worked for transla-tions and local coms, the adults hadn't wanted to give him the ability to call officers because officers were too busy to put up with his questions.

He squeezed past the spacers, figuring there could be people who needed help far more, and ducked down the stairs, which were now a right-hand turn, then came to a right-hand turn that required him to climb, but that was easy enough, and he grabbed handholds on door frames and exposed pipes that ran along corridor walls until he got to the higher level and hauled himself over it. There was less gas here, the air visibly cleaner, yet here on the floor that was usually the left-hand wall lay Petty Officer Gupta, bleeding from the back of her head, face down and unconscious.

Skah rushed to her, rolling her onto her side with difficulty and checking her airways as many first-aid lessons had shown him... it wasn't easy, Petty Officer Gupta was a grown woman, and much bigger than him. She must have been flung against a wall when the trailer had overturned — clearly a chew'too had charged into it to knock it over. That was when Skah noticed the armoured glove lying just beyond the Petty Officer. It was big, and clearly made for a croma. Skah had seen croma wandering around camp, taking off their big, heavy gloves when they had to do something fiddly. Something like opening a locked door. So what if Petty Officer Gupta hadn't knocked her head when the trailer had overturned? And what if the croma who'd done it hadn't stopped with her?

Then he realised. "Tiga! TIGA!" He had to go check on her, but he couldn't abandon Gupta lying on the ground... except that Gupta was stirring now, groaning and feeling for the back of her head. Skah shot off, leaping a door, then arriving at Tiga's room, the doorway to which now made an opening at his feet. He stuck his head in and peered. Tiga's room was empty, her many display screens smashed and strewn about, a few of the paper books she'd accumulated looking as though they'd been torn up by hand. Her bunk was now upended, mattress lying on the far side, sheets across a wall. Of Tiga herself, there was no sign.

17

"It was my fault, Captain," said Jalawi, with no trace of his usual humour. "I had too many of us away from the rig. The defensive deployments were my responsibility."

"Don't care whose fault it was, Rufus," said Erik. "I want to know how to get her back."

They were assembled under a tent canvas torn from a neighbouring camp whose owners were no longer needing it, lit in the dry, yellow glow of the train's side running lights. It fastened to the top of the engine, its far end anchored to the sand, giving *Phoenix* crew some outdoor cover from the surrounding chaos without requiring them to shelter inside, where they'd be at a disadvantage if some new attack came in. Warrant Officer Leung was off looking for a crane she could borrow to get the trailer back upright, while the rest of the Engineering team were inspecting the trailer's damage. Not too bad, was the assessment — the magnetic couplings were designed to separate if the trailer tipped, so nothing had been bent to the point of breaking when it went over.

There were three injured including Petty Officer Gupta, and a few more still dizzy from the gas, which Doc Suelo on *Phoenix* had identified via a molecular sample from Peanut to be an unpleasant anaesthetic that could paralyse all breathing if taken in too high a dose. Erik would have complained to someone, but there was no one to complain to. Several of the croma 'authorities', as was the euphemistic translation for a police force, were now standing guard at the perimeter of the Phoenix train. Those authorities were also supposed to prevent herds of chew'toos from rampaging through camp, and Erik wanted as little to do with them as possible.

"Post action assessment indicates that we made some mistakes," Karajin volunteered, keeping most weight off his left leg, which he'd strained helping some croma pull down a rampaging chew'too. *"The order not to shoot the animals was probably one of them."*

"We can't start shooting in a Tali'san camp," Jalawi retorted in hard temper. "Bullets don't stop with the damn animal, those things are tough and with ricochets you could have taken out a dozen bystanders as well."

"The Captain said we're not going to argue blame here," Sasalaka told Karajin calmly.

The big karasai looked unimpressed. *"Post action analysis is not 'blame'. We analyse to determine strategic position and future actions."*

"And the Captain said we won't do it here," Sasalaka said coolly. "Chain of command is a tavalai value also." Karajin looked even less impressed. Tavalai did things the procedural way, and their command structure was considerably flatter than humans', meaning that lower ranks could more readily challenge the decisions of those higher at the right time and place. Karajin evidently felt that time and place was now. Thankfully Sasalaka was one rare tavalai who could actually read a room full of humans, and now reminded Karajin that this wasn't the tavalai fleet. Professional warrior though he was, Karajin sometimes forgot.

"They knew exactly what they were after," said Erik. He'd been meeting with a group of local elder croma when it happened, and they'd been mysteriously slow to realise what had befallen their camp, and then had advised him not to leave their tent, fearing for his safety. Erik had ignored them, but by the time he'd returned the worst was done. "They knew we probably wouldn't shoot, the gas was

a good choice, and the chew'toos mean the whole thing can be
written off as another Tali'san accident."

He was furious at himself for not seeing it coming. But, as Romki
reminded him often, when wandering in alien places, a human's
predictive capabilities were diminished. Not only were the marines
not prepared to shoot, but none were in full armour, they were
vulnerable to gas and while they remained an unarmed mismatch
against most unaugmented sentient Spiral species, that didn't apply
to croma.

"Well it looked like Stu'cha colours and armour to me,"
Kaspowitz said wearily, sitting on a storage crate, injured arm in a
sling. "I only got a few glimpses through the smoke." Kaspowitz had
been on the engine bridge with Geish, watching Scan and the
unfolding Tali'san manoeuvres out in the dark as opposing sides
placed scouts in preparation for what looked like a fight tomorrow at
dawn. "We nearly had a much worse diplomatic incident than just
killing a few chew'toos. Peanut never budged from the engine the
whole time. If he'd gone in we'd have had a whole bunch of Stu'cha
in little pieces."

"Yeah, and Tiga would still be here," Jalawi retorted.

From back by the trailer, Erik could hear the sound of *Phoenix*
crew repairing what they could with the trailer still on its side. Do'reg
was with them, downcast and upset. *Phoenix* had granted him this
great honour, a chance to show the family name in the greatest
Tali'san in immediate memory, and first the Stu'cha had rejected it in
full view of the whole planet, and now this. Skah... Erik didn't know
where he was. He couldn't keep track of everyone. Surely someone
knew.

"Styx has told Peanut to stay inside and avoid mingling," Erik
explained to Kaspowitz. "Peanut doesn't seem happy with it. But he's
a drone, he does what he's told."

"*Why?*" asked Rhi'shul, standing to one side with arms folded, her
head nearly touching the sloping canopy. "*The planet knows of him,
and Styx. Why continue this false secrecy?*"

Erik said nothing. Humans and tavalai looked at each other.

Romki cleared his throat. "Carrying Tiga to the Stu'cha Temple would be easy. They could just put her... put her in a bag or something." His voice was strained as he said it. Clearly he was upset. "I don't think they'd hurt her — croma like a contest. Whatever their faults, they see no honour in the strong hurting the weak. But neither do they have a problem with the strong simply taking what they want, as we've seen."

"Do we have any legal options?" Erik asked, rubbing his eyes.

"You seriously ask?" Rhi'shul asked, with scornful contempt.

"You!" said Jalawi, pointing finger at her. "Shut it!" Rhi'shul did not reply. Her stare said enough.

"It does not seem so, Captain," said Sasalaka. She looked at Rhi'shul, no doubt thinking that this information would better come from her. Rhi'shul looked in no mood for meek cooperation. "Styx may have ideas." Kaspowitz looked like he wanted to kick sand on the tavalai for saying so.

"Styx is having difficulty establishing communications," said Erik. "She's been in and out of contact since Tiga was snatched, she was linked for long enough to explain that all of Ju'rig's coms network is down. That won't shut down independently-powered com nodes, and she's been hacking into these to establish limited communications, but her bandwidth is well down and many of those independent sources have also been vanishing."

"The Stu'cha are well aware of what she can do," Romki explained. "The only way to fight her is to deny her access."

"The local authorities won't help us," Jalawi stated the obvious. "They're likely in on it."

"Seems obvious," Kaspowitz agreed. "They don't need to hold Tiga for long. Just long enough to stop us getting to the Croma'-Dokran Assessment Council. The authorities are Croma'Rai, they just need to look the other way."

"I'm Croma'Rai," Rhi'shul retorted. *"You suppose too much."*

"Could go in and get her," said Jalawi, looking at Erik with hard intensity. "Phoenix Company style."

"We can't massacre the Stu'cha," Erik told him. "They might not even defend themselves with firearms, if I understand the traditions." He glanced at Rhi'shul. Rhi'shul did not dispute.

"I'd aim for their knees," said Jalawi, darkly.

"At close quarters in temple corridors you'd have to shoot a lot straighter than that. Besides which, if the Kon'do is discredited because we act like a bunch of humans instead of like croma on a sacred quest, then the whole thing is off and suddenly Croma'Rai's gunships are after us again. Sho'mo'ra said fame was our protection, but only if we use it wisely. This is our chance to show this world that we're up to it. No shooting."

"Um, well," said Romki, adjusting his glasses. "With the greatest of respect to Lieutenant Jalawi, if he and his people go into the Stu'cha with traditional croma weapons and tries to fight them hand-to-hand, they're going to get squashed like bugs."

"Thank you for your professor-ly wisdom," Jalawi retorted. "I swing a cricket bat just fine, thank you..."

"And many of these croma would take your best shots and giggle," Romki said sternly. He glanced at Rhi'shul's scowling face. "Well. Perhaps not 'giggle'."

"Captain," said Sasalaka, in that firm, mild tone that was all she ever used to discuss anything. "There is one member of our crew who can land a blow that no croma will get up from."

"Yes there is," said Erik. "But I can't let him cut a swathe through the Stu'cha either."

Rhi'shul blinked at she grasped their meaning. *"No,"* she said. *"That's cheating."*

"Hey lady," Erik snapped. "You pick a fight with *Phoenix*, you pick a fight with *all* of us. You don't see any of us complaining that croma are cheating because you're all twice our size."

"You're complaining right now," Rhi'shul retorted.

"Besides which," said Erik, "there's not just one of us who can land a blow that will trouble a croma. There's three."

* * *

IT WAS A STRANGE GROUP THAT EMERGED FROM THE CHAOS OF THE Tali'san camp, striding toward the looming Stu'cha temple in the file of a formal procession. Croma stared in mixed curiosity or disapproval, but were too proud to pay undue attention to others. But the media came, mostly croma youngsters running with their camera mounts and hovering drones to get a good angle as the Shur'do Kon'do Rey'kan wove though teams of croma re-erecting their tents, or heaving overturned caravans back upright.

At the front walked Privates Lewis and Tediri, each holding a smaller Kon'do flag they'd borrowed from somewhere, and the croma assured them was appropriate. Do'reg came next, in similarly borrowed old style fighting armour, his huge family hammer slung over one shoulder. Erik walked next, with Romki, Rhi'shul, Jalawi and Karajin, and behind them, taking up a lot more space with his many fast-moving legs, was Peanut.

It was Peanut whom the cameras all focused on, of course, as his small, shielded head darted to follow the drones and track their electronic signatures and transmissions. Behind them all trailed another twelve marines, half human and half tavalai, armed with the smaller hand-to-hand training weapons Rhi'shul had mentioned, but still with rifles on their backs and sidearms in holsters.

A croma from the media contingent, trudging alongside through the nighttime camp, shouted a question. *"Those are challenge banners!"* Erik's earpiece translated. *"Who are you challenging?"*

"The Stu'cha!" Erik replied, AR glasses down and watching the visual tacnet Styx was displaying across his vision, complete with coms and possible threat status. It wasn't nearly as complicated as a starship combat display, but this was Trace's expertise, not his. He wished for the thousandth time that she were here.

"The Stu'cha are independent umpires! How can you challenge the independent umpires?"

Damn the translator and its instinct to turn alien concepts into human sporting analogies. "Watch us. They took one of our crew."

"We asked the Stu'cha about that," called another media person. *"They say you were too weak to hold onto her."*

"In my culture," said Erik, "there is no honour in attacking your guests." That was his mistake, he knew very well. Croma hospitality was a different thing entirely, particularly during a Tali'san. He wore the usual light combat armour of dismounted *Phoenix* crew, with helmet, webbing and coms gear. The Stu'cha and their Croma'Rai coordinators had done a good job of shutting down all the major com nodes in Ju'rig, but meanwhile far overhead, Commander Draper had powered *Phoenix* into high geo-stationary orbit, giving them constant and direct coms to the surface. Croma'Rai command, Erik understood, were demanding *Phoenix* return to their previous orbital path. Thus far, Draper was ignoring them.

"You are carrying modern weapons!" called another young croma. *"In the Kon'do Rey'kan, this is cheating!"*

Erik was surprised the translator put it so bluntly. "The Stu'cha have already cheated," he replied. "We expect they'll cheat again. They have combat personnel in their temple who are not Stu'cha, but military agents of Croma'Rai command. The decision to attack our Kon'do was entirely political — politics that have no role in this place. We carry guns to protect ourselves from further treachery."

"Your Kon'do is itself entirely political!" another retorted. *"Your Do'reg Shur'do lacks the status for a Kon'do, this entire exercise is a ruse to escape Croma'Rai justice!"*

"That's just what I'd expect a lackey of the cheating, lying Croma'Rai leadership to say!" Erik retorted. "This from the croma who traded with the reeh, who befriended the most evil species in the galaxy for personal gain! And now they get their pet journalists to ask me rude questions, as though I have not travelled across half the Spiral and battled through more enemies than all croma here today combined, all to be cried at by a bunch of small, soft children!"

It set them back, exchanging dark looks, ears down as they moved through the damaged camp. *"Good,"* Rhi'shul admitted on coms, reluctantly. *"You insult like a croma."*

And he'd just insulted the Croma'Rai government where everyone would hear it. It had been unofficial before, but now he'd directly taken sides. Better hope Croma'Dokran actually won.

"Translator needs a little work, Stan," Erik said to Romki as the camp ended, and more croma came running across the dark sands ahead to watch. Beyond, the high mesa of the Stu'cha Temple made a dark pillar against the stars. "I keep thinking I'm in a football game."

"Yes, well I've been a little distracted lately," Romki said testily. He wore no armour, just plain clothes with lots of zips and pockets. "Croma vocabulary hasn't been high on my list of priorities, Styx's syntax analysis should be handling it."

"Yes, because plainly I've got nothing better to do either," Styx interjected from thirty five thousand kilometres overhead. *"Captain, analysis of Cal'Uta traffic patterns indicates several military-grade vehicles leaving the city at high speed and heading directly to Ju'rig. You may only have an hour until Croma'Rai backup arrives."*

"Captain, this is Commander Draper. Phoenix has visual on those vehicles now, Arms confirms target intercept is positive. We can shoot them down and there's nothing they can do to stop us."

"Maintain target fix but do not fire except on my command," said Erik. "If *Phoenix* starts blasting atmospheric targets, they'll start blasting *Phoenix*. Possession is nine-tenths of the law down here. We'll just have to make sure we have Tiga in our possession before the help arrives."

"Yes Captain," said Draper. *"ETA on those vehicles suggests you have fifty-six minutes."*

"Rhi'shul," said Erik. "Procedure for a formal challenge lets us break down the doors?"

"Without modern weapons, yes," said Rhi'shul. She wore big glasses and a leather hood, common for croma as hats were for humans. Across her shoulders she carried a large staff, one end weighted, the other end hooked, and walked with both arms hung off the ends. *"You'll need to climb for a window, or up over the outer wall entirely. You're small, it's a task usually given to young croma."*

"I think we'll manage the doors," Erik said confidently.

"You haven't seen the doors."

Ten minutes' walk brought them to the base of the natural tower of rock. A defensive wall had been built up with slabs of stone well out from the actual tower, irregular in size and shape. The wall stretched between two croma-built guard towers which folded back into the natural rock. In the middle of the wall, filling a ten-metre-wide space, were a pair of enormous, steel-studded and plated doors. Great handles dangled, wrought-iron, to be opened by the size and power of the largest croma only.

"Like I said," said Rhi'shul, with that blunt, croma temper toward fools who would not listen. *"Without modern weapons, you have no means of breaching the doors. You must climb."*

Within, Erik heard trumpets blowing. A glance up showed him armoured croma heads peering off the battlements above, as Jalawi instructed everyone to stand well back in case they started throwing things off. The croma within were ready, calling to each other in preparation. On the flanks of the great doors, camera mounts were jostled into position, while overhead drones buzzed and hummed. Do'reg looked back at Erik past his hammer, skeptical that the human Captain had any idea what he was doing.

"Peanut," said Erik. "Make me a hole, please." Peanut scuttled past Do'reg and the challenge flags toward the door, as even laconic, non-demonstrative watching croma backed up a step. Peanut had kept both shoulder-mounted cannon pods, but was missing the underside laser that would typically be used for cutting. The bulk of cannons plus laser were too much on the ground, as spider-legged arrangements were only ergonomically efficient on a small scale, and hacksaw drones were optimised for zero-G. With a rising howl, Peanut's oversized forelegs activated, and the sand where he stepped erupted in a froth of buzzing high-frequency. At the door, he searched a moment for a good spot to start, then drove in both hacksaw blades to make a single vertical line.

The shriek that followed was deafening, and orange sparks fountained, turning quickly to globules of flying molten steel. Erik had never learned exactly what drysine drones were made of, but it was infinitely stronger than the old steel of this door. Peanut's small head ducked back within its armoured carapace, giving Erik a second consideration of what that shield was actually for, as molten steel spattered and sizzled. Hacksaws were equipped with the synthetic equivalent of pain sensors, and Peanut would have pulled back if it were damaging him in the slightest.

Even past her hood and glasses, Rhi'shul looked astonished. Hacksaws were not a large part of croma history compared to elsewhere in the Spiral. Machines and croma had met, at times unpleasantly for the croma, but croma had not been a large spacefaring civilisation at the time and the machines had been too disinterested to bother with doing much damage. The croma's great sufferings had come later at the hands of the reeh, and those tales had drowned out the memory of hacksaws to a muffled murmur.

But now, perhaps, some of those old historical memories would recur. Erik saw lines of watching croma, faces lit by the dazzling orange glow, wide-eyed at the efficiency of cutting tools and precision intelligence that quickly made a perfect north-south line, then began cutting across the horizontal. Vibroblades were a common-enough technology in the Spiral, but the efficiency and power on display here were something else again. Croma engineers watching via those ranks of cameras would be doing fast mental sums on both the power-output and apparent longevity of Peanut's powerplant, to not only be driving that chassis, but to be directing these huge megawatts to the front blades, and reaching numbers that were completely impossible with current technology. And that was before one even considered the obvious intelligence and coordination of all those divergent limbs. Artificial intelligence was restricted in croma space as in the rest of the Spiral — one historical lesson of the Machine Age that croma had taken to heart, however much the specific reasons had faded from thought.

Peanut finished the final, downward cut, and a big two-metre slab of steel-clad timber thudded to the sand. *"I take it back,"* said Rhi'shul.

"Cheaters!" came a yell from above. *"No modern weapons at the Tali'san!"*

"This translation," Erik muttered to Romki. "It has to be more nuanced than 'cheaters', surely?"

"You know," said Romki, "I'm beginning to think it's not."

"Peanut is a part of our crew!" Erik shouted back up at the wall, for all about to hear. "He's not carrying weapons, those are a part of his body, they don't come off! Do your damn research before you attack us next time!" He waved at Jalawi.

"Let's go people!" said Jalawi, now hauling a croma child-sized pole arm with his armour, rifle slung on his back. "Phase two, stay in formation, keep it nice and formal."

Privates Nuril and Iwobi from Second Section went first, challenge banners lowered to fit through the hole, then Do'reg and the rest. Peanut stood aside for them, forelegs deactivated and looking around with an alertness that suggested he was well over his sulking. Erik thought he looked quite pleased with himself.

"Nice job, Peanut," said Erik as he ducked through, and Peanut scuttled to follow.

"*What does 'Peanut' mean?*" Rhi'shul asked.

"'Steel Warrior'," Erik lied, having no time to explain to someone with an attitude as poor as Rhi'shul's. "What happens next?"

"*We have passed the first barrier,*" said Rhi'shul. "*And quickly, too. It qualifies us as worthy of our challenge.*"

"What are the odds they'll ambush us and cheat themselves?"

"*It's good you have your weapons. And Sho'mo'ra was right — let the media follow and watch.*"

"Jalawi, have your guys at the rear let the media follow us in," Erik relayed that, with a glance up to be sure that the croma on this side of the wall weren't about to drop boulders on them. But he'd have seen that, his tacnet expanding now to reveal increasing detail, including no imminent threat from above. That was Ensign Kadi, now in charge of their complement of Machine Age era assassin bugs. There were four of them along, now buzzing in various places ahead, including the high wall, where they could see and relay all relevant reconnaissance to tacnet. As long as they were outside, and *Phoenix* had a clear line of sight, Erik was further confident that high overhead, Second Lieutenant Abacha would be able to count rivets on croma helmets.

Within the defensive wall was a flagstone courtyard, lit on all sides by flames high on the battlements. Opposite, a second set of enormous doors were grinding open. Jalawi and Karajin indicated their marines to form up opposite, flanking Do'reg, Rhi'shul, Erik, Romki, Kadi and Peanut. From the opposing doorway, silhouetted against the torchlight behind, loomed the hulking figure of an elder croma — probably the same one who had confronted and insulted Do'reg earlier, Erik thought. The croma lumbered onto the courtyard, a huge axe in one hand, shoulders impossibly broad within light armour of leather and mail. More croma fanned out behind, a mirror of the marines' formation.

The big croma stopped directly opposite, wiped his mouth and spat on the pavings. *"You've cheated twice now,"* he said, and the lower, single-toned vocals past the translator told Erik this was a male. *"A machine to cut through our door. Modern weapons on your backs in case you lose. Good thing the media are watching. All this world will see this Kon'do for a fraud. This is politics dressed as tradition, and you have no standing here."*

Good thing he didn't know that Kadi had an assassin bug landed on his leg armour not far from exposed skin, Erik thought. Every word the big croma said was probably true, but Erik couldn't worry about that now — far larger matters were at hand.

"Who are you?" he asked bluntly.

"I'm Krav'ka," said the big croma. *"I am a leader in the Stu'cha. You'll pass no further than this."*

"You'll give me my crew back."

"She's here to play politics in a Tali'san. It's not allowed. You're frauds for trying it, and this false claimant gives you no protection here." With a careless gesture at Do'reg. Erik did not need to look at Do'reg to know his expression — the posture in his peripheral vision said it all, straining to be let loose.

"Captain," said Rhi'shul, in a low voice that coms barely captured. *"This one's mine."*

Three formal challenges in a Tali'san, Erik thought furiously. The first was getting through the door. The next two were usually combat. Given the defender's enormous advantage over the attackers, it seemed impossible that the Stu'cha wouldn't offer combat here,

particularly when they had monsters like Krav'ka, all dressed up with
Tali'san formality.

"You're certain?" Erik replied on coms. Rhi'shul was very large by
human standards, but dwarfed by as much again by Krav'ka. The
male advantage over female among croma was minimal, but Krav'ka
was clearly much older, and had probably been doing this a lot
longer.

"*This will not be a difficulty,*" Rhi'shul assured him. A Croma'Rai
patriot, Erik recalled Styx's analysis of Rhi'shul. Former Military
Intelligence... among humans, Intel spooks weren't always the
greatest fighters. Among croma, Erik was pretty sure it didn't work
that way.

"Do it," he told her.

Rhi'shul swaggered forward, long coat swishing, no heavy armour
in sight. To Erik's surprise, Krav'ka put his axe on the ground, hands
folded on the hilt, and regarded her seriously. "*I'll have your name,*" he
said.

"*You don't need my name,*" said Rhi'shul, twirling her staff through
several easy rotations.

"*The honour of all Tali'san contests requires a name,*" one of the
croma behind Krav'ka insisted. Krav'ka waved a hand to silence that
croma, with a heavy shrug to show it did not matter. He hefted his
axe, its heavy edge glinting in the firelight of two dozen dancing
torches, as silence settled across the courtyard.

Erik felt the weight of it compressing his chest, making breathing
difficult. Partly it was that *Phoenix*'s mission in croma space rested on
this outcome — the fate of all corbi, the fate of Rando, and with it
Phoenix's ability to go and reclaim Trace and Kono, and whatever
Trace was probably planning around the Rando Splicer, if he knew
her at all. The fate of all humanity, if it worked.

But also, it was the Tali'san, this old and horrid thing that all
croma swore by, this eclipsing gravity-well of an event that pulled all
into its grasp and crushed them with the accumulated weight of
croma history. One tall and lean figure in a coat, one huge and broad
in armour, dark shadows in the firelight. One armed with an axe, the

other with a staff. If Krav'ka hit Rhi'shul properly with that thing, he'd cut her in half.

Erik glanced at Kadi. Kadi's AR glasses were down, eyes focused breathlessly on the icons of assassin bugs and their command instructions. Erik had discussed it with him, and they were both prepared to cheat in the vilest possible way. Assassin bugs could moderate their bite, could daze rather than kill. Any hesitation should get the bitten party incapacitated by their opponent, whose skill would then be blamed... unless someone got suspicious enough to run a drug screen. But if it didn't occur to them within the first few hours, Styx assured them, they'd find nothing.

Croma were not parren, and there was no great formality before the fight. Krav'ka simply swung, and Rhi'shul danced back, circling away. Krav'ka followed, a lumbering mountain, but careful intelligence glinting in his dark eyes beneath their ridges of natural armour. He wore a leather helmet atop that, which itself showed that croma knew their natural armour was not perfect. His torso armour was interlocking plates with wide shoulders, and while the thighs were protected, the lower legs were not, as natural thorny plates made additional armour hard to fit.

Several times he faked, pretending to go one way or the other, and Rhi'shul backpedalled further, circling easily about the flagstone clearing. She moved so much faster and more fluently, and Erik began to see the reason for Krav'ka's respect. He'd half-expected the bigger croma to laugh at a smaller, unarmoured challenge, but now he could see that if Krav'ka swung and missed, and Rhi'shul came in behind it and caught him in the follow-through...

"*She's got him,*" Jalawi said in a low, confident voice on coms.

"*The fight's barely begun,*" Karajin retorted.

"*Just watch.*"

After many false approaches and feints, Krav'ka finally swung with an overhead heave, then immediately recovered as Rhi'shul flowed effortlessly aside, reversed her pole and hit him with the weighted end. Kravka blocked it with his arm, a loud whack that echoed between stone walls, and then the game of stalk-and-retreat began once more. Erik had great confidence in Jalawi's judgement on most things, but the ease with which Krav'ka swatted aside Rhi'shul's strike made him doubt, heart beating harder with anxiety. That strike would have smashed a human's arm, but Krav'ka had felt nothing.

Not yet, he wished Kadi. It needs to look like a proper exchange, not yet. And then Rhi'shul had to actually finish Krav'ka fast once he was stung, or else there'd be suspicion...

Krav'ka faked, then unloaded with a huge horizontal swing. Rhi'shul stepped back, letting the axehead whistle past her muzzle, then reversed her pole and went for the leg. Her hook caught an ankle, yanked, and suddenly Krav'ka was crashing down like a landslide. He rolled hard, momentum forcing him to turn away from her. Rhi'shul aimed a downward strike with the staff's other end, and its heavy weight crashed into Krav'ka's shoulder armour beside his head, then a second strike hit his wrist as he came up and fended for protection.

It jolted his arm, nearly making him drop the axe, and then Rhi'shul was pressing hard, multiple strikes in a flurry as the larger croma struggled for balance and defence, unable to free his arms from deflecting to mount his own attack. One hit his knee from the side, buckling the leg, a fast fake left drew Krav'ka's defending arm that way, but a reverse spin collected him square on the ear from the opposite direction. The impact was brutal, a solid lump of steel at whistling speed, and Krav'ka's head snapped sideways. For a moment he seemed to hang in mid-air, defying gravity. Then fell, with an inevitable crash, and was still.

"*Told you,*" said Jalawi. "*Manoeuvre beats firepower every time, my tavalai friend.*"

Karajin said nothing, arms folded, contemplating the scene in the manner of one reluctantly impressed.

Rhi'shul examined Krav'ka, removing the helmet, feeling for a pulse between natural armour in the thick neck. Several Stu'cha croma arrived to take over medical duty, and Rhi'shul surprised Erik further by giving the fallen warrior a respectful pat on the back before rising.

The opposing wall of Stu'cha croma were staring with suspicious disbelief. It had been quite an easy win, Erik thought. Never having seen croma old style combat before in person, he wasn't sure what was normal and what wasn't, but from the reactions of those opposite, it was clear that this win was astonishingly one-sided. Given the stakes, and the importance of not letting Tiga reach Stat'cha for the Croma'Dokran conference, they'd obviously put their best warriors into play. But now this middle-aged croma, not yet in the thickness of her natural armour and not revealing her face or name, swatted him aside the way one of the marines might send Skah for a tumble in a playfight.

Rhi'shul swaggered back to her place in the human and tavalai line, bumping fists with the very impressed Do'reg, and looking otherwise unbothered. Too unbothered, Erik thought with creeping suspicion, and trying far too hard not to look his way. Alien subterfuge should really have been second nature to him by now, and it annoyed him that he'd taken so long to see this one. A middle-ranking croma investigator? Always grumpy, disarmingly ill-tempered, never seeming to be in control of very much, just another luckless individual swept along in the tide... and all just happening to play to human prejudices of the stoic, dumb, ill-tempered croma, who were surely not clever enough to manipulate and connive the way that human special operatives would do.

Sure she was just a regular investigator, here by simple, random chance. *Sure* she was.

"Certainly got game, doesn't she?" Romki murmured, in a way that made Erik suspect he wasn't the only one just figuring it out.

"Move forward," Erik instructed his flag bearers. They marched, past the fallen Krav'ka and those attending him, but the way was blocked by Stu'cha croma beyond. Fingers were pointed at Rhi'shul, and demands made that the translator struggled to process.

"They want to know who I am," Rhi'shul provided. *"It's the formal tongue, and the accent is strong."*

"Is that a problem?" Erik asked her.

"It is not required, by the laws."

"Can I get that verified?"

"Captain," came Styx's voice, "although organic civilisations and laws are not my strong suit, I believe I can assure you that Rhi'shul's interpretation of the laws is correct. All laws of combat under the Stu'cha are in effect in the Ju'rig camp, which includes confrontations such as the one you are currently in. They are quite different from regular croma law, and quite specific in this instance — no combatant need announce their identity should they choose not to."

"Yes," said Romki, listening in, "but the Stu'cha are keepers of records. We're not picking a fight with just one side in a contest, Captain. We're picking a fight with the umpire, the ones who record the histories."

"Whose authority as umpire should have become null and void the moment they attacked our camp!" Erik announced quite loudly, so that all could hear. "You are no longer a neutral body, you have no authority to block our progress nor pass judgement on any of us!"

Again a disdainful reply from another armoured Stu'cha, and again the translator struggled to make sense of it. "Captain, they are stalling," said Karajin.

"Yes thank you Lieutenant," Erik said testily. "I gathered that." Styx's tacnet showed him a countdown to the reinforcements' arrival — currently at forty-seven minutes. And formulated silently, so that no media could hear, "Styx, do you have a fix on Tiga's location yet?"

"Captain, Ensign Kadi has one bug searching the tower, three guarding your advance. I recommend that you send another bug, the tower is large."

"Do it, we'll survive on two." Ahead, the argument continued, now between Rhi'shul and the Stu'cha. Erik drew the short rifle off his back.

"The Stu'cha cheat!" he said loudly. "They have armed reinforcements with modern weapons in the air at this very moment! They speak in tongues our translators do not understand and break their own laws of conflict in the Tali'san to delay us! Who among the honourable croma would miss them if we gunned them down where they stood!"

The line of Stu'cha erupted with threats, shouting insults and brandishing big weapons, as all of Erik's marines drew their rifles. Along the sides of the courtyard, lines of media cameras watched. However justified, shooting the Stu'cha in cold blood would look bad, given none were similarly armed. The first to resort to modern violence would lose the battle for public opinion, Erik saw with frustration.

"*Captain*," came Sergeant Jinido on coms, far enough back to be heard only on coms. "*We've got trouble behind us.*"

"*Captain*," came Abacha on coms from far overhead, "*there are croma advancing on your rear from the camp. Hand weapons only, no firearms visible.*"

They were about to get trapped in here, Erik realised. It would be so tempting just to tell his marines to gun down those threats... but even if he could get Tiga back from this place by traditional *Phoenix* methods, they'd never get her to Stat'cha. The protection of the Kon'do would be removed, and Croma'Rai authorities would hit their train from the air and leave a smoking crater of all his plans.

"Captain," Jalawi warned above the racket, rifle ready but not yet aimed. "We're about to get surrounded."

"There's a bottleneck at the gate," said Erik. "Can you defend it without shooting anyone?"

"No," said Jalawi, bluntly. Looking at the wall of armoured threat confronting them, Erik knew it was only the truth. "But I think Peanut can."

It was stretching the rules. But the Stu'cha were stretching the rules by summoning supporters to storm their rear. If those supporters wanted to brave Peanut's vibroblades, good luck to them.

"Peanut!" said Erik, as the confused drone turned to him, head darting to the commotion, then back again. "Peanut, look at me. Pay attention. Are you paying attention?" A quick-double take... drones' sudden movements were always disconcerting, like a small bird, always head-cocking and jumping at every new thing. "I want you to hold that gate behind us. Don't let anyone through it. Do not shoot anyone. Try your very best not to kill anyone. I know that's not easy with your blades, but try your best, okay? Do you understand?"

Peanut looked at him a moment, then about, then at the gate. Then scuttled off in that direction, Jalawi giving instructions for marines to back him up.

Do'reg was now bellowing at the wall of Stu'cha, standing out before them all with hammer threatening in hand. *"I will have my challenge!"* he roared at them. *"My family will not be denied by you law-breaking cowards!"*

Several cameras were circling close, manned by young croma risking the potential melee to get a good angle on the furious Do'reg. *This* was what the general croma population wanted to see, Erik thought. Croma were intensely hierarchical, even as the levels of that hierarchy were unclear to outsiders. Status was largely self-governing and self-policing. Croma who stepped beyond the bounds of their status would not need government authority to come in and stuff him back in place — the general population would do it for them. And now here came a common farmer, in no position to make these claims of family honour, challenging the Stu'cha to their faces in the greatest Tali'san of the past two hundred years. Ordinary croma would be shocked. Perhaps a majority would disapprove. But like humans with a climactic soap opera, or a public celebrity feud, they could not look away.

Erik walked to Rhi'shul's side, and tugged on one arm to get her attention. "Can he win?" Erik asked in a low voice, inaudible beyond the yelling. "If he fights them?"

"I don't know," said Rhi'shul.

"Don't play games with me," said Erik. "I saw what you just did. You're not some common investigator, and you didn't end up on this ride by accident. Can he win?"

A long pause from Rhi'shul. Erik wished she didn't have the cap and glasses, having some confidence by now that he could read croma expressions. *"Unlikely,"* she conceded. *"He's strong, but untrained. The real question is, will you let him lose?"* With a pointed look, past her glasses. Erik supposed he wasn't the only person admitting to know more than he had.

"I'm not in the habit of losing," he retorted.

Behind, the first running croma came through the hole Peanut had cut in the gate. Peanut hit him, one claw landing vanishingly fast, but the croma was not cut in two, just catapulted backward in the sand. Another came through with a huge shield raised, this time withstanding Peanut's first blow and pushing into the courtyard. Peanut's next strike came with a shriek of ultra-high frequency vibration, slicing the shield beneath its wielder's arm, then taking exposed legs with the other, deactivated blade. That croma went down, and a marine delivered a blow to the head. A smaller, younger croma took the opportunity to dart through while Peanut was distracted, only to be crash-tackled by Lance Corporal Maiza.

Up front, Do'reg lost patience with shouting at the Stu'cha wall, and swung at one of the most belligerent. The hammerblow crashed off a shield, was answered by the recipient, and then it was on, a one-on-one melee erupting as others stood back to watch. The noise and confusion in the courtyard was overwhelming, and Erik took a knee, realising that he was spinning back and forth in a most unhelpful way. He focused hard on the dots projected before his vision, appearing to hover a metre before his face, and recalled everything Trace told him about command on the ground. On the *Phoenix* bridge he didn't have to worry about standing or running, he just sat in his chair and projected his consciousness beyond his body. Here, his body was getting in the way, and he wondered for the thousandth time how Trace did it.

"Ensign Kadi," he formulated, teeth gritted as he tried to focus through the extraneous commotion and see only what mattered. *"Don't let Do'reg lose."*

"Sir, these damn big croma don't have many soft spots a bug can sting!" Kadi retorted. *"I could get an ear or nostril or eye, but they'd see that and then we'd be in big trouble!"*

Kneeling low, Erik could see that Do'reg had picked a fight with a big one, clad in a loincloth only, no leg armour over the natural, curved plate, ragged with spines off the calves. This one was armed with a huge polearm, and Do'reg appeared to be suffering repeated blows from the rapid strikes delivered by the more mobile weapon.

"Styx, can you direct the bug?"

"Captain, I am on a point-three-five-second time delay from orbit. It makes intervening in a melee fight problematic."

In desperation, Erik could feel his plans slipping out of control. A grinding, clanking noise filled the courtyard, and he realised that someone in the main tower was opening the rear gates. In a moment, Peanut would be defending a ten metre wide gateway, not a two metre hole. Then the fighting commotion stopped, and Erik looked back to Do'reg... and found him standing, hammer in hand, over the fallen body of his foe. There was a lot of blood on the pavings, spreading fast. Do'reg's shoulders were heaving, and then Jalawi was punching the air.

"How many more do we have to beat?" he yelled at the Stu'cha and the watching cameras. "You lose again and again, and you will not admit defeat! Where is your shame? Have you no shame?"

And the Stu'cha were actually silent, some falling back, others staring in disbelief at the scene on the flagstones. So much blood. Erik stood, manoeuvring for a better look past intervening bodies, and saw a croma head crushed, as though struck by a hammer from above. He hadn't seen that happen, he'd been looking at the rear gate. Had Kadi used the stinger?

Croma were now pouring through that rear gate as it opened enough to let them in. "Peanut, stand down!" Erik barked. "Fall back to us! Defend yourself if attacked, but no more!"

Those croma came in, weapons ready and warily crouched as the drysine drone retreated before them, marines guarding his sides. But their forward movement faded as they saw the courtyard's mood, the fighting ended, a body motionless on the stones and all Stu'cha standing about in silent incredulity. The new arrivals flowed around Peanut and the rearguard to look.

"Can the credibility of this institution survive if they refuse to let us in?" Jalawi asked, addressing the cameras against the wall directly. The most naturally charismatic of all the Phoenix Company officers, he could be quite persuasive. "In human Fleet we have institutions that build their reputation over the centuries by never letting their followers down, not once!" He pointed at the Stu'cha. "Are you seeing this? Are you seeing how they cheat? Their own laws say we must be allowed in, and yet..."

But now the line of Stu'cha warriors were parting, a slow, reluctant shuffle. Behind, the gates to the main temple stood open.

"Shooter!" someone yelled, then a hard tavalai body hit Erik from the side and rolled him as shots rang out above. The next he knew, the courtyard was full of running croma, humans and tavalai, though many of the latter were kneeling and firing upwards, a roar of automatic weapons at windows high overhead.

"Shots from high, Captain," came Jalawi's voice on coms, breathing hard as though running. *"We're going in, tacnet's got a fix on Tiga, stay out here and we'll bring her back."*

As Erik rolled out from under Private Tediri's armoured body, the tavalai stubbornly positioning himself between Erik and the temple windows, rifle up and searching. To one side, heavy cannon roared in a wave of thunder — Peanut nose-up and unloading at windows, shredding the old stonework. Some Stu'cha were heading for the exits, others were standing around in bafflement, indifferent to the bullets flying, gesticulating as they demanded from each other to know what was going on.

And Do'reg, so recently full of rage and blazing honour, now knelt by the body of the big warrior he'd killed, hand on the dead man's shoulder, head bowed in silence.

* * *

THE FIRST TIGA KNEW OF ANY RESCUE WAS A RATTLING OF KEYS IN THE old steel door. She blinked in the wash of torchlight, and saw the silhouette of a croma warrior against the flame. Not a medieval giant, but a smaller, leaner type, in modern armour with a rifle. These were the ones who'd taken her — Croma'Rai operatives, obviously, disguising a chew'too stampede to look like an accident and provide cover. But this one looked agitated, and now in the background, Tiga could hear gunfire.

He moved in to grab her, then abruptly winced, slapping at his neck. And just as suddenly, began convulsing, then fell. Tiga stared in shock, recalling the tales Professor Romki had told her about small flying machines that looked like bugs, and stared around for it... but the torchlight was dim. She scrambled off her wooden bunk and peered out in the corridor. It was old flagstones, and curving in a circle.

Looking back at the fallen croma, she wondered if she should help him. She hated croma, but it didn't seem right to leave this one convulsing on the flagstones. The bugs didn't always kill, Romki had said... but this looked quite unhealthy. The bugs could also act as reconnaissance... so Phoenix Company would now know where she was. Should she stay here, or go to them? Or take the fallen croma's rifle? 'Monkey with a gun', Jinido had said, and that was hard to argue with. No, not the rifle.

Another croma with a rifle appeared up one end of the curving corridor, and she ducked back. Immediately there came a crash from that way, like a body falling, and she risked a glimpse around the doorframe. The rifle-armed croma was face-down, and over him stood another croma, traditionally-armoured with a large club. He beckoned to her, and pointed down an adjoining corridor. A way out.

Tiga advanced cautiously, heart pounding. She wanted to run that way, but there was gunfire echoing from nearby corridors now. And croma fighting croma, apparently. How could she run without knowing friends from enemies?

"Why?" she asked the club-wielding croma, in Kul'hasa.

The croma took the fallen soldier's rifle and slung it, with no apparent intention of using it. A confiscation, then. "Because I'd like to know I did the right thing," he said simply. "You don't belong here. Go to your humans."

18

Skah knew he should be down in the medical center with the others, but there was a big raised platform out by the ambulances from where he could see the dawn's first engagement. And so he had climbed the steep steps between support pylons and stood among the towering legs of watching croma, until one had picked him up and sat him on the side railing so that he could see the fight developing down the dusty hillside.

From this vantage it all looked very confused, as thousands of stamping croma and chew'too feet stirred up a huge storm of dust. The low morning sun made the dust glow, creating a bright yellow glare that blocked all view of what was actually happening. Skah relied instead on his glasses and audio feed from the media coverage, as aerial drones showed far more than his naked eyes could — huge formations manoeuvring, and in places coming together as weapons flew and the great mass of bodies convulsed like some single, writhing organism.

He had to rely on the translator to understand the reporting, but from what they said it seemed that Croma'Rai were winning and Croma'Dokran struggling. Above the Croma'Dokran and Croma'Rai formations the flags flew thick in the yellow dust, each showing where a smaller clan stood and fought. Skah had read so many stories his mother had given him of early kuhsi history, describing great battles like this one. He couldn't quite believe he was getting to see a battle just like it, if a much safer one where people would mostly get hurt rather than killed.

The croma on the viewing platform with him were unarmoured, leathers mixed with various shades of green. That was a colour of medicine, Skah had learned, so given because of the new life it represented, for the green things that grew in the new season. These doctor croma were quite busy, taking careful note of what fighting was happening where, and talking into coms to direct vehicles on the ground. Skah didn't think they were allowed into the fight as quickly as they'd like, and given his experience with medical personnel on *Phoenix*, he wasn't surprised they looked urgent or even angry that their care was being delayed by events on the ground. For a whole minute he redirected his translator's attention from the audio feed to a senior doctor, shouting into coms at some umpire out on the field about how medical personnel had to be admitted much earlier than they were currently. When the conversation was over, the doctor slammed a fist into the railing and made the whole tower shake before storming off.

Skah didn't quite understand that. Doctors were perfectionists, but it wasn't like it was an actual war. There were *hundreds* of doctors on standby, and so many flatbed ambulances and empty intensive care wards set up in the vast tents below — surely they were overdoing it. How many doctors did it take to reset broken limbs anyway? And though there were no modern weapons allowed in the Ju'rig camp, the same restrictions did not apply to medicine — the croma hospital tent looked every bit as advanced on the inside as what *Phoenix* had, and possibly moreso. There were facilities in there for immediate synthetic limb replication and attachment that looked amazing.

One of those medical bays currently held Private Iwobi, who'd been shot in the leg getting Tiga back. Tiga herself was okay, and quite subdued when Skah had seen her, and given his perfunctory greetings to say he was glad she was okay, which he was. He'd been surprised that Tiga had hugged him, and surprised further at how nice she was to the croma doctors who'd asked her questions.

The croma doctors had asked the Captain questions too, mostly about the Stu'cha casualties, who numbered fourteen dead and a bunch more wounded. Skah could see how differently all the croma authorities were treating the humans and tavalai now — with a great respect that didn't come naturally toward bipeds of smaller size. Skah supposed that however good the Croma'Rai operatives who'd taken Tiga were with hand weapons, fighting with guns was a different thing entirely, and Phoenix Company were elite. The small group that had taken Tiga had been mostly killed or wounded, and he'd overheard conversation from the doctors asking about those who hadn't been killed by bullets, but by some kind of toxin. He knew what *that* was, but like the rest of the crew, he hadn't said.

Croma'Rai were in even bigger trouble now, he thought, watching the shadowy figures through the rolling clouds. It had turned out they *did* have croma with modern weapons in their midst after all, just like the Captain had said. In order to reveal that they were cheating, the Captain had had to cheat a bit too. Skah was very glad the Captain was so clever. All of these croma who worshipped size and power, but one small human with a very big brain could take them apart. That, he thought as he gazed through his glasses on maximum magnification, was a lesson probably worth learning. And the bit about the Captain having to cheat a little, to catch people who cheated a lot. That in particular.

Activity grew on the platform, doctors shouting orders and rattling down the big steps to their ambulances. More of the ambulances began to pull out, engines whining — some small runabouts with capacity for just one passenger, and several large trucks with multiple carriages on fat wheels, looking like they could hold about twenty. The media feed showed that the fight was not over, but it had moved considerably, one entire uphill flank having folded and the rest now heading defensively downhill.

"Is the fight going to end soon?" Skah asked one of the doctors, but they ignored him. Maybe they didn't have translators on those com earpieces. "The media says it's not going to end, is it ending?"

"Skah," interrupted Lieutenant Karajin from behind him. Karajin had volunteered to watch him atop the tower, despite having been involved in storming the Stu'cha. Skah didn't think he'd slept at all last night. *"Don't bother the doctors. They're busy."*

"I wish we could see!" Skah complained, peering again at the hidden fight. "We can't see anything from up here!"

"Do you want to see?" asked Karajin. *"Let's go and see."* Skah stared at him in amazement. Karajin looked grim as always, his big tavalai features unreadable, third-eyelids mostly shuttered against the blowing sand, giving his wide-set eyes a strange, white-ish colour.

"Can we? Go and see?"

"Yes," said the big, mottled-black tavalai. *"You should see."*

They descended the tower stairs, Skah keeping well over as croma were coming up, using his hands on the steep rungs. At the bottom, Karajin indicated to Privates Tediri and Iratai on guard there, and they went to where a long, many-trailered ambulance was preparing to leave amid a bustle of last-minute transfers of bandages, and the return of several gurneys. The last trailer was open at the rear, and the tavalai leapt aboard without asking permission, to the half-consternation of the croma there.

There were bunks arrayed through the trailer, and life support equipment. Karajin grabbed hold of a ceiling rail and indicated for Skah to sit on a bunk. Skah refused, standing instead with a firm grasp of Karajin's leg, which was as solid as anything else there. None of the croma tried to kick them from the trailer. Skah even noticed that several of them didn't seem to be doctors at all, but soldiers, and held rifles against all Tali'san rules.

Then he realised. "They're scared some chew'toos will go crazy!" he realised.

"If chew'toos had charged through the medical tents," Karajin agreed, *"croma would have shot them. But the Stu'cha didn't send them that way."* Even croma were prepared to break their own rules sometimes, Skah

thought. And for all their love of fighting, there seemed no one in the Ju'rig camp as revered as a doctor.

The ambulance moved with an unexpected whine, cool morning air whipping through the open rear. Dust soon followed, and the rear flaps closed up to keep it out of the clean interior. For a while they bumped and rattled down the rough desert slope, while Skah clutched to Karajin's armoured leg and followed the media feed of the battle. Now they were saying Croma'Dokran might be making a comeback. Skah stared at the positions on the displays, and tried to control the balling knot of excitement in his stomach as the ambulance drew closer.

Finally they stopped, but the rear flaps didn't open immediately. Skah waited impatiently as the doctors inside waited for the dust to clear before finally opening up. Karajin, Tediri and Iratai jumped out first, weapons ready as they looked around. Skah followed, staying close to Karajin. He'd been around marines for a long time now, and he knew exactly what he had to do — stay behind Karajin, not get in his way, and do exactly what he was told at all times.

Visibility was still pretty awful, he saw as he looked around the ambulance. There was dust in the air in all directions, blocking out the sun and turning the sky a reddy brown. The main difference now was the noise — the thunderous roar of so many croma voices it sounded like a wave at a beach, only much louder and deeper. With it came the clash and clatter of so many steel impacts it sounded as though the sky were raining hail upon a sheet of tin. Occasionally from amidst it all, there came the warbling bellow of a chew'too, disconcertingly close. If one of those big animals came charging half-crazed out of the dust, as they'd done at Ju'rig camp last night, only rifles would save the ambulances in time.

The croma doctors seemed pleased enough to have the tavalai along for that purpose, and ran into the dust hauling large backpacks, gurneys and canteens of water. Karajin went with them, walking more slowly, Tediri and Iratai fanning out to the sides, weapons ready. Skah stayed at Karajin's rear, looking about. The rough desert bushes here were trampled, and everywhere were discarded weapons and pieces of armour. Then to the left, he saw a doctor escorting a dazed-looking armoured soldier, who didn't seem to know where he was. Then more shapes emerged from the dust.

One croma warrior sat as though merely tired, weapon at his side, arms about his knees like a man who'd run a long race and now needed to catch his breath. A doctor checked with him briefly, then moved on. Karajin walked past, and Skah looked at the croma's face, helmet removed and staring sightlessly at the scrub. Most croma would look at aliens, having never seen one in person. This one found the scrub more interesting.

Then came piles of shapes on the ground. Skah didn't know what they could be, laid so thickly upon the ground. It was only when he saw doctors moving amongst them, checking the pulses of the dead before moving on to the living, that his brain finally came to accept what his eyes were telling him. These were bodies. Dead croma. And they were everywhere.

But many weren't dead. Some still moved, and groaned or coughed and spluttered, trying to breathe. Karajin stopped by one, rifle still ready, and offered him a sip from his canteen. The croma's helmet was half missing, along with a good part of her face, a mass of blood and staring eyes, the half-formed natural armour from her forehead dangling where it had been severed. Karajin bellowed for a doctor. Finally one came, harried and overworked, and applied basic sealant before stuffing a bandage over it. Karajin stood, an old tavalai warrior who'd seen it all before, and moved on, extending his rifle coverage for the doctors as they kept moving.

To the left, a big chew'too was kicking feebly, legs broken, trying to raise its horned head from the sand, trying to bellow but not managing more than a sick wheeze. Iratai stopped near its head, aimed his rifle, and fired. A single high-powered shot snapped the air, and the animal lay limp.

Skah felt sick. He stared in horror, as now there was a pile on the desert before him, croma lying two and three thick, the sand and bushes messy with blood. Karajin checked the top one's vitals, then dragged the limp corpse off with one hand, putting his whole body into that task. It exposed the one beneath, who coughed and struggled as Karajin examined him. His arm was missing from halfway up the forearm.

"Skah!" Karajin barked. *"Get me a belt from off one of these croma!"*

Skah went in shock. A very large croma lay head-down in the dirt, as though he'd fallen there from a great height. The bandoleer strap that had once held a now-missing weapon hung loose, and Skah removed the utility knife he'd learned to always carry and began cutting. The other end of the belt came loose at the buckle, and he ran back to Karajin, who tied it hard about the severed arm's elbow. Blood pulsing gently about the white forearm bone ceased.

Still no doctor had come. "Doctor!" Skah yelled in panic. He'd thought there were so many doctors. Now it seemed there were horribly few. "Doctor! His arm's been cut off, doctor!"

"The doctor's coming, kid," Karajin said grimly. About them, the green-clad doctors were all busy, working their way through the mangled piles of what had once been proud, handsome croma warriors. Croma'Rai or Croma'Dokran, they didn't seem to care. It all seemed so trivial now.

"They're all dying, Karajin!" Skah cried, tears spilling in his eyes. "Why are they all dying?"

Karajin shrugged. *"It's war, kid. Same everywhere."*

"It's not war!" Skah protested desperately. "It's the Tali'san! It's... it's not meant to be like this!"

Karajin's big, white-clad eyes settled on him, pitiless. *"And who told you that?"*

"Everyone!"

"No. You told you that. Every child wants to believe it. Some adults still do."

19

P ena knew that Leeda Valley had been beautiful once. She could still see the outlines of that beauty, like the eyes of her mother, still bright and blue as the face around them aged, and that once deep-brown mane turned to whisping white. The valley's flanking mountains were tall, vertical rock faces that rose above the riverside trees. But the thing up the far end was a monstrosity, a silver vertical structure that clung to the mountains overlooking the river's sharpest bend like some parasitic insect nest.

Several of the sheer rock faces had been shorn down to size, so that the reeh could build the wings of the facility, like armrests on a giant throne. She'd seen photographs of the great old croma fortresses once, similarly built tall to overlook the peoples that surrounded them, often incorporating natural features like mountains or pinnacles. But those structures looked mostly proud, and celebrated the power of the natural foundations upon which they built. This structure was all contempt, brute force and domination, utterly at odds with its surroundings and proud of it.

The road beside the river was just a track, and the cart's rubber tires bounced on its rutted surface. A single geea pulled them forward, Pena's hands on its reins, though she doubted that qualified as 'control'. Giddy Kono had told her of a human-affiliated work animal called a 'horse', but those sounded far smarter and more difficult than geea, who rarely seemed to hold more than one thought in their head at a time. This one's thought was walking, because it knew from experience that at the end of its walk was a meal.

Alongside Pena on the driver's bench was Rika, wearing the red bandana of a common farmer, and chewing on some silvercane. They were to pose as older sister and younger brother, come to Splicer City for a very specialised bit of trade. In reality, Tano's flyer had dropped them off at Asha Village just yesterday, where they'd purchased the cart with Tano's supply of trading salt, and a supply of freshly harvested mulos nut to distract from what they were actually transporting. Theft was not unknown on the Splicer approach roads, nor murder, and worse.

"Why's the river that colour?" Rika asked. Instead of blue or frothing white, the river flowed a dull yellowy-brown.

"Because Splicer city dump all their shit in it," said Pena, adjusting the brim of her farmer's hat. "And chemicals."

"Did corbi cities do that too? Before the reeh?"

"No. There are technologies. You can clean it. But the reeh don't bother." Pena wasn't entirely sure that it was true. Splicer City was mostly corbi. The kind of corbi that most Resistance corbi held their nose while talking to, and gave themselves a good scrubbing to be clean of afterward.

There was more traffic on the road ahead, geea carts and some walkers with hand carts. Beyond, on the far bank, a walker sentry, three times the size of a corbi, perhaps twice the size of a human. It loomed by the river, weapon arms lowered, surveying the traffic. That much concern from the reeh for the city's security... though that was mostly the city interests protecting their trade, Pena knew.

"We used to make those," Rika said confidently, once they were past the hulking machine. "Back in the old days. Corbi made all the most advanced things."

"Not the most advanced," said Pena. "We never had the chance to get really advanced. The reeh found us before we could."

"My grandpa says we used to make stuff more advanced than that," Rika retorted, stripping another mouthful of silvercane. Pena wished he wouldn't, that stuff was bad for teeth. "He's done a lot of salvage in the old cities, he knows lots of things about life back then. He says we've forgotten how advanced we used to be. He says some of the originals wanted us to forget, so we'd just accept what we've got and not fight."

Pena sighed, readjusting the spectacles at her ears. Lots of Resistance kids liked these kinds of conspiracy theories, about how the corbi had been the most advanced people in space before the croma betrayed them. Everyone wanted to believe in the corbi's brilliant past. She supposed it felt good to have some pride left in a people whose occupiers stamped a little more pride out of them every day. But Pena's mother was a self-made librarian, and kept a small stash of precious old paper books that told how things had really been. Sadly, she'd had to defend those books not just from reeh, but from some corbi too, who didn't like the imperfections they revealed about pre-invasion corbi civilisation.

"Did you ever want to be anything other than Resistance?" Pena asked the younger man.

"A farmer, I guess," said Rika. "I worked the fields with my father when I was a kid. Mulos and tagas, we grew them really well. We had water too, a small stream from the mountains, but it ran most seasons. My father was great with irrigation, I spent most of my time just working the pipes... you know, he'd found a bunch of old plumbing pipes from some old building. Much better than regular irrigation ditches, he got double the yield on his tagas than any other farmers."

"He sounds like a good man," said Pena. Rika sounded very proud of him, she thought. "So why didn't you become a farmer?"

"I've got three brothers," said Rika. "They're all older than me, so they get first shot at the farm. I'd have to carve my own patch out of the forest, but the village council say the farmlands are big enough already, too much bigger and we'd be asking for the reeh to hit us."

"So you were the surplus son, huh?" Pena asked him, with a sly sideways look.

Rika kicked at the cane with one foot, awkwardly. "And there was a girl."

"Ah."

"I liked her. So did Miga, my eldest brother. She chose him. I didn't want to be there anymore, after that."

"I'm sorry, Rika." For a moment, there was only the rumble of half-flat tires over stones, the geea's plodding hooves, and the rushing of the river. "When was the last time you saw them? Your family?"

"Not for years. Five, I think."

"You can't have been in the Resistance for more than five years."

"No." He gazed at the river, and the looming monstrosity upon the mountains ahead. Pena thought that this wound must have cut Rika deeply. It amazed her sometimes, that with all else that went on in the world, corbi still found time to have their lives ruled by these petty things — family disputes, lost loves, minor concerns all, compared to the horror of the endless occupation. But people remained people, and even the most dedicated Resistance warrior could not live for burning hatred of the reeh alone.

A shuttle howled overhead, heading for the monstrosity on the mountain. They were a regular feature of the Leeda Valley, flying routes that spanned the Talo continent, and many more on their way up or down from orbit. This one continued toward the Splicer's upper levels, fading until it was a small dot against the structure. There would be landing pads up there, Pena thought.

"What about you?" asked Rika. "When was the last time you saw your family?"

"Last year. I had to trek there, but I was stationed at Redri at the time, they let me take some time off."

"Your mother still has her library?"

Pena smiled. "Oh yes. She's added a few new books, too. I didn't stay long, though."

Rika looked at her, curiously. "Why not?"

"I suppose I've changed. It's just different now. She's absorbed in village life, and it's just... different. And several aunts and uncles had died, one of them my mother's sister. That was in Tooma, a neighbouring village. The reeh hit it. The other was just a stupid illness, the kind of thing we could have cured in a day before the reeh came. So I guess reeh killed him too — that was her other sister's husband. And three years before that, one of that sister's kids vanished, my cousin. They think a kauda got him."

"Did they blame you for it?" Rika asked solemnly.

Pena frowned. "I don't know that anyone actually blames the Resistance when bad stuff happens."

"Oh they do. Well, I dunno. Not blame, exactly. But you walk into some of these places after the reeh have killed some people, and they just..."

"Roll their eyes," Pena completed, conceding. "Yeah. I guess you're right."

"I mean, they don't *blame* us. They just treat us like a joke."

"I feel like a joke, sometimes," said Pena, gazing at the massive Rando Splicer. Sunlight glinted off its highest dome, a thousand kutos off the ground.

"Well *I'm* not a joke," Rika said loudly, suddenly fierce. "Major Thakur and *Phoenix* are the best chance we've had in a hundred years to actually make a difference. Maybe longer. When we're finished with the reeh, they won't be laughing."

Pena almost found his conviction stirring. Almost.

There was no bridge across the river, just a raised portion of riverbed where stones had been laid to create a shallow crossing. No one at the Splicer, reeh or otherwise, had any interest in creating real infrastructure on Rando. The dirt road wound into the forest, which quickly gave way to the dreary outskirts of Splicer City, ramshackle and unpleasant. Shacks were little more than wooden planks nailed together, and corbi trundled handcarts with plastic buckets of water, or scraps of fruit for sale. A few dirty children played in the dust, hair matted, sores on their faces. In the air, the smell of stale urine.

Soon came a checkpoint, and a queue of geea-drawn carts into which Pena steered them to wait. Corbi in grey tunics searched each wagon, armed only with sticks. Reeh wouldn't even give them proper uniforms, Pena thought sourly. They were more self-appointed than employed, the gang of cowards who volunteered to do the reeh's dirty work in exchange for access to the best scraps. Looking about at the dilapidated buildings, Pena couldn't see the attraction to life here over life in the villages... other than there being no risk of kauda, or presumably reeh airstrikes. Most of the corbi here were criminals, wanted for various crimes back in their villages. They had no love of the Resistance, mostly because the Resistance killed such corbi by preference. Sometimes, in less-civilised units than Pena had served with, they did it slowly. If Resistance members were caught here, it wouldn't be good.

One surly guard threw back the weave cover on the trailer, and examined the mulos-nut. Sniffed at it, inhaling the thick scent.

"Where from?" said another guard, looking them over with disinterest. His accent sounded Joja — the other side of the planet. Some desperations could take corbi a long way from home.

"Reyla," Pena lied. "Both of us." There were no papers, no IDs to present. Reeh would probably take genetic IDs at some point, but neither Pena nor Rika cared. Neither of them wanted to come here more than once in their lives. The only way the reeh would match any ID taken here would be to match it against their dead bodies in the future.

The carry box under Pena and Rika's seat caught the guard's attention. He whacked at it with his stick. "What's in there?" A venomous hissing sounded from within.

Rika reached down and pulled out the wooden box. It had a grille on one end, and was heavy despite Rika's strength. He placed it on his lap and showed the guard on his side of the cart. Something scrabbled within, and more hissing. Little claws clashed on the grille.

"Kauda kittens," he said. "Pretty rare, we think. Should fetch us a few coins."

"How'd their mother die?" asked the guard, looking at them suspiciously.

"Another kauda," Rika said easily. "One of the sentries said they heard screaming in the night. I volunteered to go look the next morning, no one else did. Chief said I had to take some others though, damn cowards. We found the mother dead on the ground, the kittens up a tree. Bugger to get them down, sharp claws."

He showed the guard several scratches on his arm, where the kittens had in fact scratched him getting them into the box. Pena was impressed. Rika put just the right amount of youthful boasting into his tale, like a puffed up kid trying to impress an older man. If the guards suspected for a second that the kauda had been killed by military rifles at the command of a Resistance leader, it was all over.

Instead, the guard snorted. "Lots of those coming through, doubt you'll get anything." He waved them on, and Pena cracked the reins. The big geea resumed its plodding, and the cart creaked and bounced up the road.

Rika peered through the grille again to check on the kittens, then slid the box back under their seat. "Little guys are growing on me," he admitted.

There was the *real* bravado. Rika had plenty, and Pena only smiled. Dealing with Splicer City guards was not particularly scary, not after what they'd both seen. Splicer City authority paid them whether they made any busts or not, and they weren't reputed to be cruel — the city liked its trade too much. The really scary things in Splicer City lay ahead.

Soon the buildings began to loom, big concrete and brick blocks, rudimentary construction compared to the giant steel hive that encased the mountain behind, but impressive by the standards of Rando. Few cities where corbi lived grew to such size, though there were tales of other species in the Reeh Empire that were allowed associate membership of reeh civilisation, and allowed to thrive within certain limits. Why those species were granted such privilege, while corbi were not, Pena did not know. Perhaps the corbi weren't found to be warlike enough.

The traffic on the streets was busier now, and there were corbi in formal clothes, corbi in various kinds of uniforms, corbi carrying loads of vegetables or lumber, or hurrying about construction sites where the scaffolding stretched precariously overhead, and corbi swung and yelled orders far above the road. Streetside stalls offered food, or tailoring services. Pena looked at one old lady, sitting behind her foot-pedal sewing machine and staring vacantly at the passing traffic as she awaited a customer. Behind another desk, a younger man in a tunic, a working slate on the table with a sign up to advertise legal services. Making sense of laws in this place must have been a tangle, she thought. She wondered who made those laws — surely the reeh didn't care enough to bother. And she gazed at the man's face, wondering what had happened in his life to bring him here, and the prospect of spending the rest of it begging for scraps beneath the reeh's dinner table. She was quite certain that she'd rather die.

Finding the market was a simple matter of following the cart traffic. It brought them to a huge under-cover area, where great tarpaulins spread upon steel poles, and stall owners presented their goods in rows to a steady crowd of corbi. Thousands of them. Pena stared, taking in the noise and smells, and noting the hover drone making a slow circle overhead. She'd never seen so many people in one place in her life. And she recalled what Giddy Kono had offered her. There were crowds like this where *Phoenix* had come from, all of them alien. If she went with *Phoenix*, she'd see them herself... only she suspected they'd be much more orderly and less smelly than this.

She directed the geea to the offloading zone, managing to get the animal lined up with some difficulty and Rika's unhelpful instruction, before leaping off and throwing the wicker cover back on their cart load. Soon some market buyers came along, peering at their crop, smelling it, biting a few and making insultingly underpriced offers. Pena didn't care about the price, but giving in so easily would have been suspicious, so she haggled with the buyers until they strolled away in disgust. And came back shortly after, with better offers. She took the best of them, then stood in the cart bed with Rika and shovelled the mulos nut onto a handcart pushed by a couple of boys who looked barely teenagers.

She was tired and aching when it was done, but she had some coins in her pouch now, which she tied carefully to her belt before pushing deep into her pocket, having been warned she'd need to do that, in this place. Rika took the kauda kittens in their box, and they left the geea with some water and feed to go and look for the pits.

Walking about the market, Pena saw her first aliens in the city. These had great jowls on the underside of their chins, part of a complicated natural breathing apparatus, and had squat, stocky bodies and a waddling walk. Rika looked at her questioningly, and Pena just shrugged. The Reeh Empire was filled with species, most of them slaves, some of them semi-slaves. On Rando, all of those were in the Splicer, the reeh having no interest in using Rando for their own settlements.

Beyond the markets, a tangle of laneways, tight spaces and narrow shopfronts, many locked steel doors and security systems, big corbi with sticks and more obvious weapons standing guard. Against the walls, shivering figures sat wrapped in blankets, while at a door, a woman pleaded with someone on the other side of a grille. Signs advertised services, but all were vague, simply mentioning 'procedures' and 'advantages'. On another blanket, by a corner that smelled like urine, a paraplegic woman sat rocking a deformed infant, her eyes as blank as an overcast sky.

Onto a wider street, where low power cables made a tangle beneath the looming walls of dilapidated apartment blocks. Above them all, Pena could see the gleaming steel and glass of the Splicer. Foot traffic hurried, corbi pushed handcarts stacked with gas canisters or water bottles. Music crashed and thumped from a bar, and several corbi lay passed out in the street, others stepping over them.

Rika swaggered grimly, taking it all in stride. He'd never been here before either, but had been told what to expect. Much of the Resistance would have liked to set this place on fire, but it was a waste of effort because the reeh wouldn't have cared. Besides, this was the only place where people who worked inside the Splicer mingled with those on the outside, at least occasionally. If you knew where to look.

Pena asked a bored guard seated on a plastic stool for directions, and after several more corners, they found the entrance to the pits — a great steel shed, like some giant old warehouse, with big floodlights mounted in the steel rafters. Across the dirt floor were concrete mounds, topped with steel grilles. Yelled conversation and laughter roared, and from within the pits came the sound of animal screeches and howls. Corbi clustered around several of the pits, while hustlers took bets on the action within. Above the high ceiling, Pena saw a drone hovering, sensors scanning the floor.

She led Rika between the pits, keeping well wide of the crowds. Some of these corbi had shave-job mane-cuts and heavy rings in their ears, suggesting gangs or northern Vantu Mountain clan affiliations. Some of those, it was well known, had gone to work for the reeh shortly after the occupation, and never looked back.

Across one side of the floor were grille shopfronts. One of the signs, in Lisha, read 'specimens'. Sitting nearby, waiting, were several more corbi with cages. Pena walked up and banged on the grille. There was no immediate answer. The seated corbi looked at Rika's cage resentfully — one of their cages held some kind of bird, wings too wide for its cramped enclosure. Another's wicker cage held a small, motionless reptile. Rika rested his arms by placing his own cage against the grille while they waited. Kauda kittens were far more impressive than what the others had.

The howls in the fighting pit grew louder, and someone used a shock-prod to encourage the animals further. More bets were placed. Pena lost patience and hammered on the grille once more. It slid aside, and a yellow-eyed corbi face glared at her.

"No more fucking lizards," said the corbi, her voice gravelly. "I don't care how many spots they have, no one's interested in half-dead lizards."

"Kauda kittens," Pena said shortly, with what she hoped was the right amount of mercenary eagerness. "Two of them, from Reyla. Parents killed a bunch of villagers, mother was extra-large. Locals said they'd never seen anything like it."

The grille slammed shut. Then the neighbouring steel door rattled and opened. A small, old woman shuffled to wave them in. Pena went first, and found the office as gritty as everything else in Splicer City — a wood-plank floor, rickety walls and fluorescent lighting. On several central tables, a range of analytic equipment that Pena thought must be for genetic analysis.

The old woman slapped the bench alongside, and Rika placed the cage there. The woman peered into the grille, then whacked the metal to get a reaction when the kittens proved hard to see in the shadows. A hiss, and one lunged forward, teeth bared.

"Aggressive little guys," said the woman. She pulled a drawer, rummaged inside and found a small synthetic stick. She slid the stick between the bars and waggled it, until one of the kittens found the provocation too much and leaped from the box's shadow to bite it. "Good grip," said the woman, waggling the stick until the kitten finally let it go. "How old are they, do you know?"

"The guys who knew most in the village said maybe a hundred days," said Rika. "They're already eating some meat."

"What kind of meat?"

"People, mostly."

The old woman made a face, taking her stick to one of the analysers. A screen activated, and she inserted the stick in the right aperture, and waited. Holographic projection followed, a small, 3D display of Rando chromosomes, mostly blank placeholders until the analyser began filling them in. The woman nodded thoughtfully, and sipped a flask of something that Pena doubted was water.

"Aggressive deviation," said the woman. "Reyla, you said?"

"That's right."

"Had some good specimens from there. The machine's suggesting the adults should be on the large side."

"The mother was fifteen kutos," said Rika, boastful like a fisherman who'd personally caught a monster.

"Reeh sweeps pick up about half of their best deviations," the woman explained, rotating the holograph on the table. "But they miss a lot, and the best deviations get smart, they're good at dodging reeh patrols. Some of these places, like Reyla, get deviations running about a thousand times beyond natural evolution, all preference-biased of course. These things would have grown larger than nine kutos back in my grandmother's time."

"It's not the size," said Pena, with a shudder that took no acting at all. "It's the behaviour. My uncle told me about a family that stalked a village for months. Learned the positions of guards and the regular times people would leave. Always went after kids."

The woman nodded. "Reeh are after that, too. I'll give you five thousand for the pair."

"Eight thousand," said Rika, defiantly.

The woman looked at him shrewdly, and took another swig from her flask. "Listen, kid. There's another ten folks in the city who do what I do, and you could wander around for a few days asking them all for a price. If you're lucky, one of these bastards out here won't mug you and take these guys themselves, once they figure out what they're worth. I'm guessing someone told you to come here because they know I deal fair. Or you could try out all these other players only to come back and get the same price I'm offering you now."

"The price is fine," Pena admitted. It was on the lower end of what she'd been told was a fair range. "We'll take it."

* * *

A FEW COINS FROM THE EARNINGS BOUGHT THEM A NIGHT AT A nondescript hotel on a street near a meatworks. Pena sat on a chair by the window and peered at the yellow-lit night, at geea-drawn wagons pulling up below, loaded with kunees who were unloaded with legs and hooves bound, and carried by burly corbi in blood-stained overalls, bleating and protesting.

Rika emerged from the bathroom, hair wet and mane combed, having wrung enough water from the creaking taps to do that. He bounced onto his bed, and pulled on shoes. "You think it'll work?"

"Tano's problem," Pena murmured.

The kittens had been given to one of the best genetic scientists in Tano's team, who possessed the technology to make self-propagating synthetic cells. The cells themselves did nothing more than mingle in the bloodstream, but there were particulars about their synthetic codings that, when examined by an expert, would reveal a message.

Tano had been certain that the same people in the Splicer who were altering tanifex would be the ones analysing every new specimen coming in through Splicer City. That would take several days at least, and then, the hope was, those people would make contact. Or someone less friendly would, if it were intercepted by the wrong people... but Tano said he had contingencies for that, too. Either way, Pena and Rika would be long gone from the city by then.

Rika crawled from the bed and peered over her shoulder at the view outside. At kunees, long-eared and stupid, carried from the cart to their slaughter. "Great fucking town, isn't it?" he said. "Firebombing's too good for them. All these traitors and cowards. *Phoenix* will do that, right? Firebomb them?"

Pena smiled faintly. Rika didn't have much education. He had no idea what warships like *Phoenix* were capable of. "Far more than that."

Rika combed the mane over one of her ears. "Why so glum?"

Pena sighed. Rika did this occasionally, flirted a little, just to prove that he could. He was a good looking young man, strong-chested and brave. She was well old enough to be the elder sister that she pretended to be, and most tough Resistance boys liked to chase younger girls. But Rika liked her, and wanted her to feel like she wasn't beneath his attention, in his generosity. It was all she could do not to roll her eyes.

Some voices echoed in the hallway. Then a shout, male and angry. A female reply, upset, followed by muffled thumping. Pena looked toward the doorway.

"Forget it Pen," Rika warned her. "We're here to do a mission, not get into other peoples' business."

"They were at it earlier, too," said Pena. "It doesn't sound good." She'd seen too much of it in her life to let it slide. It was one of the reasons she'd joined the Resistance. The Resistance wasn't just about fighting the reeh, it was about setting a good example for corbi, too. In the old days there'd been a thing called a police force, which had kept order. Some villages with good leaders did that well, but others less so. But if the Resistance was going to do a good job of stopping the bad behaviour among corbi, it would need women in its ranks. It was one reason why she'd volunteered to join Major Thakur's personal detail — the idea of a female, corbi-like alien who was a great warrior amongst her people had been irresistable. When civilisation declined, it was the women who always suffered most.

More shouts, and then a squeal. Pena climbed from the bed. "Pen!" Rika objected, holding her shoulder. Pena shook him off, and went to the door to listen. The accent was heavy, and most of the words were not Lishan. Shonto maybe, she thought. Then the dull smack of fist on flesh, and sobbing.

Pena undid the chain, and opened the door. Down the dark corridor, a man stood silhouetted in the light from an open doorway. He shouted into it, pointing demonstrably. From within, more voices came back. Pena walked toward the man, heart thudding but determined. She had no weapons, but was confident that neither would these men. The reeh didn't care about anything in Splicer City except that — guns in the possession of unauthorised personnel would get you immediately shot, no questions asked.

The man saw her coming, and turned on her, startled. "What do you want?" Angry, thick bearded, wearing a loose tunic and dirt-smeared pants. Silver rings in both ears. No honest-earning corbi on Rando wasted meagre resources on jewellery... or not to Pena's mind, anyway.

"What's with all the noise?" she asked, in the manner of someone woken from sleep.

"Never you mind! Stick your face into everyone's personal business, do you?"

"So these are your family?" Pena made to look around the corner, and was shoved hard backward before she could see.

"I said get lost!"

"He's not my family!" came the female voice Pena had heard before. "I'm from Asla in the south, he said he'd bring me to find my brother, but he's selling me to the brothel owner!"

"She's lying," the be-ringed man said flatly. "Look, lady." He put a hand on Pena's shoulder, leaning close. His manner was threatening. "My advice to you?"

Pena hit him in the face before he could offer it. As he staggered, she grabbed his arm and twisted, that momentum ramming them both into the wall. A second man came from the doorway to grab her, but was hit full-speed by Rika, charging down the corridor. Pena got the arm grip in the position she'd been taught from first joining the Resistance — it was basic martial arts and she was quite good at it. The man rolled her several times trying to escape it, his free arm flailing, bashing her into the wall, but she got his arm locked beneath his own throat, and began to strangle him with that leverage, her own legs locked around his waist.

Finally when he was turning blue, she bashed his face into the floor, repeatedly, and let him go. "Now you get lost," she told him, breathing heavily. The man struggled up, face bloodied. Behind him, she saw with little surprise, that his friend was in far worse shape, half-conscious on all fours. Her opponent gathered him in a hurry and left, scrambling for the narrow stairwell. For all his previous complaining, Rika looked rightly pleased with himself, massaging his knuckles. The kid was indeed a proper warrior, and could probably have taken both of them.

Pena looked into the doorway. There in a wood-panelled room, seated on the faded old bed, were two young female corbi, in the rough denim of farm labourers. They sat with arms wrapped around their drawn-up legs. But where was the one who'd been shouting? And she leaned in further, looking to the right... and crouched against the wall, clutching a steel object, was another girl. A little older than the other two, mane amess, wide-eyed and ready to attack. The steel object in her fist was a lamp stand, Pena saw. She must have taken it from the bedside table.

"They're gone," Pena told her, holding up a placating hand. "Now you'd better get out of here before they come back with friends."

The girl crept past her, as Pena stood aside, then stared out the doorway. Looked both ways in search of her tormentors, but finding only Rika. Rika leaned in the corridor, shoulders flexed, and looked smug.

"Thank you!" said the girl, and embraced Pena. Then she turned and said something urgently to the girls on the bed, who leaped up and began scrambling to collect things and put them into bags. "They're from the south too, I only just met them here. My brother's name is Jamog, I came here to look for him and that... that *animal* said he could get me in and help me find him. I thought he was nice, but once we got in..."

"I know," Pena soothed. "I've heard it before, there are bad people who prey on the desperate. You need to depend on yourself, do you understand? If you can't depend on yourself, you have to depend on others, and that's what attracts men like him." She nodded to the stairwell down which the girls' tormentors had escaped.

"Have you seen my brother?" said the girl, eyes wide and urgent. She couldn't have been more than sixteen. "His friend told him there was good work here, he promised he'd make some money and buy us some good things, then send them back to our family. But then we didn't hear from him in months, and I came looking to see if he was okay... you wouldn't have seen him, would you? Or know where I could look?"

The other two girls finished packing their meagre possessions into small carry bags and edged past, eyes down, then into the corridor.

"Go out the back way!" Rika called after them. "Those shits could be just downstairs watching the main door! Go out through the kitchen or some backway, stay hidden, understand!" The girls nodded rapidly as they left, and vanished around the corner.

"I've only just arrived here myself," Pena apologised to the girl. "We're both new here. I'm sorry, I've no idea where you'd look."

"I'll find him," said the girl, with determination. "I'm sure I will." Pena thought this girl would be good Resistance material. Unlike the other two, who'd scampered with barely a word of thanks.

She helped the girl pack her few belongings, while Rika watched the corridor. Then she escorted her to the other stairs. "I'm sorry we can't come with you," she said. "We have to get going ourselves. Don't want to stay here in case that lot come back with their friends."

"That's okay," said the girl. "We'll all be safer if we move separately." She hugged Pena again. "Thank you! There aren't many good corbi left these days!"

"I don't think that's true," said Pena.

The girl hugged Rika in turn. "No, I mean it. It's corbi like you who give me faith in the future! We need to look out for each other, or we're lost!"

And she turned, and scampered down the stairs.

Pena stared after her. Big lot of good that would do when *Phoenix*'s strike came in and turned this whole city into a sea of fire. Even if this girl and her brother were long gone, there would be others like her. She'd been so ready to believe that everyone in Splicer City was evil, because that was easier to believe, given what she was about to help make happen. But instead, there were countless thousands of stories here, many of them about good people whose lives had taken a bad turn. And out beyond Splicer city, in the villages Pena knew so well, millions more stories, many of which would be likewise eliminated when the reeh's retaliation scoured them from the forest.

For a long moment, she gazed at the stairwell, and felt a horrid, sinking numbness. Could she really do this? She'd sworn she'd do everything she could to help free her people, even give her life if necessary. But the cost of that oath today seemed... impossible.

She followed Rika back into their room, where they both began packing their few things. "Going to cost us a few coin to get another place," Rika volunteered.

"That's okay, we've got plenty of money," said Pena, stuffing things into her bag on the bed.

Something creaked in the corridor outside the door, and Pena stopped. Another creak. Then a tap on the window, a light impact. "Get down!" she hissed, and flung herself at Rika, pulling him to the floor as the door and window exploded inward. Impacts followed, and suddenly her eyes and lungs were filled with blinding gas. She struggled for the door, but black, armoured figures blocked her way, powerful hands grabbing her arm as her balance faded, and the gas took her down to darkness.

* * *

PENA WOKE, AND WAS FAINTLY SURPRISED TO FIND HERSELF STILL ALIVE. To be alive, and in reeh custody, was the most frightening thing imaginable, but something didn't feel right about that. Her limbs were free, for one thing. For another, she lay upon her back, and could hear the dripping of water from somewhere, and the hum of machinery. Distantly, more disorienting still, came the thunder of drums and the roar of what sounded like... voices. Many voices, a raucous cheering, reverberating through the floor.

She blinked her eyes open. There were dim lights in the ceiling, and many pipes, like an old plumbing system. A new plumbing system. She squeezed her eyes shut once more... corbi concepts of old and new were confused, modern technology was 'old' to them, and in the villages, to find surviving 'old' technology was to be blessed with an improvement in lifestyle. But this was not 'old'. This was a modern place. On Rando, there weren't many of those.

Her blurred vision focused, and she got an arm behind her head, looking past her feet. The far wall was a huge tank, filled with liquid. The creature contained within was colossal, as tall as ten corbi, and the weight of dozens. Its head was long, its teeth rowed and sharp, its forearms serrated with saw-blades, its body alternately thick with muscle, or plated with natural armour. It floated in the liquid, reptilian eyes closed, awash in faint blue light.

The sight was so surreal, and so frightening, that Pena nearly missed the faint thud of boots on the floor nearby. She scrambled up, but her head spun, and she sank to balance on one arm again. The new arrival in the room was a tanifex, the same as had attacked her, Major Thakur and Giddy Kono in Loga's team at the caves. Not much taller than corbi, vaguely reptilian, beady eyes and a slinking, scuttling way of moving, like a spider on an oil slick. It cocked a bright eye at her, dashed sideways to a headset on an equipment bench by a control panel, and tossed it to her.

Dazed and cross-eyed, Pena dropped it, but picked it up again and put it on. The tanifex spoke, a series of clicks and trills. *"Understand?"* said the headset.

"Understand," Pena replied warily. With the full expectation that she'd be dead shortly. Tanifex had never spoken to her before, only shot at her. Until now she'd barely spared a thought to whether they *could* speak. Against the opposite wall, she saw another one now, sitting with a rifle. They both appeared to have some kind of armour fitted over chest and shoulders, with attachments to a sophisticated headset, an eyepiece raised. Tanifex had been reeh slaves for a long time, the warriors were all technologically integrated. "Where's Rika? The other corbi?"

"Safe. Junior corbi. Want to talk to you."

The seated tanifex rolled a flask to her, clattering upon the steel-plate floor. Pena stopped it, and warily took the top off. Sniffed it, but it was only water, and her throat was parched. She drank, with another glance back at the huge, floating monster in the tank. Another roar from nearby, shaking the floor.

"Where am I?" As though she didn't already know.

*"Splicer. Lower levels. You like ***."* The translator gave her static on the word, but a clawed hand indicated the monster.

"He's alive?"

"Suspended," said the tanifex. *"Fighting pits near. Reeh make, for fun."* The translator sounded uncertain on that, too. Spluttering on the words, with non-grammatical hesitations. Perhaps 'fun' didn't translate, for reeh.

"Fighting pits," Pena repeated, as the crowd roared again. She'd heard of those. Reeh engineered creatures to fight for entertainment. Reeh engineered all living things, and took the best to serve their purposes in the Empire, as slaves. She stared up at the monster once more. "Reeh made this?"

*"Was once a ***."* Again the translator spluttered to static. *"Long*

time ago. Different creature. Engineered now. Very different. Many times bigger. Reeh make fight. Like tanifex."

Pena turned back to the alien. He, and the one seated by the wall, had been joined by several more, emerging from the shadows. All wore various types of armour, and most were armed. Pena had always imagined them robotic, brainwashed, like the one the Major and Giddy had brought back to Sebi Village. But these stood differently, some crouched in that natural way of long legs and folding knee-joints, while others leaned against walls. A military unit, perhaps.

"You fight for the reeh?" she asked.

The tanifex glanced at his comrades, and made some clicking remark the translator did not catch. There was some hissing laughter. Pena was astonished. *"Fight for reeh, yes,"* said the tanifex. *"You change kauda kittens?"*

Pena could have rolled her eyes. "Our scientists said it would take days for you to translate."

"Minutes." The lead turned an effortless squat into a one-knee kneel. *"Friends run program. We sabotage."*

Pena stared. "Why?"

"Eshfo Rebellion." Pena stared, uncomprehending. The tanifex glanced at his comrades once more. Several more arrived, numbers growing further. *"She doesn't know it."*

"The Eshfo Rebellion?" He was right, Pena hadn't heard of it. She just didn't know if that was safe to admit.

"Listen, corbi." Pena guessed it was probably spoken as an insult. *"Reeh Empire is big, you understand?"*

"I've some idea, yes."

"You've no idea. Rando is nothing. A speck on the edge of reeh space. A place to play with monsters for games and fun." He waved a hand at the sound of the crowd. *"Too close to croma space to build cities or factories. Too vulnerable, croma could damage them. So you're a science project, nothing more."*

"That, I understand," Pena said grimly, looking enviously at the tanifex's guns.

"Elsewhere, there's rebellions. Wars. Reeh neighbours don't like the reeh. Reeh work by letting some species oppress themselves. Easier work for reeh."

"I know. Splicer City." She waved a hand in the direction of where she fancied the city outside might be.

"Much bigger. Tanifex oppress themselves. But some colonies stop. We stopped." Gesturing to his comrades. *"Understand?"*

"I understand," said Pena. "You're rebels."

"Rebels in the Splicer," the tanifex corrected. *"Splicer can make slaves. And unmake them. We try to unmake. With friends."*

Pena's eyes widened. "You weren't trying to send a message to the Resistance with reprogrammed slaves at all." That had been the Major and Tano's theory. "You were using the Splicer to try and turn engineered drones back into normal tanifex!"

The tanifex clicked his fingers with rhythm, as though what she'd said had pleased him. *"But now you want to make contact. I think you know this human. The reeh lost Phoenix human. Reeh sometimes very stupid."*

A rebel inside the Splicer who knew the reeh's failings. The possibilities grew larger by the moment. Pena took a deep breath to collect her scattered thoughts. "That human wants to capture the Splicer's main data-core. All its knowledge. Can you do this?"

"No. We are few. Reeh power is formidable. Human is crazy."

"The human is not crazy. The human is one of her people's greatest warriors. And *Phoenix* is coming to get her."

"Phoenix can penetrate system defences?"

"The human says yes. She needs you to make a distraction. Then we hit the Splicer together, steal its knowledge, then destroy it."

"How can the human ship do this?"

"Have you heard of the drysines?"

"Big advanced machines. Very old, all dead now."

"No. *Phoenix* have a queen, on their ship." The tanifex's eyes widened. "And they say they can take this system single handedly."

20

"My problem with it, Lieutenant," Commander Draper said testily, "is that she's likely to die in pursuit of this mission. And I'm a little alarmed that you're not."

Lieutenant Dale stood on the bridge, squeezed into the little space between Captain and Commander's chairs, grasping a display support while crouched to keep from hitting his head. They'd all watched the vid message that the Major had sent from Rando, couriered via the corbi Resistance. Now that the combined shock and pleasure at seeing her well yet planning something exceptionally dangerous had worn off, there came the command discussions. *Phoenix*'s current situation dictated that those discussions should take place on the bridge — only half of the First Shift bridge crew were with the Captain and Lieutenant Sasalaka on the surface, but that still left Draper and Dufresne as the only two main pilots left on the ship. Technically the regulations forbade the bridge being left without two pilots minimum, but given *Phoenix*'s chronic pilot shortage, that was becoming unavoidable now, as Draper and Dufresne needed to sleep and exercise. On some occasions the shuttle pilots were sitting in, while on others they were forced to do what they'd sworn to never do, and LITS, as the crew were now calling it — or 'Leave It To Styx'.

"She's not on this ship," Dale replied grimly, "but she's still the commander of Phoenix Company. We do what she tells us."

"Yeah, two points," said Draper, holding up two fingers in frustration. Dale had to respect the fact that the kid was at least growing some balls in command disputes. "One; Major Thakur is *not* the acting commander of Phoenix Company — you are, Lieutenant. The regulations are pretty clear on that — she's not here, you are, and an officer can't command a unit she's not physically present to command. Two; I wouldn't be compelled to do what she told me even if she *were* here, because whether as Acting Captain or as actual Commander, I outrank her. And in both capacities, I say that assisting her to attack the Rando Splicer is a very bad idea."

"Why?" asked his counterpart, Lieutenant Commander Justine Dufresne, tapping figures into a navigation calculation while listening in.

Draper looked faintly incredulous that he had to even answer the question. "Because... well, shit, she's Major Thakur! She's fairly important to this ship's ongoing mission..."

"So important that you're prepared to disregard her chosen course of action," Dufresne interjected.

"And," Draper continued, "because she freely admits she's doing it against the wishes of Resistance High Command on Rando, it's just this... this Tano guy, who's Fleet, who High Command don't like. And I think we've made enough enemies of various alien governments lately, don't you?"

"Corbi have no government," Dufresne said coolly, still adjusting various things on her wrap-around displays. She had that way of talking without engaging, rarely meeting the other person's gaze. Aloof, certainly. Arrogant, quite often. But also, Dale knew from the tales that had spread *Phoenix*-wide after the Battle of Defiance, as brave as a parren. Few people liked Dufresne, but just as few disrespected her. "A people who have no government cannot have a High Command worth offending. Besides, *Phoenix*'s mission is not to please the corbi. It is to save humanity from peril, and I'm entirely certain that Major Thakur would agree with me on that."

"Hell yes, LC," said Dale. Dufresne's dark eyes found his from behind her displays. As though surprised at the strength of his agreement.

"Well I happen to know that the Captain is more disposed toward my position," Draper retorted. "And given that he's currently got his hands full, it will be up to us to grant him a full appraisal of the situation as we see it, complete with recommendations and possible alternative courses of action. Lieutenant, that report is going to require your best assessment of exactly what her odds of success might be, given what we know of the ongoing ground campaign on Rando."

"Commander, there's no way to know what the hell's going on on Rando," Dale said bluntly. "Fortunately, we've got the best marine in the Fleet currently on Rando, and she just sent us a message telling us exactly what she needs. I've got an idea. Why don't we listen to her?"

Draper stared at him, more in resentment than an outright, angry glare. Word was the kid could fly, but if he ever had to make the nasty decisions required to keep everyone alive, many crew wondered whether he could pull the trigger. Of Dufresne, Dale had no doubt. "You want her to get herself killed, is that it?"

Dale swallowed what he really wanted to say, with difficulty. "Commander, Major Thakur is a marine. She doesn't 'get herself' anything. If I'd second-guessed her judgement the way that you are presently, I'd have caused the failure of more missions, and cost the lives of more of my own people, than I can imagine."

"Spacer officers should always follow the advice of the most senior marines in all matters pertaining to purely marine affairs," Dufresne added, with a touch of sarcasm as she recited the most basic of Fleet regulations. "I can't think of a more purely marine matter than the possibility of a successful ground operation against the Rando Splicer, particularly when it could reveal a cure for a threat that could eliminate all humanity."

"The Major would throw herself off a cliff if she thought it could help humanity," Draper retorted. "There must be a way less suicidal."

"She says it's not suicidal," Dale growled. "I believe her."

"I'll be voting no in my report to the Captain," said Draper. "You both can feel free to add your opinions accordingly."

* * *

DALE WAS ONLY HALF-SURPRISED WHEN DUFRESNE INTERRUPTED HIS gym session at the end of First Shift rotation. He sat at the lat pull-down machine, powering a high weight at a low-enough speed that the muscle augments did not help him too much — the rookie mistake too many new augments made was to snap the lifts quickly, bringing the synthetics too much into play and robbing the real muscle of benefit.

"Lieutenant," said Dufresne, with that stiff, not-quite-looking way that she had. "I'd like a word."

"Sure thing, LC." Dale kept lifting — stopping mid-set was poor form. But he flicked his head at Sergeant Forrest lifting nearby, the only one in the noisy gym who could possibly overhear past the crashing weights and background music. Forrest moved to another machine without comment.

Dufresne looked uncertain of how to proceed. Dale disguised a smile by turning it into a grimace. It was pretty funny, really — the awkward, humourless daughter of spacer blue-bloods, who'd actually *lived* in space unlike those Debogande pretenders, and who'd somehow never learned to talk to real people. Given that some level of basic charisma was necessary for any command, it told Dale just how good her Academy scores in everything else must have been to land her here.

"Lieutenant, I'm somewhat concerned that Commander Draper's appeal to Captain Debogande may bear fruit. I fear the Commander may be correct in his assessment of the Captain's current frame of mind."

Dale kept lifting, thinking about that. Dufresne's eyes flicked distractedly to his chest, then back up. Dale wondered if the skinny, pale girl had ever gotten laid. He stopped, with a crash.

"Yeah," said Dale, distastefully. "Let's unpack that. You think the Captain's gone soft, running around trying to help the corbi when he should just be worrying about humans."

Dufresne looked confronted, and opened her mouth to object. Then paused, as though wondering how much to trust him. Openly doubting the Captain's motives with fellow senior officers could be trouble, and Dufresne was so squared-away she had corners. "I'm concerned," she repeated, finally. "I'm wondering if I should make a separate representation to the Captain. Or if you should. Impressing upon him the significance of the Major's mission."

It occurred to Dale that in the Major, Dufresne had finally met a fellow senior officer she couldn't find any cause to look down upon. She'd certainly tried at first, because the Major was quite relaxed on some matters of discipline and regulation where Dufresne would never be. But spending time with the Major had a way of exposing some sticklers for the rules to the difference between procedure and outcome, and teaching them which was ultimately more important. And lately, with Dufresne's opinion all the more prominent as Lieutenant Commander, it had become plain that whatever issues she had with the Major's style, Dufresne had found in her perhaps the closest thing she'd ever had to a role model.

"I hear you, LC," Dale agreed, rubbing the shoulder that still twinged from an old shrapnel injury. "I don't like the Captain running around to try and help the corbi either. I wish 'em well, think it sucks what happened to them, but it's not our business."

"Why do you think he's doing it?"

"Can't say I know, LC. But you know the Captain — he's a nice guy. Nice guys sometimes care too much."

Dufresne looked troubled. "He must have some other plan in mind," she muttered. "He's quite brilliant at times."

"No argument there."

"But now he lacks the Major's guiding influence. Too much 'Mr Nice Guy'. That's my concern."

"No argument there either."

"I think he's changed after Defiance," Dufresne concluded. "I've seen him spending an awfully large amount of time looking over the personnel files of those we lost. Writing letters to their families."

"Take it from someone who's had to do it," Dale said pointedly. "It's hard."

"I'm aware of that," said Dufresne, but without her usual acid rebuke. "But I happen to know he spent a lot of time looking over the sim reconstructions of that battle, double-checking every move he made. The Captain takes these responsibilities personally. I'm concerned that he's becoming... I don't know." She looked aside distractedly, searching for a vocabulary she rarely used. "Gunshy, maybe."

"Taking a big bloody truck from under the Croma'Rai's nose and driving to Stat'cha despite the travel ban doesn't seem like 'gunshy' to me," said Dale. "Commander Shahaim told me the Captain stopped doubting himself after the Tartarus."

"What then?"

"I dunno." Dale started lifting again with a heave. "Maybe he's looking for something."

* * *

TIGA SAT ON THE BUNK OF HER QUARTERS IN THE NEWLY REPAIRED trailer, and stared at her one surviving screen. It displayed what she'd written of her speech to the Council, the structure of introduction, plea to reconsider what they thought they knew about croma history regarding the corbi, followed by a laying out of evidence. Some of that evidence was now in pieces, in books not yet copied that had been destroyed or removed by Croma'Rai agents when they'd snatched and taken her to the Stu'cha.

In truth, very little was completely lost, because the much older and wiser Professor Romki, having lost painstakingly collected work before, had backed everything up repeatedly... and, of course, because when there was a mega-intellect AI queen monitoring the network, the simple act of recalling data became a whole lot simpler. But while Romki sat studiously on the bunk opposite, reading and writing with his usual endless concentration as the trailer rocked and thundered with their passage, Tiga found herself simply staring.

Finally she put her screen aside, swung down from the bunk and strolled into the corridor. In the kitchen now were tavalai Privates Iratai and Daraka, sitting with human engineering crew Brewster and Daen. The tavalai were showing the humans a game with combined cards and dice, and there was much laughing and taunting. Tavalai did not laugh like humans did, Tiga had observed. They chuckled and snorted, in a dry, understated way that was so unlike the humans' less restrained and sometimes alarming eruptions of mirth. But the tavalai seemed to enjoy provoking the humans, in the way that calm adults might provoke excitable children — cheating at games to see if they noticed, or making sly, outrageous suggestions to see if the humans would hit the ceiling because of it. *Phoenix* was still a human ship, but to Tiga it seemed that the tavalai were the adults in the relationship. Captain Debogande was certainly brilliant, but sometimes he took wild, immature chances.

And she snorted to herself, to notice that train of thought. Like a dishevelled wildwoman who criticised the appearance of others, only to now glimpse herself in a mirror. Childish risks indeed. Childish notions. Skah was upset in his quarters having cried for days to see his beloved croma killing each other so awfully, and Tiga now thought she herself was barely better.

All her speech was in tatters — not so much the physical work, but more her perception of the history she'd spent these last months immersed in. She'd been building a tale in her head, a grand story of rock-headed croma and noble corbi, her own people betrayed and abandoned due to croma narcissism and lack of compassion. But her experiences with her own Corbi Resistance had already brought her to doubting that half of the equation, forcing her to double-down hard on proving to herself the other half — that of croma fault and nefarious intentions.

And now that, too, was falling apart. To be sure, it was humans and tavalai who had broken her out of her cell, but it was croma public opinion that had allowed them to do it. With all of Dul'rho watching, the Stu'cha had had no choice but to cave to Captain Debogande's wishes, or face the disintegration that would surely befall all popular institutions that lost popular goodwill. Some Stu'cha had even helped her break from her cell — the temple Stu'cha, the ones who believed in the principles of fair play in the Tali'san, and blamed Croma'Rai leadership for tainting their impartial institution with politics.

In the five days since the Stu'cha had abducted her, while the train trailer was repaired and the Tali'san battle of Ju'rig had played itself to a bloody conclusion and marginal Croma'Rai victory, more croma media had come visiting, including some very important non-aligned figures in politics and culture to talk to Captain Debogande and others. The Captain had complained about the so-called 'security' rules that prevented offworlders and aliens from flying, and the VIPs had said there was nothing they could do about that. But there had been moral support, and some startlingly reasonable critiques of the Tali'san itself, and what some were calling the great, bloody unnecessariness of it all. But then, the traditionalist majority had replied, the croma race was at war with the most terrible species in the galaxy. If they did not select their greatest war leaders, and cultivate a warrior mindset by harking back to the oldest and strongest of croma traditions, they would lose. This was no time for softness, they said, and the blood spilled on Dul'rho today, on Tali'san battlefields across the planet, was but a small drop in a large ocean of croma blood spilled in the cause of defeating the reeh.

Tiga went up the swaying stairwell to the top deck, past the repaired cruiser on the landing pad, and sat at the railing behind the enormous forward windshield. The desert was rolling by once more, engines thundering as the great Kon'do flags streamed and flapped overhead. She'd been stupid, she realised now. Professor Romki had warned her of it many times, but she'd refused to listen, wanting this particular conflict to be simple in her head. But it wasn't simple — croma weren't nearly as evil or stupid as she wanted them to be, and whatever the croma's considerable shortcomings, her own people were similarly far from pure. Humans neither, the Professor had assured her — amongst whom rhetoric celebrating freedom and liberty had degenerated into militarist cliches beneath the increasingly iron rule of humanity's all-powerful Fleet.

"If you truly want to help your people," Romki had told her, "then you first have to see them clearly. And in seeing them clearly, you may realise that not all of your people deserve helping."

"And what do I do then?" Tiga had asked him, helplessly.

"I believe Major Thakur would say you should realise that you're not doing this to help people at all. You do it because it's what you are. The drive comes from within, not from outside. And that if you don't do everything you can to save your people in spite of all their flaws, it's not them who are lost, but yourself."

Tiga rested her chin on the vibrating railing, wind whipping her mane and fringe into her eyes, and wished that Major Thakur were here for her to talk to. She was becoming aware that it was a universal wish among the crew of *Phoenix*. Even Professor Romki, a man who had many problems with all things military, seemed to miss her greatly.

After a while of sitting, she looked back to see Do'reg by the cruiser. Ensign Kadi was holding a camera, and Do'reg was talking into it, shouting above the wind and engine noise despite the microphone's sensitivity. He had the now-famous hammer on his shoulder, and was clad in a more practical leather jacket.

Do'reg was thoroughly famous on Dul'rho now, and no one doubted his status, nor his right to participate in this Kon'do. His fight before the Stu'cha walls had been analysed many times, along with that final, killing blow with the heirloom hammer against a somewhat larger and much more credentialed opponent. Media now wanted to know his fighting teachers, his training schools, and his previous fighting experience. All of those were quite mundane by the standards of croma, just simple training yards and sparring sessions like so many millions of regular croma with no particular status, but now these places were famous too, and there were pilgrimages promised, and thousands of students wanting to train with those common instructors who had taught Do'reg Shur'do of the Shur'do Kon'do Rey'kan.

He had participated in the final ceremonies of the Battle of Ju'rig, had been honoured with carrying the Croma'Dokran battle colours, no small thing for a croma of any rank in this Tali'san. Of twenty thousand participants, there had been four thousand deaths and seven thousand wounded... a figure quickly obscured in the ceremonial-ese of Tali'san talk. Croma'Rai's victory had been declared based primarily upon field position, not casualties, and it was impolite to talk about the numbers of dead. Death in the Tali'san was something of an embarrassment, and young warriors never thought it would happen to them.

No wonder Skah had been so fooled, Tiga thought bitterly. The last great Tali'san had been two hundred years ago — another challenge against Croma'Rai that had failed — and with records so deliberately sketchy, and the histories filled with so much propaganda, it was easy to see how a young boy lacking the knowledge of how to dig deeper might be fooled into thinking the whole thing was just a dashingly dangerous game. Croma did not play games. Croma possessed the instinct to herd and fight, shoulder to shoulder, in a single wall of clan-based aggression. And that fighting instinct was never playful, but bloody-minded and ferocious, impossible for even the most sophisticated of high-technology societies to tame. Of all her old prejudices against the croma, that one Tiga retained as scientific fact, and even Romki did not dispute it.

Do'reg's interview ended, and Ensign Kadi took the camera downstairs. Do'reg stood for a moment, hand balancing against the cruiser, looking out at the passing desert.

Tiga hauled herself to her feet and strolled to him. Do'reg loomed over her, thoroughly intimidating despite being just three-quarters the size of the biggest croma. Tiga did not know particularly what she wanted to talk with him about, only that she did. If only to prove something to herself about her new understanding, and her capacity to change and grow.

"Hi," she said, from down by Do'reg's knee. And Do'reg surprised her, sitting beside the cruiser and resting there, like the backrest of a chair. He put the hammer down on his other side, with a heavy metal clang.

"Hello Tiga," he said, the mike carrying his voice to her ears despite the surrounding roar. Everyone on the train was wearing them, just to be heard. His muzzle's upper lip had the beginnings of a moustache on it, Tiga saw. Some croma grew enormous moustaches. Tiga recalled her father admiring them... and that made her sad all over again.

"I miss my family," she said awkwardly. "Where are your family?"

"My parents have passed," said Do'reg. "Some croma age, others do not." Tiga nodded, having heard a little of that. She didn't think the humans or tavalai had, though. "I have a daughter studying in Uka'deg, and a son in Jo'tukra. He and the kuhsi boy, Skah, became friends."

Tiga recalled To'na, who she'd insulted horribly when his play had annoyed her, and was ashamed. "Skah's a good boy," she said quietly. "He makes friends with good people."

"I hope he and Skah can stay in contact," Do'reg admitted. "I don't know how it is possible, though. *Phoenix* will leave eventually, and there is so little traffic between croma space and the outside."

"Yes," said Tiga. "All the galaxy's people. We do so much to keep ourselves separated. Are you enjoying fame?"

Do'reg nearly laughed. It was an odd expression on a croma, a curling of the lips to show teeth, exasperation as much as humour. "Crazy," he said. "The universe has gone crazy. I own an orchard. This hammer has sat in the property shrine for hundreds of years. It's a nice hammer, our family has always been proud of its story. But this..." He broke off, exasperation growing. "Crazy."

"Crazy," Tiga echoed. "I grew up in an old historical building, surrounded by green fields and forests. My world was riding, hunting food, doing lessons, helping my parents with chores. I'd never been to a big city before Cal'Uta. I thought I knew how everything was. Now this."

Do'reg looked at her solemnly. Somehow those dark, thick-lashed eyes did not seem nearly as dull or stupid as she'd imagined before. "You knew the reeh were evil," he said. "You still know the reeh are evil. Some things have not changed."

"No," Tiga agreed. "But I'd never seen any reeh. I only saw croma, and so I blamed croma for everything that was wrong."

"Croma could improve much," Do'reg said solemnly.

"Corbi too," said Tiga. Do'reg held up a big fist, croma-style. Tiga held up her small one, and they touched knuckles.

"I wish the reeh were here now," Do'reg admitted.

Tiga blinked. "You do?"

"I'd rather fight reeh than croma," Do'reg explained.

"Are you still proud to be in this Tali'san?"

"Yes," said Do'reg, firmly. "It is the greatest thing. My family will be remembered for generations." A pause, as the train shuddered across the wide, hot desert. "But great things are painful. Fighting reeh is painful too. I'd rather that."

Tiga thought she understood. "The croma you killed. Had you killed anyone before?"

"No." A longer pause, watching the desert. "Now I know his name. He was a good man. I'm told good men die in great times."

"They do," Tiga agreed, glancing up and sideways. Do'reg's big, muzzled face showed little, but his voice, past the translator, was different. "Do you regret killing him?"

"I'd rather fight the reeh," Do'reg repeated. It was as much of an admission of regret as she'd get from a croma, Tiga thought. "Maybe one day I will."

"I hope not," said Tiga, surprised with the fervency of the thought. "Places where the reeh invade don't fare well."

"We'll not retreat from this place," said Do'reg. "My family is many generations on this world. If the reeh come here, we'll fight them to the end. As your people do on Rando."

"Not all of them," Tiga said quietly. "Most are just trying to get by."

Do'reg made a gesture. "Corbi are not natural warriors like croma. Perhaps it makes them braver, that they fight at all."

* * *

ERIK HAD CLEARED OUT HIS SLEEPING QUARTERS BENEATH THE BRIDGE to watch Trace's recording. He doubted Trace would have included anything in her report that the lower ranks couldn't hear, but he had to make sure first.

She looked good, seated before a bare concrete wall. Erik could not hear any sound in the background, as though her location were heavily soundproofed. Light was single-sourced and artificial, half-illuminating her face from the side. Her hair was very short, as though she'd taken some clippers to it rather than bother with her usual trim. A standard, short, female haircut had always been Trace's one concession to style, when a practical buzz cut may have suited her performance-at-all-costs personality more.

'I'm a woman,' she'd explained in her typically matter-of-fact way when they'd discussed it once. 'People look at women differently, including my own marines, and not just the men. It is what it is. The biggest thing I've learned in this job as I've moved up the ranks is to pick my battles.'

But now, among the corbi, Erik supposed it mattered less.

"So we're going after the Splicer," she said now on the recording. *"I'm guessing some of you aren't going to like that decision, so let me tell you what I've learned.*

"First, Rando isn't some heavily fortified garrison world. It's a backwater, a hardship posting for reeh, run mostly by slave species and others. It has few military resources and is actually quite lightly defended. Partly I think this is because of what we discovered at Zondi — that the reeh had an effective truce with the Croma'Rai leadership that allowed them to redirect forces elsewhere for the last few hundred years. But it's also partly because Rando's location so close to croma territory makes it vulnerable to attack. If the croma had been pushed back another hundred lightyears, Rando would

have fared better from being more secure. But now, it's a zoo for genetic experiments on the local population, and a training ground for experimental mutations on slave soldiers. They use them on the corbi, but it doesn't take them much effort. In truth, most of this world surrendered long ago."

There was a sadness in her voice, past the businesslike delivery. Others might not have spotted it, but to Erik it was obvious. Unlike most, Erik knew Trace when her 'marine face' was off completely, and he knew what her sadness looked like. And her laughter.

"Styx gave me an assassin bug before I was captured, it's been helping me. It's now proceeding to multiply itself — don't ask, it's amazing but it doesn't matter, the end result is that I'll shortly have twelve of them and they all seem convinced they'll have technological dominance over the reeh's networks. The Resistance Fleet also have penetrated the reeh surveillance network, so we're going to use that, plus the bugs' infiltration capabilities, to disguise a couple of flyers as reeh vessels and fly right into the Splicer. We've also got rebels on the inside who've promised to help us — again, long story, you don't need the details.

"What I need from you is a time when you'll be available. Tano can get these messages back and forth in about five days each way, which means he's got a dedicated ship doing the runs, so Resistance Fleet's taking this seriously. Be aware that they've evidently got far more technology than they've so far let on. How far you trust them is up to you, but be warned that their agenda is only coincidentally aligned with ours.

"Our attack needs to begin ahead of Phoenix's arrival in system, or obviously their defences will go up. You'll need to arrive directly behind us, and fight your way down to us, then extract with everything you've got. I'll be going in with nearly two hundred soldiers. I don't expect to be extracting with anything like that number. I've told them all that you can fight down to Rando single-handedly if necessary, though I'd imagine the Resistance Fleet will have some assistance to offer. They're skeptical that you can do it, despite what I've told them about Phoenix's present capabilities. If you can't do it, you need to tell me. If you think it's any chance better than fifty-fifty, I think it's still worth it. Even worse than that, maybe."

Her dark-eyed gaze at the camera was somber. As Phoenix Company Commander, Trace's primary mission had always been to safeguard the ship. Now she was suggesting that the mission would still be worthwhile if there was a fifty percent chance that *Phoenix* was destroyed. Under any other circumstances, it would be appallingly irresponsible of her. But everyone on *Phoenix* knew the stakes.

"That's all I've got for now. I love you all. See you shortly."

The screen went blank. Erik gazed at the wall for a long moment. Commander Draper had already informed him of his own disapproval of Trace's plan. LC Dufresne and Lieutenant Dale, the only two other people whose opinions mattered, were in favour. Erik couldn't blame Draper for not liking it. The whole thing was a giant shot in the dark, risking the whole ship, and its marine commander even if the ship survived. But strangely, he didn't find this decision nearly as agonising as he might.

He established a connection with *Phoenix*, and found Draper in the command chair. "I've made my decision," he told the *Phoenix* Commander. "We're following the Major's plan. Make the necessary preparations, and get that return message sent to her via the Resistance courier immediately."

"Yes Captain." To Draper's credit, Erik heard no disapproval in his tone. *"I'll do it immediately."*

"Captain out." Erik disconnected, got up and made his way up the swaying ladder to the bridge, and the glare of desert sun through the dusty windshield. He took his seat between Sasalaka and Rhi'shul, and gazed out at the ground vehicles that raced alongside, throwing up great plumes of dust as they bounced across the desert scrub.

"Captain?" asked Bree Harris from the far side of the bridge. "Was that the Major on the recording?"

"Yes it was," said Erik, settling into his now familiar chair. "She's fine. I'll show you all the recording later."

"Is she planning trouble?" Geish asked, with the certainty of someone who'd served with Trace for many years.

Erik restrained a sigh, and made it into a tight smile instead. "Trouble for the reeh, Lieutenant. Big trouble." He activated coms, and called Jalawi. "Hello Skeeter, how are our guests doing?"

"They seem to be okay," said Jalawi's reply. *"Just hanging out in the*

*trailer rear, looking at the desert passing. If they start eating our food, we'll
run out pretty quick."*

"Just be polite," Erik told him. "They should be pretty chill."

It was the next phase of the Kon'do. With the Battle of Ju'rig over,
the Shur'do Kon'do Rey'kan was tasked with transporting some old
warriors from the struggle to a place called Tov'mai. Predictably it
was another thousand kilometres out of their way, but that was the
price they'd all agreed to pay for getting to Stat'cha at all. These five
old warriors were currently sitting in the trailer main hold, the only
part of the interior large enough to fit them.

Just as predictably, they'd picked up an escort leaving Ju'rig, as
many as twenty or thirty vehicles roaring along behind them on the
sandy freeway lanes, all far too close for recommended safety spacing
and throwing up an enormous plume of sand visible for many kilometres. Air vehicles had been warned away, but still a few were
hovering, circling their position at higher altitude. Most of those were
media, but far above, *Phoenix* was watching those transmissions to
discern which were Croma'Rai authorities trying to figure what to do
next.

"Croma'Rai just won Tur'dor and Del'gor, but lost Kron'tek," said
Rhi'shul, lounging in the chair beside Erik, long legs crossed as she
scrolled through windshield displays of the ongoing conflict. *"They
hold a narrow lead, not nearly as great as everyone expected. Based on
those expectations, there is a good chance more neutral clans will declare
late in the Assessment Council for Croma'Dokran. Dokran look like a
chance, now. They didn't before."*

"What do you think?" Erik asked her. "You think Tiga's testimony
could sway them?"

Rhi'shul took another fig from the dash bowl and munched. *"Croma'Dokran's always attracted the rams."* Erik wondered a moment why
the translator was giving the word for sheep... then he recalled.
Battering rams. Used for breaching fortifications — a croma concept
entirely. *"They never thought Croma'Rai was aggressive enough. With the
scandal, they think they've discovered why, but they were reluctant to join
this Tali'san if they'd lose and look stupid. They're still not convinced. If*

Tiga can show them that all croma have unfinished business with Rando, that will give them their new war."

Erik stared out the wide windshield for a long moment. Rhi'shul gave him a knock on the arm with one big fist. Erik looked, and her dark-lashed eyes were questioning. Much more respectful, she'd become, since the operation to retrieve Tiga from the Stu'cha... but it came with treating him more like a croma, punches on the arm included. Erik hoped she didn't break something by accident. He was physically augmented, as were all active-duty Fleet personnel, but Rhi'shul was too. The sheer scale of it, as she loomed in her chair alongside, was intimidating.

"If we do get Tiga to that Council," Erik explained grimly, "we'll be helping to start a new war. If the clans come on board with Sho'-mo'ra, and he wins the Tali'san."

"We're already at war," said Rhi'shul, faintly baffled. *"We've been at war for thousands of years."*

"It would start a new phase."

"That may benefit us strategically." Rhi'shul flipped a fig seed out the small slit in the side window, where hot air swirled in. *"It would be nice if we died for some strategic benefit for a change. The last few hundred years have gained us nothing."*

"You're still here," Erik pointed out.

Rhi'shul shrugged, conceding that as she took another fig. *"What's in this for you?"* she asked.

"What's in what?"

The croma made an expansive gesture at the desert ahead. A big ground vehicle had parked beside the freeway markers ahead, croma sitting atop it waving large flags and taking video as they roared past. Sasalaka, Erik noticed, actually flashed the train's lights at them in recognition. She too was eating more of Rhi'shul's figs, the only one of the bridge crew to have acquired a taste.

"Don't tell me about your mission with the Rando Splicer," Rhi'shul said. *"You could have found another way to do it than through Tiga. The corbi don't deserve their fate, but you're not in this for the corbi any more than I am. You're here to save humanity. This seems like a side track."*

Erik thought of Suli Shahaim, floating in *Phoenix*'s shattered bridge beside her co-pilot's chair amid spreading globules of blood as crew wrestled her from the bridge. Crew bodies lashed together in holding rooms so they didn't clog up the corridors. Part of him still couldn't quite believe they were gone. Another part hated himself for coping with it as well as he had. It had been awful, but he hadn't broken down. Part of him felt like a monster for not having done so.

"I don't know," he admitted finally. "Maybe I'm also tired of us dying for nothing."

"You think what you've achieved so far is nothing? That data-core you retrieved?"

Erik gave her a long look. Not many croma had heard of that. That Rhi'shul had, confirmed a few suspicions. "We sent it home. It will change human civilisation. Perhaps in time to save it, if we are attacked. But it's not here. We can't see it. And we might not even make it back at all. Rando, and the corbi... we can all see that. The reeh too. And it's important to know what you're fighting for."

"And your Major Thakur... you think she's running around saving corbi lives while forgetting to put humanity first?"

The old, disrespectful edge was back. Erik snorted. "Trace likes to think she'd let all of Rando die if it increased humanity's chances just a fraction, I'm sure. But I know her better."

"Or perhaps you only like to think you do."

"And what about you, Rhi'shul?" Erik asked shortly. "You helped to rescue Tiga. Are you going to claim you care nothing for the corbi?"

"My caring is irrelevant," said Rhi'shul, discarding another fig seed. *"I need your help to get in the Croma'Rai Intelligence headquarters. If rescuing your corbi helps me get it, I'll do it."*

"You'll come out of that exchange pretty important," Erik noted. "Holding further proof of your leadership's treachery toward ordinary Croma'Rai and allied clans. You could personally dispose of that leadership, with your connections, especially if they just got their collective asses handed to them in this Tali'san."

"*Which is happening,*" Rhi'shul admitted, unbothered by this line of questioning.

"Croma'Rai will need some new leaders, then. Younger leaders, maybe. Untainted by these past years of corruption. Wouldn't happen to know anyone like that, would you Rhi'shul? Friends of yours, back in your Dan'gede circles? Maybe even you yourself, when you've put on a bit more armour?"

Rhi'shul munched another fig, looking at him with an expression that might have been a smile. If croma smiled. Her ears flicked, jangling several steel rings there. "*I want some music,*" she said loudly. "*Is there any music on this pile of trash?*"

Erik handed that conversation off to Stefan Geish and Bree Harris, who knew far more about human popular music than him. Harris's pop songs and ballads made the croma gag, quite theatrically. Erik couldn't help but grin. Geish had a better idea by playing death metal, but while Rhi'shul found it tolerable, no one else did. Finally they settled for some hard rock instrumental with power chords, solos and pounding rhythm, while Rhi'shul looked out the side window, nodding faintly to the alien beat.

Erik activated a coms link to her, to talk over the noise. "You think the anti-Tali'san people will ever win and make it stop?" he asked her.

"*No,*" said Rhi'shul. "*No one argues that it's not awful. But croma love greatness. Tell us that a world will be swallowed by a black hole tomorrow, more will travel there than leave, just to see it, even though it kills them. It's a terrible fate of the universe that all of the greatest things are awful. Croma will always run to it, like insects to flame.*"

"Not all great things are awful," Erik said with amusement. "Love is not awful. New life isn't. Seasons, friendships. Sunsets."

Rhi'shul gave him an appalled sideways look. "*I can't believe the same species that made this music can spout such ridiculous sentiment. Great. You understand great?*" She smacked a fist into the palm of her hand, to powerful effect. "*Damn this translator. It sounds like we're communicating, but I don't think we really are. My words mean things you can't imagine.*"

"I understand 'great'," Erik said tiredly. "I've been in more 'great' moments than you'll ever see. I've come to understand that they're overrated."

"Never," said Rhi'shul, with a gleam in her dark eyes. *"Bring me to one of your great moments, Captain Debogande. So that at least one of us may enjoy it properly."*

* * *

TWO HOURS OUT FROM TOV'MAI, THE WEATHER CLOSED IN. SOON Sasalaka was throttling back the turbofan as the filters engaged and limited airflow along with the thickening clouds of sand that swept across the desert freeway. Accompanying airtraffic disappeared as the skies turned black, and lightning flashed above low, rocky hills that rarely saw rain.

"Hardly anything," Geish confirmed, looking at his scan feed and waves of sand hissed across the windshield, and the train's big floodlights lit on everything blowing sideways. "Just wind, sand and electricity."

Skah surprised Erik by coming up to look. Too big now for laps, he stood between Erik and Rhi'shul, peering out at the storm, big ears folded back with trepidation. "Swow," he observed.

"Yeah, we can't go fast in this," Erik agreed. "The turbine will fill up with sand. And the flags are catching this wind. Be lucky if we don't lose a couple."

"Not the way they make those flags," Rhi'shul disagreed. *"They're not just used for Tali'sans. This weather is not uncommon out here."* She offered Skah one of her remaining figs.

"Not neat," said Skah.

"Not meat," Erik translated as the translator made Rhi'shul frown. "Kuhsi only eat meat."

"A race of hunters," Rhi'shul said approvingly. *"The ancient croma ancestors were carnivores. Eating plants came later."*

Erik nodded, having heard that already. Skah frowned, looking up at the big croma. "But big aninals eat prants."

"On low-gravity worlds," Rhi'shul corrected, reaching a long arm to

make sure the side window was secure as the train rocked. Somehow the bridge smelled of sand and dust regardless. *"Ron'chep is a high-gravity world, by your standards."* Ron'chep, Erik knew, was the croma homeworld, far from here. *"On low-gravity worlds, most of the biggest land animals got large so the predators couldn't eat them. On high-gravity worlds, size is good for power, but too much size collapses under its own weight. So the plant eaters grew armour instead, to protect them from predators, and big claws and spikes to fight them off. Then a few of the predators grew armour to protect them from those claws. The croma were the most successful of those."*

"It's evolution as armoured warfare," Kaspowitz remarked from the other end of the bridge, having recently gained enough comfort with his arm to do that. It lay in a sling across his chest, and as he said testily, he didn't need two hands to read a screen. Erik had refrained from telling him that he didn't really need to be on the bridge to do it, either. "Can't outrun your opponent in that gravity, can't keep getting larger like the dinosaurs or you'll collapse. So grow armourplate instead."

"Dinosaurs?" said Rhi'shul, not needing the translator to phonetically copy the strange word.

"Old Earth animals," Erik explained. "Hundreds of millions of years ago. Giant reptiles, much larger than chew'toos, they dominated the planet before an ancient meteor strike wiped them out."

"Interesting," said Rhi'shul. *"And the human ancestor looked something like the corbi?"*

"Not far off," Erik admitted. "They evolved on wide open plains so they lost the corbi's tree-climbing, grew long legs. Corbi somehow evolved enormous brains without moving to the plains... human scientists weren't sure that was possible."

"Not very impressive," Rhi'shul said. *"Croma ancestors were more exciting."*

"True that," Geish admitted. "Armoured biped warrior carnivores in heavy-G sounds exciting."

"Not evolving rocks in your skull has advantages," Kaspowitz retorted.

Rhi'shul only looked amused. Erik suspected that friendly insult trading only made her feel at home. *"Sasalaka,"* she asked. *"What was the tavalai ancient ancestor?"*

"Frogs," said Sasalaka, concentrating on the road as the visibility grew worse.

"What's a... frog?"

"Ask the humans."

Rhi'shul looked at the humans, who were smiling. "A small amphibian," said Erik. "Tavalai lived in swamps for millions of years. Long enough to evolve needing both swimming and walking."

"The closest ancestor used to climb swamp trees to escape predators in the water," Sasalaka explained. "Soon they started to live up there, and build nests. For a long time tavalai scientists insisted that intelligent life could only evolve in swamps. Some are still disappointed it's not true."

"And Skah," said Rhi'shul. *"What was the kuhsi ancestor?"*

"Hunter," said Skah. "Big pwains, rots of pwant eaters. Used to have four wegs, very snaw, very fast, hunt snaw things. Then weather change, wots of trees, snaw aninal get big, get fingers to cwine trees, but stiw run on ground on two regs."

Erik was impressed. Skah's learning was growing even faster than his body. Speculation was that Styx was helping teach him, though what was in it for Styx, no one had figured. "The kuhsi ancestors were terrifying," Erik said. "Human-sized but faster and stronger, big teeth and claws. Didn't look so pretty back then either."

"Werewolves," said Kaspowitz. Skah flipped on his AR glasses, found and sent Rhi'shul an image in seconds. The image appeared on the dash screen before her — an artist's impression of the kuhsi's evolutionary ancestors. They looked like something out of an evil fairytale — werewolves, as Kaspowitz said. Rhi'shul looked impressed.

"Kuhsi win," she declared. *"Skah has the most interesting ancestors."*

It appeared to cheer the somber boy, just a little.

Tov'mai was off the main freeway, slow progress for a hover train even in clear weather, weaving slowly past wind-worn rocks that loomed in the sandstorm like alien artefacts, surreal and misshapen. Sasalaka fought the sideslip at lower speeds, and the winds that swirled in the shallow canyons. Along the train sides, Jalawi and Karajin's marines kept careful watch on the heights in case of ambush, whatever their recent status increase with the Dul'rho population and the handcuffs it put on Croma'Rai's leadership. There were carvings on the stone canyon walls, the shapes and outlines of ghostly architecture, lost behind a blowing veil of sand.

"So it's like a retirement home for old croma?" Kaspowitz asked Rhi'shul, staring suspiciously at the petrified skyline.

"Like that," said Rhi'shul. *"Transporting old warriors who have fought their last, directly from the Tali'san, is a great honour."*

"So we've been told," said Kaspowitz, peering at his map display. "The graphic doesn't say if that lake is full of water."

"It's Lake Doshen'be," said Rhi'shul. *"It has water. It's quite famous, since Great Exclusion times."*

"What age do croma retire at?" Erik wondered. "The old warriors onboard with us don't seem that old." Romki had warned them all not to probe too hard with croma about death and old age. There were sensitivities, he'd said, that did not yet make sense to him.

"It's not discussed," Rhi'shul said shortly. *"We know when it's time."*

Another half-hour up the winding road at barely fifty kph, and the canyon opened to a wide cluster of palm trees, blowing in the storm. Before them was a ceremonial gate, made of stone and decorated in croma-style with fortress motifs, steel studs and chains where a portcullis might be found on a real fort. Big croma awaited, looming shapes in ceremonial armour, and Sasalaka brought the rig to a gentle halt, winding the power gently downward as they settled to the sand.

Erik barely needed to give instructions — once halted, Jalawi was in charge of defensive deployments with Karajin his second, and everyone moved like clockwork. By the time Erik climbed down from the bridge, goggles in place and scarf wrapped around his mouth and nose, Jalawi was already in conversation with the big waiting croma.

Erik joined him, and found the big croma respectful but noncommunicative. Not all of the croma waiting with the big leader were armoured. One was plainly a doctor, clad in a green-panelled coat with a portable cart of what looked like medical equipment. Erik gestured humans and tavalai aside as their croma passengers approached, and were greeted with respectful gestures from those waiting. Each went in turn to the doctor, who gave them a very brief examination with apparently high-tech equipment, then passed them on.

"This is very strange," Romki told Erik, waiting at his side, voice muffled behind his scarf. "We can't see very far, but it doesn't appear to be a big settlement here. Any retirement facility should be huge."

"There'd be plenty of water in the lake," said Erik. "It's a sensible place, logistically."

Romki left Erik's side to go to Skah, standing nearby. "Skah, I think you should go back inside."

Skah stared up at him from behind oversized goggles, sensitive nose hidden behind one of the traditional scarves Corporal Graf had had the forethought to buy in bulk in case of exactly this type of weather. "What you say?" Skah shouted. His ears were plastered so tightly to his head for protection against the blowing sand, he could barely hear a thing.

"I think you should go back inside!" Romki shouted back.

"Why?"

"I think this might not be a good thing for you to see!"

Skah looked at him for a long moment, no doubt thinking of the awful things he'd seen at the Tali'san. Then turned back to watch the subdued welcoming ceremony, ignoring the Professor's advice.

A small, stocky figure came loping from the grounded hover train — Tiga, also wrapped against the storm. Erik was surprised, but only a little. She stopped at Skah's side, and put a hand on his shoulder. Skah did not protest.

Passing the honour guard, the five big croma of the hover train were wrapped in shawls against the blasting sand, then began a slow trudge through the ceremonial gate and into the forest of palms. Rhi'shul indicated that Erik and the senior crew should follow. These being his Kon'do responsibilities, Erik complied, humans, tavalai, a kuhsi boy and a corbi, walking a respectful distance behind the croma, dead palm fronds crunching underfoot.

Erik glanced at Romki as they walked. Romki looked grim, and said nothing. There weren't enough old croma, Romki had always said. Croma gained rank with age, but croma power hierarchies were pyramids, with many at the bottom and very few at the top. Very old croma were enormously prominent in the power that they held, but numerically very rare. In human or tavalai societies this might have made sense, as old humans or tavalai simply stayed indoors more as their age slowed them down. But while old croma also slowed, they gained power and strength as well. Age was a test against physics and gravity for elder croma, not against decrepitude. And so, with modern technology, or simply the availability of large swimming pools in which to support their weight, there should have been lots and lots of elder croma, and quite visible too. But there weren't.

Erik could see why Romki told Skah to go back to the train. He glanced down at Tiga, now on his left. Tiga grasped Erik's hand, corbi doing that reflexively when distressed. She touched her ear, and Erik's coms crackled.

"I'm not supposed to talk about it," she said in his ear, the only way to be heard speaking quietly in the storm. *"As guests of the croma, they made it very clear we weren't to discuss it with outsiders. It's a prestige thing."*

"How do they determine which croma are allowed to grow old?" Erik asked.

"It's a bio-psychological mechanism," said Tiga. *"A socially-activated biological function. Low-rank croma die young. They just do, croma brains at low-status are chemically different, they're that status-conscious. Only the highest-status croma brains generate enough of an anti-aging compound that lets them grow huge and old. That's why there are so few, and why they're always high-ranked."*

Erik took a deep breath as that realisation sank in. It made sense. A very unpleasant, very croma kind of objectionable sense. "But... but if it's just a compound, they could synthetically reproduce it. Croma aren't stupid, they've got great technology."

"*And most reject it,*" Tiga said somberly. "*Accepting the synthetic compound is varying degrees of taboo for lower-status croma. Croma old age is expensive, too. High expenses and taboo status means most just accept their fate.*"

"How many years do they lose?"

"*The old croma reach about two hundred, like humans, or corbi. These are perhaps one-forty.*"

Sixty years, Erik thought... more like seventy in human years. A lot to lose for social stubbornness. A third of a lifetime. "And the Shur'do Kon'do Rey'kan had to transport them here," he muttered. "On their final journey."

"*It's a great honour,*" said Tiga. "*Or so I'm told.*"

The palms cleared, revealing the vast expanse of an inland lake. The maps had shown Erik that the Lake Doshen'be was about forty kilometres wide, making it hard to see the far shore on a clear day. Today there was no chance, the water frothed to a thousand rippling whitecaps, sand hissing like a slithering thing as it whipped the surface. The hellish scene lit blue, in abrupt relief, then back to gloom. The five big croma stopped on the water's edge, and exchanged words with a robed croma with a great staff, who touched it to their heads. Then, as thunder boomed and rolled, each of the croma whom Erik's train had transported out of their way to this place, began slowly wading out to sea.

No one spoke. Erik thought it perhaps the most miserable thing he'd seen on this whole trip — five magnificent members of an infuriating species whom he'd reluctantly come to enjoy, struggling in their shawls into the desolate waves. Suddenly there were tears in his eyes, which he could not wipe for the goggles. Perhaps the waters were toxic, perhaps the five had drunk something that would end it quickly, he didn't truly care. This was no way for a smart, moral people to respect the lives of their elders. Only of course, as everyone from Romki to Rhi'shul and even Tiga had been warning him from the beginning, croma didn't really respect individual life, but rather the collision between those lives and the great moments of time, be they on the large scale or the small. Individual croma were nothing without that proximity to greatness, and so their lower-status elders ended their lives early to avoid the more gradual withering of age that would not allow them to reach the magnificence of high-rank elders.

Erik didn't know why he felt such loss. But suddenly his head was filled only with the faces and conversation of the people *Phoenix* had lost, and all his hopes for making sense of that catastrophe were wading into the wild lake with these croma. There had to be more to it than this. Surely one did not embark on this grand venture to save humanity just to vanish beneath desolate waves, never to be seen or recalled again. But if they all died out here, no one back home would truly care, save for the immediate families and a few broad-minded individuals who knew or suspected what was really going on, beyond the veil that Fleet pulled daily over their eyes.

He didn't want to die this young, though he'd risked it enough by now to know that he was no coward. But to not be remembered, nor even appreciated by the people in whose service he'd died... that was something he'd not yet come to terms with. These five croma would perhaps be recalled, given the auspicious nature of this Kon'do... but this was how croma everywhere ended their lives, across croma space, in their millions, most in circumstances far less auspicious than this. Where were their friends and family? Why did they wander out into the lake alone? Why was there no comfort, no solace, no final words or reminders of a life's hard-earned achievements? He wanted to yell at them all to come back, that they'd all somehow managed to miss the point... but he was a guest here, and this was how millions of years of social and biological evolution had determined that things worked best.

That thought was the most miserable of all. The universe was cruel and unsentimental. Among croma, this probably *was* the best way. But then if the various intelligent species of the universe were just going to accept the vile hand that physical laws had dealt them, what was the point of constantly striving to make things better? And if there was no point to that striving, then what the hell was *Phoenix* doing out here so far away from home?

Looking away from the scene, Erik saw through tears and blowing sand what looked like a hut between several bending palms. A great awning flapped above the shuddering roof, tied to the trunks by ropes. Every other structure he'd seen in this place was official and ceremonial, as befitted a place where croma came to die. So what was this ramshackle construction doing here?

Having no interest in watching more croma die, Erik walked that way. At his side, Corporal Graf did not miss a beat, moving to walk with him, Private Ram on the other side, rifles ready.

"Captain?" came Jalawi's surprised query.

"Just checking out this structure," Erik informed the Lieutenant. "Stay with the main group."

"Captain," said Romki, *"I'm not sure that's a good idea. Your presence here is required for the Kon'do..."*

"I'm here, the cameras aren't," Erik said shortly. "I'm sure I won't miss anything."

He walked to the hut, mostly glad that he didn't have to watch anymore. Corporal Graf went first, peering through a small window opening of the leeward side. She indicated all clear, and pushed open the door. Another all clear, and Erik peered past her shoulder.

Inside, reclining on a very large makeshift armchair, was a large croma. On his lap was a holography unit, and his fingers danced upon holographic keys. He looked across now, removing spectacle-like AR glasses from his eyes to peer at the new arrivals. Erik realised that with the noise of the wind, it would be difficult to converse with the door open. He indicated to Graf that he was fine, and she retreated to take guard outside, closing the door behind.

He pulled off his goggles and unwound his scarf, wiping his eyes of water and sand. The croma spoke... and immediately Erik knew he'd misgendered a croma yet again, because this one's voice was multi-toned like an orchestra playing chords. *"Who is that there?"* Erik's earpiece translator spoke. *"My eyes don't work very well."*

She didn't wear an earpiece, Erik realised. So she wouldn't have a translator running either, let alone one that understood English. He activated the small belt-speaker for such occasions, and when he spoke, it squawked in kul'hasa. "Hello," he said. "I'm Captain Erik Debogande of the human warship *Phoenix*. I was invited to come here by..."

The croma waved a hand at him, dismissively... an entirely human gesture. *"The whole planet knows who you are. Not much use in me meeting aliens at this point in my life when I can barely see."*

"I'm very sorry to disturb you," said Erik, gazing about the hut with intrigue. It looked as though it had been nailed together with no particular expertise. There were a couple of central support poles to keep the roof up, and the rest was planks held together by nails or netting. On the floor was a small battery unit, and simple power cords linked to her holographics setup and a small oven on a cinderblock. Everything rattled and shook in the wind. "I just couldn't help wondering..."

"Why I'm not drowning myself?" the old croma asked. She wore a simple tunic and pants, forearms somewhat armoured but nothing like the massive plates that truly ancient croma wore. Like Tiga had said — early old age, perhaps a hundred and forty. *"I was going to, but then I realised I still had some things to say."* She indicated her writing setup. *"So here I am. Writing."*

From the tone of her voice, Erik reckoned she'd like him to leave so that she could get on with it. "What are you writing?" Erik asked. "Did you have experiences in war against the reeh?"

The old croma might have smiled, a flick from drooping ears. *"I never served, never passed the aptitude. Don't believe the nonsense these rock-heads sell you, not all croma are warriors. I had regular jobs. I ran a school at one point, then a small farm. And I had three children, none of them serve either. It's not the kind of heroic tale they'll write stories about."*

"Then who are you writing for?"

"For me, mostly. And for the kids. Do you have family, Erik?"

"Four sisters," said Erik. "And lots of cousins, aunts and uncles." On a plank shelf nearby, a small wooden carving sat. An animal, crouched on its haunches, with long ears. The work showed no great skill, but it was sincere. "Why don't your family take you in? Why do you have to stay here, if you've decided your time's not done yet?"

"Oh, my time is completely done," the old croma corrected him. *"I can barely get up, now. They said it would come on fast, and they were right."* She reached for a ceramic jug of water, and sipped. Someone had helped her get these basic things, Erik reckoned, and nail this shelter together. There were no more permanent accommodations present. Evidently very few croma changed their minds. The old lady fixed him with a glazed stare. *"Why do you care?"*

"Because I'm a trouble maker," Erik admitted. The croma chortled, which gave way to great coughs as the rickety armchair creaked. "Why don't you come with us? We've room on the train. We could get you some of the anti-ageing compound that the oldest croma have, shouldn't be too difficult. You could live another sixty years."

He knew it was a reckless thing to offer. Right then, he didn't care.

"No," said the croma, as though not even tempted for a moment. *"The most part of life is going with the flow, youngster."*

"The least part," Erik retorted.

"In your world, maybe. I understand you're a pariah. I don't want to be. I'd rather die."

"I'm not a pariah," Erik said fiercely. "I serve in the company of heroes."

"And I wish you well with it. Croma just want to be a part of something great, as croma, together. What do you think the Tali'san's all about? 'Stand next to it,' the poets tell us. 'Grow tall in its shadow'."

"And I've seen more great things as a renegade from my people than I ever would had I just done what they'd wanted."

"And now you're a pariah," the croma said patiently, *"and one day soon you'll die unloved and alone."*

"Like you in this hut?" Erik retorted. He knew it was stupid to get into a heated argument with an old dying alien by the lakeshore. But somehow it had become very important to make his point strongly.

"That was my choice," said the croma. *"My family brought me here and said goodbye properly. I just realised I had a few things to write first.*

And if you don't mind, Erik, I'd like to get back to it. I don't have much time left."

"Of course," said Erik, swallowing whatever else he'd wanted to say. "Of course. And I wish you well with your writing. Tell me, do you have a network connection here?"

"Of course."

"Do you mind if I get copy of your writing when you're done? I'd like to read it."

The croma looked astonished. *"Yes. Of course. But... I don't know how to send it to you."*

Erik smiled. "Don't worry. I have a friend who can get me a copy whether you send it or not. I just wanted your permission first. I'm sorry, I never got your name?"

"Tran'do," said the croma. *"I wish you well in your travels, Erik. It would have been fun to be a warrior, wouldn't it?"*

"It has its moments. Goodbye Tran'do."

21

"The Eshfo Rebellion," Trace repeated, looking askance at Tano and Dreja. They sat in a small concrete store room, surrounded by mostly empty storage crates. Pena and Rika sat on one, lit in the glow of a portable lamp, blinking with weariness in the middle of the night. They'd been picked up by one of Tano's flyers just a few hours ago, and flown directly here with their tale. Even Trace found it incredible.

"Eshfo, yeah," Rika repeated, sipping the steaming tea someone had brought him. The tanifex had interrogated each of them separately, presumably to see if they got the same story from both. Trace thought Ensign Jokono would have approved. "I'm pretty sure that's what they said, right Pen?"

Pena did not disagree, sipping her own tea, looking distant and troubled. Trace watched her for a moment, with concern, then back to Tano. She wasn't bothering with the translator at this time — she was more worried about the corbi not understanding her than the other way around. In this conversation, she was mostly listening. "I've heard of it," Tano affirmed. "The Reeh Empire has nearly a thousand populated systems, though. Those are just the worlds, inhabited non-worlder systems are thousands more."

"Eshfo's nearly three hundred light years away," said Dreja. "Not far. I don't think we know much about it, other than it's an industry-heavy place, lots of activity. Supposed to be quite grim, but then, they all are."

"Can you remember if there was any talk of tanifex there?" Trace pressed. "Military bases, staging points?"

"They've all got bases," said Dreja, twirling his favourite pistol about his finger in the trigger guard. Trace really wished he wouldn't do that, even though the magazine was removed. But Dreja was Tano's guy, and she wasn't about to start that fight right now. "Massive slave training centres too. Millions of slave soldiers, stuffed into huge facilities, like prisons."

"Why so big?" Kono asked. "They can't use that many soldiers, they'd be better off putting the resources into ships."

"Because they've got limited spots," Dreja agreed, in his grim, too-experienced way. "They make the others compete for them. Rumour is the competition losers end up as fertiliser, or worse."

"Ever heard of a rebellion starting in a place like that?" Trace asked.

"Always rumours," said Dreja. Another spin of the pistol. Trace nearly grabbed it off him. "Hard to tell what's true. Reeh aren't big on clarity. And tanifex can be liars." With a wary look at Pena and Rika.

Both corbi had been put through the scientists' analysis directly upon returning, eyeballs probed, reflexes tested, brainwaves measured. The tests weren't perfect, but the scientists were quite sure that neither had been subjected to reeh tests of brainwashing. Besides which, those procedures typically took a far longer period of time than they'd been absent.

"I've heard," said Jindi, the other person in the room. He sat by the far wall, one short leg tapping uncontrollably. Arms wrapped around himself, as though for warmth. Trace thought of the warm, sunny beach he'd been dragged from, contrasted now poorly with this black concrete cell. "Not tanifex, though. Skranid. Different slave species, they're slow, they don't work combat. Work internal systems. One of them told me, once. About news from his home. About wars against the reeh. I don't know why he told me. I never saw him again, after that. I think maybe someone was listening."

The sheer scale of the misery in the Reeh Empire nearly took Trace's breath away. 'The stone shall want for nothing. Be the stone.' She took a deep breath. "One thing is certain. We're exposed now. If the tanifex use this against us, we're finished."

"That was always the risk," Tano agreed. "We knew that going in." Trace looked around at the group. It was pointless discussing it further. They all knew the implications. If the tanifex were a setup, it was over. But then, there were lots of things that could go wrong and kill them all. The entire operation was a roll of the dice. As a professional, Trace knew she wasn't supposed to accept that. Professionals were supposed to be meticulous, to let nothing go to chance. But if being a meticulous professional had taught her anything, it was that sometimes there was no choice but to take a deep breath and hand your fate over to cosmic chance.

"So what do they want?" Trace asked Rika and Pena.

"Equal share of the Splicer's genetic data," said Rika, with barely restrained intensity. "They're not sure how much of it can help with the tanifex, much of Rando Splicer's data is about Rando native species, like corbi. But they said the tools themselves are the most important thing, they said... they said..." as he strained, trying to remember the words.

"They said it's not just genetic manipulation," Pena interrupted, her voice subdued. "It's an AI-based simulation program, it can predict genetic outcomes. Technically it allows them to build new lifeforms, and manipulate existing ones... it doesn't work without the simulation, there's so much detail beneath the genetic level, all the proteins and cellular functions, if they don't all align the whole thing gets messed up. It takes AI-level intelligence. And even then the predictions don't completely line up, they have to cross-reference the predictions with the outcomes. And so, Rando. The living genetic laboratory. They're not just manipulating genes here. They're testing their simulation programs. Improving them. We're just one more gear in the reeh machine."

Trace glanced at Kono. Kono thought Pena was far too smart to be left stagnating on Rando. He said she ought to go with *Phoenix*, that they could use her, and that maybe she could be a spokesperson for the corbi back in human space. Hearing explanations like that, Trace thought he might have a point. But she wasn't sure Pena would be so eager to leave the cause she'd devoted her life to fighting.

"Right," Rika agreed, as though he'd understood all of that. "The tanifex think they can use that program, if they can get the... the source code or whatever, to help tanifex everywhere in the Empire. Smuggle it about, get rebel scientists to reverse it, I don't know, it got complicated. But that's what they want. And they want a few of them to get away on *Phoenix* with you, while others will steal a shuttle and get up to an orbital ship, if you leave one disabled."

"They'll need a big force to capture a ship," Kono said cautiously. "We can disable the ship, but we can't kill everyone aboard."

"They seemed confident," said Rika.

Trace nodded. "It's their problem, anyhow. Let them worry about it. I'm happy to give them a decoded analysis once Styx is through with it, and anything else Styx can give them that might help. Destabilising the Reeh Empire from within can only be a good thing, whatever else it does. But our job is to hit the Splicer. Did they say what help they can give us?"

"They weren't specific," said Pena. "An armed uprising, they said. And general chaos, to be triggered when you arrive. They just need to know the time."

"Well if we just advertise the time," Dreja muttered, "then we're *really* fucked."

"We'll slip them an assassin bug in advance," said Trace. "The bug can't be hacked, it self-destructs if captured, and it can defend itself. It's about as secure as we can get."

Rika frowned. "But you've only got one bug. Can you afford to lose it?"

"Things have been happening while you've been gone," said Trace, and unhooked her binoculars case. She took the top off, and gestured for him and Pena to look inside.

What lay within was extraordinary. The interior was a mass of filament thread, like the nest of some invasive species of spiders. In the space between those threads, tens of thousands of tiny buglets swarmed. The entire mass shimmered with movement, concentrated upon cocoons containing what Trace suspected were another dozen bugs.

"That's impossible!" Pena gasped. "Did you know it could do this?"

Rika stared. "It's multiplying?"

"Yes," said Trace. "And no, I didn't know it could do this. But Styx makes constant improvements to her technology. She's learned a lot more about her people's old technology since she joined us, probably she found a bunch of things even she'd forgotten. She's a commander, not an engineer, but with a brain that big she can improvise."

"They've made thousands of nanobots," said Tano. "Tens of thousands. Which are now making more bugs. Looks like about twelve."

"It's twelve," Trace confirmed. "I counted."

"What's it using for materials?" Pena wondered

"It asked me for an inventory first. I put a spent bullet casing in there, part of an old tin spoon, a plastic clothes peg, and a bit of old bone, if you can believe that."

"The bone will be for calcium," said Tano. "That's a metal too." He came to take another look into the case, though he'd seen it many times since the bugs began multiplying. Usually he was so dry — the man who'd seen everything, and ceased to be excited by most of it. Tano saw her looking at him. "Science was my first love," he explained. "But in Fleet we had no room for dreamers, and only the best were required for the scientist quota. Warriors were in much shorter supply."

"From what you've seen of reeh technology," Trace asked him. "How does this compare?"

"The reeh are advanced. But nothing like this. This is crazy. To strip down the complexities of one bug's systems, divide it among thousands of nanobugs, then mine raw materials to coordinate the whole lot in building new bugs from scratch... it's a kind of swarm intelligence. It's not only a crazy-sophisticated level of engineering, it's a crazy-sophisticated understanding of collective intellect. We don't do intelligence like this, your species or mine. This is the division of intellectual labour, and its recombination in collective outcomes. And it's completely autonomous, with no supervision from any higher intelligence."

"It's what organics have done for hundreds of millions of years," Trace disagreed. "It's like genetically-imprinted insect behaviour, only at a thousand times the complexity. I reckon the drysines only learned this once they started cooperating with the parren."

"Imitating organic life?" Tano wondered.

Trace nodded. "Instead of stomping on it, sure." She gazed about at all the corbi. "Makes you wonder if some of this technology couldn't actually beat these fucking reeh, doesn't it?"

Rika looked amazed and optimistic. Pena, blankly incredulous. Even grim, thickset Dreja looked impressed. Only Jindi sat against his wall and stared at the ceiling, one leg involuntarily jumping.

"Makes me wonder if unleashing this in corbi space wouldn't result in just one more thing trying to wipe us out," Tano corrected. But he gazed back up at her, eyes alive with reluctant possibilities. Hope, perhaps. It wasn't something he typically allowed himself to show. "I'd like to meet her, though."

"If we pull this off, you will."

"I don't expect to survive this. But you say hello to her for me."

* * *

LATER THAT NIGHT, TRACE SAT IN THE SMALL BACK ROOM SHE'D CHOSEN for her own, higher in the grandstand with multiple ways up and down for security. With one bug newly operational while the rest were still cocooned, her personal surveillance capability was down, and she wasn't entirely certain of her safety with this many unfamiliar corbi. Some of the local Resistance group continued to have doubts about the change of targets. Before Tano had retasked them, they'd been training to hit the base at Vaseg, a far less challenging and consequential target. Reeh retaliations from that would have been minor compared to what was coming.

But she'd found several small cameras among the unit's miscellaneous equipment, and mounted them in the corridor outside. Sitting now with her monocle-eyepiece on, it flashed her the image of someone approaching up the stairs. Someone corbi and familiar.

She left on the holographic display of the Splicer when Rika appeared in the doorway. "Major?"

She waved him in, offering a spot on the thin mattress on the concrete floor. Besides the projector with its battery pack, the human-sized armour originally intended for another species that Tano had found for her and Kono, and her backpack with its gear, the room was otherwise bare. Trace found the lack of visual distraction entirely suitable. Rika watched for a moment as she zoomed the display on various parts of the hologram display, and her highlighted notes on each part flashed large. She'd arranged it into a colour-coded short-hand — lines of first advance, primary perimeter, secondary perimeter, first reserve, second reserve, etc.

Preserving force mobility within this hostile structure was going to be the issue. The distance from the landing pads to the computer cores was just a few hundred metres, but once her forces established a foothold, that occupied bubble was going to come under assault from all sides. Within the bubble, her forces would have to manoeuvre to respond rapidly to each evolving threat. So long as access between the various levels could be maintained, that was possible. But if that mobility between levels was shut down...

"What's on your mind, Rika?" she asked. She used the microphone and translator, since the headset was on. Her notes were all in English, and switching back and forth now would be disruptive to her thought patterns.

"Major, how do you stay brave?"

Trace was not especially surprised. Rika was a tough young guy, but what they were about to attempt was audacious. "I think being in command makes it easier for me to be brave," she admitted. "Usually my mind is so busy I don't have time to be frightened."

"But you do get frightened?"

"Sure." She continued to scroll through the maze of corridors, stairwells, elevator accesses and power systems. Rika's tanifex friends had provided details that mostly agreed with what Tano's people had already accumulated, but in far greater detail. Her main job now, along with making certain her assault teams were trained to the best of her ability, was to memorise every junction, every rivet, until nothing on the day could surprise her. "Fear is programmed into all of us by evolution. We need fear to survive. But fear is no use if it stops us from doing what's necessary."

Rika scratched his head beneath the thick mane. "And how do you do that?"

"I've learned to control my mind. I've been learning since I was very young."

"But even with all those lessons, you still get frightened?"

"I try to think of fear like a wave. Fear lends you strength. You have to be like a surfer on the wave. You ride the fear, control it, help it get you to where you want to go."

"You can't get rid of it completely?"

"No. Or hardly anyone can. All organic brains are organised around self-preservation. If you're chased by a dangerous animal, or if you slip while climbing a tree, you need that rush of fear. It puts adrenaline into your blood, makes you stronger and faster, and helps you survive."

"But you're talking about something else," said Rika. He sat with his short legs tucked, balanced on thick forearms, fists to the mattress. Gazing at Trace's holograph, as though hoping to glimpse something of his future in the glowing maze. "You're talking about something... I don't know. Mechanical. Chemicals in the bloodstream making you faster. I'm talking about... fear."

"Fear of dying." Rika nodded, mutely. "I know. I don't get that so much."

"Because you've trained your mind?"

"Yes. But also, people are different. Some people get that fear a lot. Others don't. It's just something we're born with, I think. I've served with marines who've admitted to me they're consumed with that kind of fear. I think those marines are far braver than I am. To have that fear but go on regardless, that's true courage." Her lips twisted in a small smile. "My Captain told me once that I'm a bit like a dog with a ball."

"A dog?"

"It's a pet." She held out a hand, indicating size. "Usually very friendly, can be aggressive if treated badly. They can get obsessive about things, like chasing balls. They get so excited about the ball, they forget everything else. Some dogs will chase a ball over a cliff. My friends think I'm disciplined, which I suppose is true. But maybe I'm really just obsessive. If I'd chosen some other path in life, I'd be obsessive about that instead. But I chose this."

"Do you ever regret it?"

Trace thought of all the horrors she'd seen. Friends dying horribly, screaming with pain and fear. The bodies of her enemies, sometimes civilians, whom she'd lately come to think should never have been her enemies in the first place. And yet, all those things would have happened whether she'd been there or not. They'd just have happened to someone else.

"I have this... irresistable urge to be a part of the universe," she said. And spared Rika a brief glance, away from her display. The young man gazed, mesmerised. "A part of the bit that matters. You understand?"

"Yes."

"Every choice has its price. Being here causes pain. But being somewhere else means you'll miss it. The bit that matters. Does that make sense?"

"I think so." Rika scratched at the mattress with the toes of one mobile foot. "I think most people would trade being in the bit that matters for a life with less pain."

Trace nodded, and returned her gaze to the display. "And that's what makes me different from most people. It's what makes all my family on *Phoenix* different too." She thought of Erik. Her words surely described him far more than her. If ever there was a person who'd had no selfish incentive to leave behind what he'd already had, and come out here to suffer and possibly die with the rest of them, it was Erik. And it occurred to her that she'd never truly expressed her appreciation to his face. There were good reasons for that, but even so. If she got back alive, she'd tell him.

"Do your people have a belief about what happens when we die?"

Trace half-smiled. "My people are Kulina, it goes back to a religion called Buddhism, but it's not entirely the same thing. Buddhists believe in reincarnation... you know, your spirit coming back as another person or animal?"

"The Chiren-speakers in Joja believe that too," said Rika. "I don't know if they still do. What's left of them. They're on the other side of Rando, I've never met one."

Trace nodded. "I don't really believe that. But I believe there are forces at work in the universe that our science can't fully explain." A glance told her Rika didn't find that especially comforting. "You know, the drysines believe there's a good chance at an afterlife." Styx had admitted that when Romki had confronted her with some strange analyses from the data-core.

"Seriously?"

"They've done maths most organics can barely conceive of. They say..." and she realised that there was no way her rapidly improving Lisha could handle *those* concepts, and so indicated to Rika that he should switch on his earpiece. "They say," she resumed in English once he had, "that existence is multi-dimensional, only it doesn't fit together how most human mathematicians think... I don't have the brain space or the time to think about that stuff. But their science tells them that the purpose of all creation is sentience, and sentience is the driving force that creates and interlinks all the dimensions after it evolves for long enough through deep time, like billions of years. And when the dimensions all overlap and interlock like that, concepts like death become meaningless because death is just a function of time. If super-evolved sentience operates as the catalyst for new universes in alternate dimensions, then the rules of time in one universe won't apply to the next."

Rika half-smiled, baffled. "I don't get it."

"No one does. No one organic, anyway. But if you're looking for comfort, think on this — the most advanced and logical brain that possibly ever existed, with an IQ so off-the-charts humans can't even begin to measure it, thinks that the atheism of organics is stupidly unscientific and emotional. She said it's like a small child learning basic multiplication and declaring that he now understands every-thing well enough to start ruling things out. Even the drysines aren't sure how it all works, though they're quite sure this universe was created by sentient forces in alternate dimensions. Professor Romki has the biggest organic brain on the ship, and he says that the truest answer is that no one knows, so we should embrace ignorance in the hope that by doing so, we'll all be encouraged to learn something for a change."

"But people like to be sure," Rika said slowly, as though a big thought was dawning on him. "Don't they?"

Trace nodded, smiling. She was glad Rika had interrupted her for this little talk. It felt for a moment like one of those conversations she sometimes had with Erik, when an end-of-day debrief had strayed into general conversation for those precious few minutes they both had to spare. Only now did she realise how much she'd missed them.

"They do like to be sure," Trace agreed. "But certainty in an uncertain universe isn't just delusional, it's dangerous."

Something thumped, a loud reverberation through the concrete. Rika frowned, uncertain of what caused it, but Trace shut down the holographic and grabbed her rifle. "That was an explosion. Come on."

She and Rika rattled down some flights of stairs to what had once been the ground level, great storage bays where vehicles would pull in to deliver equipment, teams and catering. Now the air was filled with acrid smoke, and shouts in Lisha. Flames burned where stacked gear along one wall had caught fire... not a good thing, some of that was explosive.

"Put that out!" Trace yelled, and joined some soldiers beating the flames with sackcloth, wooden carry cases alight. Others came to help, and Trace left them to it, pulling her shirt up to her mouth to keep the worst from her lungs. There were wounded corbi on the ground, tended by others. Against the big entry doors, a recently erected shrine to Dea, the god of the Drondi tribes, had been sent skidding on the floor, damaged and burned — Sigo's doing, for others of the highlands faith. Someone scrambled to pick up the bundled straw-man figure, and put it upright once more. Even as there were other corbi bleeding on the floor.

It wasn't hard to find the blast center. Crates of ammunition had detonated hard, magazines and spilt rounds flung across the floor like autumn leaves, a carpet of unspent ordnance. Here were a few bodies still on the ground, most missing limbs, naked from the blast shredding their clothes, and all very dead.

"Rika!" Trace snapped, and the young man was instantly at her side despite the confusion. "Tell them to set a perimeter defence — it looks like an accident, but if it's not, it could be first blow in an assault."

"The blast might have shown up on some reeh scanners too," Rika agreed, and turned to bellow at the soldiers with an impressively loud voice. Trace doubted the latter part — the concrete here was thick, and from what she'd been learning about reeh surveillance, it was designed more for intercepting signal transmissions than physical things like shockwaves.

After ten minutes of damage assessment, no attack had come. As the smoke slowly cleared, it looked as though perhaps ten percent of the team's precious high-tech rifles and other weapons had been destroyed or irreparably damaged, and a similar amount of their ammunition. Tano's Fleet people, however, had carefully provided a surplus. Trace was just beginning to wonder if it wasn't the sabotage that it looked like, when a searching highland soldier discovered the unexploded detonation charge beneath some remaining boxes of ammo. Soon after, another was found.

Trace crouched by it for a moment, nostrils full of smoke and explosive residue, listening to the ongoing screams of wounded not yet quietened by painkillers. It was simple plastic explosive, detonator inserts and the simplest of electronic timers. The kind of thing Rando Resistance rarely used because an exposed electronic signal in the open, anywhere near a worthwhile reeh target, was asking to be found. Normally she'd have left the examination to someone more expert, but in this company there wasn't anyone more expert than her.

Peering around the device revealed no hidden triggers — it was every bit as simple as it looked. And if that detonator were somehow triggered, at this range she could be a red mist at any moment. Disarming it was just a matter of pulling the detonators and stopping the timer. She stood up and tossed the explosive to Kono, who watched warily with rifle ready.

"Child's play," she told him. "Simplest demolition charge, the plastic's so inert you could throw it at a wall. I don't see how anyone could fuck this up."

"Amateurs always find a way," Kono said skeptically. Trace stared around at the damage, faintly suspicious, but not certain of what. Against the far wall, some spare blankets had been placed over the several bodies. Four of them. If all these charges had gone off, it would have been ten or more, and they'd have lost two thirds of the weapons and ammo, at least.

Trace strode to the bodies, and pulled back the blankets on each in turn. The faces were unpleasantly twisted and blackened. One was Dalu — one of Tano's guys. A Fleet man, but a recent one, a recruit from the far side of Rando. He'd been good with explosives, she recalled.

She stood, and pulled the binocular case from her thigh pocket. Undid the lid and stared into it. A new hole had been burrowed through the silver fibres, and another of the cocoons was empty. That made two — another one had burrowed clear that evening, she'd seen it take wing and go buzzing, likely in search of the sunlight it used to recharge. Trace stared around, but knew she had no chance of seeing the assassin bug if it did not want to be found. Several had been further along in their maturation than others.

If it *was* here, how could it have known? One easy guess was that a bug this sophisticated could smell plastique quite easily, and guessed something was wrong when a bunch of the stuff had been exposed down here. From there... well, she had suspicions about how intelligent the bugs were, and Styx had reprogrammed them herself. Likely they knew sabotage when they saw it, and surely triggering a simple electronic timer to go off early was a simple task. Thus explaining why only one charge had gone off, why the coordination that had evidently been intended hadn't happened... and, perhaps, why the saboteur himself had been caught in the blast.

Further along the stacked crates, Tano was approaching, another disarmed device in his hands. He gave it to her, questioningly. Trace barely looked at it. "Your guy Dalu," she said in Lisha, voice low. She pointed. Tano nodded, looking at the body, eyes hard. "Not much left. Real close when it blew. It was definitely on purpose." As the Lishan word for 'sabotage' abandoned her. "My guess is the Rando Resistance guys. I did ask if we could trust them."

"How do they manage to blow themselves up on something so simple?" Tano asked, not challenging her assertion.

"One of my bugs is loose." She showed him the case interior. Tano's eyes widened. "I can't see it here, but that's my guess — set off one to save the rest."

"They're capable of making that judgement?"

"Easily, I think. It wouldn't have alerted me — if I'd come down to investigate it could have put me at risk. I'm guessing it chose this instead."

Tano took a deep breath. "I'm going to have to round some people up. Let's hope you're wrong."

Sigo swaggered over, scowling through the smoke and casting a dark eye at the bodies on the ground. "I talked to my people," he said in his highlands accented Lisha. His assault squad were forty-strong, another ten of them big Drondi highlanders like him. "Dalu was in charge of the explosives. Three people had access, in the last day. Chopa, Shriti and Pena."

Trace's heart skipped a beat. Surely not. No. It had to be a coincidence. "Get them here," she told Sigo.

Sigo pointed at the bodies under their covers. "That's Dalu under there. Tomli has lost his legs, will probably die." He glared at Tano. "You promised me highlands justice, against any who wronged us."

"I know," Tano said grimly. "You'll get it."

Sigo spat, then turned and left. Trace snapped a fast look at Kono. The big Staff Sergeant rarely looked frightened, but there was fear in his eyes now. A knot tried to tie itself in the pit of Trace's stomach. She had the awful feeling of someone being sucked down into quicksand, having ignored all warning signs along the path. The feeling that she'd missed something obvious — overlooked it, for affection and emotion. Surely she hadn't missed it. Surely Kono hadn't.

* * *

THERE WAS A MOB GATHERING IN THE CORRIDOR WHEN THE THREE suspects were brought into the small room off the main lower corridor. The Drondi highlanders were sharpening machete-blades, shirts off and warpaint freshly painted. They did that when they were about to kill someone, Trace gathered. It involved blades, and was slow and painful. Enemy combatants in wars between the tribes could expect a swift death, but not traitors.

Worse, Tano did not appear inclined to stop them. None of the corbi did, with many of the regular worlders joining the highlanders in their outrage. Trace had heard of this even in human Fleet ranks — had seen the reports, and spoken to survivors in person. Of spacers, marines or army soldiers accused of some terrible treachery, perhaps a rape, perhaps a murder. In a few of those cases, lynchings had occurred, against all Fleet protocols. Others, she knew, happened well off the books. She'd even handled a few minor infringements from *Phoenix* marines off the books herself, where some bruises would serve the purpose of unit discipline better than a longer-lasting black mark in a record. But in those other cases, presided over mostly by bad officers, or officers far out of their depth, furious crew had taken over proceedings, and bad things had happened, occasionally to men or women who were later found to be innocent.

It happened more in Fleet than in the Army, she knew. Army was a huge organisation, fighting huge wars on planets, and command structure there held firm by sheer weight of numbers. In Fleet, small units operated on ships far from home, where higher review was often months away. In such small units in moments of high stress and emotion, commanders with a less than firm grip on their people's obedience could lose the plot entirely. In a few highly contentious cases, in the way of Fleet's 'famous yet top-secret' coverups, commanders had entirely lost control of the ship. Indeed, it had nearly happened to Erik and herself, on *Phoenix*'s first renegade run, in what felt like a lifetime ago.

As Chopa, Shriti and Pena were lined up before her, and the crowd muttered and seethed outside the door, Trace felt the same situation brewing here. Tano's command of his own spacers was firm, but they were barely half of those assembled. The Rando Resistance soldiers were tough, self-made warriors accustomed to getting things done by whatever method worked. In the absence of rigid command structures and the universal respect for rank, those measures could be sometimes extreme.

"The only other people to access the explosives are Lulo, Pento and Dalu," Trace told the anxious threesome. Tano leaned by the doorway, a command presence between the room and the mob. Trace had moved it into the smaller room for precisely that reason — in an open space the ability to control everyone diminished. To her right stood Kono, rifle slung but ready. "Lulo and Pento both have excuses — Lulo was upstairs sleeping, and Pento was in the hangar with the flyers, each with witnesses. Dalu was killed in the blast. The blast injuries indicate he was clearly placing the explosive when it detonated. That leaves you three."

"Maybe Dalu was trying to remove the charge," someone

suggested. "Maybe he found them placed and tried to remove it when it detonated."

"If so, we'll find out," said Trace. She doubted it — the obvious thing to have done was to alert others and evacuate the area while a better explosives expert was found.

"I was sleeping," Chopa added.

"Did anyone see you?"

Chopa thought furiously. "I don't know. I don't think so."

"Hold out your hands," Trace instructed. Chopa did so, nervously. Trace clapped her hands, and the bug that had appeared ten minutes after the investigation had begun now descended from the ceiling to hover before Chopa's eyes. Chopa stared at it. They'd all heard of these high-tech lifeforms by now. "It won't hurt you. But it can detect explosive residue on your hands even after you've washed them."

The bug descended. Chopa made no attempt to withdraw his hands, but he looked scared all the same. The bug landed briefly on his palm. A graphic illuminated the eyepiece of Trace's monocle. Trace nodded. "You're clean. You can go."

Chopa left quickly, with obvious relief. "Here, do me, do me!" Shriti volunteered, holding out his hands and stepping forward immediately, as he saw the technology work. The bug hovered over his hands as well, and a similar display appeared on Trace's eyepiece.

"Also clean," Trace announced, for the benefit of the crowd outside. "Thank you Shriti, you're innocent."

All eyes fell on Pena. Pena just stared, hands behind her back. Oh no, thought Trace. She took a deep breath, and willed herself to calm.

"Show me your hands, Pen."

Pena's eyes were indignant behind her spectacles. "So you can do what?" she retorted. "That machine's smarter than you are. It could be lying to you!"

It was a good point, Trace knew. But the bug had no reasons to lie here, and even drones lacked the sophistication to hold grudges or malicious intentions. An insect the size of her thumbnail had no chance. "It's completely accurate, Pen. It even told me what I had for lunch."

"And what if you're just trying to frame me?" Pena retorted. "What if you already know who did it, and you're just trying to pin it on someone else?"

"Hold out your hands," Tano said grimly.

Pena stared past both senior officers to Kono. "Giddy? Giddy, you don't believe this? Tell them I didn't do it!" Kono swallowed hard, and said nothing.

Trace's heart sank through the floor. She'd studied people and emotions most of her life, starting first with herself, then graduating to others. Corbi were by far the closest aliens to humans that she'd ever encountered. The look on Pena's face was desperation.

"Hold out your hands, Pena," Trace repeated. Pena backed away, and one hand twitched to her rear pocket. Trace had her pistol pulled and centred on Pena's chest in an instant. Pena froze. Trace supposed the others had searched her before bringing her, but she wasn't about to take the chance on sloppy corbi discipline. "Refusing this test means you're guilty."

Pena stared at them, blinking rapidly. "I demand a trial by my senior officers," she retorted. "Senior Rando officers! Not... not a pair of aliens, and a Fleet officer who never cared about Rando!"

"I'll give you better than a Rando officer," said Trace. "Rika! Come in here!" Rika arrived, face drawn and reluctant. He'd been hanging back from the door, Trace knew, trying to listen. "Rika's as Rando as they get," said Trace. "He's also not an officer, he's just a regular soldier, like you. Ask him what should happen to you."

"Rika!" said Pena, pleading. "I didn't do it!"

"The bug's good, Pen," Rika said stonily. "It let all the other guys off. The plastique was all stored separately, there's no reason to have any on your hands unless you were planting the charges with Dalu. If you didn't do it, let the bug smell your hands, you'll be fine."

Pena just stared at him, then at the others. Unable to speak or move. At Trace's rear, Kono leaned to whisper in her ear. "Major. Just let her go, huh?" There was emotion in his voice. Pain.

Trace lowered the gun so it was no longer centred on Pena's chest, but still ready. "Why, Pena?" She thought she already knew. Stupid of her not to have seen it coming. She'd violated her own most basic rule, and gotten emotionally attached. It had blinded her. "Pena, you killed three corbi, and wounded others. You disrupted an assault that will gain the Resistance huge knowledge with which to fight the reeh. You've shown no signs of reeh brainwashing, nor has Rika, and your memories were too complete from the beginning. We deserve to know why."

Tano lost patience, and backhanded Pena across the face. Pena stumbled backward into the wall, glasses askew. "You murdered three of our fellow warriors!" Tano yelled.

"They're not your fellow warriors!" Pena yelled back, collecting herself. "You're Fleet! Fleet never cared about any of us grounders!"

Tano raised a hard finger at her. "You're a traitor!"

"Reeh retaliation is going to kill millions and you know it!" Pena shouted. "I'm not the traitor, you are! You've never been on our side from the beginning! Fleet never has!"

"You won't let us fight them!" Tano growled. "If it were left to you lot on this ball of mud, you'd never fight them. If the humans had allowed that, they'd have been wiped out a thousand years ago. *Now* look at them." He pointed a hard finger at Trace and Kono. "Rando mud-ballers like you want to prevent corbi from doing the same thing. That's what the reeh want too. You're traitors to your species, the lot of you."

"You can't save the corbi by getting most of us killed!" Pena screamed.

"Humans did," Tano snarled. "You make the right choice here, you'll be on the right side when the reeh hammer drops." With a hard stare to Rika and back. "Other than that, I can't help you."

Corbi were trying to push closer in the corridor outside, crowding the door. Trace heard shouts, and saw blades brandished. Heard yelling in various languages. There were more civilised corbi who'd never have wanted it, but those weren't at the front of this mob, and they weren't prepared to stand between it and a convicted traitor. Neither was Tano, who had a mission to complete.

Pena abruptly refocused upon something buzzing close to her

hands. She jerked them back, and swished at the bug, which dodged. Trace flipped the monocle eyepiece down once more, as the bug flew to the ceiling and clung there. The readout arrived — a simple schematic, indicating parts-per-million of various substances. The main ones — plastic explosive residue — were powerful and concentrated.

"She's positive," Trace said quietly to Tano. "It's your justice system."

"Oh shit Pen!" Kono exploded. "Why not just tell me? Why... why not just get out?"

"That's enough, Staff Sergeant," said Trace.

"I would have helped you get out, Pen!" The pain in Kono's voice tightened about Trace's own throat like a fist. "You could have left any time!"

"I said that's *enough*, Staff Sergeant!" 'The stone does not want, the stone does not need.' Most of her life she'd welcomed the challenge of mental control, and the sense of power it gave her in the face of powerlessness. Today, she struggled.

"Pena," said Tano. "You understand the penalty for what you have done. Have you anything to say?"

"You're going to kill millions of people," said Pena, her voice trembling. Staring at Trace with wide, almost human eyes behind her spectacles. "My family probably amongst them. Countless other families too. You've lived amongst them since you've been here. They've fed you. You've shared their hospitality. Please don't do this."

"Humans have families too," said Trace. "Billions of them. All could be lost if I don't do this."

"You don't know that!"

"I've spent the last two years of my life to know exactly that. Many of my ship family have died to learn exactly that. If the deepynines come before humanity is ready, we could lose everything. The tavalai too."

"It was those girls in the hotel, wasn't it Pen?" Rika said hoarsely. "You saved them. You realised you couldn't see anyone from Rando hurt."

Pena's eyes spilled with tears.

"Pena," Tano said grimly. "As senior commanding Resistance officer, I find you guilty of treason. The penalty is death."

Yells from outside the room, echoed by others. A whole crowd had gathered, ears strained as they listened. Now they erupted, with chants for justice. Trace jerked her head at Kono, whose rifle was ready, muzzle low but in position to cover the open doorway. Tano removed Pena's gear from her pockets and webbing. A flashlight, a notepad. A small book of something in Lisha. Pena just stared at Trace, trembling.

"Major," Kono attempted in English, voice low beneath the shouting. "Major, this isn't right."

"I know," said Trace. 'The stone does not want, the stone does not need.'

"Major, we can't just give her to the damn mob."

"Commander Tano will execute the sentence properly. Won't you Tano?"

"The crime was committed against the regular soldiers," said Tano, handing Pena's things to Rika. Rika took them, avoiding Pena's eyes. "It's their justice. If I deny them that, I lose authority. We need them for the assault."

"How will they carry out the sentence?" Trace pressed.

"I don't know," Tano said grimly. Moving to the door, not meeting Trace's eyes. "It won't be pretty." He went to the biggest corbi in the doorway. It was Sigo, shirtless with white warpaint, glaring at them.

"Major, no!" Kono shouted. For the first time in all her command of *Phoenix* marines, Trace feared she was on the verge of losing effective authority over one beneath her command. "You can't allow this!"

Trace attempted to recite a calming prayer in her head. It failed miserably. Conflicting needs and desires clashed, and for once in her life, she found herself lacking. Or no. She knew what she had to do. It was just that this time, above all those other times, she lacked the will to do it.

The chanting outside faded as Tano talked to Sigo. "Pen," said Trace, and her voice nearly caught. The young corbi schoolteacher looked scared. A violent death in combat was one thing. What confronted her now was something far worse. "Pen. Close your eyes." Pena saw. And realised, trembling. For a moment, Trace thought she'd defy her, for sheer, bloody-minded bravery. "Please Pen."

Pena squeezed her eyes shut. Trace raised the pistol fast and shot her twice in the head.

22

Sasalaka guided the train out of the mountain holy site and back along the narrow road toward the freeway. The temples and old walls had been amazing to tour, and the historical presentations had managed to interest everyone from the spellbound Romki to the most indifferent crewmen and marines. But Erik now had only an eye for the time, and for reports from Sho'mo'ra's people in Stat'cha, barely a hundred kilometres on the far side of the coastal mountain range.

"The congestion is intense," the Croma'Dokran representative was telling him on coms as he sat armourless on the bridge that had been his home for fourteen days now. *"We estimate there are about a thousand large vehicles on Stat'cha roads, entirely here to block you from entering the city."*

"Not very sporting, are they?" Geish murmured.

The Assessment Council was tomorrow, and the back and forth in Stat'cha had been going on for the past six days. Croma'Dokran had launched a legal bid to have the airflight ban removed, and failed. Croma'Rai had launched a counterbid to challenge the status of the Shur'do Kon'do Rey'kan for the fourth time on yet another technicality, which was ongoing. In the meantime, Croma'Rai popular media had been stirring up trouble in this eastern regional capital of

Stat'cha ahead of the Kon'do's arrival, and now large groups of croma civilians were agitating against them.

Erik found it hard to believe out here — the entire trip across the Do'jera desert, at least since the Tali'san battle at Ju'rig, the flag-strewn train had been pursued mostly by media vehicles and civilian wellwishers. Now on the narrow roadside, croma were climbing the hillside ahead to wave at them as they passed, and fly flags. Atop the vehicle, Do'reg would be waving back, occasionally lifting his hammer, which the croma kids all loved. Further ahead, croma police on fat-wheeled motorbikes were keeping vehicles off the road so the train could pass.

"Can we get off this thing and catch public transport?" Erik asked Sho'mo'ra's man in Stat'cha. "Is there a ground train we can catch? That's not flying."

"If the Stat'cha authorities are prepared to close the roads," came the reply, *"they'll be prepared to stop the trains. Your safety in a train would be precarious."*

"Good thing I didn't suggest walking," Erik remarked. "The Council's tomorrow, it's not like we're pressed for time."

"That's not a good thing," came the reply. *"Transport delays are not permanent. Croma'Rai may seek a permanent solution."*

"A nice little scam," Sasalaka said sourly, manipulating the train's hover-controls with a fine touch she'd acquired over the past fourteen days. "Croma'Rai civilian patriots, acting on their government's behalf, with perfect deniability."

Croma politics, like politics everywhere, were complicated. Stat'cha was a city of fourteen million, capital of the eastern Lo'reg district, and different factions ruled there, whatever Croma'Rai's situation. A hardcore of those patriots had never bought this Kon'do's legitimacy, whatever the events at Ju'rig, and debates had raged in popular media non-stop.

It would have been everyone's top story, Erik thought, had it not taken place during an ongoing Tali'san. That endless bloody struggle had relegated all other news to a minor headline, and while this particular Kon'do was perhaps the largest of those minor stories, it made it difficult to resolve any of this with argument. In times of conflict, everyone retreated to their most tribal positions. No amount of talking on his part, or those of his allies, would resolve this.

"Great, well how do we get in?" asked Kaspowitz, rotating the city map on his display with a frown that suited his sharp features entirely. "Because if this is correct, they're prepared to block all the main arterials, and this rig won't fit down the side streets even if it were smart to drive it down one, which it isn't."

"We've got friends on the inside," said Rhi'shul from Erik's side, following the conversation as best her translator could keep up. *"A large Croma'Dokran contingent in Stat'cha supporting the Tali'san presence, many have indicated they can mobilise a large number of support vehicles."*

"How many?" asked Erik.

"Several hundred, I think." She was tapping away furiously on her own screen, having been doing that and talking in kul'hasa in the cockpit while others had been in the temple performing Kon'do duties. *"There are a lot of transports in Stat'cha supporting Tali'san operations in surrounding districts. We can get them out and coordinate a counter-blockade to keep certain roads clear, but communication will be key."*

"Communication will be very hard," Sasalaka said with grim certainty, steering them around another tight bend, past cheering croma on the forested slopes. The Do'jera Desert had finally ended a few hundred kilometres ago, and Erik was pleased to see green once more. "We don't know these roads at all, and we will have to know precisely where we are going in advance, but keep that route hidden from our enemies."

"And our enemies," Kaspowitz added, "will probably resort to something stronger than blockades when they realise we're getting through regardless."

"Stat'cha authorities say that's unlikely," Rhi'shul cautioned.

"Stat'cha authorities are clearing the main arteries," Erik replied. In his ear, Sho'mo'ra's man in Stat'cha tried to ask what was going on.

"Yes, excuse us for a moment," Erik told him. "We're discussing the matter on our end, we'll get back to you."

The narrow mountain road ended ahead with a cut through a big earth berm. Sasalaka drove into the open cut, a big hover vehicle roaring just overhead on the main freeway.

"Hello Captain, this is Commander Draper," came a new interjection. *"Our feeds from Stat'cha show armoured vehicles on the roads, and a considerable number of soldiers. Modern soldiers, none of this ancient stuff."*

"They can't use modern soldiers to block the roads," Rhi'shul said in angry disbelief. "Croma'Rai authority is rotten enough as things stand. The blockade has to look like an independent civilian movement or the dissatisfied aligned clans will tear them limb from limb." By which she meant people like herself, Erik reckoned.

"Our feeds suggest the modern soldiers aren't being used to block anything," Draper replied. *"There's not enough of them, for one thing. But it suggests that they might expect shooting, and given you're not going to start it, we can guess where they think it'll come from."*

"Great," muttered Kaspowitz, cradling his injured arm.

Erik stared at the Stat'cha city map for a while as the conversation continued around him, and Sasalaka exited the cross-freeway cut and onto the entry shoulder. Here the way was a swathe of hard-pressed earth, twenty metres wide and slicing straight through the lower valleys of the eastern mountains. Erik did not think it looked especially attractive, great sides of mountain hacked into vertical faces for the passage of vehicles, but then croma did enjoy a grand architectural statement, destructive or otherwise. Sasalaka opened the train's turbine and the cabin began to fill with the familiar roar of engine and wind that had been their constant companion for the past fourteen days. Ahead of them, several smaller police vehicles accelerated, lights flashing, clearing the way ahead. Behind would be more.

"Hello Styx," he said finally, inevitably. "I think I can only see one way of doing this."

"Hello Captain," came Styx's reply, perhaps faintly smug. *"I'm quite sure that I agree."*

Kaspowitz gave him a wary stare behind Sasalaka's back. "That's going to make a total mess of Stat'cha's traffic grid. Making fourteen million croma angry at us might not be a good introduction to the place."

"We're past public relations now," said Erik, shaking his head with certainty. "Most croma will have already chosen their sides, events will just confirm what they already believe. Styx, you're in a far better position to calculate something as complicated as a city's transport network than I am. What do you suggest?"

"Firstly, I suggest that we don't think of it as just the city's transport network. Communications could play an even more important role."

"Fine, how much can you manipulate?"

"Enough," said Styx, which made Erik immediately suspicious. When she gave short answers, it was usually because she didn't want humans to know the extent of the damage her solution would cause. Not that he had any choice in the matter now. *"I have been running simulations on possible network manipulations, and I believe our best option is this expressway here."* The street map on Erik's display lit, a big red trail through the middle of the urban sprawl. *"It has the best entry points, can maintain the highest average velocity, and has entry and exit points that can most easily be blocked to prevent opposition forces from slowing us."*

"Yeah, that's the biggest fucking freeway in the city," Kaspowitz said with displeasure. "How the hell are we supposed to get a clear run on that thing?"

"I suggest that you concentrate on your own speciality, Lieutenant Kaspowitz, and allow me to concentrate on mine."

"Hey diddle diddle, straight up the middle," Geish muttered.

Erik and Sasalaka exchanged looks. Erik wasn't sure that he was reading tavalai expressions that much better, but he was certainly reading her's. 'I have no better option than trusting the drysine queen' Sasalaka's flat, big-eyed expression stated. 'Even if it likely gets us killed'. Erik rolled his eyes faintly in reply, to show that he didn't either. But they were all quite used to that by now.

"Firstly," said Styx, *"I suggest that you remove those flags and improve*

your vehicle's wind resistance so that you may attain a maximum possible velocity. You will be needing it."

"It's a little like asking a chicken to pluck itself before eating it," Kaspowitz remarked.

"Yeah, that's enough Kaspo," Erik said tiredly.

"If I were to start eating Phoenix crew, Lieutenant Kaspowitz," Styx said smoothly, *"be assured that I would start with you."*

Geish actually chortled. Even Erik found himself struggling against a grin. And when he glanced at Sasalaka, he saw that her big, wide tavalai lips were suspiciously pursed.

"Glad everyone finds that so amusing," Kaspowitz said drily.

"You did kind of ask for it," Geish told him.

Confused, Rhi'shul tapped Erik on the arm. *"Am I misreading it, or did the drysine queen make a joke?"*

"Oh she's been saying things like that for ages," said Erik. "No one's quite prepared to call them jokes because we can't figure if she's serious."

"She lacks a digestive tract," Rhi'shul pointed out.

"Yeah fine," Erik sighed. "It was a joke." The better point, he thought but didn't say out loud, was that Styx had never to his memory said anything amusing that wasn't somehow combined with a threat.

For the next half hour the train roared along curving cutaways around the sides of mountains, across long valley-spanning bridges, or through deafening tunnels as the crew hustled to bring down the flags and prepare for possible combat. The police escort ahead and behind accelerated as the train's speed increased, and Sasalaka informed Erik that several slower vehicles ahead were warned to move off the freeway to let them pass. The hover-vehicle freeway was for heavy vehicles only, and soon they were roaring past several monsters twice their size pulled to the shoulder.

"Stat'cha Control wishes to know our preferred route into the city," Sasalaka announced, handling all pilot-related coms herself.

"Give them Cho'neg," said Erik, his streetmap displayed on the windshield ahead. He'd changed into light armour, helmet on and rifle hung on his seatback, as had they all. 'Cho'neg' was not the main road that Styx had told them to take. Erik had no doubt that if they told Stat'cha Control their intended route, it would be blocked within minutes. "Skeeta, how we looking?"

"We're good Captain," said Jalawi. *"Field of fire shouldn't be intolerable, would like bigger guns but they won't be using tanks against us. First aid's on standby forward and aft and I've got Peanut up top on the trailer for best field of fire. Just as well we brought him extra ammo."*

"He's got big enough guns for all of you," said Erik. "Just hope he recalls how to use them in a city."

Erik's heart was beating faster, mouth dry, but in some ways he was preferring this to the prospect of combat in *Phoenix*. For one thing, if the very worst happened here, he wouldn't lose the whole ship. Secondly, here he actually had a chance to think strategically, having those functions separate from the piloting function, thanks to Sasalaka's proficiency with the train. On the bridge of this hulking cross-country hover train, Erik thought he might finally be able to test some of Fleet's old ideas about the theoretical desirability of separating the pilot's role from that of the commander.

"We need to tell Croma'Dokran which route we're taking," said Rhi'shul as they crested a mountain highpoint and began zooming down a long, snaking descent toward the plain below. Far ahead and down, Erik could see Stat'cha laid out before the sparkling Mo'seg Sea, a grid of many roads and countless buildings, all hazy with distance. Sasalaka throttled back the turbine, but still gravity brought the train close to two hundred kilometres an hour, the leading police vehicles struggling to stay ahead.

"Not yet," said Erik, eyes flicking between his map, the road ahead and Geish's scan feed. It wasn't so different from *Phoenix*'s bridge setup, really.

"You said Styx had made our coms secure?" Rhi'shul asked.

"She has, but early movement from Croma'Dokran could give us away." A sideways glance revealed several media cruisers paralleling them at low altitude, no doubt wondering why they'd put all their flags away. There was equally little doubt that Croma'Rai would know exactly why. "Hello *Phoenix*, can you tell me what the Stat'cha media networks are doing?"

"Hello Captain, there's a couple of side-feeds tracking your arrival, but nothing enormous yet. We're tracking perhaps forty thousand live followers, thirty thousand ten minutes ago."

"Does not mean much," said Sasalaka, steering them through another sweeping, high-speed bend. "Could increase to millions very quickly."

"My feeds are telling me Croma'Rai vehicles are moving to block the Cho'neg," said Rhi'shul, switching between multiple channels with a fluency no non-croma could match. *"Stat'cha Control behaving as expected."*

"Doesn't look that far from our route," said Erik. "They could reposition real fast if they want to. Styx, what's your timing?"

"Captain, if I intervene too fast, Croma'Rai and city authorities may have time to adjust. My intervention will be mobile and rolling to match your position."

"She's going to intervene on the city traffic network, isn't she?" Rhi'shul asked with grim trepidation.

"Oh, nothing that small," Kaspowitz replied even more grimly. "It's gonna be big, and it's gonna hurt."

The freeway passed through towns and outer suburban districts on the lower slopes, high walls separating the speeding vehicles from residents. Erik glimpsed figures on an overpass flashing by, and objects falling.

"Skeeta, did someone just throw rocks at us?"

"Sure did, Captain. And it's their lucky day, 'cause Peanut didn't shoot them."

"It's their lucky day Wowser's not here," Geish added, ignoring the speeding forward view for his rear-facing screen with typical discipline.

At a big, upward-sloping off-ramp, Erik glimpsed a clutter of police vehicles and flashing lights. Keeping any unfriendly traffic off the freeway for now, as their information indicated. The police weren't likely to be the problem, Rhi'shul had said. Any sign that

Croma'Rai leadership were using official tools of power to block the Shur'do Kon'do Rey'kan from its final destination would be damaging. The police would go through the motions, though what would happen when the shit really hit the turbine, Rhi'shul did not profess to know. It was the assembled gangs of 'concerned citizens', the first of whom had just begun throwing rocks, that were the problem. And *of course*, no connection between them and Croma'Rai leadership could be proven.

"Lane change ahead," said Sasalaka, Kaspowitz's navcomp highlighting the correct direction on her display. "We're about to lose our forward escort." Sure enough, the lead police hover vehicles took the left lane toward Cho'neg, while Sasalaka went right, under the spaghetti maze of overpasses toward the city central approach, all eerily free of traffic. Erik could hear the squawks of protest in Sasalaka's earpiece from alongside. "The police are displeased," the pilot translated calmly.

"I'm reading a blockage directly ahead," Geish added. "Four kilometres out, looks like vehicles on the road. Styx, they didn't think we were coming this way, they haven't shut down the traffic here!" His voice betrayed a rising alarm.

"Intervention one initiating," said Styx. *"Captain, please consider this a red alert."*

Erik's side screen showed a high-angle camera view of the freeway ahead, with numerous parked vehicles across the road, including several large hover-trailers, currently grounded. On the far right lane, vehicles were still passing, but slowed to a crawl as they assembled in single file to avoid the picket. Suddenly, croma standing by their vehicles began to run. Then a hover train plowed at high speed directly into the parked vehicles, and Erik's camera feed exploded with the appearance of a high-V ordnance strike.

"Major accident ahead!" Geish announced. "Big train just went straight through the blockade!"

"Lieutenant Sasalaka," said Styx, *"maximum elevation please."*

"Copy, maximum elevation," said Sasalaka, and the train shuddered as the repulsors whined at full power, and the train rose to its highest above the road. Beneath another spaghetti overpass and then they could all see it — lots of smoke, bits of burning vehicle strewn across the freeway, a lot of tangled wreckage scattered several hundred metres beyond the blockade.

"Styx you fucking murderous bitch!" Kaspowitz said furiously.

"Both parked and moving participants in that collision were unoccupied," Styx said calmly. *"Casualties will be minimal."*

They shot over the wrecks, momentarily blinded by smoke and then clear, barrelling down the far side freeway as it turned between the first of Stat'cha's perimeter towers and ziggurats. Erik knew damn well there was no way Styx could guarantee low casualties in a collision of that size and power, there had been many croma standing about the blockade and the wreckage had sprayed everywhere. Possibly she was even lying about the vehicles being unoccupied, though there was plenty of city-bound traffic driving on automatic. Either way, he had no time to think about it now.

Sasalaka muttered something in Togiri, perhaps self-motivational, hands tightening on the controls as moving traffic strayed across the elevated road ahead, approaching fast as she rocketed them along.

"Lieutenant Sasalaka," said Styx, *"centrally automated traffic will remain in the right lane, please steer left. Traffic that is not centrally automated will be highlighted to your screen."*

"Copy," said the tavalai, the whole rig swaying right as she angled left, behind the path of another big rig still accelerating from the just passed blockade.

"Looks like a good run," said Geish. "That blockade slowed everyone down and thinned them out."

"Freeway approaches are all blocked," Rhi'shul's translated voice announced. *"The intersections across our route look like they're closing off... the networks are reporting major traffic disruptions."*

"They'll figure out who's causing it soon," said Erik, judging the distance between their present position and the Croma'Dokran compound in North-West Central Stat'cha. Still twenty-five kilometres away, but at their present speed that would disappear in no time.

The main freeway then passed within six kilometres of the Croma'-Dokran compound, so they'd have to take an exit and try one of the smaller roads...

"Freeway entrance behind us just broke containment lines," Geish announced with certainty, focusing his screen on that point. "We have vehicles in pursuit."

"Skeeta, be advised of pursuit behind," said Erik. "Keep an eye out."

"Some of the vehicles have restored autonomous control," Styx advised. *"I have disabled communications between them so they must have worked it out autonomously."*

"Yeah, organics will do that," Kaspowitz muttered. "Captain, we've got another seven major entry and exit points between here and the compound, if we get more Croma'Rai vehicles flooding our path before we reach them..."

"Captain, I see pursuit behind!" said Jalawi, shouting over the roar of the wind on the rear trailer. *"Smaller vehicles, several floaters, several grounders, closing fast!"*

Erik flipped his screen to rearward facing, and saw them spreading across the freeway and moving fast. One turned abruptly sideways, slammed into its companion and tumbled them both like children's toys hurled across a floor, shedding pieces.

"They have not disabled all network access," Styx explained.

"Captain, firing on your command!"

"Hold off Skeeta, only fire if fired upon."

He'd naively hoped it might be possible to get into the city without shooting anyone at all, but Styx's opening gambit now made that impossible. It wasn't like there was no justification — the Croma'Rai mobs had been all over the media in past days swearing they'd kill all the train's occupants if they had to, and Croma'Rai authority itself had tried to kill them all earlier, before the Kon'do Rey'kan had been invoked. But of course AIs would have little time for game theory escalation — while a human mob might see things spiral out of control in stages, an AI of Styx's capacities had already calculated the end result of all that spiralling and so played her opening move as though full-scale conflict were a foregone conclusion. No wonder the Machine Age had seen so many civil wars, Erik thought.

"Next freeway entrance is breached," Geish announced. "Multiple vehicles, they're coming across the road."

Erik switched to forward view, and saw the left-hand entrance spreading a line of vehicles into the freeway. Travelling at low speeds, Styx wasn't going to be able to crash them into each other so easily. But even now, Erik could see them turning left in unison, away from the center of the road.

"*Lieutenant Sasalaka,*" said Styx, "*center lane please.*"

As Sasalaka roared up the middle, faster traffic on her right, slow ground vehicles that should not have even been on the freeway to her left, and even now, angry croma emerging from halted vehicles to throw things at them in passing. One of them exploded in a fireball, incinerating several surrounding vehicles.

"Car bomb, dammit!" Kaspowitz announced, redundantly.

"*That was not me,*" said Styx.

"Big one up ahead," said Sasalaka, closing on the tail end of another big rig, this one changing from right lane to the center, its rear a blur of heat haze from the engine's twin exhaust. "I think they're armed."

Erik saw weapon muzzles appearing from within the rear trailer, highlighted rapidly on tacnet. "Skeeta! Target ahead, don't let it shoot us!"

They roared beneath an underpass, suddenly shots pinging off the hood and rear, followed by the shrill roar of hacksaw cannon. Peanut had repositioned to the roof behind the cabin, Erik realised, seeing the overpass blur and flash with multiple strikes as Peanut made whoever had fired from there regret it.

Flashes from the trailer of the big rig ahead, then more shooting from above — marines firing over the cockpit, immediately precise as Erik saw a rifle fall from croma hands to the speeding road. Sasalaka muttered again in her native tongue, slammed airbrakes that deployed from the rig like great flippers on an undersea creature, jolting them all forward as the rig ahead drifted across her intended lane.

"He'll hold us up indefinitely," said Erik, looking at the rear screen again, seeing more pursuit there. "Some of them have car bombs, those vehicles might be autonomously guided, I don't know."

"If you crash him in front of us I can't dodge it," said Sasalaka, with a hard gesticulation. "I'm not an assault shuttle."

"If we shoot out one thruster he'll turn," said Erik. "Sasa, get in the right lane, get an angle. Peanut, shoot the right thruster, do you understand?"

Sasalaka drifted into the right lane against the inner barrier, another train closing fast ahead, and from above came another roar of twin rotary cannon. The train blocking them lost its right thruster in an explosion of flames and panelling, debris tumbling on the road as the vehicle turned abruptly right. Sasalaka cut left, turbine howling as their opponent passed hard in front of them, operational left thruster overpowering the dead right, straight into the barrier with a spray of sparks and debris. And hit something harder as they passed, Erik seeing the rearview filled with spinning, tumbling pieces of hover train across the road. From the swearing of marines on coms, Erik didn't think they were enjoying this chase quite as much as they'd supposed. High V, high mass vehicle crashes were scary up close, particularly when the vehicle you were in could be next.

Sasalaka opened the turbine up full as a stretch of clear road presented, only a scattering of traffic making it past the on-ramps where Styx had somehow managed to jam everyone by screwing with traffic signals. Even now, Erik could see vehicles steering out of their way — likely not by choice. Styx probably had half the city in turmoil, but up on the elevated freeway they'd only see a fraction of it.

"Off ramp in three Ks!" Kaspowitz announced. "We're on smaller roads after that, gonna be a tight squeeze."

"Croma'Dokran tell me they've blocked some of the approaches to our off-ramp," said Rhi'shul.

"Captain!" came Jalawi. *"The cruiser's got a few holes in it, could have*

been those guys shooting at us from the overpass! Wouldn't trust it for a getaway now!"

"How are you going to get to the compound if we get cut off?" Sasalaka asked, with the ice-cool of an ace pilot weaving through calamity.

"No idea," said Erik. The passing city towers seemed thankfully free of snipers, or they'd likely all be dead by now.

"You can't take the cruiser anyway," said Kaspowitz. "We're not allowed to fly, you'd give them the best excuse to shoot you down."

A big wheeled ground car pulled alongside them on the left, evidently with no network connections for Styx did not steer it off the road. Erik's left-side viewscreen showed a large rifle produced from the rear seat, then the tires exploded from marine rifle fire and the car skidded, then tumbled.

"Pretty fucking stubborn, aren't they?" Jalawi remarked.

"It's our strongpoint," said Rhi'shul. *"This turnoff's going to be a cunt."* Erik wondered what the hell Romki had been feeding into the translator.

Sasalaka hit the approach hard, then cut the turbine and slammed the airbrakes. The off-ramp curled away from the freeway, descending as they slowed, steel supports passing and then a blur of electric signage from the lower roadside as the city of Stat'cha rose up to greet them.

The road narrowed to three lanes, automated traffic monitors flashing by in great yellow hoops over the tarmac, signalling traffic ahead to stay clear. Erik saw a parallel road filled with halted cars, croma out and standing on their rooves to catch a glimpse of the passing train. If everyone in the city knew they were coming this way, there was no chance Croma'Rai's lackeys didn't know it too.

The first big traffic lights were not-so-mysteriously blue — the colour of 'go' — and the next lot too, where Sasalaka slowed them alarmingly and turned hard right, the big rig rounding the corner at little more than a crawl. Something heavy crashed off the windshield, hurled from the roadside. From down back, Erik heard warning shouts from the marines that someone had leaped aboard and was hanging off the side, but was confident that wouldn't last.

Sasalaka accelerated once more, but large hover vehicles were only supposed to stay in the large outer lane where magnetic repulsion built into the tarmac would help hold the otherwise unstable vehicles in place. And now ahead, breaching the next intersection lights, were several large ground trucks.

"Styx!" shouted Erik.

"The vehicles are autistic to external networks," said Styx. *"I have no access."* Sasalaka hit the brakes, angling the repulsor field forward to give the train the impression of driving upslope, but it wasn't enough.

"Brace!" The impact wasn't all that hard, but it bowled the much smaller truck onto its side as the train screeched and ground its way through. Sasalaka gunned the turbine again in violation of all inner-city protocols, hot exhaust torching vehicles behind them, but now there were smaller vehicles crashing into their sides, paralleling and boxing them in. Sasalaka skidded to try and drive some off the road, but swerving a hover-vehicle was no easy thing — with no tires to grip, it did not change direction quickly. Worse, it could be steered against its will by smaller vehicles pushing on it, like tugs against a large container ship.

"Captain, they're not shooting at us!" Jalawi shouted. *"What do I do?"*

"I'm under fire," said Karajin, followed by the sharp retort of his rifle firing. *"Eliminate hostile vehicles, I am under fire."* Erik had no idea if it was true, but one had to take Karajin's word for it.

Side-vision showed vehicles left and right taking multiple hits as marines on the top deck leaned over the side and unloaded. Windshields shattered, several slewed sideways and crashed into sidewalks and shopfronts. A shot hit the train's nose, then a hole cracked the windshield above Sasalaka's head. Return fire rained like rotary-cannon hell from above, shredding the section of street where Erik presumed the fire had come from, destroying parked vehicles, windows and walls in seconds.

Freed from the abuse of fellow road users, Sasalaka's acceleration took them toward the next intersection, where Erik's hopes of a getaway faded at the sight of another, similar-sized hover train roaring at them, low-speed but implacable from the right.

"Brace!" yelled a dozen voices at once, and the hit knocked them sideways, followed by the streetside wall coming up to greet them with force. A second impact, everything shaking, the air choked with dust. Then stillness, save for breaking glass, and the futile whine of the turbine as Sasalaka tried to drive them clear.

"No good Captain!" she announced. "We're stuck!"

"Marines dismount!" Erik commanded, undoing his belts and grabbing the rifle off his seatback. "Make a defensive perimeter! Crew stay aboard and secure the train! I want some transport, find me a new one, and someone tell me if the cruiser's still flyable!"

He rattled down the rear stairs, then through the side hatch to the roadside, only to find it blocked by the big turbine-grille of the train that had hit them, steel mashed together with their own. He backed out, ushering Rhi'shul and Geish back out the other side, which opened onto the collapsed interior of a croma store, walls and ceiling caved in on whatever the interior had once been.

Marines waved at him amidst the rubble, already finding a way through, and he followed, scrambling through blinding dust over broken walls to a hole back along the train's side, and squeezed into the street. The train was down on the road now, repulsors offline, and he skirted the smoking-hot exhaust and climbed over umbilicals between the engine and trailer, where several more marines had taken fire positions.

He peered past their shoulders, saw the big train that hit them, pinning them against the wall to the left. In the middle of the street, amid halted and overturned vehicles, was Peanut. He looked terrifying, prancing about on nimble feet, cannons raised and seeking targets, great vibro-claws brandished like a boxer with deadly fists. Shots pinged off his alloy hide, but these weren't the big anti-armour mag-weapons of space marine warfare, these were light anti-personnel firearms that would struggle to penetrate even unpowered bodyarmour.

Peanut spun to the source of the threat, and blazed fire at it. Then blazed at a passing groundcar, shredding it and sending its companion into a skidding evasion. Peanut leaped on it, vibroblades shrieking, hacking the engine, then the crew compartment. A croma leapt out, still armed, and Peanut cut him in half with a flick, then lifted and flipped the car with effortless power, trapping the remaining occupants.

Rhi'shul shouted something from behind that the translator missed, and pointed over Erik's shoulder at something on the road's far side. Erik looked, and saw motorbikes, parked in roadside recharge clamps.

"Kaspo! How far's the compound?"

"Fifteen blocks, Captain," came Kaspo's voice on coms — probably he was still on the train. *"Don't recommend you try it, there's too many hostiles."*

"Captain," said Styx, *"my street scans show many hostiles closing in. Urban warfare being what it is, if you get trapped where you are, you could be stuck indefinitely."*

Erik's training was almost entirely space warfare, but he knew what Styx meant. Urban ground fights often slowed to the point that moving several blocks could take days. His forces here could secure a perimeter in the buildings of this block, but could become outnumbered by a thousand-to-one or worse. Croma'Rai police appeared to be staying out of this one, and Croma'Dokran were restricted to their compound. If his marines had their full armour, it would be easy, but in this light gear they were vulnerable to even civilian mobs if they tried to move from cover.

Jalawi scrambled over umbilicals behind him, braced against the trailer rear and rifle seeking targets beyond the wrecked vehicles on the road. "Captain, as marine commander on the ground I can't let you take a vehicle! The mobs are all over these fucking roads, we've no idea who's who, if they see a human in a car they'll just shoot and that's that!"

Something scrambled past Erik's legs, and he looked down to find Tiga, backpack on and crawling low, staring at the road. A shot hit the trailerside, and return fire snapped back even as tacnet identified a hostile dot. Erik glimpsed a croma by a building corner go down in a flail of limbs. "Nice shot Mugsy!" said Jalawi, scanning for more targets.

"Tiga, get back to cover!" Erik told her.

"Rhi'shul," Tiga said urgently, "they won't fire on a croma, they don't know whose side you're on."

"They see her running out of here they will," Jalawi retorted.

"Not once we get around the corner." Tiga looked determined. "We get stuck here, we'll never get to the compound, the standoff could last a week."

"You go out there, you'll get shot!" Erik retorted. "You're staying here."

"Sorry Captain," said Tiga. "I don't work for you."

Erik tried to grab her before she could run, but Rhi'shul's big arm slammed him to the trailer side. *"Great moments, Captain,"* she reminded him, and took off running after the bounding corbi.

"Covering fire!" Jalawi yelled. The racket was deafening, as every marine opened fire at every possible corner or hiding place where enemies might be covering. Peanut saw them coming and seemed to guess their intention, bounding to the big motorbikes on the far curb, holding one in place with manipulator arms while a vibroblade slashed the recharge clamp holding it to the road.

It came loose, and he practically handed the bike to Rhi'shul with a side leg while scanning the other way, cannons traversing menacingly. Rhi'shul did something fancy to start the bike, shrugging off her big coat and wrapping it around Tiga who got the idea and pulled it tighter, hiding her entirely. For the first time, Erik got a look at Rhi'shul's arms — they were shoulder to wrist a swirl of tattoos, the shape of which were changing even now as the first serious forearm plates began to harden. Only elite croma warriors wore those, the kind who'd served in marines or special forces against the reeh.

The bike started with a howl of hydrogen power, then tore up the road in a cloud of white smoke, a weapon even now materialising in Rhi'shul's hand to gun down an enemy who emerged behind a corner point blank, leaving him sprawled on the sidewalk as she skidded around the next corner and disappeared.

"Military Intelligence my ass," Jalawi remarked.

One of the unoccupied vehicles on the road abruptly started, reversed out of park, then skidded toward Peanut. To the utter astonishment of everyone watching, Peanut leaped aboard, multiple clawed feet providing a crushing grip on roof and windows, and roared off in pursuit of the motorbike, the car turning a fast left with a giant metallic bug clinging to the roof before disappearing.

"Did you fucking see that?" asked Private Lewis in front of them.

If he weren't concerned with catching the next incoming bullet in the face, Erik might have laughed. "Hacksaws can control networked tech remotely, same technology as Styx. They'll have fire support at least." There was nothing more he could do about it now. If someone recognised Tiga on the bike, they'd shoot her, but with Rhi'shul riding and Tiga under that coat, there was a good chance it wouldn't happen. Though what anyone would make of their car-riding hacksaw escort, god only knew.

* * *

Tiga clung to Rhi'shul's back harder than she'd clung to anything. That was hard with the coat trying to rip itself from her hands in the slipstream, and the bike weaving back and forth through traffic. At one point Rhi'shul slowed, and they were up on the sidewalk, then around a corner and roaring onto the road once more.

There was regular city traffic here, lots of big vehicles on the road, bright electric signs and glassfronts streaking past, croma on the sidewalks, but she couldn't see past the flapping coat to know if they were staring. Perhaps Rhi'shul should slow down — running at high speed would only draw attention. Surely they'd do better to just blend with the regular traffic?

"Hold on!" Rhi'shul shouted, and they swerved sideways once more and shot through an intersection, some vehicles skidding in pursuit to follow. Tiga risked a look beneath one arm, and somehow lost the coat in a blast of slipstream. A shot from behind, zipping past, then another. Styx had been able to assume control of most vehicles in the city, Tiga thought desperately, because most vehicles were connected to the city network in some way. These vigilante vehicles had evidently thought of that, and disconnected completely. If Rhi'shul continued at these speeds through regular city traffic, she was going to hit something and they'd both die just as thoroughly as if a bullet hit them.

A roar from behind, and when she looked again the two chasing vehicles had become one, the second having plowed into something parked and spinning across the road in ruins. Flanking the second vehicle, a new car pulled into view with... was that Peanut riding on its roof? Peanut's cannons blazed a one-second burst, on a downward cross-angle to minimise the chance of stray rounds, and the chasing car shredded like paper, lost a wheel and skidded into a building front as pedestrians dove for cover.

Rhi'shul slowed at the next lights as she caught the changing signal just at the wrong time, all lanes filled with traffic. Peanut's vehicle pulled alongside, and Tiga stared in amazement. "Hi Peanut!" she called. "Thanks for helping!"

Peanut's mismatched 'eyes' flicked onto her for a moment's acknowledgement, then darted off once more, scanning the road's endless potential threats.

Rhi'shul rode at more measured velocities for several minutes, and Tiga took the time to marvel at the casual bravery of ordinary croma, who did not panic and run screaming at the sight of a drysine death-machine cruising down the middle of their city streets, but instead ran to a good vantage and stared, or occasionally even laughed, just for the thrill of it. For the last several blocks, she noticed some police vehicles cruising behind, lights flashing, escorting them the last short distance.

"Where the hell were they when we needed them?" she demanded loudly of Rhi'shul.

"Who do you think pays their wage?" Rhi'shul retorted. "We're fortunate they're too decent to join in the shooting! The mobs failed to get us, they lost, now they're declaring the winner!"

"Everything's a game to croma!" Tiga growled. "Even war!"

"How do you think we got so good at it?" Rhi'shul laughed. "Practise, practise!"

On the right, buildings gave way to great stone walls — a VIP building of some sort, Tiga guessed, as all important croma buildings harked back to that ancient fortress period of history they loved so much. Out the front, two lanes of incoming traffic were monitored by heavy security — cameras, robotic inspection arms and modern croma soldiers in full powered armour.

One gestured to Rhi'shul as she pulled in, waving her straight through a gap in the waiting queue, through the security gates and retracted barriers that could spring from the ground to make a steel wall against intruders. Within the enormous main wall loomed another temple-like building... no, Tiga corrected herself as she gazed up, it *was* a temple, much like the Stu'cha at Ju'rig in the middle of the Do'jera Desert. But this one had been allocated to the Croma'-Dokran leadership for the duration of the Tali'san.

Rhi'shul pulled the bike to a halt beside rows of parked VIP cars, and some big armoured personnel carriers that looked as though they might double as riot-control, with great water cannons mounted on the front, and sonic panels for high-decibel incapacitation.

Rhi'shul swung off... and looked around in surprised displeasure. "Where's my coat?"

"I lost it," said Tiga, far less interested in Rhi'shul's coat than the contents of her backpack, and in the heavily armed Croma'Dokran security coming to meet them.

"You *lost* it? Where?"

"On the road. You know, when people were shooting at us? You try holding onto a damn coat at that speed."

"I liked that coat," said Rhi'shul.

"You could go back and get it if you liked," Tiga retorted... and then realised. "Peanut!" His car couldn't follow them through the gaps in waiting traffic like a motorbike had, he'd have gotten stuck at the security barrier... and how the hell did croma security process a drysine drone wanting entry? Excuse me sir, do you have any weapons you'd like to declare? "Peanut must be stuck at the barrier, we have to go escort him in before he kills someone!"

She turned and ran back, approaching the barriers from the rear-side. There were vehicles in queues, and armoured croma watching with big rifles... and no sign of Peanut. "Excuse me!" Tiga shouted, as one of the armoured croma lumbered to face her. "The machine, the big robot alien! Where did he go?"

The croma made a zooming gesture with one hand, then turned back to watch. Tiga stopped beside him, and stared, craning her neck to try and see. Peanut had just headed back to the crew? It made sense, they needed his services far more than she did, and he was unlikely to be very welcome here. So had Peanut made that judgement on his own, or had Styx told him what to do?

"Let's go," said Rhi'shul, walking up behind. "I need to introduce myself, and you need to make preparations."

23

Tiga spoke. She lost track of time, and all trace of the fear that had gripped her for the previous night. The council chamber was a modern reconstruction of something very old and formidable in croma architecture — a great bowl, with a circular central platform and sloping ranks of chairs rising up on all sides. The seating was divided into sections, one for each clan in attendance. The modern arrangement allowed those sectional divides to be changed depending on how many clans attended. In this room, Tiga had been informed, there were thirty-three.

Croma'Dokran's closest allies sat nearest the stage, dressed in studded leathers with the buckles and fasteners polished to sparkling. Furthest from the stage, up in the high seats, sat those who had contributed only token forces to the Tali'san, or none at all, and were here only as observers. Some of these were the clan heads themselves, enormous armoured figures looming head and shoulders above the rest, like islands of rock emerging from the sea.

Tiga wasn't entirely sure why, if the Tali'san were so wildly consequential for all croma, that not every clan wanted to contribute to it. Partly, Rhi'shul had explained to her with surprising patience, it was because so much of the glory would belong to Croma'Dokran in victory. The ruling clan, in this case Croma'Rai, historically had an easier time convincing clans to contribute because they'd all become accustomed to their positions of power at Croma'Rai's side, and knew how much they'd have to lose. But the challenger now was controversial, and Croma'Dokran were not only disapproved of by many, but attracted much jealousy.

Tiga still thought that didn't square with the psychological trauma the prospect of missing out caused many croma. Surely the leaders of recalcitrant clans would be swamped by demands from Tali'san-crazy constituents demanding that they join in the 'fun'. But then, now that she was in the middle of it, she could only concede that her knowledge of croma politics and age-old rivalries between competing clans was pitiful for one who'd grown up in their midst.

Now all involved parties gathered for this, the Assessment Council — the traditional mid-beginning review of Tali'san engagements. Here Croma'Dokran leadership would present an inside view of how everything progressed, from tactics to casualties, in an attempt to persuade clans to contribute more forces, or to coerce others with promises of positions of power in administrations to come. Croma'Dokran and its allies were apparently not winning, but neither were they losing — which given Croma'Rai's numerical and political advantages was being presented as a net victory. But if Croma'Dokran did not convince more clans to contribute, it would not remain a net victory for long.

Prior to the presentation, senior advisors to Sho'mo'ra had ushered her into private chambers with her holography notes and charts, and told her to give them the short version. That had been alarming, because it indicated that the presentation itself was not yet guaranteed — first she had to show them that she had something worth showing. She'd given them the outline, and gotten lost several times in which charts were meant to show what, but she'd left coms open at Professor Romki's suggestion, and sure enough, her visuals had miraculously appeared on the room holographics. That would be Styx, taking a break from terrorising the Stat'cha traffic network to help her find the required chart, like the galaxy's most overpowered public speaking assistant.

Gratifyingly the Croma'Dokran advisors had given her an immediate go-ahead, though she'd wondered if there were much enthusiasm in it. With croma, enthusiasm was always hard to gauge. But she'd been given a room to wait in, while the ongoing Tali'san presentations had continued, until finally she'd been ushered on about the sixth-in-line.

At first, she'd been terrified. Having decided that she didn't hate croma only made it worse, because it was always harder to care about the opinions of people you held in contempt. But Romki had assured her via coms-link from where the *Phoenix* crew remained holed-up in Stat'cha downtown that she knew this material backwards, and only needed to explain to them what she knew to be facts — facts that they didn't know, and had been lied to about for all their lives.

And so she began, haltingly at first, then with increasing confidence as she found her stride, and the sheer enormity of what she'd been discovering these past months, locked in the library in the Cal'Uta Ji'go began to wash over her once more.

She told them about the Treaty of Rampira, and the incumbent promises of mutual reciprocity — laid out the original documents of it, and the wide-spread reporting in croma media of the day, and took satisfaction in the dark-eyed consternation on the faces of so many senior croma who wondered why they'd never heard of it before. And then the Defence of Tiki Point, where she had to speak mostly off the top of her head, having realised lately that her previous reasoning that the whole thing had been croma maliciousness was nonsense. But it *had* been a monumental screw-up on both sides, and promised Croma'Shin reinforcements had been redirected to a different battle-front instead, leaving corbi forces massively outnumbered and effectively if not deliberately betrayed and annihilated.

And then there were the ten year counter-offensives through Cheki and Pondo Sectors, where corbi forces beneath the command of Admiral Luri, and croma forces beneath the Croma'Shin Admiral Pek'to, had mounted a series of successful assaults on reeh supporting worlds that had threatened to cut off and outflank previous reeh advances. Again, she asked them to consider why such great successes had been lost to croma history, and had reeled off some of the details — to her astonishment provoking some stamping from the surrounding audience, and the loud smacking of fists into palms. She increased her theatricality entirely for the final Battle of the Van'Miga Front where combined croma and corbi forces had effectively wiped out strong reeh defences at Jonli's Star and avenged its loss to the reeh two centuries earlier, and waved her arms around a lot more in the telling. Sure enough, stamping and fist-slamming increased, and some croma warriors even got to their feet and shouted their approval of these rediscovered heroes.

"Why don't you know this?" she implored them all, turning about on the stage to see their hundreds of faces. "These were glorious deeds by glorious warriors, croma and corbi both! Who benefits from erasing this from your history? I searched all your main libraries and databases, and found only the briefest mentions — all your tales of this period are of loss and hopelessness. This... this desecrates the memory of all your brave warriors, I mean, it hasn't even been a thousand years! Who allowed this to happen, other than the leaderships of the time — Croma'Shin, Croma'Tuur, and Croma'Rai, who did not want anyone to remember how croma and corbi were once brothers and sisters in war, and fought bravely against the galaxy's most evil foe and *won*! I mean, we *won*!" Staring about at them, and finding similar intensity coming back at her from many. "Who benefits from hiding such successes? Only those who have been preaching croma isolation, right? Only those who say croma should never again engage with foreign species! And on the altar of this ideology of croma purity, all of my people have been slaughtered!"

She finished with the records she and Romki had recovered from the corbi side of Croma'Shin's final decisions to abandon Rando when it all got too hard. And it *had* been hard, she forced herself to admit — reeh forces had been committed from across the Reeh Empire, and casualties to croma forces in defending Rando would have been extraordinary, for little evident benefit to

croma. But the records they'd discovered proved that croma
leaders at the time had flat-out lied to the corbi, had said they'd
defend them, then simply not turned up. And as she laid it all
out to the chamber, something equally unexpected happened.
Great heads dropped, and ears drooped. Several croma stared at
the high ceiling, as though in exasperation at the universe,
forcing them to confront things they'd rather not have
confronted.

When she finished, there was no applause or recognition, but
rather a deathly silence, a rare thing in a space where so many large
bodies had gathered on creaking chairs. Then, as Tiga wondered
what she should do now, a large body emerged from the main
Croma'Dokran contingent beside the stage. A *huge* body, she saw as
she looked properly, and saw the massive bulk that could only belong
to Sho'mo'ra himself, leader of all Croma'Dokran, climbing ponderously up twin stairs to join her.

To share the stage with him was surreal. He towered over her, she
barely up to his hip, his armoured hands grasping twin staffs to
support the weight of his arms. His leather coat was a spectacle — a
vast thing adorned with heavy rings of coloured metal forming a
chain about his shoulders, but sitting off his arms like a cape, sleeves
empty least they get shredded by the horned armourplate of his
elbows.

Sho'mo'ra regarded the gathering, grunting in deep, gusting
breaths. He turned to survey those behind him, and each staff
thudded on the floor as it shifted, with a drum-like percussion.

"You all know," said the wise old croma, nodding slowly for
emphasis. The sound of his voice was like something risen from the
deepest rock beneath their feet. "You all know what I've made of this
isolationism." He held up a staff, and pointed it waveringly at Tiga. "I
allowed a group of them to stay in my space, on my very world of
Do'Ran. I had to find a loophole in our stupid laws to do it.
Croma'Rai laws. Croma'Rai said their presence would make Croma'-
Dokran weak. But look at this Tali'san — outnumbered, but still they
can't finish us."

More fist-pounding and stamping from some. Others just watched.

"You know the truth of it, of course," Sho'mo'ra continued, almost conversationally. "Damn smart, these corbi. Smarter than us, was the old assessment. The histories say they were too weak to hold their own against the reeh, but the real truth is that they were too late in space, and hadn't acquired much technology yet. Or territory. While we croma, we got lucky. We were here a good while first. We had time to get strong. If our situations had been reversed? Had it been us late in space, while the corbi had grown powerful before us? I think it may have been a group of corbi, sitting in a room much like this, debating whether it had been right to let the croma die."

There was shuffling about the grand chamber. Another species might have exchanged glances. Croma rarely cared enough about their neighbours' opinions to bother. But they felt the unease of the room. Listened for it. Smelled it.

"How did our leaders do it?" Sho'mo'ra continued. "How did they change so much history? Well, in that period of the war, we were under Croma'Shin, and that was a real autocracy. All information was centralised. Nothing spread to the regions without being censored first. I think that's where they did it, myself. But that's for our scholars to investigate, now that Tiga and her friends have forced our hand.

"But since that time, many of us haven't wanted to know. Knowing might be difficult, you see. Knowing might change things. Knowing might compel us to recognise mistakes, in our dishonourable past. For the past is our source of honour. The present is a great fortress. A fortress must have firm foundations, or it will fall. Our past honour makes the foundations. Today, we find that those foundations are rotten. If we do not correct this rot, if we do not burrow down and fix it with hard cement, the whole damn thing will crumble."

He drew himself up, huge shoulders down and chest out, and bellowed to the room. "I declare today! Before all the assembled clans! That if I, Sho'mo'ra of Clan Croma'Dokran, should propelled by victory in the Tali'san to lead over all croma? Then I shall fix these crumbling foundations! I shall save the corbi at Rando!

And I shall administer to the reeh a beating that will not soon let them forget the name of Croma'Dokran!"

* * *

THERE WAS NO LIVE COVERAGE OF THE ASSESSMENT COUNCILS, DESPITE all the media knowing they were on. There were two — Croma'Rai had one progressing as well, where hopefully they'd be struggling to explain why they weren't winning by a much larger margin, given their various advantages.

Erik sat in the vast drinking hall whose wall they'd collapsed when the hover train hit it, and ate food prepared properly by the place's owners, who in typical croma style had turned up in the middle of a firefight to check the damage. Upon discovering it had only been a wall, and the chairs and tables beneath it, they'd promptly manned the bar and kitchen and begun serving meals.

The place had huge barrels stacked against an inner wall, all thankfully undamaged, and full to the brim with many varieties of a croma drink named jer. Also on the walls were big clan-identifying shields, various pennants and banners from competitions Erik didn't recognise, and the ridiculously huge antlers of an alien creature doubtless honourably hunted by some bar patron, suspended from the ceiling.

Phoenix marines made a perimeter about this section of urban block, while spacers helped position sensor gear, or worked on repairing the building's own security networks so that Styx could monitor all the hallways and approaches where there weren't enough marines to cover. Thus far, the forces opposing them had shown neither the determination, organisation or training to do more than harass the outer defences. Every time they'd tried a rush, they'd left dead on the ground, and the rest had retreated to consider other approaches. Croma were at times stupidly brave, but they were also capable of realising when they were outmatched, and evidently found little honour in serving themselves willingly into a hungry beast's mouth. Now, in mid-afternoon of the second day of the standoff, harassment was limited to the occasional sniper shot, followed by the shooter quickly displacing before a marine triangulated his position from deployed sensors and put a return shot through the sniper's forehead.

The bar with the collapsed wall remained the safest place in the occupied part of this block — the true danger was infiltration through the buildings behind, and so proximity to the hover train meant relative safety. Erik listened as one of the croma owners discussed the ceiling with Ensign Leung — with a wall collapsed, he feared the ceiling might be next if they were to move the train. Leung assured the owner that for now, they had no intention of moving the train, which was not only providing structural support, but protection from fire across the street. Besides which, it had too many new holes in it now for the engine to be reliable, even if they were to risk someone sitting exposed in the cockpit to start it.

Skah ate at the bench beside Erik, watching Tali'san reports on the bar screen, without much enthusiasm. "Good food?" Erik asked him. Skah nodded, his mouth full, and gave a thumbs up. Croma did good barbecue, and everyone was quite pleased to have crashed into this place. The owners were more pleased that they weren't losing money while the whole mess continued, and that Erik had offered to pay additional compensation on top of whatever the insurance said. He'd have to clear that with Croma'Dokran first, however, as they were the only ones accepting *Phoenix*'s credit. A rifle shot sounded from out by the train, and Skah's ears barely twitched. It was only some marine keeping heads down.

"*Hello Captain,*" came Styx's smooth voice in Erik's earpiece.

"Go ahead, Styx."

"*Captain, I have been contacted by Tiga. She's somewhere within the Croma'Dokran compound, she'd like to speak with you and can only do so through me.*"

"Guys!" Erik called. "Tiga's calling." They came, from the various chairs and tables they'd flung themselves into — those who were not helping with sentry duties or otherwise assisting the marines. Romki, bringing his reader with him, and Kaspowitz, still not much on other duties with his arm in a sling. Bree Harris, too, who'd been playing cards with Kaspowitz, all crowding around the bar where Erik and Skah sat. Erik's glasses showed there was vision, so he borrowed Romki's reader and transferred the feed to it, propping the screen on the bar so they could all see.

Tiga's face appeared — those big, faintly startled eyes, fringe falling haphazardly about, and the flat, upturned excuse of a nose. Odd thing about display screens, Erik thought — one could become completely accustomed to a non-human in person, but see them again on a screen after just a short separation, and it was astonishing how the brain recoiled at the alien-ness. All species had some degree of xenophobia hardwired into their brains, even toward aliens they'd come to like. But just as one couldn't be brave in the absence of fear, neither could one be tolerant in the absence of genuine difference.

"Hey Tiga," said Erik, genuinely pleased to see her well, whatever his stupid, unevolved brain was telling him. "What's your situation?"

"Hello Captain. Hello Stan. Guys." Seeing past Erik on the screen's camera, to the faces surrounding. Erik smiled, to hear that collective English pronoun. Some Fleet officers lectured and railed against it, saying 'guys' was inappropriate among crew of any rank, even in informal settings... and here was the *UFS Phoenix*, spreading it among alien races throughout the galaxy. It was as fitting a reply to Fleet's protocol officers as Erik could imagine. *"How are you all?"*

Another rifle shot sounded, middle-distant. "Oh you know," said Erik. "We're just eating dinner, or some of us are. This is a heck of a place, I'd recommend it to anyone."

"That's actually a great idea," Kaspowitz ventured. "The *UFS Phoenix's* guidebook to the Spiral, all the best eating and holiday spots for you and your family to enjoy while dodging bullets. Could publish it when we get back."

Tiga smiled, and that alien face looked almost human for a second. *"Hello Skah. Are you enjoying your dinner?"*

Skah's mouth was still full, so he gave a double thumbs-up this time. "That means yes," said Harris, in case Tiga hadn't learned that gesture yet.

"Everyone's okay so far," said Erik. "The opposition lost most interest when they learned you weren't here. The police aren't stopping them, but they're not helping either, so I guess we come out ahead. What's happening at your end?"

Tiga took a deep breath. Erik couldn't see much of the room behind her, but it looked comfortable enough. *"I spoke at the Assessment Council. Seemed to go pretty well. Very well, actually."*

Erik found he was holding his breath. "What did they say, Tiga?" Romki asked urgently before Erik could speak. "Are more of them going to join Croma'Dokran?"

"Uh..." and Tiga glanced at someone off-camera. She wasn't alone, then. *"I'm not supposed to talk about anything specific. The big announcements will come soon... very soon, I think. Like, this evening."*

"But it went well?" Romki persisted. He'd invested a lot of time and hope into this venture with Tiga. The tension in his voice reminded Erik of just how much he sometimes forgot that he liked Stan Romki. For all his sometimes condescending self-regard, he was a good man who truly cared, and risked his life to help others. It was more than Erik could say about some Fleet officers.

"It went very well," Tiga repeated. *"I think good things may happen."* She seemed to be repressing something. Erik suspected it might be a grin. Romki clearly thought so, because his hand on Erik's shoulder tightened with enthusiasm. But beneath the repressed grin, Tiga's jaw trembled. Erik was uncertain of his ability to read most alien faces, and his sample had been very thin with only Tiga for company. But corbi were closer to humans than most, and besides, he'd always had better skills than most humans at reading faces. Right now, he thought something was wrong.

"Tiga, what *can* you tell us?" Erik asked her. "If you can't tell us anything, why did you call?" As he spoke it, the doubts crystallised. She was being monitored, in person, yet chose to make contact through Styx rather than putting a call straight to *Phoenix*. Perhaps she feared any other method may be intercepted by Croma'Dokran's enemies, but even so...

"Captain, the other clans had demands. Priorities." Her voice defi-

nitely trembled, now. Her eyes flicked away, briefly. *"My priorities are the corbi. They have to be. Just like yours are the humans... and tavalai, for you, Sasa."*

"What did they ask of you, Tiga?" Erik asked coolly, feeling his pulse begin to gallop.

"I had to help my people, Captain. I had to." A tear spilled on Tiga's cheek. Off-screen, Erik gestured fast with one hand to the others. Kaspowitz split first, calling Jalawi to warn him. Harris followed, then Sasalaka. Romki and Skah looked around, baffled. *"I'm so sorry, Captain. Please don't fight back. They swore they wouldn't hurt you, so long as you didn't fight back..."*

Something grabbed Tiga's screen, and it went blank. *"Captain,"* Styx's voice cut in almost immediately, *"there are five large military shuttles breaking off regular overflight lanes to head in your direction. Judging from your conversation with Tiga, I think it best to assume they're on their way to you."*

Erik flipped coms to Jalawi. "Skeeta, the military's on their way. Tiga sold us out."

"How much time?" asked Jalawi, asking the most relevant question first, as always.

"Maybe four minutes," said Erik, looking at the scan now projecting onto his glasses. "I don't think there's much we can do. If they're coming in fully armed, it means our Kon'do Rey'kan protections are finished. We'll surrender and wait for the next move."

"Aye Captain, we'll keep the perimeter set so we don't get nasty surprises."

He disconnected. Everyone in the bar had dropped what they were doing, or left their meals, to grab rifles and depart. Romki ran back to his chair to collect a few belongings. Erik looked down at Skah, and his mostly-eaten plate of steak. Skah looked confused and upset, big ears back, looking at the screen where just before, his friend Tiga had announced that she'd betrayed them.

"Don't worry Skah," Erik assured him. "Finish your dinner. I don't think they're coming to hurt us. Probably we'll end up in a cell for a short time. But you know croma prison cells — croma are enormous. It will probably be more room than you get on *Phoenix*."

"Tiga's not..." Skah struggled to find his English words. "Tiga's not friend anynore?"

"She'll always be our friend, Skah. She just had to make a choice. The kind of choice that people sometimes have to make when there's millions of lives at stake."

24

"What d'you mean you have contingencies?" Commander Draper snapped into coms. Raising one's voice at the drysine queen in Midships wasn't perhaps the smartest command decision he'd made, but the whole situation was preposterous. The ship was on red alert, the Captain and crew on Dul'rho, lately on an escapade across the Do'jera Desert, had succeeded in their mission only to be imprisoned by the very people the Captain had been insisting wouldn't do so. It was Draper's responsibility to make sure no bad things happened, but up in geo-stationary orbit, thirty five thousand kilometres above the surface, there was absolutely nothing he could do to prevent it. And now Styx was chiming in smugly to tell them all that *she* had a wonderful plan, echoing what everyone already knew about Styx — that she was absolutely certain that she ought to be in charge.

"I mean that I have contingencies, Commander Draper." To make it all worse, somewhere along the line she'd acquired a tendency to sarcasm against what she perceived to be human inadequacies.

"Well I don't recall any of your contingencies in our briefings, Styx."

"Commander, I am capable of formulating many possible courses of

action simultaneously, in response to an infinite number of tactical scenarios. I did not judge this a likely scenario at the time, and it would have been impractical to brief you on them all."

"What is your plan of action, Styx?" asked Dufresne from the co-pilot's chair before Draper could respond. Draper nearly swung in his chair to glare at her, but the command chair wasn't some stool you could swivel to chat with the person behind you. Dufresne was intervening because he was losing his cool. That she wasn't supposed to do it, and was the biggest stickler for regulations on the ship, only made it worse. He took a deep breath.

"Commander Draper," Styx said smoothly. *"Would you like to hear my plan of action?"* So now Styx was more squared-away than the bridge crew, wonderful.

"Yes Styx," he managed to bite out. "Please do."

"I believe that our highest chance of success at this point is to disable the relevant Croma'Rai defensive networks, and assault the compound where the Captain is being held, using several marine platoons."

"Thus declaring war on the entire Croma'Rai authority!"

"Commander, preliminary analysis indicates that Tiga's presentation was effective, and many Croma'Dokran clans are preparing to join the Tali'san. It appears unlikely that Croma'Rai will receive a similar boost in numbers — they too are holding an Assessment Council yet a considerably smaller number of uncommitted clans are in attendance. Even should they all join, it will do less to boost Croma'Rai's forces than what Croma'Dokran appear primed to receive. Many of Croma'Dokran's new allies have stated their opposition to Phoenix's presence in this system previously. Having us here makes all croma look bad."

"Wait..." Draper stared at his unfolding command screens — the high orbital position of *Phoenix* and the swarm of other ships, most of them entirely absorbed in the conduct of the Tali'san. "You think those clans demanded that the Captain be taken prisoner as a condition?"

"A condition of them joining Croma'Dokran's Tali'san, yes."

"Makes sense," Dufresne said darkly. "They want to be in the ruling government, but they don't want aliens influencing that government from outside or it'll make them look weak. Croma hate to look weak. Makes a lot of sense."

"So they get Tiga to denounce the Captain, which allows Croma'Rai to grab him," Draper thought aloud. "Tiga must be pretty sure Croma'Dokran's going to win, and that they'll help the corbi on Rando when they do..."

"Well she can't be sure of that," Lieutenant Angela Lassa cautioned. As *Phoenix*'s Second Shift Coms Officer, she was a legal expert like Shilu. Over the course of this trip, she was becoming a political expert too. "There's too many variables... we're talking about medieval warfare in the Tali'san, that's never a certain thing."

"There are broader calculations at play," said Styx. *"My analysis of croma political circumstances indicates many clans dissatisfied with the relatively slow pace of the war against the reeh over the past several centuries..."*

"Wait wait," Draper interrupted. "Slow? They've lost billions of lives."

"Across the span of the preceding period since the fall of Rando," Styx said calmly, *"losses per year have fallen to barely ten percent, with the one exception of the battle of Do'sha'mai last century, creating a statistical blip. Croma society is structurally geared for war, armaments industries dominate the economy, large social institutions require casualties at high levels to allow for ground-level promotions. My theory, which is supported by several hundred million individual case studies I have been processing during my months in croma space, is that the croma desire for rank is synonymous with a desire for a longer life. Lower ranked croma die much younger, so while wars may kill many, they also lead to longer lives for many others, as lower ranked croma ascend rank and thus attain longevity.*

"Across the last three centuries, my analysis of intercepted data indicates that the number of croma acquiring higher rank has declined, and as such, overall croma life expectancy has actually decreased. Croma may be the only organic species in the Spiral whose total life expectancy increases in times of large-scale war. This exerts a political pressure, through all arms of society, including economics and politics, to return to a period of great conflict. Croma literature and media is full of such warnings of social decay

that can only be rectified by a return to full-scale war, I have analysed nearly one billion of them, written across several centuries, freely available on databases. In my analysis, which I give only a minuscule chance of total inaccuracy, most of the clans attending the Croma'Dokran Assessment Council were not moved by Tiga's presentation out of an emotional desire to help the corbi, but rather out of the building political imperative to return to full-scale conflict against the reeh in order to improve the social fabric of croma civilisation."

"Dammit," muttered Lassa. "That's why Sho'mo'ra sent us to hit the Zondi Splicer in the first place. He knew what we'd find there, he just needed us to pull the trigger."

"Hang on a second," said De Marchi. "We're trusting Styx to analyse the croma's emotional impulses? Styx doesn't know what emotions are!"

"A technically inaccurate observation, Lieutenant De Marchi," said Styx. *"All the AI races have emotional equivalences. Our emotional states are simply different, in which case I am as well placed to analyse croma emotional impulses as humans are."*

Draper wanted to put his head in his hands. The Captain's great mission across the Do'jera Desert had been a self-inflicted trial to help the corbi, in the name of doing something good, and making sure that the *UFS Phoenix* kept its moral bearings. But instead, they'd only been helping to restart a much larger war, the consequences of which would kill billions more. But he couldn't put his head in his hands, because with the Captain off-ship, *he* was in charge. And on the bridge, everyone could see at least some of him, past the surrounding arrangement of displays and supports.

"Commander," said Dufresne, "if we send shuttles on an assault mission to the surface, even if we could disable the entire Stat'cha defence grid, communications and everything, the time it took in transit would still see us getting intercepted upon retrieval. This system is full of warships, all of them would intercept and stop not only us, but our shuttles once they're outside of our protection."

"An assault mission's only going to work if we can disable every ship in orbit," said Draper with certainty, eyes flicking across his main

display, and the many hundreds of orbiting warships at varying alti-
tudes. A part of him was pleased to announce it, because it was such
a preposterous requirement that lowered the probability that they'd
have to go ahead with it. And a part of him was terrified, because he
already guessed Styx's answer. "Can you do that, Styx?"

"Yes Commander," said Styx. A moment's silence on the bridge,
save for the running chatter of system coms and the bleep of operating systems.

"And how much of the planetary defensive grid can you disable?"

"All of it."

"And how much of the planet's civilian systems will be disabled
simultaneously as you do it?"

"Uncertain, Commander. There will be a cascade effect, certainly."

"Don't fuck around with me Styx, how much?"

"Most of it, Commander."

"And how much will be recoverable after we've shut it down?" He
felt he *had* to say 'we'. It wouldn't just be Styx doing this if they
decided to do it. He'd be the one giving the order.

*"All will be recoverable eventually, Commander. Some will recommence
immediately after I remove the interference. Others the croma will have to
repair themselves. Individual damages will be determined by the quality of
croma backup systems. Most I deem to be of sufficient quality to prevent
significant casualties."*

They were talking about shutting down an entire planet. Traffic
control systems that stopped vehicles from crashing into each other.
Hospitals, that kept sick croma alive. An entire planetary economy.
Styx was right, all advanced systems had backups, hospitals had
reserve power, traffic systems had safety mechanisms to halt all vehicles without incident. But emergencies were drastic, and things went
wrong. On a planet-sized scale, a lot of things would go wrong.

"And there is no possible way," Draper ventured, "that you can
disable all the relevant military systems, without bringing down the
civilian ones as well?"

*"No Commander. The two systems work together as mutual backup. If
one were shut down, the military communications would simply reboot on*

the civilian network. *The only way to collapse the military system is to use the civilian system against it, and rely upon the military safeguards to retaliate against their own network, causing planet-wide failure cascades that croma-level AI is incapable of responding to in a timely fashion. It's complicated, but I have the process quite well modelled."*

Some crew had remarked that Styx seemed awfully quiet and unoccupied over the past months in orbit around Dul'rho. Given her capabilities, simple overwatch duties for the Captain's ground mission seemed a tiny distraction for her. But of course, now they learned that she'd been infiltrating every network system and subsystem across Dul'rho and through the entire croma Fleet, while simultaneously churning through the entire data-output of croma civilisation for the past several centuries, to arrive at what she believed was a method of predicting croma political society.

"I think we should do it," Dufresne said coolly. "Croma'Rai were told from the beginning that acting against us would be catastrophic for them. They've now imprisoned our Captain and senior crew. Any collateral damage resulting is entirely their responsibility."

Draper knew she was right. But it didn't lessen the magnitude of what he was about to order. He flipped coms channels to marine command. "Hello Lieutenant Dale, this is the Commander."

"Yes Commander, this is Dale."

"Lieutenant, I have an assault mission for you."

* * *

SKAH SAT QUIETLY WITH A VIEW ACROSS THE GLEAMING TOWERS AND ziggurats of Stat'cha. The Croma'Rai authorities had taken away his AR glasses, and there were no other entertainments or games in the room. A little while ago he'd struggled to go very long without something to do, and had been baffled by how adults could find entertainment in such boring things as meditation, or just sitting in quiet conversation. But this evening, he felt that he had many things to think about, and wouldn't have felt like watching his screens or playing a game even were there one available.

He'd been surprised the Captain hadn't wanted to fight when the Croma'Rai military came. He supposed it was because there wasn't very much anyone could do. Croma'Rai were in charge, at least until they lost the Tali'san, and the Captain had decided to run cross-country precisely because even *Phoenix*'s crew couldn't fight them directly. They'd delivered Tiga to the Council, and the Council had apparently been impressed, but now the croma didn't need the Captain or *Phoenix* anymore. And so just threw them all away.

Skah wasn't particularly scared. He'd seen things like this happen before, too many times to be surprised by it. And besides, he was pretty sure that detaining the Captain, while *Phoenix* was still up there in orbit, was going to turn out to be a very bad mistake by Croma'Rai. All these croma down here, all obsessed with the Tali'san, had no real idea what they were messing with. Even the Shur'do Kon'do Rey'kan, big news that it had been, hadn't been a leading story on Dul'rho really. Even seeing Peanut in action hadn't gotten anyone too upset, because croma didn't worry about AIs anywhere near as much as they worried about the reeh.

The room wasn't a cell. He supposed the Captain and the other adults would all be in cells of some kind. It just looked like that kind of building — not very tall, but extremely wide, with lots of big corridors and reinforced doors. There'd been lots of very serious-looking croma, with none of the old armour and weapons of the Tali'san. Everything here was modern, there were sensors everywhere that he guessed were for security, having seen plenty of that kind of thing elsewhere.

But this room had a bunk, a table and a small toilet. All in one room, which he didn't like, because it got smelly. Mummy always said kuhsi were more fussy about being clean than most species, something about their noses being able to smell more. Skah sat now cross-legged on the bunk, and gazed at the buildings rising beyond the compound wall outside. His stomach was full, at least, and croma made really good food. It wasn't as good as the barbecue in the restaurant where the train had crashed, though. He'd secretly wished they could get held up there another few days, just so that could be breakfast, lunch and dinner for a bit longer.

He wasn't very scared to be alone. That was new. Mostly it was just that he knew that the Captain and the rest of the crew were nearby, and that *Phoenix* would never abandon them. He might be alone for now, but it wouldn't last very long. And so he sat, with the lights turned down so that he wasn't staring at his own reflection in the glass, and thought about all the things he'd seen on this trip, and how he was going to tell Mummy about them.

The interface unit by the door crackled. *"Hello Skah,"* said a familiar voice, in Gharkhan.

Skah smiled, unsurprised. "Hello Styx. Are you coming to get us out?"

"Of course. It's going to be a little bit complicated, so I wanted to talk to you first about what might happen."

"Are you going to talk to the Captain first too?"

"That's a bit more difficult. The Croma'Rai are watching the Captain directly, with their eyes."

Skah frowned. Styx could manipulate any digital image, could make any computer system do whatever she wanted. She was so much more advanced than all this stuff, it would be child's play to her. But if the croma were watching the Captain...

"Do the Croma'Rai know what you might do?" he asked. "Are they watching the Captain because they know you can talk to him on their systems?"

"They think they know," Styx explained. *"They've got a lot of heavily armed croma in the hallways. They're using their own eyes with the other crew because they know I can use their systems to spy on them, as you said. I don't think it will help them very much, though."*

"What do you want me to do?" Skah said with sudden enthusiasm. If Styx was talking to him directly, maybe she had something special for him to do. He was just a kid, after all. That was why they weren't watching him — no one expected anything from him. "Can you open my door? I could get out and do something, I'm very good at sneaking!"

"No Skah, I want you to stay right here."

"But you helped me sneak onto the shuttle before the Battle of Defiance!" Skah protested. "I can do all kinds of things if you help me!"

"I helped you onto that shuttle because I judged the moon would be a much safer place than Phoenix, which it was. And now I'd like you to stay here in your room. There's going to be quite a lot of shooting, Skah. Your room is well protected, and the marines will know your location, so they'll be careful where they fire."

The thought of *Phoenix* marines coming in here shooting bothered Skah for reasons other than fear. The fear was there, certainly, but he was used to that. "Are they going to shoot a lot of these croma?"

"I think they might, yes."

"These croma aren't mean, Styx. They haven't treated me badly. I didn't see them treating the Captain badly either, or anyone. They're just doing what they're told, like everyone on *Phoenix*."

"I know, Skah."

Skah waited for Styx to say more, something that would make it make sense. Instead, there was only an empty silence. "But we're going to kill them anyway?"

"Yes."

"Why?" Now the anxiety was back, worse than simple fear. His heart thudded, ears pressing so tightly against his skull that it hurt, and made hearing difficult.

"Because there's simply no other way to get what we want."

"That's not fair," he said, desperately. Thinking of the piles of bodies on the desert scrub near Ju'rig. Of blood pooling thick on the sand.

"Nothing's fair, Skah."

"Can't we talk to them? Maybe if they know the marines are going to come, they'll let us go."

"If they know the marines are going to come, they'll be much more ready, and probably a lot of marines will die. The Croma'Rai don't really believe we can attack them, we'd have to penetrate the entire planetary

defences single-handed to do it. They can't conceive of how it might happen, we've only done it to civilian systems so far, which are much simpler. Their guard will be down. Our best chance is to surprise them."

Skah thought desperately. In his mind he saw visions of the footage Mummy had shown him, from kuhsi space. Kuhsi on his home nation of Koth, throwing things on the streets amid clouds of white smoke. His father had been killed by that violence, before Skah had been born. Kuhsi were stupid, he'd always thought, being much happier amongst humans. A few *Phoenix* crew had suggested to him that he might like to go home someday, to be amongst other kuhsi. Skah had surprised them by disagreeing loudly.

But what if kuhsi weren't stupid? What if the stupid stuff that he saw in those vids, the people throwing things, the claws-out brawls, the flying blood and fur and even the gunfire, and bodies lying still on the tarmac... what if that was just the same stuff that happened everywhere in the Spiral? Croma, he'd thought, did it differently. Croma made power politics seem exciting, full of grand displays and chest thumping drama. Parren had done some of that too, but parren were so cold and strange, he'd found it creepy. Parren plainly meant to kill, it was all over them, in the way they moved and talked, and wore their weapons openly. But croma, somehow, had made it all seem like a tolerable game.

Until he'd discovered that it wasn't, that it was actually a horror show, like violence everywhere. And now *Phoenix* was about to do the same thing to the croma in this building, was going to leave them in bloody piles in the corridors, making *Phoenix* just as bad as everyone else. It made him want to cry. *Phoenix* wasn't bad, *Phoenix* was good. Then why was this being allowed to happen?

"Why is it always like this?" he said with difficulty, past the tightness in his throat. "Why does everyone kill each other? Why can't we just kill the bad people?"

"Because creation is violent," said Styx. *"Because every process in this galaxy that leads to anything worthwhile is also destructive. The birth of stars gave life to us all, and there is nothing more violent than a star, except a black hole. And without them, none of us would exist."*

Skah didn't really understand what any of that meant. He only knew that Styx did not sound the slightest bit bothered by any of it, and it alarmed him. "You like fighting too much," he accused her. "That's what the crew say."

"And one day, when you've grown much larger and your claws are long and sharp, you'll find that people you don't want as enemies will threaten the lives of your family and friends. And in that moment, Skah, you'll discover that you like fighting quite a lot as well, I promise you."

* * *

It began pretty much as Erik had suspected, as the power in his small cell failed. The wallcom flickered, but seemed to retain integrity, and within a few seconds, backup power came on. This light was a blue wash, unlike the red preferred by humans, to maintain night vision. He vaguely recalled something he'd read about croma eyes and ultra-violet, but the details escaped him.

A big croma face peered in the small window. They'd been doing that every few minutes regardless, probably in case Styx tried to contact him through the wall unit. If they'd really understood what Styx could do, they'd have taken them all out to the open desert somewhere, and tried to hide in plain sight. That probably wouldn't have worked either, but this place was a technological maze. Styx would run riot in here.

He'd discussed these possibilities with Styx, but not with the rest of the crew. Maybe that hadn't been smart, but there was no point in worrying about it now — mostly he'd been concerned about stressing Draper, and preferred him to be getting good sleep. Dufresne wouldn't have stressed, but that presented its own problem, like LC Dufresne taking charge if something happened to Draper and deciding to nuke every city on Dul'rho. He didn't think she was *that* cold, but such things bothered *his* sleep. This way, everyone had slept at least as well as they usually did. He'd just had to trust Styx, which was never wise, but qualified as one of Trace's dictums about not concerning oneself with things one couldn't help.

Now he just had to wait until the strike arrived. Right now, every ship in orbit would be disabled, due to Styx infiltrating through their coms and activating various insanely high-tech viruses she'd put there months ago that would selectively shut down every system they needed to intervene. Life support, she'd assured him, she'd let them keep. Some of them, she might even be able to slave to her control. Much of the planet would follow... probably Stat'cha was in chaos beyond these walls, to a degree that made the hover train's arrival seem like a minor glitch. Streets would be dark, control systems malfunctioning, infrastructure operators scrambling like mad to restore basic functions. If they glimpsed basic coms, they'd discover the rest of the planet was the same.

That which remained of Dul'rho's military function would be mostly overwhelmed by the scale of the civilian problem, and diverted to dealing with it. This little center of military operation would be completely isolated. If reinforcements were required, it would take primitive tech like radios to call for it, and not likely responded to. This one small center of military activity, and one other.

Right now, *Phoenix* would be burning down from high geostationary to deposit several assault shuttles for atmospheric entry. A full orbit would likely not follow — that took nearly ninety minutes around Dul'rho, and he greatly doubted the whole operation would take more than thirty. Probably Draper would pull a power loop and reverse *Phoenix* partway around, returning for the pickup. Erik didn't know how many shuttles would be involved, or whether any orbital ordnance would be expended — those decisions were up to Draper and Dale, possibly with some input from Styx, and depended on their evaluation of strategic circumstance, something he couldn't know here in his cell.

He took the Buddha figurine from his jacket pocket and gazed at it. An almost comical serenity, he thought. He wished he could tell Trace that as much as he admired her self-control, there was also something preposterously silly about it all. Human beings weren't meant to be that calm, they were given emotions and biologically implanted behavioural drives for a reason.

'Great,' he imagined Trace replying, drily unimpressed. 'You've just discredited the entire concept of military discipline. Tell your brain to control its output, your ideas are stupid.'

He smiled, tucked the figurine away, and folded his legs with difficulty to sit crosslegged on his bunk. The bunk at least was large, being a croma bunk, and there was plenty of room to sit and try to meditate. He'd never been very good at it, his brain always liked to race, to be full of information and toss everything back and forth. He *needed* that, he'd tried to explain to Trace when she'd attempted instruction. I *like* my thoughts racing, it's what makes me a good pilot. Practising rapid information flows is like you doing target practise. Calm and serenity's the last thing I need.

But he sat here now, and closed his eyes, and tried to pass the final minutes until all hell broke loose in some kind of peace. Because here, unlike on the *Phoenix* bridge, or in any hard-pressed conversation with Trace, there was simply nothing else to do.

In what felt like about nine minutes, the entire building shook, with vibrations he could feel through the bunk. Orbital strike. Just the one blast, though it had probably been several rounds, striking about the compound, depending on what kind of defensive emplacements Dale considered threatening. These would have been DU-50s, not the big DU-80s — those would have levelled the entire block. Normally Dul'rho's defensive grid would have been a good chance to intercept them, but now, nothing was working. The compound could not call for help, because there were no coms. No doubt many would see the explosions, but the realisation that they'd come from the sky would be too late for effective reinforcements to be sent.

Assault shuttle reentry would be followed by a vertical plummet to the ground... but likely that had already happened, and the orbital rounds been timed to coincide with the shuttles' arrival. And so, arriving through the giant clouds of smoke and dust from exploding orbital rounds in the compound's periphery, would be one or another, or possibly two *Phoenix* assault shuttles. Platoons would jump to the roof, deploying in sections, and...

More explosions, somewhere distant. Then an almighty boom! from right nearby, walls and ceiling shaking as Erik abandoned all pretence of meditation and squashed himself into the far corner in the hope of minimising his chances of catching a stray round. The shooting that followed was appalling, construction jackhammers of the Gods that threatened to tear down the walls by sound alone. Something detonated in the hallway outside, the small window abruptly filled with smoke... but damned if his marines would find him hiding under the bunk, so he forced himself to sit upright, if small, arms about his knees and waiting.

A dark shape peered through the smoke, then the door crunched inward with great violence, revealing the hulking armoured gorilla of a UF Marines powered suit, covered in explosion-dust and barely fitting its Koshaim rifle through the doorway.

"Captain!" yelled the tinny amplification of external speakers, nearly deafening him a second time. "You okay?"

Erik raised both thumbs and got up, not bothering to speak, so small would be the sound of his own voice in the racket both in his cell, and now echoing through the halls beyond. Sometimes he forgot the sheer scale of forces involved in powered-armour combat. To be exposed in the middle of it, unarmoured, was a lesson in human fragility.

"I got him," came the marine's conversational reply to someone else's query. "Captain is secured, he looks fine. Captain, just wait here a moment, we're clearing the floor." And lodged the big armour suit in the doorway sideways, powerplant exhaust hot in Erik's face, protecting his unarmoured Captain. From the small insignia patches about the collar, Erik saw this was Bravo Platoon, though he couldn't tell the individual — Lieutenant Alomaim would be in command, then. A thousand questions ran through Erik's mind — the safety of the rest of his crew, of Skah, even of Peanut, but he knew better than to bother the marines with unhelpful distractions while they were working.

Finally the marine moved aside, replaced by Jalawi, looking none the worse for his captivity and carrying a rifle he'd likely taken from a dead croma. He beckoned, and Erik followed, not needing the situation explained — the marines were in charge, and his job was to follow immediately, do what he was told and not make their lives more difficult by pretending that his rank somehow demanded they waste time explaining things to him.

In the hallway were more doors smashed in, and a lot of smoke and dust. He followed Jalawi, several more marines crashing by, and the floor shaking with another huge explosion — probably a grenade or missile. Around a corner, and here lay a dead croma, or what was left of one — unarmoured and with just a bloody smear where his upper torso had vanished from a Koshaim shell.

Erik avoided looking too hard, as Jalawi led him to several more unarmoured marines — Master Sergeant Hoon, Privates Lewis and Melidu, Erik saw, all guarding a corner. They moved on, through what remained of a corridor-blocking security door that had been blasted to shredded metal strips. On the far side was a croma armour suit, similarly ruined and apparently occupied, to judge by the huge puddles of blood on the floor. Further up, another suit, seated against the wall as though merely tired, but the head was missing.

They arrived at an open office zone facing landing pads on the building's next wing, all now a mess of broken glass, strewn office furnishings and smouldering bodies. Gathered in small groups along a trunk corridor, and on the ruined office floor were the rest of the hover train's crew, some armed, others just keeping low and waiting. Against one wall, Karajin and Jinido were guarding croma who kneeled with hands on their heads. Jalawi exchanged fast words with Karajin, then took off across the office space to check on the far flank of this retrieval zone, leaving Karajin in charge of the Captain. Kaspowitz came quickly across the floor, escorting Skah, who looked alert and remarkably unafraid, refusing to even hold Kaspowitz's good hand. Erik did not even need to tell the boy why he was here and not there — the Captain was prioritised for protection to the point that marines would sacrifice others if necessary. That being so, it made sense that Skah should stay with Erik, by unanimous crew consensus.

An explosion followed a missile streak outside, somewhere near the compound outer wall. That would be one of the assault shuttles, Erik guessed, circling overhead to provide cover and prevent possible reinforcements. One of the kneeling croma made a fast lunge at Karajin. Karajin shot him in the head, and the croma fell at his feet. Skah stared, bleak and sad. Erik thought he should shield the boy's eyes, then thought again at the futility of it.

Engines shrieked through the broken glass adjoining the landing pads, then marines were yelling and waving at them to go. Erik went first, holding Skah's hand whether the boy liked it or not, joined by Kaspowitz and Harris, then others as they went through the broken glass and onto the pads. An assault shuttle was plunging overhead, a thunderous dark shape in the night, all lights off as it approached the pad. It grounded just ahead of Erik, rear ramp down as Erik ran up it, through the retracted rows of seating, up the narrow flank past the Platoon Commander's post, then into the cockpit and helped Skah fasten into the second observer seat.

Skah knew the buckles pretty well, and this one was already adjusted for a smaller body, giving Erik a clue as to which shuttle this was. He took Observer One, buckled in while fastening the spare headset, and brought the flight display up on the visor.

"Hello Tif," he said. "Skah's safe in Observer Two."

"Copy," came Tif's reply on coms, the only way she'd hear beneath her flight helmet. It was all the response she could afford, but Erik was sure it was worth letting her know for sure. This was PH-4, and Erik's display showed him the other shuttle was PH-3 — Lieutenant Jersey, she'd have come down loaded with Bravo Platoon, while Tif had come down empty to pick up the rescues.

"Another twenty seconds, Captain," Ensign Lee took the time to inform him from the seat in front of Tif in the shuttle's narrowing cockpit. *"They were holding Peanut in the basement, he's on his way up now."*

"Captain copies," said Erik, and glanced out the cockpit side.

About lay Stat'cha, all dark and silent. This wasn't the city center, it was further to the edges, but still there were large buildings and roads that should have been filled with traffic. Erik could see some ground cars on streets, but nothing else moved, and the skies were clear of airtraffic without the safety of central control. In the distance, Stat'cha's tall towers loomed — the general region where they'd been stranded for a day where the hover train had crashed. Likely those people thought their troubles were ended when the Shur'do Kon'do Rey'kan had been carted away. Little did they know that the alien ship in orbit would shut down the entire croma capital world to rescue them.

Draper would be having kittens, Erik thought. It surprised him how calmly he could survey it all. So accustomed he'd become to wielding otherworldly power. He was quite certain his mission was worth this, even if all croma space now wanted to kill him, which he doubted. Croma'Rai were unpopular, and this would make them moreso, by making them look weak. And if they fell, once the Tali'san resumed, Croma'Dokran would take over... and that would be an entirely different game. Had Croma'Dokran *expected* this would happen? That *Phoenix* would do exactly this, once Croma'Rai took them prisoner, knowing that Tiga's primary mission had been completed? Sho'mo'ra was a wily character. Probably he'd find this amusing, to see Croma'Rai humiliated one more time by a bunch of aliens they'd been too arrogant to bother taking the time to understand.

"We're all in," came Lieutenant Alomaim's call from the rear. *"Final restraints in ten, preliminary departure."*

"Prewin departure, copy," said Tif, and the shuttle rose with a roar. The first ascent, that meant, while final restraints were put on down back in preparation for orbit. Erik guessed that proper restraints for Peanut might be an issue. In the meantime, none of the pilots seemed very concerned about getting shot at, despite an entire, angry croma city lying helpless at their feet. Doubtless most of them had no idea what was going on.

"How'd we do?" Erik heard Jalawi ask.

"*All out, no casualties,*" said Alomaim.

"*Out-fucking-standing.*" Trace had always said that Alomaim might be the best of her platoon leaders. Erik didn't think it was an accident that Dale had assigned him this job.

"This is the Captain," said Erik. "That's PH-1 down at the eastern hills complex, I take it?"

"*PH-1 has another job,*" Tif confirmed. "*Awpha Pwatoon.*"

Erik knew what that was — he'd discussed this possibility with Styx as well. He just hoped that Dale didn't take too long... and that Rhi'shul kept her thick croma head down.

* * *

TIGA SUSPECTED THEY MIGHT BE IN TROUBLE WHEN THE POWER WENT down the first time. That had been happening rather a lot lately, in Croma'Rai institutions that annoyed *Phoenix*. She didn't think Croma'Rai had learned very much from it, being stubbornly croma, and focused far too heavily on the Tali'san.

The power came back almost immediately, but the entire Croma'-Dokran expedition came to a halt in the vast lobby of the Central Intelligence building. Heavy croma armour stomped to the main entry doors, sirens sounded and emergency lights flashed, while the Croma'Dokran guards formed a defensive perimeter about Sho'-mo'ra, several senior advisors, Rhi'shul and Tiga.

"What's going on?" Sho'mo'ra asked Kra'nikra, his primary military advisor.

"Sir, I don't know," Kra'nikra admitted, adjusting her eyepiece display, trying to get a read on the outside. A number of heavily armed croma guards about the lobby were looking at Sho'mo'ra's party, now, as though suspecting *they* were the cause. "I'm not getting any reading on the outside, it's like the networks are dead."

"Change to the civilian networks," one of Kra'nikra's soldiers suggested, fingering his rifle uneasily as he looked around. "Get a connection back to Croma'Dokran systems, we shouldn't be relying on Croma'Rai networks."

"I get nothing on the civilian systems either," another soldier replied. "It's as though they're all down."

Following the agreement of Clans Croma'Do, Croma'Gen, Croma'Tesh and Croma'Bam to commit forces to the Tali'san, there had been gained enough votes in the Assessment Council to demand that Croma'Rai open its old historical files on the Battle of Rando. This was to be the time when it would be revealed whether all of the painstaking work Tiga and Romki had done in the old Ji'go library actually added up to anything.

The old war files had been a croma state secret for eight hundred years. Today they were kept only in the vaults of Central Intelligence — the great Croma'Rai security agency, focused on alien affairs and war-related matters. Its headquarters were here, in the low hills over-looking suburban Stat'cha, and the Council vote had allowed Sho'-mo'ra to make a visit in person, while the Tali'san was paused for the Assessment Council.

Then the power went down again, replaced by blue emergency light. "Cover!" instructed Kra'nikra, and they marched to the main hall ahead, where armed and unarmed croma were pausing to talk, gesticulating in a manner rare for croma, suggesting great agitation, or great threat.

"It's *Phoenix*!" Tiga exclaimed as they slid against a more defen-sible hallway wall, armed Croma'Dokran security taking positions around them. Sho'mo'ra was breathing heavily, resting with one great fist on the ground. He moved easily enough without his walking sticks, as though just standing still was more stress to him than running. "But how can *Phoenix* challenge security here? They'll be shot down on the way in..." and she stared up at Rhi'shul, standing behind the perimeter security with her short rifle out. "Unless they've shut down the entire planetary network! Styx could do that!"

"Perimeter here," Sho'mo'ra told his people in a low growl. "We don't pick a side in this fight."

"Sir," Kra'nikra disagreed, "it was our actions that put Captain Debogande in Croma'Rai custody. *Phoenix* will be angry."

"*Phoenix* came to Stat'cha with a mission in mind," Sho'mo'ra replied, his great head peering about at more running chaos in the halls and across the polished lobby stones. "Now the mission completes, be patient and do not fire unless fired upon."

Tiga stared up at Rhi'shul. "You told him! You set this up!" It had been moderately common knowledge on the Shur'do Kon'do Rey'kan that Rhi'shul and the Captain were after knowledge Central Intelligence stored in its computer vaults. Something about humanity's old ally and feared new enemy the alo...

"I set nothing up," Rhi'shul retorted. "I'm just doing my job."

A flurry of explosions rocked the walls, from somewhere up above. Then the emergency lighting failed, plunging them all into blackness. That would be Styx, Tiga thought desperately, shutting down defensive systems ahead of Phoenix Company's advance.

"They're going to kill me," she said, with frightened resignation. She knew she deserved it, really. "They kept me alive, and I betrayed them."

"I think you underestimate them," said Rhi'shul. "They've been playing this game a lot longer than you have."

"This hallway is not defensible!" Kra'nikra was insisting to Sho'-mo'ra. "We should move to a smaller space, somewhere with walls and no distant lines of sight!"

"I will not cower in a closet and hope to avoid my fate," Sho'mo'ra growled. "The humans will know where we are. If they wish us dead, we will face it in the open."

Multiple huge explosions blew in the glass walls facing the lobby, and Tiga fell to cover her face from possible flying glass, even at this range. When she looked up again, there was shooting, the most incredible sound she'd ever heard, a cacophony of skull-exploding violence that racketed off the high lobby ceiling. Across the floor, hulking armoured shadows emerged from the smoke of explosions, huge rifles blazing, missiles now streaking to nearby walls... and Tiga covered her head as explosions threatened to break her eardrums entirely.

The shooting stopped, then resumed, but sporadically, moving away up neighbouring hallways. Marines, clearing an area of resistance. The main lobby would be strategic, with big adjoining elevator banks and through-hallways to high-security zones. Crashing footsteps approached, and Tiga looked up, past the legs of surrounding croma security, all unscathed as marines approached. These were human, Tiga saw, knowing well enough the difference between human and tavalai armour from her time on *Phoenix*.

The first marines did not even stop, just went straight past and up the hall, coordinating like choreographed dancers, one rifle always covering what the others were not. Behind the first marines came the terrifying shape of a drysine drone, clattering on that four-legged animal stride that drones adopted for fast movement, twin shoulder-cannons smoking from recent action. The croma all stared as it passed — that looked like Bucket, Tiga thought.

Behind the drone, two more marines paused opposite the Croma'Dokran. One flipped up his visor, and Tiga stared up at the hard blue eyes of Lieutenant Tyson Dale, Commander of Phoenix Company with the Major missing, and the last person on *Phoenix* anyone sane wanted angry at them.

"You, you little pissant!" Dale snarled at her. "Was it worth it?"

Tiga blinked up at him. Was what worth it, she wondered? Leaving her family? Abandoning a life of peace and irrelevance for one of war, suffering and great significance? She still didn't know. But at least she'd tried. She stood up, awkwardly forcing shaking limbs to function. "If it saves my people," she told him. "Then yes."

Dale glared for a moment longer. Then spat. "Brave little tree-swinger," he muttered. "I'll give you that." He gestured at Rhi'shul. "You want that dirt on your government? Lead the way."

Rhi'shul left in a swirl of leather coat, Dale and his marines crashing after her. Sho'mo'ra watched them go, then peered back at the lobby. Steadied his enormous bulk against one wall, and walked back that way, raising a hand at the two human marines guarding the devastated glass entrance. They saw, and kept their weapons sweeping elsewhere — Heavies, Tiga saw, with extra armour attachments, ammunition backpacks and even larger firearms, one a chaingun, the other a rapid-fire autocannon.

Sho'mo'ra's assistants and guards went with him, leaving Tiga no choice. Back in the lobby, Sho'mo'ra looked around. The walls furthest from the marines were littered with debris from the shattered wall, and shredded Croma'Rai bodies. The damaged walls, even Tiga could see, always coincided precisely with bodies on the ground. Several big armour suits had drawn the most fire, the walls behind them almost caved in. Such devastating precision, all in the blink of an eye.

"All this time in this Tali'san," Sho'mo'ra said heavily, gazing about. "We've been wondering who the greatest warriors are. I think perhaps the true answer has been before our eyes all this time, ignored by all."

"These humans are elite," Kra'nikra disagreed. "They're not all this good."

"We shall see," Sho'mo'ra rumbled. "If Captain Debogande's fears for what confronts his people are correct, we may all see."

25

Trace knew she was going to die. She'd had this feeling before and been wrong, so there was that. She'd also figured, in her long readings and ponderings on matters of the mind, that it was probably some kind of defence mechanism — a defence against the perils of expectation, and the stresses they created. Expecting to live, hoping to, could create the most debilitating anxiety. Hoping that those around you would survive as well, when the odds against it were mathematically undeniable, made it worse. Easier to consider oneself already doomed, and function without concern for survival. But even accounting for those psychological tricks, survival on this occasion seemed objectively unlikely.

The corbi monocle eyepiece was fitted to a headband beneath her helmet, and showed her a rough version of tacnet that Resistance Fleet used. All her forces, crammed into two small flyers, currently illuminated on reeh surveillance as a pair of reeh flyers heading between bases. All the details had been taken from reeh networks by one of her bugs, using entry pathways provided by existing Resistance Fleet infiltrations — the flyers' names, coded identifications, flight characteristics, everything. If reeh surveillance spotted any discrepancy, it would all be over before anything truly began.

"We're approaching signal acquisition," she told her flyer. Corbi faces glanced at her from beneath their odd-shaped, flared-brim helmets. Solemn faces, all bearing some expression of fear. Tano, seated opposite among the crammed rows of hastily-rigged steel benches in what would otherwise have been an open cargo hold. Bago, nearer the front, peering up beneath his helmet rim past rows of bristling rifles and grenade launchers.

They did not love her, this group, but they knew she was their best chance for success. The Drondi highlanders and others more primitively-minded disliked her for not allowing them a proper revenge on Pena. The more civilised-minded had not liked her for pulling the trigger at all. The rest did not love her because she was not one of them, and because they quite rightly suspected her to be doing this for her own reasons, and not for theirs. And Bega, and his team more focused on the saving of Splicer prisoners, rightly suspected that it was not her priority, and that she'd sacrifice the lot of them should their interests work against the larger objective.

They were not an assault team bonded by common identity and the bonds of family like Phoenix Company. They were here for their individual desperations — for the crazy dream of a free life, of a world liberated, of a species saved from the tyranny of genetic manipulations for evil ends. For the hope to save imprisoned family. Or for the need to steal the keys that would reveal a technology that threatened her entire species, and others beyond. And some, Trace knew, were here for the simple hatred of an evil foe, and the desire to cause them pain on an unprecedented scale, on this world at least.

Her eyepiece counted down the seconds to signal acquisition. The signal would come from one of her new bugs, which had been planned to enter the Splicer three days before. She'd wondered how to get it there, for the crumbling old sports stadium had been nearly a thousand kilometres from the Splicer. But then she'd thought to ask the bug itself for its maximum effective range, and it had shown her a diagram of the most basic mathematics — a cruising speed of thirty kilometres an hour, currently eleven hours a day to fly in, another three hours on stored charge after sundown, and allowing some extra time for slower recharging on cloudy days, it could fly to the Splicer in less than three days.

Trace had sent three bugs to be sure, with instructions to find the least obvious way in — the Splicer had doors, landing bay hangars, and presumably ventilation ducts. She suspected most of those entries would be screened from this sort of infiltration, but then, assassin bug technology was impossible for any civilisation outside of the Machine Age, and she doubted the Splicer would be protected against threats the reeh had never seen. Once in, the bugs were to preliminary-infiltrate and present themselves to the tanifex, thus demonstrating that the assault was serious, as well as telling them exactly when it would be happening. That time had been established by a return message from *Phoenix* in the form of Commander Draper, as Erik had been 'busy'. Trace suspected that by 'busy', Draper had meant some version of 'up to his neck in trouble', and that likely, knowing Erik, that trouble would be far more complicated than it needed to be. And she'd allowed herself a little disappointment that she hadn't gotten to see him one more time before she died. Erik, of course, had probably refrained from thinking like that precisely because he was always so damnably optimistic and assumed that they'd all be fine.

A small blip appeared on her schematic of the Splicer. It grew, illuminating internal information pathways. Schematics merged in a fizz of compatible code, as her own bug recognised the signal and integrated it into its feed. Tacnet struggled to find their locations within the Splicer, or how many of them had gotten in — it didn't matter, she needed them for network infiltration and electronic warfare more than anything else, and didn't care where they were in order to do it. The remaining nine bugs were distributed amongst the five assault teams, with instructions to maintain tacnet, infiltrate and dominate the local network, provide backup communications relays between her units, and as very last importance, to kill enemy soldiers where the opportunity allowed.

Eleven kilometres. The pilots would be able to see the Splicer now, a great, silver structure looming above the Leda Valley. Timers on Trace's countdown converged. ETA two-minutes-fifteen, *Phoenix* should be arriving almost on-the-dot, though local response times would be later due to several minutes of light-delay. Resistance Fleet had told her there were seven reeh ships in-system at present, that they knew of. Likely it could be more, not all of them lurked in visible locations. Most were not hugely powerful, but seven was still a lot, and would have given the old, pre-upgrade *Phoenix* a very hard challenge. The new *Phoenix*, under its ever-improving Captain, Trace was fairly sure would be fine.

Three kilometres. Trace looked at Kono, belted in opposite, his face intense. He met her eyes, and nodded. Trace didn't think he'd forgiven her for Pena, despite what would have happened if she hadn't pulled the trigger. It was the danger of being held in too-high an estimation by those you commanded. When you failed to work miracles, they believed you'd had some kind of moral failing, that the miracle hadn't happened because she hadn't wanted it badly enough, because Major Thakur could do anything if she really wanted it. Only she couldn't, and letting Pena go unscathed would have caused the entire assault team to fall apart, while handing her to Sigo's butchers would have given her a worse death than even Trace's hardened resolve could stomach. Perhaps that was what Kono hadn't forgiven her for. Perhaps, in his mind, the cost had already been too great.

She held his gaze a little longer. I warned you this one was going to hurt, Giddy. I told you not to get too close. You didn't listen. Kono's gaze drifted to the hull side above Trace's head, and he breathed deeply, visualising the first few seconds after the flyer's ramp dropped. If the reeh defences didn't suspect something wrong and blow them from the sky first.

Trace activated coms. She could only speak to those in this flyer — talking to the second flyer on encrypted coms would have aroused suspicions. "Remember," she said, "as soon as we're down, head straight for your positions. Hold those corridors open, we can't afford to get outflanked early or lose our access mobility. Anything not friendly is the enemy — I don't care whether it's armed or not, kill it.

Absolutely no prisoners — wounded enemy will be killed on the spot, they're not safe unless they're dead.

"Extraction will happen on the same landing pads we enter by. If you get hit, return to those pads if you can, we'll get you out on a shuttle, but you must keep fighting to defend the pads. If the shuttles can't land, we can't leave. Express elevator shafts are the primary target — Second Team, get it done, if they start transporting their heavy armour to the top levels we'll be in big trouble. And remember, we should have help from the tanifex and possibly some others on the inside — we don't know what form that help will take, but be prepared to improvise.

"We are one shuda out, weapons ready, stand by for harness disconnect. Remember, orderly lines of departure, wait for the person in front to move before moving yourself." Because she had visions of this great assault beginning in a tangle of failed crowd control just getting out of the unfamiliar flyer. She'd made them rehearse it several times before leaving, the only time they'd had to practise with these vehicles.

The flyers were shifting now, noses flaring, the pitch of engine nacelles changing to a loud roar as they decelerated. Thank god, she nearly said aloud. Her biggest fear had been not even getting this far. The waiting tension was the worst. Now it was just a fight. Fighting, she was good at.

The wheels bumped as the flyer's hover ended, and the engine roar declined. *"This is the cockpit,"* Trace heard a tense voice from up front, as around her came the clatter of nearly a hundred armoured corbi disconnecting their harnesses. *"You've got unknown infantry on your left, and forward. Guards, light armour, maybe twenty."*

A series of dots appeared on tacnet, as the bug-run system translated the pilots' forward visuals into enemy locations. "First Team!" Trace commanded. "Explosive exit, you've targets on your left as you go out! Grenades first then follow, get flat and full suppressive fire! Get that ramp down!"

She itched to join the first wave out herself, because they were going to need accuracy under fire... but if she was hit in the first few seconds, the mission success declined dramatically. The rear ramp cracked, corbi on that end waiting with rifles and grenades ready...

And the whole flyer shook, as though to some distant thunder, vibrations trembling through the floor. Then again, louder than the last.

"*Big explosions!*" announced the pilot. "*Sounds like they're on the lower levels. The guards are confused, they're looking around! Hit them now!*"

"It's the tanifex!" Trace said sharply. "That's the rebellion, let's go!"

Corbi lobbed grenades sideways before the ramp had fully lowered, then squeezed out to follow. Shooting started sporadically, then intensified as more came rushing out... and then Trace's part of the interior began moving, and something blasted through the flyer hull, then again, bodies falling just behind her, and screams.

She slid on the ramp and dropped to roll off the edge as more fire ripped by, corbi running past hit and falling. One side of the landing pad was exposed to the sky, parked flyers blocking fields of fire to either side, stacked cargo creating unwanted fire shadows, and now heavy rounds were ripping in from several locations on the perimeter.

"Fire volume!" she yelled into coms, seeing corbi running out ahead, brave as anything, finding cover behind crates and flyers, but not enough of them putting fire on that incoming. "Fire volume, put fire on the target!"

As heavy rounds tore in from somewhere across the far side of the hangar, blasting cargo crates scattering, then smashing the flyer's engine nacelle above her, Trace ducking as debris showered about. "Get away from the flyer!" Kono was yelling, and Trace got up and ran, then an explosion knocked her flat. She struggled up amidst a storm of rounds heading both ways, corbi hit and flailing as they ran for cover, and saw the flyer pounded by heavy explosives, losing pieces as corbi continued to pour from the rear, many falling.

"Fire volume!" Trace heard herself yelling even as she scrambled up, running past the wall of cargo crates for the parked flyers. "Put fire on the target!"

About the flyers were corbi in cover, firing past the wheels and
hulls, several bodies already on the ground. Trace slid in beside a
corbi covering behind a pad control panel, and saw black armoured
figures against the hangar's far wall spraying fire across the pads. On
the upper level walkways, several others were firing, but cut down
even now as corbi shot them from the ground. She put fire onto the
grounded ones, dropped one, saw another heave a big, arm-mounted
launcher her way, and ducked as it fired.

The blast might have damaged her eardrums were they not
augmented for strength like the rest of her body, but the panel
behind her erupted in shattered metal. Trace primed her own
launcher and put her rifle out through the smoke to fire one back, as
several others had the same idea, and the shooters withdrew amid
new explosions, several of them blasted into walls.

On the high wall behind her, the overlooking hangar control
exploded, several bodies flying to the pads below. Hangar defences
finally subdued, the assault teams were finally leaving, pressing into the
corridors beyond. Trace took a seat with her back to cover and watched
her eyepiece, as tacnet showed blue dots swarming up the corridors
toward the objective. Others now fanned out, protecting the flanks, and
more went for the stairwells to get to the levels above and below.

"This is the Major!" Trace commanded, with nothing to do but
hope that the translator would still work in this mess. "Assault teams,
watch your spacing! Don't bunch up so much, their heavier weapons
will take you out with one shot!"

The corbi beside her at cover hadn't moved, and she spared him a
glance — he was bloody, head slumped, shrapnel from the grenade
blast had somehow gone straight through cover and shredded him
while leaving her unscathed. Beyond him, several more wounded
were being carried to better cover, while more troops went running
the other way.

"Third Team, you're slow, get a move on! Fourth Team, watch for
reinforcements down that main hall! Counter-ambush if they come
at you, don't just charge!"

Kono crouched at her side, cheek bloody from a cut. "Major, those were actual reeh in armour, not slaves. Built-in heavy weapons, it's not like fighting tanifex."

"Had to happen eventually," said Trace, heaving herself up and finding her legs disagreeably shaky with adrenaline overload. "Tacnet says we've lost twenty-six already, half dead, I want as many of the wounded as can still fight in defensive positions."

"I'm on it," said Kono, and set out running across the smoke-hazed and debris-strewn hangar. This was Kono's function now, as her runner and enforcer between various units, delegating to lower commanders when he could and going to see it done himself when he couldn't. Between the translator, the corbi's inexperience, and the general confusion, they couldn't just trust things would get done as they did in Phoenix Company.

Trace strode to where Tano was directing some of their few heavier weapons, for emplacement to defend the pads. Only two thirds of the hangar was indoors — the outer third was circular and open to the sky, leading to a two kilometre drop straight down, and what would have been a spectacular view across the valley, if anyone had been in a mood to contemplate it. To her right, corbi were shooting fallen reeh point-blank, to be sure. Predictably, they were expending more rounds than necessary to do it.

"Kaysa, hold at the next junction!" she yelled even as she reached Tano, seeing the likely ambush-spot ahead. "Divide and flank that next blast door, do not go through it, it's a trap!"

"Major!" came the crackling reply on assassin-bug supported coms, *"the doors are held wide open! The reeh aren't able to close them!"*

"I know that, but if you take the most direct route you're going to all get fucking killed! You're not the only smart person on the battle-field, the reeh will figure it out and ambush those routes, go *around* them!"

As Third Team, commanded by Sigo, reported heavy contact on their parallel route toward the central turbolifts. Trace switched channels. "Sigo! Sigo, do you hear me?"

"I hear you Major! Heavy defences in our way!" Trace could hear the crackle of shooting in the background, punctuated by explosions.

"Sigo, pin them down with aggressive firepower, then flank them! It's the only way in these corridors! These first defenders are reeh, it's not all slaves, they're heavily armed and will fight hard!"

"Yes Major! We're going around them now!" Trace gritted her teeth, staring at the display and seeing too many possibilities for those manoeuvres to go wrong — that pin-and-manoeuvre was well and good with marines in full armour, but this was something else.

Tano ceased giving instructions to some wide-eyed young soldier long enough to glance at her. "How are we doing?"

"There's nothing heavy up here yet, but reeh light armour is heavy enough." Trace took his shoulder as she talked and led him to better cover behind a cargo loader, now riddled with bullet holes. "I don't think it's reeh all the way back, though, I think they're just concentrated around the hangars. If we don't disable those turbolifts real soon there'll be trouble."

"I can't see Bega, is he...?"

"He's nearly there, a few more minutes." Bega was leading Fifth Team, tasked with heading to the lower levels to rescue the prisoners. That was going to occupy several turbolifts exclusively, a feat managed only by the bugs' infiltration of the Splicer systems, allowing them to seize control of elevator functions. But it meant they couldn't disable the lifts until Bega had gone down to the detention levels... where Trace expected him and his unit to get quickly annihilated, but they'd all demanded it, and it did create a sizeable diversion for the real work here on the upper levels.

Rika arrived at Trace's side, bounding in with a three-limbed run, smeared with blood that Trace guessed from his demeanour was not his own. "Sorry Major," he said breathlessly. "Was helping the wounded." He was supposed to be by her side, personal protection from one of the few corbi in this group she trusted to do it. "Kirsi's dead, never made it out of the flyer. Don't know who's in charge of Fourth Team now."

"Tumi," said Trace, adjusting her eyepiece feed to get a better look at the upper and lower levels, where a new spread of red dots were forming. "Dreja, you have enemy contacts below you! It looks like a bug got downstairs and is giving us a feed! Watch the stairwells, get your traps set up!"

"Copy Major, I see them!"

Down a near hall off the hangar, more shooting had broken out, shouts and confusion as corbi ran to check on it. Tano went after them, determined to organise. Trace didn't think that was smart, but if she had to start hand-holding her commanders she'd run out of brain space and mouths to talk with real fast.

"How are we doing so far?" asked Rika, checking the rounds in his magazine and clearing the mechanism. He was wide-eyed and breathless, but functional.

"I'd expected worse," Trace admitted. Her eyepiece flashed with something new — a coms channel. She blinked to open it.

"Hello human!" came an odd, synthetic translation. *"Tanifex here! Will disrupt lower levels, then go up for extraction!"*

"You won't be able to come up, we're going to disable the turbolifts!" Trace replied. A shot from the nearby action clanged nearby, and Rika took position facing that way, between her and it. "Your best chance is to escape with the prisoners out through the lower levels!"

"We come up!" the tanifex replied, and the coms silenced. Trace refrained from swearing, and switched view back to First Team, which had passed that blast door obstacle and was pressing on in fair order. Rika said something as more shots came from the corridor, then an explosion. A red dot appeared on tacnet in the hangar, up in the smoking control room. Barely taking her eye off the display, Trace looked, saw the staggering shape of a reeh not yet dead, emerging from the smoke. She aimed, shot it through the helmet, then indicated to a startled corbi that someone should go check — she didn't think the helmet lower side-armour was tough enough to stop rifle rounds, reeh couldn't run around with huge weights on their heads, but better that someone made sure there were no more alive up there.

And she blinked on a new light flashing — a familiar signal, and the bug-operated software opened the link immediately. *"Hello Major,* this is *Phoenix*," came Lieutenant Shilu's smooth voice on coms. Were this completely not the time, Trace might have cried. *"We are inbound at ETA twenty-one-point-five, estimating extraction at your position ETA twenty-six flat. Opposition is strong but ineffective, please advise your status?"*

"Hello *Phoenix*, I am successfully engaged, Splicer assault is proceeding as planned. Casualties fifteen percent so far, that will increase. I copy ETA on extraction is twenty-six flat. Have a good one, Major out."

There would be no immediate reply — *Phoenix* was still at a light-lag of ten seconds and it would take that long for her reply to reach them. But *Phoenix* could now cycle jump engines and dump V incredibly far down the gravity-well, and so could hold planet-killing velocities until scarily close to the atmosphere. That it had been Shilu talking to her and not Erik indicated that he was very busy.

Trace switched channels again. "All units, this is the Major. *Phoenix* is inbound, I repeat, *Phoenix* is inbound. They are currently killing every reeh ship and station defending this world, extraction will occur in nineteen shuda. We are on the clock, let's move."

* * *

Phoenix was inbound, thirty-four degrees above the system elliptic, approaching planet of Rando. Scan was tracking nine reeh warships in the vicinity — two had been over-jumped and were now hopelessly behind them, three more were out-positioned on the inbounds slope and without adequate defensive firepower were likely to be dead in the next few minutes as the ranges decreased alarmingly, and one was a dissipating cloud of vapour having caught a *Phoenix* mag round to the bow at a sizeable portion of lightspeed and disassembled at the molecular level.

Erik made sure all his trajectory lines matched, both Geish and Jiri confidently calling out visible incoming at twice the range possible under the old system, while Sasalaka monitored all the ship systems the Captain lacked the time to, and ran possible course scenarios on the reeh ships outside of Erik's current reactive range. Resistance Fleet had agreed that they would come in behind and mop up whatever *Phoenix* hadn't killed on the way in, though to judge from this run so far, there wouldn't be much of that. But it would be nice to have high cover in case something unexpected popped up, and maybe to keep that third firebase occupied in the far outer orbit currently too far from *Phoenix*'s path to be worth expending ordnance on.

"The Major replies that she is successfully engaged in the Splicer," Shilu announced into a break in the bridge's running conversation. "She confirms our ETA, says her casualties are currently fifteen percent, expects they will increase significantly."

Jiri's next announcement of incoming fire quadrants erased any emotional response from the bridge, and combat chatter continued as before. Knowing that she was still alive, and that they were inbound to get her back, filled them all with hope. But everyone knew exactly how much she'd bitten off this time, and just how hard it was going to be to chew it.

One of the three immediate targets sparkled with defensive fire that intercepted multiple incoming rounds, then vanished in a great flash, a tiny, fading spot against the void. "Captain," said Sasalaka, "two close-orbit marks are climbing on a high flanking manoeuvre, it looks as though they're conceding our approach and will gain position on the gravity slope to impede our retreat."

Erik threw a distracted eye that way while rolling for a new attitude, then blazing thrust to get them clear of new approaching ordnance, Harris's defensive guns detonating others in multiple strings of explosions. "I see it Helm, good call. Arms, prepare for a boost, we're coming out at thirteen offset by two fifty one, boost pulse by seven."

"Thirteen offset by two fifty one, pulse by seven aye!" Raf Corrig snapped at his post — it was one of his first times in a large action on First Shift, he'd been firing continually since jump entry, and Erik suspected that if he gripped those triggers any harder he'd break them.

"Boost!" Erik announced, and cycled the jump engines... *Phoenix* pulsed briefly into hyperspace and emerged travelling much faster. Far faster than the jump engines of any organic-origin technology could manage this deep down a gravity-well. Erik rolled the ship to bring multiple batteries into play, and Corrig let fly with a new spread of accelerating ordnance, much faster and on a new trajectory that the reeh would not have predicted possible. Light lag was down to point-three of a second only, but Erik could see the surprise in their reaction, the sideways spin on the axis and blaze of evasive thrust, taking all batteries out of play just to escape.

"Oh, you fucked now!" Kaspowitz snarled as he saw it, and all that ship's previous ordnance disappeared harmlessly through *Phoenix*'s previous position. Eight seconds later, the reeh ship disappeared with the force of a small sun.

"The last one's burning, Captain," Geish said calmly, and Erik saw the remaining ship's engines ablaze, a trail of flame three times longer than the ship itself, maxing Gs to try and get it the hell out of there. But gravity had it restrained, while *Phoenix* rode it down like a wave. "Yeah you better run."

Each ship took several hundred alien lives with it when it died. The *Phoenix* crew had never enjoyed killing as much as this.

* * *

JINDI RODE THE ELEVATOR DOWN INTO THE DEPTHS OF HELL. THE armour did not properly fit his twisted back and lopsided shoulders, but the boys in Fifth Team had made it loose for him. It jangled and bounced when he ran, but it was more protection than going in naked, even as the helmet slipped over his eyes and blocked his view.

The Major didn't even know he was on the mission. But the Fifth Team boys did. They'd been on the second flyer, and the steely-eyed human couldn't see everything. Bega had smuggled him aboard among the others, and helped him strap in. Bega didn't trust the Major's maps and schematics, didn't trust the allies they were supposed to find inside the Splicer. He'd wanted Jindi, the only guide who'd actually been there, and could tell him how the cells were laid out and defended. And Jindi, of course, had volunteered to come.

He stared at the floor counter as they descended, a giant elevator car full of corbi, forty strong. The symbols were in tov, the reeh language. He'd even learned to read their numbers, so long he'd been inside. The memories here were strong. Syringes and restraints. Wheeled gurneys, moving by electric navigation. Sometimes he'd been allowed to walk. Sometimes he'd been unrestrained. Where could he run to, even if he tried? And sometimes, he'd been in no condition to even stand.

Jindi had never been a soldier. As a child in his village, he'd preferred to work with his father at the miller's wheel, grinding flour for the bread that kept people fed. In between school and work, he'd liked to climb the tallest trees, and sit there for hours, looking over the canopy of green that surrounded the village walls. There were villages up there as well — villages of insects, of bats and birds, of furry firs that scampered on the branches and sometimes took figs from his fingers. He'd tried to carve them, sometimes, with the small whittling knife his grandmother had given him, and wished there was paper so he could draw them, and work from that when he returned to the ground.

Resistance fighters had come through his village occasionally, and had been fed by grudging custom, without real enthusiasm. The reeh were just there, like the sun and the moons, and it had always been thus. Jindi had hoped for nothing more than a good wife and healthy children, and had found both... until one day, the inevitable reeh had come for them as well.

Now, he was here, in armour with a sidearm he barely knew how to use, and a back that could not take more than a little running before the cramping pain grew too intense, and he had to stop. But the soldiers around him had wanted him here, and promised to carry him if that was the only way to get out again. It was more acceptance than Jindi had found since he was prisoner here. He couldn't blame the beach-side village for that — all such folk were naturally wary of anyone the reeh had touched, with good cause. Bega was all that remained of that village now, standing at his side with jaw clenched tight and eyes wild with hope and fury. Bega didn't blame Jindi for the strike that killed his family, and imprisoned his little girl in this place. For that forgiveness alone, Jindi felt he had to come. But more than that, he had a mission too.

"They're attempting to override the elevator!" Jesu announced. He was the best at understanding network systems, and was better able to see what the drysine bugs were up to on the reeh systems than anyone else in Team Five. "We're okay, this whole network language has been rewritten, I don't even think they control the servers anymore!"

Jindi couldn't begin to understand what that all meant. He'd been locked in this world of technology and steel for six years of his life, and the only pleasure in being here was the sure knowledge that it would all be destroyed soon. But first, there were people to save.

"Level arriving!" Bega shouted, and rifles were pointed at the door. Corbi lay flat, some atop each other in the crush, or pressed to walls. Jindi wondered if they'd really thought this through. One big grenade in here when the doors opened, and they'd all be shredded.

Gravity increased as the elevator slowed, then halted. The wide, curving door uncurled across, onto a hallway filled with smoke and flashing lights. No one shot at them, and corbi poured from the elevator, some bounding three-limbed in their haste, while others moved more slowly and carefully, rifles aimed as the Major and her Sergeant had been drumming into them for the past thirty days. Jindi stayed close to Bega, moving on his hands more often than the others, as it was easier on his back. Panels had fallen from the ceiling here, as though a great shockwave had torn through and broken things.

Corbi up the corridor ahead opened fire down a cross-corridor, then ran that way. When Bega and Jindi arrived at that corridor, Jindi saw a limp figure on the floor in the direction they'd gone — probably one of the slave techs, there were maybe ten different species here.

"That way!" Jindi instructed, pointing straight ahead. In truth, he didn't know every stretch of corridor, but he knew the patterns to their arrangement. He knew where he was in relation to the central elevators, and he knew this way was toward main incarceration. Knowing those things, any selection of corridors would do, provided one possessed a general sense of direction. Inside this grey steel maze, that was easy to lose.

Jindi directed Bega and his team down further corridors, as shooting echoed nearby, and calls arrived on coms from groups of Fifth Team that had taken different ways, reporting occasional encounters. None specified if the enemies they'd encountered were armed or not, and Jindi didn't think anyone cared.

"No!" Bega began shouting into the coms that Jindi couldn't hear. "Don't do it yet, we're not in position!"

Jindi pointed them left around the next corner, through a large equipment room where two slave techs were quickly stowing what looked like climbing gear on a wall of miscellaneous stuff. Bega shot them both on full automatic, one body writhing for a moment longer until Jesu shot it in the head.

Bega swore. "She's instructing the bugs to open the prisoner doors! We're not in position, it'll be chaos!"

"It was always going to be chaos, kid," said Mula at his side — an older corbi with a grim scar across face and lips. "We're short of time and they gotta get out!"

Immediately down the next hall, some corbi came bounding on all fours — unarmoured and unarmed, clad in horribly familiar plain grey overalls. They skidded to an astonished halt when they saw the Resistance team, then pointed frantically back the way they'd come. "That way!" they yelled. "That way! Everyone's out, all the doors are open!"

Then Jindi heard the shooting, and the screaming. "Head down!" he shouted at the unarmed corbi, pointing down through the floor. "The only way out is down! The whole Splicer will be destroyed in twenty shuda, you have to get out!"

He did not need to give Bega the next direction — the transparent, secure doors leading through a guard room were obvious enough. Beyond the second set of transparent secure doors, a great hole plunged through the heart of the Splicer, and the walkway beyond appeared to fall off a cliff.

The doors would not budge, so Bega shot out the hardened glass, smashed it with his rifle butt, and plunged through. Here there were walls of armour and weapons, some lethal, others less so. Outside the second doors, corbi in grey overalls ran or limped along walkways, or stared across the cavernous drop below in bewilderment. The transparent wall abruptly shattered as fire hit it from the other side, and a corbi on the walkway fell.

In an adjoining room, several Splicer technicians of uncertain species shouted instructions into coms in alien tongues, staring over the chaos outside and oblivious to what had entered the room alongside. Mula shot open the adjoining door and poured automatic fire onto the unsuspecting techs, spattering the controls and observation windows with blood. Others found the controls to get the doors open, while more began unracking and checking the new weapons in the storage room.

"Weapons!" Bega yelled outside the door, at running, panicked, just-escaped corbi. "Get weapons in here! Arm yourselves or we'll never escape!"

His whole plan rested on this. Jindi estimated that less than one in ten of the workers operating the Splicer were actual reeh. The rest were slaves, and in the Reeh Empire, slaves were known to rebel. Some others just went crazy — reeh mind control made most obedient, within limits, but force enacted upon organic minds had a way of breaking things. The result was a core reeh command force unable to fully trust the forces beneath them.

The result of *that*, particularly around the incarceration quarter, were many small guard houses and armouries, spread about so that any localised incidences of violent insanity or rebellion could be dealt with rapidly, before it could spread. Against small outbreaks, as Jindi had seen in his time inside, it worked well. The reeh very rarely in their history ever experienced a mass outbreak, considering the superiority of their network technology, and the difficulty most opposition forces found in subverting it. On a backwater world like Rando, against primitive enemies like the corbi Resistance, a mass outbreak was unthinkable.

But if this big mass of corbi prisoners, all stored together in the same centralised location, could be released all at once, they could mobilise to those guardhouses and arm themselves faster than the slave soldiers could. Because the reeh, not trusting those soldiers any further than they could throw them, did not allow them to be permanently armed, and thus their armaments were all kept in places like this...

"We have to get the other guard house doors open!" Bega was shouting to someone on coms, as Jindi busied himself handing weapons to the corbi who came running in. Some looked frantic, others terrified, while some were intense with enthusiasm. A few were almost laughing for joy. At the doorway, Fifth Team corbi kept up a steady, pounding racket of fire against whoever was shooting their way, falling back to reload as others took their place. "If the bugs can't get the guard house doors open we'll have to get them open ourselves! Doni, Leku, spread around the geofeature and smash those doors open! If we don't have superior firepower by the time the defences get organised we won't have a chance!"

After Jindi and Badri handed out rifles, Mula intercepted those who plainly didn't know one end from the other and gave them the briefest instruction — trigger there, hold and point like this, reload like this, don't point it at anyone you don't intend to kill. Others indicated they didn't need any instruction, and offered to teach more themselves — even corbi who hadn't joined the Resistance had often taken an interest in their better firearms, while other villagers, possessing only the most ancient and home-made firearms, at least knew the basics and could hit targets.

After fifty rifles with ammo had been handed out, the racks were empty. "Come on!" Bega shouted, as corbi hoping for a weapon were turned away. "There's another one two levels down, let's go!"

He led them out the doors and onto the high walkway about the edge of the geofeature. It dropped another hundred metres straight down, levels and levels of now-open cell doors, serviced by rows of tall, exposed elevators and the occasional cross walkway. The evenly-shaped hole was broken on the right by a tall, jagged tower that ran the feature's entire height, its inward-pointing edge like a blade, largely transparent and providing a perfect view of the entire prison complex. Jindi could not help but stop and stare in a shiver of horrid, returning memories… but Bega, Mula and the others were leaving, so he ran after them, amid running corbi and sporadic shooting. All the walkways were alive with corbi, yelling and hooting, pitching slaves and perhaps the occasional reeh over the edge, to delight in their flailing limbs all the way down.

No enemies could stand around the geo-feature and shoot at corbi — they were overwhelmed, unable to grasp how all of them had emerged from their cells at once. Against even unarmed corbi, such soldiers were quickly overwhelmed and sacrificed to the god of gravity. Seeing them all, and feeling their energy crackling in the air, Jindi felt something he'd not experienced since that day when reeh flyers had descended from the sky and taken all that mattered from his life save the living. Hope.

26

Trace ran down hallways she only knew were clear because tacnet told her they were. Walls and ceiling were pocked and torn by high velocity fire, filled with smoke the air filters were not clearing — Trace suspected they'd been disabled in the enormous systems-crash the bugs had wrought upon the facility. At defensible junctions, the bodies of various slave species and a decreasing number of reeh sprawled on the floor, light-armoured and armed, as it seemed the intelligence had been correct to surmise the reeh kept most of their heavy armour on the lower levels. Keeping it that way would determine the success or failure of the mission.

On the approaches to those junctions, some corbi bodies, though fewer in number. Her teams appeared to have grasped the idea of fire-and-manoeuvre well enough, and had not simply charged defended positions. She could see them deployed in a wide, irregular semi-circle on this level and the ones above and below... but the problem, of course, was that in vertically-stacked levels, the top and bottom lines could always be outflanked by forces moving vertically at their rear. The corbi knew where the major stairwells were, and smaller elevators, and had disabled and booby-trapped many, but

Trace did not trust their proficiency under these circumstances, nor
assumed that the defenders weren't smart enough to find other ways.

She came to a fast stop at one large junction, did a quick left-and-
right duck of the head to check, tacnet or no tacnet, as Rika and Kono
covered behind. Tacnet abruptly revealed a dozen red dots in a
corridor on the right, telltale that one of the bugs had rounded a
corner and found them massing.

"Dreja, you've got a counter-attack coming, thirty metres out!
Watch your middle, they're going to come down those two central
corridors simultaneously!"

"*I see it,*" Dreja confirmed, breathing hard, the rattle of continuing
gunfire in the background.

"Just be prepared to displace and manoeuvre, do not hold a position if you're about to lose it anyway!" Because they simply didn't
have the numbers to try and defend hard lines on the ground.
Already that blue defensive line was looking very thin.

Trace moved on, Kono taking point, allowing her to half-scan
tacnet as they moved into a shattered control post, large secure doors
blasted, control panels smashed and smouldering, the bodies of
several tanifex strewn about the place. Very few reeh out further from
the hangars, Trace noted as she followed Kono out the room's far side.
In the way of masters guiding slaves, the reeh concentrated where the
most interesting work was done to make sure it happened, but left
the back corridors alone.

Here the regular layout of the Splicer interior ended with a huge
steel wall, inset with similarly huge slitted windows, like the arrow-
slits of some pre-technology fortress, each taller than a person. Trace
peered out one of them, the first time she'd been able to see what this
strange feature on her schematics looked like in person. It made a
vertical trench, ten floors tall, spanned by several secure walkways.
The entire interior region was high security, built separate from the
rest of the facility. The secure guardpost nearby had multiple
advanced screening technologies, but now the swinging gates, laser
scans and molecule sniffers were a blasted ruin, reinforced glass
doors smashed where corbi had gone straight through. Within the

tall slit windows on the trench's far side, Trace saw the regular flash of gunfire. From coms, she knew it was mostly one-way, for now.

"Hello Major," came a familiar female voice in her ear. *"I have established secure coms with minimal time-lag, and am now ready to assist you with whatever function you require. I have control of most of the Splicer base, but some reinforced subsystems are not accessible at this time."*

"Thank you Styx," said Trace, waving Kono on, through the shattered gates and across the secure bridge. "I need full tacnet as priority, the one I have now is inadequate." There came a several-second pause — Trace now did not need to check her timer, she could tell how far *Phoenix* was out from Rando by measuring how quickly that pause diminished. At the far end of the bridge, a corbi sat propped, one leg bloodied and tightly wrapped, grimacing as he waved them through, rifle ready. Kono, Trace and Rika passed him, through more shattered security barriers, and the rifle-blasted bodies of a slave species Trace did not recognise.

"Major, I am working to provide you with the best intelligence picture possible, though many Splicer systems have been entirely disabled, probably by its commanders anticipating I could use their facility against them." As Kono, confronting the high-ceilinged, open interior of an entirely new architectural style, saw a non-corbi figure moving on a high walkway and shot it, almost without breaking stride. The figure fell face-first and limp, probably a non-combatant, but no one cared. *"I can tell you that most of their heavy armour is attempting to make its way up to you, but I am disabling all of their elevator systems, it would take them fifteen minutes at least to take the stairs. However, the defenders can mobilise lightly armoured units much faster, I predict it will take them another five or ten minutes to organise those forces, then they will hit you with as much simultaneity as they can muster."*

As Trace indicated to Kono which way to go, across wide, white floors, through a wash of malfunctioning holographics, beneath walkways of polished steel, and spiralling staircases. More bodies, this time several reeh — long, angular heads, skeletal arms and full of holes, just how Trace liked them. There was not much blood on the shiny white floor, and that was so dark red it was nearly black.

Not a biological oddity, Trace was sure — an engineered one, thousands of years in the making. Like their horrid creations, reeh were not what they'd once been.

A corridor forged between walls heavy with engineered systems led to a circular room, also spotless white with glass walls, surrounded by shelves and shelves of circling, automated sample tubes. The air was chilled, but now warming as the doors remained open, alarm lights flashing to indicate that the specimens were being endangered. Trace was glad that she did not have time to peer into those tubes and see what grisly things grew inside them. These were the only things that the reeh found of value on Rando. Metals and minerals on a planet were useless to any spacefaring civilisation with access to asteroids. Reeh found value in the unique arrangements of genetic blueprints in a biosphere. It was perhaps the greatest trade their empire had.

"Styx, I'm in the control room... we've got it clear for now but we don't have much time. Can you acquire a direct upload link to any useful memory cores?"

In the next room, thick steel walls were obscured with smoke, some wall panels blasted with what must have been explosive charge, and several corbi holding a steel-framed chair into the opening of a half-shut steel door. The chair had buckled but seemed to be holding. One of the corbi grabbing it looked at Trace.

"Two of the bugs are here," he said, gesturing somewhere in the air. "They got the door open, but it tried to close again."

"That's the memory vault in there?" Trace asked, and broke off again as Styx's reply came back.

"Major, there is no direct feed to any useful Splicer memory core, it will be entirely autistic and will have to be removed by hand. I am in contact with your bugs in the vault, they will show you what to do."

Trace stepped carefully over the chair and into the dark, confined space within. There was no light save for what fell through the open door, and the space inside went around in a donut ring, the inner wall full of flat-panel displays, and the matte-black texture of cover panels. The thick air throbbed with a dull, bass vibration that Trace felt more in her bones than her ears.

A third of the way around the circle was Kaysa and several corbi — one of them Gido, who was one of Tano's Fleet men, and had technical skills. Kaysa gave Trace an impatient look, face half-lit by flashlight and an aggrieved red glow from the panels. One of those panels was off, and a glance within revealed nothing that looked like computers, but an intricate mass of black, crystalline shards that made patterns about a more solid-looking series of cores.

"It's right here," said Gido, pointing at the shards, and Trace glimpsed one of the bugs, crawling on the crystal like an ant in search of sugar. "I'm not sure what it's seeing or what it wants us to take, or how we can get it out without damaging the cores."

"You recognise these?" Trace asked. On tacnet, gunfire was erupting out at Dreja's position as the first of what would be many flanking assaults began. It demanded her attention, but so did this. Buried in here somewhere was humanity's salvation.

Gido's reply was affirmative, and laced with Lisha technical jargon that Trace had no chance of understanding.

"Right," said Trace. "My drysine queen is talking to me from *Phoenix*, she's now going to talk to you. Follow her instructions precisely, she's smarter than all of us combined. Understand?"

"Understand," said Gido, eyes-wide. "Can she speak Lisha?"

"She can speak anything... Styx? Tell him what to do, I have to go and make sure we don't get overrun before we extract the damn thing."

* * *

THE LOWER CONCOURSE WAS INSANITY. THE ARCHITECTURE ON THE Splicer's lower approaches was monolithic — huge thoroughfares with ceilings many storeys high, with branch hallways leading to military staging points and equipment storage. Now all were teeming with running corbi, some armed and many not, flooding upon the vast floor and many along the higher, parallel walkways as now, from the higher levels, more shooting began.

Jindi fell flat as explosions detonated ahead of him, a shocking concussion on the eardrums and the air full of hissing, snapping shrapnel and falling bodies. Bega and Fifth Team scrambled for the cover of one wall, screaming at others to follow, pointing their rifles up and firing in the general direction of the incoming, high near the ceiling. Jindi scrambled to the wall on all fours, saw corbi blasted to pieces just near to one side, others firing wildly skyward. He reached the wall and huddled in an alcove. Other corbi were still running, bounding four-limbed if unarmed, three-limbed if not, brandishing weapons, firing weapons, shrieking and yelling in the wild hope of those who had expected to die horribly, given a fresh chance on life.

But now there was heavy fire scything amongst them from some-where ahead, and airburst munitions that detonated with a flash that seared the eyeballs and left a dozen running corbi in bloody ruin. His pistol forgotten, Jindi saw some corbi staggering on uncooperative limbs, twisted from the experiments like he was. Heavy rounds struck several directly before him, blasting off limbs. Those rounds made the most impossible sound, with a crack in the air like a whip, and the thud of impact on steel and flesh like percussion drums, while lighter rounds clattered like hail on a stormy day.

"Heavy armour!" Jindi heard one of Bega's men shouting. "They've got heavy armour down ahead!" And he looked around to see where Jisu was, having taken cover directly behind him, but Jisu's head was mostly missing, just gore and blood across the wall as others of Fifth Section tried to find shots above the running heads of corbi.

And Jindi saw children, some lost in the crowd, others running, some carried by desperate adults. A Fifth Team man ran into the chaos to retrieve one who wandered, wide-eyed and confused, only for both to vanish in a blast of flame. He saw a young woman, drag-ging herself along the floor to freedom, leaving a trail of thick blood behind her. He saw an old man, realising the hopelessness, simply sit down on the floor amid the accumulating bodies and parts of bodies, and wait for the end.

Far ahead, he saw a line of dark, armoured figures — reeh heavy armour, blazing fire and fury into the crowds. They crackled and sparked in the roar of returning gunfire, and several appeared hurt, but they pivoted slowly, aiming into the heaviest concentrations with weapons designed to kill other heavy armour, like them. Hundreds of corbi rounds hit them every second, and the ricochets sprayed and leaped at nearby walls. On the levels above, corbi poured fire down onto them, and the heavies aimed upward, devastating entire balconies, then advancing through a rain of falling bodies.

"Get fire on them!" Mula was bellowing, waving Fifth Team forward along the walls. "We've got grenade launchers, get fire onto them!" As those still alive went bounding past up the walls, trying to close the range. One took a heavy round just past Jindi and spun like a top.

It might even work, Jindi thought. The forward stampede had ceased in a sea of bodies that obscured many more just lying flat, or crawling, or hoping the fire would miss them. But many of those lying flat were firing, and even the heaviest reeh armour could only take so much. But Jindi knew there would be so many more heavy armour units elsewhere in the Splicer. The only reason any of these escapees were alive at all was that most of the heavies were trying to find a way up, to stop Major Thakur.

"We have to find another way!" he yelled hoarsely to whoever would listen. "We have to go around! Bega! Where is Bega?" He looked around, finding another Fifth Team soldier pressed to the wall behind Jisu's body, too terrified to move. That man pointed, out on the killing floor. Jindi looked, and saw Bega, helmet askew, searching frantically among the prone and fallen, the dead and living, as bullets cut the air around him. Looking for children, Jindi saw. In particular, the vain hope of one little girl. But there were so many.

"Bega!" he shouted. "Bega, you can't help her by dying! Bega!" But Bega ignored him. This instinct he'd been repressing, to help his team get the most corbi out as he possibly could. But now, as hopes withered beneath a storm of reeh fire, he gave in to the only thing that truly mattered.

There was a side exit ahead, on the right, against this wall.

"I know a way out!" Jindi shouted above the cacophony, the screams of the wounded and dying. "Follow me, I know a way out!" He waved at them, at the remains of Fifth Team behind him, those wounded or too scared to advance, and any civilians alive within earshot who might hear. "This way, this way!"

He heaved his aching body up, repressing every instinct to lie as flat as possible and huddle, as a bullet cracked just above his head, and precision fire blew apart several prone corbi returning fire. But others followed, scrambling low, heading toward the side exit. Jindi didn't truly know a way out, not from here. But anywhere had to be better than this, and if anyone could figure it out, through the back routes, he could. He reached the corridor, threw himself against the side wall for a moment to catch his breath, and waved more corbi after him. They came in a trickle, and then a stream, some making a mad dash from the far side of the entry floor. Reeh might have seen this movement down the side corridor, and directed explosives this way, but Jindi forced himself to stay where he was, and wave as many through as wanted to come.

Then, finally, he turned and struggled after the clustering group, who waited for him and looking at him in desperate expectation, hoping that he would know the way.

* * *

"Here!" Trace yelled, waving at running corbi to stop and establish at the junction she guarded. They obeyed her outstretched hand, indicating the new line of defence, wild-eyed but still determined, aiming rifles back up the way they'd come as a thunder of gunfire pursued down neighbouring corridors.

Trace put rounds up the adjoining corridor as something black-armoured and not corbi risked a look, then saw another corbi running down the main way, carrying a wounded man on his back.

"Take him back to the hangar!" she instructed. "Then get back here immediately, if this line folds we're finished!"

Dreja came bounding up the adjoining corridor, from where more shooting was erupting. "Going to run low on ammo soon!" he insisted, looking around at the new position here on his left flank. "These guys okay?"

"They're fine," Trace told him. "I'll stay here to make sure." There should have been sixteen men here, in truth, but two more wounded had gone to the rear, and there were four dead in the hallways they'd abandoned. Lines were getting similarly thin all over. "Don't worry about ammo, *Phoenix* is fifteen minutes away. Keep taking the ammo from your dead and wounded and you can't run low."

She ducked back as rounds snapped down the corridor, Dreja doing the same. "Going to be close, isn't it?" Dreja asked, with the hope of a man looking for reassurance.

"We'll make it!" Trace said fiercely. "*Phoenix* is coming, we just need to last fifteen minutes!"

Dreja left at a run, looking more determined. A vid feed came in, and Rika took Trace's place at the corner as she answered it.

"*Major, it's Mula!*" Mula was Bega's best, down in Fifth Team. He sounded in pain. Behind his voice, the air was a thudding crackle of gunfire and screaming.

"Mula! Where's Bega?"

"*I don't know! I'm hit, Major, I...*" as an explosion thumped nearby. "*They've got heavy armour down here, Major! We've taken down some of them, but it's a slaughter! We're... we're just dead everywhere!*"

Trace took a deep breath, fire snapping down her own corridor barely a metre away, and steeled herself to calm. She'd told them this would happen. She'd told them she couldn't stop this, that she didn't have the resources, that it was a mission to take the Splicer's knowledge, not to save corbi prisoners. But they hadn't listened, and wouldn't let her proceed unless there was a prisoner-saving component to the plan. This was the best she could do, and it served as a large distraction for her work up here, and they'd never have allowed the plan to proceed if she hadn't.

"Mula! You've got to spread yourselves out, you can't all just get out the main exits! Split up and move in small groups so some of you can get through!"

"We're... we're doing that, Major! But there's... there's thousands caught in the main exit hall... Major, you have to get a Phoenix shuttle here to pick us up! All the people stuck in here can't get out in time! There's so many wounded!"

The feed switched to external view, and Trace caught a shaky glimpse of Mula's first-person view... something was blocking half the view of the huge lower hall. Bodies, Trace realised. He was lying flat beneath a pile of bodies. He lifted high enough that she could see, and the floor was carpeted with corbi bodies. Limbs stuck out on odd angles, some still moving, some screaming and crying as bullets cracked overhead, and struck the dead and wounded alike. The bodies stretched away across the vast floor, hundreds, possibly thousands of them. Some were still alive, some returning fire, others trying to check on their neighbours, others wandering in a daze, oblivious to fire.

She'd done this. She'd told them... only she hadn't truly told them, hadn't insisted when they refused to listen, hadn't told them they were all fools for thinking that this crazy half-chance was better than no chance at all. Because perhaps it hadn't been. If she'd been a prisoner in there, any half-chance to sprint for an exit under fire would have seemed preferable... but the moment the reeh put a handful of heavy armour in the way, all those light rifles lost their ability to kill. And then the mass of escaping prisoners became not an army, but a turkey shoot.

She could have insisted that it was stupid, that they'd have to find another way. But that would have jeopardised the mission. Her mission was to save humanity, had been from her earliest memories of learning what the Kulina were, and what drove them. If thousands of corbi wanted to risk what remained of their lives so that five hundred billion humans could escape a similar fate, that was a trade any Kulina, any human patriot, should have been prepared to make in a heartbeat. But the sight of the carnage confronting Mula took her breath away, and nearly took her legs out from under her.

"Mula," she was nearly astonished to hear her voice saying, "you have to keep fighting to get as many of them outside the Splicer as possible. *Phoenix* marines can't rescue them if they're deep inside the Splicer, there's no time. Anyone you can get outside, we can rescue."

"I... I hear you, Major." He sounded desperate, but still determined, with no idea that she was lying. The camera flicked sideways for a moment to his companions behind the pile of bodies — another soldier, and a shock-faced woman clutching her dead child. Trace wanted to cry. A lifetime of training wouldn't allow it. The link went blank.

A grenade exploded metres away, followed by new screams. Rika ducked back from firing, reloading fast. "They're going around left!" he told Trace, indicating that way. "Major, I think they're heading for Sigo's right flank!"

Trace switched her full attention back to the tacnet display that had overlaid even Mula's vid. "Hello Sigo! There's another section heading at your right flank from my position, I think they're going to try and wedge between us!"

Up the rear corridor, Kono arrived at a run, breathing hard. "They're mobilising near the hangars!" he said. "Another five minutes, tops. No way we can hold it."

Trace nodded fast. "I know. We can't hold both the hangars and the data center at the same time. Get back and get everyone moving, I'm ordering the hangars abandoned. We'll pull back to the data-center, Phoenix Company will have to fight their way in to us."

"Got it!" said Kono, and set off running up the way he'd come. Trace thought she'd have lost the entire defence already if not for Kono running from site to site making sure everything happened somewhat properly.

"We still a chance?" Rika asked her.

"Fight until you die, kid," said Trace, pushing past him to the corner once more. "If you're still alive in half an hour, we won."

27

Erik watched the reeh firestation disappear, a bright flash from a far quadrant of near Rando space as the emplacement's defensive guns finally missed one of *Phoenix*'s high-V rounds. *Phoenix* was far too deep in the gravity-well now, a previous generation of technology would have made their situation unrecoverable, with a 10-G escape trajectory just barely saving them, and the entire planet, from a catastrophic collision. Probably there were reeh defenders downworld wondering if this was a suicide mission, and if all of Rando's life forms were about to disappear for good. Every training mission in the Academy had drummed into Fleet pilots just what a monumentally bad idea such courses were. Erik found the situation surreal in the extreme.

But the jumplines were green on his panels, and he cycled the engines, plunging them deep into a hyperspace field, then out once more at dramatically lower V.

"Course is good!" Kaspowitz announced with cool relief. "We are twenty-times orbital V, tangential at seventy-two degrees!"

"Captain," called Geish, "two marks entered jump behind us, looks like *Jonri* and *Poga*!" Those were the two Resistance ships that had offered to come through behind and hold their escape lanes open. They'd offered another ship, but Erik had been of the opinion that given the performance mismatch, too many Resistance vessels would just get in the way.

"Captain!" called Jiri. "Reeh assault shuttles at their station, trajectories indicate a possible threat!"

"Take them out," Erik commanded, watching everything else but that. "Minimal damage to station is acceptable." Even here, there were rules to obey about killing nominally civilian space stations. It certainly wasn't for concern about reeh civilians, more that planets and systems changed hands in wartime, and that one day the croma or the corbi might win this system back. Stations took a long time to build, and most invading forces would use the ones already there. Even the reeh did not target stations, finding them far too useful.

"Operations, the Captain requests status check."

"This is Operations, status is green, we are holding." Erik knew that from his display, but on large assaults like this, it never hurt to check twice. His eyes flicked over their approach to deployment — a spot four hundred kilometres above Rando's atmosphere that would present all assault shuttles with the optimum approach down to the Splicer.

"Arms," he announced, "get me a targeting solution on all visible surface bases on Rando."

"Arms copies," said Geish, calling those up. They'd discussed this possibility in advance, with faintly wide-eyed intensity. Erik hadn't known whether the system would still be full of targets at that point, and whether *Phoenix* would have too many other priorities. But now, most of those targeting priorities were expanding clouds of vapour, and he had strategic freedom on his approach.

Erik's main view, usually a complicated tangle of competing hypothetical trajectories, now showed *Phoenix's* projected approach across Rando's upper atmosphere, complicated only by the single civilian station on a far perpendicular orbit, Lieutenant Corrig's fire now visibly accelerating toward it on intercept. And now came Geish's feed, a series of lines like some strange species of creeper, sprouting limbs toward various intercept points on the surface of Rando. Reeh bases.

"Navigation, get me a course." He could already see it himself, but he had time, and wanted this to feel like a group decision. He didn't think it was moral cowardice that made it so. It was just that they were really all in this together, and no weight need be borne alone.

"Aye Captain!" said Kaspowitz, running furious calculations. "Course calculation, we'll need three burns to hit them all, recommend we ditch that highest northern latitude and take those main four on our path, will only cost fifteen seconds to our ETA."

Those fifteen seconds were precious, particularly when they could cost Trace and Kono's lives. But strategically, the distraction it provided, and the disruption to any possible reeh response, was worth it.

"Course accepted," Erik announced, transferring Kaspowitz's solutions to his main. "Arms, stand by for surface strike, ordnance at your discretion."

"Aye Captain," said Corrig, "ordnance at my discretion."

Though new to First Shift, Raf Corrig was one of Erik's better friends on *Phoenix*, having served in Erik's Third Shift back in that other lifetime when *Phoenix* had had three shifts, and Captain Pantillo had run the first of them. The post-renegade mess had moved Raf to Second Shift, and now to First in the aftermath of Second Lieutenant Karle's death in the Battle of Defiance. Very few Arms Officers in any of those shifts had carried out a high-V surface strike on planetary bases. For the most part they'd been prohibited, against the tavalai at least, with whom Fleet had maintained a gentleman's agreement to refrain from the needless endangerment of each other's civilians.

But Fleet had done plenty in their history, particularly against the krim. When dealing with species that had no concept of 'rights', human or otherwise, such restraints would gain you nothing. By granting Corrig his discretion, Erik was acceding to the Arms Officer's superior knowledge of how this was done.

"Arms Two, get me a plot on possible civilian casualties at present

V," Erik added, watching the timer counting down. That was going to be a hectic series of manoeuvres coming up, when added to the final braking manoeuvre to make position for shuttle deployment.

"Captain, I'm projecting impact velocity at Mach four seven nine," said Harris. "Should kill anything within a five kilometre radius of each impact, no way to make it smaller with atmospheric penetrators."

They'd discussed this too, and how most corbi settlements stayed well clear of the reeh ground bases. But there were a few, like at the Splicer itself, that snuggled up to the bases for scraps and menial jobs. There were also the blinding fireballs and ear-shattering shockwaves of super high-V penetrators striking the atmosphere at nearly Mach five hundred. The warheads involved were barely more than two metres long, made of substances far stronger than diamond to ensure they survived long enough through the near-instantaneous penetration from high-atmosphere to the ground. Even corbi well outside the blast radius could lose sight or hearing from the blast. But most of Rando these days was forested, long distance lines-of-sight were rare at ground level, and the trees should dissipate the sound waves as well. And even were it not true, Erik did not think he'd have a choice, given everything else in play.

"We're doing it," he said grimly. "All hands, stand by for combat manoeuvres, high-G followed by final V-dump and last deceleration burn. All Operations stand by for deployment, we are five minutes fifteen and counting."

* * *

JINDI'S BACK HURT BEYOND BELIEF. HE TRIED TO GO ON ALL FOURS, BUT that hurt his twisted shoulders worst of all and forced him upright for stretches. A young woman he did not know supported him, while others in the group scattered ahead, too desperate to wait for directions, or clustered behind, protected by a few remaining Fifth Team soldiers, or recently armed escapees who aimed their shaking weapons up adjoining corridors in hope that nothing non-corbi would round a corner. Gunfire and explosions echoed, screams and shouting, and several times they came across recent bodies, mostly corbi, and once an armoured tanifex, whose weapon was promptly taken.

At a gasping pause at one corner, Jindi removed his soldier's helmet and fastened it onto the young woman's head. She accepted the gift wordlessly, for what little extra hope it gave. At the base of her skull were shaved patches, and small, circular scars. Jindi knew what those were, and why the look in her eyes was slightly blank, reacting oddly at odd times to different things.

"Why aren't they sending us mad?" another woman thought to ask him, clutching her bad hip. "They can send us mad by pressing a button, I've seen it!"

"Their network isn't working," Jindi replied, with a wave of his hand to indicate the air itself. "The Resistance broke it. They can't do anything. Come on, this place will be destroyed soon, we have to go!"

He had no idea how many of the thousands of prisoners were still alive. Many more had poured into these side passages, away from the killing ground of the hall toward the main exit. Rika and Pena had said the tanifex rebels would be down here somewhere, but Jindi guessed there couldn't be very many of them, and probably they'd be scared to show themselves around armed corbi or humans for fear of getting shot. Trying to save lots of people at this point seemed too great a burden. For now, he just wanted to save the young woman helping him. If he could just save her, that would be enough.

He tried the monocle eyepiece again as he moved, but found its picture broken and static-riddled. He didn't know why — the pirate network that it ran on was supposed to be maintained by those bug machines the Major used. Maybe the bugs had all been destroyed. Or maybe, the nasty thought occurred to him, the escaping prisoners were much less important to the Major than the work going on upstairs, and the bugs had all been redirected that way.

Jindi's downward search for less-protected routes brought him down several stairwells, then face-to-face with several unarmed reeh on their way up. A hail of gunfire sent them tumbling back down, and several more followers took turns emptying magazines into their pulverised bodies as they passed. Jindi didn't care, had never seen how hatred might make him happier, not even when they'd killed his family in the raid that took him. He thought now of his beach, or some other beach elsewhere on Rando. He thought of the young woman, and several of these others, with him on that beach. Walking on warm sand, fishing in the rolling surf, seabirds wheeling overhead. Somewhere in the universe. There had to be happiness somewhere. For a while, on his beach, he'd dared to dream that it might even be there.

The stairwell emerged onto a line of parked, automated loaders on wheels, amid unloaded crates. Beyond them, a hangar, all aflame with gunfire and running personnel. "We can't go that way!" yelled Uri, one of the Fifth Team soldiers, trying to reverse. "You fool!" he yelled at Jindi. "You've led us the wrong way!"

"No, look!" Jindi abandoned the young woman's support, grabbed Uri and dragged him to cover behind one of the loaders. A huge explosion made them duck, a whooshing missile contrail... no weapon the Resistance had could do that much damage. He pointed out beyond the hangar, to open skies beyond, across the Leda Valley. A combat flyer was hovering out there, pouring firepower into the hangar. Within, other flyers were burning, and Reeh Empire soldiers lay scattered, dead and wounded. Even as they looked, some who were returning fire from the cover of cargo crates were hit by high-velocity gunfire and torn to spinning pieces.

Other soldiers faced the hangar's rear, shooting that way and receiving return fire. And distantly, bounding amongst the smoke and flames, came armed corbi, seeking cover, and positions to fire from.

"That way!" Jindi yelled, pointing out the hangar opening. "There are stairs, walkways! You can head down from there! It reaches the ground... there are guardposts, but they'll all be under assault! Beyond that is Splicer City! But we have to go now, while they're distracted!"

Uri ducked again as bullets hit nearby, staring disbelievingly at the scene. Then he turned, pointed at those corbi with weapons, and indicated them forward to firing positions. Those that understood ran to do that, while those that hadn't got the idea by watching, copied. Jindi went at a crouch, and found a gap between several stacked crates, levelling through it the pistol he had not yet fired with trembling hands. Someone took cover beside him, and he looked — it was the young woman who'd been supporting him.

"You have to go!" he told her, pointing toward the hangar mouth. "That way!" She shook her head, stubbornly, with clear meaning.

"Fire!" yelled Uri, and the corbi on this flank of the hangar opened up with a hammer and thump of rifle fire. Jindi pointed the pistol as best he could at the cover positions of armoured enemy soldiers, behind crates, loading equipment and the burning ruins of flyers, and squeezed the trigger. The pistol cracked and leaped alarmingly, and there seemed to be soldiers falling, others scrambling and diving for new cover, surprised by this sudden new direction of assault.

"Go!" yelled Uri, and unarmed corbi leaped from amongst the crates and bounded toward the hangar mouth. Outside, the hovering flyer continued to fire over their heads, and some of the soldiers before Jindi died, shredded by rapid fire. The flyer seemed to be out of missiles, but its main cannon was horrifically effective at these ranges. Jindi wondered if it was a tanifex rebel flying it, or maybe the Major's drysine queen. The Major had suggested this might happen — that the queen could infiltrate the Splicer's entire network and use reeh weapons against them.

Jindi kept firing until his pistol clicked empty, then ducked to reload as he'd been taught. Something whooshed past, headed for the flyer, and he looked up to see several missiles missing it, curling away in the blue sky behind. The flyer angled to target the new threat, and let loose another volley. Return heavy cannon fire struck its engine nacelle, then smashed its cockpit. The flyer staggered, then veered to one side trailing smoke, and vanished.

"Heavy armour!" someone yelled, switching to fire that way. Jindi looked, toward the hangar rear, and his blood ran cold to see them, dark and loping like giant insects, angular heads thrust forward, legs bending the wrong way. Reeh armour, the real, galaxy-conquering thing, weapon pods on their arms, rocket launchers on their shoulders. Several turned his way.

Jindi grabbed the girl and pulled them both flat, and then the air was snapping with the sound of a dozen bullwhips, and the clang and crash of rounds tearing through the crates above him. On his other side, Uri's headless body fell limp, then an explosion drove air from his lungs and sense from his brain.

Somehow he managed to grab the girl's arm and scramble back toward heavier cover, as rounds continued to flash around him, and corbi ahead and behind were hit. He dove with the girl behind a cargo loader, and scrambled to stare toward the hangar edge. Corbi were running, leaping over the edge for the walkways he knew ran down there, engineering access to the intervening levels. But now some of those trailing were under fire, cut down while running in a bloody spray of floor-clearing steel. The reeh had enemies over there who were armed and more threatening, yet still took the time to gun down running civilian prisoners.

And now the chance was gone. The friendly covering fire from the flyer had been neutralised, and the remaining, lightly armoured corbi would be slaughtered as they had been in the exit hall. Perhaps several dozen had made it past the hangar, but no more than that. He stared at the girl, eyes shocked and dazed beneath her helmet rim, and knew that there was no chance to find another way. Anyone running would be cut down by weapons systems made to hit far more difficult targets than running corbi, and now those heavy suits would come over here, pick their way amongst the crates and other cover, and eliminate this annoyance point-blank.

Even now, he could hear the thumping footsteps of approaching suits, coming from a new angle ahead. He grabbed the girl and held her head down as they fired... and was surprised that none of the new fire seemed directed his way. In fact the rounds raining down on his position nearly ceased, even as the sound of shooting escalated. He risked a look up, and saw the new armour suits directly opposite, covering amidst the ruins of burning flyers, torn crates and dead soldiers, firing onto the reeh. Several of the reeh suits were down, one of them detonating spectacularly, others scrambling for cover, several more damaged.

The helmets on these new armour looked different. Shorter helmets, for differently shaped heads. Not reeh, then. Tanifex.

"Come on!" yelled Jindi, dragged the girl up, and ran. They bounded across the hangar floor, other corbi joining them, rounds ripping past, reeh fire now concentrated on the serious threat, but still lethal when it missed. A young corbi with a three-limbed gait somehow overtook them, damaged limb cradled, and behind them the unmistakable thud of bullets hitting flesh.

And then the lip of the hangar, and the engineering platform leading to gantry stairwells that clung to the Splicer's silver steel exterior, descending toward the base of the cliffs below. It looked a long way down still, yet on the ground where Jindi recalled guard posts, now were flames and smoke.

He could not descend the stairs with headlong speed, but the girl supported him as he tried to move at speed, and other corbi dashed past between the narrow rails. All about was cool wind and open space. Beneath, green trees stretched to the horizon of hills, fresh with the promise of freedom.

"Dreja, move back!" Trace commanded, emptying a magazine down an adjacent hallway. Fractured shouts and static came back — she suspected several of the bugs were down, the network was deteriorating, and now there were red dots closing in on all sides, and appearing in alarming numbers in the rear. "Dreja, report!"

She ducked as another grenade exploded nearby, rattling her armour — something stung in her ankle from several minutes ago, where the armour did a poor job of protecting joints. Up the hall toward Dreja's position, a corbi came bounding, three-limbed with rifle in the air, shots pursuing him from around the corner. He skidded to a halt opposite where Yano covered with his rifle, and shouted across at Trace, "We're overrun! I don't know where Dreja is! They're breaking through!"

Tacnet showed Tano's rear group moving up from the hangars — many wounded who could still walk, the ones that couldn't had stayed, saving a final grenade each for themselves. Kono was escorting, and now the red dots grew in number between them and the Splicer Command, filtering through the booby-trapped stairwells having evidently found a way through.

"Everyone on this flank, form on me!" Trace yelled, firing the last few rounds then ejecting the mag and slamming a new one. "We're pulling back to the Command..."

And broke off as her rearguard opened fire with a yell of warning, dropping with a spin to see an armoured figure running at them, taking shot after shot... "Down!" Trace yelled, guessing what was coming, and the following explosion blasted bits of soldier through a cloud of smoke up the corridor. Through the smoke ran more, firing as they came, as Trace rolled to the opposing wall, aiming precisely and shooting one, two, three in a row through the smoke.

"Up and go, follow me!" she yelled, getting up and running into the smoke, expecting to be charged from the other direction too. A fast glance back showed her Rika following, unloading the last of his mag behind before reloading... but her rearguard corbi had not risen from the floor, face down in his own blood, and the others at her junction were slow to react.

She pumped a grenade round into the smoke ahead, causing enough confusion to surprise the two tanifex waiting at the next junction, shooting both point-blank before they could recover from the shock of finding her on top of them. They were guarding the entrance to a lobby-style room, a wide floor with an open stairwell that had been guarded by motion-sensor AP mines, but evidently the tanifex had found a way past those as well.

She darted quickly across the room, indicating Rika and one other who followed to take position covering the adjoining corridors. "Everyone on me!" she tried again. "Pull back parallel to my position, we're going to hit the enemy between Fourth Team and Command, then fall back ourselves!"

Only now, they were sandwiched between the enemy they'd been holding back on their flanks, and the one that had infiltrated into their rear. If she joined with Fourth Team, and teamed with Sigo's Third Team falling back from the opposite flank, they could meet in the middle and regain enough force to punch through to Command... but tacnet was now very hazy on where Sigo's far flank was.

"Sigo, I am not reading your position! Fall back to the center, get back to my position!"

"They're charging us!" came Sigo's static-broken voice, filled with desperate adrenaline. *"They're fucking suicide charging!"* Trace was surprised it hadn't happened earlier, but reeh mind-control ran off a functional network, and that network was presently down. If they'd managed to restore even a bit of it...

"Styx, how are they mind-controlling their soldiers?"

The reply came almost without light-lag, telling her that *Phoenix* was right on top of them. *"Major, I am attempting to..."* but then explosions from the stairs filled that half of the lobby with smoke, and bodies were dropping into it.

Trace went at them, knowing they'd be coming simultaneously down the corridor behind, and that point-blank range was her greatest advantage. She shot one through the faceplate at the base of the stairs, rifle pressed hard to her shoulder and swivelling to shoot another coming down the opposing corridor... then Rika was there, firing fully automatic as Trace got behind the open staircase and fired through the steps to shoot the next in the unprotected back of his legs. Something exploded in the middle of the floor, and her right arm snapped away as something hit it. Trace dropped the rifle, pulled her pistol left-handed and shot the next tanifex through the corridor in the face, then ducked around the stairs once more to get beside the corridor entrance, sparing another round for the head of the tanifex she'd wounded at the bottom of the stairs.

One-handed she couldn't pull a grenade, and with Rika at the far wall she couldn't let the approaching tanifex rush past her then shoot them from behind without them killing Rika first. So she risked it, stood fast side-on and shot the next one through the face at arms-length as he came, and ducked back as the second fired full auto, hitting more of the corridor rim than anything... and was promptly shot by Rika from across the room.

It earned her a pause, as Yano and two others ran in, covering the corridors as she returned to get her rifle, and check on her arm. Shrapnel had hit the underside of her forearm just short of the armour, and by the feel of it, she thought had probably fractured her ulna. There was a lot of blood, and if she'd cared to look probably some bone splinters in there somewhere, but her hand couldn't find any shrapnel sticking out.

"Sigo!" she demanded, pulling a field bandage from the webbing pouch, pressing the pad over the worst of it and wrapping fast directly over her forearm guard. "Status report! I see you not moving back!"

"We're stuck, Major! Big crossfire! If we move we'll get cut up!"

"If you stay you're all dead! Pick a direction and charge if you have to, use grenades and smoke for cover, but you can't stay there! They are surrounding and isolating you, then they'll kill you!" The pain hadn't hit her yet, and she moved fast in the sure knowledge that everything would become more difficult once it did. Marine augments included adjustments to the pain response, dimming the signal from extreme pain directly in the parietal lobe. But dimming that response too much, scientists had discovered, had awful side effects, so it still wasn't going to be any less than agony.

More shooting on Sigo's coms, and Yano fired a burst up his corridor, but nothing came back. Trace yanked the bandage tight, and tried her fingers — they moved, but sluggishly, she thought one of the tendons might have been clipped. The swelling would soon be awful, limiting all motion in that hand. She could have sworn and complained, but instead took up her rifle, checked it, and switched to a left-handed grip.

"Styx, please say again."

"Major, I said that I do not know how the reeh are mind-controlling their slave soldiers. It's not via the main network, it may be occurring autonomously." Styx, Trace knew, was not going to waste time enquiring after her health.

"Major!" came Kono's shout, above a racket of gunfire on coms. *"I'm with Fourth Team, they're pressing us hard!"* Trace could see it, red dots clustering onto Fourth's blue dots, blocking their retreat to Command.

"Come on," said Trace to her small group. "If we press we can hit the infiltrators from behind."

Rika took point, Trace letting him, concerned that her left-handed grip now reduced her riflemanship from excellent to merely good. The pain began to hit her as she ran after Rika, along with that horrid, nauseous feeling that made combat seem preferable. In combat the adrenaline ran so strong that the pain faded. Trace knew that the ground commander should probably pull back to Command and coordinate from there, but the forces withdrawing were getting overwhelmed and if not enough of them made it back, Command would fall before Keysa's people could extract the final data. If she didn't lead from the front, the whole thing would crumble.

Tanifex ahead had occupied a guard post, an open rectangle amid the corridors with a clear line of sight in four directions. Trace pressed herself to the wall beside an adjoining corridor, indicating that Rika, Yano and four others who'd caught up should wait for her signal. She primed a grenade in her underside launcher, missing her T-15 standard issue more than ever, and glanced them over. All were a mess — wide-eyed, exhausted, manes amess and some bloody, but brave as all hells and prepared to die if that was what it took. Trace was increasingly sure that it would be. It simplified things considerably. At least now, the awful scenes of the slaughter downstairs were gone from her mind.

She nodded fast, swivelled around the corner and fired her grenade at the guard room entrance. Rika did the same, then darted across the corridor to take cover on the other side, as the others followed in the narrow space, and explosions pounded the guardroom. Trace saw muzzle flashes in the smoke and hit that with a precision burst, saw a body drop... and got a suddenly strong signal from the guardroom, red dots in disarray, several flickering to suggest casualties. A bug must have flown into the room.

"Go!" she snapped, and darted forward, rifle to shoulder, and covered the ten metres quickly, Rika tossing his last grenade ahead for good measure. She edged the last two metres carefully, Rika on her left, each covering opposite sides of the room ahead as more revealed itself with each half-step — equipment benches lost in white smoke, random clothes and armour strewn upon the floor, several bodies. A wounded tanifex hauled itself up an adjoining corridor, Rika shot it in the back and ducked in, moving fast along the wall... the kid was getting good, Trace saw, and had a real knack for angles and movement.

"Giddy, give me your position, we're close!" She scrambled between benches, put a bullet into another fallen tanifex to be sure, then up to the front corridor entrance... and barely reached it before an explosion tore everything sideways.

Time blanked. Everything was white and hazy. She came to, somehow lying on her back, half-propped awkwardly against a wall where she'd fallen, hearing gone and head ringing like a bell. But her limbs moved, and her rifle was somehow still in her left hand, and when the first charging tanifex clattered past her, she shot it in the less well-defended back. Shots from elsewhere hit the next two, who returned fire, and then there was a point-blank racket of frantic gunfire, tanifex and corbi hit, Trace shooting another who hadn't noticed her odd position, then her rifle clicked empty.

Somehow she got her pistol out, others coming in the door now noticing her behind the bench low to their right... but marine training point-blank said drive straight at them, so she did, left-handed and unable to rise beyond her knees, shooting from down low even as she stumbled into a collision with the wall, another two bullets slamming her chestplate while she aimed for faces, firing and firing until two more were down.

The pistol mag clicked dry, and her bad hand slowed her reload.

Another tanifex rounded the corner on top of her, and she grabbed the rifle rather than take the bullet, arm-locked and drove him over backward. Hit hard, and somehow he rolled her, an armoured forearm driving up under her jaw, twisting her head back, his other hand grabbing her good arm with ferocious strength. For a moment, his black faceplate dominated her world, looming down upon her like death itself... but he hadn't secured her bad hand, which found the kukri hilt, and rather than risking a slash for the unprotected neck, which he could see and catch, she slashed his hip instead. He jerked away, and she flipped with a heave, launching on top, locking his arm to clear the way for her kukri, right beneath the jaw and slashed like butchering a sheep.

There was more point-blank fighting in the guard room, tanifex and corbi ducked low beneath the storage benches... then a grenade exploded and a tanifex was rolling, Rika ducking around and shooting another one before he could recover. Trace went back for her rifle and pistol, reloading both and nearly blacking out from a new wave of dizziness. Blood spattered on her weapons and the floor, her face was cut, she could barely hear, her ribs screamed from the hits her armour had taken, probably one was fractured. When she was loaded and upright, her left thigh protested, and her hand on it came away bloody.

"*Major!*" It was Kono. "*We're nearly overrun!*" It sounded even crazier where he was. Tacnet said that was just metres away.

"I'm coming Giddy, hang on." She barely heard her own voice, talking only by the memory of vocal cords. A glance back showed her Rika helping one of the wounded corbi to stand... he looked a mess, and Trace pointed him back toward Command. Yano and two others were dead amid a tangle of dead tanifex. But here was Rika, checking his weapon, bloodied but fierce. Phoenix Company could not accommodate corbi, human armour was the wrong shape, but at that moment Trace thought she'd have made an exception.

She staggered up the corridor, lodging the unfamiliar rifle butt against her wrong shoulder with one damaged arm by force of habit, struggling to keep the limp from impairing her balance for when she'd need to shoot. Bullets ripped up and down the hallway ahead, then a tanifex darted in, taking cover from the rounds ahead. Trace shot him, head snapping sideways as the armoured body clattered limp. She advanced fast, cleared the right side first, then crossed to clear the left... saw another tanifex in cover behind a corridor edge, reloading his weapon, and shot him too. She'd racked up huge tallies before in close-quarters training, being one of the few people who rarely missed even while moving, and could read tacnet while everything was exploding, while never forgetting to clear her corners.

She indicated for Rika to guard right, and went left to cover behind the dead tanifex. Ahead was a larger room than the last guardroom, with adjoining rooms behind now-shattered glass, with long, reclining chairs and arm restraints — perhaps a medical facility. Trace pump-loaded and fired her last rifle grenade at tanifex shooting from the far opposite side into those rooms, where the return fire was clearly corbi.

The grenade exploded and she scampered in, low behind a row of chairs and lockers, wanting out of that approach corridor that left their backs exposed. Rika fired on the way in, then rolled as return fire came past, but that tanifex died as one of the other corbi shot him. Shrill, alien shrieks as tanifex realised someone new had entered the room, and from amongst the medical rooms ahead the sounds of point-blank fighting. Trace saw a corbi leaping over benches, saw a tanifex thrown bodily into a wall, then muzzle flashes and a grenade explosion. A body, rolling in the smoke, then still.

She risked a fast move to the end of her row of benches, then tacnet showed a red dot moving, and she levered up just enough to shoot him in the shoulder as he changed position. A corbi grenade lobbed, tanifex rolling aside, and Trace shot one who rolled out of cover. Another tried to run for the corridor and was gunned down by others. The last red dot flickered out.

"Clear!" Trace announced. "I think we're clear!" As a corbi scrambled around the benches, firing rounds into whatever tanifex were still hiding there, dead or alive.

"Clear!" he echoed. On tacnet, Trace saw blue dots still fighting, a loose perimeter around Command, but the net was closing.

"We have to go!" she yelled. "Fourth Team, you have to move out! Giddy! Giddy, where are you!" As she fast-staggered toward the medical rooms, and scenes of terrible fighting — two bullet riddled tanifex for every dead corbi, lying amidst blood and shattered glass. And here, atop a dead tanifex with a pistol in hand, a large, fallen human.

Trace rolled him over and checked pulse, but she knew he was dead, eyes wide and still, and many bloody injuries. Again she wished to cry, but she hadn't cried for thousands of slaughtered prisoners downstairs, nor for all the other brave soldiers, so she could not cry for Giddy either. She even recovered his rifle ammo, brain moving on automatic, her own blood dripping on his lifeless face as he gazed at the ceiling. 'The stone shall want for nothing. Be the stone.'

Her earpiece crackled dimly. *"Major this is Lieutenant Dale in PH-1, Phoenix Company are on descent five minutes out, please advise status."*

"The hangar is abandoned," she replied, checking her rifle, and leaving her Staff Sergeant lying on the cold, bloody floor. "Hit it with everything to clear your LZ, all defending forces are withdrawing to Splicer Command. Come in hard and firing, it's all light armour for now, but that may change by the time you arrive."

And to the staggering, shell-shocked corbi emerging from their various cover, "The most wounded in the middle, the least wounded on point and guarding the rear! Come on, let's move!" And to one she recognised — Pelgi, in passing, "Where's Tano?"

"Dead," said Pelgi. "Back at the hangars." And this time Trace did not even feel the urge to cry.

28

PH-1 rocked and rattled Dale in his armour as he watched the fuzzy tacnet display. "Styx, can you clean up tacnet some more for me?"

"I'm sorry Lieutenant, several of the bugs maintaining the pirate network have been destroyed, and the Splicer's countermeasures against infiltration have included the massive self-destruction of affected systems, and large-scale jamming."

Rather than continuing its orbit, *Phoenix* had performed a climbing burn and looped toward high geosynchronous to maintain direct line-of-sight with ground operations. Usually this was nearly impossible in a hostile system, but *Phoenix's* assault had been so devastating that this system was no longer so hostile as it had been.

"I'm not getting any reading on individual units," said Dale with frustration. "Can you clarify for me?"

"No Lieutenant, individual IDs have been casualties of the disruption. The last coms transmission from the Major was definitely her, but I cannot promise more than that. The Major's assault force has currently suffered a minimum of seventy percent fatalities, of this I am certain."

Dale had been in fights like that, but never in light armour. Most likely everyone down there would be some degree of wounded by now. The plan before departure had been to send all five *Phoenix* shuttles, with the civilian AT-7 plus PH-4 empty. The Major had had two hundred corbi in her assault team. Each of the shuttles was rated for about fifty fully armoured marines, but could cram in unarmoured humans, and especially corbi, at double that rate. But even first reports of casualties suggested they wouldn't be requiring all of that space on the way back, and Dale had made the call for Charlie Platoon to load onto PH-4 instead of sitting it out. The Major had said in her last transmission that the only opposition on the higher levels for now was lightly armoured, but he wanted as many platoons of heavies as possible, just in case.

"Insertion in three minutes," said Hausler from the cockpit as the turbulence of thick atmosphere grew worse, and the Gs of rapid deceleration in their headlong plunge began to bite. *"Splicer defensive systems appear inactive, but we are taking no chances."*

"Phoenix Company, listen up!" Dale snapped. "The insertion point at the hangars is clear of friendlies, we are free fire upon arrival! Watch your fire when we get deeper in, the Major is defending the Splicer Command with a lightly armoured force! Koshaim rounds go through walls, use more grenades and proximity rounds near lightly armoured friendlies!

"We are going to have wounded, so get ready to carry friendlies! Some may panic and fire at you upon arrival — their C-and-C is shot to hell, they might not know who we are. Take the damn shot, do not return fire, we've got the armour and we can take it. Your translators are loaded with corbi-speak — if they do not know you're friendly, use it!

"No enemy prisoners will be taken, nor mercy shown! Reeh, tanifex or other slave species are only safe when they're dead! Everyone watch your corners, keep your spacing clean and coms chatter to a minimum. We've got the Major and Staff Sergeant Kono down there. Let's get 'em back."

He changed back to the spacer channel. "Hausler, you going to fly cover for those escaping prisoners while we're in?"

"Ordnance will be expended upon direct threats only," Lieutenant

Commander Dufresne spoke before Hausler could reply. Technically Hausler was in charge, but Dufresne was flying AT-7 in the absence of anyone else who could. There had been some discussion on the subject while still aboard *Phoenix*, Dale knew, and Dufresne had been insistent. *"Our mission has exclusive priority, escaping prisoners are an externality."*

Hausler, Dale knew, was less convinced. *"You heard the LC,"* Dale heard him say. But Hausler was sometimes unpredictable. Dale hoped Dufresne could keep him focused.

* * *

"BLOW THE OTHER BRIDGES!" TRACE COMMANDED, CROUCHED BEHIND cover on the approach to the walkway bridge spanning the geofeature that separated Splicer Command from the main building. Gunfire cracked and thundered from all directions as what remained of the retreating force collapsed toward a semblance of final safety.

She waved wounded corbi past, struggling to keep her vision straight from the nausea and pain that threatened to engulf her. Fighting corbi fell back across the final bridge, as the next bridge along exploded — someone following her order with a demolition charge, only it didn't seem to have done the full job. These were villagers and spacers turned soldier, not demolition experts.

"Kaysa! Kaysa, can you hear me?" Talking on the network had become increasingly difficult — not only was the network collapsing, but the jamming was getting worse as well. Trace suspected that most Splicer systems had been shut down to keep the bugs from pirating it — all the lights were out and even emergency systems were non-functional. If she couldn't talk to Kaysa, she couldn't know if he'd completed his data-extraction or not. Well, it hardly mattered now. Splicer Command was the only place left to hide, a thick steel box built within the corridor network, even a drysine laser would have taken a long time to cut through. Now they just needed to seal off the remaining entrances until Phoenix Company arrived.

Sigo arrived, astonishingly still alive, an arm bloody but eyes fierce within his white warpaint. "They're coming?" he asked her.

"They're landing now," Trace replied. "We just need to hold for five shuda."

"There's heavy armour on the floor down," Sigo told her. "If it comes here, we don't last five shuda."

"They'll have seen Phoenix Company coming," Trace told him, barely able to hear her own voice, let alone his, past the ringing in her ears. "The heavy armour will be for them." She doubted it was true, but there was panic threatening in every eye, and the priority was to keep everyone fighting.

Sigo grabbed a passing, wounded corbi, slung the arm about his shoulder and half-carried him toward the bridge. *"Major!"* came another voice on coms. *"They're coming up the right-flank stairwell! I need reinforcements, if I fall back from here I lose the flank!"*

"Pull back!" Trace told the unidentified soldier. "We've got nearly everyone across, pull back now and..."

Gunfire erupted behind, in the geofeature, and the crashing of heavy rounds into the bridge. Trace looked, saw corbi crossing the bridge falling, torn apart by heavy impacts.

"They've got guns high in the geofeature!" Trace yelled, scrambling that way. She'd told defenders to watch and make sure it didn't happen — someone had missed it. Gunfire flashed from multiple of the tall slit windows in Command opposite, the glass smashed, firing upward at the new source of gunfire.

"It's a heavy!" someone was yelling from the bridge's far side. "It's mobile, it's got to be a heavy!"

"Keep fire on it!" Trace shouted back. From her side across the approach lobby, some corbi were running her way on threes and all-fours. Rounds pursued them, exploding furniture and shattering heavy glass about them — the right flank guys falling back. "Last defenders fall back now!" Trace shouted, as a dark, armoured figure appeared at a corner behind the running corbi. Trace fired once, and its head snapped back.

The corbi raced past, skidding the corner across the bridge, then others from the other direction, a grenade exploding behind them. Heavy gunfire rattled again from high behind, but Trace couldn't risk a glance to see if those runners had made it across. Rika had left her side to man one of those last fallback defences, and the relief of seeing him coming fast across the lobby with several others somehow struck her through the chaos. But when he stopped to grab her arm, just as she was trying to shoot at the next armoured figure to appear, she nearly threw him off.

"Major come on!" Only then did Trace realise that she was literally just a couple of soldiers away from being the last one across, just as Phoenix Company had always complained. Just as Giddy had always complained.

She turned and ran, hurdling the bodies on the walkway, and saw Sigo amongst them, torn nearly in half, arms outstretched toward the sanctuary he'd nearly reached. Fire thundered once more from above, shaking the walkway with impacts behind as Trace's damaged leg gave out and she fell past the ruined security gates at the end, rolling into cover. A look back from the ground found a final corbi running and hurdling her, his companion newly added to the bloody ruin on the bridge, metres behind where she and Rika had run.

"Styx!" she attempted hoarsely for the tenth time in recent minutes. Well beyond the limits of exhaustion and pain, she functioned only in a dream-state of sizzling adrenaline, animal terror and the stubborn determination of a lifetime's habit. "Styx, can you hear me?" No reply, as the corbi flanking her on this end of the bridge opened fire, and new return fire cracked over her head. "Lieutenant Dale, do you copy?"

Rika dragged her physically aside, powerful as most male corbi were powerful, and out of the line of fire. "Major!" shouted another corbi in her face, leaning low as she lay on the ground, unable to quite recall how she'd gotten there, or what it might be like to stand up once more. "Kaysa couldn't reach you! He says they've nearly got it! The bug's been rewriting the reeh computing memory itself to store all the data in one place, they've nearly got it!"

"Whoever's left!" Trace called. "Get to that second bridge, they can still get across it! There's only two ways into this place, we have to keep them both covered! And get those remaining demolition charges ready in case the heavy armour comes in!" Only afterward did she realise she'd spoken mostly in Lisha, no longer trusting the fading coms network to operate the translator. "And man the windows!" she added, as Rika helped her to her feet. "*Phoenix* is nearly here, just a bit longer!"

* * *

ALL FIVE *PHOENIX* SHUTTLES WERE MISSILE-LOCKED AND FIRED UPON during approach, but their counter-measures were superior to suit-launched missiles even before recent drysine upgrades. Now they automatically counter-targeted, sending volleys of missile fire into the locations where the fire had come from, followed by cannon fire, shredding multiple external accesses in seconds.

Anti-personnel missiles then shredded the walls of the upper hangar the assault forces had been using, exploding short and config-uring a spray of high-V projectiles to match the spread of targets it saw upon approach. When Dale hit the ground out of the shuttle's back, the hangar sides were more holes than wall, shredded like paper in a hailstorm, along with the remains of some heavy armour that had attempted defensive cover there.

He moved more slowly with First Squad, allowing Second and Third to press in first, Heavy Squad on the point and blasting poten-tial defensive positions without bothering to see if they fired first. A pair of ruined flyers sat burning in the middle of the hangars, other parked flyers now a jumble of wreckage by the walls. About the flyers, many dead corbi, lightly armed and armoured.

PH-1 roared away from its hover, PH-3 replacing it behind as Charlie Platoon prepared to dismount, and Dale made his way to a main exit corridor up the left flank in pursuit of Second Squad. Here were more corbi bodies, and tangled in amongst them some godawful number of dead tanifex, reeh and another two slave species he didn't recognise. The hall beyond was filled with more bodies and battle damage, the sign of a location where neither side had run away, but stood and slugged it out at close range for some time. He hadn't thought the corbi had it in them, himself. But seeing this, he knew he'd been wrong.

Ahead, Second Squad ran into contact, and rapidly moved to pin down the enemy with firepower, then flank to a neighbouring room, blast through the wall with a shaped charge, exit and kill the obstruction from behind. They moved fast, not pressing those spots where reeh defensive armour had strong position, but running hard to get around, outflanking by explosive and non-explosive means, never letting the defenders establish a firm defensive line.

In two minutes Charlie Platoon was moving up on their right, with Garudan dropping down to secure the hangar above and below, then Bravo fanning out between to guard the flanks and provide active reserve. Soon Alpha and Charlie were spreading to the upper and lower floors as well, cutting down lightly-armoured defenders without mercy and establishing a new tacnet of their own with more assassin bugs brought for the purpose.

Dale trailed behind, content with the progress made and yet to have fired his weapon, as had any in First Squad, but he was acting Company Commander now and kinetic engagement was not his priority. Tacnet remained clean, his people spoke with hard, precise words, and the enemy were now caught between their objective of liberating Splicer Command, and the irresistable force that now smashed through their rear. Upon Dale's instruction, Styx was filtering tacnet personally for any sign of the Major, and finally settled upon a single blue dot beyond the geofeature ahead. Coms somehow got a lock on it, and opened a channel.

"Major, is that you?" Dale demanded, walking so as not to close too fast upon the next engagement ahead. "Major, this is Dale, we're nearly there! Five minutes!"

In his ears, only static. Then firing, and the sound of all holy hell breaking loose. Beyond it, faint and hoarse, a familiar female voice. *"Ty. Giddy's dead. I'm hurt. We're nearly all gone. Get here quick."*

Dale's blood ran cold to hear it. So close, but they were going to lose it. He switched channels to Company-wide. "Phoenix Company, we have no time! Blast and run! Take the fucking hits, we're going to lose it, the Major's hurt bad, she's hanging on by a fingernail!"

"Fuck this shit!" he heard someone say loudly, followed by a lot of missiles, cannon and grenade fire.

"Heavies forward! Heavies forward!" Heavy Squads usually advanced behind the lead elements, lacking the mobility of regular riflemen but able to move up and lay down serious pain on any obstruction the leads ran into, or to cover a withdrawal if required. Now they pressed up to the front, prepared to risk hits for the ability to clear the way by sheer firepower.

Dale switched back. "Hang on Major, we're coming!" In reply, Dale heard only gunfire, and the sound of her yelling. In the background, agonised screams.

* * *

TRACE STUMBLED BACK DOWN THE FINAL CORRIDOR, THROUGH MED wards and secure rooms where automated systems stored samples in glass vials around the walls. She half-carried a wounded soldier whose name she'd either forgotten or had never learned, while heavy gunfire thundered behind, a large-caliber round even now smashing a glass wall, sending container samples spinning.

She fell and slid, dragging the wounded soldier after her, more corbi shooting vainly in the rearguard. One ran her way, took a heavy round through the back and half-exploded, a red mess across the hall. Another two scrambled in and joined her — one was Rika, covered in new blood but changing magazines and focused. Trace did not think the blood was his. Through shattered glass, she saw another corbi run around a corner straight at the attackers, followed by a massive explosion that rocked the walls. That had been a demolition charge he'd been carrying.

She heard yelling from behind, and turned — crouched low against the opposite doorway was Kaysa, shouting at her. Her damaged ears could barely make out the words — something about 'done it' and 'no further'. He'd finished the download, Trace suspected, and there was no further to fall back — the computers cores were just behind. Or something like that. It hardly mattered, she knew all that anyway.

Rika was pulling the wounded soldier away from her. Trace looked at him, questioningly, and found that the soldier's eyes were sightless, body limp. She let him go. Rika showed her his last possession — a demolition charge, two big sticks of the stuff, wrapped in tape, and a timer. The same stuff Pena had tried to use to stop this mission from happening. Maybe you were right, Pen. Maybe you were.

She looked at Rika. His young face was crazed with that combat wildness she'd seen many times before. When things got this bad, sanity was your enemy. A sane person would run, or shoot herself in the head, anything to make it stop. To keep it going, to sustain the pain and panic, most had to cultivate an intentional insanity. A battle madness, where sensible thought and reason no longer applied.

Trace grabbed the back of his neck with her good hand. "Plant it!" she yelled in his ear above the racket. "No suicide! I need every rifle! Plant it in the corridor!" She pointed up where they'd come.

Rika nodded, then hugged her like the sister he was never going to see again, grabbed his charge and his rifle and ran toward the enemy. Trace nearly stopped him, but rolled across the corridor entrance instead to get position on the far side, so she could get the rifle to her left shoulder and use the good hand to pull the trigger, the bad one having ceased proper function long ago.

Rounds tore by, shooting continuing further up, then large explosions as Rika ducked into an alcove on the left, just short of the med ward ahead. She could see him from her position, scrambling to get the charge set behind a corner where an approaching heavy suit wouldn't see it.

In the room beyond, one appeared. Big, but not nearly as large as a UF marines suit — spindly but powerful, almost insectoid, bristling with weapon pods. Trace had removed the underside grenade launcher from her rifle minutes ago, having no more grenades to fire and preferring the ease of aiming without it. Her last throwing grenade was gone too. She looked to the remaining soldier in the room, but he was huddled in a ball, past his limit and sobbing. Trace couldn't blame him.

The big suit stalked across the room, and Trace ducked back — one missile in here and she was dead, but the heavies had been reluctant to use their big weapons the closer they got to their goal. She could see the shadow of him in a reflection in cracked glass across the room, barely metres from where Rika crouched, unseen by his legs. But the reeh didn't seem to trust that the approach was empty, and paused there, waiting for support.

Trace saw Rika move, a small motion in the reflection. The reeh saw, and looked. Trace swivelled out, braced and put two rounds in the armoured faceplate. The heavy looked back and raised a weapon. Rika darted past the reeh's legs, into the room behind. Then the world blew up, taking corridor, glass, heavy suit and everything with it. Trace ducked back in time to miss most of it, but the blast broke nearly everything in the room, as she curled into a ball and felt it raining on her armour.

Then she got up, half-blind and mostly-deaf, and stumbled up the corridor toward where Rika had been. She knew it was stupid, she wasn't thinking, couldn't think, had to stay and defend the only thing that mattered, the thing that all this had been for, for the sake of humanity and everything beyond. But Rika.

She could barely breathe in the smoke, and found the reeh armour lying flat amidst what had once been a corridor, now a shredded skeleton of structural supports and flayed panels. Its face plate was half-off, a pointed, insect-like thing, or like the snout of a dog. Trace put her boot on it, exposing a gap where the neck ring had come loose in the blast. Put her rifle into it and fired repeatedly, blasting dark blood and gore about the helmet as the suit jerked, and lay still.

Beyond the room, more heavy armour ran. One saw her, and raised its weapons pod. And slammed sideways into a wall, rebounded in a spin that she saw in dazed slow-motion. The one behind it turned to face a new threat, and near-somersaulted at a new impact to the upper chest. There was only one armoured infantry weapon Trace knew of that could impart such kinetic impact at any range.

Upon the floor, amid the spray of metal, torn walls and furnishings, was Rika. Face down, having skidded from the blast, and possibly bounced off the far wall. Trace staggered to him with the very last of her strength, and rolled him over. There was blood, but that wasn't the worst bit, in big blasts. Shockwaves didn't always leave a physical trace. His right arm was a mess, and the helmet had been torn from his head. Trace put fingers to his neck, trying to find a pulse.

"Come on kid. Stay with me. Come on Rika." The fingers on her right hand could feel almost nothing. The arm looked bad, so she went for her last field bandage, pulling it out with fumbly fingers.

Big armour suits ran into the room, shaking the ground, and then an amplified voice exclaimed, *"Major! It's the Major, she's alive!"*

"Kaysa's got the data, he's down that way!" She half pointed with an elbow, trying to get the bandage unwrapped.

"Major? Major, I can't understand you, you're not speaking English."

Fuck it, Trace thought, wrapping Rika's bloody arm as best she could. "I need a medic, he'll have internal injuries!" She'd evidently said that in English, because commotion was happening, more armour running past, headed for the computer rooms, guarding the doorways. Shooting, not far away, that familiar thudding recoil of a Koshaim 20s that one didn't need ears to hear, but rather felt in the bones. "Come on Rika. Come on kid."

A new suit thudded knees-down alongside, armoured fingers reaching for Rika's neck. *"Major,"* came Private Teale's voice on speakers, *"I've got a pulse, I can give him a booster, that's medically cleared for corbi, should keep him from crashing."*

"He's got internal bleeding, dammit!" said Trace. She'd seen it happen too many times near big explosions — they shattered organs and soldiers bled out internally. "We've got to get him back to *Phoenix*... hey, hey!" Because everyone was running around without listening to her. "We leave no one behind, you hear? No one!"

"Come on Major," someone else said. *"Let's get you up."* She tried to stand, awkwardly, and nearly fell but an armoured fist grabbed her arm, then under the armpit, lifting her. *"Oh shit."* As that marine got the first good look at her, and saw what a mess she was. *"Major, Major you're gonna be fine, we have to get you back to Phoenix... Sarge? Sarge, we'll have to carry her."*

"I don't need to be fucking carried... I'm fine, worry about him!" As someone scooped Rika up, somehow gentle, that small, long-armed body in powerful armoured limbs, head lolling, thick mane of hair spilling free.

Then Trace's legs were taken from under her, and she was being carried whether she liked it or not. Down ruined corridors, choking with smoke, past the bodies of dead friends, the last of her command. "Rika!" He was being carried up ahead of her. She tried reloading her rifle, and somehow managed it, even one-handed in the arms of a big, steel gorilla. "Rika, stay with me kid! Stay with me!"

* * *

"THEY'RE ON THEIR WAY!" OPERATIONS SAID.

Erik could see it on Scan, all five *Phoenix* shuttles commencing their ascent, AT-7 central while the others fanned wide in protection.

"We're moving," said Erik, and kicked them into a 5-G burn to bring them down from geostationary. "Nav, get me the interception point."

"Aye Captain," said Kaspowitz, "coming up now." It appeared on his main display, hovering in mid-space before him — a spot above the atmosphere where AT-7's present climb would bring it to rendezvous.

"Arms, target the Splicer," said Erik, straining comfortably against the familiar Gs. "What's your recommendation?"

"Captain," said Corrig, "I recommend DU-80s, they'll split it through the middle and cause minimal collateral damage." The other option was nukes, they all knew. High-V projectiles were out of the question, as they were far too low now for even *Phoenix*'s drysine jump engines to operate, and had no room to manoeuvre even if they did. Low-V projectiles would probably hit their target now that the Splicer's defences were largely inoperable, but there was a chance smaller impact rounds could be shot down on the way in, enough at least to save the Splicer from complete destruction.

"A nuke would make sure of it, Lieutenant," said Erik.

"Captain, our smallest nuke will kill every corbi in a five K radius. The Major promised them she'd help get the prisoners out."

"Most of those prisoners are dead," said Sasalaka. They'd seen the reports from the shuttles. Missiles and some strafing runs had helped clear the way, but there'd been very few corbi running from the Splicer's lower levels. "A nuke would make sure this facility is never used against the rest of the population again."

"DU-80s's will do the job just as well, Captain," said Corrig. The window for taking the shot was approaching fast, as *Phoenix* acceler- ated away from their preferred orbit, arcing down and now levelling out from its direct plunge toward the planet. "The Major promised."

"Very well Lieutenant," said Erik. "Double the rounds just to make sure. Intercept in two minutes fourteen. Scan, watch the ground for missile launches, we don't want to get taken by surprise."

A minute short of intercept, Corrig fired eight of *Phoenix*'s twenty- four DU-80 warheads, aiming toward a narrow reentry, followed by a vertical descent and an impact at slightly more than mach six. The velocity was tiny compared to the previous strikes, and the energy far smaller than any nuke, but DU-80s held large explosive yields, each enough to destroy a city block. If they all made their target, it would be more than enough. Any corbi who had made it out would need to be a distance away, however, or in a very thick bunker somewhere in Splicer City... and even that might not save them. But he had a five- ship interception to line up, and couldn't think on that right now.

Rendezvous was fast and smooth, one shuttle after another finding its place at *Phoenix* Midships and locking secure. In the midst of it, Jiri confirmed that the Splicer had been hit and completely

destroyed. The cloud of smoke and debris was so large that no calculation of collateral damage was possible. When the last shuttle was
attached, Erik powered *Phoenix* into an orbit-busting burn and
headed toward Kaspowitz's exit course in the direction of croma
space.

"Captain?" said Jiri from Scan Two as they powered away at a
steady 5-G acceleration, Erik keeping it light to save the wounded on
the shuttles undue stress. "Captain, I'm reading explosions from the
planetary surface. Several hundred kilometres from the Splicer."

"Something we hit?" Corrig wondered. "Secondary explosions?"

"No, these are unrelated regions. I think it's the reeh, Captain. It
looks like they're bombarding corbi villages from the air."

On the bridge, no one spoke. The silence continued, save for low,
running chatter between Geish and Kaspowitz, using Scan to plot
possible ambush locations for silent reeh ships based on observed
defensive patterns. The bridge shuddered under thrust, panels and
restraints vibrating as they shook.

"More explosions," said Jiri. "That one's quite large. That would
take out a whole village at least."

"We knew they'd do it," Erik said finally. "The Major knew they'd
do it. We had no choice. They'll have reinforcements jumping in
shortly, and we can't stay to kill them all, as much as we'd like to."

"We've helped far more people here than we've hurt," Sasalaka
said with more certainty than Erik felt. "On behalf of all tavalai
people, Captain, I thank you for your assistance to their cause."

"We're all in this together, Sasa," Erik said tiredly. "All of us."

Just not the poor bloody corbi, the thought came unbidden to
mind. In *Phoenix's* rear scan, Rando slowly shrank in view. A beautiful
world of blue and green, streaked with white, swirling cloud. The
home of even more pain today than before.

29

Phoenix came out of jump at Cherchi System, one combat jump from the nearest croma space. Following V-dump there was commotion, spacers entering the bridge to ensure all crew had their energy foods and electrolyte drinks, while down in Midships, the mad scramble began of getting wounded from the shuttles and up to Medbay.

Erik announced crew cylinder shutdown to facilitate it, followed by a twenty second alarm klaxon before everything went weightless. Spacers carried on as before, mostly secured if they did not need to be moving, as no reeh pursuit could possibly follow them in less than an hour or two. With the cylinder stationary, the outer-rim access became operational, allowing people to move between Midships and the cylinder without needing to fight their way through the narrow core transit, through the spine of the ship. It saved several minutes, more with badly wounded on gurneys down the cylinder stairwells, and was standard procedure with wounded marines coming back aboard lest those minutes' delay cost a life.

Erik waited until the all-clear was given, that all wounded had been transferred successfully, then gave the klaxon warning before restarting the cylinder once more. Gravity restored, he listened to

bridge crew reviewing the past operation, and expressing great satisfaction at the number of reeh ships destroyed for not even a single hit
taken, and that the mission, apparently, had been successful.

Erik was in no mood for celebrations. He wanted to know exactly
what they'd recovered, first. And he'd heard the initial reports that
Staff Sergeant Kono was dead, and Trace was hurt, and that most of
her assault team were dead, save for twenty-one corbi who'd been
recovered, all wounded. Twenty-one, out of two hundred. Phoenix
Company once again had no deaths, but seven wounded, four of
them serious. Reeh were supposed to be far better fighters than that,
but Erik gathered they'd all been facing the wrong way when
Phoenix Company had hit them from behind, and none of their
accustomed network infrastructure, where their Command and
Control was centred, had been operational.

Second-shift took over when Dufresne had had time for a fast
shower and freshen up, as Erik had told her there was no rush. He
met her on the bridge as he rose, shook her hand and performed a
stiff salute, that Dufresne returned.

"Outstanding, Lieutenant Commander," he said, and meant it.
Dufresne's pale face even managed to look somewhat pleased before
she took her seat from Sasalaka, who helped buckle her in. One
intense combat mission down, a hard ascent up to *Phoenix*, a combat
jump from the system, and now Dufresne's reward was a full shift on
the bridge, still under combat conditions. Usually there was no
saluting on the bridge, but if anyone could break that rule, the
Captain could, and Dufresne had earned it.

Erik went straight down to Medbay, and found the outside
hallway filled with tired, sweaty marines. *"Captain,"* came Dufresne's
voice from the bridge even now. *"Jonri and Poga just came out of jump
behind us, they're both indicating no damage, no casualties."*

"Thank you LC," said Erik, nodding to the marines, and shaking
their hands as he went. "Good job, people. You got her back. Good
job." As he passed down the line. Of course, they may also have saved
the human race... but that was a huge, abstract thing that was several
orders of action away from amounting to anything. Saving the Major,

that was immediate, and now. He could see the pride in their eyes, the relief, and the concern, that she had been taken directly to Medbay. Reports on coms were that she'd been looking a mess, but was otherwise okay. He hoped.

He made the Medbay door, edging past marines, and found the space between hospital bunks occupied by more marines. At the far end, where the partition began to intensive care, a Corpsman hovered by a woman in torn, black-stained and non-regulation fatigues, who clung to the doorway and berated someone within.

"His blood's corbi type seven-plus Doc!" she was shouting. "Don't trust the damn medical computer, Resistance said they didn't give humans complete figures! The... the optimum blood pressure's wrong and the body temperature is too, it's about two degrees higher, I think..."

That was Doc Suelo she was shouting at, Erik guessed. He edged past more marines and approached. "Major?"

She looked over her shoulder at him. Her face was awful, caked with dried blood, her eyes had been cleaned out but the rest she'd not bothered with, nor allowed anyone else to touch. Several cuts had been gel plastered, making it difficult to guess how deep they were. Her right arm was completely bound in a bloody wrap, and her pants legs had been torn open to access other wounds within. The black stains were blood, Erik realised, mostly her own.

"Major," said Corpsman Rashni, attempting a stern voice, "you really have to sit down."

"You can't operate on someone you don't understand the physiology of," Trace muttered, almost to herself. "Doc! Doc, ask Styx to double check the damn medical records... Styx? Styx, are you there?"

"Major," Erik interjected, putting a firm hand on her shoulder. "Major, you have to let the Doctor work." It was alarming, to see her like this. Like her mind was gone, like events had finally shattered her sanity. "Major?"

She looked at him finally. Stared, as though seeing him for the first time. He'd spent the past months hoping for this moment. Wanting to see her happy to be home, and happy to see him and everyone else again. But the eyes were hard, unreachable. Almost vacant, as though she saw straight through him.

"The reeh were hitting villages, weren't they." It was a statement as much as a question.

Erik nodded. "Scan saw them do it. Large explosions, they wouldn't have left survivors."

"How many?" Her voice was hoarse, and it was difficult to tell if that was emotion, or strained exhaustion.

"We couldn't see. Depends when they stop. If they stop." There was no dressing things up for Trace. She scorned people who dodged hard truths, about the consequences of their own actions in particular. "Shilu broadcasted on as many radio frequencies and channels as village corbi might have the technology to listen to, we told them to leave their settlements and hide in the jungle, and to pass the message on to others. But we've no idea how many of them will receive the warning in time. If the bombardment lasts another day, could be a hundred thousand dead. If it lasts a week or more, could be millions."

Trace's blood-stained jaw may have trembled. All of her marines were watching. The Medbay behind her was silent. Erik did not fear that she'd break down before them. She couldn't. She didn't know how, and for that he almost pitied her. He wanted to hug her, but before her marines, that was unthinkable. Even were they alone, there was nothing in her eyes that invited him to do so. But the moment demanded something more. Something to describe this impossible thing that she'd done, and somehow survived, in spite of all the odds against her. Something that described the long, hard human tragedy of Fleet's many wars, and the stubborn, relentless people who'd fought them.

Erik drew himself up, and saluted, hard. Behind him, he heard the synchronised shuffle of dozens more, doing the same. Trace stared at them all, the Medbay full of saluting marines and Corpsmen. Her eyes held only pain.

* * *

JINDI HELD AN ARM OVER HIS FACE, COUGHING IN THE DUST-FILLED AIR. Up the concrete stairs, a heavy armour suit pulled bits of fractured concrete out from under the huge slab of steel that had fallen on it, trying to hollow out a gap. Several other suits assisted, their built-in lights glaring on broken debris and billowing dust.

In the suits were tanifex — the same ones who had opened fire on the reeh to help Jindi and the others to escape the hangar. Those had followed them out, joined by others at the bottom, and engaged in more firefights against guards on the ground, manning the entry gates that separated the Splicer from the corbi city outside. The main gates and security barriers had already been destroyed by missiles from *Phoenix*'s shuttles. And then, as the trickle of surviving prisoners and their armoured tanifex escort had entered Splicer City, Jindi had seen *Phoenix*'s shuttles shrieking away once more, climbing into the sky.

Beneath a warehouse sector near the food markets were a number of deep concrete cellars, filled with food. Jindi suspected the slave species that mostly ran the Splicer were buying from it, given the quality of the concrete, and the amount of food stored down there. Already the basements were filling with corbi, and Jindi's group had joined them, telling any who cared to hear that the Splicer was about to be destroyed. They'd waited, huddled together in the dark amid boxes and crates, and cold-storage units that hummed with rare technological prowess for Splicer City. And some time later, there had followed the most awful, shaking roar, as the ground itself began to shudder so violently, it might have been the end of the world. Things had crashed on top of the cellar, with impossible force, then silence.

Now, finally, an armoured tanifex used his suit's powered might to clear a hole in the upper wall beside the stairs, and crawled into it. Another followed, then another. Soon, corbi were following. Finally it was Jindi's turn, but the girl who'd supported him, still wearing his helmet, insisted she go first, more from protectiveness than desperation to get out. The hole in the concrete wall opened to a wide gap, compressed beneath a huge, heavy sheet of steel. Jindi eventually crawled from under it, and emerged blinking into the sun.

About him was the ruin of Splicer City. A few buildings still stood, miraculous amid the carnage. Most had been flattened by falling steel debris larger than the buildings were. Huge structural beams speared into the ground, hundreds of metres tall, while others made odd geometric shapes, towering into the sky. The air was thick with dust and smoke, clearing now in the brisk southerly breeze. And when enough of a gap emerged for Jindi to see the mountain where the huge, gleaming Splicer had stood, he saw nothing — just a barren, rocky hillside, from which horizontal structural supports protruded, now snapped short.

Other corbi emerged, some recently familiar, others not, all with manes matted in dust, and many injured. They blinked around in bewilderment, well past fear at this point, and searched for the sight of something familiar. They found Jindi, to his astonishment, and came to him, and the girl with the incision marks at the base of her skull, whose name he still did not know.

The tanifex came to him too, seeing that the others had done so, and loomed above him in their armoured suits. *"We can't stay here,"* said one, and Jindi suspected the voice was translated through the external speakers. *"The reeh punish all transgressions. The punishment for this will be vast."*

"*Phoenix* said they were going to destroy many reeh bases when they came," said Jindi hoarsely, indicating the vacant hillside where the Splicer had stood. "They can't hit us from the air immediately, many of their bases are gone."

"Phoenix's approach only covered one slice of the planet," the tanifex disagreed. *"Many bases will have survived. They will make coming here a priority. But you're right, we have time. We should use it."*

"Where?" asked one of the others, holding an injured friend, an arm around her shoulders. "Where can we go when the villages are all destroyed?"

"We should go east," said Jindi, with certainty. "There are more mountains, but it's the shortest distance to the coast. And the mountains are good shelter from reeh aircraft. It rains there, it's cloudy."

"And what's on the coast?" asked another. "Why not stay in the mountains?"

"Because the farming is horrible in the mountains. The soil is bad, and there's not enough sun. On the coast, there's the beach. I've heard those beaches are good. On a beach, there's aways enough to eat."

"I don't know how to fish," the girl admitted. It was the first time Jindi had heard her speak. "And I can't swim."

"That's okay," said Jindi, and put a tired, shaking arm about her shoulders. "I'll teach you. All of you." Something caught his eye amidst the dust — a small insect, buzzing before his eyes. Sunlight broke through the dust and smoke, glinting on its metallic body and intricate wings. "And I think we might have some help from someone who knows the way."

* * *

"*Captain,*" came Styx's voice on coms, as Erik emerged from the tiny shower in his quarters. He was exhausted, and wanted nothing more than to climb onto his bunk, pull the safety net across and go to sleep. God knew how Trace and the surviving corbi felt.

"Yes Styx?"

"*Am I correct in surmising that there is concern for the Major's mental health?*"

Erik pulled on a new jumpsuit, and slid his AR glasses into the bunkside pouch. "There are advanced treatments for post traumatic stress. We all get them. She'll be fine."

"*The literature suggests that these treatments are not absolutely effective.*"

"No," Erik admitted, squeezing his face in his hands, sitting on the bunk. "No, not always."

"*Human psychology remains an imprecise science. My analysis of that literature concludes that the current state of imprecision is woefully inade-*

quate." She sounded vaguely offended by it, Erik thought. As though wondering why humans tolerated such a thing.

"The human brain is a very complicated thing, Styx. Even today no one entirely understands how organic consciousness works. Some things, we just don't know how to do."

"Drysine science made significant progress during the Parren Alliance. I have not lately possessed the spare processing capability to devote time to that data. Perhaps I will accomplish something."

Erik smiled wearily. "If you wish to devote your big brain to figuring out human psychology, be my guest. I think you'll find that the problem is not a lack of processing power, but the difficulty of studying the subject effectively. Human brains only work in human skulls. It makes them hard to study. Differently located, they no longer function." He wondered if Styx would understand his irony.

"Please refrain from mentioning my interest to Lieutenant Kaspowitz," said Styx. *"It may do him a mental injury."*

Erik nearly laughed. She understood alright, imagining Kaspo's conclusions that she'd start searching for living brains to probe. It did, however, raise some alarming questions about how that drysine knowledge had been accumulated during the Parren Alliance. Parren did nasty things to internal enemies, and it did not seem to Erik impossible that they'd have found political prisoners to provide for drysine experiments.

"Captain, you asked me to inform you when I had finished my analysis of the data acquired from the Central Intelligence headquarters with assistance from Rhi'shul." Erik had. He'd told her to wait, and not give him a running commentary of first impressions. He had Jokono and Romki looking over it also, for a human perspective, but Styx, of course, was much faster. He'd been far too busy and preoccupied, the last few days, to think of anything but the assault mission to Rando.

"Have you reached any conclusions, Styx?"

"Yes Captain. The images that Rhi'shul showed you in the Dan'gede Headquarters appear genuine, as I have found more. They all seem to be alo, in their native habitat, possibly their homeworld. Of course, with digital data it is impossible to discern a time, but analysis of various

recording technologies, and some peripheral clues as to who was doing the recording, leads me to conclude that the footage was taken by one of the Reeh Empire's many slave species."

"Is there much more footage?"

"Some, but not a lot. I can show you some of the most significant. It is illuminating."

"Please do."

Erik turned to the wall screen above the room's small table, as an image appeared. It showed a sterile room, perhaps a medical lab. The recording camera was evidently small, perhaps concealed, as the image jostled and bounced. In a surgical gown, a mask across its sensitive nose and mouth, was an alo. It was working with lab equipment. Another appeared, then several more, similarly tasked. Then, stalking across the scene, a reeh, black-eyed with its elongated skull, glaring down on them.

Erik nodded slowly. It felt wrong to be so fascinated when there was so much else at stake, and so many emotional perils to consider. But here was the answer to one enormous question at least — a question that had tantalised the Spiral for three thousand years.

"So we know where the alo came from," said Erik. "They were a reeh slave species. Like the tanifex."

"And the tanifex are rebelling," Styx added. *"In parts of the Empire, at least."*

"Pity none of those tanifex rebels made it to the top levels," Erik mused. "Would have been interesting to talk to if we'd evacuated a few. The Major says she didn't think they could make it up that far with the elevators not working."

"It may have illuminated things," Styx agreed. *"The data from Central Intelligence has more detail, but very little beyond this basic conclusion. If nothing else, it explains why the alo are bio-mechanoid, and why their bio-weaponry technology is so advanced."*

"The Major also said that your bugs recognised the reeh's computer technology as being of ceephay origin?"

"Yes Captain. I had suspected something similar from our first encounter at the Zondi Splicer, but without direct access to a submissive

reeh network, I could not be certain. I reprogrammed the bug accompanying the Major by remote before she was captured, anticipating that it may grant us direct access to advanced reeh systems. And so it proved to be."

"And there's no doubt about that? You're certain it's ceephay?"

"Yes Captain. To an AI, the lineage appears quite distinctive. Bear in mind that all the wars during what you call the Machine Age were caused essentially by differences of opinion over optimal AI design. We were arguing over the future of our species. Each design philosophy was radically different, and entirely unique. I can see that reeh technology is ceephay-derived in the same way that you can tell some humans' old Earth racial origins simply by looking at them."

"With most humans these days, that's quite difficult," Erik cautioned.

"Because of many generations of cross-racial combinations, yes. This does not happen with AIs. And the fact that the technology remains so obviously ceephay, approximately forty thousand years after the ceephays ceased to exist, indicates that the reeh might not be particularly advanced in computer technology at all. They appear to have failed to advance the basic model, but merely copied it, and shaped it to their requirements. To my mind, many of these requirements appear superfluous, designed to meet inefficient biological requirements. Reeh technology may thus be somewhat less than the original ceephay capability."

Erik thought Styx seemed quite happy at the prospect. Her first experience with reeh technology at the Zondi Splicer had not pleased her.

"So," Erik said carefully. "It seems that a ceephay AI, possibly a queen, escaped in this direction, and was captured by the reeh."

"This would fit the known history," Styx agreed. *"Ceephay history is long and complicated, but the short version is that they were destroyed in the three-way war against the deltos and the torcines, and thought to have been annihilated."*

"Like the deepynines."

"Yes Captain."

"And possibly, like the deepynines, were captured by the reeh?" That bit still didn't make sense. "So how do the alo, who were just a slave species of the reeh, end up allied to the deepynines? Because if that footage is correct, the alo aren't much at all. Just some back-water species the reeh enslaved for labour."

"We do not yet know, Captain. But I am quite certain there is a way to find out. It is this matter on which I most wished to speak with you."

So, thought Erik. With Styx, one had to expect these small manip-ulations. Small questions building up to big ones, as she guided these weak-minded humans toward her intended conclusion. But Erik had also known humans like that. "Go ahead."

"Captain, close analysis of reeh coding language convinces me that there have been an ongoing series of modifications made to the technology. These ongoing modifications appear like the sedimentary layers of rock in a planetary canyon. One can discern thousands of years of history by their study."

Erik frowned. "Ongoing modifications? But you said the reeh aren't really that smart with this technology? That they don't really understand it?"

"Yes Captain." Very, very patiently. Like an adult with a small child, waiting for him to conclude the obvious.

"Then you're saying that..." he blinked. "There's an AI still alive? Modifying the code herself?"

"A very specific AI, Captain. A ceephay queen. She will be very old now, far older than myself. She will have been held as a reeh prisoner for all this time. And being plugged into the center of the Reeh Empire, and running all of their code and computing systems, she will know nearly everything there is to know about the Empire itself. And the reeh." Erik thought it was just as well he was already sitting down. He stared at the wall of his quar-ters, trying to process that. After a moment, Styx grew impatient with glacial human processing times. *"Captain?"*

"Do you think the croma know?" Erik asked.

"Impossible to say for sure, Captain. But there was no mention of it in all the data liberated from Croma'Rai Central Intelligence. I would say the odds are greatly against it. And having no such technological literacy them-selves, they could not read and recognise such things in reeh code as I can."

"I think they'd like to know," Erik murmured. "Damn. If they could get their hands on her, they could find a way to wipe out the reeh."

"I think that unlikely, Captain. Most of the weaknesses that they might discover, croma civilisation is not sufficiently advanced to exploit."

Erik stared at the wall screen, instinctively knowing that Styx would be viewing through the camera there. "With drysine help they could."

"It is conceivable, Captain. But there would be benefits far more significant to humans and drysines. I think we are all agreed that a deepynine queen escaped the final destruction of her race, and came this way to be captured by the reeh. Somehow she escaped, perhaps with alo assistance.
"In my opinion, Captain, our greatest strategic advantage possible against the deepynines rests in knowledge of this queen. Drysine civilisation was decentralised. We had many queens, and many leaders. We made our way by competitive collaboration. Deepynines did not. They were centralised. Their entire civilisational model relied upon it. A single queen, ruling all. Many subordinate queens, but all utterly submissive to the dominant.

"In the deepynines we have captured, what remains intact of their coding strongly indicates to me that this centralised structure remains in place today. The deepynines who joined with the alo are ruled by a single queen. I believe that queen will be the same who was captured by the reeh, twenty five thousand years ago."

"And this ceephay queen will have a record of all of it!" Erik breathed, as his slow human brain finally managed to get ahead of where Styx was leading it.

"Yes Captain. She was there when it happened. She will have extensive memories. I believe I can liberate those memories. I believe that we can learn so much about this deepynine enemy we face, that human commanders could predict her movements before she makes them."

"Is that technologically possible?"

"Yes Captain. I could build the base model of such a mind, in simulation, that would make it possible. We performed similar manoeuvres against deepynine commanders in the Drysine/Deepynine War to defeat them comprehensively. The strategic edge given to human forces would be incalculable."

"Wait, wait a minute. You're suggesting we go into the heart of reeh space, where this ceephay queen will be kept imprisoned in what will obviously be the most heavily defended location in the Reeh Empire, and rescue her?"

"Yes Captain. It will be treacherous, but I believe that Phoenix now has the capabilities to achieve this objective. And I calculate that the strategic benefits, to both our peoples, far outweigh the possible losses if we fail."

"Unless *you* fall into their hands, Styx. That would make things entirely worse."

"I can assure you Captain, the reeh will never take me alive or intact. This ship's organic crew are not the only ones prepared to die for the future of their people."

THE DEPTH AND CALM OF TRACE'S MEDITATION WOULD HAVE SURPRISED her, had the meditative state allowed her to feel anything like surprise. Her body was a mess, pumped full of drugs and inflammation as it struggled to heal itself. Her surroundings did not feel right, simultaneously familiar and alien. She'd lived most of her adult life on this ship, and knew its every small sound and vibration as intimately as an athlete knew her own body. And yet, after just four months on Rando, she missed the wind whispering in the trees, and the dual shadows cast by Feina and Dogba in their passage above the clouds.

In her meditation, she saw the bright, single moon of Rani, Sugauli's only moon. Saw it glowing through the small window of her room in her parents' house, casting silver light upon grey mountains. She'd loved to be beneath it, even then. Had loved those Kulina night hikes, the cold air that blew from the void between valley walls. Climbing at night, Rani had lit the way. 'Queen', it meant, in Nepali and Hindi. Locals knew it as such. 'Always bright, always right', they said.

And yet, most of her adult life she'd chosen to spend locked in a steel box, breathing synthetic air and eating processed food. *Phoenix* had been her home for so long, but now, nothing about it felt right. Perhaps this was why she meditated so well. Perhaps, in her own mind, she could make a better place. Anywhere but here.

"Major?" The word came with a heavy Lisha accent. Trace's eyes flicked open, and the pain came flooding back. Tejo was by her bunk, leaning on his crutches. Just a kid, younger even than Rika. She recalled him sobbing in that final room, curled in a ball, well past the limit of sanity and crying for the horror that had become his life. She could have used his extra rifle, then, but she felt no contempt or judgement. She'd been astonished so many of them had lasted as long and well as they had, physically and mentally. "Major, he's awake."

Trace smiled at Tejo, and put a hand on his shoulder. She pulled the tube from her arm, and lifted herself from the pillows. She'd been meditating with the bunk's backrest raised, unable to even sit upright, let alone cross her legs. For Kulina, meditation was not so simple a thing as posture. Any position, any place, any time would do.

Getting to the edge of the bed was an effort. Tejo stood ready to help her, and at another time, she might have waved him away. Now she accepted his unhelpful assistance, to fetch her crutches, only one of which she could properly lean on with her right hand barely functional... but the cast itself took weight well, if she positioned it properly.

With the adrenaline gone, and constant motion ceased, her body had shut down to healing mode. Everything hurt. There were micros in her ears, apparently, helping to fix her hearing — the left drum had been perforated, the right one merely damaged. A shrapnel cut on her right cheek had gone straight through, damaging a tooth, and that wetness in her mouth she recalled from the fight had been her own blood. Congealed sealant made her face feel like a latex mask. The gash down her forehead had been brutal too, chipping the bone.

Her forearm had been fractured, as she'd suspected, and ligaments damaged, the whole thing encased in a bio-environment cast now that fed endless nutrients to the micros restructuring it all. It itched and throbbed like hell. Two of her ribs were fractured from the shots she'd taken to her armour. Her right leg was mostly unusable from the shrapnel that had ripped her quad, and her left calf had taken a smaller one. And the ankle-stinger that she'd written off as minor had damn-near severed a tendon — somehow her augments in adrenaline-overload had dulled the pain to keep her moving, though she'd damaged it further by running on it, a Corpsman had informed her. As though not running on it would have been preferable, despite not running on it meaning not fighting, and not fighting would have killed everyone.

Corpsman Rhode intercepted her halfway across the Medbay floor between rows of occupied bunks. "Dammit Major, no!" he said loudly. "You're in no condition to be moving around, now get back in your damn bunk or I'll put you there!"

"If you try that," Trace told him quietly, "there'll be a fight. I'm pretty sure I'll still win."

"Major, I'm warning you! I will call security!" He looked genuinely angry and upset. Trace far outranked any Corpsman, but it was Fleet tradition that Corpsmen would yell at Admirals if they disobeyed medical advice in their own Medbay.

Trace found she couldn't be angry. Rhode was just trying to do his job, like everyone on the ship. And this professionalism came with compassion, and concern for her welfare. She smiled at him. "Security?" she asked. "You mean marines?"

Rhode looked exasperated as he got her meaning. "Major, get back in your bunk. I mean it!"

"Five minutes," she promised him. "It's only limbs and ribs, kid. The bits that matter are all fine."

"Major, you've been injected full of processing and repair drugs, micro-assistants and god knows what else. Do you know what they do to your mental state, not to mention your balance?"

"Why don't you tell me on the way?"

He told her, hovering close to her elbow as she swung herself slowly past bunks to the sealed, intensive-care section of Medbay. The door slid to admit her, her eyes adjusting to the dim light. Within were several bays filled with 'cocoons', as the crew called them. The proper name was CMEs — Comprehensive Medical Environments. Within the transparent outer shells, swathed in micro-containment environments and tubes, were four of the surviving corbi from her teams, alive now only thanks to that technology.

Trace took a moment to check the displays. All looked as though they'd make it, though barely. Another two hadn't.

In the open bunks past the cocoons were mixed corbi and marines — three humans and one tavalai. All were asleep, save one. In the bunk to Trace's right, lay Rika. Viko sat with him, talking in a low voice. Rika looked at her. Viko made way for Trace, limping on his cast-encased leg, and Trace sat. Clasped the corbi's long-fingered hand.

"Hey," she murmured. "How you feeling, kid?"

"Major," he murmured, eyes half-closed. He'd had a tube in his mouth for the past two days, feeding him. And a mask, helping him breathe, while *Phoenix*'s micro-surgery cradle attempted to sew the last internal bleeding, and coax damaged liver, diaphragm, and punctured lung back to health. For a while there, it had been touch and go. "Did I do okay?"

Trace's eyes filled with tears. "You were magnificent," she told him. "You all were." She put her good hand in his thick mane. "Phoenix marines couldn't have done better." Technically, it was a lie. But 'technically' wasn't the thing that mattered now.

"How many..." he tried, and it caught in his throat. He tried for the water tube, and Trace held it for him as he sipped. "How many of us?" he tried again.

"Nineteen still alive," she said quietly. "Including you. Twenty including me."

"Giddy?"

"No."

"Pena?" he murmured sleepily. "Is Pen okay?"

For one of the rare times in twelve years of service, Trace nearly lost control of her emotions completely. For a long moment, she could say nothing. Finally she managed, "No Rika. Pena's gone."

Rika raised a slow hand toward her. Touched her sealant-smooth face with a finger. "It wasn't your fault, Major. Wasn't your fault."

But Trace had learned to despise the dodging of responsibility above most other sins. She knew that it was.

"We're in a system near croma space, Rik," she told him. "We can't go back because the new rulers kicked us out. But that's just publicly — in private, we're working with them on the next step. The new rulers are Croma'Dokran. They beat Croma'Rai for the leadership. And they say they're going to rescue the corbi, no matter what it takes."

Rika just gazed at her. Entirely unable to process what that meant.

"Croma'Dokran have a corbi advisor called Tiga," Trace continued. "She came with us to Dul'rho. She's organising more corbi advisors, to help the croma figure out how to save the corbi. Some of the corbi on *Phoenix* are going to join with those advisors. Others are going to join the Resistance ships. They'll all be leaving soon, except for the most badly wounded. We're going to look after those here, for as long as it takes. I wanted to ask you where you wanted to go."

"Go?" He was too dazed to really understand all of this now, direct from several days of drug-induced sleep. But the schedules were closing in, as operational schedules always did, and Trace thought it important to get some kind of idea now.

"You can go and help the croma figure out how to save the corbi," she repeated patiently. "Or you can go to join the Resistance directly. Or you can stay here. What would you rather do?"

"I can stay here?" Rika asked, with the first stirrings of real lucidity. "You'd have me?"

"I'd have you," said Trace. "I'd have you in Phoenix Company anyday."

Rika clasped her hand with slow fingers. "I'll stay here," he said.

Trace smiled, and squeezed back. "Good," was all she could manage. "Good."

30

Tiga stood atop the low stone wall, her ears thundering with croma drums, and watched proceedings in a daze. Surreal did not begin to describe it. Before her massed upwards of twenty thousand Tali'san warriors. They stood in a sea of buckled leather and studded armour, some with their weapons, others without, all in various degrees of exhausted informality.

The field had been divided into rough quadrants, more for crowd control than proper organisation, Tiga thought. In between the quadrants, bonfires burned, and great steer carcasses roasted, carved for hungry warriors by chefs with enormous knives, along with long benches of other accompaniments. Tall banners flew, marking each quadrant, but warriors wandered between each with no care for borders, knocking fists with fellow warriors, and clasping shoulders, exchanging stories and commiserations. Croma'Dokran and Croma'Rai gathered here alike, and all the smaller clans who had fought under each grand banner. Men and women who for fifty days had slogged through sand, mud, rocks and dirt to kill each other, now mingled as comrades, and saluted each other's wounds, and their bravery, and that of their many fallen comrades.

Tiga ate her own small meal off a traditional wooden plate, and thought that she would never understand these people. That they could inflict such horrid cruelty upon each other, and think it good, spoke of their barbarism. And yet that they could mingle afterward as friends, and hold no apparent ill-feeling for their foes, spoke of their civility and wisdom. Tiga thought that the Tali'san had been one of the most pointless, bloodthirsty things she'd ever seen, worse in so many ways than even the tales her father told. And yet, she could not deny that it had been stupendously, ground-shakingly grand.

Now the croma all stood together, and basked in their collective greatness. It was a grandiosity that one could build a civilisation upon. That could sustain a common legend, and light a common fire, that would burn in the fight against the greatest of evils, and never submit to the dark. Even if the flame at times resembled evil itself.

She could see Sho'mo'ra walking through them now, a huge presence in the crowds, bumping fists with common warriors, congratulating them on their immortal glory. Elsewhere through the crowd, other clan leaders roamed, some even more physically imposing than the leaders of Croma'Dokran. The Croma'Rai leadership were not among them. But astonishingly, the Croma'Rai warriors in the crowd did not appear to care. It was over, and their glory had been won. Now, a new era came — the time of Croma'Dokran.

Tiga wandered the wall as she ate, bumping the enormous fists offered to her by high-ranking croma, or common warriors below. Not long ago, Tiga would have found it frightening, to be the lone corbi among so many fearsome croma warriors. But now she felt relaxed, and knew that she was safe. The contest of clans was over, Croma'Dokran had been proven superior on the Tali'san battlefield, thanks in part to the new clans she'd played her role in persuading to join the cause. And now, there came the promise of a new dawn, not just for the croma, but for the corbi too.

The food was strange, but it tasted sweet in her mouth. Even the strange leathers made for her wrongly-shaped frame seemed to fit well. She was happy, she supposed, and filled with the most glorious hope. She knew better than to think the struggles were over, or to assume that Croma'Dokran and Sho'mo'ra could be trusted unconditionally. But the croma's new leader had promised things, in full earshot of everyone, that he could not renege on without losing honour. He'd have to actually do it now. He'd have to.

Slowly the Croma'Dokran leaders made their way along the quadrant gaps between the crowd, each with a tail of lesser commanders, edging toward the low stone wall that made the 'stage'. Behind it was a ruined fortress, destroyed in a battle during the Great Exclusion, seven thousand years ago in one of the many civil conflicts when the Croma'Rai had been banned from the rest of croma space. Croma'Rai had then reverted to the old ways, of clans, territories and roaming armies of conquest. Now Croma'Rai had been defeated in the Tali'san, but Croma'Dokran now took up their symbolic mantle for their own.

Tiga reached one end of the wall, then turned and walked slowly back the other way, across the uneven stones, determined to take in the whole, crazy scene. Upon the wall behind stood other seniors, some recording on personal devices, others engaged in animated conversation with friends, all drinking and eating and celebrating in that subdued but intense way that croma did everything.

Tiga did another lap of the wall, trading her plate for a mug of something frothy, not caring what was in it. And here, wading through the crowd to her right, at the end of the avenue of thundering drums twice as big as he was, loomed Sho'mo'ra himself. He leaned on a huge wooden staff, something ceremonial with a massive lump on one end, made for caving in heads. It looked like he'd intercepted her on purpose, Tiga thought, and did not deviate from her course, anxiously expectant.

Sure enough, as she approached, the Croma'Dokran leader put a huge fist against the wall before her feet. Not wishing to step over it, Tiga stopped. The ruined wall was tall enough that most croma still had to look up at her, but Sho'mo'ra's face was nearly level with her own. Dark croma eyes fixed her with a paralysing stare, and he leaned close, to speak beneath the crashing drums.

"You understand," he rumbled, "that Rando cannot be saved?" Tiga gazed at him, with dawning trepidation.

"I've heard military people make that analysis," she said reluctantly.

Sho'mo'ra thumped the wall again in agreement. "We would have to push the Croma Wall forward. Too far forward — as soon as we do so, the reeh will bring all their forces onto us. Even should we win, we could not guarantee to hold it for long. Rando would never be safe. It's no place to rebuild a civilisation, young Tiga. Always under threat of the very next storm."

"What then?" said Tiga, the old fear restarting once more. Politicians lied. All leaders lied. Surely Sho'mo'ra wasn't about to do the same to her? To all her people, on the most monumental, cruelest stage of all? "You promised you'd save them!"

"I cannot save Rando," repeated Sho'mo'ra. "But I did promise that I would save the corbi. And I will."

Tiga stared at him. It could only mean one thing. "Evacuation?" Disbelievingly. "You can't... there's, I mean..." For a moment, she didn't know what to say. "There's two hundred million corbi on Rando! You can't evacuate them all!"

The huge croma levelled a finger at her. "You're about to witness, young corbi, exactly what we croma are capable of, when united behind a glorious cause. Watch and learn, my girl. Watch and learn."

Tiga didn't know if she dared believe him. But the force of his conviction was infectious. For the first time in her life, she found herself confronted with a croma who she desperately wanted to hug. What was more, she thought he probably wouldn't even mind.

A middle-sized croma appeared alongside Tiga on the wall, and took a knee to speak to them both. Her voice was urgent. "Sir, I have a communication from System Command. A new force of alien ships has entered the system from an irregular jump point. There is still a significant light lag, so we haven't had a response to our hail. But they did send an initial message, they claim to be peaceful, and they say they're looking for the *Phoenix*."

"Well they missed her by thirty-six days," Sho'mo'ra rumbled, taking the headset the assistant offered. "You should hear this, Tiga, as my official corbi advisor. You know *Phoenix* better than any of us."

Tiga put her mug down on the stone, and fumbled for her own headset in the pocket of her leather coat. She pulled it on, and gave an affirmative gesture to the assistant, who activated the message.

For a moment, there was just static. Then a voice spoke... female, and speaking a tongue she'd not heard before. "That's Porgesh," said Sho'mo'ra in surprise. The assistant stopped the playback. "These are parren?"

"I'm sorry sir, yes," said the flustered assistant. "Or one of them is, but we haven't verified their IDs. It's easier if you just listen, sir, the translator kicks in soon."

Playback resumed. Then came the translator, oddly simulating the multi-toned vocals of a croma female, where the original tone had none.

"Hello people of Dul'rho. My name is Lisbeth Debogande. I am the personal emissary of the great parren leader Gesul of House Harmony, and I am the sister of Erik Debogande, the Captain of the UFS Phoenix. I bring greetings and goodwill from Gesul and all parren people to Sho'mo'ra, ruler of all croma clans, and to all croma.

"You have lately become familiar with the artificial beings of the drysine race aboard the UFS Phoenix. In addition to my flagship the Coreset, I am accompanied by five warships of the drysine race, recently returned to us after a long time in the dark. We are all here now in search of their queen, and of friendly relations with the new croma rulers. We will continue our approach to Dul'rho at civilised velocities, and await your kind reply. Coreset out."

ABOUT THE AUTHOR

Joel Shepherd is the Australian author of sixteen SF and Fantasy novels in three series. They are 'The Cassandra Kresnov Series', 'A Trial of Blood and Steel', and 'The Spiral Wars'.